blue
rider
press

ALSO BY DANIEL PRICE

Slick

The Flight of the Silvers (The Silvers—Book One)

The Song of the Orphans (The Silvers—Book Two)

THE SILVERS—BOOK THREE

DANIEL PRICE

BLUE RIDER PRESS | NEW YORK

THE WAR OF THE GIVENS

blue
rider
press

An imprint of Penguin Random House LLC
penguinrandomhouse.com

LIBRARY OF CONGRESS CATALOGING-IN-PUBLICATION DATA
has been applied for.

ISBN 9780735217911 (trade paperback)
ISBN 9780735217904 (ebook)

Printed in the United States of America
1st Printing

BOOK DESIGN BY TIFFANY ESTREICHER

For Ricki

A QUICK NOTE FROM THE AUTHOR

The book you're holding in your hands (or e-reader, as the case may be) took six years to complete. Health problems, plus the chaos of the pandemic, threw an endless series of hiccups and hurdles into an already lengthy process. The fact that *The War of the Givens* demanded, at gunpoint, to be 784 pages long didn't make it any easier.

Many of you readers have been waiting since 2017 for the conclusion to Hannah and Amanda's saga, enough for some of you to ask "Hannah and Amanda *who?*"

I wouldn't blame you for forgetting certain details. And luckily, I have you covered. Go to **danielprice.info/recap** for a whole mess of refreshers about *The Flight of the Silvers* and *The Song of the Orphans*, including an illustrated plot summary (with stick figures and everything!), a character guide, and a glossary of all the terms and concepts that have been introduced over the course of the series.

Of course, if you *really* wanted to get your head back into the story, there's no better way than to reread Books One and Two before starting *The War of the Givens.* But for those of you who don't have the time or patience, the recap materials on my website are just a click away.

Thank you again for your patience and understanding. At long last, the wait is over. The Silvers have reached the end of their journey. I hope you enjoy this final trip through the crazy little world I created.

PROLOGUE

In the bygone days of old New York, in the northernmost quarter of Brooklyn, there had once been a nine-acre luxury garden buried deep in the heart of a slum. It had been created in 1890 by the assemblyman Winthrop Jones, a lifelong Brooklyn resident who'd grown dismayed by the concrete and unsightly squalor that had spread like blight across his neighborhood. He'd spent months of his life and half his own fortune carving a scenic oasis in the middle of the district, a welcome splash of nature among the endless rows of tenements.

Sadly, Winthrop fell to consumption in 1891, just weeks before his park could be unveiled to the public. His dying request to the city of Brooklyn: *Keep it clean. Keep it pure.*

To honor him, the mayor christened the place Winthrop Park and hired a full-time staff to maintain it. Patrolmen roamed the tree-lined paths, their eyes peeled for hoodlums, beggars, and anyone else who sought to sully the grounds with their mischief. The park was a proper place for decent folk, and damned if it wouldn't stay that way.

On the fifth of October, 1912, a young man hopped the iron fence at Russell Street and cut a diagonal path across the ryegrass. Though he'd never caused anyone a lick of trouble, Freedom Williams had no illusions of being welcome here. He was seventeen, Black, and built like a wrestler, with oversized fists that hung at his sides like mallets. In the light of day, his presence would have sent every cop in the area into a state of high alert. But at five A.M. on a brisk and wintry Saturday, there was no one around to assume the worst about Freedom. He had all of Winthrop Park to himself.

His face lit up in a bright, contented grin as he basked in the peace and quiet. He shared a two-room flat with his mom and four siblings, and spent sixty hours a week on the busy floor of the ironworks. This was the only time of day when he could actually think. The fact that his shortcut shaved five minutes off his commute was just the icing on the cake.

At five past five, as the first hints of dawn began to creep above the tenements, a man's throaty cough yanked Freedom out of his thoughts. He looked to his left at the shelter pavilion and saw a figure crouched in shadow at the base of a pillar, just ten feet away.

"Holy mercy!"

Freedom jumped back, his heart pounding savagely. "Sorry, uh—"

He took a shaky step forward, struggling to make heads or tails of the fellow. He was a bald white man of considerable size, in a tweed cap and jacket that were similar to Freedom's. A day worker, from the looks of him. He might have even hauled iron at the foundry. That didn't explain what he was doing here in the cockcrow hours, with a bottle in his hand and an unstrung look about him.

He's got a storm in his eyes, Freedom's father would have said. *Best keep your distance.*

Freedom took a clumsy step back. "Apologies, sir. I didn't mean to holler. I just wasn't—"

"*Złodziej.*"

"Pardon?"

The stranger shook his last drops of whiskey into his mouth, then rose to his feet. At full height, he was even larger than Freedom had guessed—six foot eight and packed with muscle. The man made Freedom look like a child. And he was only getting madder.

"*Jesteś złodziejem.*" The giant gestured furiously at Freedom's right arm. "*Nie chce mi się wierzyć, że kupiłeś ten zegarek za swoje pieniądze!*"

Freedom raised his palms. "Look, mister, I don't know what you're saying but I don't want no trouble, okay?"

"*Oddaj mi zegarek, a możliwe, że cię nie skrzywdzę.*"

"I'll just be on my way."

"*Powiedziałem oddaj!*"

The giant struck his bottle against the pillar, shattering half the glass. Though Freedom knew full well that he should be running, he couldn't help but gawk at the bottle's odd remains. Instead of sporting a crown of jagged teeth, like it did in the cartoons and picture shows, only a single fat shard extended from the neck. The thing looked more like a garden trowel than a weapon.

Still sharp enough to cut you, Freedom thought. *Run!*

He fled to the north and the mad giant followed. Freedom hadn't been chased in a donkey's age, not since he outgrew his abusers. But the old childhood lessons remained burned in his memory. *Don't look back. Mind your feet. And find a way out of his sight.*

Unfortunately for Freedom, the park offered little in the way of cover, and it was hard to mind his feet when the sun was still a stranger. His left foot caught on a root of a tree and sent him toppling to the grass. Freedom barely had a chance to right himself before a huge hand grabbed his coat by the collar.

"Wait!" Freedom pleaded. "Please!"

The giant clamped the back of his neck and pulled him in close. Freedom struggled in his grip, gagging at the man's pungent stench. His clothes smelled like sweat and yesterday's garbage, with a little piss and whiskey thrown in for good measure.

"Sam to na siebie zesłałeś."

The giant raised his bottle-blade, his eyes wet with tears. In a better state of mind, Freedom might have asked him what he was crying about. He wasn't the one who was about to get gutted. He wasn't about to leave a mom and four siblings with no last hope of paying the rent.

And for what? Freedom had to wonder. *What the hell am I dying for?*

He closed his eyes in cringing dread, but all he felt was release. The giant had abruptly let go of his neck and was now screaming bloody hell about something.

Freedom opened his eyes just in time to catch the strangest thing he'd ever seen: his would-be killer flying backward through the air, as if gravity had gone sideways on him. The giant flailed and twisted helplessly as his body careened toward a lime tree.

But then a sudden glow silhouetted him: a twelve-foot sphere of blinding white light. By the time Freedom dared to uncover his eyes, the spectacle was gone. There was no glow, no giant, just a faint and smoldering mist around the base of the tree.

Freedom looked around the park in a dull, mindless stupor. "What . . . what just . . . ?"

"It's all right," said a voice from behind him. "He's gone."

He turned around and saw a short young woman sitting idly on a bench—a platinum blonde in odd attire. She wore loose gray slacks as if she were a man, and her sleeveless blouse seemed scant for mixed company. She had no hat or coat of any kind, despite the weather.

"What just happened?"

The woman casually picked some lint off her pants leg. "Some maladjusted lunkhead thought it was a good idea to rob you. I disagreed."

Freedom studied his savior in puzzlement, his breath still coming in gasps.

This strange little pixie was ninety pounds at best. She couldn't have possibly thrown that ogre.

She looked to the east at the coming dawn, then patted the slats of her bench. "I only have a few minutes. Let's talk."

"Look, ma'am—"

"Don't you dare 'ma'am' me."

"Miss—"

"Don't do that either," she said. "You call me Ioni or you don't call me anything."

It suddenly occurred to Freedom that he was having one of those dreams his sister had read about, the kind where you know you're dreaming but keep doing it anyway. There was even a fancy name for it, though damned if Freedom could remember it.

He took a deep breath, picked up his cap, then lingered near the bench in hesitation.

"Begging your pardon, miss . . ." He corrected himself in the heat of her glare. "Ioni. There are folks 'round here who'll wear my hide if they see me lolling with a white woman."

Ioni furrowed her brow indignantly. "I'm not white. I'm Spanish-Korean."

"You don't look it. And they won't care."

"There's no 'they' here, Freedom. Just us. Even if there were bigots lurking about . . ." She flicked her hand at the misty lime tree. "You saw what I did to Nelek."

"Who?"

"Big guy. Polish. Tried to kill you with a broken bottle."

Freedom sat on the bench, a good four feet from Ioni. How did she know the giant's name? How did she know *his* name? And what did she do to that lunatic?

"I didn't kill him," Ioni attested, as if she could read at least some of Freedom's thoughts. "I just whisked him back to his flat on Henry Street."

"*Whisked* him."

"My folksy way of saying 'teleported.'"

Freedom's stomach churned with stress. He may have dropped out of school in the middle of eighth grade, but he still knew the natural order of things. No one, not even the Spanish-Koreans, went around "whisking" people.

Ioni slumped on the bench with a look of distant gloom. "Truth be told, I feel sorry for Nelek. He has a defect in his hypothalamus that makes it hard for him to sleep. He's never had a good night's rest in his life and it's made him kind of . . ."

She wound her finger near her ear, as if that was supposed to mean something to Freedom.

He did a sudden double-take at her. "Wait. Did you say he was *robbing* me?"

"Trying to."

"I got nothing worth stealing."

"You sure about that?"

Freedom suddenly remembered the way Nelek had pointed at his wrist. *Of course*, he thought. *I'm a fool and a half.*

He pulled back his coat sleeve to reveal his one flashy trinket: a 1909 Wilsdorf & Davis military bracelet watch. He'd acquired it last year after saving the life of a drunk and grateful Englishman, but it wasn't the treasure it appeared to be. The brand name was forged. The watch hands were tin. And the band was made of silvertone, a pale imitation of the real thing. Nelek would have gotten twenty cents for it at the most.

Freedom unclasped the watch and stashed it in his pocket. "My mama said I was asking for trouble by wearing that."

"Wise woman."

"The wisest," said Freedom. "A boy my size puts some white folks on edge. So she taught me to keep my head down and always be respectful. It's saved me a lot of grief, that's for sure."

Ioni sighed at the ground. "I'm sorry. These aren't the best of times."

Freedom suddenly noticed her own wristwatch, the most puzzling thing he'd ever seen. It broadcast the time in glowing red digits. No hands. No dial. No painted-on numbers. To Freedom, it was a thing of pure madness, like a Christmas goose that cooked and carved itself.

Ioni smirked at his bewildered expression. "It's digital," she explained, as if that meant a thing to Freedom. "Light-emitting diodes. You won't see these until at least the 1970s."

"What are you?"

If Freedom's mother had been there, she would have smacked him for being rude. But his life was getting crazier by the moment and it put a real crimp in his small talk.

Ioni's smile deflated. "You picked the wrong day to ask me that."

"I didn't mean to insult you."

"I'm not insulted. I just . . ."

Freedom watched her guardedly as she mulled over her next words. "There's only one thing I ever wanted to do with my life," she said. "And now that I finally have the job, all I want to do is quit."

"Why? What do you do?"

Ioni bit her lip in contemplation before looking at Freedom again. "I'll answer your question if you answer mine first. There's something I've always wanted to ask you."

"Always? We just—"

"How did you get the name Freedom?"

He lowered his head and stroked the scar on his palm, a year-old burn from a cracked iron mold. "It was my dad's name. He was born on Emancipation Day."

"Wow," said Ioni. "That's beautiful."

"Beautiful." Freedom chuckled cynically. "He spent his whole life hauling iron at the foundry. Six days a week, twelve hours a day, ever since he was a boy. The only difference between him and a slave was nine cents an hour and a couple less beatings."

Ioni nodded solemnly. "But you took his job when he died."

"I had to."

"No you didn't. You could have run away and lived your own life."

Freedom looked at her aghast. "What kind of man leaves his family like that?"

"A selfish one. That's my point. It's easy to be weak in times like these, but you did right by the people who need you. That isn't something that happened to you. You chose to be good."

Ioni dipped her head, her voice a low mutter. "Meanwhile, I do terrible things to backwater Earths. I destroy whole cities, just so my employers can see what happens next."

Freedom shook his head. "There's nothing about you that makes a lick of sense to me. I just know I'm still breathing 'cause of you. You saved my life and you don't even know me."

He'd expected his words to lift her up. Instead she looked even more despondent.

"I only did it to make myself feel better," she admitted.

"Didn't seem to work."

"No, it didn't. Let's try something else."

She waved her hand in a curious manner, like she was petting an invisible dog. An orb of light filled the empty space. By the time it faded, a brand-new object had materialized on the ground: a brown leather suitcase that looked big enough to fit a full-grown sheepdog.

"It's yours," Ioni said. "Open it."

"I don't . . . I mean . . ."

"It's no trick. No trap. Just a simple gift for a man who deserves one."

Anxiously, Freedom hoisted the heavy suitcase onto his lap, popped the latches, then gasped at the bounty inside. "Mother of God!"

He slammed the lid shut and cast a nervous look around the park. "Are you crazy?"

"Maybe," Ioni said. "But the money's real and it's all for you."

Freedom opened the suitcase again and flipped through a pile of twenty dollar bills. There were about a hundred in each stack and there were *hundreds* of stacks.

"Four hundred thousand dollars," Ioni told him. "That should tide you over for a while."

"A while?" Freedom laughed with disbelief. "I couldn't earn it in a hundred lifetimes."

Ioni smiled. "Guess Nelek picked the wrong time to rob you."

"I'm sorry. I can't . . . I can't take it."

"Freedom—"

"You don't understand. If anyone finds out—"

"They *won't*," Ioni promised. "You're a clever guy. You'll know where to hide it and when to use it."

Freedom emitted a noise that fell somewhere between a squeak and a cackle. He could barely wrap his mind around the life-changing implications. Ioni was right. If he spent the money cautiously, in little dribs and drabs, he could take care of his family for the rest of their days without raising suspicion.

Only one question remained.

"Why?" he asked Ioni. "Why do this for someone who never did nothing for you?"

"That's not the way I see it. But if you don't feel right about taking a gift from a stranger, there's something you can give me in return."

"What's that?"

"Your wristwatch," she said. "I was going to ask you for it anyway."

"Why? You already got one."

She lazily shrugged her shoulders. "I could always use another."

Though Freedom was thrown by her request, he removed his watch and handed it to her.

"There," she said. "Now we both got something out of the deal."

While Freedom locked up the suitcase and clutched it tightly against his chest, Ioni turned her attention upward. The clouds above the eastern rooftops had turned a dull shade of orange, enough to paint the trees of Winthrop Park with a fiery luminance.

Freedom took her in with gobsmacked reverence. "He was right."

"Who was right?"

"My dad. The only time he ever whupped me was when I said the world was getting worse. He told me how his father had been born in chains, how *his* father had been sold up and down the southern coast. But my dad, he didn't see none of that. He lived a better life than all that came before him. And he swore to me that I'd live a better life than him."

Freedom cast a vacant look at the tenements, a tremulous crack in his voice. "I never believed him until now."

Ioni rose from the bench, a dull new sadness in her voice. "I'm afraid I have to go, Freedom, but there's one more thing I'd like you to do for me. Not a demand. Just a request."

"Anything."

"I want you to stay right here for at least twenty minutes," Ioni told him. "Don't go home. Don't walk around. Don't worry about anyone giving you trouble. You'll have this entire park to yourself. So just sit right here till the sun comes up and think of all the wonderful new things you'll do with your life. Can you do that for me?"

Freedom nodded. "Sure enough, but—"

She placed her hands on his cheekbones and gave him a tender kiss on the lips. Though a part of him still wondered if he was dreaming all this—*A lucid dream*, his mind suddenly recalled. *That's what my sister was reading about*—he was able to cast the thought aside and simply enjoy the moment. He was sharing a kiss with one of God's blessed angels. For all he knew, he was kissing God herself.

Ioni broke away, looking as blue and stricken as anyone Freedom had ever seen.

"You seem so down," he noted. "Wish there was something I could do for you."

She gave him a weak smile. "It was nice just to talk to you. The job does get lonely."

"You still never told me what it is you do."

Ioni blew a heavy sigh before proceeding down the walkway. She stopped in place after fifteen feet, then gave Freedom one last look over her shoulder.

"I change things," she told him. "I change worlds."

A flash of light enveloped her, blinding him. By the time Freedom could see through the dancing spots, Ioni was gone. Fat plumes of mist rose from the little patch of concrete that she'd been standing on.

"God have mercy . . ."

Freedom did as she requested and stayed right where he was. His head was so muddled and bubbling with thoughts that he could scarcely remember his own name, much less go anywhere. He craned his neck and glanced around the heavens, until he felt reasonably certain that the universe had no more surprises for him today.

By the time the sun came up at 5:54, all the mysteries of the morning were sealed away in a box, giving Freedom full latitude to think about his fortune and all the things it could buy him. A nicer home with a room of his own. A belly full of first-rate meats. He could even get some better clothes and take a girl out on the town. The sky had cracked wide open for him and revealed a future of bright possibilities.

A quick, sudden flash caught his attention from the east, as if someone were reflecting sunlight off a mirror. Freedom turned his head and saw a peculiar glow just forty feet away from him, near a young plane tree that, unlike its red-leafed siblings and neighbors, had yet to change shade with the autumn. Now it was boasting an even more unique attribute: an orb of light the size of a baseball, dangling from a branch like some divine biblical fruit.

Freedom stood up and cautiously approached the anomaly. On closer inspection, the orb wasn't attached to the tree . . . or anything, for that matter. It floated five feet off the ground, as bright and steady as the moon itself, but what *was* it? Freedom had had his fill of craziness for the day, and if he hadn't been in such good spirits, he might have run to the nearest exit.

Instead, he took a nervous step closer and squinted into the light. "Ioni? Is that y—"

The orb exploded in every direction, a dome-shaped eruption that enveloped the park in a heartbeat. It silently expanded for three and a half seconds, until it was tall enough to split the clouds and wide enough to cover half of New York City. From space, the blast looked like a bright eye opening on the edge of North America. From the Jersey horizon, it looked like a second sunrise.

To those who saw the Cataclysm with their own two eyes, it looked like the end of the world.

The dome of light dissipated, leaving nothing behind but bisected buildings and a circular field of ash. From the upper reaches of Central Park to the southernmost corner of Flatbush, from the heart of Queens' Astoria district to the river's edge of Hoboken, the city had been reduced to its barest carbon elements. There was no one alive within five miles of Winthrop Park. Not until a spherical portal opened up in midair and a lone young woman stepped out into the wasteland.

This time, Ioni had come dressed for the climate. A translucent forcefield covered her body, protecting her from the tiny flakes of ash that floated all around her. It didn't escape her reckoning that some of those flakes had once been Freedom Williams, Junior.

Crying, Ioni looked to the future and saw a breathtaking change in the strings. All across the nation, all over the world, the story of humanity was being rewritten on the fly—an alternate timeline full of panic and change, knowledge and temporis. She could already hear the excited chatter of her employers as they marked the cascading effects of her genocide. One of them even had the nerve to congratulate her.

Ioni switched off her neural link and permanently disabled her chipsets. She was done with the institute, done with the job, done with her family and all of her friends. If any of them wanted to find her, they could come back here to the mangled past. She was going to stay on the new Earth she created and witness firsthand the consequences of her actions.

She reached into her pocket and retrieved the watch she'd bought from Freedom, paid with cash that he'd never get to spend. Ioni had given him a little taste of bliss before dying, which was a hell of a lot more than her other victims got.

She secured his watch around her wrist, right next to her digital timepiece, and then began to walk through the ashes. By the time she'd reached the northern edge of Brooklyn, she could see all the way into the next century—new people, new nations, new gadgets, new problems. But something looked wrong on the distant horizon, a few clicks past the turn of the millennium. Something . . .

Ioni stopped in place and gasped. She saw an unprecedented crisis a hundred years from now, a tangle in the strings that threatened every life on this Earth. She could only catch quick flashes from her vantage: three tall and fearsome beings from the future she'd created, plus several dozen refugees from her own native history. The conflict would spread like fire across the globe before converging on the streets of an empty American city. Ioni couldn't even begin to guess what would happen in San Francisco, but the little bits she saw were terrifying. It looked a lot like the end of all futures.

It looked a lot like war.

PART ONE

THE LAST SILVER

ONE

The Levitar was a marvel of modern transportation, a jewel in the crown of the Central American Union. While the rest of the world only dabbled with the concept of flying trains, Mexico and its partners jumped in with both feet and built the model for all future skyrails. From the hills of Tijuana to the towers of Panama City, commuter trains shuttled at nine different altitudes. More than twenty million people rode the Levitar each day. It was the cheapest, fastest, most reliable way to travel the Latin territories.

At high noon on Friday, the twentieth of July, a ten-car trendelaire left the platform at Tampico and flew a straight northern path up the Gulf Coast. Unlike the usual trains, which were covered from roof to bumper in animated advertisements, this one was black, with dark, mirrored windows. Most of the locals who saw it assumed, quite correctly, that it was a government transport. Some even guessed that it was Seguridad Interna, Mexico's most elite and high-powered intelligence agency, behind the shaded glass. But why in the world were they going north? There was nothing up there but the tempic wall of Texas, and the Americans got *very* nervous about flying objects near their border.

Ten minutes after its departure, the trendelaire climbed to two thousand feet and banked a left toward Nuevo León. In this rural area, at this elevation, Seguridad had the sky to itself. There was nothing to see on the telemetry screen except an old weather drone and a pair of black-bellied whistling ducks.

Had the pilot looked out the window at just the right moment, she would have noticed a subtle distortion in the air, like a heat ripple. By the time the train passed beneath it, the anomaly had turned into a fiery white teleportal: thirty feet wide, three microns tall, and completely immune to gravity.

A four-seat aercraft emerged from the underside, then followed the train at shifted speed. The Owl wasn't anyone's idea of a sleek and elegant vessel. It resembled a pair of child's binoculars, with unsightly antennae sticking out from all sides. Integrity hadn't designed it to win any beauty contests. It was a tactical stealth shuttle, impervious to thermal, radar, and infrared detection. Its lumiflaged chassis made it transparent in flight and almost perfectly invisible while hovering.

The Owl caught up to the trendelaire, then swooped above the roof of the tail car. The weird little ship was easy to pilot. On a better day, Caleb might have even enjoyed himself. But the risks and enormities of the current situation were enough to stick a shiv in his *joie de vivre.* He was flying a woman and two kids into the crosshairs of Mexican soldiers, on behalf of a U.S. spy shop. Caleb couldn't have been less qualified for this *fakakta* mission, yet the strategists believed, and the augurs agreed, that he was the best chump for the job.

His dark-haired companion leaned forward in the navigator seat, her brown eyes filled with dread. Unlike Caleb, who'd let half his muscles turn to flab in the comfort and safety of the underland, Eden had managed to stay fit. She actually looked like a badass in her black ballistic armor, though Caleb could see from her stiff and anxious pose that she wasn't a fan of aer travel. Her myoelectric hands had already crushed the hell out of her armrests.

"Watch your speed," she grumbled.

"I'm watching."

"If you overshoot—"

"Eden. I got it."

A crackling voice filled their earpieces, his words too garbled to understand.

"We didn't catch that," Caleb said. "Repeat."

Seventy miles to the north, in the small Texas town of Laredo, Peter Pendergen adjusted his radio's temporal converter. "I was just telling our dear Miss Garza to have faith."

"Faith." Caleb chuckled bleakly. In another life, on another Earth, he'd been a congregational rabbi. Then a devil named Azral came to Tarpon Springs, Florida, and slapped a platinum bracelet on his wrist. Now here he was on the other side of creation: an orphan, a breacher, a swifter, a fighter. And though he never said it out loud, lest he break the heart of his poor dead father, Caleb had also become an atheist.

The Owl passed the trendelaire car by car, until it was five yards above the roof of the engine coach. Now came the hard part. Caleb de-shifted the shuttle, switched to manual thrust, and watched the landing monitor closely. He had to move in perfect lockstep with the train while descending as gently as a housefly.

"Here we go." Eden looked to her squadmates in the back seat. "You ready?"

The boy and girl nodded in unison, their expressions obscured by their tinted face masks. They were both so short and wiry that Caleb couldn't tell them apart in their tactical gear. All he knew was that they were way too young for flying train robberies.

The Owl was six inches above the engine coach when Caleb activated the landing struts. They stuck to the roof with a clamorous *thump*.

"Damn it!" Caleb yelled.

Eden peeked out her window. "Maybe they didn't hear us."

"They heard you," said a second voice on the radio, her tone as cool and sharp as her Sudanese-British accent. "We just lost our advantage."

Caleb muttered a curse. Melissa Masaad was a certified expert at making him feel bad, but he knew he deserved it. She'd warned him over and over not to jump the gun on the magnet clamps.

"What do we do now?" he asked Melissa.

"We stick to the plan. We just do it faster. Eden—"

"I'm on it."

Eden rushed to the back and pulled the lever for the exit hatch. As cool wind and sunlight flooded into the cabin, Caleb turned to his younger teammates. "Stay behind Eden. Watch your step. And whatever you do, don't look down."

"We know what we're doing," the girl brusquely replied. "We've been doing it longer than you."

Eden took her first step onto the train, her magnetic boots clacking against the steel roof panels. She was just about to summon her temporal energy when something caught her eye from the distant west: a towering mountain that she had no trouble recognizing.

Her mouth went slack behind her face mask. "*Increíble . . .*"

She'd been born and raised in another world's Mexico and wasn't expecting to see anything familiar. But there it was: the Cerro de la Silla, looming above the city of Monterrey, just the way she remembered it. In a weaker state, she might have convinced herself that she was home again, but . . . no. The Earth she knew was nearly two years gone. This was just a distorted reflection.

Melissa sighed impatiently. "Eden . . ."

"I'm working! I'm working!"

She pressed a button at the base of her wrist, summoning thick gloves of tempis over her prosthetics. It was an unfortunate necessity for a woman of her talents. She'd lost her original right hand in a superheating accident and lost the original left one to frostbite.

Eden cleared her mind of all distraction, raised her right fist to chest level, then bombarded the roof with a cone of concentrated heat. The center steel panels changed color in quick succession, from gray to red to blazing hot yellow.

Caleb watched her from the back of the Owl. "Wow."

Eden wasn't part of his Platinum crew. She was one of the eight orphans from Austin, Texas—the ones who'd received iron bracelets. While the other Pelletier groups had evolved into families, the Irons had only become more polarized over time. The progressive half followed Eden's lead. The Good Ole Boys swore fealty to Ben Hopkins. It broke Caleb's heart to see the group split along old fault lines, though he made no bones about whom he liked better. He'd side with Eden every time, and moments like this were why.

After liquifying a six-foot swath of roof panels, Eden used her subthermic hand to cool the hole's molten edges. The engine car had been successfully breached.

Now it was the tempic's turn.

Before Eden could even speak the boy's name, eight white globs came shooting out of his fingertips. They hit the roof with dull wet thuds, then immediately began to wriggle. Within seconds, they expanded into their full-grown forms, their dead white eyes fixed on their creator.

"Goddamn," Eden muttered.

The kid was the last surviving member of his orphan group: the ill-fated Golds of New York. He was born Ahmad Bradshaw, but no one called him that anymore. On this world, among these people, he only answered to one name.

Melissa watched him through Eden's helmet camera. "Heath, don't forget to—"

"—block the door," he said. "They know."

A shudder ran up Eden's spine. There were few things in the world she found creepier than Heath's tempic men. They were all six feet tall and broad in the shoulders, with sinewy limbs that moved differently than the average person's—*savagely*, as if they'd all been raised by wolves. Stranger still, they each had the same gratuitous "hairstyle": a long white mane, always tied in a ponytail. From what Eden was told, the men were modeled and named after a dear friend of Heath's, a guitarist he'd never stopped mourning.

The Jonathans dropped through the hole in the ceiling and attacked the soldiers in the engine car. Eden heard six seconds of gunshots and Spanish exclamations, and then nothing.

"It's over," said Heath. "They're down."

Caleb chuckled in dark astonishment. "Kid, remind me to never piss you off."

"Cut the prattle," Melissa said. "You all have your orders."

While Caleb prepped the Owl for takeoff, Eden and the teenagers climbed down into the train. In hindsight, it was an unfair fight: four hapless grunts in bodysuits versus eight indestructible golems. By the time Eden arrived, the soldiers had been relieved of their weapons and immobilized by the Jonathans. Heath's remaining four minions formed a makeshift barrier at the rear door, and not a moment too soon. Armed goons were trying to force their way in from the second car. Eden didn't put high odds on their chances.

She approached the control console and checked the status on the main screen.

"Code-locked?" Melissa asked.

"Code-locked," Eden confirmed. "How'd you know?"

"Standard procedure. How persuasive are you feeling?"

"Very." She turned to the prisoners and addressed them in Spanish. "Which one of you is the pilot?"

"I am," said the woman of the quartet, a diminutive speck compared to her squadmates. But she certainly knew how to glower with the best of them. Her glare could have melted walls.

"We're not here to kill anyone," Eden assured her. "We just want your cargo. Give us the control code and no one gets hurt."

The pilot barely opened her mouth before another soldier yelled at her in Spanish. "Don't you dare, Rosa! I'll kill you myself if you help this traitor!"

Eden looked at him confusedly. "Traitor?"

"You have no accent. You're as Mexican as us. What did the *caucás* offer you? Money?"

Eden shook her head. "You have no idea what's going on. You don't even know what you're carrying."

"I know you work for Integrity, the worst people on Earth. They poisoned a village in Nicaragua. Women. Babies!"

Eden didn't doubt it. "Listen—"

"No! We'll die before we help you! So just go ahead and—"

A thunderous boom filled the train car. The soldier's belly burst with blood. Eden turned around to see the girl on her team fire a second shot from her sidearm, then a third. By the time she finished, each male soldier had a .38 slug in his stomach. They all fell howling into the arms of the Jonathans.

Heath looked to the girl in horror. "What are you *doing*?"

"Are you crazy?" said Eden.

Caleb listened to the ruckus through his earpiece and sighed. The Coppers were weird, the Irons were fractious, and Lord knew the Platinums had their fair share of issues. But none of the orphan groups—*none* of them—were as complex and mystifying as the Silvers of San Diego. And none were more worrisome than the youngest of their number, an angry little hellcat named Mia Farisi.

Seventy miles away, in the dank and dusty warehouse that served as the Laredo command center, Melissa ordered her medical team to get the revivers ready. She shot a thorny look at Peter. "If those men die, I'm holding you responsible."

"Me?"

"You're her teacher. Her mentor."

Peter scoffed. "She surpassed me months ago."

"You told me I could rely on her."

"You can," he said. "She didn't shoot those men for kicks. She's got a plan. Just trust her."

Melissa looked to the back of the room, at the shadowy form of Zack Trillinger. She could see from the crack in his poker face that he didn't entirely share Peter's confidence.

Up in the skies of Nuevo León, Eden brusquely pulled Mia aside. "Whatever you think you're doing—"

"Just shut up and follow me." Mia holstered her pistol. "I need you to translate."

She pulled off her helmet, tossed it aside, and then turned to face the pilot. Thirteen months of physical conditioning had changed Mia's once-angelic face into a mask of hard angles. Her hair had been cropped to a lopsided pixie cut, platinum blond in some places and lily white in others. Her new penchant for dark eyeliner—gobs and gobs of it—was enough to make her look crazed. Between her raccoon eyes and her razor-sharp jawline, the prisoners took Mia to be a thirty-year-old operative. She was just a month shy of sixteen.

She spoke to the pilot in a furtive half-whisper. "I heard him say 'Rosa.' Is that your name?"

The woman waited for Eden's translation before nodding. Mia ran a gentle finger down her cheek. "Well, Rosa, I don't know what that man said to you, but I'm sure it wasn't nice. Those guys don't think very much of you, do they?"

Eden could tell from Rosa's faltering glare that Mia had struck a nerve.

"I get it," said Mia. "There's a man out there who doesn't think much of me either. It drives me crazy, and not because I like him. I hate his guts and I have every intention of killing him."

Eden paused. "Mia . . ."

"Just *translate*."

She waited for Eden to finish before addressing the pilot again. "I can always tell when he's watching me. I feel it on my skin. And I need him to see, every time he looks at me, that I am not weak. I need him to know that he didn't break me."

Mia motioned to the other three soldiers, still bleeding in the arms of their captors. "You clearly feel the same about those idiots, so I took them out of the equation. Either they'll get reversed back to health or they'll die. If they're reversed, they won't remember a thing that happened here today. If they die . . ." She shrugged. "Then who the fuck cares what they think?"

At last, Eden could see Mia's brutal strategy. She still didn't like it one bit.

"Give us the code," Mia implored the pilot. "None of your people will know."

"*I'll* know," the woman replied in surprisingly good English.

Mia laughed and squeezed her arm. "Oh, Rosa. You think we'll let you remember this?" She brandished her gun again. "The way I see it, this ends only one of two ways—"

Rosa abruptly relinquished the code. Eden entered it into the control console, then activated the air brake.

Finally, Mia thought. She was one of the world's strongest travelers, but her power still had limits. She couldn't teleport more than a hundred miles at a time, she couldn't jump blind to an unfamiliar location, and she couldn't draw a portal on a moving object. But now that the train had come to a stop . . .

"Doorway in three," she told Central. "Stand back."

She formed a spatial link with the command center and willed a ten-foot portal onto the wall. A squad of armored Integrity agents charged single-file through the opening and relieved the Jonathans of their prisoners. The poor, anguished pilot screamed all the way to Laredo.

Melissa boarded the train from Central Command and lifted her helmet visor. "There were a dozen ways to make that pilot talk," she said to Mia. "You chose the cruelest, most reckless—"

"Cruelest?" Mia laughed. "Who do you think we work for?"

"That was the old Integrity. We're not like that anymore."

"Yeah, right. You keep telling yourself that."

Melissa frowned at her. "When we get home, I'm recommending another psychological—"

"Oh, fuck you and your headshrinks. I got the job done!"

Zack stepped through the portal, his helmet tucked in the crook of his arm. "I could hear you guys from Texas. Is this really the time?"

"No," Melissa agreed. "Headgear on, the both of you."

Peter followed Zack through the gateway, then tossed a nod at Mia. She waved the portal shut behind him. "How many soldiers in the next coach?" he asked.

"Thirteen," Heath muttered.

Caleb hovered the Owl over the roof of the second car and counted the faint blue figures on his thermal scanner. "Looks like thirteen, but I can barely see them."

"Tempic armor?" Eden asked.

"Tempic armor," Peter confirmed. The suits were cool enough to stymie the heat sensors. There was certainly no other way that Heath could count them without looking.

"Can you take them all?" Melissa asked Zack.

"Absolutely. I just need a portal."

"I got it," Mia said.

"*I* got it," Peter said.

He tossed a plum-size camera drone through the gap in the ceiling, then used his tablet computer to guide it along the windows of the second car. Within moments, he had enough visual and infrared knowledge of the cabin to forge a spatial connection.

"I'm in," he told Zack. "You ready?"

"Do it."

As soon as Peter cast a portal onto the wall, Zack thrust his hands into it and fired a glowing white burst of temporis into the neighboring coach. His teammates watched through Peter's tablet as thirteen soldiers shuddered where they stood, their personal chronologies reversing by the hour. By the time Zack finished, they were all reverted to the men they'd been at midnight. Some were back in their T-shirts and underwear. Some only wore pajama pants. All of them were sick to the point of collapse. Chronoregression was never easy on the human body. In the hands of a less experienced turner, the process was often fatal.

But in his twenty-four months on this mad sister Earth, Zack had become a master of his craft. He rigorously trained with the Gothams' best timebenders—two hours each morning, every morning. He'd even managed to squeeze in some practice on his wedding day. It was the least one could do when one had gods for enemies.

"Good job," said Melissa. She hailed Central on her radio. "Thirteen more for extraction. Wait for Mia's portal and get ready to move fast."

Mia crossed her arms in a sulky pout. "So I stay behind while the rest of you move on."

Melissa glared at her. "You're lucky I don't send you home."

The Owl's dashboard beeped in alarm. Caleb studied the new blips on his radar screen. "Uh, guys? There's a big flock of bogeys coming at us from the south."

Peter sighed at Melissa. "Their cavalry got here early."

"That's all right." She looked out the northern window at the tiny new dots in the sky. "So did ours."

Outside in the distance, twenty-one hundred feet above the flat desert sands, two aerocycle riders led an army of drones toward the trendelaire. At 12x speed, they were all just streaks to the naked eye, a V-shaped blur moving south across the firmament. A person would have to be flying right alongside them to see the sheer amount of firepower they were packing, enough to level an office building. The drones were called "stormbirds" for their electromagnetic weapons. The cycles were called "ravagers" for their .50-caliber machine guns.

The two armored pilots had a special name of their own. Long ago, when they were just little girls, their mother had called them the Great Sisters Given because she believed, even when they didn't, that they were both extraordinary. She'd also hoped to foster some unity between her daughters, who were as different from each other as night and day, and who could never quite seem to connect.

That was hardly a problem these days, as Hannah and Amanda were the tightest of siblings. Their life-or-death struggles on an alien Earth had rendered all their old issues obsolete, to the point where they could barely remember their squabbles. If Melanie Given could have seen them now, she would have cried at the love and respect they had for each other, even if she found them a little too extraordinary for comfort. The sisters had acquired biological talents that dwarfed all the ordnance around them. They didn't need bullets to raze a building to the ground.

Hannah checked the radar map on the inside of her visor. There were at least twenty red triangles making a fast but scattered course in her direction. "What are we looking at here? Drones? Fighters?"

Felicity Yu, Melissa's right-hand woman at Integrity, responded from her terminal at Laredo. Her entire cubicle had been shifted to keep pace with the Givens. "Hang on. Still waiting for the satellite snaps."

Amanda could see the trendelaire clearly: eight hundred feet of stationary target that was mostly glass on the sides. Even light weapon drones could hurt Zack and the others.

"Doesn't matter what they are," she said. "We have to take them out fast."

Felicity shook her head. "If there are people in those flyers—"

"There are on people on that *train*."

"I hear you, Red, but we need to be careful. We're already risking an international incident. We leave too many bodies and we'll have a whole new war on our hands."

Felicity spoke with a flawless American dialect, even though English was her fourth language. Integrity had poached her from the Japanese secret service, who had poached her from the Chinese, who had poached her from the Koreans. Loyalty wasn't exactly her strong suit, though she had nothing but love for her current employer. Integrity knew how to treat a young analytical genius, even one as eccentric as her. And now that they were fighting to stop an apocalypse, she was sufficiently motivated to stick around for a while.

A grainy image of a flying object appeared on Felicity's monitor. From bird's-eye view, it looked like a big silver boomerang. "Okay. Good. They're just drones. *Cimitarras*."

"*Cimitarras*," Hannah echoed. "As in 'scimitars.'"

"Don't let the name scare you. Those things are pure cannon fodder. They're barely armored, they're not that fast, and they only have light machine guns."

"Only?"

"I didn't say they were harmless. Still, the stormbirds will make snacks out of them."

"You sure?" Amanda asked.

"Trust me. I know my drones." Felicity eyed her monitor suspiciously. "Then again, so does Seguridad. They wouldn't send such a minor-league defense if they didn't—"

The radio connection died with a squeal. Hannah tapped her helmet. "Felicity?"

Amanda activated her temporal converter and opened a channel to Laredo. "Central, come in. Can anyone hear me?"

The sisters couldn't even hail each other on the network. They brought their ravagers together and raised the volume on their helmet speakers.

"No signal," said Hannah. "Those scimitar things must be jamming us."

Amanda nodded. "One more reason to take them out."

"Okay, I'll ride point with the stormbirds—"

"Wait."

"—you keep watch on the train."

"Hannah . . ."

Amanda pointed at the Integrity drones behind her, all clustered together in a blinking red state of confusion. Without a clear link to their remote human pilots, the damn things were useless: sixteen black metal stingrays just dawdling in the air like kites.

Hannah cursed under her breath. Seguridad had just given them a hell of a wedgie. Now she and Amanda had to handle all those flying Mexican bullet geysers by themselves.

The scimitars were almost upon the trendelaire. At eye level, the machines managed to look both surreal and intimidating, like Gatling guns on metal hang gliders.

Hannah looked to Amanda and saw her disconnecting her speedsuit from her ravager. "Wait. What are you doing?"

"We're not going to beat those things in a gunfight."

"No, no, no. We talked about this."

"I'll be fine. Just hang back and guard the train."

Fifty yards away, in the sixth car of the trendelaire, Zack looked out the window and saw his wife swing her leg over the seat of her aerocycle. "Oh, no, no, no. Don't you dare. Amanda!"

She leapt from her ravager and dropped out of view.

The last thirteen months had not passed quietly for Amanda Given. Over the course of one winter, she'd suffered two miscarriages, a complete nervous breakdown, and a confrontation with Esis that cost her both her arms.

But then, come February, Amanda's fortunes turned the other way—a monthlong farrago of happy surprises that brought her from the lowest point of her life to the highest. By March, nearly everything seemed to be right with the world. She was free of the Pelletiers' twisted demands. She was happily married to the love of her life. And though it took a few long weeks of trial and adjustment, her self-made tempic arms proved vastly superior to the old ones.

Best of all, Amanda had discovered a new aspect of her special ability, one that filled her days with endless joy and made her twice as fierce on the battlefield.

Solid force protruded from her shoulder blades, cutting like knives through the back of her armor and trailing her body in streams. The tendrils knitted together to form two white wings of concentrated aeris, twelve feet wide from tip to tip and marked with swanlike plumage.

There were only twenty-nine people on the face of the Earth who could soar through the sky on pure willpower. Amanda wasn't just one of them now. She was one of their best.

With a thousand feet between her and the desert, she straightened out her body and let her wings do the steering. Once her altitude leveled out, she sent a new directive to the appendages on her back, a simple command that reversed their gravitational axis. Though the aerics of the world were loath to admit it, none of them flew in a traditional sense. They merely fell with grace in different directions.

The moment she returned to twenty-one hundred feet, Amanda hooked a sharp left and made a beeline toward the scimitars.

Mia watched her from the middle of the second car. "Oh shit. Be careful."

She and the others had good reason to worry. For all her skill, Amanda's flight experience was limited to the subterranean confines of the underland, where wind wasn't a factor and the only price of failure was a broken bone or two. Here in the open, even small mistakes were fatal. And bullets still flew faster than her.

Amanda tripled the size of her tempic fists, then plowed through the nearest two scimitars. One of them broke apart on impact. The other one fell in a smoldering death spiral. The remaining eighteen drones began to turn Amanda's way as she circled around for a second attack.

Hannah kept her ravager's machine guns ready, but she didn't dare fire while her sister was in range. "It's not working."

This isn't working, Amanda thought. She didn't have time to keep playing Whack-a-Drone. She needed a new strategy, fast.

She spread her wings and forced them upward at half-strength: a hundred and thirty pounds of countergravity, just enough to keep her hovering. As soon as she fell still, she closed her eyes, bowed her head, and crossed her arms against her chest.

Hannah blinked at her, baffled. "What are you doing?"

"What's she doing?" Eden asked.

Caleb watched her blankly from the cockpit of the Owl. "Is she *praying*?"

Though her faith in God had never been stronger, Amanda wasn't calling on heavenly forces. Quite the opposite. To beat these drones, she had to take a page from the playbook of demons.

She had to think and fight like a Pelletier.

After a moment of concentration, Amanda could feel the scimitars in her thoughts, the twelve-inch liftplates that kept each one aloft. They were all made of aeris—her talent, her specialty. And now that she had them all mapped out, she was ready to get vicious.

The drones lined up Amanda in their gunsights. Zack pressed his hands against the window glass. "Come on, hon. You got this."

With a hearty cry, Amanda thrust her hands outward. Her sleeves tore to shreds as her tempic arms split into eighteen bladed tendrils. They extended through the air in multiple directions before piercing the hull of each scimitar. For a moment, Amanda looked like a madman's delusion: a flying, tentacled creature with eighteen metal pets on leashes.

She yanked her tendrils back with force, tearing crucial bits and circuitry from of the hearts of all her enemies. The guidelights of every drone went dark in unison. Their dead, smoking corpses fell spinning toward the earth.

Zack pumped his fist in the air. "*Yeah!*"

"Yeah!" Mia yelled.

Caleb shook his head in awe. "You go, *shiksa*."

Melissa lowered her head and sighed. As relieved as she was to see her best friend prevail, she feared the consequences of her actions. Seguridad now had video footage of Amanda and her talents, which spies would carry far and wide. By the end of the day, half the governments on Earth would know that chronokinetics were real and the United States had them.

But that was a problem for later.

Hannah caught new movement out of the corner of her eye: a sputtering scimitar, the one Amanda had winged in her first attack. It had somehow recovered its bearing and altitude, enough to line up Amanda in its cracked targeting lens.

"No!" Hannah turned her ravager on the drone and blasted it out of the sky. But her attack was slow by half a second, enough to let the scimitar put a dozen rounds into her sister.

Zack blanched at the sight of his wife's shuddering body. "*Amanda!*"

It was sheer divine luck that only one of the bullets hit flesh. Six of them nailed Amanda in the wings. Three of them struck her tempic arms. One lodged itself into the middle of her chestplate and another one careened off the side of her helmet. The last shot nicked the knee joint of her armor, taking a small amount of skin and muscle with it.

Amanda felt the pain of each impact, a cascading barrage that overloaded her senses and threw her body into shock. Her arms and wings all melted away, sending her willowy form plummeting toward the desert.

"Shit!" Hannah pushed her ravager into hot pursuit, just as Caleb sent the Owl into a nosedive. They'd barely halved the distance between themselves and Amanda when a ten-foot portal opened up in the sky and a small armored figure came leaping out of the surface. She tackled Amanda in midair and clutched her tightly in her arms.

As the last drone died, the radio network returned with a loud static hiss. Melissa switched on her mic. "Caleb, tell me you have her."

"Not yet. Someone's falling with her now. It looks like—"

"Mia," Peter said with a sigh.

"It's Mia," Hannah confirmed. "What the hell is she doing?"

Mia couldn't help but wonder the same thing. When Amanda fell, her thoughts went blank and she jumped through a portal without a hint of a strategy. Now she only had seconds to figure out how to turn her mindless act into a rescue. She couldn't just teleport them to the ground. They already had too much momentum. But maybe—

The Flipper, said a voice in her head.

Yes. Sometime over the past year, Mia had become friendly with the Gothams' young travelers. She practiced with some, fooled around with others, and had lengthy discussions about teleportation with the rest of them. There was a portal trick called the Flipper that, if done correctly, used gravity itself to slow a body's fall. All the travelers talked about it but, because of the sheer risk and difficulty of the maneuver, no one had dared try it. Now Mia was forced to break new ground before the ground broke her and Amanda.

Melissa gripped Peter's arm. "Tell me she has a plan."

"She does."

"She does," Zack echoed. "I think I know what it is."

He pressed the button on his transcom. "Caleb, can you hear me?"

"Copy, Zack."

"You have to shift the Owl to maximum speed. *Your* maximum, not the shuttle's."

"Uh, I can try but—"

"You'll only have one chance to catch Mia and Amanda on the upswing. *Don't* miss them."

"Upswing?"

"You'll see it when it happens! Go!"

Mia ignored all the noise on the radio and concentrated. It was impossible to make a portal, much less two of them, while her body was spinning and she couldn't tell up from down. A hot panic overtook her, paralyzing her, castigating her for the dumb, pointless death she'd just inflicted on herself.

No. Fear and doubt were the flaws of Past Mia, and that girl died last summer. This version—this *woman*—didn't surrender to weakness. More than that, she had unfinished business. As long as Semerjean still lived and breathed, she wasn't going anywhere.

Mia closed her eyes and let the wind on her skin serve as her compass. Once she became vertically oriented, the rest was simple. All she had to do was make the two biggest portals she'd ever made in her life.

Fifty feet below her, a hundred feet above the desert floor, two horizontal discs of light materialized right next to each other, each one the size of a Little League field. She didn't want to worry about wind sway throwing her and Amanda off target, splattering their bodies across the sand or slicing them in half on the edge of a portal.

Mia looked down at the rapidly approaching gateway. "Here we go," she said to Amanda. "Glad you're not awake for this."

Their bodies plunged into the milky white depths of one portal and came shooting out the top of the other. The infamous Flipper, performed flawlessly in desperation by the great Mia Farisi.

Caleb watched the two Silvers through his windshield, hang-jawed. Their terminal fall had become a rocket ascent, but now gravity was their new best friend. It was determined to slow their crazy momentum, providing Caleb with one hell of an opportunity.

"Hang on! I'm coming!"

He swooped the Owl beneath Amanda and Mia and followed them in a straight upward path. He was expanding his temporal field to encase the entire shuttle, an increasingly difficult feat to maintain, like flexing a stubborn muscle. Even with his speed advantage, he only had a few seconds at best to stage a successful rescue. One bad move would break a friend's neck or send her tumbling off the roof of the ship.

Caleb tracked his targets through the ceiling camera, positioning the Owl with tyrannical finesse. Though his faith in God had died with his homeworld, he found himself mouthing the words of an old Talmudic blessing: the *Tefilat HaDerech*, a prayer for safe travels or, in this case, safe landings.

Yehi ratzon milefanecha Ado-nai Eloh-einu veilohei avoseinu . . .

Hannah watched from fifty yards away as the Owl made contact with Mia and Amanda. Caleb had brushed up against them at the very last second of their ascent, and in just the right place. They touched down like feathers on the smooth metal surface of the roof hatch.

"He got them!" Hannah cried. "He's bringing them in."

Peter exhaled with relief. Melissa and Eden traded a weak smile, while Zack took his first breath in seconds.

"Caleb, do you read me?"

"I'm here, Zack. We're here. We're all just . . ." He chuckled maniacally. "Yeah."

"How are they?"

"Amanda's banged up and bleeding, but she's breathing well enough. Mia—" A horrible retching noise filled the background. "I think she's done for the day."

"You're all done," Melissa told him. "Get back to Central as fast as you can."

"Are you sure? I can still help."

"Just get them to the medics," Zack said. "We'll take it from here."

"All right, guys. Be careful."

Zack and Peter watched the Owl depart, while Melissa, Heath, and Eden waited anxiously near the exit. After a long, breathless moment, two Jonathans emerged from the train's seventh car and gave their creator a thumbs-up.

"It's clear," Heath said. "Let's go."

Deep in the back of the old Laredo warehouse, fifteen yards beyond the bustle of government agents, a dark-haired girl in a blue summer dress lay flat on her back across three folding chairs. At thirteen, she was the youngest of all the underland's orphans, the one least likely to talk about the old world. The psychologists assumed that she was repressing her memories but she had no problem with the past. She simply found the future to be a hell of a lot more interesting, with its branching roads and wild chain reactions. Even the smallest of gestures could ripple through time and change millions of destinies at once. She'd once moved the apocalypse a whole day forward just by kissing Heath on the cheek.

Her name was Nadiyah Al-Marri, but everyone here knew her as the young prophet See.

She peered up at the ceiling with busy eyes, her thoughts moving laterally across the strings. She was supposed to be scanning the next few minutes for trouble but her vision had become distorted, fuzzy. That was odd. The immediate future was usually the easiest part to read, like the top line of an eye chart. Either her mind's eye needed a contact lens or something in the future was causing static.

A crystal clear image suddenly emerged through the haze. See sat up with a gasp. "Oh no!"

All the agents in the warehouse stopped to watch the young Copper as she made a mad dash through the bullpen. She skidded to a halt at the edge of Felicity's cubicle.

"I have to talk to Hannah! It's urgent!"

Wide-eyed, Felicity handed the girl her transmitter, then opened an all-channel on the radio. If their augur was panicked, then everyone needed to know.

See paced the floor in a taut little circle, her long curls bouncing with each step. "Hannah, can you hear me? Hannah, come in!"

A tinny voice crackled over the speaker. "I'm here. What's going on?"

"You have to get to the back of the train. Park on the roof. Hurry!"

"Why? What—"

"Just go!"

Hannah floored her aerocycle, grumbling. See was the second-most powerful augur they had, but her communication skills fell somewhere between R2-D2 and Lassie. Sadly, their number one prophet was unavailable to help them, as usual. Last Hannah heard, he was bumbling around the Hawaiian Republic, yet another cryptic waypoint on his messianic solo quest.

See watched Hannah on the telemetry screen as her aerocycle landed on the roof of the tail car. "Okay, now get off the bike and move to the back of the train."

"Sweetie, are you absolutely—"

"Yes, I'm sure! Hurry!"

As Hannah ran across the roof, she caught a strange flash on the inside of her visor, a fat cluster of radar blips that only appeared for half a second. "Wait. Is that—"

"Yeah." Felicity saw the same thing on her computer and knew exactly what it meant. "Speed fleet. Brace yourself."

A squadron of aercraft suddenly de-shifted behind the trendelaire—sixteen vessels of identical build, all huddled together in a wall formation. Hannah had expected to see jet fighters under the circumstances, but these bulky brown warships were something else entirely. They looked less like planes and more like—

"—tanks," Hannah said. "They have flying tanks."

The DS-10s were unique to Central America, a modern spin on an old army classic. While the chassis were all salvaged from decommissioned ground tanks, the weapons, wheels, and interiors had been thoroughly refashioned for twenty-first-century combat. Its girded aeric liftplates allowed the DS-10 to fight in virtually any environment—on land, on sea, up in the sky, even deep underwater. The "DS" stood for *donde sea*, the Spanish term for "anywhere."

Hannah didn't have to wonder if these flying metal war beasts, these Peter Panzers, had people inside them. Each one looked big enough to hold a pilot and two gunners.

"Just stay where you are," Felicity told her. "We'll take care of them."

Twenty feet behind Felicity, in a four-by-four cluster of temporally shifted cubicles, Integrity agents strapped on their remote pilot helmets and synched up with their stormbirds.

Felicity wasn't encouraged by See's expression: a prescient dread, as if sixteen geese were about to take on a herd of rhinos. "Our drones are weaker," Felicity admitted. "But they can fry all the tanks' electrical systems if they get close enough."

See shook her head with a gloomy expression. "They won't."

Hannah had a front-row view of the carnage as computer-guided missiles took out half the stormbirds in seconds. Another three were obliterated by the DS-10s' plasma cannons. Their powdered remains fell like snow over the desert.

Melissa stopped at the front of the train's eighth car and gripped Peter's arm. "Escape door. Now."

"We can't give up. We're almost there."

"Just do what I say."

He grudgingly opened a portal to Laredo. Melissa hailed Hannah on the radio. "Listen to me. When the last drone falls, this train will be Seguridad's next target. I know how they operate. They'd sooner destroy their precious assets than let another country have them. Do you understand what I'm saying?"

Two more stormbirds succumbed to guided missiles. Hannah thanked her stars that she'd listened to See. If she'd been on her ravager when the big tanks came, they would have blown her out of the sky.

"It's all right," she told Melissa. "I can stop them."

"You better be sure because there's no one left to catch you if you fall."

"I know."

"And if you miss even one of those—"

"Melissa, I *got* this."

"That's all I needed to hear." Melissa motioned to Peter, who waved the portal shut. "Let's keep moving."

Heath pressed his head against the window in a futile attempt to watch the battle.

"She'll be okay," Zack assured him.

"How do you know?"

"Come on. It's Hannah. When has she ever lost a fight?"

Heath moved away from the window, grim-faced. "Everyone dies eventually."

Zack ushered him forward, sighing. The boy had made huge strides since Jonathan's passing, but his thoughts still wallowed in a pitch-black cloud of fatalism. Now that Hannah had become his emotional lifeline, he was all but convinced that she was the next one to fall.

The final stormbird almost succeeded in reaching a DS-10, but was stopped at the last second by an explosive charge. As the booming noise faded and the last drone fragments fell out of view, Hannah faced the tanks alone from the trendelaire. She could practically feel the hard stares of her adversaries, every pilot and weaponeer.

That's right, she thought. *You don't know what to make of me. But you saw what my sister did to your drones and now you're kind of nervous.*

Hannah clenched her fists, her fingers crackling with raw temporic energy. *You should be.*

She thrust her arms at the fleet of tanks just as they fired their missiles.

There had once been a time, not that long ago, when Hannah shared the same power as Caleb: a timebending swifter, able to dash around all obstacles in a quick and windy blur.

But then in May of last year, while saving a friend from a horrible fate, she'd pushed her power past its limit and caused permanent damage to her brain. Now she couldn't accelerate herself without suffering one consequence or another—a seizure, a blackout, a blinding headache, or worse. The Integrity doctors warned her that her next speed run could kill her. So she retired her talent and let mechanical shifters handle all her velocity needs.

But she could still bend the clock the other way, an extreme deceleration that made even the fastest objects move like garden slugs. Her slowtime field could be cast onto any target, be it a single human being or a fleet of enemy warships.

The skill was entirely unique to Hannah. And it didn't hurt one bit.

She formed an invisible cloud of temporis in the air, freezing every DS-10 in place and slowing all their missiles to a crawl.

See followed the action through Hannah's helmet camera. "She did it! She got them!"

Felicity double-checked the monitor, just to confirm that the whole fleet was in stasis. "Wow. Sixteen tanks in a big bowl of time soup. That's a new one for my diary."

Hannah lifted her visor and took a deep, relieved breath. "Mine too."

"You all right?" Peter asked her through the radio. "The strain—"

"No strain. I'm fine. There's just one problem."

"The missiles," Felicity guessed.

"The missiles," Hannah said. "I can slow them down but I can't stop them."

Melissa traded a nervous look with Zack. "How much time can you buy us?"

"Four minutes," Hannah estimated. "Five, tops."

Eden jerked a thumb over her shoulder. "I can run back to the engine room. Move us out of the way."

Peter shook his head. "If those missiles are target-locked—"

"They are," said Melissa. "There's no evading them. We'll just have to—"

"Look out!" Heath shouted.

He'd been the only one to notice the anomaly behind Melissa, a patch of blurred, distorted air in the vague shape of a human. Melissa barely had a chance to turn her head before the invisible stalker rammed a tempic sword through her back. The blade burst out through the armor plating on her stomach, then retracted into its creator's hand.

"No!" Heath sicced his Jonathans on the assailant, but none of them responded to his command. The minions stood like white wax statues, all paralyzed by unseen forces.

See watched from Laredo with wide brown eyes. The static in her foresight had vanished in an instant, revealing everything that had been hidden from her. She grabbed the transmitter with both hands. "Zack, look out! She's coming for you next!"

The more the assassin moved, the more Zack could see her outline. She stepped over Melissa's crumpled frame, then lunged toward Zack in a vaporous haze.

"Shit." He raised his hand for a temporal attack but stopped himself at the last second. In these close quarters, with his loose energy, he was at risk of hurting a friend. And if that friend just happened to be Peter, then they were all as good as dead. His portals were their last and only hope of getting off the train alive.

It was the peak of irony, or perhaps just cruelty, that the assassin used the exact same attack that Zack was suppressing: a concentrated dose of temporis, focused squarely in the vicinity of Zack's right hand.

He screamed in pain as his fingers aged several weeks ahead of him—an unprecedented agony, like having his flesh stripped off with hooks. He fell to the floor in a half-conscious stupor, his hand rotted black, his body a jumble of screaming cross-signals.

"Stop!" Eden yelled, for lack of a better plan. Like Zack, she couldn't unleash her power in here without subjecting a teammate to friendly fire . . . or friendly ice. "Who *are* you?"

The assassin relinquished her cloaking field, revealing a slim young woman in a knightly suit of armor. The plating was made of cloudy green stone, like jade or dyed marble, but the pieces all connected together seamlessly. The joints bent and flexed as easily as cloth.

Eden struggled to process the creature in front of her. "I'll ask again—"

The assassin's helmet split open and folded in on itself, until it was nothing but a strip on the back of her head. The woman behind the armor was ghastly to look at. Her skin was a bloodless shade of white, with dark, inky veins that stained her neck and temples. Small square protrusions littered her forehead, as if someone had planted a crop of subdermal devices. Even more unnerving was the color of her eyes, a green so bright and unnaturally vibrant that they practically glowed in daytime.

She's not with the Mexicans, Eden thought to herself. *She's barely even human.*

Two cars down and ten feet above them, Hannah tried to make sense of the din in her earpiece. "Felicity, what's going on in there?"

Felicity blanched at the view from Eden's camera. "It's under control," she lied. "You just focus on those tanks."

The assassin turned her emerald eyes onto Peter, then spoke in a voice flecked with odd and hollow distortions. "I have a message."

"So do I," said Peter, as he pulled the trigger on his .38.

He'd been hiding the pistol behind his back, its barrel aimed at a four-inch portal. The bullet came down through a spatial breach in the ceiling and struck the assassin on the dead top center of her skull.

The woman turned to Peter in round-eyed shock before her body tumbled forward in a heap. But instead of crashing against the textile carpet, she fell straight through it like a ghost. Her body passed out of view, leaving nothing behind but a spatter of blood.

Heath looked to Peter, slack-jawed. "You killed her."

"Had to. We don't have time for that gobshite."

He opened a portal to Central and hailed them on the radio. "Medics, come quick. We have two people here in bad condition."

He turned to Eden. "You and Heath keep going. I'll catch up."

"What, just us?"

"That boy is an army all by himself. Go!"

Eden and Heath moved on with the Jonathans just as the first two medics arrived through the portal. They lowered their stretcher at Melissa's side.

"Zack first," she said with a croaking rasp. "Hurry."

"He doesn't look as bad."

"Look again," said Peter. "He's been rifted."

The mention of the word jolted Hannah's concentration, enough to let the missiles lurch forward several yards.

"Oh no. Peter, how bad is it?"

"Hannah—"

"He's my brother-in-law! Just tell me!"

There were few injuries more dire than a temporal rift wound, when a body was forced into two different speeds. The process unleashed pure hell in the bloodstream, a host of new problems from ruptures, to clots, to life-threatening embolisms. Since temporal injuries were functionally irreversible, the only way to treat a rift victim was to put them in a hyperbaric oxygen chamber and pray the bubbles in their blood didn't kill them. Even with prompt medical care, Zack only had a ten percent chance of surviving the next five minutes.

Peter watched the medics as they ferried Zack back to Central. "If all goes well, he'll only lose the hand," he told Hannah.

"When will we know?"

"Darling—"

"Don't."

"There are folks right here who'll die a lot sooner if you don't hold those missiles."

The thought wasn't lost on Eden as she hurried her way through the second-to-last train car. She didn't want to die at twenty-five, and certainly not here in the skies of *Otroméxico.* But if the universe had taught her anything these past two years, it was that it didn't give a shit what she wanted. It didn't owe her a long life or a happy ending or a single damn answer to the mysteries it posed. *We do as we do*, the fickle gods insisted. *Deal with it.*

Heath followed her down the aisle, his hands clenched at his sides. "This is it."

"What?"

"The last door," Heath said. "It's locked."

Eden looked ahead to the end of the car, where an octet of Jonathans waited impatiently by the exit hatch. Unlike the sliding metal doors of the other coaches, this one was thick and electronically sealed.

"Call your men back," Eden said to Heath. "It's about to get real cold."

The nearest missiles were now fifty feet from the trendelaire, close enough for Hannah to see the lettering on the warheads. She tried to bend the clock further in a favorable direction but her temporal bubble had become too large to bully. It resisted her at every turn, threatening to burst right open if she kept pushing it.

"Speed it up," she told Heath and Eden. "We're almost out of time."

"Working!" Eden yelled. It took twenty-two seconds to freeze the door to a brittle state, then another sixteen for the Jonathans to smash it to pieces. As the last chunk fell, Eden stepped through the ice mist and into the final cabin.

What if the intel was bad? she wondered. *What if we went through all this shit for nothing?*

But then she saw four bunk beds through the haze. A wardrobe. A lumivision. A kitchenette. Two couches. And in the center of it all stood the object of the mission: eight young women of Latin American descent, dressed in white jumpsuits and clustered together defensively. From the looks of things, the train car had been their prison for weeks.

Eden studied the arm of the captive in front, the thick white bangle that hung around her wrist. Though the material looked like gleaming white stone, it had the same size, shape, and build as the old iron bracelet that Eden used to wear. Any doubt about the intel was long gone. These were the people they'd come to find.

The Pearls of Guadalajara.

Eden raised her hands in peaceful accord and carefully approached the new orphans. "It's okay," she told them in Spanish. "We're from your world."

The nearest missile was twenty feet from Hannah when she finally broke a sweat. "Peter . . ."

"I know. I know. We're hurrying."

He'd caught up with his teammates thirty seconds ago and opened a portal on the wall. Despite the looming deadline, Eden had a hard time convincing the prisoners to step into the breach. They studied it with matching looks of terror, as if it led straight to an even worse hell.

"It's all right," Eden assured them. "It's perfectly safe. Look!"

She motioned for Heath to cross through the portal but he stubbornly shook his head. "I'm not leaving without Hannah."

"Oh, for Christ's sake . . ."

Peter carried him through the gateway and then came back alone. He glared at Eden. "Tell them the train's about to explode!"

"*El tren está—*"

"We *heard* him," said the oldest-looking captive, a long-haired brunette of striking beauty. "But we've been fooled more than once. Why should we trust you?"

Eden was thrown by her strong Cuban accent. She'd assumed all the Pearls were Mexican.

She relinquished her sidearm to the woman. "Take it. If you don't like what you see on the other side of that portal, you can shoot me in the face. Just *go*!"

The Cuban examined the gun in tense dilemma before addressing her people in Spanish. "They're really nervous. I don't think they're lying about the train."

Peter did a double-take at the woman's thick bracelet, a much different breed than the others. It looked less like pearl and more like metal. And not just *any* metal. Silver.

"What's your name?" he asked her.

"Ofelia."

"Ofelia, we went through six kinds of hell to find you. Some of us got hurt along the way. If we don't get you off this train, then you'll be dead, I'll be dead, and my friends will have suffered for nothing. We need to leave now. I'm begging you."

Ofelia nodded anxiously, then looked to her fellow prisoners. "Okay. We're going."

She steeled herself with a deep breath, then charged into the portal. One by one, the other prisoners followed.

Peter waved them through the gateway. "Come on. Come on. Hurry."

"How's it going down there?" Hannah asked him over the radio.

"All good. I'm coming for you next."

"How? You can't see where I am and you can't jump blind."

"I've got a camera drone somewhere," said Peter. "I just need—"

"There's no *time.* I'll just use the ravager."

Peter scoffed at the idea. "That's a surefire way to die."

"The bike goes fast."

"But *you* don't," he reminded her. "Not like you used to."

"Peter, if you don't trust me after everything we've been through—"

"Of *course* I trust you."

"Then trust me to get to that bike."

The last of the Pearls escaped to Laredo. Peter swapped a heavy look with Eden, then motioned for her to leave.

"You better be right," he told Hannah as he followed Eden through the portal. "Godspeed."

Hannah snorted bleakly. It wasn't God's speed she needed. The missiles were almost upon the train. The ravager was twenty feet in the other direction and would take at least four seconds to start up. But if she managed to shift without seizing or fainting—

Don't do it, said a ghostly voice in her head. *You'll die.*

Hannah couldn't tell if he was speaking through her earpiece or her own crazy thoughts. But she had no trouble recognizing his soft, drowsy cadence.

"Theo? How—"

Forget the bike, he insisted. *If you want to live, you only have one option.*

"But—"

Jump, Hannah. Right now.

"There's no one left to catch me."

Yes there is. Do it!

Hannah threw up her hands, flummoxed. She didn't know where he was or how he was talking to her, but if anyone had earned her trust, it was the mighty Theo Maranan.

She closed her eyes and took a running leap off the side of the train.

Hannah was fifty yards beneath the floor of the tail car when her time bubble popped and twenty-one missiles struck the trendelaire at full speed. She only managed to catch a glimpse of the carnage, a popcorn string of conflagrations that enveloped every passenger coach.

By the time the flare-ups ended, only the engine car remained intact. It rocked back and forth in a frantic struggle between its antigravity system and the thirty-one tons of skeletal wreckage that pulled down on its chassis. After a sputtering moment, the liftplates gave out and the last remains of the trendelaire fell toward earth in a vertical line.

Well, shit, thought Hannah as she tumbled through the sky. What if she had fallen for a mean and simple trick? Between the Pelletiers, Ioni, and the psychotic Evan Rander, there was no shortage of people who could spoof Theo's voice. But no, the Pelletiers still needed her to make a baby for them. Evan wouldn't kill her without gloating about it. And Ioni? She may have been strange and occasionally shifty, but she'd been nothing but nice to Hannah. She gave her a hell of a pep talk nearly two years ago, on one of Hannah's worst days on the new world.

There are some events in life that are so reliable, we don't bother predicting them, Ioni had told her. *The sunrise. The full moon. The rainbow after a storm. These are all things that can't be stopped by mere mortals. You know what the augurs call them?*

Hannah could only shake her head. That was when Ioni held her hands and breathed a smiling whisper into her ear.

Givens.

A cool white force suddenly overtook Hannah. The tempis enveloped her body so delicately that she barely even felt it until it stopped her short, six hundred feet above the ground.

Even with an armored chest, the inertial impact squeezed half the air out of Hannah's lungs and made her black out. When she came to, she was rising faceup through the air, her view of the sun eclipsed by a small, oddly shaped aercraft. The rear hatch was open and a woman leaned out the back. Hannah could recognize her just by her lithe silhouette.

You're kidding me.

Amanda pulled her sister into the Owl and gently placed her in the back seat. "You okay?" she asked. "Is anything broken?"

Hannah struggled to speak through winded breaths. "I thought . . . I thought you guys . . ."

Amanda closed the hatch and clutched her shoulders. "It's okay. Just breathe."

"I thought you guys left."

"We came back," Caleb said from the pilot's seat. He jerked his head at Amanda and Mia. "Your sisters insisted."

Hannah slumped in her chair, exhausted. "Of course they did."

As the DS-10s made a collective dive for the shuttle, Mia opened a new portal in the sky. The Owl disappeared through the twisting folds of space, out of the smoke and haze of northern Mexico, and into the skies of Altamerica.

TWO

On March 11, 1913, one week into his third term as president of the United States, Theodore Roosevelt took a group of local journalists on a walking tour of the new Manhattan. It had been five months and six days since a mysterious conflagration razed half the island to the ground. There was little to see below 96th Street but endless fields of blackened soil, a rustic grid of half-paved roads, and flag-marked construction sites.

Roosevelt motioned to the many labor crews, urging the press to imagine, just *imagine*, the splendorous city that would rise from the ashes. "It'll be the marvel of the modern world," he proclaimed. "The greatest comeback in the history of man."

"But, sir," said a rumpled old columnist from the *Evening Journal*. "How can you say with certainty that there won't be another Cataclysm?"

Indeed, Roosevelt had won the 1912 election by promising what Woodrow Wilson wouldn't: an inviolable nation, impervious to Cataclysms and other biblical acts of terror.

It wasn't until the week after his inauguration, while standing among the seedlings of the new Union Square, that he formally revealed the keystone of his plan to keep America safe.

He called it the National Integrity Commission, an elite new intelligence service comprising the country's best law enforcers and scientists. Armed with an unlimited budget and freed from constitutional constraints, the agency would have carte blanche to protect the United States from foreign threats, be it a hostile nation or an otherworldly menace. In addition to keeping a vigilant eye on America's hidden enemies, Integrity would unravel the mystery of the Cataclysm and expose every twisted soul behind the atrocity.

"Even if the culprit is God himself, our agents will find him and bring him to justice," Roosevelt promised the reporters.

But for all of Integrity's skill and resources, its people proved powerless to solve a crime of such magnitude, an attack that went so far beyond the limits of modern knowledge that it might as well have been magic.

Stuck for clues and under hard pressure from Congress, Integrity began rounding up anyone who looked even remotely suspicious: immigrants, radicals, dark-skinned idlers, all the scapegoats and boogeymen of the fractured American psyche. Thousands of innocent men and boys were hauled away to black-site interrogation centers, where they were beaten and starved without a shred of legal recourse.

By the time Roosevelt died in 1922, the agency he'd created had become the opposite of what he'd intended it to be: a symbol of fear and unchecked corruption, a scourge among the people it was sworn to protect. Even politicians were afraid to speak out against Integrity for fear of becoming its next "person of interest."

In August 1931, after nationwide riots broke out in protest of government abuses, President John Nance Garner fired ninety percent of Integrity's staff and refashioned the agency into an international spy ring. Its new directive: to keep a close watch on major foreign governments while subtly advancing American interests abroad. The operatives didn't have to be ethical in their pursuits. They just had to be quiet.

Within three years, Integrity ceased all activity inside the United States, at least as far as the public knew. A secret domestic unit continued to hunt for the perpetrators of the Cataclysm, their eyes squarely fixed on America's supernatural fringe. Every storefront psychic, every telekinetic spoonbender, every self-proclaimed Martian was investigated. In these wild times, any one of those nutters could be real. And any real freak had the potential to cause damage.

In August 1971, a man named Alexander Wingo sparked a whole new breed of paranormal legend when he published an exposé about a secret American society of superpeople. These timebending metahumans—or *Gothams*, as Wingo dubbed them—had been genetically altered by the Cataclysm and could break the laws of nature in a dozen different ways. Yet instead of seeking fame with their incredible talents, they lived a clandestine life in Quarter Hill, New York, eighteen miles north of Manhattan. By Wingo's guess, the Gothams had been infesting the town since the late 1930s, passing themselves off as mundane suburbanites while breeding new and more powerful mutants.

Though the majority of the public dismissed Wingo as a crackpot, Integrity placed undercover operatives in every pocket of Quarter Hill society, ingratiating themselves among the longtime locals while rummaging through their safes and drawers. Aside from a few closet Wiccans and a higher than average number of foot fetishists, the agents found nothing out of the ordinary. They could only conclude, after twelve months of fruitless effort, that these so-called Gothams were as real as wood elves.

It wasn't until recent times, after the orphans and Pelletiers began wreaking supernatural havoc across the nation, that Integrity finally learned what Alexander Wingo had been shouting all along: there were timebenders living in the suburbs of New York, and they were a hell of a lot smarter than anyone realized. Not long after Wingo exposed their secret existence, the Gothams found a clever new way to avoid public scrutiny, a one-of-a-kind hideout buried eight hundred feet below the basements of Quarter Hill.

They called it the underland, and it was a marvel: twenty-two million cubic feet of space, with sixteen streets, fifty-four buildings, an artificial sky, and all the privacy the Gothams could ever want. On the surface, they suppressed every hint of their special abilities. But down in the underland, beyond all prying eyes, they could spread their wings, cast their portals, twist the fabric of time without any fear of exposure. It was the only place on Earth where they could truly be themselves, and it served them well for a whole generation.

But then in May of last year, on the clever hunch of a senior agent, Integrity performed a deep radar scan of the Quarter Hill subterrain and discovered the clan's greatest secret: the town beneath the town. The agency had already seen enough evidence of the Gothams in action to consider them a national threat. Suddenly they knew exactly where to find them.

On June 12, a day that would become known as Red Sunday to some, Integrity burrowed into the underland and staged a takedown of the Gothams. Thanks to the careful planning of the siege leader, Oren Gingold, two hundred and fifty soldiers managed to subdue eleven hundred chronokinetics on their own territory, without spilling a drop of blood.

But then things went wrong, *very* wrong, and war broke out beneath the streets of Quarter Hill. By the time the smoke cleared, more than a hundred Gothams lay dead in the village, along with half of Integrity's invasion force. Gingold himself had been the very first to fall.

The incident created a quandary for both the Gothams and Integrity. Neither side wanted a repeat battle, yet neither one could live under the continuing threat of the other. Thankfully, Cedric Cain, Integrity's new director, a man installed that day by the president of the United States, proposed a fair compromise: a conditional alliance that allowed the Gothams to live freely while providing full access to the U.S. government.

"Work with us and we'll work with you," Cain promised the Gothams. "Tell us your secrets and we'll help you keep them."

Now, thirteen months and eight days after the events of Red Sunday, the Gothams still struggled to adjust to the arrangement. Integrity had changed every facet of life in the underland, from the armored thugs who guarded all the entrances to the scientists who monitored every chronokinetic in action. Strangers with top-clearance security badges came in and out of the village at all hours, prying into the Gothams' most intimate business while treating them all like circus seals. *"Show me that thing you do with your tempis." "Let's see how fast you can run to that lamppost." "Come on. Just one more lumis trick."*

Even worse were the physical changes that Integrity had inflicted upon the village. The old gymnasium was gone, replaced by a three-story ziggurat that served as the agency's field office. The banquet hall had been converted into a bunkhouse for federal goons and eggheads. And God only knew what Integrity was doing with the augurs' former guildhall. Everything but the front door had been sealed up in tempis. No one was allowed inside except top-ranking government officials and a few select orphans and Gothams.

But there was one new building that no one complained about: the government-run health care clinic that replaced the old vivery. For four generations, the Gothams had to rely on painkillers and folk remedies for their power-related ailments, as there were scant few doctors on the surface they could trust. Now, thanks to Integrity, the clan had access to some of the world's top specialists. The clinic had already saved the lives of two dozen timebenders whose special ability had turned on them, including Hannah Given. If a neurologist hadn't gauged the full extent of her brain damage, she would have kept on swifting until it killed her.

At midnight on Friday, eleven hours after the Pearls of Guadalajara were rescued from the Mexican government, the waiting room of the clinic was jam-packed with orphans: seven Platinums, six Irons, and the whole Copper septet. They were all relative latecomers to the underland, the ones who'd arrived in the aftermath of Red Sunday. Many of them had nearly fled during those tense early days, when frictions between the Gothams and Integrity threatened to explode into a second war. But two people above all others had convinced the orphans to stay: Melissa Masaad, their government liaison and ever-dependable den mother; and Zack Trillinger, their fellow alien, who always had a way of making bad situations seem manageable.

Now that very same pair lay unconscious in the emergency room, surrounded by doctors and their closest companions. None of the orphans could rest until they knew for sure that Melissa and Zack would be okay. Unfortunately, it had been sixty-eight minutes since the last update. The lack of news was starting to become ominous.

The waiting room fell into an anxious hush as Felicity Yu emerged from the ER, still dressed in the same orange shirtdress that she'd worn to Laredo. By now the orphans had become used to her radiant outfits, a contrast to the dull gray blazers and blouses of the other Integrity agents. Felicity figured she might as well wear what she wanted to wear, as people were going to stare at her anyway. It wasn't often they laid eyes on a six-foot-one Korean woman, one who strayed from the bounds of their narrow gender concepts.

But these orphans had come from a more progressive Earth, which Felicity found refreshing. Half of them had had at least one transgender friend or relative. Even the few that seemed uncomfortable around her had been decent enough to keep their thoughts to themselves.

Felicity looked around at the twenty clustered timebenders. "Where's Eden?"

"With her boyfriend," replied a Platinum, a freckled young lumic named Sarah Brehm. "She told us to call her as soon as there's news."

"There's news," Felicity said. "Melissa's awake and she's finally stable. The doctors say she's out of the storm."

The orphans eyed her warily, as if she was bracing them for bad news.

"No update on Zack," Felicity admitted. "He's been in surgery for the last three hours, so—"

"What kind of surgery?" asked a man in the back.

Felicity had to lean to the side to see Ben Hopkins crouching in the corner, accompanied, as ever, by his White Iron buddies. At thirty-two, Ben was the oldest of the orphans and the only one built like a bona fide superhero. Though he was consistently polite in his folksy Texan way—all *yes, ma'ams* and *no, sirs*—he had a palpable mistrust for the people he considered different from him, even the ones from his own world. That made him a particular headache for his government handlers, half of whom were women of color.

Felicity tossed him a cool nod. Though he had never been openly hostile to her, he wore the same evincible look of distaste that made her stop video-calling her father.

"The rifting gave him blood clots in a number of veins and arteries," Felicity explained. "The surgeons have to fix each one or Zack's in big trouble."

"What about his hand?" asked Cesar Osorio, one of Eden's Brown Irons. "Last we heard, they were talking about—"

"It's gone," Felicity said. "The doctors had no choice. There was too much dead tissue."

The orphans cursed among themselves, for reasons Felicity could understand. Though Zack was loath to admit it, he'd become something of a role model to his people, a shining example of resilience. He threw around old pop culture references without a hint of morbidity, as if the memories of his world made him stronger, not sadder. And he treated the looming apocalypse with an enviable amount of detachment. To hear Zack say it, it simply was what it was. If they saved the world, great. If not, ¯_(ツ)_/¯.

Most impressive of all, he made punchlines out of the Pelletiers, though few had suffered more at their hands. To be near Zack was to be reminded every day that you didn't have to surrender to the madness of the universe. You could still be a semblance of the person you were.

Except now the universe had gone and done it: claimed the drawing hand of a born cartoonist, an especially cruel fate for Zack, as if an assassin had been sent to murder his spirit. It didn't take a genius to figure out who'd hired her.

"Pelletiers," an orphan said through a thick Creole accent. "This is their devilry."

Everyone looked to the left side of the room, where a muscular woman with a faded buzz cut sat nestled among her Coppers. Johanne Sylvain had been an Olympic athlete on her native Earth, the first female swimmer to ever compete for Haiti. Then everything changed on a cold July morning and she found herself lost in another world's Seattle, the lone adult in a group full of teenagers. Why the Pelletiers chose her for that particular bunch, she had no idea. She'd never had any younger siblings. Never so much as babysat.

But she nurtured the young ones all the same—strengthened them, gave them all new names and purpose. Even now under the aegis of the federal government, the kids still took their every cue from her. She was the mother of the Coppers, and she would gladly let this whole world die if it saved the lives of her children.

Mother looked around at the other orphans, See's sleeping body still cradled in her lap. "That woman who attacked Zack and Melissa, the one with green armor. She wasn't with the Mexicans. Is there any doubt who she works for?"

The room fell into loud, nervous chatter. Felicity waited patiently for it to subside. Both she and Melissa had learned not to stop Mother when she was on a tear. She was a passionate woman, loyal only to her children, and the most dangerous orphan alive. Her spherical portals could swallow whole buildings and teleport them into the sea. Worse, the scientists feared that she had yet to reach the limits of her potential. For all they knew, she could destroy half a city. Integrity had been created nearly a century ago to stop people just like her.

As the cross talk showed no signs of fading, Felicity raised her hands. "Guys, *guys*, listen to me. Amanda and the rest of Zack's people are sitting in the next room. They're even more stressed than you. The last thing they need is a commotion in here. Please?"

The orphans quieted down. Mother nodded obligingly. "Forgive us. We're all on edge."

"And for good reason," Felicity said. "But there won't be any news until morning. So please, go home. Get some rest. If anything changes, I'll call you."

Grudgingly, the orphans rose to their feet and filed for the exit. Only Ben Hopkins went the other way. He weaved a path through the shambling exodus until he reached Felicity.

"You know I rarely agree with Mother, but she's right. If there are a new bunch of Pelletiers running around, we got problems."

Felicity tried to pat his arm, but he moved away like she was toxic. The skin of her face turned a hot shade of red and she swallowed the urge to scream at him. *You're a tempic transphobe from another world and you think* I'm *the freak?*

Instead, she forced a cordial smile. "Look, I'm not saying you're wrong. I'm just saying let's consider all the evidence and counterevidence before we—"

"*Counter*evidence?"

"You didn't see the woman who hurt Zack. I did. I watched her right on camera and I saw her do something that no Pelletier would ever do."

"Yeah?" Ben asked. "What's that?"

Felicity matched his cold, hard expression. "She died."

By Saturday morning, the doctors had become optimistic about Zack's chances. His vital signs were improving by the hour and his skin had turned a healthier shade of pale. At noon, he was officially declared stable and moved to a private room.

The nurses had pumped so many painkillers into him that he woke up feeling like a vaporous presence, a man-shaped cloud drifting slowly above the bed. Integrity agents wasted no time debriefing him, talking endlessly about things he wasn't even remotely ready to process. It wasn't until Amanda entered the room that his eyes popped open and his mind snapped awake. Last thing he remembered, she was getting riddled with bullets in the skies of northern Mexico. Yet there she was in all her glory, a gorgeous sight in her white blouse and denim shorts. He might have taken her for an apparition if he hadn't noticed her new knee brace.

Zack reached out to touch her, only to find exactly what the government handlers had been nattering about: a bandage-wrapped stump at the end of his right arm.

He surveyed the space where his hand used to be. "Oh."

By midafternoon, he was all stocked up on kindness and sympathy. Everyone who came to see him, from the sisters of his heart to the Gothams he could barely stand, seemed to be working off the same script. *Look, you'll be fine. The prosthetics here are amazing. You've seen what Eden can do with her hands. You'll barely notice the difference.*

It was only his latest visitor, a broody young Gotham named Mercurial Lee, who had the nerve to be glib about his condition.

"Art-wise, you're fucked."

Zack smiled wanly. Mercy had never been one to temper her words, especially around him. In their sixteen months of mutual acquaintance, their lives had become chaotically intertwined, a spiraling path that took them from enemies to friends to lovers to ex-lovers.

Then, just when they thought they could settle into camaraderie, the Pelletiers had forced them into a twisted arrangement, one that brought them back to the bedroom for the purpose of conceiving a child.

That had been an awful time for Zack and Mercy, to say nothing of Amanda and Peter, who'd been roped into the same accord. Luckily, the situation had become a lot less tangled. Semerjean had inexplicably released Zack and Amanda from their commitment, while Mercy had found love with an entirely different orphan.

Caleb stood behind her chair, his large hands clamped around her shoulders. "Come on, hon. His art's not fucked. Once he gets his new hand—"

"Doesn't matter," said Mercy. "He won't be able to feel the pencil, and he needs that touch if he wants to draw anything worth a damn."

Caleb sighed at Zack. "Don't mind her. She spent half the morning puking."

"Yeah, I'm in a shit mood," Mercy said with a pout. "Doesn't mean I'm wrong."

"You're not wrong," Zack admitted. He held up his good arm. "I'll have to draw with Lefty here, which I figure will take some adjustment."

"Some?" Mercy scoffed. "It'll take years to get back to your old skill level. Years you don't have."

"Okay," said Caleb. "I think he's had enough sunshine from you."

On the contrary, Zack preferred her brutal honesty over the cheesy platitudes he'd been getting *ad nauseam*. And if anyone had earned the right to paint the whole world black, it was Mercy. She was five months pregnant with Caleb's child, a Gotham/orphan hybrid who was destined to die on a lab table. For Mercy, the only thing worse than being a broodmare for the Pelletiers was being their enemy. They'd made it very clear what would happen to her and her family if she didn't do what they wanted.

Mercy shook a finger at Zack. "Okay, fine. You want sunshine? Think of Rebel."

"That's not usually where I go for happy thoughts."

"Me neither," said Mercy. "But he had a metal hand like the one you're getting. And he smacked the shit out of Esis with it."

Zack nodded amenably. "And nearly blew up Semerjean."

"Right. See? There's your upside. Think of all the new ways you can hurt those fuckers."

Zack heard the sound of his wife's uneven footsteps. He gestured at the door. "It's okay. I get all the inspiration I need from that one."

Amanda limped into the room with two covered trays of food. As she laid out the plates and drinks on the side table, she tossed Mercy a cynical look. "He's already said it six times."

"Said what?"

"'How can I complain about one missing hand when my wife lost both her arms?'"

"It's true," said Zack.

"I took days to cry about it," Amanda reminded him. "You barely gave yourself an hour."

Zack looked away with distant gloom. "Your situation was different."

"*Much* different," Mercy stressed.

"Doesn't matter." Amanda weaved her way around Zack's IV tubes and sat hip-to-hip with him on the bed. "We have plenty of food here," she told Caleb and Mercy. "Help yourself."

Mercy clumsily rose from her chair, her right hand pressed against her baby bump. "Can't. Got an appointment down the hall with Agent Dumbass."

"That's *Doctor* Agent Dumbass," Caleb joked.

"He keeps telling me to do all these things for the baby, as if I care. As if I'm even gonna *meet* the kid."

Amanda sighed despondently. "Hon . . ."

"I'm fine," Mercy insisted.

"I'm here for you whenever you need me. You know that."

Mercy looked away, her voice barely a whisper. "Of course I do."

Even in his opioid haze, Zack could hear the undertones in both women's voices, a guilt from Amanda and a resentment from Mercy. The two of them had been sisters of the same cruel burden, but only one of them had broken free.

Amanda watched Mercy as she disappeared around the corner. "I hate this."

"She's strong," Zack said. "She'll manage."

"I'm more worried about you." Amanda touched the bandage along the stump of Zack's arm. "If we still had those discs—"

"Sweetheart, don't."

In June of last year, at the end of Red Sunday, the Pelletiers came to the underland to make an ill-fated deal with the survivors. As a gesture of good faith, Esis presented Amanda with a hundred pieces of healing technology from her era, each one able to perform a single medical miracle, from curing a case of Alzheimer's to healing a rifted limb.

Unfortunately, Amanda had only managed to use four of the devices before she had her big fight with Esis. As if removing Amanda's arms wasn't enough, Esis had remotely destroyed the healing discs as a petty "fuck you" to the woman who broke her nose. Now the machines were just powder in the Integrity science lab, sixteen pounds of pure silver sand.

"They must be pissed at us again," Amanda said. "Why else would they send that creature?"

Zack shrugged. "I don't know. If they didn't want us finding the Pearls—"

"—they would have put up more of a fight," Amanda said. "This has to be about something else. Something in the future."

"Hey, you know what would be nice?"

Amanda nodded her head with a feeble half-grin. "Not talking about the Pelletiers."

"I'm sorry. I just can't today."

"You don't have to apologize, and you don't have to explain."

Amanda fiddled with the band of her wedding ring, a gold and diamond loop that hung limp at the end of her necklace. The unique nature of her hands made it impossible to wear rings the traditional way. The tempis was always changing shape, shifting at will to become hammers or spatulas or whatever else she needed at the moment. The only thing she couldn't change about them was their temperature, always fifty-five degrees Fahrenheit, like a brisk autumn day. There were times she felt like she was touching Zack with a corpse's fingers. But he never complained about it. Not once.

She saw Zack studying her mechanical knee brace, her newest and least welcome accessory. Her anterior cruciate ligament had been shot to hell in Mexico. The surgeons had already scheduled her for a new bionic replacement.

"We keep losing pieces of ourselves," he said.

Amanda rested her head against his. "We're still alive. Still together."

Zack nodded weakly. "And it's a damn good thing because I'm really going to need you. I think it's finally . . ."

He reluctantly replayed his talk with Mercy, her harsh but accurate assessment about his art. *It'll take years to get back to your old skill level. Years you don't have.*

Zack chuckled, his voice choked with tears. "I think it's finally starting to hurt."

Amanda extended her arms all around the room, pressing buttons and pulling cords until everything was just right. Soon the door was closed, the blinds were drawn, and Amanda was spooning her husband on a soft, flat bed. After twenty-five beeps of the electronic heart monitor, Zack became lost in a deep and solid slumber.

Amanda held him the whole time, her eyes wide open, her addled mind filled with thoughts of Pelletiers. And babies.

Once upon a recent time, there had been a quiet street in the southwest corner of the village, a cobblestone cul-de-sac with six wooden cottages. The Gothams had used them to sequester their worst troublemakers—the ones who used their powers for harm, the ones who couldn't be trusted to act discreetly in public. It was the underland's only bad neighborhood, and the stigma of living there had been strong enough to scare most Gothams into behaving.

In May of last year, the houses were given over to the clan's first guests: six Silvers and two Golds who had forged a tenuous peace with the Gothams. While a few of the locals, like Carrie Bloom and the late Yvonne Whitten, went out of their way to befriend the new tenants, most of the clan kept a wary distance. Some of them called the cul-de-sac "Freak Street," a name that Zack found so hilariously ironic that he immediately used it himself.

Six weeks into their stay with the Gothams, the orphans of Freak Street suffered three devastating losses. First David Dormer, the dauntless young Australian who'd been with the Silvers from the start, was exposed as a traitor and a secret Pelletier. Then Jonathan Christie, Hannah's lover and Heath's closest friend, was shot dead during the chaos of Red Sunday. Lastly, Theo Maranan, the long-suffering augur of the group, left his friends to embark on a Holy Grail vision quest, a pilgrimage that he insisted on taking alone.

The orphans barely had a chance to mourn before twenty-three strangers came stumbling into the underland—all the Platinums, Coppers, and Irons who'd been lured to the village by a Beatles song. There weren't enough houses to accommodate the newcomers, and the Gothams, still reeling from their own tragic losses, were in no condition to help.

Luckily, Integrity had all the resources they needed to build a new sanctuary for the orphans. They bulldozed the entire cul-de-sac and replaced it with a luxurious compound—forty-eight flats in six glassy towers, with a clubhouse, a commissary, two swimming pools, and a fitness center. Even Melissa and her team of government liaisons got their own fancy building: a three-story office/apartment complex that was the envy of the other agents.

Now the once disreputable sector of town had become its nicest property, and nobody called it Freak Street anymore. Integrity had dubbed it the Orphanage in honor of their favorite timebenders. And damned if the name didn't stick.

At 10:25 on a Sunday night, the commissary was virtually empty. Heath and See sat back-to-back in neighboring booths while Ashley Nielsen, one of Integrity's full-time orphan handlers, gathered a late-night snack at the salad bar.

Mia watched them all from a rear corner table, a lime-green bottle of Vegi-Milk in her hand. The stuff tasted like lettuce on wet graham crackers, but it was surprisingly refreshing, especially after an hour on the treadmill. Though the back of her tank top was drenched in sweat and her leg muscles throbbed with resentment, Mia felt a gratifying heat in the core of her being, as if her last few stubborn ounces of softness were finally melting away.

A charcoal sketch fell off the edge of See's table. Heath picked it up from the floor and studied it. See had drawn a square-chinned man, one whose neck was nearly as thick as his head.

"Who is that?" Heath asked.

See shrugged. "I don't know. He keeps popping up in my visions."

From the quick and distant glimpse that Mia was able to catch, the man looked like Bobby Farisi, the oldest of her four brothers. But unless See was suddenly glimpsing dead people in her foresight, it was probably someone else.

Heath passed the sketch back to See. "It's a good drawing."

"Thank you," she replied in a perfectly casual tone. Though Heath couldn't see it, her wide, blushing grin practically lit up the rest of the dining room.

Incredible, thought Mia. The girl was head over heels in love with Heath, and admitted it to anyone who asked. But whenever she was around him (and See found many excuses to be in his vicinity), she was as cool and composed as a dowager. More than that, she knew all of Heath's prickly pet peeves and triggers, and avoided each one with finesse. She was playing a long and patient game with him. And by all external clues, she was winning.

When Mia once asked her how she handled her crush so deftly, See had smiled at her like the answer was obvious. *I do what the future tells me.*

If anyone could appreciate the sentiment, it was Mia, though it'd been well over a year since any of her future selves had written her. They must have all concluded, as she did, that there was no point messing with the past. It never made her life any easier, only sadder. Plus, as Mia had demonstrated time and time again, there were much better uses for portals.

Everyone in the dining room turned their heads as the front door swung open. Agent Nielsen nearly dropped her salad at the sight of the new arrival.

"Director! Wow. If I had known you were coming—"

He cut her off with a breezy wave. "No worries, Ash. I was just checking up on Melissa."

Mia snorted derisively. She'd come to know Cedric Cain over the past thirteen months. The man never *just* did anything.

He tipped his fedora at the kids in the corner. "Heath. See."

Though Heath responded with an indifferent grunt, See nervously looked away. Mother still mistrusted Cain, which meant that all of the Coppers did.

Cain took off his hat and smiled charmingly at Mia. "And there she is, the Great Train Robber. May I join you?"

"Only if you don't smoke."

He pulled his empty hand out of his coat pocket. "Well, that answers my next question."

Cain took the chair across from her, a towering presence, even when seated. Between his steel-blue eyes, his chalk-white hair, and his six-and-a-half-foot frame, he could have been a nicer version of Azral Pelletier. Caleb once joked that Cain was secretly Azral's father, a gag that Mia didn't find particularly funny, as she knew damn well what Azral's father looked like.

She took a deep swig of her Vegi-Milk, her eyes never breaking from Cain's. "So. How are the women?"

Cain looked at her askance. "The women?"

"The ones we rescued on Friday."

"Oh, the *Pearls*."

Mia bristled at his choice of words. She'd tried for weeks to get Integrity to drop those factional terms—all Pelletier labels that, like the bracelets themselves, had been forced upon the orphans. Sadly, no one seemed to share her outrage. "Just roll with it," Peter had advised her. "None of my people ever asked to be called Gothams."

Still, she would have rather been called a bitch than a Silver, and she had a middle finger ready for anyone who thought otherwise.

"They're doing okay," Cain said of the Pearls. "We'll give them a few more days to get adjusted before we integrate them."

Mia nodded. "It'd be nice if they could join us on Tuesday."

"Right. The party."

"Party." Mia chuckled darkly. There were many ways to mark the two-year anniversary of an apocalypse. A party wasn't one of them. Then again, Hannah, who had taken charge of planning the event, was determined not to make it a sobfest. There'd be food from the old world, games from the old world, a whole mess of upbeat music. Who knew? Maybe it *was* a party.

Mia studied Cain cynically. "Okay. Let's get it over with."

"'It' being . . . ?"

"Don't play dumb. I know why you're here. I shot three guys in Mexico and now you're all worried about me."

Cain's handphone chirped impatiently. He checked the screen before putting it facedown on the table. "You think we're overreacting?"

"It was strategy," Mia insisted. "We needed the pilot to give up a code. I got it from her."

"And those men you shot?"

"Healed, just like I knew they'd be. That's why I aimed for their stomachs."

"Gut wounds can still kill."

"Well, it didn't kill them, okay?" Mia glared out the window. "Fuck. You're acting like it's the worst thing anyone at Integrity has ever done."

Cain smiled wistfully. "It's not even in the top million."

"Then why are you and Melissa giving me shit?"

"As you said, we're worried about you. You're an extraordinary girl in many ways, but there's an anger in you—"

Mia opened her mouth to protest, but Cain cut her off. "A *righteous* anger," he stressed. "You have every reason in the world to be mad."

"But?"

Cain looked away with a heavy sigh. Mia could see how badly he wanted a cigarette. "But your anger's made you reckless," he said. "Reckless in a way that's going to cost someone's life. And I'm not talking Mexican soldiers. I mean someone from our side. Maybe even you."

Mia fought the urge to throw her chalky green drink at him. She'd stopped a flying train and risked her life to save Amanda. Yet all she got for it were lectures and recriminations.

Which prompted a new question. "Why do you care?" Mia asked. "You're the head of a government agency. You meet with the president twice a week."

"Twice a month," Cain corrected.

"Why even bother with me?"

Cain checked on the others in the dining room. While Agent Nielsen and See made a conscious effort to pretend they weren't listening, Heath kneeled on his seat and watched Cain and Mia directly. The boy had never been much for pretense.

Smirking, Cain turned back to Mia. "You know, it's funny, in a not-so-funny way, how the mood in this place never changes. Every time I come here, I feel the tension. Gothams, orphans, and government agents, all clustered together in an underground pressure cooker. While I'm glad as hell you're not killing each other, I don't see you bonding over the one thing you have in common, the one thing that separates us from everyone else."

Mia nodded in grim acknowledgment. "We're the only ones who know how fucked we are."

"We're the only ones who know the threat," Cain said, more delicately. "If the public finds out that the sky's coming down, it'll be chaos. That's why most of the agency is still in the dark. My daughters don't know. I haven't even told the president."

That last part was news to Mia. "You don't trust him?"

"I don't trust his people. In any case, there's nothing he can do for us. I'm taking all my cues from Theo, and he doesn't mince words about what we need: a lot more orphans."

"And a few less Pelletiers," said Mia.

Cain nodded. "This world will never be safe as long as they're here. You've been face-to-face with Esis, spent months in the company of Semerjean. That makes you a valuable asset to us. As far as I'm concerned, you're one of the most important people on Earth."

He slumped in the chair with a gentle shrug. "*That's* why I bother with you."

Mia wasn't sure if she should laugh or cry. She could remember a time when she was absolutely no one, some chubby little nerd in the back of the classroom. "Look—"

Cain's handphone vibrated again. He shut it off and stuffed it back into his pocket. "I have to deal with that in a minute, so let me cut to the chase. I'd like to set up a meeting between you and a good friend of mine."

"I've already *talked* to therapists."

"She's not a therapist. She's the press secretary of a U.S. senator."

Mia looked at Cain bemusedly, as if he just delivered the punchline to a very obscure joke.

He shrugged. "If we lived in a smarter country, she'd be president by now. But we don't, so she's not. In any case, there's no one on the planet who's better suited to help you."

Mia arched an eyebrow. "And if I don't talk to her?"

"Then we'll have no choice but to bench you from all future missions."

Mia laughed. "Bullshit. You need me. I'm the only traveler who can make portals in midair. Everyone else, even Peter—"

"—needs a hard, flat surface," Cain finished. "Yes. That was indeed the case."

"Was?"

"One of the Pearls is a traveler," he matter-of-factly informed her. "Makes free-floating portals, just like you. Though she doesn't have your experience, she's already proven to be a fast learner. Peter says she has real potential."

Mia's mouth dropped open. "*Peter's* training her?"

"Of course he is. He's a terrific teacher. You said so yourself."

Mia shook her head. "No, no, no. He wouldn't do that to me."

"To you?" Cain snickered. "He may think the world of you, but he still has his priorities straight. The fate of the Earth comes before your pride."

Mia jumped to her feet. "Fuck you."

"I'm giving you a chance to make things right. Go see my friend. Talk to her. She'll help you with your—"

Mia waved a man-size portal into the air, then vanished into its milky white depths.

"—anger issues," Cain finished.

The disc shrank away. Cain pulled a cigarette out of his pocket tin and flicked a flame on his lighter. "Guess I know where she's going."

A hundred and twenty yards to the east, in the top-floor suite of Orphan Tower Five, two young Gothams kissed in the dim light of the living room. They were both sixteen and, like most of the souls in the underland, they figured they only had a few more birthdays left. Needless to say, they had a lot of living to do before the world ended. Without that pressure, who knew? Liam Pendergen and Sovereign Tam might have just stayed friends and guildmates. But after trading affections for nearly a week, their minds and desires had become fully entwined. All they wanted now was more of each other, *all* of each other, every minute of every day.

Sovereign closed her eyes and sighed with pleasure as Liam planted a trail of kisses up her scarred, slender neck. She was also a thermic and, just like him, she carried the marks of old mistakes. But now his long gloves were off, her turtleneck sweater was on the floor, and they'd never felt less self-conscious about their burns.

She threw a cursory look around the Pendergen apartment, the only Gotham flat in the Orphanage. "Why do you and your dad still live here?"

Liam pulled back to look at her. "Why shouldn't we?"

"You're not on the run anymore. You could go back to your house on the surface."

The boy thought it over a moment. "I don't know. We've been living with these guys so long, they're practically family."

Sovereign smiled teasingly. "Yeah? You ever think about knocking it with one of the breacher girls?"

Liam shook his head, laughing. "First of all, 'breacher's an outdated word. A *Rebel* word."

"Ooh. I've been schooled."

"Secondly, half of those girls are Coppers. And the Coppers are, uh . . ."

"Crazy," said Sovereign.

"I was going to say 'odd.'"

"My dad thinks they're all crazy here."

"They're not," Liam said. "But they all lived through our very worst nightmare. The fact that any of them are functioning at all is . . . I don't know. I just have a lot of respect for them."

Sovereign stroked the side of his face. He'd grown several inches in the past year and change, and was sporting even more of his father's good looks. "You are the sweetest, cutest thing," she said. "Why did it take us this long to get together?"

Liam grinned. "No idea. I'm just glad we did."

He leaned in closer and breathed a nervous whisper into her ear. "By the way, and I'm totally fine if you say no to this—"

"Yes."

"You don't even know what I was gonna say."

"You were going to ask if we could take it to your bedroom," Sovereign said. "I knew your question. Now you know my answer."

A portal opened in the middle of the living room, blinding the two young lovers with harsh white fluorescence. They sat up on the couch, startled.

Liam only needed a glimpse of the silhouette in the portal to see who was crashing his flat. "Mia? What are you doing here?"

She stormed across the carpet without so much as a glance in his direction. "Where is he?"

"Sleeping. What's torking you now?"

"None of your goddamn—" Mia stopped and did a double-take at the half-dressed blonde next to Liam. "Sovereign? Wow. When did this happen?"

Sovereign hid her chest and neck behind a large couch pillow. "None of *your* goddamn."

"You're still pissed about Regal?"

"Of course I am! You took advantage of her when she was confused."

"Confused." Mia scoffed. "I still have hickeys on my—"

"I don't want to hear it!"

"Your sister's gay, Sovereign. Deal with it."

Mia stormed down the hall and pounded on the door of the master bedroom. "Peter!"

She waited five seconds, then charged inside. "Hey!"

Peter sat against the headboard, his lap and legs hidden under a pair of queen-size pillows. He took in Mia through bleary eyes. "Sweetheart, unless there's a crisis—"

"You're training my replacement?"

"—it can wait till morning."

"*My* replacement. And you didn't even tell me!"

Groaning, Peter palmed his face. Even in the low light, Mia could see the thin white scar across his chest, one of the many wounds he'd earned while protecting the Silvers.

"She's not your replacement," Peter said. "She's just someone who needs training."

"Well, Cain just said he doesn't need me anymore."

"I'm pretty sure there's more to that story."

"Yeah. He basically—"

"I didn't say I wanted to hear it," Peter curtly replied. "Not tonight. And certainly not while you're in a lather."

Mia threw her hands up, then took a few steps into the room. "Look, can't we just—"

"You don't want to do that."

"What?" She froze at the sight of his naked hip, then immediately turned around. "Oh my God!"

"I warned you."

"I thought you were wearing something!"

He shook his head. "I don't wear anything to bed."

"You don't even have a *blanket*?"

"Must have fallen off the side."

Red-faced, Mia hurried back into the hallway and looked down at the floor with cupped eyes. "Fine. We'll talk about it tomorrow."

"Smart choice."

"Shit. I really *do* need therapy now."

"Next time you'll know not to barge into bedrooms."

Mia closed the door behind her and teleported back to her apartment. Peter could feel her journey in his senses, like a warm, soft finger brushing gently across his thoughts.

He turned his head to the left. "She's gone."

A woman stepped out from the darkness of the closet, naked beneath the wrap of Peter's plush comforter. "You think she saw anything?"

"Nothing she ever wanted to see."

"You think she saw *me*?"

"Darling—"

"Don't."

Hannah sat down on the edge of Peter's bed, her dark eyes dancing back and forth in thought. "Don't call me that."

THREE

Six months prior, in the middle of January's angriest blizzard, an orphan, a Gotham, and a government agent took a midnight trip to the surface. They left Quarter Hill in an agency Griffin and flew six miles north to the Bear Mountain Nature Preserve, a sprawling alpine wonderland that, in warmer seasons, served as one of southern New York's most popular hiking destinations. The observation park at the top of the mountain offered stunning views in all directions, from the skyline of Manhattan to the floating inns of Croton-on-Hudson.

But in the cold, black depths of winter's night, there wasn't a human soul to be found. The summit was desolate, a howling void of wind and snow that offered no view of anything but the steam of your own breath.

Hannah couldn't think of a better place to host a meeting with the devil.

Melissa landed the aerovan in the middle of the park and opened the electric side hatch. A rush of cold air filled the Griffin, stinging every inch of Hannah's face and flooding her mind with second thoughts.

"You sure you don't want me to stay?" Melissa asked her two passengers.

Peter tightened the hood on his winter coat and stepped out into the blizzard. "I wouldn't advise it. He's not your biggest fan."

"Nor yours," Melissa said. "If this goes bad—"

"We'll be fine," Hannah assured her. "The worst he'll do is say no."

Melissa watched her bleakly as she grabbed her supplies. "For your sake, I hope he does."

She wished Hannah and Peter the best of luck, then left them alone on the mountain. They immediately got to work planting eggbulbs in the snow, a long and tedious undertaking that made the minutes pass like hours.

Once the two-hundredth bulb was finally placed, Peter flipped a switch on a wireless generator. The eggbulbs came to life in synch, emblazoning a cool blue name across the summit.

DAVID.

Hannah unfolded two lawn chairs and placed them around a portable heater. "Have a seat," she told Peter. "He won't show up for at least a couple of hours."

"You think it'll take him that long to see it?"

Hannah laughed bitterly. She knew that Semerjean had been watching them from the moment they left the underland. But he was a vain son of a bitch with an inflated sense of superiority. He wouldn't simply come running at the flash of a Bat-Signal. He'd make his summoners wait in the freezing cold until they remembered their place on the food chain.

An hour passed, and then another, and another. By four A.M., Hannah's nose had gone numb behind her double-wrapped scarf and she could feel the biting cold beneath her visor. Peter suggested they pack things up and call Melissa.

"Just wait," Hannah insisted. "He'll be here."

At six o'clock, when the coffee ran out and the faint light of dawn began to peek between the lowest clouds, Hannah finally saw the gap in her logic. If Semerjean was watching, then he already knew what they were going to ask him. Maybe his frigid silence *was* the answer. Maybe he'd been saying no all night.

Hannah stood up with a weary groan. "All right. I guess we can go."

Peter clutched her arm. "Wait."

"What?"

He gestured at a patch of snow just twenty feet away. "Someone's coming."

A ten-foot portal split the air, exactly where Peter was pointing. Hannah's heart skipped a beat at the handsome young man who emerged from the light. It had been seven months since Semerjean stopped pretending to be David. Hannah would have expected him to revert to a more distinguished age, one far more befitting a patriarch. But there he was, still wearing that face—*that* face—the face of a boy she'd loved like a brother. He still resembled David in so many ways that Hannah had to fight to keep from crying.

As Semerjean closed the portal behind him, Hannah finally noticed his clothes. He wore a simple black oxford shirt over loose denim jeans, a casual ensemble that would have left anyone else shivering. If the freezing cold bothered him, he did a fine job hiding it.

Semerjean studied the eggbulb array with wry amusement. "'David.' Interesting. You couldn't use my real name?"

Peter drank him in through slitted blue eyes. "We didn't have enough bulbs."

"Oh, I don't think that's true. I think you're just nostalgic."

"Nostalgic?" Peter scoffed. "I didn't like David any more than I like you."

Hannah clasped his wrist. "Peter . . ."

"No, let him speak," said Semerjean. "It's nice to finally clear the air. I lost count of the number of times I had to stop myself from killing you, Peter. Living with you was the most painful part of my job."

Peter grinned vindictively. "If you thought that would hurt me—"

"On the contrary, I knew it would please you. This is a friendly gathering, is it not?"

"No," said Hannah, her arms sternly crossed. "We need to talk about Amanda."

Semerjean lost his smile. "Right. Yes. We heard about her unfortunate, uh . . ."

"Miscarriage," Hannah said. "Her second one."

Semerjean brushed the snow off his shoulders. "We're sorry for her loss. That wasn't the outcome any of us wanted."

"But you let it happen anyway," said Peter. "You people see the future better than anyone. You knew she was about to suffer."

Semerjean jerked a doleful shrug. "There were . . . mitigating factors that prevented us from interfering."

"Interfering." Peter laughed venomously. "That's all your goddamn family does."

Hannah gripped him by the coat sleeve. "Stop."

"But as soon as Amanda needs your help, you suddenly have respect for her boundaries. That's rich. That is just—"

"Peter, *enough.*"

Hannah suddenly regretted bringing him along. As the father of both of Amanda's lost children, he had every reason to be upset. But he was blowing their chance to get help.

Peter threw up his hands in frustration, then retreated back to the comfort of the heater. Semerjean waited until he passed out of earshot. "We *couldn't* intervene without destroying the very purpose of those pregnancies," he told Hannah. "We need them to be as—"

"—natural as possible," she finished. "Yes. We know."

Semerjean had explained it all to Mia last June, in the middle of Red Sunday. The Pelletiers were looking to breed the perfect mutant hybrid, a child of two Earths who'd provide the genetic material they needed to cure a fatal disease called "terminus." It was their world's last affliction, the final obstacle between humanity and immortality. So they brought ninety-nine orphans to the world of the Gothams, with the intent of merging their DNA.

With each orphan subgroup, the Pelletiers took a different approach. For the Pearls, it was *in vitro* fertilization. For the Golds, it was apomictic parthenogenesis, a form of engineered cloning. Semerjean hadn't said anything about the Coppers, Platinums, or Irons, but he'd been painfully clear to Mia about what the Pelletiers wanted from her clan.

"Now the Silvers . . . oh, you were a challenge. We knew from the start that we needed to trust one group to the hands of nature—a natural conception, a natural mutation, a natural immunity to terminus. My wife and son looked to the strings and were very encouraged by what they saw. If their forecasts are right, then you represent our best chance for success. The sisters especially."

In their arrogance, the Pelletiers had thought that they could manipulate the Silvers into breeding with the right Gothams, a complicated mating game orchestrated from the inside by Semerjean himself. None of it had worked out the way he hoped, especially with Zack and Amanda. After much frustration, the Pelletiers stopped toying with subtle machinations and resorted to outright thuggery.

But all they got from their threats so far were two failed pregnancies and one broken Silver.

Hannah looked to Semerjean pleadingly. "Amanda can't do this anymore. She can't. I've known her all my life and I've never seen her this bad."

"We're well aware of her emotional state," said Semerjean. "And believe it or not, we empathize. If she needs a respite before trying again—"

"No, you don't get it. She *can't* do this again."

Peter rejoined them, calmer but no less astringent. "You force her to carry one more kid and she'll slit her wrists. That's not just talk. Our augurs foresee it. I'm guessing yours do too."

"So what do you propose, then?" Semerjean inquired. "You didn't come here just to beg."

"Don't be coy," Peter said. "You already know what we're offering."

"Yes, but I need to hear you say it. How can I expect you to honor the deal if you can't even speak the words?"

Hannah traded a dark look with Peter. They'd already decided that it would be better to hear it from her. The hard part now was looking in the eyes of a man she hated and swearing a pledge that she hated even more.

"Peter and I will make you a child," she told him.

Semerjean wound his finger impatiently. "If . . ."

"You let Amanda and Zack go."

He shook his head with a scornful laugh. "And there it is, the sticking point."

"What are you talking about?"

"He speaks of Trillinger," said a stern female voice.

Hannah and Peter turned around, startled by the woman standing behind them. Esis had come to the mountaintop without any fanfare. No portals, no lights, no puffy clouds of smoke. She simply melded into the scene as if she'd been there all along.

She circled into Hannah's view, an elegant sight in her waistcoat and scarf. There was something off about her presence, though—a clashing ambience, as if she'd been superimposed from a much brighter backdrop. Stranger still, the falling snow didn't seem to stick to her. It fluttered right through her hair and clothes.

A projection, Hannah guessed. *She's not really here.*

One look into her deep black eyes was enough to convince Hannah that she wasn't all there either. By now her madness was legendary, the stuff of nightmares for everyone in the underland. But there was a subtle new frailty to her movements, a noticeable waver that Hannah hadn't seen before. Maybe the disease that was killing all her people had advanced in recent months. Maybe she was closer to the end than anyone was willing to admit.

Esis moved to her husband's side, her hard gaze locked on Hannah. "You ask us to absolve two couplings in exchange for one. Even a woman of your limits can see the flaw in that."

Hannah shook her head, confounded. "I thought you knew about Mercy."

"What of her?"

"She has a new boyfriend, Caleb Brooks. He's one of your—"

"We know who he is," Semerjean snapped. "We already approved of their union. It frees Mercy from the burden of sleeping with Zack. It doesn't free him from *his* burden."

Esis nodded in agreement. "He must make arrangements with another fertile Gotham."

"No!" Hannah cried. "You can't do that!"

"Of course we can," said Semerjean. "Zack himself agreed to the terms."

"It was a deal made at gunpoint," Peter growled. "If you think that's fair—"

"Fair?" Esis laughed. "He'd be dead a dozen times without our aid. We gave him life. We gave him freedom to be with his lover. All we ask in return are two nights a month with a woman he finds attractive. How is that remotely unfair?"

Hannah was so angry, she couldn't feel the cold anymore. She took a step forward and pointed her finger at Esis. "You kidnapped Zack. Tortured him for days, then threw him to Rebel to get tortured some more. And all because he fell in love with the wrong woman."

Esis sighed with forced patience. "Child . . ."

"They've both put up with enough of your shit. Just leave them alone!"

"We're not entirely opposed to the notion," Esis replied. "But what you offer is not enough."

Peter shrugged. "What the hell more do you want from us? Twins?"

Semerjean palmed his face, exasperated. "*Kan'uil teil-a*, you are so very dense. Allow me to spell it out for you."

With a wave of his hand, he summoned a pair of lumic holograms, the two young souls that Peter held most dear on this world.

Hannah drank in the images of Mia and Liam, stupefied. "You can't be serious."

"You leave my son out of this!" Peter yelled.

"Your son would be dead if it wasn't for me," Semerjean said. "I leapt out of an aerstraunt, at great discomfort, to save him from a gruesome fall. Do you think I did that because I *like* him?"

"I swear to God—"

Hannah held him back. "Peter. *Peter!* Stop! It doesn't matter. It's not happening." She looked back at the Pelletiers with seething contempt. "Even if we wanted to, we'd never get Mia to agree to it. Not in a million years."

Semerjean almost looked hurt by her assessment. "You overstate her spite for us."

"You *understate* her spite for you," Peter said. "She'd sooner die than help you, 'boy.' You only have yourself to blame."

"Enough."

The voice seemed to come from everywhere, a thunderous bass, as if God himself had stepped in to arbitrate. Though Hannah couldn't see him, she could easily recognize his haughty tone. He wasn't God. If anything, he was living proof of a cold and senseless universe.

Azral approached his parents from behind, looking just the same as he ever did in his ash-gray suit with a tieless, open collar. Like Esis, he seemed to be a vivid projection. The falling snow passed through him without a care in the world.

Hannah wished she could be as cavalier, but her heart pounded painfully at the sight of him. The last time she saw his fierce blue eyes was the last time she saw Jonathan.

He flicked a dismissive hand at Hannah. "These negotiations are pointless. This girl has proven herself to be untrustworthy. Any pledge she offers will be broken at the slightest whim."

Hannah clenched her jaw, struggling to maintain her composure. She'd been a halfway decent actress once. If she couldn't keep a level head, the least she could do was act like someone who could.

She took an angry step toward Azral. "*You're* the one who can't be trusted! I'd be pregnant right now if it wasn't for you!"

Azral sneered at her assertion. "That's absurdly false."

"The last time we spoke, I swore I'd have a baby with whoever the hell you wanted. All you had to do was let Jonathan live. But you had Evan kill him anyway, and for *what*?"

"You broke your word."

"How? I didn't even have time!"

"You broke your word in every string of the future," Azral said. "Every single one."

It took all of Hannah's strength to not use her power on him: a fatal blast of forward-time, aimed right at his little black heart. Even in her rage, she had no illusions of hurting him. All she'd do is piss off the family, which was an awfully quick way to stop existing.

Peter rushed to Hannah's side. "Just give us a moment," he told the Pelletiers.

He retreated thirty feet with her and spoke in a hushed whisper. "Look, this is all going sideways. Let's not lose sight of the reason we're here."

Hannah peeked over her shoulder at the Pelletiers. Peter must have been crazy if he thought they couldn't hear him.

"We have a chance to save Amanda right now," he told Hannah. "We just have to cut Zack from the deal."

"No."

"He'll survive."

"It's not about survival," Hannah said. "It's about finally pushing back. If we don't draw a line, they're just going to keep at it. They'll come for Liam and Mia, then Theo, then Heath, then all the rest of our people. And when they're done with us, they'll come right back around for Amanda again, because who the hell's going to stop them?"

Peter closed his eyes. "We'll deal with that as it comes. Listen to me . . ."

As he continued his argument, a woman's voice flittered into Hannah's thoughts: *Don't lose hope. You have everything you need to free Zack and Amanda.*

"What?"

"What?" Peter asked.

Hannah blinked at him distractedly, then shook her head. "Nothing. What were you saying?"

"I said your sister's the one we need to save. We won't get another chance."

He's wrong, said the ethereal voice. *There's a reason why Azral's so bitter toward you. He's looked to the strings and he knows you're his best hope for success. You have power over him and his life's work, and he's deathly afraid of you knowing that.*

Hannah's mind spun in frantic circles. She knew the voice of Ioni Deschane when she heard it, but she didn't know if she could be trusted. This was, after all, the same woman who'd told Mia to shoot Esis in the head, a disastrously bad piece of advice that had terrible consequences for Mia and the girl she loved.

Just wait, Ioni warned Hannah. *In five days' time, the Pelletiers will accept the terms of your offer. They'll give you Zack and Amanda. But not now. Not here.*

Peter eyed her warily. "Hannah?"

You need to walk away.

"Hannah, are you with me on this?"

Her eyes narrowed to icy slits as she hurried back toward the Pelletiers. She stopped in front of Semerjean, her expression firm and resolute. "I want you to leave Zack and Amanda alone. You get the fuck out of their lives for good and I promise you—"

"Hannah . . ."

"I *promise* you that Peter and I will make you a child. That's the deal on the table."

Semerjean gravely shook his head. "Unacceptable."

"Then I'm sorry to have wasted your time."

Hannah pulled her handphone out of her pocket and autodialed Melissa. "We're done here. Pick us up."

Semerjean chuckled. "Hannah, please. I've been acting far longer than you. I can tell—"

"It's no act," Esis bitterly declared. "The strings are clear. She has truly wasted our time."

With a brusque little gesture, she severed her own projection and disappeared from the scene. Azral leveled one last glare at Hannah before popping away like a soap bubble.

Alone again among his former companions, Semerjean reopened a portal. He took one step toward it before turning around. "I have to be honest, Hannah—"

"Since when?"

"—I didn't think much of you in our first days together. I found you vapid, weak, illogical, and needy."

Hannah turned her head, grimacing. "Oh my God. Just go away."

"But then you surprised me with your hidden strengths," he continued. "There are times when you were flat-out brilliant. And if you had successfully arranged a deal with us, it would have been one of the most selfless acts a sister has ever done for another."

Semerjean shrugged with lament. "Shame we couldn't make it work."

He took a half-step into the portal, then sneered over his shoulder. "Tell Amanda I'm sorry for her losses, and that I wish her the very best of luck with her next pregnancy."

Hannah didn't have the strength to curse at him. She was far too thrown by the glint in his eyes, a look so cold and utterly malicious that she felt like a fool all over again. How did he manage to trick her for so long? How did she not see through his act?

The portal shrank away. Hannah and Peter remained where they were on the mountaintop, without talking or moving or even looking at each other. They merely stared at the ground, their bleak expressions shrouded by the hoods of their jackets, until the light of Melissa's Griffin pierced the dark veil of the storm.

If Hannah came to regret anything about that meeting, it was that she didn't tell her sister about it. At the crack of dawn on Friday, five days after Hannah and Peter returned from Bear Mountain, Amanda crept out of the apartment that she and Zack shared, then descended into the network of tunnels beneath the village. There, in a musty old storage chamber that no one had used in years, she formed Esis's name in large tempic letters and held it aloft in the air.

Though she had barely put any thought into it, her summoning ritual proved a lot more efficient than Hannah and Peter's. Amanda didn't have to gather up a box of lumic eggbulbs or smuggle herself to the top of a mountain. And she didn't have to wait more than fifty-two seconds before her demon of choice arrived in person by portal.

Unfortunately, the conversation didn't go half as well as either of them had hoped. What began as a volley of snarling unpleasantries devolved into shouts and invective. Ironically, it was one of Esis's tamer remarks, an offhand reference to a miscarriage as a "setback," that drove Amanda into mindless violence. Before either one of them even knew what was happening, Amanda's fist lashed out and struck Esis in the nose, breaking it.

It was a one-in-a-million punch on Amanda's part, and the last thing she ever did with her flesh hands.

Twelve hours later, while her sister lay sedated in the underland health clinic, Hannah trashed her own bedroom in a fit of self-loathing. If she had listened to Peter instead of Ioni, Amanda would still have her arms and a semblance of hope. Hannah had screwed it all up, and now Amanda would never be—

"Okay."

The voice had come from the other side of the bedroom, but there was nothing there but an upended dresser. It wasn't until Hannah faced the mirror on the wall that she saw Semerjean standing right behind her reflection.

"Your deal is accepted," he coolly informed her. "Amanda and Zack are free."

She spun around to confront him, but he still wasn't there. By the time she checked the mirror again, his face had overtaken the picture.

"Now, Hannah, listen to me very carefully, because I'm only going to say this once. We are formally done with the rest of your brethren: your sister, her lover, that spiteful little girl I once adored, and the 'messiah' Theo Maranan, who's become as useless to us as he is to the rest of you. They're nothing to us now. We'll no longer heal them when they're dying, or save them when they're imperiled. And if they get in the way of our grand design, we will not hesitate to kill them."

His voice fell a sharp octave. "*I* will not hesitate."

Before Hannah could even formulate a response, Semerjean spoke again. "As far as we're concerned, you're the very last Silver. Don't disappoint us. And, Hannah?"

He leaned forward in the mirror until his vengeful face filled the whole frame. "Don't ever summon us again."

FOUR

At the whispering end of a hot July Monday, six minutes before midnight, the sky above the underland turned a deathly shade of red. The lumic projection of evening stars transformed into a collage of memorial photographs: the hundred and seventeen Gothams who were brutally killed on Red Sunday. For the third time this month, anonymous hackers had sabotaged the skycaster to rain the mother of all guilt trips on Integrity, and it worked. Even Hannah, who'd never done harm to any of the victims, felt a pang of contrition. If she'd moved a little faster that day, fought a little bit smarter, maybe some of those Gothams would still be alive.

Peter stepped out of the bathroom to find her standing half-dressed at his window, her body lit in a macabre crimson glow. "They're at it again, huh?"

She grabbed her pants off the bed. "I should go."

"Gotta get home before the husband gets suspicious."

Smirking, Hannah flipped him off. During her six long months of clandestine trysts with Peter, only Heath, her flatmate, took notice of her late-night absences. She hated lying to him about them, but the boy was terrible at keeping secrets, and there were others among them who wouldn't take kindly to her Faustian bargain with Semerjean. Mia would pitch a holy fit. Zack would feel guilty. Liam would get stressed. And Amanda? Dear God. She'd pledge her womb all over again in a desperate attempt to save Hannah. She'd never be able to live with her little sister's sacrifice. Never.

Hannah gestured at the wall of Peter's bedroom, the usual place for her exit portal. "Well?"

"Hang on." He took her by the hand. "One last bit of business."

Hannah smiled softly, then let him pull her into an embrace. Despite the strategic nature of their union, Peter insisted there was room for affection in the process. "We don't have to pretend to be more than we are," he'd told Hannah. "But we care for each other. We *like* each other. It'd be nice if we showed it once in a while."

If anything, he'd understated her regard for him. This was a man who'd risked everything, even the love of his son, to keep the Silvers safe. He sheltered them for months at his own expense, became a criminal fugitive right alongside them. And he never stopped believing in the world's salvation, a hope that had carried Hannah through many dark days. There wasn't a doubt in her mind that she loved Peter Pendergen. It just wasn't the kind of love that typically resulted in babies.

Peter pulled back to look at her. "Sorry again about that whole 'darling' thing."

Hannah shook her head. "I overreacted yesterday."

"I don't say it to put a claim on you. It's just a silly little—"

"Peter, it's *fine*."

"I just don't want to make it harder for you than it already is."

Hannah scoffed at him. "You think I'm suffering?"

"I think you deserve all the love and happiness your sister has," Peter said, "instead of a gobshite arrangement with a creaky old Irishman."

Hannah rolled her eyes. "First of all, you're not even forty. Second, you're a *hot* Not-Forty. So take that 'creaky old Irishman' shit and stuff it, *darling*."

"But—"

"*Third*. Look at me." She pushed him down on the edge of the bed, then rested her hands on his shoulders. "I don't want what Amanda has. I never did. Love and marriage look great on her, but they don't go well with my skin tone."

Peter eyed her skeptically. "I saw the way you were with Jonathan."

"I loved him," Hannah admitted. "I might have even been *in* love with him. I don't know. But I don't think it was a lifetime thing. He was a drifter, just like me. In the best case, we probably would have lasted two or three years before becoming good friends."

"Wow," said Peter. "That's not something I expected to hear."

Hannah shrugged. "I'd never say it to Heath. I feel bad even saying it to you."

"You shouldn't."

"Well, *you* shouldn't feel bad about me," she said. "I like these nights we have together. It's the easiest part of the deal." Her face turned grim. "It's the shit that comes after that worries me."

Peter nodded in agreement. "I pray to God every night that you don't get pregnant. Now I'm worried it's working too well."

Hannah shared every bit of his concern. He'd managed to knock up Amanda twice in five months, but half a year with Hannah had produced absolutely nothing, not even a false alarm. If the Pelletiers were getting impatient, they hadn't said a word. They certainly couldn't fault Hannah and Peter for lack of trying.

Five and a half minutes after the sabotage started, the undersky reverted to moonlight and stars. The moody red glow disappeared from the window, not a moment too soon for Hannah.

"That's my cue," she said. "You gonna give me a ride home or what?"

Peter opened a portal to her flat. "Consider yourself ridden."

Hannah sneered at him. "Cute. You know, you're awfully smug for a hand-me-down."

"Now, now. Let's not bring your sister into this."

More than anything, it was the thought of Amanda that kept Hannah feeling good about the arrangement. She'd been on the brink of suicide six months ago. Now Amanda was a revitalized woman, with new arms, new wings, and a new joy of life. One look at her smile was enough to convince Hannah that she was doing the right thing. And who knew? Maybe her baby, if she ever managed to conceive one, would be a winning ticket for the Pelletiers. Maybe it would finally get the bastards to pack up their stuff and go home.

Hannah kissed Peter, then took the shortcut back to her apartment. All the flats in the Orphanage had the same layout and furnishings. Aside from a guitar and a few feminine touches, Hannah's bedroom was a perfect clone of Peter's—extravagant, vast, and a little bit cold, just like the agency that built it. Hannah could only imagine how much Jonathan would have hated this place. He would have hated a lot of things about Hannah's life now.

As the portal closed behind her, her bedside clock rolled over to midnight. A holographic bubble informed her that the date was now Tuesday, July 24.

"Oh shit."

Hannah had been dreading this day for months, the darkest of dark anniversaries. Their world was officially two years gone, and there was no sky big enough to hold the faces of the dead.

Integrity couldn't have picked a worse morning to take the skycaster offline. While technicians installed a new security upgrade on the console, the projector beamed a blank white screen above the village. The orphans woke up to the same bleached sky that had hung over their world two years earlier, the first eerie harbinger of the apocalypse to come.

Even the most hardened survivors were rattled by the callback. Some broke out in blubbering tears while others managed their grief more sublimely. Heath closed all his window blinds and played "Eleanor Rigby" on his synthesizer. Mia teleported to the underland's gun range and shot twenty paper men in the face. Caleb went topside to a Quarter Hill synagogue and picked a philosophical fight with a rabbi. Eden got drunk. Ben Hopkins smoked pot. The Coppers followed Mother's cue and went back to bed.

Only one of the orphans took her anguish to the source. Forty-five minutes after their work began, the Integrity technicians jumped in shock when a furious redhead swooped down from above and landed atop the aerial projector.

Amanda glared at the duo from her high perch, her wings folded upward in a predatory V.

"Put the sky back. *Now.*"

Within moments, the white canopy reverted to sunshine and clouds, and Amanda was back in the air. Her handphone rang from the pocket of her sweatpants. She fished it out and pressed the receiver to her ear. "Please tell me that wasn't your screwup."

"I had nothing to do with it," Melissa insisted. "You, however, left two government workers in need of clean underwear."

Amanda suppressed a sinister grin. "I might have overdone it."

"I'm sorry for any distress they caused. Their timing was . . . unfortunate."

"Well, at least Zack missed it."

"How is he?"

Amanda looped around the clock tower and took a bird's-eye view of the clinic. Zack had been in surgery since seven A.M., getting his new Gelinger Mark VI prosthetic hand installed. Though the doctors assured Amanda that it was a low-risk procedure, it would take six hours to run all the necessary wires up Zack's arm and connect them to the right muscles.

"I don't know," Amanda told Melissa. "They only just started."

"If you're looking to pass the time, I have a job for you and Hannah."

"Yeah? Anything fun?"

"Afraid not," said Melissa. "Those orphans we rescued from Mexico aren't doing well."

"I'm sorry to hear that. What can we do?"

"There's a woman among them who, despite her protests, has become their leader of sorts. But she's having a hard time of her own. If you and Hannah could talk to her, maybe give her some guidance and helpful perspective, it would benefit the whole group."

"Of course." Amanda banked left at the upper wall of the dome. "I've been wanting to meet the Pearls anyway."

"She's not technically a Pearl. She's the other one."

"The other one?"

Melissa paused, baffled. "Has no one told you about Ofelia?"

"No," Amanda said. Between her multiple knee surgeries and Zack's crippling infirmity, she'd barely left the clinic in days. "Why is she 'the other one'?"

"I'll explain when you get here."

At half past nine, the sisters met Melissa on the north side of the village, in the squat concrete ziggurat that served as Integrity's field office. The southern wing of the second floor had been converted into temporary housing for the Pearls of Guadalajara. Each bedroom had a solic dampener that could suppress any or all powers with the flip of a switch. Another switch flooded the area with torpolone, a fast-acting knockout gas used by riot police and dentists.

Hannah only needed thirty seconds in the monitoring room to understand the precautions. One of the Pearls was having tremendous difficulty controlling her tempis, while another kept erupting in bursts of colorful light. A third one sported numerous splints and bruises on her limbs, all high-velocity impact wounds that brought back painful memories for Hannah. That poor girl must have been the swifter of the bunch.

Amanda leaned in to study the struggling young tempic. "Wow. She reminds me of me back in the early days. How are they all such, uh . . ."

"Amateurs?" Melissa said. "It's not by choice."

She lowered herself into a desk chair, wincing behind her sunglasses. Though the doctors expected Melissa to make a full recovery from her reversal, her body still reeled from a host of minor maladies, everything from Achilles tendinitis to extreme photosensitivity.

Amanda rushed to Melissa's side. "You all right?"

"I'm fine. Just a little anemic."

"Did you take your iron pills like I told you to?"

"Yes. Stop fussing."

Hannah sneered at the sickly sweet sight of them. Amanda and Melissa were cut from the same cloth, two natural-born paladins with an excess of virtue and a matching uptightness. They'd instantly clicked in the underland and become the closest of friends. Though Hannah had tried to forge her own rapport with Melissa, their conversations only seemed to come in two flavors: small talk and secrets. Melissa was the only one who knew about Hannah and Peter, while Hannah was one of the rare few souls who had the dirt on Melissa's romance.

Amanda kept her puzzled attention on the Pearls in the monitors. "It's been two years. How can they just be discovering their powers?"

"They were reversed," said a voice from the hallway.

Eden shuffled into the monitoring room, exhausted. As the only other Mexican from the Pearls' native Earth, she was the perfect ambassador to the group. But the job came with long hours, high tension, and the occasional bodily harm. Amanda could guess from her red, bleary eyes that she'd just been caught in the lumic's lightburst.

"You okay?"

Eden collapsed onto the couch in the back of the office and draped her arm over her eyes. "They're like puppies. Sweet, exploding puppies."

Amanda's brow crinkled. "When you say they were reversed—"

"She means a lot," Melissa replied. "From all available evidence, we believe they were regressed twenty-three months."

"Holy shit." Hannah heard from Peter that the Pearls had been timewiped, but she hadn't known the extent of it. To turn the clock back that far on someone without killing them took a godly amount of skill. No doubt the Pelletiers were behind it, but why?

Amanda studied the Pearls with new sympathy. "So as far as they know, they've only been on this world four weeks."

"They've been oriented," said Melissa. "But there's nothing we can do about the missing time. Everything that happened to them has been permanently undone."

Hannah suddenly felt the strong urge to cry, and she wasn't even sure it was over the Pearls. Her emotions had been running raw all morning, even before she saw that stupid white sky. The anniversary must have been hitting her harder than she expected. All at once, she wanted to punch a window, weep like a child, stab Azral in the neck, and hide under a blanket. More than that, she wanted to tell Amanda everything about what she'd been doing with Peter, and why. She couldn't handle the secrecy anymore.

Amanda studied the monitors through slitted green eyes, her voice dripping with venom. "Reversing those women was probably the nicest thing the Pelletiers ever did for them."

Eden lifted her head off the couch pillow. "You think it was a *good* thing?"

"I think it was a blessing," said Amanda. "It's no coincidence that the Pearls are all women. They were specifically brought here for fertilization. Hell, they were probably kept in a breeding cage, just spitting out babies, and not just for twenty-three months. The way the Pelletiers mess with time, it could have gone on for years. Decades. Would *you* want to remember that?"

Hannah had to bite her lip to keep from crying.

"I wouldn't," Eden admitted. "But it still doesn't make sense. If the Pearls are so valuable, how did they end up with the Mexican CIA?"

Amanda shrugged. "I guess the Pelletiers knew we'd rescue them eventually. Now they have eight more orphans in a village full of Gothams. At some point soon, they'll stop being passive-aggressive about it and force us all to breed."

Hannah kept a tight, impassive expression while her inner self howled with grief. For all of Amanda's miraculous recovery, she still had scars from her ordeal. Worse, she was probably right. There was nothing to stop the Pelletiers from pulling her back into the mating game, especially if Hannah couldn't give them a child.

She fidgeted with the plastic card in her pocket, the driver's license of a long-dead orphan. Hannah had been holding on to it for nearly two years and never thought she'd need it for anything more than posterity. But the arrival of the woman named Ofelia Curado gave it all new meaning and purpose.

"So which one is she?" Hannah asked. "The one we're meeting with."

Melissa motioned to the long-haired brunette on Monitor 5. "That one. The traveler."

The sisters leaned in for a closer look. While most of her companions flailed and fretted, Ofelia sat calmly behind an executive desk, her feet propped up and a cigarette in her hand. She moved her arm in lazy waves, summoning dish-size portals into the air. Despite Melissa's assertion, Ofelia didn't look like she was having a hard time adapting.

"Can you bring her in for a close-up?" Hannah asked.

Melissa zoomed in on Ofelia's face. Even in her run-down state, she was a strikingly lovely woman, with flawless bone structure, a cute button nose, and the most soulful brown eyes Hannah had ever seen. She looked like a classic Hollywood movie star, just biding her time in a Malibu rehab clinic.

"She's beautiful," Amanda said. "Looks older than the others."

"She is," Melissa replied. "By at least a decade."

"A thirty-year-old Cuban in a group of young Mexicans," said Eden. "Definitely the odd duck of the pack."

"Will we need a translator?" Amanda asked.

Melissa shook her head. "She's lived in America half her life, most recently San Diego."

Amanda turned to her, wide-eyed. "She's from San Diego?"

"That's why I wanted you and Hannah to talk to her," Melissa said. "You have more in common with her than anyone else. Look."

She centered the camera on Ofelia's right wrist. One quick glimpse of her shiny metal bracelet was enough to brief Amanda on the news she'd been missing. It seemed Ofelia Curado wasn't a Pearl at all. She was the last of the Silvers to be found.

"Hello, sisters."

Ofelia had been fully prepared for visitors. By the time Hannah and Amanda reached her office-turned-bedroom, she had two folding chairs set up for them. She sat up straight behind her manager's desk, with her hands pressed together and a preemptive look of skepticism, as if the Givens had come to sell her rainbows in a jar. Her dark eyes bulged at the sight of Amanda's tempic arms, but she quickly recovered her poise.

Hannah was nowhere near as subtle in her gawking. Seeing the silver bracelet on camera had been jarring enough. Seeing it up close after nearly two years was a cold, hard slap in the face, even worse than the sky that had mocked her this morning. The universe seemed determined to make her relive the apocalypse, bit by ugly bit.

Ofelia beckoned them inside. "Please. Sit."

"Uh . . ." Amanda paused at the door, her attention caught on a thin gray cot that had been deliberately placed out of camera view. It was currently occupied by one of Ofelia's fellow refugees, a small young girl in a white T-shirt and sweatpants. She slept without a twitch or shudder, even with all the bustle in the room.

"Don't worry about Rosario," Ofelia said. "She was having a hard time, so I gave her some of my sedatives. She won't be waking anytime soon."

Amanda wasn't comforted. "I'm not sure that's safe."

"Are you a doctor?"

"I was a nurse."

"Well, I was a talented opioid addict," Ofelia replied. "I know what I'm doing."

Hannah couldn't help but enjoy her rich and smoky voice, garnished with a pleasing accent that made every word flow like music.

"If it's all the same to you," said Amanda, "I'd like to check her vitals."

"Be my guest, but I don't—" Ofelia froze as Amanda's right hand stretched across the room and pressed two fingers to Rosario's neck. After a few seconds, her arm shrank back to normal.

"Okay," said Amanda. "Her pulse is good."

"Mine isn't," Ofelia said. "I thought your arms were just covered in tempis for some reason."

"No. They're solid."

"I don't even know how to react to that."

As the sisters took their seats, they noticed a long, gauzy bandage on the underside of Ofelia's forearm. The wound was so fresh, Hannah could smell the blood and antiseptics. The scents didn't usually nauseate her, but now they threatened to bring her breakfast back with a vengeance.

Ofelia lit a new cigarette and took a long puff, her brown eyes fixed on Hannah. "So you're the swifter of your group."

Hannah struggled to suppress her queasiness. "I *was* a swifter. Now I'm a slower."

"That's a thing?"

"It is now."

"You're both very strange." She narrowed her eyes at Hannah. "You also look familiar. Did we meet in San Diego?"

Hannah shrugged. "We might have. I don't know. It's . . . been a long time."

"Not for me." Ofelia shook a finger at her. "I know for a fact that I've seen you somewhere. Give me time. It'll come to me."

Hannah traded a nervous look with Amanda before taking a deep breath. "So, listen—"

"Given," said Ofelia. "That's an Irish name, isn't it?"

"For us it is," Amanda replied.

"Well, you've certainly got the look down, all green-eyed, pale, and pretty." Ofelia studied Hannah again. "You, on the other hand, could almost pass for Latina. Are you two really sisters?"

"I take after my mom," Hannah explained. "Amanda got all our dad's genes."

"Genes." Ofelia took a long hit of her cigarette. "I hear that's why the Pelletiers chose us. We all have a . . . *¿Cómo era la palabra?* . . . a *mutation* in our brains, and that it runs strong in families."

Hannah knew where she was going with this. Ofelia had a genetic sibling of her own and she was working up the nerve to ask about him. She was right to be afraid.

"It's similar to what the Gothams have," Amanda said. "You know about them, right?"

"Oh yes. Peter's told me all about his people."

Amanda's eyebrows rose. "You know Peter?"

"Of course. He's been helping me with my portals. He didn't tell you?"

"No, we're not, uh . . ." Amanda tensely shook her head. "We don't see a lot of each other."

"He's a good man," said Ofelia. "And he says good things about the two of you. I hear you both played a big part in saving us from the Mexicans."

The sisters acknowledged her with humble nods. "It was a group effort," Amanda said.

"Well, I'm grateful all the same."

Ofelia checked on Rosario, then blew an angry puff of smoke at the wall. "Four long weeks on that fucking train, always moving around from place to place. At every stop, new people came on and off. Soldiers and scientists. Men. Always men. They took care not to hurt us, but they still weren't kind. In hindsight, it's a miracle that none of us were raped."

She fell into her thoughts for a moment, then whisked a small portal into the air. "If I'd known about this, I could have saved us myself."

Amanda shook her head. "Wouldn't have worked. They were blocking you with solis."

"Solis." Ofelia laughed. "Aeris, tempis, slowers, swifters. It's like something out of a comic book, the kind my brother used to read."

Hannah's hand clutched tightly around the driver's license in her pocket. "We were the same way. It took us weeks before we could wrap our heads around it."

Ofelia's expression turned sour. "Is this where it starts?"

"Where what starts?"

"The pep talk," she said. "I'm not dumb. I know why you're here. Melissa thinks I can't cope."

"Is she right?" Amanda asked.

Hannah cringed at her sister's directness. She'd been a veteran of war for so goddamn long that she forgot how to deal with rookies.

"You tell me," Ofelia fired back. "You were a nurse. You know how to read people."

"Not like I used to," Amanda confessed. "I see a real strength in you." She pointed at Ofelia's bloody arm bandage. "But I also see a deep vein cut—"

"An accident," Ofelia insisted. "Peter warned me that portals have sharp edges. Last night, I learned it the hard way."

Amanda thought about it for a moment before giving her the benefit of the doubt. "Then I made a bad assumption. I'm sorry."

"No need to apologize. Given everything, it was a good assumption." Ofelia took another look at Amanda's tempic limbs. "Since we're talking about arms, may I ask how, uh . . . ?"

"I picked a fight with the wrong woman," Amanda curtly explained.

"I'm sorry to hear that."

"Don't be," said Amanda. "It got me out of a bad arrangement."

Hannah felt sick all over again. Earlier that year, on the eve of Zack and Amanda's engagement, Semerjean had appeared in their flat like a phantom and confirmed their hunch that the Pelletiers were done with them. They were free to be together with no strings attached. Whenever Zack or Amanda tried to question their good fortune, someone—usually Hannah or Peter—urged them not to overthink it.

Ofelia opened her mouth to say something, then looked at the camera self-consciously. "I suppose I am in over my head. As much as I try, I still can't trust these government people."

"They won't hurt you," Amanda insisted. "Even if they want to, we won't let them."

"You're not loyal to Integrity?"

"Our people come first," Hannah assured her. "And you're part of the family." She flicked a hand at her silver bracelet. "Hell, you're even part of the *nuclear* family."

Ofelia fumbled awkwardly with the bangle. "Then I have to tell you, sisters, that this isn't the first time I've been under observation. I have a long history of emotional problems."

She finished her cigarette with a trembling hand, then crushed it against the desk.

"But I was doing just fine before everything changed. I was six months clean. I had a good job, a girlfriend. And then suddenly . . ." She threw up her hands. "I'm stuck on a world that doesn't make sense, full of people I don't know who are looking to hurt me. I've got a doomsday behind me, a doomsday ahead of me, and twenty-three months of blank space in between. I stay up nights wondering what was done to me, but I'm pretty sure I don't want the answer."

Hannah wanted to cry all over again. This woman had every reason in the world to be depressed, plus a few new ones she had yet to learn.

Ofelia glanced over her shoulder at Rosario. "The only people who share my plight are these girls, and even they have an easier time handling it than I do. Some of them think this is just a weird dream. Some of them say that it's all God's plan. And some just believe that it'll all work out somehow. I wish I had their optimism, but if there's one thing life has taught me repeatedly, it's that there's no one up there looking out for us. We're all on our own."

As tears rolled down her lovely face, Amanda shot a sharp look at her sister. Someone needed to be putting their sympathetic hands on Ofelia—*warm* hands. Not tempis.

Hannah moved around the desk and kneeled at Ofelia's side, her nose once again filled with the sickening scent of blood. "Listen to me . . ."

"No." Ofelia yanked her arm back. "As long as you keep stuff from me, I can't trust you."

"What am I keeping from you?"

"I don't know. But *she* does." Ofelia gestured at Rosario. "The girl's a prophet. She sees all kinds of things. Some are so bad, they have to sedate her. Others are just . . ."

Ofelia snatched another cigarette from her pack. "She said you'd be coming with bad news in your pocket, but she wouldn't tell me what it is." She laughed darkly. "I keep wondering about it. I mean what can be worse than what's already happening? What is there left to take from me?"

Hannah swapped a dark look with Amanda before retrieving the license from her pocket. She put it down on the desk in front of Ofelia, but kept it hidden beneath her hand.

"I was playing it by ear," Hannah admitted. "I didn't know if I was going to show it to you or wait for another day."

Amanda nodded heavily. "We want to make things better for you, not worse."

"I understand that," Ofelia told her. "But if I'm truly part of the nuclear family, then you're going to have to trust me."

Hannah closed her eyes and breathed a heavy sigh. Of all the days to be revisiting this topic, why the hell did it have to be today?

"You were right about the mutation running strong in certain families, like mine."

Hannah lifted her hand and revealed the license. "And yours."

Ofelia gasped at the face on the card, a handsome man of Cuban descent. Hannah had been carrying around the driver's license of Jury Curado for nearly as long as she'd been on this world. But she hadn't thought about him in months, not until she learned Ofelia's last name.

"My brother!" Ofelia took the card in her hands, her eyes wet and glistening. "I thought he was dead! I mean . . ."

She glared at Hannah. "No. If Jury was alive, there'd be no force on Earth that would keep him from me. You're trying to tell me—"

"I'm sorry."

"—that he was here and now he's not."

Hannah pulled her chair to Ofelia's side of the desk and sat inches away from her. Her nausea had come back in full force, enough to make the room spin.

"I didn't know him," she confessed to Ofelia. "None of us did. He was supposed to be part of our group but . . ."

"Someone killed him," Amanda said. "Just minutes after he arrived on this world."

Ofelia turned to her, horrified. "He's been dead *two years*?"

Hannah squeezed her wrist. "I'm so sorry."

"It doesn't make sense. If you never met him, then how do you know about him? How did you get his license?"

"There, uh . . ." Hannah steeled herself, then shot her sister a pointed look. *Let me explain it*, she silently urged her. *Just me.*

"There's a man from our world named Evan Rander," Hannah began. "He's also one of the Silver group but he isn't anything like us. He's a psychopath. And he has a really weird ability that lets him . . . relive his life on this world. The same five years, over and over and over again. He plays it differently each time."

Though Hannah was looking down at her knees, she could feel every watt of Ofelia's stare. She wanted this all to make sense *now*, and Hannah just kept fumbling around.

"In one of his earliest run-throughs, Evan . . . fell in love with me. Or whatever passes for love in his sick brain. But I didn't love him back and he's hated me ever since. I must have had something special with Jury in those other timelines, because whenever Evan starts over again, he kills him right away. He doesn't ever want me to meet your brother, but he wants me to know exactly what I'm missing. That's . . ."

Hannah tapped Jury's photo. "That's how I got his license. I'm so sorry."

"Stop apologizing," Ofelia snapped. "You don't owe us anything."

"That's not true. I feel partly—"

"You are *not* responsible," Amanda interjected. "None of this is your fault."

"She's right," Ofelia said. "I've had my share of stalkers. Men who believed they were entitled to me and wouldn't take no for an answer."

She raised the hem of her T-shirt, revealing a two-inch scar on her abdomen. "One of them stabbed me. Do you think it was my fault?"

Hannah shook her head. "No."

"Then stop saying you're sorry."

The room fell into a brief, awkward lull as Ofelia finished her cigarette.

"My husband went through the same thing you're going through," Amanda told her. "He had a brother on this world that he never got to see."

"Were they twins?" Ofelia asked.

"No."

"Did they grow up with a rapist for a father? Did they flee to Miami in a little wooden boat?"

"Ofelia—"

"You know nothing about what I feel. Jury was everything to me. To think that I could have had him here, that I could be seeing him right now . . ."

She looked back to Hannah and exposed her knife scar again. "Do you know what happened to the man who did this?"

Hannah nodded miserably. "I'm guessing your brother happened to him."

"Very good. Now, what was done to the man who killed Jury?"

Hannah was ashamed to tell her that Evan was still alive, still at large, still hurting people without a shred of compunction. Integrity had fed his image through every law enforcement database in the world, but he hadn't registered a blip in more than a year. It was hard to find a man who could undo his own mistakes. Even the augurs were helpless.

"We don't know where he is. But I will find him," Hannah promised Ofelia. "He's taken more than one man from my life, and he has a lot to answer for."

Ofelia picked up her brother's license. "May I keep this?"

"Of course."

"Thank you," said Ofelia. "And thank you for telling me about Jury. I know you were afraid it would send me over the edge, but it actually did just the opposite."

She held up the license, her dark eyes narrowed to slits. "You just gave me a reason to go on."

In a stronger state of mind, Amanda might have reminded both Hannah and Ofelia that vengeance had a way of backfiring on people. Her tempic arms were proof enough.

Hannah was just about to say something when Ofelia suddenly looked to her with wide-eyed revelation. "*Godspell!*"

The sisters reacted with matching blank faces. "What?"

"That's why you look so familiar! I saw you onstage in a production of *Godspell*."

Hannah had no idea why she found that so funny. Maybe it was the weird and heavy mood she was in. Maybe it was just the timing. Or maybe it was the fact that Ofelia was right. Once upon a time, somewhere deep on the other side of creation, Hannah had performed in cheesy, low-budget musicals. The memories were so quaint and utterly silly that they brushed like feathers across the most ticklish parts of her mind. What began as a giggle became a loud chortle, then exploded into a guffaw.

Then suddenly her nausea came back with a fury, enough to drive Hannah back to her feet and send her running out of the room.

Amanda rose from her chair. "Hannah?"

Hannah had just barely made it to the sink of the nearest bathroom when she tossed up the remains of her breakfast. While her face dripped with sweat and her vision danced with spots, she rinsed out her mouth with cold water. She hadn't thrown up in ages, not even last Friday, when she'd tumbled a thousand feet through the windy skies of Mexico. Maybe her frazzled nerves got the better of her. Or maybe she'd picked up a flu. The underland was a veritable germ incubator. All it took was one sniffly Gotham.

Or maybe . . .

No.

Wide-eyed, Hannah examined herself in the mirror. Over the shoulder of her reflection, above the thermic hand dryer, was the faint and handsome visage of a devil she knew.

Semerjean beamed a teasing smile at Hannah. *"Well, well, well. What do we finally have here?"*

Amanda knocked on the bathroom door. "Hannah? Are you okay?"

No response. Amanda peeked around the hallway to find Ofelia and four Pearls looking back at her with nervous curiosity. She gripped the door handle tight enough to bend it.

"Okay, Hannah. I'm coming in."

She opened the door to a half-fouled sink, plus a line of strange markings on the mirror. Someone had burned a black word into the glass, a diagonal scrawl of finger-traced letters.

CONGRATULATIONS

White-faced, Amanda turned her head and saw Hannah crouched in the far corner of the bathroom, her fingers trembling, her face drenched in tears.

"We had to do it," she cried. "We had no choice. You were dying." Hannah covered her face with her hands. "You were dying."

By the time Ofelia caught up with the sisters, they were huddled together in the bathroom, their pink and white arms wrapped tightly around each other. Ofelia could only assume from the way they both wept that someone had just died on them. She would have never guessed in a million years what Amanda and Hannah were really crying about: the unexpected spark of life, a brand-new Given brought into creation.

FIVE

The Tams had a bit of a self-esteem problem. They were the second largest family in the Gotham clan, full of smart and attractive people. But aside from the occasional powerful augur, they were all mediocre timebenders. Their tempics could barely dent a wall, their swifters were the slowest in the guild, and the half-formed illusions of the family lumics were the butt of village in-jokes.

Unable to compete on a genetic level, the Tams chose wealth as their battleground. Their augurs were forced to learn market economics, a potent combination of foresight and insight that forged them all into killer stock traders. Their early investment in Prior Chronolectrics, the first American company to offer kitchen juves, had turned the Tams into billionaires, while their poor fellow Gothams were only earning hundreds of millions.

To this day, the Tams never stopping lording their net worth over others. Their palatial estate in the Heaven's Gate district of Quarter Hill was twice the size of the next largest property, with the greenest lawns, the bluest pools, and the whitest of white marble fountains. Whenever their kinsmen tried to one-up them with opulence, the Tams simply added another wing to their mansion. They'd planted a flag on their one hill of dominance and God help anyone who tried to take it from them.

Mia had gone to their house on five separate occasions and was shocked by its vastness each time. Regal Tam's closet was the size of Mia's apartment, with enough clothes, shoes, and accessories to fill an outlet store. Luckily for Mia, she was a similar height and build as Regal, which gave her hundreds of outfits to borrow.

For a trust fund girl with superpowers, Regal dressed with surprising humility. There was nothing in her wardrobe that was too ostentatious, though her fondness for paisley and bright flower patterns left Mia with only a few dozen tolerable options.

She emerged from the closet in black slacks and silver boots, plus a black-and-silver bander that, on another world, would have been called a tube top. "How's this?"

Regal sat up in the canopy bed, half-naked beneath her cashmere comforter. Like her younger sister, Sovereign, she'd inherited some of the more enviable traits of her family bloodline: a sharp mind, a strong jaw, a pair of radiant blue eyes, and a complexion so flawless that she might as well have been airbrushed. In a different community, she might have been considered preternaturally blessed. But here among the Gothams, she was a low-grade swifter and an unabashed sapphic. That pretty much made her a misfit.

Mia wasn't encouraged by her disapproving look. "What? You don't like it?"

"You look great," Regal said. "But it's kind of outdated to wear a bander with pants. And by 'kind of,' I mean 'very.'"

"What am I supposed to wear it with?"

"Short wraps," said Regal. "I have dozens."

"I don't do skirts."

"Okay, so go like that. It's an orphan party. They won't know you're antiquing it." She pointed at Mia's torso. "But at least wear a jacket."

Frustrated, Mia beckoned to her. "I'm already late. Just pick one for me."

"Fine." Regal dashed across the room in a streaking blur and vanished into the closet. She emerged two seconds later in a bathrobe, with a cropped silver jacket dangling from her hand. "I hope you're not just using me for my clothes."

"Of course not," said Mia. "Why would you think that?"

"Because I don't see you for weeks on end. And when we do kick around, you never stay."

Mia slipped her arms into the jacket sleeves. "I told you I had somewhere to be."

"Then you should have come here earlier." She watched as Mia twirled a slow 360. "Yeah. That definitely fits the occasion."

Mia examined herself in the mirror and smiled. Regal was right. The jacket made her outfit perfect for tonight's special gathering—not too formal, not too casual, and still a little bit sexy. It wasn't every night that she got to meet eight new women from her world. Better to start on a good first impression.

Mia kissed Regal on the lips. "Thank you. You're a lifesaver."

"Happy to help," she said, with an expression that suggested anything but.

Mia opened a horizontal portal to her bedroom and dropped her old clothes into the disc. "You're right. I should have come here sooner."

"Don't get me wrong. I'm always glad to see you."

"But?"

Regal shrugged. "I don't know. Maybe it's just the end of the world talking, but I don't want to spend the rest of my life having quickies. I see how happy my sister is with Liam . . ."

Mia rolled her eyes. "They're children."

"They're the same age as you."

"I've been through more than they have," Mia said. "I've seen what falling in love gets you. Trust me. You don't want it."

"And if I do?"

"Then you don't want it with me."

Mia waved a new portal to the underland. "I'll bring your clothes back tomorrow."

"Keep them."

"Regal—"

"You said you're late, so go. Be with your people. Have a nice party."

Mia stepped halfway into the breach, then briefly turned around. Somewhere deep in the back of her mind was the perfect thing to say to Regal, but she couldn't seem to find it. Her thoughts were stuck, as they often were, on the fractured glass image of Carrie Bloom.

"It's not a party," Mia ended up saying. She took one last look at the splendor of the Tam house, then retreated back into her dark little underworld.

The music could be heard from every corner of the Orphanage—a hard, thumping bass that rattled all the windows, garnished with Heath's dulcet voice. Mia only had to take a step out of the portal before she recognized the song he was singing: Billy Idol's "Dancing with Myself," a rather upbeat tune for such a grim anniversary. Mia's father used to play it whenever he worked in the garage. The image of his love handles jiggling, her older brothers giggling as he swayed his hips to the rhythm . . . God. She hadn't even joined the shindig yet, and she was already wallowing in old-world nostalgia.

Suck it up, Mia told herself. *You're not a weakling. You can handle this.*

As she drew closer to the clubhouse, she could see through the windows. The don't-call-it-a-party party was clearly in full swing, with a dozen people dancing in the middle of the room. Beyond them, the Great Remains, Heath's merry band of musical orphans, were rocking out on a tempic stage: Joey Fehrenbach on lead guitar, Mateo McGraw on drums, the Copper named Shroud on a double-neck bass, and Heath himself on keyboard. Hannah usually joined them as a vocalist and guitarist, but Mia didn't see her with them.

"Bullshit!" someone nearby shouted. "You could have talked her out of it!"

Mia easily recognized Amanda's voice. It was coming from the alley between the clubhouse and the commissary, just slightly out of view. For a split second, Mia feared that the sisters were having a fight, but . . . no, she could always feel Peter when he was near. His aura was like a beacon in her traveler senses. He was the one in Amanda's gunsights.

"She knew the risks," Peter insisted. "She didn't care. You were in trouble. This is how she wanted to help."

"It's not what *I* wanted," Amanda fired back. "I never wanted this for her! If I had known—"

"You would have stopped us," Peter said. "Exactly why we didn't tell you. Hang on."

"Don't you dare walk away from me."

"I'm not. Just give me a sec."

Shit, thought Mia. In all her distraction, she forgot that Peter could sense her just as easily as she sensed him. He emerged from the alley and shot her a cynical look. "You snooping on us?"

"No." Mia crossed her arms defensively. "I was just going to the thing."

"All right, then. Keep going. We'll meet you inside."

"Is everything okay?"

"Nothing you need to worry about," Peter assured her. "We're just having a talk."

"You're having a *yell*. If this is serious—"

"Mia . . ."

Amanda stepped into view and leaned against the brickface. Though she looked perfectly lovely in her white cocktail dress, Mia could read every line and shadow on her face. They'd been on this world for just twenty-six minutes when they'd first met each other, and they'd been together every day since. Mia *knew* Amanda. Whatever was eating her, it was big.

"Please tell me what's going on," Mia implored her. "If someone's hurt—"

"No one's hurt," Amanda said.

Now that Mia thought about it, the last time Amanda was this upset was when Caleb knocked up Mercy. "Holy shit. Is someone pregnant?"

Peter gritted his teeth. "Damn it, girl. Just let us talk."

"Okay, *fine*." Mia walked away, fuming. "Excuse me for thinking I was part of this family!"

She pushed through the swinging glass doors of the clubhouse and took a quick look around. There were at least three dozen people scattered about: nearly all the orphans in the underland, plus most of their government handlers. Mia even spied a few Gothams in the mix, all the native timebenders who, through friendship or more, had become entwined in the lives of the orphans. Mercy sat in a dark corner booth, her hand clasped protectively around the wrist of her brother, Sage. Liam and Sovereign sucked face by the snack table, oblivious to the rest of the world. Noah Rall, one of Zack's best friends from the turners' guild, was having an intense-looking discussion with Eden. They'd been dating for three months and were getting pretty serious, despite the fact that she was an orphan and he was a Gotham. The last thing either of them wanted was to make a baby for the Pelletiers. But what if all their protective measures failed? What if she was the pregnant one?

The Great Remains finished their song and were mightily applauded. Heath briefly conferred with his fellow musicians before mumbling into the microphone.

"Okay. We're gonna play some more Beatles."

Nearly everyone in the room broke out in laughter, to Heath's chagrin. He'd be the last one to admit that he was obsessed with the Beatles. To him, it was just common sense. If you liked music from the old world, if you liked music *at all*, then you acknowledged the Beatles as the greatest band of all time. To think otherwise was simply fallacious, like thinking two plus two equals Coldplay.

"This one's for Jonathan," Heath muttered into the microphone.

All the chuckles in the room suddenly came to a stop and a maudlin hush fell over the crowd. Mia could feel hot tears pricking her eyes. *Damn it, Heath.*

The band began playing "Here Comes the Sun," rather beautifully as far as Mia was concerned. But it wasn't exactly the best tune for grooving. The orphans on the dance floor scattered to the periphery just as Mia was trying to scan the room for Zack.

"Mia!"

Felicity Yu approached her from behind, dressed, as ever, in a brightly colored pantsuit. "Look at you, all fashionably late." She scrutinized Mia's outfit. "Well, you're late, anyway. What is this, Eighties Night?"

Mia batted her arm. "Shut up. I look good."

"You do," Felicity said. "If I had your adorable figure, I'd be wearing the same thing."

"Where's Melissa?"

"Headache," Felicity said with a sigh. "Thus it falls on me to play Chaperone-in-Chief."

Mia looked around. "It's a lot more festive than I was expecting."

"You say it like it's a bad thing."

"I don't know," Mia admitted. "I mostly just came here to meet the Pearls."

"Well, you're half in luck," Felicity said. "Four of them are here. The other four are . . . what's that expression again?"

"Not ready for prime time."

"Not ready for prime time," Felicity echoed with a laugh. "You people have the best jargon."

A sharp new aura penetrated Mia's consciousness, a traveler she'd never felt before. The mysterious Ofelia was somewhere in the room, but Mia couldn't get a lock on her.

Felicity gripped her shoulder. "Listen, uh, that Bloom girl stopped by earlier."

Mia's heart lurched. "Carrie?"

"Yeah. She walked the room for a couple of minutes and then lit off. Guess she was hoping to find you here."

Mia palmed her face. "*Goddamn* it."

"You're just leaving a trail of broken hearts, aren't you?"

"No. That's not . . ." Mia didn't have the strength to explain it. Carrie wasn't one of her quick-fling conquests. She was a loss. A big one.

Felicity saw the sorrow in Mia's eyes. "Sorry. I didn't mean to tease. I only wish I had more of your courage."

"It's okay. I just . . ." Mia scanned the room again. "I have to find Zack."

Felicity pointed to the right. "Last I saw, he was over there with his buddies."

A salvo of cheers rose up from that direction. Mia weaved through the crowd to find a mob of orphans clustered around a table, all smiling down at the one man who was seated. Though Mia couldn't see Zack's face from her vantage, she had a perfectly clear view of his new hand, a sleek black prosthetic that looked like something from the twenty-third century.

"Okay," Zack told his audience. "For my next trick, I'll attempt something I've never been able to do before: the infamous Vulcan hand salute."

Caleb gaped in mock horror. "People have *died* trying that."

"I don't think it's covered in the warranty," Ben Hopkins teased.

"Some things are worth the risk, my friends." Zack looked around. "Is everyone ready?"

"Just do it, you ham."

"All right. Here goes." With exaggerated effort, Zack squinted at his myoelectric hand until the fingers split apart in a perfect V.

The onlookers cheered. Zack brandished his hand with beaming triumph before catching a glimpse of Mia. His smile went flat.

"That's it," he told Caleb and the others. "Next show at ten o'clock."

As the others dispersed, Zack drank in Mia through tired gray eyes. "Well, well. Look who finally showed up. Nice abs."

"Nice hand." Mia sat down next to him and poked his metal wrist. "Does it hurt?"

"Nope. It's just a big dead weight at the end of my arm. But it seems to be working, so . . . hey."

Mia patted his shoulder. "You'll get used to it."

"Carrie was looking for you."

"I know!"

"Just talk to her already," Zack said. "Stop being a wuss."

"I may be a wuss but you're a sucky husband."

"How am I a sucky husband?"

Mia jerked her head at the entrance. "Amanda's right outside and she's super upset, while you're in here doing hand tricks."

Zack replied with a dismal shrug. "She wanted to talk to Peter alone."

"She looks ready to smack him," Mia said. "What the hell's going on?"

Zack tapped his new fingers against the table, his eyes dancing in dilemma. "It's not my news to give."

"Can't you just tell me?"

"Mia, do you trust me?"

"Oh, don't pull that."

"Do you trust me?"

"Of course I do!"

"Then take the night to enjoy yourself," Zack urged her. "Mingle. Dance. Reminisce on good times. And if all that fails, then hook up with someone."

Mia rolled her eyes. Zack saw her as a teenage Casanova when the truth was much simpler. There were a lot of lonely people in the underland who had come to believe, with very good reason, that life was crushingly short. Anyone could get laid in this environment. All you had to do was be direct.

Of course, it didn't always work the way Mia had hoped. She'd broken the hearts of two different Coppers, enough for Mother to declare her *persona non grata*. And there were three Gotham lesbians who'd told her to lose their number. From the way she'd left things with Regal, it would probably soon be four.

Mia looked to the far side of the clubhouse, where Sovereign nestled lovingly against Liam. "Do you think I'm psychologically unfit?"

"For what?" Zack asked. "That jacket?"

"For going on missions."

"Oh." Zack chuckled. "You saved Amanda's life. You won't get any shit from me."

"Right! See? But Cedric's benching me until I talk to someone."

Zack nodded. "He's trying to push therapy on me too. Guess he thinks we need it the most."

"That's bullshit."

"Is it?" Zack asked. "There are times when even I get worried about us."

"What do you mean?"

Zack lifted a flap on his mechanical wrist and toyed with the fine motor settings. "When's the last time you thought about Rebel and Ivy?"

"Why would I?" asked Mia. "They're dead and no one misses them."

"*We* don't miss them," Zack said. "But ask any Gotham and they'll tell you what amazing, wonderful people they used to be. Everyone looked up to them."

Zack studied the square of four divots on the back of his flesh hand, a scar from his time as a Pelletier captive. "Then You-Know-Who crashed into this world and took everything Rebel and Ivy had—their friends, their cousins, their whole entire future. Esis killed Ivy's babies while they were still in her womb, just to teach her a lesson."

Mia didn't like where Zack was going with this.

"Whatever you think about Rebel and Ivy," he said, "they had every good reason to hate the Pelletiers. But they let that hatred ruin them. By the time we met them, they were both batshit crazy. Everything that was good about them was just . . . gone."

Zack slumped in his chair and watched the band play. "Whenever I get worked up about the Pelletiers, I think of Rebel and Ivy. I don't want to become like them and neither should you."

Mia looked away with a wounded expression. "You really think I'm that bad?"

"No," said Zack. "But you're not as good as you used to be."

"Mia!"

Hannah beckoned to her from the other side of the dance floor, a lovely brunette at her side. At long last, Mia had a fix on Ofelia Curado, but all she wanted to do now was punch someone.

She stood up from her chair. "I'm sorry you feel that way."

Zack shook his head with wincing regret. "Don't listen to me. I'm in a shitty mood and I'm not thinking straight. Even if I was, I have no business telling you how to be."

"No, you don't," Mia said. "And while you may miss the fat, stupid girl I used to be—"

"Mia . . ."

"—*I* don't."

"You were never fat or stupid," Zack bleakly insisted. "That was just Future Mia talking."

"Yeah, well, I'm her now. And she was right about all of it." She looked to Hannah. "See you later, Zack."

Mia walked across the empty dance floor. She was only halfway to Hannah when the Beatles song ended and the audience fell into lively applause.

Hannah smiled at her brightly, as if everything was right with the world. Mia could only assume from her blithe and sunny demeanor that she was completely removed from this pregnancy drama, the one that had turned half their family into moody jerkwads.

"You're finally here," Hannah said to her. "I've been talking you up all night to Ofelia. She was starting to think you didn't exist."

The moment Mia looked at Ofelia, she forgot her resentments. The woman had been pretty at a distance, but up close she was a celestial vision. Her eyes, her lips, her *traveler's aura*. She was a fragrant rose on the portal network. Even her emotional pain was gorgeous.

Ofelia shook her hand distractedly. "I've heard a lot about you."

Mia kept shaking her hand, silent and slack-faced, as if she'd been hypnotized.

"Uh . . ." Hannah pulled Mia's hand away. "This is the part where you say something nice."

"You are seriously hot and I'm hoping you're gay."

Hannah frowned at her. "Not *that* nice."

Ofelia laughed. "You're a bold one. How old are you?"

"Sixteen."

"She's *fifteen*," Hannah insisted.

"I'll be sixteen next month," Mia said. "But with all the shit that's happened to me, I might as well be thirty."

Ofelia smiled at her. "I like you, Mia. I look forward to getting to know you. And while I consider myself to be mostly gay, we're going to have to settle for friendship because—"

A high scream rose from the west side of the clubhouse, bringing the music and chatter to a halt. Mia looked to her left and saw a petite young stranger clutching her head in agony.

"Rosario," said Ofelia. "She must be having a vision. I should, uh . . ."

Hannah patted her back. "Go."

As Ofelia rushed to her friend's side, Hannah looked to Mia in astonishment. "'You're seriously hot and I hope you're gay'?"

"It was a compliment."

"It was borderline harassment," Hannah said. "She's been having a hard time. She doesn't need that from you."

"It's not a big deal," Mia fired back. "I already moved on."

"Good."

Mia suddenly caught something in Hannah's expression, a rigidness in her jaw that usually meant she was stressing about something. Now that Mia thought about it, she'd seemed a little too cheery earlier, more than an evening like this warranted. Maybe she wasn't so far removed from this great and secret crisis. Maybe she was right in the middle of it.

Ofelia escorted Rosario out of the clubhouse, leaving an uncomfortable silence in their wake. Heath waved for Hannah impatiently from the edge of the bandstage.

"Guess I'm on," Hannah said to Mia. "Gotta go."

"Hannah . . ."

Mia caught her arm at the edge of the stage ramp. Hannah turned around and looked at her expectantly, but Mia was caught between two competing questions. After a few stumbling moments, she settled on the easier one.

"Are you okay?"

Hannah glanced at her with confusion, as if Mia had suddenly asked her if she was still right-handed. "Of course I am. Why wouldn't I be?"

That was all Mia needed to confirm her worst suspicion. With one exaggerated look, Hannah had just answered both her burning queries. She was definitely the pregnant one, and she was definitely not okay.

. . .

The room broke out in riotous applause as Hannah took the stage. She was, like Zack, a well-respected figure among the orphans—the one who always seemed to have her act together, the one who could always be counted on to lend a sympathetic ear. More than that, she was an endless source of existential optimism, and expressed all her hope with conviction. When Hannah spoke of the world's salvation, she sounded like a true authority on the matter, and for good reason. There was no one on Earth who knew the great messiah better. There was no one who believed in Theo more than she did.

Plus, she could belt out a hell of a tune. As much as the others enjoyed Heath's singing, it was Hannah who was the true marquee star of the Great Remains. She didn't just mimic the voices of dead singers. She put her own passionate spin on the songs from the old world, and brought them to life in ways that Heath couldn't.

Hannah took the microphone, her electric guitar in hand. "Thank you. Wow. You guys are so nice. Now, before I begin a long set of showtunes—"

The audience chuckled. A few of the orphans booed.

"Oh, fuck you," Hannah joked. "One of these days, you'll let me do it."

She caught Mia's eye for a moment and then tensely looked away. "Anyway, before we get back to the rock and roll, I want to clear something up. Everyone feels weird about calling this a party, for reasons I totally get. I mean it's been two years, *two goddamn years*, since the sky came down on the world we knew and took nearly everything from us. And there isn't a single one of us here who can say it's been easy. We've run, we've fought, we've struggled, we've bled. And we've lost people. We've all lost some very good people since we got here." Hannah tapped her wooden fretboard. "This guitar belonged to one of them. I've been practicing it for hours a day and I'm still nowhere near as good as he was."

Hannah paused as Amanda and Peter reentered the clubhouse. Mia noticed the brief, heavy look between the sisters.

"So why have a party on this shitty anniversary?" Hannah asked her fellow orphans. "Well, for starters, we have eight new people here in the underland—good people, *our* people, right here where they belong."

The crowd clapped loudly, though the remaining Pearls in the room looked like they wanted to sink through the floor.

"But there's more," Hannah continued. "I'm reminded of something my brother-in-law once said to me, and I remember it clearly because it's the only smart thing he's ever said."

The audience snickered at Hannah's quip, then flat-out laughed when Zack flipped her a metal middle finger.

Hannah smiled. "Glad to see it working. And in all seriousness, Zack's brilliant. He said that a world only dies when there's no one left to remember it. I never forgot that. I mean, really, it's so incredible when you think about it. A world only dies when there's no one left to remember it."

He'd actually said it to Mia, not Hannah, but the quote somehow got around. Mia didn't mind being written out of the story. The last thing she wanted was all eyes on her.

Hannah took a deep breath before continuing. "So the next time you feel weird about calling this a party, I want you to remember that beautiful thought. We're not here celebrating the death of our world. We're celebrating the fact that it still lives and breathes through all of us. We're here, we're alive, we're together, and we remember. *We remember.*"

The orphans broke out in their loudest cheers yet, though there were more than a few moist eyes among them. Even some of the Gothams had to bite their quivering lips.

Hannah brushed away her tears and smiled at the crowd. "Okay. This is the part where I stop talking. I love you all, my brothers and sisters. And I hope you enjoy this beautiful song." She readied her guitar, then nodded at her bandmates. "Hit it."

The orphans in the clubhouse hollered with delight as they heard the familiar opening chords. Hannah and Heath had spent weeks re-creating "With or Without You"—the standout hit of U2's fifth album—from memory, until they had a note-perfect music sheet. Those in the audience who knew and loved the song were initially jarred by Hannah's feminine take on the vocals. But within a few moments, the discord faded and the melody carried them home.

Mia retreated into the ladies' room and washed her hands, her thoughts spinning furiously around Hannah's new conundrum. In hindsight, it all made perfect sense: her nighttime "walks," the little flecks of secrecy in Peter's aura, the Pelletiers' inexplicable amnesty for Zack and Amanda. A Faustian bargain had been made behind closed doors, and Mia knew exactly which devil wrote the contract. The part she couldn't wrap her head around, and made her absolutely livid the more she thought about it, was how Hannah and Peter could have trusted Semerjean after all the shit he'd pulled.

A toilet flushed and Sovereign emerged from a nearby stall. As always, the young thermic was dressed in a tight, sleeveless turtleneck, the only kind of top that could flatter her figure while hiding her burn scars.

As Sovereign rinsed her hands in the sink, Mia caught her scrutinizing gaze in the mirror.

"I know," Mia growled.

Sovereign furrowed her brow. "Know what?"

"That no one wears banders with pants anymore. It's an outdated look. I'm aware."

"That's not why I'm staring," Sovereign said. "I'm just noticing your clothes look an awful lot like Regal's."

"Oh." Mia smiled. "Yeah. Good eye. I borrowed them an hour ago."

"You were in my sister's bedroom?"

"I was in your sister's everything."

"You're vile."

Before Mia even knew what she was doing, she pushed Sovereign against the wall and squeezed her hands around her woolly collar.

"Get off me!" Sovereign yelled. "Are you *crazy*?"

Mia let go of Sovereign, her thoughts lost in a jumble of other people's concerns. *"You're not as good as you used to be." "There were a dozen other ways to make that pilot talk." "Your anger's made you reckless. Reckless in a way that's going to cost someone's life."*

Sovereign hacked a throaty cough and glared at Mia. "When I tell my father what you did—"

"—he'll probably buy you a pony," Mia said. "That's all your family's good for. I'm sure your money will be a real comfort when you all die screaming in two and a half years."

Mia retreated several steps, then turned around to Sovereign. "Go back to the party. Have a good time. And if you ever call me 'vile' again, I'll drop you down an elevator shaft."

She opened a portal beneath her feet, then disappeared through the floor.

She emerged fifty yards to the south at the gated edge of the Orphanage, landing feet-first into a flower bed. Mia had thought, or at least hoped, that the dirt would comfortably break her fall, but the impact was murder on her ankles. She stumbled forward on a broken boot heel, then toppled hands-first onto a walkway.

"Ow! Shit!"

Mia closed her portal and scrambled back to her feet. Her palms were scraped, her legs were throbbing, and her pants were flecked with soil.

That's what you get for making a cool exit, she thought. *At least no one saw the landing.*

"That looked painful," said a woman in a lovely accent. "You couldn't use the door?"

Mia turned around to find Ofelia sitting alone on a curb, looking like a femme fatale in her moody lamppost lighting, a smoldering cigarette in her hand.

"I thought you went home," Mia said.

"Home?" Ofelia snorted. "Those offices aren't my home. I can't bear to go back there. At least not yet."

"Where's, uh . . . ?"

"Rosario." Ofelia blew a fat puff of smoke. "I let the government people walk her back. They're just going to sedate her, anyway. She doesn't need me."

"Is she okay?"

"She'll be fine." Ofelia smiled softly, then patted the curb next to her. "Come sit with me."

Grimacing, Mia hobbled her way to Ofelia, but left a respectful space between them.

"Sorry if I made you uncomfortable earlier," Mia said. "Wasn't my intention."

Ofelia laughed. "Are you kidding? It was the best part of the night. First normal thing that's happened to me since I got here."

Try as she might, Mia couldn't find the strength to smile. She still heard Sovereign echoing around inside her head. *You're vile. You're vile.*

"A lot of people are telling me I have issues," Mia said. "I'm starting to think they're right."

Ofelia waved her off. "Please. You should have seen me at your age."

"You were bad?"

"I was broken." Ofelia took another hit of her cigarette, a faint malaise in her eyes. "I gave myself to men and women of low character. They treated me horribly and I convinced myself that I deserved it. It wasn't the happiest time of my life."

Mia tensely shook her head. "That's not what I'm doing. At least I don't think so."

"I believe you," Ofelia said. "Peter said you're the smartest girl he's ever known. I can see it in your eyes and the way you talk."

Mia finally managed to laugh, though it was black as tar and filled with self-loathing. "If you knew *my* past, you wouldn't think so. I've made some of the dumbest mistakes a person can make. I fell in love with a boy who didn't even exist."

Ofelia nodded uncomfortably. "David."

"Yeah," Mia said with a sigh. "Guess Peter told you."

"No. Melissa."

"Melissa." Mia scoffed. "She's one to talk. She's dating a man who barely exists."

"She didn't say you were dumb," Ofelia assured her. "Just betrayed."

"I was both."

The distant clubhouse erupted in cheers. Hannah had finished her U2 song to resounding approval from the audience.

"You ever fall in love with a girl?" Ofelia asked her.

"Yes," Mia replied. "That didn't end well either."

"What happened?"

"Same thing that happened to you," Mia said. "She was reversed two years by 'David.'"

She could see from Ofelia's dark, busy eyes that the topic didn't sit well with her. "Why would he do such a terrible thing?"

"To hurt me," Mia said. "I fired a gun at his wife's head and he couldn't let that go unpunished. So he reversed Carrie right in front of me. Made me watch as she went from the fourteen-year-old girl I loved to a twelve-year-old who didn't recognize me."

"Coño." Ofelia blew smoke through gritted teeth. "That's monstrous."

"That's Semerjean," Mia said. "He told me to be grateful that he didn't kill her. Meanwhile, Carrie had to find out all over again that her mother's dead and the whole world's ending."

"Has she learned about you?"

Mia toyed with her broken boot heel. "She must have heard from someone that we were close, because she keeps looking for me. She wants me to tell her about everything she forgot, but . . . I don't know."

"Why *don't* you?" Ofelia asked. "You can fill in all the missing pieces for her. You can even start fresh. How old is she now?"

Mia shrugged. "Don't know. Probably close to the age she was when I met her."

Ofelia gripped her arm. "Mia!"

"You don't understand!"

"You said you were in love with her."

"I was. I am. I don't know!"

"There's no excuse," Ofelia insisted. "That girl you love is still alive."

"You don't *get it!*" Mia jumped to her feet. "I tried to kill Esis!"

"Yes, and you were punished for it."

"By Semerjean," said Mia. "I didn't tell you what *she* did."

She pressed down hard on her scraped left hand, using the pain to distract her from her emotions. If the dam cracked now, there'd be no fixing it. She'd become Past Mia all over again, that weak and weepy child.

"I should have known how stupid it was," Mia said. "To think a .38 pistol could kill a woman like that. Esis caught the bullet in a little time portal, and she promised me that it'll come back someday. Right in the head of someone I love."

"Mierda." Ofelia blinked at Mia in astonishment. "Can she even do that?"

"Yes," Mia assured her. "She pulled the exact same trick on a man named Rebel. A bullet he'd fired at Esis in autumn came back and killed his wife in the spring."

"Oh my God . . ."

There was something about Ofelia's reaction that helped Mia gain control of her own. She stuffed all her emotions into a box, then slapped a big metal lock on the latch.

"That's why I won't get close to Carrie again," Mia calmly explained. "That's why I mess around. It's not a phase and it's not normal. It's just . . ." She shrugged despondently. "It's just the way things are."

Ofelia shook her head in astonishment. "My God. You weren't kidding. All the shit you've been through, all the burdens you carry. You may not be thirty years old, but . . ." She shook a tight finger at Mia. "You're sure as hell not a kid anymore."

That was the nicest thing anyone had said to Mia in ages. For the first time tonight, she actually felt good.

"I hope we do become friends," Mia told Ofelia. "I think there's a lot you can teach me. And as a traveler who can make floating portals, there's definitely stuff that I can teach y—"

"Who is that?" Ofelia asked.

She pointed to the distant front entrance of the Orphanage, where a lone male figure approached in silhouette. It wasn't until he passed under the bright cone of a lamppost that Mia's eyes popped open in recognition. She covered her mouth with both hands.

"Oh my God!"

Ofelia studied her reaction, thrown. "Is that a good or bad—"

Mia vanished into a portal, emerged sixty yards down the road, and flung herself at the ambling man. He stumbled backward on wobbly legs.

"Oof. Wow. What a welcome. Hi, Mia."

She hugged him tight, her dark eyes spilling tears. "Hi, Theo."

SIX

He'd been a ghost in their lives for thirteen months—the prodigal prophet, wandering the Earth on a never-ending quest for knowledge. He'd sent his friends postcards from distant lands and texted them whenever he was back in the States, but his messages were always vague. *"Doing fine." "Feeling good." "It's beautiful here." "Miss you."*

Even on the brief and rare occasions when he returned to the underland, Theo never revealed much about his progress. Was he at least getting *some* of the answers he was looking for? Had the future become any clearer? He wouldn't say. All his friends knew, all they *needed* to know, was that the story wasn't over. There was still an elusive string of time where he and his people helped stop the apocalypse. Theo wouldn't rest until he found it.

But with each new visit, he'd seemed more and more distracted, and his behavior on the road had become erratic. In September, he was arrested for setting his rental house on fire. In December, he was hospitalized after overdosing on mescaline. The following month, he paid a Canadian doctor to put him into a coma and keep him there for two weeks. Though he insisted that there was a strategy behind each of his actions, even his staunchest defenders were starting to worry about him.

Now suddenly, after six long months of minimal contact, Theo had made a surprise return to the underland, and he'd never looked more wretched. His hair was overgrown beneath his woolly gray cap, his clothes were stained and riddled with holes, and he had the untamed beard of a caveman. It hadn't even occurred to Theo to clean himself up before seeing his friends again. He'd been grubby for so long, he just accepted it as his natural state.

He could feel Mia's eyes on him as she followed him down the walkway. "I'm fine," Theo assured her. "Just a little roadworn."

"Roadworn? You're missing a tooth."

"Oh. Yeah." He touched the gap where his upper left canine used to be. "I got into a fight."

"With who?"

"No one you know," he said with lament. Just one minute back and he was already lying to the people he loved. "Why are *you* scuffed up?"

Mia looked down at her dirt-stained pants. "Made a bad portal exit."

Theo could tell there was more to the story, but he didn't bother to ask. He was too busy reveling in the bright spots of her future. She had a hell of a surprise waiting for her in August, one so joyous that Theo was afraid to tell her about it. Better to wait until the event became more certain. He didn't want to get her hopes up for nothing.

"Thanks for saving Hannah, by the way," Mia said.

Theo stopped a moment, unsure if she was being sarcastic. "What?"

"Last Friday in Mexico, when you got inside her head. She would have never jumped off that train if you hadn't convinced her. How'd you do that, anyway?"

"Uhh . . ." Theo had no idea what she was talking about. He'd spent most of that day in a Honolulu hotel, eating cold fried chicken and watching Japanese war movies. "I'm not entirely sure."

"Well, it saved her life." Mia squeezed his hand. "God, it's so good to see you again. It feels like it's been years."

"Yeah. It does." He took in his surroundings with dull, listless eyes. After all his time on the surface world, the underland seemed phonier than ever. The projected stars, the recirculated air, the sun-starved trees that continually needed reversing. The place was as fake as a movie set, and it was far more vulnerable than its residents cared to admit. If the Pelletiers ever declared open war, they could crush the whole village in seconds.

Mia gestured at the glass cube building where the orphans' government handlers lived. "Maybe you should see Melissa first. Dump your stuff and rest a while."

There was nothing Theo wanted more, but he couldn't. Something strange was going to happen in ten minutes and forty seconds, right inside the clubhouse. He needed to be there for it.

"That's okay," he told Mia. "I'm getting my second wind."

Theo's heart pounded as he drew closer to the party. He could already hear Hannah getting her best Deborah Harry on, a rocking rendition of Blondie's "Call Me." Five minutes from now, she'd tell him what a challenge it was to bring the song back from memory, and she wouldn't explain it calmly. She and Theo were about to have a rough reunion, for reasons he couldn't discern.

Mia broke away from him to talk to a woman he'd never met before: a willowy brunette in loose white sweatclothes.

"Ofelia, this is Theo, our good friend and our very best hope for the world. Has anyone told you about him?"

Ofelia eyed him skeptically. "*Everyone's* told me about him. Uh . . ."

Mia smiled at her bemused expression. "He usually looks better."

Theo didn't hear a word of their exchange. He was too distracted by the bauble on Ofelia's wrist: a shiny silver bracelet that looked just like the one he used to wear, only . . . different. There was some invisible, nebulous quality about it that rang every bell in his foresight. The bracelet was an object of power in the strings, with the ability to change millions of futures. But would it save lives or claim them? And why would a dead Pelletier trinket be so—

Mia snapped her fingers in front of his face. "Theo!"

He fell out of his thoughts. "Huh?"

"We're going inside," Mia said. "But before we do, you should know this hasn't been the best day for some of us."

"What do you mean?"

"You don't see it?"

Theo grumbled in his thoughts. The future was a wall of a billion TV screens, each one jumping from channel to channel. No one, not even the Pelletiers, could see everything that was coming. No matter how many times he explained it, his friends still thought he was omniscient.

"I have no idea what you're talking about," he said.

Mia shrugged. "Okay, well, you'll find out soon enough."

"Can't you just tell me?"

Mia looked away with a dismal expression. "It's not my news to give."

Theo was too tired to push the matter, and too self-aware to play the hypocrite. He was sitting on more news than he knew what to do with—the good, the bad, the bittersweet, plus a few little tidbits that had yet to be categorized. And there was one ticking bombshell at the top of the pile, the very same one that had sent him running back here. He wasn't even sure how to process the information, much less share it. All he knew for sure was that time was their enemy. The endgame had already begun.

Hannah was halfway into a stellar performance when Theo stepped into the clubhouse. After two weeks of screwups and frustrating rehearsals, all the stars had aligned on the Great Remains' cover of "Call Me." And for four blissful minutes, every note hit its mark. The song was so well done and so infectiously dynamic that it brought two dozen people onto the dance floor—Gothams and Integrity agents, White Irons and Brown ones. Even Mercy Lee, who shared all of Hannah's reasons to hate the world, mixed it up with the revelers.

Then the swinging doors opened and the musicians onstage got their first clear view of Theo. Joey Fehrenbach faltered on his electric guitar. Mateo McGraw dropped a drumstick. Shroud stopped playing his bass entirely, and Heath stood agape behind his synthesizer.

Hannah looked to the door, then froze in shock. Her microphone only barely picked up her squeak of a voice. "Theo?"

Within moments, the entire room was silent as forty-two people stared at him.

Theo knew their reaction was all his fault. In indoor light, he looked utterly horrid. His skin was jaundiced from poor nutrition. His eyes were hooded from lack of sleep. Stress hives had broken out across his hands and neck. All of that might have been forgiven if it wasn't for the look on his face.

Theo gazed across the room in slack-faced horror, as if he'd just seen the whole world's medical chart and realized that it was beyond saving.

Except he wasn't looking at the Earth's dark future. Only Hannah's.

"Theo." Mia tugged his hand impatiently. "*Theo.*"

"What?"

"You're freaking everyone out."

"Oh." He forgot about the weight he carried with these people, the ones who knew about the Earth's terminal illness. To them, he was the so-called savior, the face of the future itself. To see that face in its current state was more than a little ominous. It was like watching Jesus Christ come back to Earth and run screaming for the nearest fallout shelter.

Theo glanced around at the anxious crowd, his palms raised in appeasement. "Sorry. I've been awake for thirty-six hours and I'm not exactly, uh . . . look, I'm okay. *We're* okay. It's the same deal as ever. I'm just here to join the party."

He turned to Zack and forced a flippant grin. "Are you nailed to the floor or are you just not happy to see me?"

Zack closed the gap between them and hugged Theo tightly. "Of all the shitty entrances . . ."

"I know," Theo said. "What the hell's up with Hannah?"

"We'll talk about it later."

"What was she *thinking*?"

"*Later.*" Zack pulled back to look at Theo's clothes. "You're, uh, still being funded, right?"

Theo nodded wearily. Integrity gave him all the money he needed and then some. He was just lazy. Plus, his haggard appearance kept the normal folk away. He was traveling the world to think and prognosticate. The last thing he needed was small talk.

He touched the black metal surface of Zack's new hand. "Ah, shit . . ."

"It's all right. It works."

"That's good," said Theo. "Because I have an important job for you and Heath."

Amanda cut between them and wrapped her tempic arms around Theo. "My turn."

"Hey, beautiful." Theo was floored by her amazing recovery. Last time he saw her, she was still recuperating from a nervous breakdown. But now she looked stronger than ever.

And there was something new in the folds of her future, a faint pink mist that smelled like—

"Ioni."

Amanda looked at him confusedly. "What?"

Theo was livid. He'd been trying to track down Ioni for more than a year, but she was stubbornly determined to avoid him. He'd even burned down his rental house while he was still inside it, just to get her to come save him. It didn't work. All she did was trick the fire department into getting there early.

Now there she was, dancing on Amanda's strings. Ioni was going to crash into her life real soon. But why?

Amanda waved for his attention. "Theo?"

"Sorry. I, uh . . ." He looked her over again. "I can't get over how good you look."

"I wish I could say the same," she replied. "Are you still taking mescaline?"

Theo mentally cursed Melissa for ratting him out. "Only when I have to."

"Theo—"

"That's not why I look bad. Trust me."

Theo wasn't the first augur to use psychedelics to enhance his visions. And in his defense, he'd gleaned some extremely useful intel while high. He'd exposed a Chinese mole in Integrity's upper ranks, then stopped a Gotham extremist from killing dozens of agents. Most recently, he'd told Melissa exactly where she could find the Pearls of Guadalajara, right down to the train's flight schedule. As far as Theo was concerned, the mescaline was worth the occasional side effect. Who knew? It might even help him save the world.

He spent the next few minutes trading warm greetings with the others: Peter and Liam, Mercy and Caleb. He nearly sprained Heath's back hugging him. He'd missed the boy terribly and would have kept on squeezing him if See hadn't interrupted.

"Theo!"

"Hey! There's my favorite augur."

The poor girl looked like she was on the verge of panic, for reasons Theo could easily guess.

"I see it too," he assured her. "Don't worry."

"But it'll be here in—"

"I know. It's all right. I've got it covered."

The portal was six minutes and four seconds away from opening, but it wasn't any cause for worry. No one would be popping out of it. No one living, anyway.

"So . . ."

He turned around to find Hannah standing right behind him, with a smirk on her face that looked equal parts stern and facetious. "Are your feet nailed to the floor?" she teased. "Or are you just not happy to see me?"

Theo threw his arms around her, struggling to keep his emotions inside. His relationship with Hannah defied all classification—more intimate than friends, less physical than lovers, and far too complex to be a straight-up sibling bond. All he knew was that she was a load-bearing wall of his universe. That was what made his premonitions so painful. It was so damn hard to look at her when her future reeked of death and Pelletiers.

"What have you done?" he whispered.

Hannah pushed him away, furious. "That's how you greet me?"

"Hannah . . ."

"After all this time, *that's* how . . ." She looked around self-consciously, then made a brusque hand gesture, like she was pulling an invisible lever. All the conversation in the room suddenly came to a halt and everyone in the clubhouse froze where they stood.

Everyone but Hannah and Theo.

His skin crawled with goosebumps as he checked on the others. They weren't entirely stilted. Hannah had merely slowed them down to a hundredth of their normal speed.

"Wow," he said. "How are you doing this?"

"How do you think?" Hannah pulled him in closer. "I left a bubble of space around us, but it's not that big. So keep your arms down and *do not* wander."

Theo still couldn't get over the magnitude of her feat. As a swifter, she'd never been able to shift more than one or two people at a time. Now she'd drowned the whole clubhouse in her slowtime field and she wasn't even breaking a sweat.

He looked back at her, bug-eyed. "This is dangerous. You could rift someone."

"Do you see that coming?"

"No, but—"

"Then maybe you should trust me," she said. "You know, we weren't just twiddling our thumbs here. Some of us got stronger."

"And pregnant."

Hannah's hot glare could have cooked him alive. "Jumping right into it, are we?"

"Look—"

"No, *you* look. I was having the time of my life when you came in and ruined it. Do you know how hard it was to get that stupid song right? All the botched chords and music sheets, all the arguments with Heath over the D-minor key . . ."

Theo did in fact know those things. He'd already foreseen that part of the argument. More than that, he knew that she was deflecting. She didn't need foresight to see the risks of her plan. And she didn't need Theo to make her feel worse about it.

"I'm sorry," he said. "It just threw me for a loop."

"Yeah? How do you think I feel?"

"Except you signed up for it. You and . . ." Theo turned to the sluggish form of Peter before looking back at Hannah in amazement. *"Him?"*

"Very good, Sherlock."

"When did he become the universal sperm donor?"

Hannah shrugged. "I needed a Gotham I trust and respect. He's been really good about it."

"Yeah, I'm sure he's been a great sport about sleeping with you."

"Better than you were."

"What?"

"We couldn't do the friends-with-benefits thing for more than a week before you flipped out," she reminded him. "It's been six months with Peter and we've never had a fight."

Theo palmed his face, frustrated. The circumstances were so different; she was comparing apples and chain saws. And she was bringing up the ancient past when he was trying to get her to look the other way.

"Which one?" he asked her.

"Which one what?"

"Which Pelletier did you make a deal with: the liar, the robot, or the crazy one?"

Hannah's voice dropped to a mutter. "You know which one."

"For fuck's sake. *Why?*"

"You saw the way Amanda was. I had to do something!"

"If you had just called me—"

"*Called* you?" Hannah laughed. "When should I have done that? While you were in Japan, while you were in England, or while you were in your self-induced coma?"

Theo was about to pace the floor when Hannah caught his arm. "*Don't* wander."

"You think I wanted to be away this long?"

"I don't know. Even when you're here, you're barely here." She swept a hand at the hindered orphans. "You're a stranger to these people. You don't even know half their names."

"Of course I do."

"Yeah? Which one's Sarah Brehm?"

Theo scanned the crowd before sneering at Hannah. "Okay, I don't know *all* their names."

"Goddamn it, Theo. This is the only family we have."

"And this is the only world we have," he countered. "Sorry if I put that first."

Her guilty reaction only made him feel worse. In truth, he could have come back fifty times without compromising his mission. He chose to stay away, and he wasn't even sure why. Maybe he was sick of being seen as a savior. Maybe he wanted to see the world before it ended. Or maybe there was a darker reason, one that Ioni had hinted at long ago:

It's a lonely road we travel, my dear. We lie to the people we love. We manipulate them. And sometimes, when there's no other choice, we throw them to the wolves. We do horrible things for the greater good. It doesn't make it any easier.

Yeah. That was probably it. Theo had glimpsed the road to salvation, enough to know that it was covered in blood. Good people would have to die for the sake of the future. Many of them were in this room. It was probably better that Theo didn't know their names. Just seeing the shadow of death on Hannah was enough to crack his heart to pieces.

"The Pelletiers once put something in my head," he told her. "A tiny little jammer in the middle of my brain. It kept me from seeing all the things they didn't want me to see."

"I remember." Hannah did a double-take at him. "Wait, *kept*, as in past tense?"

Theo nodded. "Yeah."

"You said it couldn't be removed without killing you."

"No, but it could be disabled. All I had to do was shut down my brain for a couple of weeks."

Hannah's mouth went slack in revelation. "Your coma . . ."

"That's why I did it," Theo said. "I had to break the hold they had on me. And it worked."

He fidgeted with the rash on the back of his hand. "I don't see everything, but I see enough. I know that sometime in the future, long before your baby's due, they'll swoop in and take you."

Theo looked away miserably. "They won't bring you back."

Hannah hemmed and hawed before clenching her jaw with resolve. "I always knew that was a risk. I did it anyway and I'd do it again." She pointed at Amanda. "*Look* at her."

"I see her," Theo said. "There isn't a doubt in my mind that you saved her. But she can't handle the sacrifice you're making, and neither can I."

"Theo, *listen* to me." Hannah looked at him with moist eyes. "You have one job to do, and you know what it is. Focus on the big picture. Let us handle the rest."

There were at least a dozen other things that Theo wanted to say to her, but they were running out of time. The temporal portal was now two minutes away from arriving, and See was inching closer to the gap in Hannah's slowtime field.

"You should de-shift them," Theo said.

"I will." Hannah cupped the side of his face. "I just need to hear one thing from you."

"What?"

"That you're back for good," she said. "Because I'm looking at you, sweetheart, and you're a mess. You need us as much as we need you."

He clasped her arm and smiled weakly. "Did I forget to tell you how much I missed you?"

"Just tell me you're done traveling."

"I'm not," Theo admitted. "But I'm done traveling alone."

"What does that mean?"

"I'll explain it all tomorrow," he promised. "We have a lot to talk about."

Hannah nodded thoughtfully, then released everyone from her slowtime field. Most of them carried on talking, oblivious to the half-second temporal shift. Others blinked with a sense of disorientation, as if a frame had skipped in the movie they were watching. Those who'd been looking directly at Hannah and Theo knew that something odd had happened. They'd jittered in place like hummingbirds before falling into pace with the rest of the world.

See splayed her arms out wide in frustration. "Theo!"

"I got it. I got it." He climbed onto the stage and took the microphone off the stand. "Uh, can I have your attention?"

Melissa darted across the Orphanage in her flimsy white slippers, her pajamas half-covered beneath a short coat. She'd been fast asleep and dreaming about dolphins when Felicity called her. The news had been surprising, to say the least.

He's back.

Melissa was mystified. She had just spoken to Theo twelve hours earlier, while he was still in the Hawaiian Republic. From everything he'd told her, he was planning to stalk Merlin McGee at his summer house until the great prophet gave him an audience. Something bad must have happened—or was *about* to happen—to bring Theo back in a hurry.

By the time Melissa reached the clubhouse, the party had taken a peculiar turn. Everyone stood in a cluster on the left side, behind a short tempic barrier of Amanda's making. Their eyes were all fixed on the same distant wall, as if they were watching a special news bulletin. But Melissa couldn't see a thing besides plaster. What on Earth was going on?

She looked to the solitary man on the bandstage. If there was a reason for Theo to be standing there with a microphone in his hand, looking as sick and begrimed as a bus stop beggar, Melissa couldn't find one. The scene was so surreal and utterly dreamlike that she half expected to see dolphins.

Theo noticed her in the doorway and gave her a gap-toothed smile. "Hi!"

The right side of the clubhouse suddenly exploded in light, a blazing white fluorescence that made everyone shield their eyes. Melissa peeked through her fingers at the large new portal on the wall. It had popped up right where everyone had been looking, but it was different than the usual travel door. This portal had a ring of white fire around the edges and made a loud whistling sound, like a boiling tea kettle. A strong wind blew through the turbulent surface, pelting everyone with dust and debris.

Half the people in the room began to shout and cry. "Don't panic!" Theo told them. "It's *not* an attack. It's just a random time portal. Keep your distance and you'll all be fine!"

Despite his assurance, Melissa could see the four travelers in the room—Peter, Mia, Mother, and Ofelia—writhing in pain. Now that she had a chance to think about it, it seemed likely that one of them was indirectly responsible for the breach. From what Peter had told her, travelers were limited in their temporal aim. They could only connect to the places they've been, and only when their past self was in the vicinity. The future version of one of those four people was ripping open a door to the present.

Melissa had a good guess who it was. She cupped her hands around her mouth and shouted into the wind. "Mia!"

It was no use. The girl was all the way at the front of the crowd, clinging to the tempic barrier with an agonized cry.

Melissa was halfway to Mia when two dark figures came flying out of the portal. They hit the floor like ragdolls, then rolled all the way into Amanda's barrier. Before anyone could get a good look at the intruders, the portal shrank away. There was no more whistle, no more wind, nothing on the wall but a giant round scorch mark.

The spectators at the front of the crowd leaned over the tempis to peek at the new arrivals.

"Don't touch them!" Felicity yelled. "Do *not* touch the bodies!"

Melissa wasn't as quick to assume they were dead, but it was a pretty good guess from the looks of them. Their skin was charred from head to toe—*blistered*, like they'd been boiled and broiled in quick succession. Yet despite all their burns, their clothes were covered in patches of frost. A dry-ice mist emanated from their skin.

Peter hadn't minced words about the gruesome effects of time travel. It was never anything less than fatal, and always an ugly way to go. If anything, he'd understated the case.

"Don't worry," said Theo. The room was so quiet that he didn't need the microphone anymore. "Even if those bodies are people we know, they're from a future that's always changing. It doesn't mean anything about anyone's fate."

"Speak for yourself," Zack retorted. "They're both my size."

Size was their *only* discernable feature. Their hair was gone. Their clothes were scorched. Their faces were blackened horrors. But they were clearly both men from their height and build. Melissa could think of at least six other people who shared their body measurements.

Hannah was the first to discover their other strong characteristic. She covered her mouth in disgust. "Oh God, that *stench*."

Soon everyone in the room could smell it: a pungent mixture of burnt hair and overcooked meat. Half the crowd moved away from the corpses. Others fled for the exit. Mercy charged into the ladies' room and retched up her dinner.

Only Peter and Mia remained at the forefront, their wide eyes fixed on the cadavers. Mia leaned over the tempic pony wall and took a dazed look at the nearest victim.

"Wait," she mumbled. "I think that . . . I think he's . . ."

Theo watched her anxiously from the foot of the stage. "Mia, don't."

Melissa's eyes went round. "Mia!"

The burnt man opened a cloudy gray eye and seized Mia by the wrist. She barely had a chance to yell before Amanda sprang to action. A sharp white spike protruded from her fist, impaling the stranger through the head. He let out a low and guttural groan before his last breath escaped him and he fell completely still.

The crowd broke out in hyperactive cross talk. Orphans tripped over each other on the way to the door. Only the shrieking high whistle of Melissa Masaad got everyone to stop and look at her.

"All right, *listen*. This party is over. Everyone who isn't a government agent, please proceed calmly through the front exit. My team: report to me."

She threw a conflicted look at Theo as he approached the exit, then heaved a sigh at the bodies. "We have work to do."

By Gotham standards, the incident wasn't all that strange. There'd been hundreds of travelers in the history of the clan, each one with billions of future incarnations. Inevitably, some of them had chosen to send objects back to their past selves—a note, a gift, an item of purpose. In 1982, Ford Rubinek received a completed, published copy of the novel he'd just started writing. In 1991, Ruby Rosen gained the next two hundred issues of her favorite comic book. In 2003, Jayne Ryder got a cutout clipping of her oldest son's obituary, a detailed spoiler that helped her save his life.

One of the Gothams had even received his own corpse from the future—several of them, in fact. Magnus Tam had been determined to become the world's first living time traveler, and believed that all it took was the right kind of shielding to survive the rigors of the trip. Luckily, he had an endless supply of future selves to weed out the bad ideas. He'd found corpses of himself in metal armor, tempic armor, thermic armor, pressure suits. At long last, when the bodies stopped coming, he decided that it was his turn to risk his life for glory. He traveled back through time in a Faraday cage and died just as horribly as his predecessors. On the upside, he helped the Magnus Tam of another timeline rule out Faraday cages as a good idea.

Melissa had no idea what caused this latest portal. All she knew was that she had two burnt bodies in the clubhouse and a messiah waiting for her back home. After forty-six minutes at the scene of the crime, she left Felicity in charge and hurried back to her apartment.

Theo paced the living room rug, wearing nothing but Melissa's red bathrobe. Though the shower had done wonders for his appearance, his mental state seemed worse than ever. He was so lost in mumbling ruminations that he didn't notice Melissa walk in.

She dropped her keys on the kitchen counter and studied Theo from afar. "So . . ."

He stopped in place, distracted. "That portal was Peter's. A future Peter's."

"I know," Melissa said. "Mia texted me. Said she recognized his energy signature."

"I think one of the bodies might be his too."

Melissa nodded patiently. "She seems to fear that as well."

"Hey, what's the name of that other woman?"

"What other woman?"

"The one with the silver bracelet."

Melissa eyed him suspiciously. "Ofelia."

"Yeah. Ofelia. We're gonna have to cut her hand off."

"What?"

"Just for a little while."

Melissa threw her arms up, exasperated. "Theo!"

"What?"

"You just pop back here without a word of notice. You don't tell me what's happening. You don't even say hello."

Theo looked at her woundedly. "I said hi in the clubhouse."

"Try it again."

With a thoughtful nod, he closed the last inches of space between them. He cupped the sides of her face and planted a warm kiss on her lips.

"Hi, sweetheart."

Late last August, not long after Theo's first trip home, Melissa had met with Cedric Cain for an off-the-record meeting. She'd made awkward small talk for several moments before getting to the point. "Against my own better judgment,

I have become . . . involved with Theo Maranan. While I know it violates the conduct code between government employees and assets, I don't believe our relationship will hurt my job performance. We plan to be discreet in our dealings and, given the scope of his task, I imagine this'll mostly be a long-distance courtship. Still, if you believe it makes me unfit to serve in my capacity as—"

Cain had stopped her right there. He didn't give a flying fig about conduct codes or indiscretions. He only had one concern: "Will it hurt *his* job performance?"

On the contrary, Melissa strongly believed that it would help. Theo needed someone to keep him grounded in the present, someone to hold him together and share his burden.

Cain had contemplated the situation for a minute before rendering final judgment. "I'm not sure four shoulders are enough to hold the weight of the world," he'd said. "But they're certainly better than two. Do what you need to. Follow your heart. But for God's sake, Melissa, tread carefully. He's the only savior we have."

As Melissa had guessed, most of the relationship was conducted by phone. She and Theo rarely spoke for less than an hour a day and she flew out to see him on the rare occasions when she could get away. She'd guided him through his first trip to London, made love with him on the shores of Belize. She'd bailed him out when he was arrested, and sat at his side through his self-induced coma. They'd shared so much, and yet she could still feel him keeping things from her.

"I don't have a choice," he'd told her. "Every word I say about the future changes it."

Melissa pulled away from Theo. "Why didn't you tell me you were coming back?"

He closed his eyes, sighing. "Because if I told you that, I'd have to tell you why. And I wasn't ready to have that conversation."

"Are you ready now?"

"No."

Frustrated, Melissa took off her short coat and hung it in the closet. "I hate when you do this."

"Do what? Keep you out of the loop?"

"Yes. We agreed not to hold anything back from each other."

Theo scoffed at her. "You're one to talk."

"What does that mean?"

"You didn't tell me about Hannah and Peter," he said. "You knew what they were doing for six whole months and you kept it from me."

Melissa looked away guiltily. "She told you, huh?"

"No, you did."

"When?"

"Tomorrow morning."

"Lovely." Melissa sat down on the couch and kicked her feet up on the coffee table. "She specifically asked me not to tell you."

"Yeah, because she knew I'd yell at her."

"She was doing what was best for her sister."

"At the cost of her *life*," Theo said. "I've seen her strings. I know what's coming."

"The future can be changed," Melissa reminded him. "You say it all the time."

"Well, this one can't, okay? When Hannah goes down, Amanda will fall apart. And when *she* falls apart, there goes Zack. One by one, they'll all go to pieces. And I can't save them. I can't save a fucking thing!"

He looked down at his quivering hands. "I've wasted so much time chasing bad leads. It's my fault. Everything that happens—"

"Enough." Melissa jumped to her feet and took Theo by the hand. "We're getting into bed."

Theo resisted her pull. "I'm not exactly in the best shape to—"

"Look again, prophet."

"Oh." He nodded in understanding, then followed her to the bedroom. "Guess you haven't been doing too well either."

"Well, considering what happened to me in Mexico . . ."

"I'm sorry about that," Theo said. "If I had been there, maybe you and Zack—"

"Stop it." She took off her wristwatch and clambered into bed. "You've been walking a hard road for as long as I've known you. I can see the toll it's taking."

She crawled under the covers and nestled against him. "Whatever you think your plans are tomorrow—"

"I can't."

"It's just *one* day off," she said. "One day to rest and recharge."

"I *can't*, Melissa. We don't have time."

"We still have two and a half years to stop what's coming."

"No, we don't."

"Of course we do. You said—"

"It's ten weeks."

Theo sat up in bed and pressed his fingers to his temples. "That's what I came back to tell you. Everything we knew was wrong. We only have ten weeks."

Melissa stared at him unblinkingly, her face a mask of stone. "What?"

SEVEN

Ofelia died in the middle of the night. Or so she believed, anyway.

She couldn't think of any other reason why she was standing on the most beautiful beach she'd ever seen, wearing a white silk dress that was completely foreign to her. The sun peeked out over the watery horizon and grinned in vibrant colors. Ofelia couldn't tell if it was rising or setting. She watched it closely for several minutes, yet it insisted on staying right where it was prettiest.

"Huh."

She scrolled back through her memories, looking for clues as to how she got here. Last thing she remembered, she was drunk in the apartment of one of the orphans—Bill or Ben, whatever his name was. He was very, very Texan and very, very muscular, and he'd been nothing but gentlemanly in his flirtations. And the fact that he had whiskey . . . well. She drank his booze until she forgot all her troubles. There may have been some halfhearted horseplay. Nothing memorable enough to keep her awake.

I'm probably dreaming, she mused to herself, before quickly dismissing the notion. Her subconscious was an ornery bitch, warped by years of trauma. The last thing it would ever do was take her someplace nice.

Ofelia turned around and did a double-take at the huge and stately mansion behind her, one of the plushest homes she'd ever laid eyes on. Spanish roof. Roman columns. Windows galore on the beach-facing side. A place like that would have cost millions on the old world. In Heaven, only the nuns could afford it. Ofelia didn't think for a moment that she belonged here. She'd been an addict, a thief, a self-destructive basket case, a lifelong weight around the neck of her brother. That last part alone earned her a tin shack in Purgatory.

As she moved closer to the mansion, she could see familiar figures on the veranda. The sprightly young Pearls, all seven of them, lounged about without a care in the world. Aida and Jackie frolicked in the pool while Lauren did a flip off the diving board. Diana and Mari ate lobster from a buffet. Arianda read a book in a cozy-looking recliner. And Rosario, sweet Rosario, played with Labrador puppies on the sand. Like Ofelia, they were all dressed in flowing white garments. Most of the girls had telling bulges in their bellies.

"What . . ." Ofelia watched in shock from the edge of the property as an eighth woman emerged from the manor: her own pregnant doppelgänger. The other Ofelia tousled Rosario's hair and then loaded a plate at the buffet.

Ofelia stood frozen in place, slack-jawed. "What the hell is this?"

"Forgotten history," said a voice to her left.

She turned her head to see a young blond stranger in a button-down shirt and slacks, a man as beautiful as his surroundings. Ofelia remembered him from their brief encounter in San Diego. His cool blue eyes were the last thing she'd glimpsed before the universe went crazy.

"You." Ofelia took a nervous step back. "You're that Pelletier. David."

"Semerjean," he corrected. "David was a fictional character."

Ofelia knew for sure now that she wasn't dreaming. And the balloon just popped on her Heaven theory. "Where are we?"

"Lárnach," said Semerjean. "My family's central base of operations, a thousand meters beneath the South Pole."

Semerjean smiled at Ofelia's bafflement. "The environment's just a calming illusion. Convincing, isn't it?"

"What am I doing here?"

"Depends which you you're talking about." Semerjean gestured at the other Ofelia. "*She* was here to help us."

"Help you make babies, you mean."

"Yes."

"This is where I was for twenty-three months."

"More like fifty-three," Semerjean said. "Time moves faster here."

"And where are the men who, uh . . ."

Semerjean chuckled. "Only the Silvers are expected to conceive naturally. You were fertilized *in vitro*."

Ofelia looked down at her wrist, only to find her bracelet gone. "I thought I was a Silver."

"That was the original plan." Semerjean wagged a finger at her. "But you and your bad luck forced a last-minute change."

"What do you mean?"

He conjured a small image of twelve jumbo jets in flight. "Seven hours before the end of your world, there was an electromagnetic disruption. Every machine on the planet went dead for ten minutes."

At Semerjean's command, the illusive jets dropped out of the sky in unison.

"The odds of a plane crashing into your building were eighty-seven million to one," he told Ofelia. "But there it was in your future: your quick and fiery death. So I hurried back to your apartment—"

"Hurried *back*?"

"Yes. I'd already given you your bracelet while you slept."

That was news to Ofelia. All she remembered was waking up in the middle of a blackout, looking for answers in the glow of her cigarette lighter. Then suddenly Semerjean showed up out of nowhere, looking harried and annoyed. He'd blinded her with pulsating light. The next thing she knew, she was in another world's Mexico, a prisoner of a flying train. If she'd had anything new or sparkly on her wrist, she'd never noticed it.

"The Pearls had already been gathered at that point," Semerjean said. "It made more sense to put you with them."

Ofelia aimed her bitter look at the ocean. "I could have been with my brother."

"He wouldn't have been with you for long."

"Fuck you!"

"Ofelia . . ."

"We could have faced this world together, but you let him get killed by a psychopath. Why?"

Semerjean sighed with a look of regret. "There are decisions my wife and son have made that I don't entirely agree with. If it were up to me, Evan would be dead and Jury would be alive. But I'm just one voice of three."

"That's bullshit." Ofelia looked back at her other self. "This is all bullshit. I would have never agreed to have children for you."

"Suffice it to say we convinced you."

"How? By threatening me?"

Semerjean gestured at the Pearls. "Do any of those women look threatened to you?"

"Okay, fine. Then you drugged us."

"Drugs would have jeopardized the pregnancies," Semerjean said. "As would excessive stress. So we filled your days with luxury and comfort. We gave you everything you needed here, even a purpose."

"A *purpose*?"

"You're helping us save trillions of souls. All the people of my era and all their future offspring. When else in your life have you ever done anything so noble?"

"And what of *my* offspring?" Ofelia asked. "What did you do with the babies I made?"

Semerjean dipped his head in contemplation, as if her question came with multiple answers. "I could lie to you and say they're living rich and healthy lives, but science can be . . . ruthless in its demands. All I can assure you is that they never felt a moment of pain."

Ofelia closed her eyes, sickened. "Why are you showing me this? Why am I even here?"

Semerjean stuffed his hands in his pockets and idly kicked the sand. "You met someone at the anniversary party, a prophet named Theo Maranan. What did you think of him?"

Ofelia shrugged. "I didn't have enough time to form an opinion."

"Yes you did."

"Okay, yes, I thought he could use a shower. And he wasn't anything like I expected. From the way people talked about him, I thought he'd look like Jesus or something."

Semerjean grinned. "Don't let appearances fool you. The man's full of surprises. But all that talk of him being a savior?" He shook his head. "Even Theo knows it's a lie."

Ofelia tried to adjust the strap of her dress but she couldn't seem to get hold of it. "What does any of that have to do with me?"

"Everything, I'm afraid. Through his own good intentions, he's leading you all to ruin."

Semerjean sighed at her skeptical expression. "I know what you've heard about me and my family. I'm sorry to say that most of it is true. We've done terrible things in our search for a cure, and we'll do plenty more before we're done here. But we offered a deal to your people last June, one that would have ensured a long-term future for every man, woman, and child in the underland. Did anyone tell you about that?"

Ofelia shook her head. "No."

"Of course they didn't. Let me show you something."

With a wave of his hand, the whole scene changed. Now the two of them were standing at the edge of a grassy cliff, looking down at a city nestled snugly inside a valley. The place was unlike anything Ofelia had seen. The buildings were all made of crystal and tempis, and were designed in a style that she could only describe as "alien." Half the buildings looked like modern art sculptures. One of the towers had a waterfall spouting out of it. Another four carried a massive park on their shoulders. The entire valley was so achingly beautiful that Ofelia didn't believe it existed.

"You're looking at an image of a city from my era," Semerjean told her. "Novo Belém."

"Novo Belém?"

"Portuguese for 'New Bethlehem.' It's buried beneath the Mantiqueira Mountains of Brazil. The sky's an illusion but everything else is real. It was built a hundred years before I was born and was widely considered to be a paradise at the time."

Semerjean peered down at the city with a wistful look. "But society evolved and Novo Belém didn't. As time went on, the amenities became limited by modern standards. Inferior. It survived as a slum for fifty more years before being abandoned for good."

Ofelia eyed him skeptically. "*That's* what you people call a slum?"

"It's all a matter of perspective. An ancient Roman would marvel at the condition of your cities. No corpses, no lepers, no rivers of excrement. Even the toilets would look clean by their standards."

Ofelia was thrown by his extreme condescension. How did he play a Silver for so long?

"In June of last year, we offered Novo Belém to the orphans and Gothams," he said. "A far better underland than the one they have now. They'd have all the space they'd ever need, all the resources they could possibly wish for."

"Forever?" Ofelia asked.

"Well, they'd likely reach capacity in a few millennia. By then, they'd be ready to integrate."

Ofelia couldn't picture what life in Novo Belém would be like. She was too busy thinking about the cost. "And in exchange for this city, we'd have to make more babies for you."

"Yes," said Semerjean. "The old-fashioned way, I'm afraid."

"You know I'm mostly gay, right?"

"You're in bed with a man right now."

Shit. Ofelia didn't remember it going that far. She must have really been messed up.

"It's a moot point anyway," Semerjean said. "Our offer was rejected."

"Why?"

"Because everyone in the underland listens to Theo, and Theo believes there's a better way. But he's been misled."

"By who?"

"Her." Semerjean conjured a ghostly image on the cliffside, a small young woman in a T-shirt and jeans. "Ioni Anata T'llari Deschane."

Ofelia studied her closely. For a woman with such an alien name, she looked like any one of a million cute blondes. "Who is she?"

"Even we don't know her full story," Semerjean admitted. "She's not from our era or yours. All we can say with certainty is that she traffics in lies. If you don't believe me, ask Mia. She hates that woman as much as she hates me."

Ofelia found that hard to believe. "So why does Theo trust her?"

"Because she tells him exactly what he wants to hear, that the apocalypse can be prevented."

"But you don't think so."

"I know for a fact that it can't."

Semerjean turned to Ofelia with a somber expression, the most earnest look she'd seen from him. "My son is a genius beyond comparison. If there was a way to stop what's happening, he would have found it. And we would have gladly fixed the problem. Our plans don't hinge on the death of that world. If anything, our ability to save it would be all the leverage we need to get your people to cooperate with us."

He gazed back upon the city. "But the damage has been done and there's no repairing it. All we can do is bring a thousand survivors to the safety of this place."

"Why not more?" Ofelia asked.

"Time travel is difficult, even for us. You saw those corpses at the party."

Ofelia nodded her head, shuddering. She'd done more than see the bodies. Through the portal, she'd felt every bit of Future Peter's agony.

"We only have the resources to bring a thousand people back to our era," Semerjean said. "Any more would risk a containment failure, which would end very poorly for all of us, in a manner you've already seen."

He flicked his hand again. Suddenly they were back at the beachside mansion, exactly where they'd been standing before.

"It's been thirteen months since Ioni's spoken to Theo," Semerjean said. "Maybe she finally realized there's no hope. Maybe she already fled. But Theo persists in clinging to his delusions. It's a long-standing pattern with him."

"What makes you think I can change his mind?"

Semerjean shook his head. "I'm not here to change his mind. I'm here to change yours."

"What?"

"Our offer," Semerjean said. "It's still available to anyone who wants it. You make us a child with a Gotham of your choice—"

"—and you'll bring me to that city when the time comes."

Semerjean nodded. "All the people who help us get to live in Novo Belém. If you prove especially helpful, we may even grant a miracle or two."

"A miracle," Ofelia said.

Semerjean summoned a life-size image next to himself, a muscular Cuban that Ofelia had no trouble recognizing.

"Jury?"

"There are parallel timelines where Evan never killed him," Semerjean said. "There are even a few where he's alive and you're not. We have the power to bring him across the strings. He'd be overjoyed to see you again."

Ofelia cried as the image faded away. Every instinct was screaming at her not to trust Semerjean, yet Theo hadn't done a thing to earn her trust either. And if the offer was real . . .

"It's a lot to process," Semerjean admitted. "You don't have to decide right now, but you will need to think it over. We've seen the future. The path Theo's taking will inevitably conflict with ours. And we've come too far, sacrificed too much, to let anyone stand in our way."

Semerjean opened a portal, then shot a grave look at Ofelia. "War is coming. Those who help us will be rewarded. Those who don't will die. Your fate is in your hands."

He was about to depart when Ofelia called after him. "Wait!"

Semerjean stopped and turned his head. She took a brief, nervous look at the other Ofelia.

"If this was such a happy time, then why did you erase our memories of it?"

Semerjean paused in momentary thought, his face an inscrutable wall.

"I said you were comfortable," he answered at last. "I never said you were happy."

He disappeared into the portal, taking all the scenery with him. Ofelia found herself standing in a dark and unfamiliar bedroom, her discarded clothes lying in a heap at her feet. She realized now, with some alarm, that her white silk dress had been just another illusion. She'd been naked in this room the whole time.

Ofelia looked to the bed and saw a large, nude man sleeping facedown on the mattress. She still couldn't remember the Texan's name, but that didn't bother her anymore. She had other things to think about. Many, many things.

By the next afternoon, she almost felt sane again. All she'd needed was a shower, a hot meal, and ten hours of sleep to put a pocket of air between her and her traumas. The portal in the clubhouse, the two ugly corpses, the dreamlike encounter with Semerjean—they all got shoved to the periphery of her thoughts, just a noisy little fuss in the background.

At four o'clock, Ofelia was finally ready to get productive. She hunkered down at her desk, extinguished her cigarette, then scrawled out a checklist on a crisp yellow notepad:

- Bug Melissa about finding Evan Rander
- Bug Melissa about getting own apartment
- See if Peter's OK, then bug him about more portal training
- Ask Mia about Ioni

She'd barely made it five steps out of her room when Melissa found her and pulled her back inside. "We need to talk."

"That's good," Ofelia said. "Because I have some things—"

"They can wait."

Melissa closed the door behind them, then sat on the edge of Ofelia's desk.

Even with her sunglasses on, the stress on her face was evident. Melissa had never struck Ofelia as a particularly relaxed woman, but she had a strong heart and a rock-hard poker face. There must have been a hell of a weight bearing down on her to make her this edgy.

"The Pearls need a leader," she told Ofelia. "One voice to speak for them and to represent their interests. You have the most life experience. You're also their best English-speaker. Will you do me a favor and please take the job?"

Ofelia eyed her warily. She had enough life experience to know that "leadership" was just another word for "headache."

"What would I have to do?" she asked.

"For starters, you'll have to keep close tabs on their issues and concerns. That means talking to them more often than you do."

Ofelia crossed her arms, indignant. "I talk with them all the time."

"Do you know what happened to them last night?"

"No. What happened?"

"We'll discuss it in the meeting."

"What meeting?"

"The one that's starting in five minutes." Melissa jumped to her feet and opened the door. "Come with me. Bring your notepad. And, Ofelia?"

She lowered her shades and looked at her through cracked red eyes. If anything, Ofelia had underestimated her strain.

"Prepare yourself," Melissa warned. "This won't be a light discussion."

Of all of Integrity's changes to the underland, none were more mysterious than what they did to the augurs' guildhouse. The entire building had been covered in tempis, its basement sealed with hard cement. The only way in was through an arduous security screening. Ofelia had to undergo three different types of body scans, then open her mouth for a rubber-gloved agent. After checking her fillings with a small electronic wand, he waved her inside.

"What the hell is this?" she asked Melissa.

"Protocol. There are only twenty people allowed in this building and everything we discuss here is top secret. You can't speak of any of it outside the war room. Ever."

Ofelia grumbled at the floor. "*Tremendo paquete.*"

"I don't know what that means."

"It means all this drama's gonna kill me!"

"If you don't think you can handle it—"

"I'll handle it. I'll handle it."

She followed Melissa down a ten-foot hallway, into a brightly lit room the size of a subway car. Down at the far end, eighteen people sat around an oblong table and chatted among themselves. Ofelia already knew some of them: Peter, Mia, Hannah, Amanda, Amanda's funny husband, and that tense-looking boy with the big hazel eyes. Hector or Heath or something like that.

At the head of the table sat the great Theo Maranan, who'd cleaned up so well that Ofelia barely recognized him. His hair was neat. His face was shaved. His clothes were clean and well-fitting. He actually looked like a regular person, though she could barely stop thinking about what Semerjean had said. *He's leading you all to ruin.*

Theo smiled at her. "Ofelia. Hey. I was hoping you'd come."

"Yeah, well, uh . . ."

She was distracted by a strange new tingle on her body—a bubbly sensation, like seltzer on her skin.

Peter smirked at her bewilderment. "Don't mind the tickle. It's just the solis."

"Solis," Ofelia said. "Like the Mexicans used to keep me from making portals."

"Yes."

"Why use it now?"

Melissa explained it as succinctly as she could. Integrity had gone to great expense to build what they believed to be—or at least *hoped* to be, anyway—a Pelletier-proof room. In addition to solis, the machines behind the walls emitted six other kinds of disruption fields to impede long-range transmissions.

"Huh." Ofelia could see from the skeptical expressions—most notably Theo's—that not everyone believed the hype about the room. Peter and Mia seemed equally doubtful. Amanda just looked miserable, for reasons Ofelia could easily understand. The solis had eradicated her tempic arms, deflating the sleeves of her T-shirt. For a woman who could fly and knock down walls, the helplessness must have been maddening.

I'll never get used to this, Ofelia thought. *Never.*

Melissa showed her to one of the last two empty seats, then introduced her around the table. There were four big Integrity honchos in the room: the head of underland operations, the chief liaison to the Gothams, the chief liaison to the orphans (Melissa), and the director of the entire agency: a shrewd-looking codger named Cedric Cain. On the Gotham side, there were two clan elders, Peter Pendergen, and a visibly pregnant woman named Mercy Lee.

The orphans themselves filled a whole side of the table—the Silvers and Heath, the young augur See, plus the leaders of the other subgroups: Mother (Coppers), Caleb (Platinums), Eden (Brown Irons), and Ben (White Irons). Ofelia flinched at the sight of the large Texan, but at least now she knew his name. From the awkward look Ben threw back at her, he was just as eager as she was to forget about their fling.

Melissa sat down next to Theo, then pushed a small lever on the table. A wall slid down from the center of the ceiling, cutting the room's length in half and sealing everyone inside.

"Thank you for all coming," said Cain. "And thank you, Ofelia, for being such a good sport. You've been forced to catch up with two years of craziness. From everything I hear, you've been holding up admirably."

"Thank you," Ofelia said with a blush. She could already see why the man was in charge. His smooth talk teemed with effortless authenticity.

Cain sat back in his chair and sighed. "Okay, we have a lot to cover today. So if we can keep the jokes to a minimum, I'd appreciate it."

Zack shrugged defensively at Cain's pointed look.

"All right," the old man said to Theo. "The floor's all yours."

Theo took a swig of coffee before starting. Despite his improved appearance, he still looked tense and painfully unrested. Ofelia wondered when he'd last gotten a full night's sleep.

"Before we get to the big stuff," he began, "a quick question for the group: How many of you got a visit from Semerjean last night?"

Ofelia's eyes went round. Her heartbeat doubled. "Me."

"I did as well," Mother hesitantly replied. "So did most of my children."

"And me," said Ben, to Ofelia's surprise. "I thought it was just a dream."

"He spoke with each of the Pearls," Melissa said. "In flawless Spanish, I'm told."

"It's not just the orphans," said Bob Howell, one of the Gotham clan elders. "He haunted at least twenty of my people. I'm guessing there are more."

"That's very disconcerting," Cain said. He turned to the head of underland operations, a middle-age woman named Leticia Gutiérrez. "Let's see if we can beef up security down here."

"What are you going to do?" Hannah asked him. "Call the Dream Police?"

Zack pointed at Cain. "See? I didn't make that joke. I just thought it."

"Those weren't dreams," Melissa told Hannah. "Semerjean was physically here."

Theo shook his head at Cain. "There's nothing we can do to keep the Pelletiers out. The only way to fight them is to counter their disinformation."

"Did he come to you?" Ben asked Theo. "Because you were Topic Number One with him."

Hannah answered on his behalf. "He didn't hit anyone who knew him as David."

"We know how full of shit he is," Mia grumbled.

"Actually," said Mother, "he was surprisingly forthcoming. He admitted mistakes his family had made. He expressed particular regret about you."

Mia laughed bitterly. "Don't believe it for a second."

"He knows how to fake sincerity," Amanda said. "A few admissions of guilt. A few strategically placed 'howevers.' Before you know it, you don't even feel like he's selling you something. You feel like you have the whole picture."

Ofelia's stomach churned with stress. "So his offer to save us . . ."

"Pure crap," Zack said. "If they ever bring us back to their world, it'll be in jars or body bags."

"*Mierda.*" Ofelia wanted to cry. All her life, she'd been a victim of silver-tongued men. She thought she'd gotten wise to them, but apparently she'd learned nothing.

Melissa typed a note into her tablet computer. "I don't want to get into the specifics now. I just need everyone who spoke with Semerjean to come see me or Felicity. We want to know everything he told you, down to the last word."

Cain nodded in agreement. "If a Pelletier says anything to you, you tell us right away. That's not something you sit on."

"That's why I brought it up," Theo said. "Because it only gets worse from here. They're going to keep trying to shake our faith, until we see them as our only hope for survival. Because once they have that . . ."

He shared a quick look with Hannah before awkwardly turning his head. "They have us."

Cain twirled his cigarette lighter in his fingers with a restlessness that Ofelia easily recognized. She was glad to see that she wasn't the only one having a nicotine fit.

"Funny you should mention hope," Ben said to Theo. "Because you haven't been giving us a lot of it lately."

Melissa clicked her tongue impatiently. "This isn't the time."

"With all due respect, I think it is. We've gone five months without a word from our so-called savior. Is it any wonder the Pelletiers see us as ripe for the picking?"

"You're right," Theo said.

"No he isn't," Zack said, his stern eyes locked on Ben. "Theo's been working his ass off, looking for answers that aren't easy to find. And it's not like he's been coming up with goose eggs. If it wasn't for him, we would have never found the Pearls."

"And how do eight Mexican girls get us any closer to saving the world?" Ben asked.

Ofelia chuckled disparagingly. "*Cabrón.*"

"Excuse me?"

"I'm Cuban, *boy.* I told you twice."

"Just ignore him," Eden told Ofelia. "You'll be happier. Trust me."

Ben ignored them in favor of Theo. "I'm just saying, the clock's ticking. The game's halfway over and you're still scouting for new players."

Theo shrugged exhaustedly. "If we want any chance of stopping what's coming, we need all the chronokinetics we can get. That's the only thing I know for sure."

"So if we get all the Pearls and Rubies and Opals and Black Gothams—"

Now it was Mercy's turn to laugh. "*Black* Gothams?"

"Those African American timebenders," Ben said. "The ones you kicked out."

"The Majee," said Peter. "And we never kicked them out. They left."

"Whatever." Ben looked back at Theo. "Say we get all these folks on board. Then what?"

"I don't know," Theo curtly admitted. "That's up to Ioni."

"Why?" asked Mia.

Ofelia was intrigued by Theo's reaction. The fact that the question came from one of his own seemed to throw him off guard, even hurt him a little. He stammered at Mia, his face racked with guilt. "Look, I know what she did—"

"No," Melissa said. "We're not turning this meeting into another referendum on Ioni. We have too much ground to cover and too little time."

"Amen," said Cain. "Let's table the questions and get to business. I want to hear everything Theo has."

"I can do that."

Using a handheld console, Theo lowered four screens from the ceiling, all custom-built electronic displays without any lumic components. They connected at the corners in a perfect square, giving everyone in the room a direct view of the same text:

Orphans

The Jades (Calgary)

The Violets (London)

The Opals (Rotterdam)

The Rubies (Osaka)

Evan Rander

Gothams

The Majee

Merlin McGee

"These are all the known timebenders who aren't currently affiliated with us," Theo explained to Ofelia. "As I said, we need most, if not all, of these people if we want any chance of surviving. We have to find them and recruit them, fast."

Ofelia raised a finger in objection. "But—"

"And if they're *not* on our side," Hannah stressed to her, "we need to make sure they don't get in our way. I know exactly who you're thinking about."

"Thank you." Ofelia had balked at the sight of Evan's name. She'd sooner let the whole world burn than make nice with her brother's killer.

"Let's start with the bad news," Theo said.

He swiped his finger across his console, triggering a change on all the displays.

~~The Jades (Calgary)~~

Half the orphans gasped or groaned. Zack mumbled a foul expletive.

"How'd they die?" asked See.

"They didn't," Theo said. "You already met one of them in Mexico."

The screens switched to a photo captured from Eden's helmet camera last Friday, an image of a woman in peculiar stone armor. She was as pale as a vampire, with thick black veins on her neck and temples. Ofelia was particularly unnerved by her eerily bright eyes, the same saturated shade of green as her outfit.

Jade . . .

"That's the woman who nearly killed Zack and Melissa," Theo said. "Her name's Joelle Legault. She's one of the nine orphans from Canada."

Caleb recoiled at her ghastly countenance. "That thing's one of us?"

"*Was* one of us," Theo stressed. "The Pelletiers have been keeping the Jades under their wing for two years—training them, augmenting them. They have at least four powers each and they're fully committed to the cause. They're basically junior Pelletiers."

Mother shook her head in disbelief. "How can they possibly work for those monsters?"

"Not sure," Theo said. "Esis might have done something to their brains. Or maybe they just fell for the propaganda. I don't know. All I can tell you is that there's no turning them back. They're worse than dead. They're enemies."

The room fell into a morbid silence. Peter gestured at Joelle's image. "Well, at least we don't have to worry about her anymore."

"Yes we do," said Theo. "I've seen her all over the future."

Eden laughed, incredulous. "That's impossible. I watched Peter kill her."

Theo shrugged. "And I know what I saw. She comes back."

Ofelia looked down the line of seated orphans and saw half of them eyeing Zack worriedly. No one in the room was happy about the Jades, but he was the only one fighting back tears.

"Is he okay?" Ofelia whispered to Hannah.

"He takes it harder than most," she whispered back.

"What, the loss of our people?"

Hannah nodded. "He thinks we're all brothers and sisters deep down, because we're all from the same cosmic neighborhood."

"He's not entirely wrong."

"He's not entirely right either," Hannah said. "Look at Evan."

Theo brought the list of orphans back to the screens. "But there's good news too."

He traced a circle around the next two names:

The Violets (London)

The Opals (Rotterdam)

"Neither of these groups are Pelletier-controlled," Theo said. "And I'm ninety percent sure they're both in London. If they're not already together, then each one knows where the other is. That makes them a two-for-one special."

"Yes, but *where* in London?" Cain asked. "We've been searching for months. Do you have any new leads?"

Theo nodded. "There's a man out there who knows exactly where the Violets are. And I know where he'll be tomorrow. There's an event in New Jersey that he never misses."

Mia scoffed at him. "You're leaving us already?"

"I'm not going at all. I'm sending Zack and Heath."

Ben pointed at Heath in astonishment. *"Him?"*

"Shut up," See said. "He's one of the strongest people we have. He's *fearless.*"

Heath eyed her strangely. "No I'm not."

"He threw a giant wolf at the Pelletiers," Peter told Ben. "Only time I ever saw them sweat."

"This isn't about power," Theo said. "It's personality. The man in question is picky about who he likes and he's *very* temperamental. Last time I saw him, he knocked out my tooth."

"Holy shit," said Hannah. "Who is he?"

"He goes by lots of names. And he's very, very shrewd. We can't have *any* government people in the area, even hidden ones. He'll know and he won't like it."

"Are you sure Zack and Heath will be safe?" Amanda asked.

"They'll be fine," Theo assured her. "But the minute we get the information we need, we have to act on it. Melissa will lead the mission to London. She's still picking out her team."

"I have them," she said. "Amanda, Zack, Caleb, and the Coppers."

Mother blinked at her, thrown. "All of us?"

Melissa nodded. "You're a formidable group and you work well together. But you'll have to do exactly what I say. London's the core of the British

Dominion, the most heavily policed city in the world. We make even the slightest whiff of trouble there, they'll hit us fast and hard."

Her warning did nothing to dampen See's excitement. "Do they still have the Tower Bridge?"

"Yes," Melissa said with a sigh. "But don't get ahead of yourself. This all depends on Zack and Heath getting the information we need."

"You're not going to London?" Hannah asked Theo.

He shook his head. "I'll be leading the other mission."

"What other mission?"

"Glad you asked."

Theo changed the screens to another photographic image: a bearded young man whom everyone but Ofelia recognized.

Peter palmed his face. "Oh Christ."

"Michael Pendergen," Theo said to Ofelia. "One of the most powerful augurs the Gothams have ever had. He left the clan a few years back to live his own life. Now everyone knows him as Merlin McGee, the great disaster prophet."

Ofelia looked at him askance. "Disaster prophet?"

"He's been predicting natural disasters for a year and a half," Melissa said. "Has yet to miss a single one. His warnings have saved thousands of lives."

"And made him world-famous," Cain added. "They practically worship him here in the U.S."

Ofelia looked to Peter. "Pendergen."

"His brother," Theo told her. "In name and spirit. Not by blood."

"Not in name or spirit either," Peter griped. "Not anymore."

"What happened?" Ofelia asked.

Peter wriggled in his seat uncomfortably. "If it's all the same, I'd rather not—"

"He bailed on everyone," Hannah said. "When all the apocalyptic shit started, Peter asked him to help and he refused."

"Why?"

Peter shrugged. "I'm still trying to figure it out."

"He's not a bad guy," Mercy said to Ofelia. "He's just . . ."

"Selfish," Amanda said. "His foresight could have made all the difference. But he prefers to do his celebrity thing."

Theo shook his head, chuckling. "I said it before and I'll say it again: he's working for the greater good. I don't know why he's going about it the way he is, but I know his end goal. He wants to save the world. And in four days' time, he'll need us."

He advanced to the next presentation slide:

Ciudad del Plata

Havana

7/29 @ 5PM EST

"On Sunday, he'll stage a press conference at a fancy Cuban hotel. That's where he'll announce a new impending disaster. I don't know what it is. I just know it'll be a doozy."

Cain leaned forward in his chair, wide-eyed. "He's not going to, uh . . ."

"No," said Theo. "He won't reveal the apocalypse. This is something more local to the United States. But I can't shake the feeling that something bad's going to happen to him at that press conference. I'd like to prevent it if we can."

"Why should we help him if he doesn't want to help us?" Ben asked.

"Because he has the answer to the question you asked earlier," Theo said. "He knows what comes next, after all the timebenders are gathered. We're going to get that information, even if we have to smack it out of him."

He looked around the table. "I want to keep this mission team small. Me, Peter, Hannah, Heath, and Eden."

"We should bring Liam," Peter said. "He and Michael were always close."

Theo nodded. "Works for me."

"I want to go too," said Ofelia. "I can help. I know Cuba."

"You don't know *this* Cuba," Theo warned her.

"How different can it be?"

"It's a U.S. state."

"The fuck it is."

"It's true," Cain told her. "It's been part of the union since 1969."

Ofelia never needed a cigarette more badly in her life. "I still want to go."

"That's fine," Theo said. "But now we're at capacity. No more add-ons."

Mia crossed her arms in a surly pout. "This is bullshit."

Theo threw his hands up. "I'm sorry you're benched. You know I'd bring you otherwise."

"It's bullshit that they benched me. I'm just as psychologically fit as the rest of you."

"The rest of us didn't choke Sovereign Tam in the ladies' room," Melissa fired back.

"You should have. She's a homophobe."

"You know what you have to do to get back on the roster," Cain told Mia. "Come see me after the meeting."

Ofelia could feel the poor girl's energies swirling inside her like a cyclone. She had so much anger, so much grief, all way beyond the confines of normal teenage drama. The fact that she was standing at all made her a heroine to Ofelia. She should have been getting medals, not sidelined.

Theo turned off the screens and rose to his feet. "We'll have to save the Rubies and Majee for the next phase. I'm still working on them."

"It's all right," Amanda said. "We're making good progress."

Peter nodded in agreement. "It's starting to look like we're ahead of the game."

"Well, that's the next thing I wanted to talk about," Theo said. "Uh . . ."

He swapped a dark look with Melissa before continuing. "Look, I've been living with the doomsday stuff for two years—the one in the past, and the one in the future. My first mistake, I realize now, was thinking they're the same. They're not."

He gestured at his fellow orphans. "Our world died over the course of six hours. This one's been dying for four and a half years. The apocalypse isn't something that's coming. It's been happening this whole time."

See bit her thumb with a terrified expression. Mother stroked her back.

"My second mistake," Theo said, "was thinking that we still had two and a half years to stop it. I figured it was like one of those bombs you see in the movies, where they cut the right wire with one second to spare. Unfortunately, it's more like a runaway train headed straight for a cliff. We can't just hit the brake at the last second. We have to start sooner—much, much sooner—or the inertia will pull us all over the edge."

"So how long do we have to fix this mess?" Cain asked. "Six months? A year?"

Melissa slumped in her chair with a heavy sigh. "About ten weeks."

The room fell into gasps and curses. It was Integrity's chief liaison to the Gothams, a man so quiet that Ofelia forgot he existed, who spoke up above the chatter. "So we still have two and a half years before the sky comes down, but only two and a half months to stop it."

Melissa nodded darkly. "That's the point of no return. If we cross that line without solving the problem—"

"—we'll have nothing to do but wait," Theo finished.

"How sure are you?" asked Zack.

"I heard it from Merlin McGee," Theo said. "Who heard it straight from Ioni. It's possible she's lying to light a fire under our asses, but—"

"What do *you* see?" Hannah asked him.

Theo tapped his arm in thought before answering. "I see everything coming to a head in ten weeks, in the streets of San Francisco. I've spent months there looking for more information, but . . ." He shrugged. "There are still so many variables, it's hard to make sense of it. The only thing I know for sure is that everyone needs to be there—the orphans, the Gothams, the Majee. All of us."

"For what?" Eden asked.

Ofelia watched Theo closely as he struggled for an answer. "I don't know," he told Eden, somewhat unconvincingly. "I just don't."

Cain typed a note into his electronic organizer before looking to Theo again. "Is there anything else you can tell us about what's coming?"

Theo shook his head uneasily. Ofelia caught his eyes lingering on her silver bracelet. "Nothing solid enough to share."

"All right." Cain pushed back his chair and rose to full height. "This new information stays among us until further notice. Don't talk about it outside this room. Don't share it with your friends. The last thing we need is a panic down here, especially after Semerjean's stunt. Can we all agree?"

Everyone nervously nodded their heads.

"All right, then. Meeting's over. Melissa?"

She flipped the switch on the tabletop, and the war room began to open. The wall had only retracted halfway when Cain ducked under it and hurried for the door. Ofelia heard the flick of his lighter, then smelled the smoke of his cigarette. The man was full of good ideas. She couldn't think of a better thing to do with her trembling hands.

She wandered off into the fringes of the underland, her last cigarette dangling between her fingers. There was a full pack waiting for her back in her bedroom, but Ofelia had no desire to go there. She supposed she could grab it through a well-placed portal, but . . . no. After that monster of a meeting, she needed to be a normal person for a while, or at least pretend to be one.

She found her way to the perimeter park and saw a familiar presence in a gazebo. Theo greeted her with a canny smirk, as if she were late for another one of their usual outings.

Ofelia cocked her head at him. "What are you doing here?"

"Waiting for you."

"How did you . . ." She rolled her eyes in realization. "You're stalking me from the future."

"It's not stalking if I get here first." He held up a notepad. "You left this in the war room."

"'War room.'" Ofelia joined him in the gazebo and took her notebook back. "Did you ever expect to be the kind of person who runs meetings in war rooms?"

"Not even a little."

"What were you before this?"

"An alcoholic fuck-up," Theo said. "You?"

"Full-time recovering drug addict."

Theo leaned on the railing and took a vacant look around the park. "I seem to have acquired a fondness for mescaline."

Ofelia nodded grimly. "I'm a sucker for whiskey now."

"Guess we'll always be the type, huh?"

"Yes, but now we're addicts who meet in war rooms," Ofelia said. "And make plans to save the world."

She matched Theo's pose on the railing and studied all the reddish-purple trees in the vicinity. She recognized them as Crimson Queen Japanese maples, but she couldn't remember where she'd learned their name.

"She has good reason to hate her," Theo said out of the blue.

Ofelia looked at him. "What?"

He tapped the front of her notebook, at the fourth item on her to-do list: *Ask Mia about Ioni.*

"Oh, right. What did she do?"

Theo sat down on a bench. "Thirteen months ago, on a very bad day, Mia had a chance to shoot Esis in the head. She's a smart girl. She knew the odds of succeeding were about a billion to one, and the cost of failure would be . . . bad. But Ioni talked her into it. She promised her that the bullet would kill Esis and that Mia and her loved ones would be protected from all consequences. So she took the shot."

"But it didn't work," Ofelia said. "Esis caught the bullet in a portal."

"Mia told you?"

"Yeah. Last night. Semerjean got mad and took it out on her girlfriend. And Esis swore to kill someone else that Mia loved."

Theo nodded darkly. "With that very same bullet."

"Did Ioni know what would really happen?"

"I have no doubt that she did."

"*Mierda.*" Ofelia glared at Theo. "And you still trust this woman?"

"I do."

"Then there's something seriously wrong with you."

Ofelia stomped out the nub of her cigarette, then concentrated on the visual details of her bedroom. Soon a small horizontal portal opened in the air and dropped a fresh pack of smokes into her hand.

Theo smiled at her, impressed. "You're a fast learner."

"Peter's a good teacher."

"You know, in some ways travelers are the opposite of augurs," he noted. "You jump straight to where you want to go. We take the long and winding road."

"Why?"

"Because every decision makes ripples in time," he told her. "Even the decision not to do anything. They all come with consequences, good and bad, and augurs see them all."

Ofelia furrowed her brow. "I'm not exactly, uh . . ."

"Okay, let's say I know that a man's coming to kill you. I warn you about it. You freak out, get in your car, and then crash head-on into a van full of kids. That's several people dead instead of one, all because I tried to save you."

He found a bottle cap on the ground and flicked it into the trees. "But I see *that* coming in advance, so I plot a different approach. This one doesn't cause any deaths, but it involves telling you a nasty lie. I might even have to break your heart a little. Is it the perfect outcome? No. But it's better than you dying or killing a bunch of kids. These are the kinds of choices we make every day. All things considered, I would have rather been a traveler."

"Wow." Ofelia lit a new cigarette, her thoughts hovering around Rosario. The poor young Pearl was still a baby augur. Is that what she had to look forward to?

Theo slumped on the bench, a distant gloom in his eyes. "I don't know why Ioni did what she did to Mia. I just know it was for the greater good. She's playing the world's most complicated pool game, and she's lining up the mother of all bank shots."

"For what?" Ofelia asked.

"For the sake of the world," Theo said. "She wants this Earth to keep on living, and she'll do whatever it takes to make it happen. If that involves lying or occasionally screwing us over, then that's the way it has to be. It's a small price to pay for saving billions of lives."

Ofelia's heart thundered. In some ways, Theo was as scary as Semerjean, but there was a fire in him that reminded her of Jury.

"Did you ever get a look at that future?" she asked him. "Where the world doesn't die?"

"Once." Theo smiled again. "Just a glimpse of it. But I still remember every detail."

"What did you see?"

"I saw Melissa," he said. "She was an old woman and she was beautiful. She was so goddamn beautiful that I can't even . . ."

His voice choked up. Ofelia had suspected that there was something going on between him and Melissa. Now she knew.

"I can't speak for the others," Theo said, "but that's a future I'm willing to die for. I'm eighty percent sure that I will."

Ofelia shook her head in dark wonder. "You Silvers are so much more intense than the others. Even your funny one has an edge."

Theo chuckled. "After everything Zack's been through, it's a miracle he's joking at all. He's an incredible guy. One of the best people I know."

For all their heaviness, Ofelia loved the way the Silvers loved each other. Had she been that close with the Pearls once, while they were captives of the Pelletiers? She didn't know and she probably never would.

Theo looked to her wrist with interest. "Ofelia, I'd like you to go to the medical clinic tomorrow and have the doctors remove your bracelet."

She glanced down at her silver bangle, seamless and seemingly indestructible. "How?"

"They'll put you to sleep," Theo said. "Then they'll either cut off your hand or break half the bones in it. Whatever it takes to pull the bracelet off."

He spoke up before she could object. "It's all reversible," he promised. "You'll be healed before you even wake up."

Ofelia was only slightly less bothered. "Is that how you guys lost your bracelets?"

"No. Zack removed ours with a little touch of temporis. They fell right apart."

"Why can't he just do that for me?"

"Because our bracelets were dead," Theo said. "They'd already shielded us from the end of the world and carried us over to this one. Their job was done. But *yours* . . ."

"What about mine?"

"I don't think it's ever been used," he told her. "I think you came here a different way."

She thought about Semerjean and all his talk about last-minute changes. Maybe the Pelletiers had brought her here themselves. Ofelia didn't remember a thing. The only question now was—

"Why does it matter to you?"

Theo tapped her bracelet with his finger. "I can't fully explain it. I just know that thing of yours is shouting at me from the future. It's swearing to me up and down that it's something I'll need. Something *everyone* will need."

Ofelia's eyes widened. "What, you think it's part of the riddle?"

"No," said Theo. "I think it's part of the answer."

Ofelia crossed to the other side of the gazebo, her frazzled mind swimming in all the recent bits of madness. Portals and corpses and crystal cities, beaches and babies and resurrected brothers. And in the center of it all, Theo and Semerjean, spinning around and around each other in a deadly dance of death. The situation seemed so high above Ofelia's head that she had no hope of ever understanding it.

Yet there was something in the hearts of the people here, particularly the Silvers, that made her kind of believe in them. And after all the turmoil she'd been through, it felt nice to believe in something.

She took a deep drag of her cigarette, then faced Theo again. "Is the clinic open now?"

"Yes."

"And you know how to get there."

Theo nodded hesitantly. "I do."

"Then what are we waiting for?" Ofelia said. "Lead the way."

EIGHT

It was barely nine A.M. in Zack's part of the world and he already had regrets. He should have dressed more appropriately for the humid summer weather. He should have left the underland twenty minutes earlier, just to get Theo off his case. He should have picked a larger car from Integrity's motor pool, not the two-door Buick Avion that looked really sleek but was actually built for Hobbits.

Finally, and he couldn't possibly have lamented this enough, he should have never let Heath take command of the radio.

Zack glared at him from the driver's seat as the boy scrolled through the stations of Spectrum 3 (Contemporary Youth). Two or three seconds of each Altamerican rock song were enough to convince Heath that he was listening to crap. But he'd been on this world long enough to know that it was *all* crap here. The music was designed to be inoffensively likeable, in flavors that ranged from vanilla to French vanilla. The singers were so bland and similar to each other that Zack imagined they were made like Heath's tempic Jonathans, an endless supply of indistinguishable white men.

Undaunted, Heath continued his search for a halfway decent song, but all he got for his troubles was a discordant patchwork of snippets. "*Oh baby, you're my—*"*"*—can't get enough of—*"*"*—under the moonlight—*"*"*—thing about you-u-u-u!*"

"Enough," Zack snapped. "You're going to give me a seizure."

Heath turned off the radio and stared broodingly out the window. Zack was flying them south along the Spirit of the Hudson—a five-lane, six-tier interstate skyway that coursed a thousand feet above the river and was composed of nothing but lumic guide rings. Though the car seemed determined to drive his knees into his rib cage, Zack couldn't complain about the view. The morning sun was out in full force, painting the skyline of Manhattan with dazzling refractions. Zack had been living so long in his underground burrow that he almost forgot about the splendors of the surface world. But he imagined he was in for a lot more reminders. If all went well in Jersey this morning, he'd be flying to London by sundown. Things were moving fast again, for reasons that continued to haunt him.

"Ten weeks," Zack uttered. "Shit. It took me twelve weeks to finish my senior art school project, and that almost killed me."

Heath kept his attention on the Manhattan aer traffic, a thousand little strands of flying black dots. "We're not supposed to talk about it."

"My senior art school project?"

"The deadline," Heath said. "We can't talk about it outside the war room."

"Come on. You really think that place is secure?"

"I just know what they told us."

"Well, it's just you and me up here. No one else can hear us."

"I can," said a voice in Zack's earpiece.

"Theo! How long have you been listening?"

"Since you turned off that horrible music," he teased.

Zack laughed. "You gonna Obi-Wan us through the meeting?"

"Nope. You got this. Just making sure you're okay."

"You could have warned me it was hot as balls out here."

"Yeah. Welcome back to the real world."

"Real world," Zack said with a scoff. He was flying a Buick over the Hudson through rings of temporal light. "Reality" wasn't the first word that came to mind.

See's cheery high voice broke in over the transcom. "Hi, Heath! How you feeling?"

The boy merely replied with a grunt.

"You're so brave for doing this," See told him. "We're all really proud of you."

Though Zack knew she was saying it out of pure infatuation, she wasn't just blowing smoke. Theo hadn't been entirely forthright about the man they were meeting, the one with crucial information about the Violets. If Hannah had known his true identity, she would have gone thermonuclear.

Zack looked to Heath in concern. "Hey, augurs, can you give us a minute?"

"Sure thing," said Theo. "Just don't slow down. You need to be there by—"

"—nine thirty," Zack wearily confirmed. "We know. We'll make it."

Their two-way connection closed out with a click. Heath eyed Zack suspiciously. "What?"

"You don't have to do this," Zack told him. "You can wait in the car and let me talk to him."

"Theo said I had to be there."

"He's asking a lot of you. More than some of us are comfortable with."

"I just want to help," Heath replied, as if it were the most obvious thing in the world. "Why? Do you think I'll get in the way?"

"No! Not at all! I just . . ."

Zack sighed through his nose, flummoxed. Whether it was therapy, camaraderie, or just good old-fashioned perseverance, Heath had grown leaps and bounds from the tempestuous kid he used to be. He no longer insisted on eating foods of a certain color, or wearing the same football jersey every day. He looked people in the eye when he talked to them and tolerated behavior that would have previously sent him into a tizzy.

Yet for all his strides, he still had a slew of emotional problems, all compounded by the tragic circumstances of his life. The people he loved kept dying on him, and Hannah's future had become . . . questionable at best. Heath had barely had a day to process her pregnancy before Theo came back and dropped the ten-week bombshell on everyone.

Now the boy was going to meet with an unremitting sociopath, one of the very worst people Zack knew.

Zack glanced out his window and saw the Statue of Liberty on her great stone pedestal, same as she ever was. The Cataclysm had missed her by five hundred and nine feet, a number that had become laser-burned onto Altamerican culture. To this day, it remained a colloquial term for the people who endured, the ones who kept surviving by the skin of their teeth. *Don't you worry about Heath now. He's five-oh-nine and doing fine.*

"Okay," Zack said. "If you say you can handle it, that's good enough for me."

If Heath appreciated the faith, he didn't show it. He merely drummed his thighs to whatever old-world rock song was playing in his head.

Zack looked at him with a sly half-grin. "So, uh, See sure seems to like you. A lot."

Heath didn't smile back. "I don't know."

"Oh, come on. She's great."

"She talks a lot."

"Everyone talks a lot compared to you," Zack said. "You just have to give her time."

"Time," Heath cynically echoed.

"You think Amanda and I hit it off right away? First time I met her, she slapped me."

"Why?"

"I might have . . . mocked her religion and everything it stood for."

Zack shrugged at Heath's disapproving look. "The world just ended. I wasn't at my best."

He tapped the steering wheel with flesh and metal fingers, his thoughts drifting through pleasant memories. "But when you're on the run and fighting for your life, you get to know the people you're with. Before long, I was looking at Amanda and seeing . . . everything. A whole universe inside her. Every time I think I have her all mapped out, I find some new and beautiful aspect of her, and I'm in love all over again."

He looked to Heath with a self-effacing smirk. "I used to be a relationship skeptic. Now I'm one of those cheesy schmucks who wants all of his friends to find the right partner. But if you're happier on your own, that's a fair choice too. Everyone's different."

The car fell into a stagnant silence. Heath anxiously fiddled with the hem of his T-shirt. "She's too young for me."

"Who, See?"

"Yeah. She's thirteen."

"So? You're close to that." Zack narrowed his eyes at him. "Aren't you?"

Heath shook his head. "I'm seventeen."

"What?" Zack had to force his eyes back on the skyway before he sideswiped another aeromobile. The kid was only five foot two and still had the voice of a choirboy. "When was your birthday?"

"A couple of months ago."

Holy shit, thought Zack. After all this time, the boy was still a vault of secrets. Zack wanted to pry more details out of him, but it would only make him uncomfortable. And Heath needed every ounce of strength he had for the unpleasant meeting to come.

A floating sign announced the upcoming exit for Elizabeth. Zack sighed in surrender, then flicked a hand at the radio. "All right. Go on."

Heath switched the band to Spectrum 4 (Classic Youth), then resumed his erratic station-hopping. Zack listened to the fragments of old and crappy songs until they crossed the Newark Bay and reached their final destination.

Elizabeth, New Jersey, had a special claim to fame, and it'd be damned if you didn't know it. No matter how you entered the city limits—by car or by train or by hand-carved tunnel—you were destined to see a sign that greeted you with a boast:

WELCOME TO ELIZABETH: THE BIRTHPLACE OF AERIS

It was true. The Severson Corporation had been headquartered there since 1963, and it was their research scientists who'd first tricked tempis into thinking that up was down. Through their once-in-a-lifetime discovery, they ushered the world into the antigravity age, and got filthy rich in the process.

These days, aeris was the only form of temporis that was still under corporate patent. Every business on Earth that made flying objects had to kick some coin into Severson's coffers.

Today, the company employed nearly a hundred thousand people and had turned a good chunk of Elizabeth into its own private compound. Zack could see it from his Avion as he descended into the city—twelve hundred acres of impeccably green campus, filled with dozens of variations of the same red-brick building. He might have mistaken it for a university if he hadn't seen the Severson logo everywhere. Their diamond-shaped "S" could have come straight from the chest of an evil alternate Superman.

Zack landed the car in a public park, then released four camera flies into the air. The Integrity drones were as small as golf balls and were equipped with spy tech that was illegal in most countries. As soon as they reached twelve feet of altitude, they activated their lumic cloaks and became all but invisible against the clear blue sky.

"You getting us?" Zack asked Theo.

"What?"

"Do you see us through the cameras?"

"Oh. Yeah. Yeah. You're coming in great."

Forty miles to the north, in a ground-floor office in the Orphanage administration building, Theo sat at Melissa's computer and kept three of the four camera flies on Zack and Heath. He steered the fourth one ahead to the park's picnic area and fixed it on a trio of tables.

"All right," he told Zack. "Go to the one at the edge of the lot, the one that overlooks the Severson campus."

"The one *what*?"

"Sorry, table. The picnic table."

"Are you okay?" Zack asked him. "You sound a little, uh . . ."

"I'm fine." Theo anxiously checked his watch. "Just over-caffeinated."

See and Amanda pulled up chairs next to him and watched the four-screen split on the monitor. "They should check for traps," Amanda said. "You know how he is."

Theo shook his head. "I'm not worried about traps. I'm worried about him not showing up."

"Who are you talking to?" Zack asked him. "Is that Amanda?"

Amanda grabbed a spare headset and put it on. "Hi, sweetheart. How you doing?"

"I'm sweating in places I'd rather not think about."

"Like New Jersey?"

"Exactly." Zack thumped Heath's shoulder. "See? She gets me."

Amanda only smiled for a moment before switching off the transmitter. "He's nervous," she said to Theo. "And the look on your face is making *me* nervous. What are you not telling me?"

"It'll be fine," he promised as he guided the cameras into position. One of them captured the Severson campus at a ridiculously wide angle, as if Theo were expecting a meteor strike.

He turned the radio back on. "Okay, Zack. Don't sit down yet."

"Why not?"

"Because reasons."

Zack glanced up at the camera. "This is feeling less and less like a Melissa production."

"It's not," said Theo. "She's busy with the London prep. I don't want her involved in this, anyway."

"How come?" Heath asked.

Theo wrung his hands as the clock changed to 9:33. "You know I love you both like brothers, right? I'd never do anything to hurt you."

"Oh God," Zack said. "I don't like where this is going."

"For the sake of the mission, I had to let something bad happen. I didn't tell you about it because I didn't want you sharing the guilt. This was my choice and mine alone."

"Theo, what the hell are you—"

"It's starting," said See.

Heath scrambled around the edge of the picnic table, his wide eyes fixed on the Severson campus. "Oh no . . ."

Zack followed his gaze but he didn't see anything out of the ordinary. Then one of the central buildings, a windowless cube of red brick and steel, began to crack in multiple places. From a distance, it looked like something out of a fever dream, a great white monster hatching from a square concrete egg.

Amanda watched the madness through the monitor. "Theo . . ."

Had she been there, she would have felt it: a massive surge of tempic/aeric energy, more powerful than any one person could produce. It punched the flat metal roof off the crumbling building and sent it spinning through the air like a bottle cap.

"Holy . . ." Zack barely had a chance to watch it land before a geyser of white force shot out of the missing roof. It rose furiously into the sky, spreading smokelike tendrils in all directions. By the time the eruption came to a stop, it was tall enough to be seen from Staten Island and strange enough to defy all classification. It looked like the corpse of a giant white willow tree, or the skeleton of a mushroom cloud.

Zack stumbled backward. "What was that? A bomb?"

"No bomb," Theo said. "Just a really bad screwup."

To understand the cause of the accident, one had to know the quandary that Severson was facing. Its patent on aeris was expiring in a year, a nine-figure loss in revenue that threatened to sink the company's stock value. The only way to keep an exclusive hold on its discovery was to develop a new and improved version of aeris and then file for a patent extension.

So the research scientists worked day and night to come up with a fresh new spin on their product, and eventually created helius. It looked and acted just like aeris, but with thirty percent more energy efficiency. Vehicles could fly an extra hundred miles before needing a battery recharge. Aerstraunts could save millions on operational costs. It was everything Severson could have possibly hoped for, except for one small hitch.

It wasn't stable.

There was a quirk in the molecular makeup of helius that occasionally caused it to expand in hot conditions. This latest explosion was unprecedented in scale, the result of an aerstraunt liftplate being stress-tested with plasma fire. Had the scientists been under a less oppressive deadline, they might have waited a few iterations before trying something that risky.

None of them lived long enough to regret their decision.

Zack and Heath watched from their safe vantage point as the campus fell into bedlam. The research lab had been completely destroyed, with half of the wreckage in flames. The displaced metal roof crashed into a neighboring building, sending most of it toppling to the ground. Workers screamed at both accident sites. Zack could hear their faint and distant cries.

"Don't go down there," Theo warned him. "There's nothing you can do."

"Goddamn, Theo. How many people just died?"

"I don't know."

"Bullshit!" Zack yelled. "You saw this coming. You probably already saw the news reports."

Theo puffed a heavy sigh. "Fifty people. Maybe more."

"Fifty?" Amanda gripped his arm. "We could have saved them all with a phone call."

"We could have," See admitted. "But then the meeting wouldn't have happened."

Theo pointed at the helius eruption. "That stupid, tragic accident is the only thing that brings him here. He comes to see it every time."

"Au contraire," said a new voice on the channel. "I actually missed it twice."

Zack and Heath turned around to see a short young man sitting cross-legged on a picnic table, a pale and skinny ginger-blond in a short-sleeve button-down and cargo shorts. He removed his shades and grinned at his fellow orphans as emergency vehicles came shrieking down the street behind him.

Evan Rander had arrived, just as Theo predicted.

Zack steeled himself with a calming breath, struggling to keep his revulsion inside of him. Though Evan was just a nuisance compared to the Pelletiers, they at least wrapped their violence in the flag of a higher cause. Evan had no such justification. Everything he did was for his own twisted amusement. He hurt people just to pass the time.

"There he is," Zack said to Heath. "Our very own psycho killer."

"Qu'est-ce que c'est?" Evan shot a flippant grin at Heath. "Well, shuck my corn. I haven't seen you in ages. How the hell are you, kid?"

Heath stood rooted at his spot, his large eyes fixed on the man who'd killed Jonathan. He didn't return the smile.

After ninety-eight seconds of splitting the sky, the helius eruption disappeared without a sound. By then the aerspace was filled with local media liveeyes: dozens of cat-size camera drones, all buzzing around the scene in a timeshifted frenzy. The accident had already become national news, destroying all of Severson's hopes for the future. Elizabeth would never go out of its way to call itself the birthplace of helius.

Evan photographed the eruption in its final moments, then took a snapshot of Zack and Heath. "Oh, lighten up. You had front-row seats to the best show of the year."

"People died," Zack growled.

"*Strangers* died, just like they do every day. Come on, man. You're a 'big picture' guy."

"That's the only reason I'm talking to you." Zack jerked his head at Heath. "The only reason he's not tearing you to pieces."

"Right. We're at *that* part of the story." Evan stashed his camera in his shoulder bag and took a seat at the nearest picnic table. "Well, I know what you want and I'll be happy to discuss it. But you gotta wine and dine me before I put out."

Evan motioned to the opposite bench. Zack paused and swapped an edgy look with Heath.

"*He* can stay standing," Evan said. "He's not here to negotiate, anyway." He pressed the receiver in his ear. "Isn't that right, Theo?"

Theo grudgingly nodded from his remote location. "Nice job hacking our radio signal."

"Hack?" Evan laughed. "I just had to know the frequency. And I have to admit I'm a little disappointed. I thought you'd be man enough to face me in person."

Theo shrugged. "The way our last meeting ended, I figured you didn't want to see me."

"Augga, please. I don't hold grudges."

"Yes you do," Amanda snapped.

"Whoa, ho, ho! If it isn't Sister Christian." Evan clapped his hands with glee. "I have so many things to tease you about, I don't even know where to begin."

Amanda sneered at his camera image. "No problem. I can be there in twenty minutes."

"Yeah. I don't think so."

"What's the matter? Not man enough to tease me in person?"

Theo covered Amanda's microphone and sternly shook his head. "All right," he said to Evan. "This is the part where we sign off."

Evan chuckled in amazement. "You let fifty people die just to talk to me. Now you're hanging up?"

"Yup." Theo turned off the transmitter, then looked to See. "Would you, uh—"

"Yeah."

Amanda watched her hurry out of the office. "Where's she going?"

"To get Hannah and Ofelia."

"Are you kidding me?"

"Look—"

"You *want* them to see Evan?"

"No," said Theo. "I want them to see Heath. Evan was right. I didn't send him there to negotiate."

Amanda eyed him uneasily. "You know I love and trust you, Theo. But sometimes—"

"I make it hard," Theo said with glum acknowledgment. "I know."

Amanda sat forward and watched her husband join Evan at the table. "If he hurts Zack—"

"He won't."

"I don't care how useful he is. I'll bring the whole sky down on him."

"Don't worry." Theo locked the cameras into position and raised the volume on the microphones. "Zack's got this."

His empty stomach churned with stress. Among his growing list of regrets for the day, he wished he'd eaten a decent breakfast. His low blood sugar was making him twitchy, filling his head with violent thoughts. All it would take was a wave of the hand to age Evan into a rotted husk, and wouldn't the bastard deserve it? He'd made Hannah's life a living hell, tortured Amanda with an electric gun, murdered innocent people all over the country. Worst of all, he'd killed Jonathan Christie and Jury Curado, two of their own endangered breed. Every orphan death was like a genocide to Zack, and Evan was hunting them for sport.

Sweating, Zack fluffed the collar of his shirt and forced his thoughts back to the mission. There was crucial information in that sick little brain of Evan's, information that could help save everyone.

Evan snickered at Zack's myoelectric hand. "Look at you getting your cyborg on. Who Skywalkered you? Esis?"

Zack shook his head distractedly. "One of her flunkies."

"Flunkies?" Evan thought it over a moment, confused. "Oh, the Jades. Right! So it was less *Empire Strikes Back* and more *Attack of the Clones.*"

"You're saying the Jades are clones?"

Evan shrugged. "I'm assuming they're clones. I don't know. I just know that killing them doesn't stop them. They always come back."

Zack fixed his scowling gaze on the Severson campus. "So I've heard."

"I told you before and I'll tell you again: you're playing a sucker's game. I offered you a better life but you said, 'No thanks, Evan. I prefer to suffer abuse and imprisonment.'"

"I seem to recall us spending time in the same jail."

"Yeah, well . . ." Evan studied the scars on the back of his left hand, the four little divots from the Pelletiers' mirror room. "That's what I get for ignoring my own advice."

Evan looked beyond Zack with a droll little grin. "So, uh, Heath—"

"Don't," Zack warned.

"What? I'm just making conversation."

"You're winding him up," Zack said. "Like a jack-in-the-box. Except it won't be a clown on a spring that pops out."

Evan laughed. "Who's afraid of the big bad wolf?"

"No wolves," Zack told him. "He's moved on from those. You set him off now, you'll get an army of Jonathans. Wouldn't *that* be poetic justice?"

Evan only flinched a moment before regaining his smug bravado. "I ain't afraid of no ghosts either."

"Tough guy," Zack said. "You've probably been through this conversation, what? Nine times already? Ten?"

Evan smiled patiently. "Five."

"So you already know that we prefer you in one piece."

"True." Evan shook a finger at Zack. "But I was mighty brave that first time."

He reached into his bag and placed a foil-wrapped sandwich on the table. "My breakfast," he told Zack. "A bacon-and-egg franklin that's gone criminally cold. Would you mind?"

"How long?"

"About an hour should do it."

Zack scanned the park for witnesses, then reversed the franklin back to piping hot freshness. Evan unwrapped the foil, smelled the steam of his flatbread sandwich, then kissed his fingertips in approval. "*Molto bene.*"

"Funny how we can both turn back time," Zack noted. "In such different ways."

"There's no kitchen appliance that can do what I do."

"No, but I knew a ten-year-old Gotham who could," said Zack. "She wasn't pleasant either."

Evan shrugged off his insult. "With great power comes great irascibility."

"Is this your fifth time eating that sandwich?"

"Sixth." Evan took an oversize bite. "Still delicious."

"Doesn't it get tedious after a while?"

"*Tedious?*" Evan laughed up a fleck of scrambled egg. "I do everything in multiple takes. If I couldn't handle the tedium, I'd be crazy by now."

Zack skirted around the obvious joke, then drummed his arm in thought. "I've already asked you that question, haven't I?"

"Yes. And you've already asked about asking."

"So let's cut the fat," Zack suggested. "What else did we talk about in those other five conversations?"

Evan smiled slyly. "You told me Hannah's pregnant."

Heath's eyes widened. Zack pursed his lips at Evan. "You're lying."

"I am," Evan said with a laugh. "But thanks for confirming my hunch."

He took another bite of his franklin and spoke through a full mouth. "She usually gets knocked up around this time, and it's pretty much always the end of her."

Theo and Amanda watched from the underland, their bodies arched in the same rigid pose.

Zack changed the subject for everyone's sake. "Is there a question I haven't asked you yet?"

"Why, yes, as a matter of fact. You haven't asked me how I've been."

"How have you been, Evan?"

"Meh. It's been a year of ups and downs. I went through a whole new experience, though. New for me, anyway."

"You treated a woman with respect?"

"That was part of it, yes. But it's even more shocking. Let me show you."

Evan pulled a photo from his wallet and slapped it onto the table. Theo and Amanda leaned in toward the monitor, but they couldn't see what Zack saw: a picture of Evan and a pretty young blonde holding hands, smiling. Their outfits told the rest of the story: his dapper tuxedo, her short white dress and rose bouquet.

Zack looked at Evan, hang-jawed. "You got *married*?"

"Last September."

"Bullshit."

"It's true," said Evan. "Rachel Hicks, twenty-six. Columbia grad. Smart as a whip. Earned *beaucoup de bucks* as a Wall Street day trader. She was jogging in Central Park one night when a loathsome man—*not* me—attacked her and . . . well, he hurt her a lot. It wasn't the first time she'd been hurt that way, and the trauma was so bad that she ended up killing herself. Her suicide note just said 'Fuck the world.'"

He looked up and saw Heath listening intently. "I read about her death in the news the next day. I liked her face and the cut of her jib, so I went back in time and I saved her."

"From the suicide?" Zack asked. "Or from the, uh . . ."

"From the rapist," Evan said. "Showed up in the park in the nick of time and broke the guy's spine with a golf club. She grabbed it from me and went to town on the fucker. By the time she finished, he looked like roadkill."

He stared at the photo in absent thought. "Though she wasn't in the best of moods, she was grateful I came along. I could have just ridden on that, I suppose, but I decided to take a chance and tell her everything: who I was, where I came from, all the cool and crazy stuff that I can do with time. I told her that the world was ending in just a few years, and that there wasn't much point to day trading."

Evan chuckled with astonishment. "You'd think she'd have me committed or something, but she believed me. She looked into my eyes, saw the truth, and said, 'Okay. What now?'"

Zack listened to him with rapt fascination. The story had changed everything about Evan's demeanor—his face, his voice, his whole body language. For once, he didn't look like a smug little gremlin. He looked like the person he might have been on the old world, before his endless time travels warped his mind and soul.

"We lived it up for a while," Evan said. "Tracked down the men who'd hurt her when she was younger and made them regret ever touching her. She took them all down with an aluminum bat and she loved every second of it. Killing bad guys made her feel alive, *passionate*. And I got all the benefits."

Amanda listened from the Orphanage, speechless. In true Evan style, the story was horrific. Yet she was relieved that he'd been aiming his malice at bad guys for a change.

"We eloped to Seattle," Evan continued. "Started saving other women retroactively, like I first did with her. It was one of best times I've ever had, playing vigilante with Rachel. Whatever strings Amanda plucks in you, this woman did it for me."

Evan gazed at his lap in absent thought before forcing a shaky smile. "But she wasn't built the way I'm built. She'd never seen the world end once, much less fifty times. If I could have brought her with me on all my rewinds, I could have gotten her to see things my way. I mean, once you realize what a joke everything is, it doesn't hurt so much, you know?"

He turned to Zack with palpable disappointment. "You *don't* know. I keep trying to teach you, but you never want to learn."

"Just tell me what happened to her."

Evan pushed aside his half-eaten franklin. "After a couple of months, she started losing her fire. Killing rapists wasn't doing it for her anymore. Nothing was. She just cried all the time and there wasn't anything I could do. And when the suicides started . . . it was rough. If she killed herself with a knife, I'd jump back in time and take away the knife. If she killed herself with a gun, I'd jump back in time and take away her bullets. It became a full-time job just to keep her alive. In the end, I just . . ."

Evan vented a doleful sigh. "I just let her go."

A long silence passed, broken only by the clamor at the Severson campus. Federal agents had arrived on the scene and were evacuating workers by the hundreds.

Evan watched the bustle before turning back to Zack. "Anyway, that's how I've been. Thanks for asking."

Theo and Amanda sat side by side at Melissa's desk, wearing the same slack expression. They'd been so enrapt by Evan's story that they didn't hear the office door open. They didn't see Hannah until she was standing right behind them, her hard brown eyes locked furiously on Evan's image.

"What the *fuck* is going on?"

She'd been eating breakfast in the commissary with Mia and Ofelia when See came rushing in. She'd assured them that Zack and Heath were fine, but there was something going on in Melissa's office that Hannah needed to know about. Something that would make her mad.

If anything, See had undersold the situation.

By the time Ofelia, See, and Mia caught up with Hannah in the office, she was already on a tear. Amanda had to hold her back to keep her from hitting Theo.

"You lied to me!" she yelled. "I asked you who this contact was. You said—"

"I know." Theo nodded at her with self-reproach. "I had no choice. I'm sorry."

"You're *sorry*?"

"If I had told you—"

"Shut up." Hannah struggled in her sister's grip. "Let go of me already."

Amanda released her. Hannah spun a one-eighty and aimed her wrath sisterwise. "How could you of all people be in on this? Did you forget all the shit he did to you?"

"I hate him just as much as you do," Amanda insisted. "If I was there, he'd be dead already."

"But you still knew."

"She didn't," Theo said to Hannah. "I only told her an hour ago."

Hannah eyed him hotly. "All this time, you've had a line on Evan. Do you know how long I've been—"

A dark, smoky laugh cut her off from behind. Five heads turned to look at Ofelia as she studied Evan on the monitor.

"This is a joke. That can't be the man who killed Jury."

Mia shrugged. "I know he doesn't look like much . . ."

"He looks like *nothing.* My brother was a cop, a bodybuilder. He could have crushed that little twerp with one hand."

Theo showed her the gap where his upper left canine tooth used to be. "See this? Evan knocked it out with a perfectly timed punch. Everything he does is perfectly timed because he has unlimited do-overs. If he screws up once, twice, fifty times, it doesn't matter. He'll keep on trying until he gets it just right. And that's the only version we see."

"He also likes to find us at our weakest moments," Amanda added. "For me, it was when my leg was broken. For Jury, it was right after the end of the world."

Ofelia threw her hands up. "If he's that dangerous, then why aren't we taking him out?"

"Good question," said Hannah. She looked at Theo again. "How many times did you meet with him?"

"Twice."

"That's twice you could have stopped him. Imagine all the things he's done since then."

"You think I'm letting him live because I like him?" Theo asked. "He's a monster. But he's a monster that we need."

"Why?"

"Because See and I can only glimpse the future. Evan's lived through every minute of it, dozens of times. The knowledge in his head can save the whole planet. Isn't that worth a little—"

"A little what?" asked Hannah. "Forgiveness? He. Killed. Jonathan. What part of that don't you get?"

Theo pointed at the computer. "Hannah, look at the screen. Look at the upper left corner of the screen and tell me what you see."

Hannah took a second glance at the monitor and reeled at the sight of Heath. She'd been so focused on Evan that she forgot about the other two people at the scene.

She looked to Theo, horrified. "Have you lost your mind?"

"Hannah—"

"What were you thinking? He's just a kid!"

"He loved Jonathan more than anyone," Theo reminded her. "He could kill Evan right now with just a thought. But he's holding back his tempis, and you know why? Because he knows that murdering Evan won't bring Jonathan back. It won't save the world. It won't even make him feel good. It'll just add another body to the pile, and he's seen enough death already."

Only See got misty at Theo's words, though it did take some air out of Hannah's wrath.

Ofelia stroked the skin of her wrist, freshly liberated from its Pelletier bracelet. "You convinced me to trust you," she said to Theo. "So if you say Evan's important to the world, then I can wait to kill him."

She jerked a thumb at the monitors. "But if I have to spend one minute with him, I can't promise you anything."

"Me neither," Amanda said.

"Or me," Hannah said to Theo. "I'm not as evolved as Heath. I *will* kill Evan if I see him. So keep that fucker away from me. And if he so much as lays a finger—"

"Uh-oh." See sat down at the desk. "Something's wrong."

"What?"

Theo and the others clustered behind See as she turned up the volume on the camera mics. The situation in Elizabeth had quickly deteriorated. Zack and Evan shouted in each other's faces while Heath pressed his fists to his forehead. From the way he shook and gritted his teeth, Hannah feared the debate had become moot. Heath was about to wipe Evan off the face of the planet, and the darkest part of Hannah cheered him on.

The trouble had started with Evan, as usual. After five straight minutes of amiable behavior, he became edgy, restless, as if the devil on his shoulder were howling at him in disgust. Zack couldn't even fathom the dysfunction inside him, the sickness that compelled him to hurt and antagonize people.

He looked to Heath with a smarmy expression. "You know Jonathan was gonna die anyway, right?"

"Holy shit," Zack said to Evan. "What's wrong with you?"

"What? I'm just trying to explain it. He was standing in the way of Hannah's uterus, so the Pelletiers decided he had to go. If I hadn't killed him right then and there, Azral would have. And it would have been a hell of a lot messier than a bullet to the brain."

He glibly turned to Heath again. "The way I see it, I did Jonathan a favor."

Zack shook his head, livid. "I'm about three seconds away from killing you myself."

"Oh stop," said Evan. "You know you're not the killing type. Neither's Heath."

"I swear to God—"

"Swear at Theo. He's the one who sent a kid to an R-rated show."

"Right," said Zack. "It's always someone else's fault. Azral, Theo, never you."

"Well, now you're just putting words in my mouth."

"I'm trying to stop your words from coming out! Everything you say is toxic. Even your pitiful story about Rachel—"

Evan stood up from the table with a menacing glare. "Careful."

Zack rose to his feet, dwarfing him. "Oh, gosh, what a surprise. You can't even take a fraction of what you dish out."

That was the moment See noticed the discussion and alerted the others to the trouble. Now six people watched from Melissa's office as Heath struggled to keep his emotions in check.

Zack hurried over to him and gripped his arm. "Look—"

Heath pulled away. "Don't touch me!"

"I just want to give you the keys, okay? Go back to the car, crank the AC, and listen to some music. I got this."

"And a fine job you're doing," Evan grumbled.

"*You* shut up." Zack looked back to Heath. "Please."

"No!" Heath looped around Zack, then confronted Evan from the other side of the table. "Why did you kill Jonathan?"

Evan rolled his eyes. "I told you. Azral—"

"Why did *you* kill him? You!"

Hannah's heart pounded furiously as Evan pondered his response—a thoughtful expression for a man like him, almost painfully sincere.

"It was nothing personal against the guy," he told Heath. "I mean he wasn't the brightest of bulbs but he wasn't stupid and mean, like Jury."

Ofelia's face went red with rage. Mia had to stop her from grabbing a headset.

"The bottom line . . ." Evan lowered his head, then shrugged in lazy surrender. "I just like hurting Hannah."

While Hannah remained as still as stone, Amanda paced the carpet. "This isn't going to work. He'll never help us. He's too far gone."

Ofelia held Hannah's arm. "We'll find him together, but you should get the final hit. If anyone deserves to send him to Hell—"

"Just wait," Theo begged. "All of you. Please!"

Zack sat back down at the wooden table and took a long, hard look at his prosthetic. "How long has it been?" he asked Evan.

"Since what?"

"Since Hannah broke your heart."

Evan retook his seat with a bitter pout. "It's more complicated than that."

"I don't care. How long has it been? Decades?" Zack tapped the tattoo on the back of Evan's right hand, a black and stylish *55*. "You've lived the same four and a half years over and over. Fifty-five times. That's . . ."

"Two hundred forty-seven years," Heath said. "And six months."

Evan glared at him. "Thank you, Rain Man, but it's actually been longer. With all the little rewinds I do, I'm probably closer to five hundred."

"Five hundred years," Zack said in amazement. "You've been carrying your grudge for *centuries*. That doesn't strike you as a little pathetic?"

"Compared to who? *You?*" Evan gestured at his half-finished breakfast. "I've eaten that franklin more times than you've made it past the two-year mark."

"Yet here I am."

"Most of you."

"Most of me," Zack admitted. "Imagine how many more times I would have survived if you had just gotten over Hannah."

"Zero," Evan said. "You would have survived exactly zero more times because you never, ever stop the apocalypse. I'm so sick of telling you that."

"And I'm sick of hearing it. You could have been our friend instead of our enemy. You could have used what you know to help us."

Evan chuckled cynically. "Yeah, that would have worked out great for me. 'Hey, guys! Did you know that David's actually—oops, hang on. Someone's disemboweling me.'"

Only Mia laughed at that. "He has a point."

"Fair point," Zack said. "You couldn't have helped us with Semerjean. But you could have helped us with the Gothams and Integrity, back when they were problems. And you can still help us now with the big mess. Between your hindsight and Theo's foresight—"

"You're wasting your time."

"Then why are you here?" Zack asked him. "You could have watched the explosion from anywhere. Why did you come here?"

Evan smiled sardonically. "Maybe you're just that charming."

"Or maybe you just miss being around your people."

"*My* people?"

"Your people," Zack said. "The few dozen of us left who'll get your *Star Wars* jokes. The ones who'd kill to watch *The Simpsons* again."

Evan looked at him askance. "Early seasons or—"

"Early and middle seasons."

"Because I'd gouge out my eyes before watching the later seasons."

"That's a little harsher than I feel," Zack said. "But I understand it."

Amanda followed their exchange with dark fascination. "He doesn't miss his people. He misses Zack."

Theo nodded. "I should have seen it sooner than I did."

Zack stood up and paced near the table's edge. "You already know what we want from you, Evan. What do you want from us?"

Evan scoffed at him. "That's the question you should have started with."

"Well, give me an answer that doesn't involve Hannah."

"My answer doesn't involve her at all."

Zack stopped a moment to study him. "You want to break the cycle."

"There you go, Sherlock."

"Get off that four-year merry-go-round."

"Four and a half," Evan said. "And it stopped being merry a long time ago. That shit with Rachel only drove the point home."

"Then *work* with us," Zack said. "If we stop what's coming, you won't be trapped. You can move on to new years, new decades, new *everything*."

"It won't work."

"How do you know if you've never tried?" Zack asked. "What if you're the key we've been missing this whole time?"

Evan glared at him. "Keys are something you carry in your pocket."

"Oh, so you'd rather live in your carousel hell than be a team player again."

"That's not what I'm saying at all, you idiot."

"Then what are you saying?"

Flummoxed, Evan stewed in his own thoughts before speaking. "I've seen what happens ten weeks from now, when even Theo admits that it's over. That final stretch is the worst for you people. You're like dead-eyed zombies. You're not even fun to tease."

Zack threw up his hands. "So what? That's our problem. If we fail, we're dead. If you fail, you can go back and start over. What do you have to lose?"

Evan shook his head in exasperation. "You just don't get it."

"I think I do," Zack said. "You've been living without hope for so goddamn long that you're afraid to try it on again."

"Fuck you!"

"Oh ho! Do I hear a nerve being struck?"

Theo couldn't help but laugh at Zack's brilliant antics. He was just as good as Evan at getting under people's skin, but his knife was sharper and far more refined. There was no one else on Earth who could have gotten this far with Evan. No one.

Zack sat next to Evan, his back against the table. "Guess we didn't reach this point in the other five conversations."

"No," Evan said. "And I'm done after this one. You've officially become tedious."

"Yeah. I get that a lot."

"And don't think I'm charmed by your self-effacing 'humor.' That shtick got old two centuries ago."

Zack shrugged. "If you want to leave, then leave. We won't stop you. Just one last question before you go . . ."

Evan nodded impatiently. "You want to know where the Violets are."

"I want to know where the Violets are," Zack echoed. "You don't have to join us. You don't have to believe in us. Just throw us a bone and we'll run with it."

"If it was that easy, I would have told you already."

"What does that mean?" Amanda asked.

"What do you mean?" Zack asked Evan.

Only Theo was starting to get a sense of the trouble ahead. This was not good news for Melissa at all. It was even worse for Amanda.

"It's not the kind of thing I can write on a napkin," Evan said to Zack. "I haven't been to London in at least nine lifetimes. My memory's sketchy and the Violets are . . . tricky. There are only five of them left and they're *very* skittish about strangers."

"What are you saying?" Zack asked.

"I'm saying I can't help, unless . . ." Evan closed his eyes with tortured reluctance. "Unless I go with you."

Amanda's tempic arms rippled with stress. "No, no, no. That is *not* happening."

See was equally flustered. "I don't want him coming with us."

Zack could only imagine their reaction right now. Like him, they'd been handpicked for the London mission. They were the ones who'd have to put up with him.

He shrugged uneasily. "If that's what it takes, we'll just have to manage. But—"

"You can't bring Hannah," Evan said. "Either she'd kill me or I'd kill her."

"She'd kill you," Zack assured him. "But she's not going anyway. It'll be me, Melissa, Caleb, the Coppers—"

"The Coppers." Evan laughed. "Oh, yay. I get to hang out with Slice, Squeak, Scrunch, and Sloopy."

See crossed her arms in resentment. "Those aren't our names at all."

"There's one more coming," Zack warned Evan. "Now listen to me before you—"

"No, no, no, no." Evan stood up and shook his head vehemently. "Not her."

"Yes, her."

"I'm not going if Amanda's going."

"Good!" Amanda yelled.

"And I'm not going without her," Zack insisted. "She and I are a package deal. Besides, she's our star player. We need her as much as we need you."

"Fuck fuck fuck." Evan paced the grass in frantic thought. "If I have to ride with Clobberella, I'm gonna need a policy."

"A policy?" Zack asked.

"An insurance policy." Evan looked up at the floating camera, the one he wasn't supposed to see. "Hey, God Girl, I know you're still watching and I know you can hear me, so here's the deal. We're gonna have a temporary truce. I don't kill you, you don't kill me. And if we get out of England with our heads still attached, I'll have information for you. Something you desperately need."

Amanda put on her headset and reactivated the transmitter. "Be more specific or go screw yourself."

Evan smiled. "Now that your sister has a bun in the oven, the Pelletiers are coming for her. But there's one way to stop them from taking her away forever. I've seen it work with my own two eyes and I guarantee it's something that none of you will ever think of."

Amanda eyed him skeptically. "And all I have to do for this information—"

"—is keep your tempic mitts off me," Evan said. "Easy peasy, lemon squeezy."

"He's lying," Hannah whispered.

"You know what'll happen if you're lying to me," Amanda told Evan.

"Yeah yeah. Save the threats for London."

Zack stood up and took a weary look at the camera. "I'll work out the details with him."

Evan smiled over Zack's shoulder. "I call dibs on the top bunk!"

"Tell Melissa we're good to go."

The next few minutes passed quietly in Elizabeth. The Severson campus had been cleared of all civilians, and the truth was finally making its way to the news. America wasn't under attack. It was just a freakish, one-time accident. Carry on and go about your day.

Heath returned to the Avion to start up the air conditioner while Zack and Evan finished their business. They spoke so softly that the microphones barely registered their voices, not that anyone in the office was listening. Theo had left to find Melissa. Mia and Ofelia went back to the commissary. The sisters retreated to Melissa's couch and slumped miserably onto the cushions.

Only See stayed behind at the desk console, though she couldn't have cared less about Zack and Evan. She steered one of the cameras toward the parked Avion, then opened a private channel to Heath.

"You okay?" she asked him.

See peeked at the sisters anxiously, then addressed Heath in a furtive mutter. "For what it's worth, I thought you were amazing."

"Why?" he asked. "I didn't do anything."

"That's not true. You shamed Evan by example. He's been mad at Hannah for centuries, over something so small in the grand scheme of things. But there you were, just a year and a month after Jonathan's death, and you put aside all your hatred. You were the better man by far. Even *he* could see it."

See bit her lip in contemplation, her hands clamped anxiously onto her thighs. "You really are one of a kind."

She cringed in the heavy silence that followed, convinced that she'd blundered in some fatal way. "I mean, it's not like—"

"Ahmad," he said out of the blue.

"I'm sorry. What?"

"My real name's Ahmad. Ahmad Bradshaw. Like the New York Giants player."

"Oh," said See. "Wow. I had no idea. Do you want me to call you that from now on?"

"No. I just . . ." He stammered from the passenger seat. "I just wanted you to know."

See smiled. "My real name's Nadiyah Al-Marri."

"Wow. I like that."

"Me too, but I also like having a new name here."

"Yeah." Heath absently fiddled with the buckle of his seat belt. "Feels right somehow."

See's handphone vibrated. She checked the screen. Mother was summoning her back to the den. Word had spread fast that the London mission was a go. Her family wanted details, *now.*

"Listen, Heath, I have to go. If I don't see you before I leave for England—"

"Be careful there," Heath urged her.

See blushed. "I was about to say be careful in Cuba. Come back in one piece, okay?"

Amanda and Hannah lazily watched her as she bounded out of the office, high as a cloud.

"What is she so giddy about?" Hannah asked.

Amanda shook her head. "No idea."

Hannah sank into the cushions and stared up at the ceiling. "He *is* lying, you know. Even if he knew something that could save me, he wouldn't share it. Not in a million years."

Amanda matched her languid pose. "I know."

"Then you know what you have to do," Hannah said. "You need to put that psycho in the ground before he puts another one of us there."

Amanda kept her head arched back, her busy eyes dancing in thought. "I know."

THE ANGEL OF LONDON

NINE

The Cataclysm was an American disaster, but its shockwave had rocked the whole planet. From nation to nation, town to town, humanity stopped dead in its tracks and reeled at its precarious new place in existence. It was suddenly living in a world where two million people could perish in the blink of an eye, with no provocation, no explanation, and no guarantee that it wouldn't happen again. For all anyone knew, New York was just the start of a multistage apocalypse.

Thousands of books had been written about the global effects of the Cataclysm, from the South American baby boom to the New Atheist movement in Europe. But nothing had changed more quickly or dramatically than the geopolitics of the era, one of the sharpest course corrections in history. Nations on the brink of war came to a sudden accord with their enemies, a domino chain of compromise treaties that altered the maps of four continents and prevented a worldwide conflict. The Cataclysm had triggered such a profound and miraculous peace across the planet that even agnostics began to wonder if it had all been part of God's plan.

Only the cynics and historians saw the great new armistice for what it truly was: temporary.

It was a truce born of fear, wrote the noted scholar E. H. Carr. *Everyone was afraid to provoke the same holy wrath that had devastated the United States. And so, like schoolyard bullies under a strict and watchful eye, the hostile nations played nice with each other, smiling for the teachers until they were once again free to indulge their baser natures.*

Indeed, by 1922, the fear of a second Cataclysm had become all but mist in the minds of the world powers. The diplomatic leaders of the previous decade were flushed out by belligerent successors, who insisted that their countries had sacrificed too much in the name of global harmony, and their neighbors had sacrificed too little. Treaties were broken one by one, sparking a nonstop chain of wars and incursions that lasted well into the 1990s.

Throughout all the strife of the twentieth century, the United States remained in an isolationist limbo. Long after it had regained its health and prosperity, it had sold off all its annex territories, raised a tempic wall along its borders, and removed itself from international affairs. When Central America fell into a multiregional civil war, the U.S. turned a deaf ear to the violence: *Sorry. Not our problem.* When the British took Haiti and the Dominican Republic: *Sorry. Not our problem.* Even when Canada, a country that had rushed to America's aid after the Cataclysm, lost half a million people to a harsh winter famine, the U.S. kept its hand on its coin purse. *Sorry,* it said to its old friend and neighbor. *Not our problem.*

Having long exhausted its goodwill among others, America stood alone today, with a repugnant reputation around the world. To most other cultures, it was a nation of crass and ignorant inbreds, not just morons but *oxymorons* for their snobby self-regard. Europeans in particular had blistering contempt for Americans, enough to make travel a nightmare for the few who ventured abroad. Visa applications were misfiled and lost. Customs agents confiscated even the most benign possessions. And should a piece of luggage end up in Belize instead of Belgium, the aerline agents offered little more than a shrug. *Sorry. Not our problem.*

But for Americans with money, the frowns turned to smiles. *Welkom! Vítejte! Bienvenido! Välkommen!* The U.S. dollar was popular in Europe, enough to prompt the creation of two dozen aerlines that catered exclusively to the rich American traveler.

The most prestigious of the lot was Windermere Ventures, a state-owned British enterprise. Their flagship vessel, the HMA *Maharani,* shuttled twice a week between Idlewild Aerport in Queens, New York, and the Richard Fairey Aerodrome in the Twickenham district of London.

Though each ticket cost as much as a semester at Harvard, Integrity loved using the *Maharani* for travel. Its onboard British customs agent was a long-time mole for the agency, and was able to provide passengers with all the paperwork they needed to pass through London's tight security. Short of building a tunnel across the floor of the Atlantic, there was no simpler, quieter, or easier way to sneak government operatives into the heart of the British Empire.

And so it was on Friday, July 27, that an Integrity agent, two Gothams, and ten orphans boarded the *Maharani* just minutes before its six A.M. takeoff. From the way Melissa had talked about it, Amanda was expecting to fly on a gold-plated luxury jet. But the *Maharani* looked more like a riverboat on the outside and a Beverly Hills mall on the inside. The four-level ship offered endless amenities, including six restaurants, three nightclubs, two spas, a game room, a fitness center, even a holographic golf course. There were at least thirty different dens for sitting and sleeping, enough for Melissa and her team to have a lounge to themselves.

While most of the group slept or relaxed with their movie goggles, Amanda wandered aimlessly around the second-floor mezzanine. She'd tried napping with Zack on one of the den's long couches, but her mind was too jittery to rest. She couldn't think of a worse time to be an ocean away from her sister, or a worse bet than counting on the goodness of Evan Rander.

This is crazy, Amanda thought. *We're risking our lives for these Violets and Opals, but why? What if they're as bad as Evan? What if they're all compromised, like the Jades?*

The other passengers barely noticed Amanda as she continued along the balustrade. Thanks to the Gothams, she knew how to dress like a rich American woman: slitted skirt, high heels, a tight and fancy waistcoat, a casual updo hairstyle that flaunted her sparkly earrings. She'd earned a few odd looks for her white opera gloves—an excessively posh accoutrement, even for this crowd. But they were still less conspicuous than the tempis she was hiding.

Yawning, Amanda leaned on the polished brass railing and scanned the action down below. The lobby floor was a giant lumic projection: a real-time map of the *Maharani*'s progress. It had only just passed the southern tip of Greenland, which meant six more hours on this overfluffed skyboat. Amanda was glad that Evan was arranging his own passage to London. She wasn't even remotely ready to deal with him.

She looked at the mirrors on the other side of the mezzanine and saw

Melissa approaching her from behind. "There you are," said Amanda. "I was wondering where you went."

"I was conspiring with our new friend, the customs agent."

"You never stop working, do you?"

"Our papers won't forge themselves."

She joined Amanda at the railing, looking elegantly dapper in her sleeveless black travel dress. Despite her upscale appearance, Amanda had already seen two British passengers mistake her for a drink server. "Colonial racism," Melissa had said with a sigh. "Only slightly more refined than the American style."

She noticed Amanda's drooped and weary posture. "Speaking of rest . . ."

"Yeah. I know." Amanda peered down at the world map again and marveled at its many changes. Korea was a single unified country while Turkey had been split into East and West Ataman. The nation of São Paulo stood in place of southern Brazil, and everything from Mongolia to Timor was marked as the Greater Chinese Dominion. "I'm still trying to prepare myself for this trip."

"Me too," said Melissa. "I was hoping to never see London again."

"You didn't like being a British secret agent?"

Melissa smiled wanly. "I was a weapons analyst. And no, I did not."

"How come?"

"Because London's a target for half the world's terrorists, and I had to study their carnage. Women and children killed by rift bombs, or cut off at the feet by tempic spring traps."

Amanda cringed at the very thought of it. "That's awful."

"England has some vicious enemies," said Melissa. "And the government's become vicious in response. The things I've seen them do to suspects, the things I *helped* them do . . ."

Melissa's voice shrank to a glum and distant mutter. "They still use some of the guns I made."

Amanda stroked her arm. "I was a mediocre nurse in a crappy marriage, and I was a terrible sister to Hannah. Should we judge ourselves by the people we were or the people we are right now?"

"I'm more worried about the people we'll be ten weeks from now, should the worst come to pass. I don't relish the thought of spending my last two years in helpless dread."

Amanda felt a painful flutter in her stomach. She could never forget the last few minutes of her Earth, the apocalyptic panic that had brought out the worst in her first husband. *I'm glad we're going to different places,* he'd said to her. *What does that say about you?*

"What would you do?" Melissa asked.

Amanda blinked at her, distracted. "What?"

"If the worst should happen, how would you want to spend your time?"

"Oh." Amanda's dark mood lifted at the thought of her current husband, a man who'd cut out his tongue before saying a cruel word to her. "I'd want to travel the world with Zack. Get the most out of life before the clock runs out. Assuming I could get him to go with me."

"Why wouldn't he?"

"I know him. He'd want to keep working. Maybe figure out a way to survive time travel, use Mia's portals to send people to the past."

Melissa nodded with a knowing grin. "That does sound like him."

"Just one of the many reasons I love him," Amanda said. "He never gives up, never—"

The *Maharani* came to a sudden stop, sending Amanda toppling over the railing. She barely had a chance to process her predicament before she found herself sprawled faceup on the lobby floor. Even in her shock, the situation felt . . . wrong. A fall like that should have cracked her skull open. Yet all she felt was a warm and pleasant numbness, as if she'd been wrapped in a thick down comforter. For a moment, she feared that she'd snapped a crucial vertebra, but her body seemed to work just fine.

Baffled, Amanda clambered to her feet and examined her fellow passengers. None of them had been thrown by the ship's hard inertia. Quite the opposite. Their stances, their expressions, even the drinks in their hands were frozen in place, as if someone had pulled the emergency brake on time itself.

"Uh . . ." Amanda glanced up at the mezzanine and saw Melissa at the railing with another woman—a tall and skinny redhead with a messy updo. It took Amanda five seconds to realize that she was staring at herself, a still-frame replica of the person she'd just been.

Oh no. She looked around the lobby, panicked. There were only three people she knew who could bend reality this far, and they were definitely not friends.

"Relax," said a voice in the distance. "It's not a Pelletier thing."

Amanda turned to the starboard foyer and saw a waifish young blonde in a strapless white summer dress. Before Amanda could even formulate a question, the girl blinked out of sight and rematerialized right in front of her.

Amanda stumbled backward. "Who are you?"

The girl brandished her wrist, revealing two parallel timepieces. The left one was digital with glowing red numbers. The right one was analog and jarringly old-fashioned.

Right on cue, Amanda realized who she was dealing with. She'd heard enough stories about the girl with two watches to form a strong opinion, and not a very good one at that.

"You."

Ioni smiled wryly. "I'll take that as shorthand for 'Nice to finally meet you.'"

"Nice? After all the things you've done—"

"You don't know all the things I've done."

"You're the one who turned the Gothams against us," Amanda reminded her. "You tricked Rebel into thinking we had to die!"

Ioni impatiently checked her watches. "A necessary evil for the greater good."

"That 'greater good' killed a lot of people."

Ioni sighed. "No one knows that better than me. Look—"

"Zack lost his only brother because of you!"

"Amanda!"

Ioni flicked her hand, summoning a bright digital readout in the air. Amanda thought it was a clockface until she saw which way the numbers were turning. It was a countdown timer working backward from six minutes.

"The Pelletiers are looking for me," Ioni said. "And they're getting a lot better at finding me. If I'm still here when that clock runs out—"

"What's 'here'?" Amanda pointed up at her frozen twin. "Where the hell are we?"

"Did Theo ever tell you about the God's Eye?"

"A little."

"Well, that's where we are," said Ioni. "It's a vantage point in the margins of time, a place to look at the strings from a distance. Under better circumstances, we'd have hours to talk here. Days." She gestured at the floating timer. "But like I said, the Pelletiers are hunting me. If they find me, I'm dead. And if I die, it's game over for everyone. *Capiche?*"

Amanda looked Ioni up and down. She didn't come across as a powerful entity. She could have been any bit player in the mundane world: the cute cashier at the local market, the perky young coed who lived across the street.

But behind the bright eyes and dimples was a hint of something older—so old, in fact, that Amanda felt intimidated. For all she knew, Ioni was an ancient power of the universe, a being with all the secret dirt on God. *His real name's Steve and he hates Unitarians. Nah. Just kidding. He never existed.*

Forty-five seconds had already passed on the timer. Amanda girded herself with a heavy breath, then suddenly wondered if she was breathing at all. If Theo was right, then her body in the God's Eye was just a visual representation of her consciousness, an avatar made of solid thought. No wonder the fall hadn't hurt her.

Amanda looked to Ioni again. "Tell me real quick why I should trust you."

"Because I have a vested interest in saving this world, and I really hate the Pelletiers. Is that enough, or should I tell you about the time I saved your sister's life?"

"When?"

"A week ago in Mexico, when I convinced her to jump off a flying train."

"That was Theo."

"That was me," Ioni said. "I only used Theo's voice so she would listen to me."

Admittedly, that made sense. Amanda had found it odd, though not entirely implausible, that Theo had forged a psychic link with Hannah.

"You know he's been waiting to hear from you," Amanda said.

"Who, Theo?"

"Yeah. Every day for the past year."

"I'm not ready to talk to him," Ioni replied. "And he's not ready to hear what I have to say."

Amanda balked at her ominous implication. "But I am?"

"You better be."

"Why?"

Ioni chewed her lip in thought before answering. "I'm sorry it took this long for us to meet. I've been watching you for a while and I like you a lot. You're a good-hearted woman, a kickass tempic, and you know how to drive Esis crazy."

"It's a short drive," Amanda grumbled.

"Yeah, well, you do it with style." Ioni wagged a finger at her. "But you've got two plans brewing in that pretty head of yours, and they're both going to end in disaster. More than that, they'll get in the way of *my* plan."

"Plan for what?" asked Amanda. "Saving the world?"

"Yes."

"That's crazy. I want that just as much as you do."

"Want's got nothing to do with it," Ioni said. "The strings don't care about our good or bad intentions. Only the results."

"And what exactly do you think I'm—"

"Don't bullshit me, Amanda. We don't have time. You're plotting two murders out of pure desperate love. The first one's Evan Rander."

Amanda froze, stuck between the urge to deny and defend her decision. "Do you know what he's done?"

"More than anyone," Ioni said. "I've seen him do things in multiple timelines. Things he'll never talk about because even he's ashamed of them."

The thought was enough to make Amanda queasy. "If I let him live, I'll be responsible for every bad thing he does. Every woman he hurts for not wanting him back. Every man who gets too close to Hannah. He's probably already planning to kill Peter."

"He won't," Ioni insisted. "I won't let him."

"Why?"

"Because I need Peter for the war that's coming, just like I need the rest of your people."

Amanda eyed her suspiciously. "What could you possibly want from Evan?"

"I don't have time to explain it. Just trust me that I need him alive."

"*Trust* you? For all I know, you've killed more people than he has."

"I have," Ioni gravely replied. "By multitudes."

"You're not making this easier."

"I'm not here to make it easy. I'm here to fix the future."

"And what about *Hannah's* future? If Evan hurts her—"

"He won't," Ioni promised. "But you will."

"What are you talking about?"

"I'm talking about your other murder plan. The bottle in your bedroom drawer."

Amanda looked away, pained. She hadn't told anyone, not even Zack, about her late-night trip to the underland's pharmacy, the methylaminopterin she'd pilfered. It was primarily used as a chemotherapy agent, but it also had a notorious second purpose.

"Abortion," Ioni said. "You're planning on slipping that drug to your sister."

The mere mention of the A-word made Amanda's spectral heart lurch. "She only got pregnant to save my life," she told Ioni. "Now she's in serious trouble. What kind of person would I be, what kind of *sister* would I be, if I didn't save her back?"

"Assuming your plan even works, which is iffy, how do you think the Pelletiers will take it?"

Amanda shook her head. "They won't blame Hannah. She doesn't know anything about it."

"You're right. They'll blame you. And what do you think they'll do to you?"

"If I thought I could trust them—"

"That's not what I asked."

"—I'd make a deal instead."

"Amanda, *what do you think they'll do to you?*"

"They'll kill me, all right? They'll kill me! I know that. You think I'm dumb?"

"A little bit. Yeah."

The timer was down to three and a half minutes. Ioni paced the lobby floor, her high heels clacking against the lumic map screen. Amanda wondered if the noise was a deliberate effect or a built-in verisimilitude of the God's Eye.

"I've spent half my life studying the people of this era," Ioni said. "On your Earth, this Earth, and thousands of others. This is an amazing stage of human evolution, because you all have the wisdom to know what's right and yet you all find excuses to avoid it. I could draw you a roadmap to a perfectly happy life and you'd still drive off a cliff."

Amanda crossed her arms with a petulant look. "Is there someone out there you truly love? Someone you'd die for, without hesitation?"

"I'd die for this Earth."

"That's a world. I'm talking people."

"So am I, but your point is moot anyway. This is a *needless* sacrifice you're making, as needless as the one that Hannah made for you."

Amanda shook her head. "I don't fault her for doing what she did. I was out of my mind and on the verge of suicide."

"Now here you are again," Ioni said. "Throwing your own life away. Except you're underestimating the Pelletiers' cruelty. Have you considered the possibility that they'll do something *worse* than kill you?"

"What are you talking about?"

"If you abort Hannah's baby, they'll take you to their home base, immobilize you so thoroughly that you can't even close your eyes. And then, after giving you a few days to think about your poor decisions, they'll bring a very special guest to your prison cell: that cute and funny guy you married."

The buzzing in Amanda's head intensified. "Stop."

"That's exactly what you'll try to say, but you can't. You'll just float there and watch as the Pelletiers torture him. And I don't mean psychological torture. I mean a high-tech spin on some old medieval classics. You'll hear screams from Zack that you've never heard from anyone, sounds you never thought a human being could make. And it'll keep on going, day after day, until all the lights go out inside of him, until you and he are both empty shells. That's when they'll finally put Zack out of his misery. But you, my dear—"

"Stop!"

"For you, the horror's just starting. The Pelletiers will take your living remains and they'll use it to make their babies. Why on Earth would they kill you when you're so valuable to them?"

Amanda turned away, her face drenched in tears. "What happens to Hannah if I don't, uh . . ."

"The Pelletiers will take her," Ioni grimly replied. "Sooner rather than later. But because she was nice enough to cooperate with them, they won't mistreat her. Not even a little. They'll keep her in as much comfort as they can until the baby arrives."

"That's *months* away."

"For her," Ioni stressed. "It might be days for the rest of us. You know how the Pelletiers are with time."

Amanda rubbed her aching temples. The pressure in her head had become an agony. "And what happens after that? They won't just let her go."

Ioni shook her head. "They might keep her in stasis and take her back to their era. Or they could just do away with her like the monsters they are. I don't know. Her future is cloudy, even to me. But I do see her again in a couple of strings. There's definitely a chance she comes back."

"How?"

"If I knew that, hon, it wouldn't be a chance. It'd be a given."

"There has to be *something* I can do."

"Not without consequences."

"Then what about you?" Amanda asked. "You helped her out in Mexico. You must have had a reason."

"I helped her because I like her," Ioni said. "And I did have a special plan for her. But if I take on the Pelletiers directly, I'll lose everything I've been working for. The world comes first. I'm sorry."

Ioni checked the countdown clock, then blew a heavy breath. "If she gets saved, and she still might, it won't be you or me who does it."

"Then who?"

Ioni's lip curled in a sardonic half-grin. "Would you believe me if I told you it was Evan?"

"No."

"Yeah. Probably not. I've only seen that in one string, and it was a real weird one." Ioni stroked her chin in contemplation. "If I were a betting woman, I'd place good money on Hannah saving herself."

Amanda scoffed, and not because she doubted Ioni. If anything, she was chiding herself for not seeing the obvious. How many times had she watched Hannah fall into peril, only to pull herself out with a fast and clever trick? She was a seasoned pro at beating the reaper. She even had experience beating the Pelletiers. And for Amanda Given, a supposed woman of faith, it seemed downright crazy not to put faith in her sister now.

She'll find a way, Amanda convinced herself. *She always does.*

Though there were a scant ninety seconds left on the timer, Ioni finally managed to look relaxed.

"I can already feel the futures changing," she said. "A lot of dark roads are closing. Thank you, Amanda, for hearing me out."

"Don't thank me yet. If Evan tries anything—"

"I understand. He's a son of a bitch and he always will be. But your husband reached him yesterday, as only your husband could. Where Evan goes from there . . ." Ioni shrugged. "If he goes the way I want him to go, then even his bad deeds will do good."

Amanda studied Ioni, mystified. She feared she'd never understand the mindset of augurs, the shapeless gray void where virtues and sins became interchangeable. She was too stuck in her old ways, too Catholic.

And yet you were this *close to killing an unborn baby*, her inner Hannah reminded her. *My child. Your blood. Don't act like this world hasn't changed you.*

Ioni clapped her hands together and flashed a pleasant smile at Amanda. "All righty then. I fixed the strings with a minute to spare. I certainly earned my taco today."

"Is this the last time I'll see you?" Amanda asked.

"Oh, no. In a couple of weeks, I'll have new measures in place and I'll be invisible again to the Pelletiers. After that, you'll be seeing a lot of me. In the real world, I mean. Not here. Although . . ."

Ioni stopped to think a moment. Amanda could see the dilemma in her eyes. "What?"

"We may have one more conversation in the God's Eye," Ioni hesitantly informed her. "If things don't go entirely as planned. If that happens, uh . . ."

Ioni sighed. "Well, let's just hope it doesn't."

Amanda didn't like the sound of that. She opened her mouth to ask another question, but Ioni cut her off.

"Take care in London. Look after Zack. Don't piss off the British and *don't kill Evan.*"

"Wait!"

Ioni nervously checked the clock. Thirty-two seconds. "Make it fast."

Amanda sifted through her backlog of questions and, in her haste, picked the least important one. "Why this world?"

Ioni cocked her head. "Huh?"

"I don't think you were born here," Amanda said. "Any more than I was. And I don't think you're stuck here either. If you're as powerful as you seem to be, then you probably have infinite Earths to jump to. So why are you risking your life to save this one version?"

At last, Ioni understood. She fiddled with the band of her digital watch, then looked at Amanda miserably. "Because this is the one I made."

The timer was down to its last nine seconds when the digits exploded in a burst of blinding light. By the time Amanda unshielded her eyes, she was back at the rail of the second-floor mezzanine, feeling light-headed, weak-kneed, and thoroughly disoriented.

"Whoa!" Melissa caught her mid-teeter. "You okay?"

Amanda studied her dazedly. "You're back."

"I didn't go anywhere. Neither did you. I think you just answered my question. Come on."

"What? Where are we going?"

"Ship medic."

"No. I'm all right."

"All right? You just got drunk in the middle of a sentence."

"I'm not drunk," Amanda insisted. "I know exactly what happened."

"Care to explain it, then?"

"I'll tell you everything. I promise. I just . . ."

Amanda could feel her arms going soft. Even her tempis was getting woozy on her. "I think I need to sit down."

Melissa helped her to the nearest window lounge, placed her into a plush recliner, then called Zack on his handphone. By the time he joined them, three minutes later, Amanda's sleeves had gone hollow and she was lost in a deep and dreamless slumber. She woke up six hours later above the eastern side of the Atlantic, just as the *Maharani* was making its final descent into England.

TEN

The City of London had a hard time deciding where it stood on the temporal continuum. The eponymous district, nestled deep in the heart of the greater metropolis, had a rich and cultured history, and the British insisted on flaunting it. While half of the streets had been refashioned with modern frills and architecture, the other half had been painstakingly preserved to reflect its look from the Tudor Age. Driving through the City of London was traveling through time itself, a yo-yo trip back and forth from the 1500s.

Zack marveled at the spectacle of Lombard Street, with its ornate Gothic masonry and dangling wooden shop signs. Though electric lights were on display in abundance, he couldn't see a hint of anything temporic—no lumic traffic signals, no tempic crosswalk barriers, no holographic mascots hawking products from their ghostboxes. For Zack, who'd grown painfully accustomed to all those things, the street was an unexpected callback to his late, great native Earth. How strange that he had to visit a foreign land to get his first real taste of home.

As the fluttercoach turned onto Fenchurch Street, the modern world came roaring back with a vengeance. Zack looked away from the window and checked on his traveling companions. As far as the British government knew, they were the students and faculty of an elite American prep school, making an educational pilgrimage through Europe. The aerline had been nice enough to rent Melissa one of their land vessels: a wheelless mini-hoverbus that, despite its aeric capabilities, couldn't fly more than two feet off the ground.

The six teenage Coppers filled the back of the coach, talking loudly among themselves while Mother calmly meditated. Caleb and Amanda sat together up front, embroiled in an intense-looking discussion. Zack assumed they were talking about Amanda's encounter with Ioni, a tale that continued to swing like a wrecking ball through his thoughts.

"You okay?" Mercy asked him from the adjacent seat.

She and her younger brother Sage were both last-minute additions to the team, a strategic gamble on Melissa's part. The boy had been a prisoner of the Pelletiers' London facility, and had even met the Violets on a couple of occasions. His limited knowledge could come in handy, especially if their asset proved . . . unreliable.

As for Mercy, she'd insisted on coming along to protect her only sibling, to the strenuous objection of Caleb. He'd reminded her, as if she could forget, that she was five months pregnant with their child. Mercy had reminded him in turn that it was the *Pelletiers'* child, which made her the safest person on the team. As long as she was carrying their precious mutant hybrid, they wouldn't let anything happen to her.

Zack took in Mercy's baby bump before making eye contact. "I'm fine. Why do you ask?"

"Because you're doing that thing again with your face."

"What thing?"

She mimicked the expression of a deeply pensive person, one who was apparently dealing with constipation in addition to heavy thoughts.

Zack chuckled. "I don't do that."

"You're doing it right now!"

"Well, I'm nervous, okay? This whole trip has me nervous." He looked beyond Mercy at her teenage brother, still wallowing in his own little world. The music on his headphones was cranked up so loud that Zack could hear its tinny residue from six feet away. "How's he holding up?"

Mercy sighed. "Still wakes up screaming about Azral and Esis."

"Shit. I'm sorry."

"He'll be okay," Mercy said. "My mom says he has decades left to him, and she'd know better than anyone."

Zack kept his glib response to himself. Prudent Lee wasn't high on his list of trusted augurs. The woman took enough opiates to make a horse go wall-eyed. "She have anything to say about your future?"

Mercy shot him a sharp look. "Come on."

"What?"

"You're one of the few people in my life who doesn't bullshit me. Don't go starting now."

"I'm just asking what your mother's seen."

"You know what she's seen," Mercy said. "You know my future."

Zack cringed at the wrath in her dark brown eyes, the same furious despair that had nearly killed Amanda. He suddenly felt helpless all over again. He couldn't save Mercy. He couldn't save Hannah. All he could do was stew in impotent rage while the ghost of Rebel taunted him in his thoughts. *Look at you. All boo-hoo-hoo over those mean old Pelletiers. You gonna keep crying over things you can't change, or are you gonna change things?*

Soon the fluttercoach reached its final destination: a stately hotel in the Tower Hill district, a half-mile north of the Thames. The Tower of London was just a stone's throw away, and beyond that: the iconic Tower Bridge. Zack would have gladly taken the chance to play tourist with Amanda if he thought Melissa would allow it. But she'd already made it abundantly clear that this was a strict tactical mission: get in, find the Violets, and then get the hell out.

As the last of the Coppers disembarked the coach, Melissa directed everyone's attention upward. "Before we check in, I want you all to look up and tell me what you see."

The twelve timebenders craned their necks in unison. The sky was a clear and opaline blue, cluttered with too many flying vessels to count.

"I see aerstraunts," said Mother.

"And aer traffic," said Caleb.

"And way more sun than there should be at eight o'clock," See added.

"The summer days are longer here," Melissa explained. "It won't get dark until nine."

Amanda scanned the lower atmosphere, her brow furrowed in consternation. "There are other things flying around up there. Little things."

"She's right," said Sky, the other aeric on the team. "I can feel them but I can't see them."

Melissa nodded grimly. "Can anyone tell me what they are?"

Zack didn't even have to guess. "Camera drones."

"*Government* camera drones," said Melissa. "The London air is full of them, and they're always watching. Always. Do you all understand what I'm saying?"

Mother took clear offense at Melissa's expression, aimed mostly in the direction of her children. "We eluded Integrity for months," she reminded her. "We know how to keep a low profile."

"Good," Melissa said. "Because the last thing we need—"

"'Ello, gov'nas!"

A small man greeted them from the hotel entrance, an ostentatious presence in his Hawaiian shirt and bucket hat, his comically oversized sunglasses. From the way Melissa grimaced, Zack figured the Hunter S. Thompson getup had been chosen just to annoy her.

Evan smacked his hands together, a devilish smile on his face. "So! You finally got here. Should we get right down to business or should we have a spot of tea?"

Evan may have been a hopeless wretch, but he knew how to pick a restaurant. The King's Lift was a marvel to Zack, a modern British gastropub that took alt-world weirdness to a whole new level. Its dining booths were individually enclosed in a cube of tempered glass and bolstered by an aeric platform. With a twist of a knob, a party could ascend into the upper heights of London, up to two hundred meters, with wondrous sights at every altitude. Even street-level dining offered incredible backdrops. The Tower Hill Gardens flanked the restaurant on two sides. At the eastern edge: a surviving piece of the London Wall, built by the Romans in AD 200.

But in the tangerine glow of an early summer evening, there was no better view than the one at the top. The city seemed to go on forever and the low red sun practically lit the Thames on fire. All the aeromobiles had their night panels on, creating a hundred glimmering streaks of light that garnished the sky like tinsel.

"Wow." Zack peered through the wall of the dining cube and admired the vibrant colors. "How'd you find this place?"

"Same way I find everything," Evan said as he speared another piece of tiger shrimp. "Trial and error, plus a whole lot of rewinding."

He'd reserved one of the restaurant's smaller enclosures, as if he'd known in advance that only five people would be joining him. Indeed, the Coppers and Sage had opted to stay at the hotel, preferring a quiet night of room service over Evan's company. Zack had extended the same courtesy to Amanda, but she'd insisted on coming along.

"I'll be fine," she'd told him. "I can handle him."

True to her word, she was the model of composure. She sat across from Evan without a hint of discomfort, as if he'd never killed a friend of hers or tortured her with a stun gun. If anything, the anxiety seemed to flow the other way. Though Evan tried hard to be his usual cheeky self, he kept checking Amanda's hands out of the corner of his eye, just to make sure they hadn't turned into chain saws.

Stranger still, he was just as nervous around Melissa, though he had no history with her. *Or did he?* Zack wondered. She could have made Evan's life miserable in a previous timeline, or even a previous version of this dinner. There was no guessing how many times Evan had relived the past hour, perfecting his jabs and witty rejoinders, testing everyone at the table to see how far he could push them.

Evan smiled condescendingly at Caleb and Mercy, the last two members of the party. Like Amanda, they'd come to The King's Lift reluctantly. From the baleful looks on both their faces, they found Evan just as awful as the Givens had made him out to be.

"What's the matter?" Evan asked Mercy. "Don't like your appetizer?"

"I don't like you."

Caleb touched her arm. "Hon . . ."

Evan's mouth fell open in exaggerated offense. "Wow. That was direct. What did I ever do to you?"

"Nothing." Mercy jerked her head at Amanda. "But I'm a big fan of that one—"

"Your boyfriend's wife," Evan teased.

"My *ex*-boyfriend's wife, who happens to be my friend. And I don't like people who've hurt my friends."

Evan chuckled. "That's real funny coming from the MVP of Rebel's death squad."

"Don't," Zack warned.

"Just saying she's killed more Golds than I have."

"Fuck you!" Mercy leapt to her feet, nearly flipping her plate over. "We thought we were saving the world. What's your excuse?"

Caleb grabbed Mercy's hand. "Look, let's just—"

"I'm fine!" Mercy straightened her blouse, then sat back down. "This prick isn't worth it."

Evan opened his mouth to say something, but then looked to Melissa and thought better of it. Zack was utterly convinced that she'd put the fear of God into him, but when? And *how*?

Caleb studied Evan cautiously. "On a friendlier topic, I have a question about your, uh . . ."

"Superpower?" Evan asked. "It's okay to say it. We're all alone up here."

"What happens to your body when you jump back in time?"

"My body."

Caleb nodded. "As I understand it, you only send your consciousness to the past. So what happens to the body you leave behind? What happens to the *timeline* you leave behind?"

Evan shrugged. "You're asking the wrong guy, rabbi. I'm never around to see what happens."

"He's not a rabbi," Mercy growled at him. "Not anymore. You know that."

"I do." Evan grinned at Caleb. "You chucked your faith when the whole world ended."

"Look—"

"I'm not teasing you, man. I get it. Believe me. I went through the same thing."

That certainly surprised Zack. "You believed in God?"

"I believed in *karma*. Even after I got here, I tried playing nice and eating all my veggies. But then a funny thing happened: this world ended too. Another seven billion people . . ." Evan snapped his fingers. "Gone. Just like that. And once again, the universe didn't care who was naughty and who was nice. The boot came down on everyone. Karma schmarma."

"You don't believe in an afterlife," Mercy said.

Evan laughed. "This *is* my afterlife. Just more of the same bullshit. But once I accepted the pointlessness of it all, I finally started having some—"

"Keratin."

Everyone suddenly looked at Melissa, who'd barely said a word all evening. She drank in Evan with wide-eyed epiphany.

"I've been racking my brain trying to figure it out," she said. "Your face has been added to the global criminal database. You should be setting off alarms wherever you go. But you found a way to trick the cameras, and I think I know how."

She reached out to touch his jaw, but he quickly pulled away from her. "You have prosthetics on your nose and chin. Thin enough to preserve your appearance but thick enough to thwart the recognition algorithms. Except the cameras in England use multispectral imaging to detect facial prosthetics, so you must have had yours specially made. A keratin-collagen compound would be fully heat-conductive, allowing you to trick even the tissue and thermal scanners."

Though Evan scoffed at her assessment, his twitchy eyes betrayed him. Melissa was right on the money and everyone could see it.

"The cost must have been astronomical," she mused. "To say nothing of the effort. It must take an hour every morning just to put them on."

"What's your point?" Evan asked.

"For a man who doesn't believe in karma, you do an awful lot of work to avoid it."

Though Amanda and the others took delight in her zinger, Zack watched Evan's reaction carefully. He could see now why Evan was afraid of Melissa. She had the power to make his life as a fugitive a hundred times harder than it already was. That gave him all the incentive he needed to stay on her good side.

A small lumic bulb on the table came aglow. The dining cube began an automated descent.

"What's happening?" Caleb asked.

"Our entrées are ready," Evan said. "A good time to tinkle for those who need tinkling."

Upon reaching ground level, the glass doors swung open and the servers arrived with food trays. As they cleared off the old plates and brought in the new, Amanda motioned for Zack to follow her. She led him to the restroom alcove and looked at him with sullen eyes. "I'm going back to the hotel."

"You sure? You've been doing so well."

She shook her head. "I can't stop thinking about Jonathan. All the good things he did for us. All the lives he saved. The man who killed him is sitting right there and he's not even a little bit sorry."

"I know." Zack took her hands and squeezed them. "I know what he deserves."

"And I know that we need him," Amanda said. "That's why I have to go. My tempis is starting to feel like it did in the old days. If I can't control it—"

"I get it," Zack said. "You want me to go with you?"

"No. You need to be here. You're the only one he listens to."

"I don't know. Melissa—"

"It's *you*, Zack. Just you. But you have to be careful. As much as Evan likes you, I think he's a little jealous. Not because you have me, but because you have someone." Amanda kissed him. "Someone who loves you with all her heart."

Five minutes later, Zack was back in the sky in his dining cube. He watched the last trace of sunlight disappear behind the horizon, then started on his codfish entrée.

"All right," he said to Evan. "Let's talk about the Violets. Where are they?"

Evan lowered his fork with an uneasy look. "I've never encountered them in this part of the timeline, so I don't exactly know."

"You said you did," Melissa sternly reminded him.

"I said it was complicated. They move around the British Dominion—sometimes with the Opals, sometimes without. But both groups work for the same organization, so it's just a matter of time before they pop up."

"What are you talking about?" asked Caleb. "What organization?"

Melissa narrowed her eyes at Evan. "If you say the British government—"

"No, no, no. That's who they're working *against*. They're part of the Scarlet Sabre."

While Melissa and Mercy nearly dropped their forks, Caleb and Zack shared the same puzzled look.

"They're freedom fighters," Mercy explained to them.

"They're *terrorists*," Melissa countered.

"They only want the British to leave their countries alone."

"So they plant rift bombs in shopping malls and kill innocent families."

"Some do," Mercy admitted. "Most don't."

"The actions of the few reflect on the whole."

"Oh really?" Mercy pointedly asked Melissa. "Because a few of your people slaughtered ten percent of mine. You sure you want to go down that road?"

Evan rubbed his hands together. "Ooh. Dinner *and* a show."

"You shut up." Melissa turned back to Mercy. "What Integrity did to the Gothams was a travesty. We flushed out every man and woman responsible. When the Scarlet Sabre does the same, then I'll reconsider my opinion."

Zack pushed away his plate, his appetite thoroughly ruined. "Let's get back to the matter at hand. How did our people end up with these guys?"

Evan shrugged. "Everyone needs a cause, man."

"They have one," Caleb said. "Why fight to liberate one or two countries when the whole planet's dying?"

"You're assuming they know that," Evan replied. "But the Opals lost their augur a long time ago, and I'm not sure the Violets ever had any. They have no idea what's coming."

"Then we have to tell them," Melissa said. She cast a stern look at Evan. "Except we don't have time to go scouring all of Europe."

"*You* don't," Evan said. "I do."

"What are you talking about?"

Evan was just about to tell her when he abruptly stopped himself. He covered his mouth as if he'd suddenly become queasy. Before Zack or anyone else could ask if he was okay, he began convulsing in his seat, his eyes rolled back and his lids fluttering wildly.

Melissa stood up. "Is he choking?"

"He's timeshifting," Mercy said. "Gemma Sunder used to shake like that whenever her future self took over."

"So we're about to meet a future Evan?" Caleb asked.

Zack nodded. "Maybe someone who's lived through the next couple of weeks. If all goes well, he'll know exactly where to find—"

Evan sat forward with a throaty cry, startling everyone else at the table. Wide-eyed, gasping, he looked around at the others. "You *idiots*!"

"What?"

"I barely made it out alive!"

"What are you talking about?" Zack asked him. "Is this about the Violets?"

"No. It's the British. They're about to come down hard on your wife."

"What? *When?*"

Evan checked the watch on his trembling wrist. "Right about now."

ELEVEN

There was an electronic file circulating among the highest levels of British government, a nine-second video that had been stolen from Mexican Intelligence. The footage, captured the previous Friday in the skies of Nuevo León, showed a white-winged woman in tactical armor battling a fleet of aerial combat drones. After crippling a pair with her large tempic fists, she split her arms into eighteen tendrils and launched them through the air like harpoons. Each one pierced the hull of an enemy, rupturing a critical processor. Thirty-two tons of advanced military weaponry: destroyed in nine seconds by a woman who shouldn't exist.

After watching the video a fifteenth time, His Majesty's principal secretary of defence held an emergency meeting with his deputies. "I don't ever want to see that . . . thing in our dominion. Find her and stop her before she becomes our problem."

Unfortunately, the woman in question had been wearing an aerocycle helmet. Without a clear scan of her facial topography, there was no way for the computers to pick her out of a crowd.

Actually, no, there was one way. England had the world's most sophisticated surveillance network, with millions of autonomous camera drones capable of seeing across multiple light spectrums. All they had to do was keep their thermal lenses peeled for a woman with cool arms—thirteen degrees Celsius, the precise temperature of tempis.

And so it was in London on a Friday summer evening that a spherical drone the size of an apple passed twenty feet above Amanda and registered her unique heat signature. An electronic alert was sent to the nearest five watch stations with double-red priority from Military Intelligence. `Subject [UNKNOWN] is wanted for [CLASSIFIED]. She is armed with unique weaponry and is considered extremely dangerous. Proceed with caution.`

Amanda was halfway between The King's Lift and the hotel when she felt a curious twinge in her spatial sense: a coin-size disc of aeris above her, the liftplate of a mini-drone. Instead of flying around on its programmed orbit, it stuck to Amanda like a distant halo. She stopped and pretended to take interest in a store display, only to feel the drone come to a halt above her. Even more worrisome, it was beginning to accumulate a posse of siblings. One camera, two cameras, three cameras, four.

Not good, thought Amanda. *This is not good at all.*

She reached for the travel phone in her pocket, then stopped herself. If she called for help now, the cameras might record her. Worse, they could trace the line back to Zack and Melissa and send a whole mess of trouble after them.

Just act natural, Amanda told herself. *They don't know you're onto them.*

She continued north up Cooper's Row, past the hotel and toward a busy four-way intersection. The City of London Medical Centre stood forty yards away on the other side of the street. Perfect. Hospitals were big, chaotic labyrinths. If Amanda was lucky, she could ditch the cameras long enough to get a call out to Melissa.

As she waited for the crosswalk signal to change, she sensed something odd among the nearby pedestrians. Two of them were wearing tempic bodysuits beneath their clothes—skintight, bulletproof, and molded with multiple weapon holsters. They pushed their way through the tightly packed crowd until they were standing right behind Amanda. She glimpsed them in the reflection of a passing van—a "businessman" and a "courier," each with their hand stuffed ominously inside their jackets.

Shit. Melissa had warned her that the British were quick, but this was insane. They must have had plainclothes agents on every street corner, just waiting to pounce on a known or suspected terrorist. She wouldn't even make it to the other side of the street.

The traffic stopped on Trinity Way and the crosswalk lit up in translucent walls of lumis. While the other pedestrians started across the street, Amanda stayed at the curb with her two new acquaintances. She'd taken full control of their bodysuits, freezing them like statues inside their own tempic armor.

"I don't want to hurt you," she muttered. "I know you're just doing your jobs. But if you knew my situation, you'd know why I can't let you take me."

She suddenly felt more tempic undersuits in the vicinity. At least three government agents were coming at her from the crosswalk, with a dozen more approaching from the east and west.

"It's over," said the operative behind Amanda, the handsome young Englishman who was posing as a courier. "We have you surrounded. There's no way out."

His partner, the "businessman," wasn't nearly as calm. He struggled and grunted inside his bodysuit. "You free us right now or I swear to Christ—"

"Shut up."

Amanda converted the two men's armor to aeris and lifted them off the ground. The agents in the crosswalk didn't have a chance to draw their weapons before their two teammates came flying at them. The whole mob collapsed in the middle of the street.

"Okay," Amanda sighed to herself. There was no hope left for a clean and subtle exit. Her only chance now was to cut loose.

She extended her arm thirty feet into the air and caught the liftplate of a flying tour bus. Every bystander in the area stopped to watch her, blank-faced, as the vehicle yanked her off her feet and pulled her south down Cooper's Row. Amanda could only imagine how she looked to the strangers below, all the muggles of London who knew nothing of timebenders. She'd be lucky if she didn't end the night as a European news celebrity.

Amanda reeled herself in toward the bottom of the tour bus until she was pressed against it. The moment a delivery truck passed on the left, she swung her way to its skirted underside, covered herself in a skin of aeris, and then blended invisibly against the bright white glow of its liftplate. She could feel the camera drones floundering behind her, stymied. They weren't equipped to chase a woman of her talents, but they were still everywhere.

What the hell do I do now? she wondered.

Her handphone vibrated against her hip. She yanked it out of her pocket and saw a new text message from Zack.

Can't call right now. We're shifted. But we know you're in trouble and we have a plan to get you out.

Amanda barely started her reply when Zack's next message arrived. **Get to the Thames as fast as you can. Don't use your wings.**

She'd already figured out that last part. Like all aeris, her wings were fluorescent. They'd stand out like beacons against the night sky. But why go to the Thames?

Fewer cameras on the river, Zack explained. **And way less light. Stick to the middle, fly low, and keep your aeris under your clothes.**

Amanda cursed beneath her tempic mask. There was no slower or more awkward way to travel than skinflight. She'd be no better than a zeppelin.

We'll meet you at the top of the Tower Bridge, Zack wrote. **If you don't see us, wait.**

A horrible thought just occurred to Amanda. What if the British had already nabbed her husband and were using his phone to deceive her?

Feeling extra paranoid, she typed. **Prove to me you're Zack.**

His response came almost instantly. **Robert Aaron Given.**

Amanda felt a cold squeeze around her heart. She'd been expecting an inside joke from him, or at the very least a *Star Wars* reference. Instead, he gave her the name of her long-dead father, a man she'd lost to cancer when she was seventeen. It was definitely Zack on the other end of the line. And from his dark choice of passphrase, he was clearly feeling anxious.

Stay safe, he texted. **Don't get killed. I like you.**

Amanda smiled feebly. **Ditto. See you soon.**

She added a quick rider before sending her message. **Wait. How are you getting to the top of the bridge?**

A few seconds passed before Zack responded. **Don't ask.**

Melissa could have punched someone. As she floated above London in a cube of glass, waiting for Evan to deliver the miracle he promised, she ruminated over the current situation and blamed herself for most of it. She should have known that the British would have knowledge of Amanda, especially after that fracas in Mexico. And she should have known they'd devise a foolproof way to detect her. For God's sake, the woman was nine percent tempis.

But you brought her here anyway, Melissa chided herself. *You chose camaraderie over strategy and now Amanda's paying for it.*

Of course, that mistake was nothing compared to the one Melissa was making now. She was putting her faith in a psychopath, a man she wouldn't trust to wash her car, much less save the life of a Given.

"Almost got it," Evan said as he typed a four-digit number into a computer tablet. "Just a few more tries."

Though the dining cubes of The King's Lift were mere elevators by function, they were still considered aercrafts under imperial British law. As such, they were required to have complete maneuverability, plus an emergency control console located somewhere on the vessel. The restaurant owners had no choice but to stash a handheld computer on the underside of each table, though the law said nothing about locking them up. So they threw each tablet inside a carbon steel keysafe and covered each safe in tempis. They weren't about to let their customers fly willy-nilly with their dining booths. They might as well give them missile launchers.

Mercy had only needed a moment to dissolve the safe's tempic casing, and Zack had easily reversed the door lock. Unfortunately, the tablet still needed an access code to function: a four-digit number that Evan insisted he could crack. But after five long minutes and several dozen guesses, he was still locked out of the system.

Caleb sat across the table from Evan, his fingers pressed against his temples. He was shifting the cube under his own temporal power, at least 60x by his estimate. Melissa had met enough swifters to know what a labor that was, like pulling four people uphill on a sled.

"You all right?" Melissa asked him.

"Yeah. I'm fine. Just anxious to get moving." Caleb pointed at the tablet in Evan's hands. "Can't Zack reverse that thing like he did with the safe?"

Zack shook his head. "Doesn't work with computers."

"The circuits can't handle chronoregression," Melissa said. "The data gets corrupted."

"Great." Caleb looked out at the Tower Hill district. "So while Amanda's out there fighting the whole city, we're stuck here trying to jump-start a fish tank."

Evan smiled glibly. "Think of it more as a poor man's TARDIS."

Melissa glared at him. "I share every bit of his skepticism."

"Tough shit, Moneypenny. We already tried it your way."

"What are you talking about?"

"I just got back from a very short future," Evan said. "Where we went down to Hammett Street and hot-wired a flying car."

Melissa's heart jumped. That was exactly the plan she had in mind. "What went wrong?"

"What went wrong?" Evan laughed. "The car sent out an Amber Alert and the Brits went 'Yakety Sax' on our asses."

"Can you elaborate in human language?"

"It means I almost died! Now shut up and let me do this."

Melissa crossed her arms, livid. "There are ten thousand possible number combinations. It'll take hours to try them all."

Evan scoffed at her derisively. "Most four-digit codes can be cracked within six hundred guesses. Just by trying the obvious. The repeaters and couplets, the birthday combos, the idiot choices like 1-2-3-4. With the law of averages, you're likely to crack it around three hundred guesses. At four seconds per try—"

"That's still twenty minutes," Caleb grumbled.

"Well, then it's a damn good thing you're shifting us, rabbi."

Mercy paced a nervous loop on the other side of the cube, her eyes locked on her handphone. "Still no word from my brother. And none of the Coppers are answering my texts."

"I'm sure they're fine," Zack said. "If trouble was coming, they'd hear it from See."

Mercy didn't share his optimism. "We have a looper and we're still flailing."

"Good point," said Melissa. She cast a seething look at Evan. "Why now?"

"What?"

"You could have jumped back to any moment in the past," she told him. "A day, a week. Even an hour's notice would have helped us avoid this mess. But you chose to show up here and now, when it's almost too late to do anything."

Evan shrugged. "What can I say? I like to keep things interesting."

"Bullshit," Zack said. "You just like it when Amanda suffers."

Though Evan refuted him with a sneer, Melissa saw a hint of a smile in his eyes. Zack was right.

"Why do you hate her so much?" she asked Evan. "Did she break your heart too?"

"No, but she pierced it a couple of times."

He entered *1226* into the passcode field and was rewarded with access to the tablet's operational system. "*Boom!* I'm in. What did I tell you?"

Zack studied the screen over Evan's shoulder. Though the interface looked as crude as an old UNIX terminal, the flight controls were clear and simple. It even projected a 3D compass to make aerial navigation a breeze.

"All right." Melissa turned to Caleb. "We're about to make a bit of a scene. The more speed you can give us—"

"I got it." He closed his eyes in concentration, until the outside world became even more sluggish. The aerial traffic of Lower Thames Street slowed down to an inchworm crawl.

"Perfect. Thank you." Melissa snatched the tablet from Evan. "I'll take it from here."

He continued to sit with his back to her, reactionless. Zack jostled his shoulder. "Evan?"

He fell off his chair in a lifeless heap, his body crashing against the floor. The others looked at Evan confoundedly as he lay dead still in the shade of the table, his eyes half-open in a trance.

"Are you *kidding* me?" Mercy kicked his ribs. "Hey, dildo! Wake up!"

Caleb looked to Melissa. "Is he messing with us?"

"I don't think so." She kneeled at his side and pressed two fingers to his neck. "I'm barely getting a pulse."

"What the hell just happened?"

"Holy shit." Zack turned to Caleb, slack-jawed. "I think he just answered your question."

"What question?"

"What happens to his body when he jumps back in time." Zack studied Evan distractedly. "I think he just sent his consciousness to the past."

Melissa rose to her feet, mystified. "You think we would have seen this before."

Zack shrugged. "We've never spent this much time with him."

"But why would he go back?" Mercy asked. "Why now?"

Because he found the code, Melissa guessed to herself.

"Because he has the code to the computer," Zack said. "Now he'll have it for us that much sooner, which will make him look more impressive, I guess."

"But we're still here," said Caleb. "Nothing's changed."

Zack scratched the scar at the base of his throat, an old war wound from Rebel. "Time doesn't move in a single line. There are forks in the road. Branches." He gestured at Evan. "Right now he's out there somewhere in the strings, making things easier for the people we were five minutes ago. They've split off into a whole new timeline, and I guess . . ."

He took another look at Evan's mindless remains. "I guess he's gone with them."

Mercy's eyebrows arched. "What, you're saying he's gone for good?"

"I don't know."

"Let's worry about it later," said Melissa. She examined the electronic controls of the tablet, then set a quick course for the southeast. "Amanda still needs us."

The dining cube moved with a creaky lurch, its lifters unaccustomed to lateral travel. By itself, the vessel couldn't fly more than eight miles an hour. There was no minimum speed requirement for aercrafts, no reason to add thrust to a room full of dishware.

But under Caleb's temporal acceleration, the glass box soared like a rocket. The King's Lift hostess looked up from her station and saw a dining cube flee in a streak of yellow light. She thought she was hallucinating until the staff technician called her in a panic. It seemed the party at Table 51 had just taken their dinner to go.

Two and a half seconds after its departure, the rogue cube arrived at its destination: the Tower Bridge of London, one of England's most iconic relics. Aside from some tempic and lumic embellishments, it looked exactly like the version that Zack remembered from his world: a double-leaf bascule stretching eight hundred feet, garnished by two Gothic towers. They were connected at the top by a pair of observational walkways which, if Melissa was right, were closed to the public at this hour. There'd only be a minimal security presence at best.

Melissa landed the cube on the roof of the left-side walkway, deep in the shadow of the bridge's northern tower. While Mercy used her solis to kill the dining room lights, Zack reversed the sliding door to an open position.

"Good work." Melissa patted Caleb's back. "Take a rest."

He de-shifted the cube with a sigh. "Feeling pretty exposed here. We couldn't have found a more private spot?"

Zack stepped out onto the metal canopy. "It's the easiest landmark for Amanda to see."

The next two minutes passed in slow, addled silence. While the others kept watch on the eastern and western flanks, Melissa sent an encrypted text message to her local Integrity contacts. There were at least three different safehouses in the suburbs of London. One of them needed to be ready, and fast.

And then what? asked a cynical voice in her head. *Even if we get out of England alive, we have no hope left of finding the Violets.*

Zack peeked over the edge of the walkway, then smiled. "There she is."

Amanda levitated up the side of the tower, her aeris radiating through her clothes. Her tempic hands had become as large as ovens, with a struggling captive inside each fist. Both men were well past retirement age, dressed in kelly green uniforms that made them look like play soldiers. The old men bellowed beneath their tempic gags, furious and terrified at the indignity Amanda had inflicted on them.

She lowered her hostages to the canopy, then touched down next to Zack. "They were out on the river," she said. "I had no choice. They saw me."

"I'll take care of them," Zack said. "You okay?"

"I'm fine. But I had to use my tempis in the middle of the city. There's no way . . ." Amanda did a double-take at The King's Lift cube. "You came here in our *restaurant booth*?"

"We didn't have a choice."

"What happened to Evan?"

"Long story," said Caleb. He cocked his head at the two writhing prisoners. "Aren't these guys a little old to be troopers?"

Melissa studied their uniforms. "They're not soldiers. They're jingos."

"Jingos?"

"Civilian militia," she said. "Deputized by the government to help patrol London. Most of them are pensioners of a certain type."

"You mean racists," Mercy assumed.

"Racists with badges," Melissa said with a sigh. "And now apparently boats."

Zack rolled his eyes. "I'll wipe their memories so we can get out of here."

"Wait." Amanda looked to the west. "Something's coming."

A small gray flightboat ascended into view, a motorized catamaran that had been retrofitted with aeris. Its underside dripped with water beads as it bobbled in the air. It must have jumped right out of the Thames.

Melissa caught a brief glimpse of two uniformed figures before one of them shined a spotlight in her eyes.

"No one move a blasted inch!" yelled a parched and raspy voice.

"We have guns and we're not afraid to use them!" yelled the other passenger.

Melissa didn't have to see them to know that she was dealing with more jingos. They were both old women and, despite their bravado, they were most definitely afraid to use their weapons.

"I can take out their liftplates," Mercy muttered in her ear. "Just give me the word."

"No," said Melissa. The fall would almost certainly kill them, and the situation didn't call for murder.

Melissa stepped forward, her hands raised high. There'd be no reasoning with these people, not as long as Amanda held their teammates in her big tempic hands. But perhaps Melissa could scare them in just the right way.

"Listen to me," she said. "This is a government operation. I'm with Military—"

"Shut it," yelled the driver. "You're not fooling anyone."

"My identification is in my pocket. I strongly advise you check it. You also might want to consider the penalty for obstructing a national security mission, under Part V, Section 9 of the Commonwealth Protection Act."

The jingos tensely conferred with each other before responding. "You can't threaten us. We're sanctioned by Parliament."

"They barely put up with you ignorant prats," Melissa snarled. "And I have even less patience. Now here's what's going to happen . . ."

She shot a quick, pointed look at Zack. He replied with a subtle nod. He was ready to reverse those women into a stupor. All they had to do was—

"Lower your guns," Melissa said. "This is your first and last warning."

"You're bluffing! We should just shoot the whole lot of—"

"Wait!" Amanda cried. "Don't!"

Melissa had assumed Amanda was pleading with the jingos, until a huge tempic fist came crashing down from out of nowhere. It smashed through the stern of the catamaran, sending both passengers spinning into the air. Amanda let go of her prisoners and reached for the other two jingos, but her long grip missed them by inches. Both women plunged into the Thames.

"No!" Melissa looked up at the black night sky, right as the Coppers materialized into view. Sky ferried them all on a platform of aeris while Sweep kept them shifted at a brisk 30x. They'd been completely invisible thanks to the lumic named Shroud, whose talent with darkness far exceeded his skill with light.

As for the tempic fist, that was all Olivia Bassin, the young Israeli orphan whom everyone called Stitch. The girl was by far the most violent of the lot, though Melissa had hoped that Mother would keep her in line.

Another mistake, she thought to herself. *Those deaths are on me.*

Mother ordered Sweep to de-shift the platform before addressing Melissa and the others from above. "Sorry we're late. We had . . . conflicting prophecies."

"You didn't have to kill those people," Melissa shouted. "We had it under control!"

Stitch snorted cynically. "Didn't look that way."

"What's done is done," Mother said. "We have bigger problems."

"There'll be dropships here in forty seconds," said See. "I've seen them! They're—"

A booming gunshot filled the air, a noise so loud it seemed to echo from all directions. Amanda turned around to check on the male jingos, but neither one of them had weapons.

"No!" Mother was the first to see him in the walkway—a Tower Bridge security guard, standing ten feet below Caleb. His smoking .38 was aimed squarely at the Coppers, and he was about to fire a second round.

"Sou là!" Mother pointed at him, prompting two of her children into action. While Stitch lashed out with another tempic springfist, the girl named Shade launched a tendril of a different force: a corrosive black matter that the Gothams called "mortis."

In the blink of an eye, the security guard was disintegrated, along with an eight-foot swath of walkway. It was Caleb's dumb luck that he jumped out of the way before the canopy crumbled beneath him.

"Stop!" Melissa cried out at the Coppers. "You'll bring the whole bridge down!"

"We had no choice!" Mother insisted. "That guard. He was—"

"Mother?"

See called to her from the edge of the platform, her skin ghost-white, her eyes wide in panic. "I don't feel right. I think I'm . . ."

Mother's eyes went wide at the stain on See's blouse, a dark red splotch in the center of her chest that spread like ink across the fabric. *"Chérie?"*

"I think I'm in trouble."

See took a shaky step backward, then fell off the aeris. Mother shrieked and jumped after her.

By the time Amanda caught wind of the drama, both Mother and See had plunged out of view. She only had a split second to witness the fleeting sight of her husband as he mindlessly ran for the edge of the walkway and dove head-first off the bridge.

Zack couldn't help but question the wisdom of his plan. Actually, calling it a plan gave it more credit than it deserved. It was an act of desperation, a Hail Mary gambit fueled purely by sentiment. See was more than just his favorite Copper, she was a pillar in the hearts of all the orphans—their youngest, their nicest, their most cherished and enduring optimist. Zack was the only one who could heal her gunshot wound, but that was only half the problem. She was moments away from a fatal impact with the Thames.

And now, thanks to poor planning, so was Zack.

Wait a second . . .

He suddenly registered the other falling orphan, a woman who'd been just as foolish as him. Except Mother had the power to buy See time by teleporting her to a higher altitude.

From the eerie way her skin began to glow, she was about to do just that.

"Wait!" Zack jackknifed through the air, struggling to catch up to her. He had to get inside her teleport field—*all* of him—or he was dead.

Make it big, he pleaded with Mother. *For God's sake, make it b—*

She exploded in an orb of pulsing light, a fifty-foot combustion near the base of the Tower Bridge. Her portal was large enough to be seen from the fringes of London, and bright enough to stop all traffic within a mile. Automobiles swerved into trash cans and light posts, while pedestrians winced in the radiance.

By the time the glow dissipated, one second later, there was a curved indentation in the lower part of the bridge, a smooth new absence in the foot of the support pier.

"My God." Melissa peeked down over the edge of the walkway and surveyed Mother's damage. "She just—"

"Yeah." Amanda grew new wings out of her shoulder blades, shredding the back of her jacket. There was only one direction Mother could have gone. Amanda prayed that she managed to bring Zack and See with her.

"Take the others and go," she told Melissa. "I'll find you."

"But—"

Amanda sprang into flight, her aeric wings leaving a bright and ghostly trail. Melissa didn't even want to think about the thousands of bystanders who were watching her. The genie was thoroughly out of the bottle now. By tomorrow, the whole world would be talking about flying super-redheads.

Far up in the sky, a mile and a half above London, Zack snapped awake from a momentary blackout. The portal jump had been hell on his system, like being torn apart by buzz saw blades and then hastily glued together. He waffled through the air with the wind in his eyes, struggling to tell the stars from the distant city lights. After four long seconds, he was finally oriented. But where were Mother and See?

Zack threw his squinting gaze in every direction, until he saw his two fellow orphans in the moonlight. They were only twenty feet below him.

"Hey!" Zack folded his arms back and made a spiraling dive toward them. "Mother!"

Mother was desperately trying to get to See, her arms cutting through the air. She'd been a champion swimmer in her previous life, one of the very best in Haiti. But the sky didn't care for her aquatic maneuvers. Up here, Zack knew, it was all about tilt and bearing. Still, for all her flailing, Mother was managing to close the distance between her and See.

"Mother, stay back! I got this!"

She did a blinking double-take at Zack, as if he were just a figment of her fevered mind. She didn't know she'd teleported him. She didn't even know he'd jumped.

"I can save her!" Zack yelled over the wind. "Get out of the way!"

Mother flattened herself to a neutral position, until the resistance created a new buffer of space between her and See.

Thank you, Zack thought. *Now comes the hard part.*

It was challenging enough to heal a stationary target, especially one in See's condition. But to heal a mortally wounded patient while falling through the sky? That was a recipe for spectacular failure, like knitting while on a trampoline.

But from the look of poor See, there was no other option. Reversal was her only hope.

Zack held himself as steady as he could and prayed for the wind to be gentle. He had to keep See's whole body in his field of vision, without a split second of interruption.

He summoned his temporis around See's twirling body until she was enveloped in a sheath of light. Zack could feel his own brain resisting him, as if it were being forced to solve a constantly changing equation.

"Come on," Zack said through gritted teeth. "Come on! *Please!*"

He didn't even know who he was pleading with. He didn't share his wife's belief in God, at least not a benevolent one. If there was indeed a divine being who was pulling the strings, then Zack imagined he'd be a lot like Esis—capricious, petty, a little bit crazy, and completely devoid of sympathy for the little people. How do you let a whole world die? How do you let even one child die and still claim to be a loving creator?

That's where faith comes in, Amanda had told Zack. *Faith in a kind and benevolent God. Faith in a plan that we can't see. Maybe death isn't the end you think it is. Maybe it's the start of a long and beautiful journey.*

Yeah, well, as nice as that sounded, Zack wasn't about to let See go. And despite his continuing lack of faith, he found himself praying for a Hollywood ending. *Just one*, he begged. *Right now. Just give me the life of this sweet little kid.*

He could feel his temporis hard at work as it knitted through every molecule of See's body. Under better circumstances, he would have known exactly how far he was regressing her. But all he could tell in his topsy-turvy senses was that she wasn't bleeding anymore. Her gunshot wound had been temporally undone. Now all he had to worry about were the side effects.

"That's it," he shouted at Mother. "That's all I can do!"

She looked down at the growing sight of London. The wind had pushed them at least a half-mile south of the Thames. They were fixing to splatter onto rock-hard ground. "Now what?"

Zack fumbled with the buttons on his mechanical hand, then activated its protective casing. The tempis would be a beacon in the mind of his wife. She'd come at them like a homing missile.

"Just hang tight," he said to Mother. "Our ride's coming."

Mother didn't have to ask who he meant. "You think she can catch us all?"

"I know she can," Zack assured her. Of this, he had no doubt. He may not have believed in Amanda's God, but he sure as hell believed in Amanda.

Mother's portal had drawn a million eyes to the Tower Bridge. Within two and a half minutes of her great white eruption, the area was declared a hazard zone and cleared of all civilians. Newsdrones photographed the bridge from all angles while federal agents in hoversuits buzzed like wasps around the upper walkways.

Melissa watched the action from a mile away, her heart still pounding a timpani beat. Even with the help of the team's two swifters, they'd only escaped by the skin of their teeth. Now they floated above the city on Sky's aeric platform: six orphans, two Gothams, a beleaguered Integrity agent, and the husk of Evan Rander. Though Shroud had once again cloaked them in a veil of last night's darkness, Melissa figured they had minutes before they were spotted by a thermal scan. Their best hope now was to hightail it out of London.

But Melissa refused to leave without Amanda, Zack, and the others.

Sky paced the floor of her flying disc, her short hair mottled with sweat. "How much longer are we gonna wait?"

Stitch glared at her. "We're not ditching Mother."

"I'm not saying we should! But I can't hold us up forever." Sky flicked her hand at a dark little patch of London, a city park from the looks of it. "Can't we just wait for them on land?"

Melissa shook her head. "Our altitude's the only thing keeping the British from finding us."

"They found us," said Sage.

Everyone looked to Mercy's brother as he conjured an image into the air: a miniaturized hologram of twelve military gunships. Sage Lee was one of the Gothams' rare dualers, the ones who were blessed with double abilities. Though he wasn't exceptionally strong as an augur or lumic, he could bring his precognitive visions to life through sound and light. As far as any of his people knew, he was the only boy on Earth who could actually ghost the future.

Melissa only needed a moment to recognize the fearsome-looking ships on display. They were Royal Aer Force Overstrands, some of the deadliest fighters in the fleet. Just one of their missiles could atomize a high school, and their 60x shifters made running away a sucker's bet.

"How long before they get here?" Melissa asked Sage.

"I don't know. Seconds."

"Let me take out their lifters," Mercy said. "I can bring them all down with one blast."

"Not without killing us too," said Melissa. "Look at what we're standing on."

Mercy glanced at the aeris beneath her feet and cursed. Her solis didn't discriminate between the temporis of friends and foes. "So what do we do?"

Melissa studied the chronokinetics around her, her mind scrambling for a plan. Only a traveler could get them out of this pickle, and they were fresh out of those at the moment.

That's what you get for benching me, teased the Mia in Melissa's head.

But the team still had a teleporter in the vicinity, a woman who could spirit them all away in a flash. Melissa just had to buy time until Mother got here.

If she gets here, her inner voice cautioned.

"Put your hands up," she ordered the others. "We're surrendering."

The orphans and Gothams shared the same dumbstruck look as she raised her hands high.

"Are you serious?" asked Sweep.

"I don't have time to explain. Just trust me."

One by one, the timebenders grudgingly followed Melissa's cue.

"I hope you know what you're doing," Caleb said to her.

"I hope so too."

Melissa looked around at her fractured crew. Six of them were minors. One of them was pregnant. All of them were victims of unprecedented cosmic cruelties. Despite all appearances, she refused to let them fall into the hands of British interrogators, where they'd be tortured night and day through methods old and modern. That was simply not an acceptable outcome.

She muttered at Mercy. "If all goes wrong, I'll speak your name. You know what to do then."

Mercy nodded in dark understanding. "They won't take us alive."

"Good woman."

The Overstrands de-shifted in a surrounding formation, a clockwork array of sleek metal jet fighters. At full size, they were even more terrifying than Melissa remembered, but it was hardly surprising that they'd been upgraded in her absence. An empire in a state of constant war needed stronger and deadlier war machines. Melissa imagined this fleet could even give the Pelletiers a run for their money. The thought of that wasn't entirely unpleasant.

Within a moment of their arrival, their turret scopes were locked on every soul on Sky's platform. Even Evan, in his crumpled state, earned a glowing red dot on his forehead.

"No one move," said a gruff male voice over a loudspeaker. *"Keep perfectly still or you* will *be fired upon."*

"We understand!" Melissa shouted. "And we surrender unconditionally!"

"Wise choice."

A dozen more aerships de-shifted onto the scene, a disparate assortment of military support vehicles. While most were content to linger outside the ring of Overstrands, a pair of bulky armored flightships made a cautious approach toward the platform.

Prisoner transports, Melissa guessed. She could feel Mercy's tense and expectant eyes on her, but it was still too soon to invoke the suicide option.

Caleb mumbled something under his breath. Melissa couldn't make it out. "What?"

"Three o'clock," he repeated.

Melissa peeked to her right and saw more ships in the distance, an entire squadron of London police cruisers. They were coming her way with a vengeance, all in pursuit of a glowing, flying object.

Oh, thank God, Melissa thought.

Amanda raced through the night on bright aeric wings, struggling to keep ahead of her pursuers. It would have been hard enough to outfly them on her own, but with three full-size passengers, it was next to impossible. See was tethered to her back on a thick tempic harness while Zack and Mother rode beneath her in her oversized hands.

Zack scanned the trouble ahead. "This'll be tight," he said to Mother.

"I know."

"You'll only get one shot."

"I *know*." Mother steeled herself with a breath. "The closer you can get us, Amanda—"

"I'm trying!" A bullet whizzed past Amanda's leg while a second one nicked her in the wing. "Just get us far away from here!"

Melissa's stomach churned with stress as Amanda and the others drew nearer. If even one of the Overstrands engaged them in combat, they'd be cut to shreds in an instant.

"We need a distraction," she whispered to Shroud. "Can you conjure up something without moving your hands?"

"Watch me."

The Overstrand pilots looked up from their cockpits as the stars disappeared by the hundreds. The absence spilled like oil across the night, until even the moon was consumed. For those in the vicinity who didn't know Shroud, the void was a sublime and captivating horror, a nightmare of a hundred possible origins. By the time the pilots stopped speculating about the anomaly, Amanda was fifty feet from the edge of Sky's platform.

"Get ready!" Zack shouted at Mother.

"Get ready!" Melissa yelled at Sky. "Keep us flying, no matter wh—"

Mother cast an explosive spherical portal, four times larger than the first one. It lit up Central London like a brand-new moon before dissipating into thin air.

The police cars in pursuit of Amanda all slammed to a simultaneous halt while thirty Royal Aer Force soldiers struggled to catch up with the new status quo. Nine of the twelve Overstrands were suddenly missing their nose cones and an S-Class prisoner transport had vanished entirely. There was no more platform in the sky. No strangers. No darkness. No peculiarities of any kind. Whatever madness afflicted the heart of London had disappeared in a flash of light.

Twenty-one miles north of the city, a half-mile above the village of Bayford, an armored Aer Force prisoner transport floated listlessly in the air, a dull gray van held aloft by automated safety measures. Its pilot and copilot sat unconscious in the front seats, their uniforms splattered with vomit. Mother's portals were rough on experienced teleporters. For the uninitiated, they were utterly traumatic, enough to throw two veteran soldiers into a deep, dark state of disarray.

Melissa hadn't bothered to check on their health. Her priority was getting as far away from their vehicle as possible. By the time the Royal Aer Force managed to ping its location, Melissa and her people were fifteen miles away.

They moved through the night on Sky's aeric platform, with Caleb providing the temporal acceleration and Shroud once again concealing them in a cloak of illusive darkness.

Shade crouched at See's side. "How is she?"

Zack pressed two fingers to her wrist. "Pulse is good. She just might make it."

Stitch grew suspicious at his wavering tone. "But?"

"But I still did a shitty job," Zack confessed. "Something went wrong when I was healing her. I could feel it."

Amanda squeezed his shoulder. "You did the best you could under the circumstances."

"That's a real small comfort if it puts her in a wheelchair."

"I disagree," said Mother. She gestured at Sweep. "He broke both his legs in a swifting accident. We thought he'd never walk again. Now look at him."

Sweep tapped the metal bars of his mechanized leg braces, a state-of-the-art gift from Integrity and a vast improvement from the wheelchair he'd been using. "I'm faster than I've ever been."

"We'll face her problems as they come," Mother said to Zack. "For now, I'm just glad she's alive."

"So what now?" Mercy asked Melissa. "We're at the top of England's shit list and they know what we all look like."

Melissa checked her handphone screen. "There's an Integrity safehouse in Bury Saint Edmonds, not too far from here. We can hide there for a night or two, until I can arrange for travel to—"

"Scotland," said a weak voice behind her.

Everyone looked to the edge of the platform, at the half-prone form of Evan Rander. He'd been so lost in quiet catatonia that the others had nearly forgotten about him. But there he was, awake and groggy, as if he'd merely woken up from a nap.

He looked to Melissa with drooped blue eyes and the ghost of a smug little grin. "The Violets will be in Scotland tomorrow. I know exactly where to find them."

TWELVE

While the British press roared about supernatural terrorists, the American news media remained snug in its own continuum. The top stories of the day were all domestic calamities: the sordid death of a drug-addicted actor, a ten-car crash on an interstate aerway, a teachers' strike, a celebrity divorce, and a salmonella outbreak caused by tainted reversible bacon.

Saddled at the end of most local newscasts was a quick update on Merlin McGee. The great prophet had scheduled a major press conference in Cuba this weekend, presumably to warn the nation about an impending natural disaster. But when pressed for details by reporters, he merely told them to wait for Sunday.

"You know what that means," said the New York–5 anchorman. "Something bad is coming."

Hannah sat by herself in the Orphanage commissary, oblivious to the blather on the lumivision. Though most of the day had come and gone, she was just getting around to having her first meal. She'd been out of sorts since her sister left, and her trip to the clinic didn't help. Now all she could think about, besides the tiny new stranger inside of her, was the fact that it was midnight in London. Amanda and the others had been there for hours, yet no one had heard a word from them. Were they in trouble? Did Evan screw them over already?

Mia spotted Hannah through the front bay window, then teleported into the commissary. "I've been looking for you. Did you get the message?"

Hannah looked at her with blinking distraction. Mia was dressed in her regular exercise clothes, but had barely worked up a sweat. She usually ran the treadmill half to death.

"No, I . . ." Hannah searched her pockets for her handphone, to no avail. She must have left it behind in the clinic. "What message? From Amanda?"

"Theo. He wants us to meet him in the science lab. Said there's something we have to see."

She noticed a curio in Hannah's hand: a glass orb the size of a golf ball. Nestled inside the sphere was a blurry white hologram of some nebulous creature, like a half-melted seahorse. "What the hell's that?"

Hannah's voice dropped to a low mutter. "Confirmation."

"Holy shit." Mia sat down next to her, her wide eyes fixed on the five-week-old embryo. "You went to the clinic."

Hannah nodded. "They scanned me six ways to Sunday, then gave me a souvenir."

Mia couldn't stop staring at the lumigram. "Wow. Crazy to think that's how we all started."

"I'm more worried about how it'll finish," Hannah grumbled.

Mia's brown eyes narrowed to icy slits, the same expression she always wore when she was thinking about the Pelletiers. "I'm sorry you're going through this."

"I'm sorry I kept it from you."

"It's good you did," Mia said. "I would have smacked the crap out of you and Peter."

"You know why we did it."

"I *get* why you did it. I just don't understand how you can trust those assholes."

Hannah shrugged with misery. "We were desperate. *I* was desperate."

Mia opened her mouth to say something, then stopped herself. Hannah figured she was censoring another tirade about Semerjean. There was nothing she could say that Hannah didn't already know. Nothing she could do to unscrew this mess.

"Has Peter seen that?" Mia asked about the lumigram.

Hannah stashed the orb back in her pocket. "No, and I don't plan on showing him."

She feared for a moment that she'd have to explain her decision, but Mia knew Peter better than anyone. The more he saw of his unborn child, the more he'd fight to protect it. Sooner or later, that fight would bring him to the Pelletiers. And that would be the end of him.

"You should have told me you were going to the clinic," Mia said. "I would have gone with you."

Hannah clasped her hand. "You're so sweet."

"Sweet." Mia laughed. "No one calls me that anymore."

"That's only because of the eyeshadow."

"I *like* my makeup."

"You look like a raccoon zombie."

Mia laughed. "Fuck you. You making Zack's jokes now?"

"Just filling the void till he gets back."

"Lucky me." Mia stood up and waved a portal into the air. "Come on. Theo's waiting."

She turned around and saw Hannah's hesitance. "What's the matter?"

Hannah didn't know if she wanted to laugh or cry. The doctors had given her a laundry list of things to avoid: cigarettes, alcohol, seafood, high heels, hot baths, paint fumes, and excessive exposure to temporis. Even a minute in a shifter could irrevocably damage the embryo. God only knew what a teleportal would do.

What Hannah found funny, in a criminally depressing way, was her reflexive desire to risk it. Just jump right through the stupid disc and spin the wheel of fate. What was bad for the baby might be real good for mama. One might even consider it a solution.

Hannah flushed away the awful thought, then tossed a sheepish look at Mia. "I think we're better off walking."

The science lab had been constructed on the bones of a Gotham playground, a two-story ovular mini-complex that had been designed with transparency in mind. The building featured an open floor plan and a belt of continuous windows, allowing any curious passerby to see everything happening inside. Cedric Cain didn't want any mystery surrounding his eggheads, no whispers among the Gothams about sinister genetic experiments. If anything, the scientists were the lab mice of the underland. They scurried around in their big glass cage, rarely acknowledging or even noticing their intermittent audience. They were too busy catching up on a hundred years of chronokinesis, all the portals and precogs and mind-controlled tempis that had officially become canon in their reality.

Hannah saw Theo before she even entered the complex, a distinct presence in his crimson hoodie and weather-beaten cargo shorts. From the way he paced the research lab, he was clearly jazzed up about something. But was it a good something or a bad something?

He spotted Hannah and Mia, and eagerly waved them inside. From the looks of it, the meeting had already started. Two dozen people stood clustered in a semicircle, including Eden, Heath, Ofelia, and Felicity. None of them seemed to share Theo's exuberance.

Hannah's heart lurched when she spotted Peter among the attendees. She gave him a warm and weary smile, her fingers wrapped tight around the lumigram in her pocket.

"There you are," said Theo as Mia and Hannah entered the lab. "Come here, both of you. I'm gonna need you in a minute."

"Uh . . ." Mia was thrown by the meeting's main attraction: a discarded silver bracelet on a lab table. Sensors were attached to every square inch of its surface, all connected to a monitor with six different readouts. The line graphs danced in frenetic peaks and valleys, as if the trinket were a living, breathing creature with vital signs.

"Ofelia's bracelet," Theo told her. "We had it surgically removed from her wrist."

"And?" Mia asked.

"That's my question," Ofelia said. "I still don't understand what you're trying to tell us."

Theo stopped in place and sighed. "Sorry. I forgot you don't remember."

"Remember what?"

"Our last day on Earth," he said. "The thing our bracelets did that day."

He looked around, then zeroed in on a lanky young orphan. "Max, you're a lumic, right?"

"Yes," said the boy. "But my name's Matt."

"Matt. Sorry. For the sake of Ofelia and some of the others, can you . . . illustrate what happened with our bracelets?"

"Uh, I suppose so. Sure."

Mia bristled as Matt Hamblin joined them at the table. At seventeen, he was the youngest of the Platinums—a handsome, intelligent, and socially awkward blond who reminded all the Silvers of David. Mia figured that Semerjean had used him as an actor's study, stealing all his best tics and mannerisms. For those who'd loved David, it was like seeing a ghost. For Mia, Matt's presence was a constant middle finger in her face.

After a moment of preparation, he created a cartoon hologram for everyone to see: a stick-figure man with an oversized platinum bracelet.

"There's only one reason we survived the end of our world," Theo explained. "The technology inside those bracelets. I don't have the faintest idea how it worked. I just know that when the sky came down . . ."

Hannah fidgeted uncomfortably as Matt simulated the start of the apocalypse. Even in crudely illustrated form, the sight of the great descending whiteness was traumatic.

". . . the bracelet created a bubble of light around us," Theo continued. "A transparent yellow orb that can only be described as a forcefield."

The Gothams and Integrity scientists all watched with fascination as the whiteness spilled harmlessly around the barrier of the cartoon man.

"Not only did it save our lives," Theo said. "It transported us across time and space, all the way to this part of the multiverse. Thank you, Matt."

Matt waved away his visual aid, then melted back into the crowd.

"Is this the best place to be talking about this?" Hannah nervously asked Theo.

"What do you mean?"

"You know." She jerked her head to the south and mouthed the words "war room."

Theo shook his head, sneering. "That place was built to make Cedric feel better. It doesn't do shit against the Pelletiers."

He picked up a second metal bracelet off the table, this one a dark and cloudy gray, like iron. "Azral built these bracelets for one-time use," he said. "The one I'm holding was taken off of Eden, not long after she, uh . . ."

"Froze her own stupid hand off," Eden dryly interjected.

"Yes. From everything we can see, it's just a hunk of metal now. No electrical activity. No temporal radiation. It did its job and now it's dead. But *Ofelia's* bracelet . . ."

Theo motioned to the lumic monitor, still dancing with vibrant activity. "This little thing's packed with power. The readouts confirm what my foresight's been telling me. It hasn't been used yet. It still has a charge."

The audience muttered among themselves, intrigued. Peter eyed Theo skeptically. "You're saying it still has a forcefield in it, one strong enough to withstand an apocalypse."

"Yes."

"And then carry someone off to another part of creation."

"Maybe," Theo cautioned. "That part's a little less certain."

Three phones suddenly beeped in unison. The Integrity agents in the room checked their screens, then hurried out the door.

"Everything okay?" Theo asked them.

"Yeah," Felicity said unconvincingly. "We'll be back."

Eden looked at Ofelia, baffled. "I don't get it. If your bracelet hasn't been used yet—"

"I don't know."

"—then how the hell did you get here?"

"I don't know," Ofelia said. "I'm missing almost two years of memories."

"We know what Semerjean told you," Theo said. "About the last-minute change in their plans. You were supposed to be a Silver, then they put you with the Pearls. For all we know, they brought you here themselves."

"But what does any of this *mean*?" asked Noah Rall, the affable young Gotham Eden was dating. "Even if it works the way you hope it does, that's only a lifeboat for one person."

"One specific *kind* of person," Peter stressed.

Mia looked at him askance. "What are you talking about?"

"Put your fingers inside the bracelet," Theo told her. "Just enough to touch the table."

Mia followed his cue and gasped at the bracelet's sudden reaction. The loop split apart into four even pieces, then snapped back together when she pulled her hand away.

"I had everyone try it before you got here," Theo told her. "It didn't open for Peter or Eden or even Heath. Just me and Ofelia and now you."

Stymied, Hannah pressed her fingers inside the loop and watched the bracelet break apart again. "Just the San Diego orphans."

Theo nodded darkly. "Just us Silvers."

Hannah reeled at the horrible implications. There were only seven people on the planet who could potentially survive the next apocalypse, and one of them was Evan.

Mia didn't hide her bitter disappointment. "Noah's right," she said to Theo. "This is nothing."

"Mia—"

"It's not even a lifeboat."

"You're not seeing the big picture."

"Me? Theo, look around. You're the only one smiling."

Theo scanned the faces in the room, all as puzzled and cynical as Mia's. Hannah's heart broke at his helpless frustration. His foresight took him to places where no one else could go, not even the other augurs. Even when he was back among the people who loved him, he was still hopelessly alone.

"We're on your side," Peter reminded him. "And we'll take our good news where we can get it. The thought of saving even just one of you—"

"This isn't about one person," Theo snapped. "It's bigger than that. I don't know when and I don't know how, but this bracelet's going to save millions of lives. I *feel* it."

Hannah got stuck on his curious word choice. "Millions."

"Yes."

"Not billions."

Theo shook his head bleakly. "The time may come when we have to accept—"

"Hey."

Felicity rushed back into the lab, harried. "I need you all to come with me."

She led the group to the other side of the building, to the little glass lounge that served as a breakroom. They gathered tightly in front of the lumivision as the mad word from England finally reached American shores.

Hannah blanched at the image on the national news, a crystal clear photo of Amanda in wingflight. "Oh my God."

The story had been rocking the world for hours: a terrorist attack in the middle of London, killing three innocent people and scarring a national landmark. But that was just the teaser to a much richer story. Soon the airwaves crackled with uncorroborated rumors, tales of great white fists knocking ships out of the sky and a redheaded woman eluding police on a hang glider. But wait, no, it wasn't a hang glider. It was something a lot more . . . unique.

At a quarter to midnight, London time, the first pictures of Amanda started hitting the GlobalNet, all taken by civilian photographers who'd been quick enough or lucky enough to catch her at full wingspan. Within fifteen minutes, the photos were on lumivision, and by one A.M., the whole world was chattering about angels over London.

Mia looked to Felicity, slack-faced. "Holy fuck. What *happened*?"

"All I know is what Melissa told Cedric," Felicity said. "The British sniffed them out and hit them hard. They all got away, but See was seriously injured."

Heath's eyes went wide. "Is she okay?"

"I don't know. I only—"

"How bad was she hurt?"

"I don't know," Felicity stressed. "As soon as I hear something—"

"Hold it." Theo held up his palm, his attention still fixed on the lumivision. The newscast had progressed into the speculative part of the story, an in-studio chat between the anchorwoman and her guest, a professor of parapsychology at Fordham University.

"Dr. Tan, what do you make of all this?" the anchor inquired.

"Well . . ." The professor chuckled and adjusted his glasses. "I think it's part of a pattern we've been seeing for a while now, and not just in England. That church in Seattle that mysteriously vanished. That huge tempic arm that saved a man's life. Tales of fast-moving people who aren't wearing speedsuits. For two years we've been hearing these kinds of stories, yet no one seems to be putting the pieces together."

"So what do you think is happening?" asked the anchor.

The professor laughed again. "I have no idea, but it's a question we should all be asking. I don't think we can dispute the fact that there are extranormal people among us. Look at this so-called Angel of London. Look at Merlin McGee."

"Shit," Theo muttered. "That explains it."

"Explains what?" Peter asked.

"I knew your brother would need help soon. I just didn't know why."

Peter reeled at his implication. "You're saying there's a backlash coming for him."

"I'm saying we can't wait until Sunday." Theo checked his watch, then cast a solemn gaze at Hannah. "We have to go to Cuba now."

THIRTEEN

The British government barely existed in Dunwoodie. The coastal village, nestled deep in the northeast Highlands of Scotland, had only one camera drone in the five-mile radius. The nearest imperial watch station was seventeen miles down the coast, in the northernmost suburb of Aberdeen.

No one was surprised by the minimal security presence. Dunwoodie offered nothing of interest to the enemies of England. No military targets. No strategic supply ports. Just twelve hundred hardworking countryfolk and a spectacular view of the sea.

The withered remains of Ceannaideach Castle, long rumored to be the inspiration for Bram Stoker's *Dracula*, stood a half-mile to the north on the edge of a grassy cliff. Though the public was normally free to explore the ruins, a tempic fence had been installed around the premises. Electronic signs warned all approaching visitors that Ceannaideach was closed this Saturday, July 28, by order of the Ministry of Defence.

It seemed the British had business in Dunwoodie after all.

Zack stood outside the barrier and waved a handheld scanner in the air. "Well?" asked his mission partner, the reedy young tempic named Stitch.

He stashed the device in his jacket. "No cameras in the sky except the ones we put there."

"Told you," Evan gloated through his earpiece. "This'll be easy, even for you."

He'd been promising his allies a cakewalk all day, but Zack didn't share his confidence. His nerves were still raw from the fiasco in London, in which three people died, See took a bullet, and Amanda became a world news sensation. Her image had become so ubiquitous in Europe that she couldn't even show her face in the boonies. That only left Zack with one tempic to work with, a girl who'd nearly killed him last year in Seattle.

Stitch willed a large gap in the shimmering white barrier, then snapped her fingers in front of Zack's face. "Hey, shithead. Wake up."

Zack fell out of his thoughts and glared at her. "You don't even feel bad, do you?"

"About what?"

"About those two old women you killed last night. That security guard on the bridge."

Stitch rolled her eyes, as if he'd just lectured her about the dangers of not flossing. "*Kol hamatzil nefesh achât mi'Yisra'êl, ke'ilu hitsil olâm malê,*" she recited.

"I don't speak Hebrew."

"What kind of Jew are you?"

"The bad kind. What does it mean?"

"'Whoever saves a life of Israel has saved the entire world,'" she said.

Zack eyed her skeptically. "And by 'life of Israel,' you mean—"

"Us, stupid. The orphans. We're God's new chosen saviors."

Sighing, Zack passed through the fence and followed Stitch up the winding path. In a better state, he might have reminded her that it wasn't exactly God who chose them. But he figured he shouldn't judge her too harshly. She'd been raised by a cult of extremists in Jerusalem and had grown up with a submachine gun in her hands. The apocalypse had only cemented her view that life was just an endless war. Take no prisoners. Kill or be killed.

The worst part: Zack wasn't entirely sure she was wrong.

Two burly young men stepped out of the castle and squinted in the high noon sun. Though they were dressed like civilians in their sweaters and jeans, Zack had it on good authority that they were both British government operatives.

The elder agent placed his hand on his sidearm. "What are you doing? This area's closed."

"We're just passing through," said Zack. "My sister and I are castle buffs. We were hoping to get some pictures."

"Didn't you see the fence and signs?"

"Look, if there's construction going on, no problem. We'll just look around out here."

The Englishman sneered derisively. "Americans, huh?"

"Yeah, but don't hold it against us."

"I have no quarrel with you Yanks. It's trespassers I don't like."

Zack pretended not to notice the sound at his feet, the faint crunch of dirt beneath Stitch's sandals. She'd cast two tempic tendrils from the skin of her heels and sent them burrowing through the ground like earthworms. Zack only needed to stall for a few more seconds.

"Come on, guys. We came a long way to see Ceannaideach."

"Ken-a-*jack*," said the younger agent, a Scotsman from the sound of him. "Not ken-a-*dack*."

"See? I'm already learning. If you just let us look around—"

"*Enough.*" The Englishman pulled out his pistol and aimed it at Zack. "You seem to have trouble taking a hint, so let me—"

A pair of tempic tendrils burst up through the stonework, a mere ten inches behind the operatives. The two men barely had a chance to turn their heads before the vines wrapped around their throats and lifted them off the ground.

Zack took out his stun chaser and shot the men where they hung. "They're out. Let go."

Though Stitch was content to let the Scottish guy fall, she kept her strangling grip on the Englishman.

"Stitch . . ."

"He's an asshole."

"So? You're gonna kill him just for that?"

"I would," Evan said over the radio.

"You shut up." Zack shot a hard look at Stitch. "Tell me something: if saving a life saves the entire world, then what does murdering someone do?"

Stitch pursed her lips in a surly pout, then let her victim fall. "You're a pansy, Trillinger."

Mother's voice broke in over the network. "Be quiet, girl, and show some respect. He's the only reason See's breathing."

"There you are," Evan said. "I hope you brought your dancing shoes, Mama, because—"

"I'm ready."

"—you're next."

A dark-haired operative stepped onto the castle's rear parapet and did a double-take at Mother. She stood on a high patch of grassy rock, right at the edge of the cliff.

"Oi! How'd you get there?"

"Same way you're leaving." She sent him away in a spherical portal. Another two guards rushed outside, only to be felled from behind by an invisible burst of electricity.

Melissa stepped out of the shadow of an overhang, a stun chaser gripped in each hand. "Two more down," she told Evan. "How many left?"

A half-mile to the south, in a dusty old building that had once served as Dunwoodie's movie theater, Evan followed the action on a bank of lumic monitors. The equipment, the weapons, even the clothes he was wearing had come courtesy of Integrity's London office. But the plan of attack was all his. He'd lived through the mission twelve times already and had fine-tuned his strategy to perfection. All it took was five orphans, one agent, and Evan's divine knowledge to clear out this group of thugs.

"Six to go," he told Melissa. "But by the time I finish this very . . . slow . . . sentence . . ."

He watched the screens with smiling delight as Caleb and Sweep took down four more guards. The swifters hit so hard and fast that their victims didn't even have time to yelp.

"Two left. They're all yours, Zacky."

Zack weaved through the dilapidated corridors of Ceannaideach, a labyrinth of weeds and ivy. He peeked through a hole in the eastern wall and caught a glimpse of the final targets. They paced back and forth in a nervous fit as they tried to hail their teammates on the radio.

"I don't want to pressure you," Evan said to Zack, "but you have ten seconds to stop them before they light the British Bat-Signal."

"I can't get a clear shot."

"Because you're not standing where I told you to. Will one of the speedsters please—"

A strong, hot wind blew through the hallway. Zack only had a moment to register the sound of Caleb's footsteps before the operatives were felled in a double stun blast.

Evan sat back in his chair with a satisfied grin. "And that's a wrap, people. We hope you all had fun storming the castle. Don't forget to tip your strategist."

"Don't get smug," Melissa said. "We're not even close to being done."

The strike team gathered in the open heart of Ceannaideach, a vast and roofless chamber that had once upon a time been a great hall. Now the place was just a lush green jungle, with foot-tall blades of grass on the floor and vines snaking forty feet up the masonry.

Caleb looked to a shady corner of the room and noticed a crumbling stairwell leading down into darkness. "Really hope our guy isn't down there. I don't do well in catacombs."

Evan chuckled. "Relax, rabbi. He's just two rooms to the north. But you have to work fast. A camera drone will be looping overhead in five minutes."

Melissa gestured at Mother and the swifters. "Gather the guards and bring them to the theater." She pointed to Zack and Stitch. "You two are with me."

Thirty yards north of the great hall, beneath one of the castle's last surviving ceilings, a gaunt-looking man in an orange prison jumpsuit sat shackled to a tempic chair. A custom leather helmet kept him blind, deaf, and gagged. Zack reeled at the skin on his tattooed arms—a sickly shade of yellow, with cuts and cigar burns marring every ink design.

"Wow," said Zack. "They really did a number on this guy."

"No less than he deserves," Melissa grumbled.

The prisoner drew a gasp of air as Melissa pulled off his helmet. "Fucking hell. It's 'bout time you bastards . . ."

He blinked in surprise at his three new acquaintances. "Well, here's a twist."

Melissa eyed him with dripping contempt. "Hello, Frederich."

As a former member of British Intelligence, she already knew everything about Frederich Michael Patrick DeVoor. The notorious South African terrorist had left a trail of destruction across the British Dominion—arson, bombings, stabbings, riftings. He never favored one style of attack and he rarely discriminated in his choice of victims. Even children who were complicit in the actions of the empire were enemies in Frederich's eyes.

In recent years, he'd joined the Scarlet Sabre and became one of their most notorious captains. The press had even given him his own nickname, a handle that he carried with pride.

He shined a filthy, gap-toothed grin at Melissa. "Please. Call me Whistler."

Zack didn't have to wonder how he came by his moniker. His laugh was nothing but a shrill and whistling wheeze, like the evil dog Muttley from those old Hanna-Barbera cartoons.

"We'll call you whatever we want," Melissa snapped. "You're our hostage now. And if you don't do what we say, when we say it, I will gladly rid the world of your stain."

Whistler scoffed. "Lady, if you think a bad attitude's gonna scare me, then you don't know what I've been through."

"I can imagine the last few months haven't been pleasant," Melissa said. "And your future's looking bleaker by the minute. You know why the British brought you here, right?"

"I reckon it wasn't a school trip."

"You were being sent back to Johannesburg," Melissa informed him. "A secret extradition, conducted far away from prying eyes. Since you're already familiar with South African justice, I don't need to tell you what they do with child-killers."

Zack wasn't used to hearing such venom in Melissa's voice. He knew she wasn't happy with this part of Evan's plan, and had to remind her more than once that it was all for the greater good. The best he could do now was step in and be the nice guy.

"But you're in luck," he told Whistler. "Your friends in the Scarlet Sabre are here. They're holed up now in the little town of Dunwoodie, just waiting for the chance to save you."

"So why haven't they, then?"

"Because we got here first," Stitch said. "Now we have you, they want you, and we're looking to make a deal."

Whistler blinked at her before laughing again. "What are you, daft? The Sabre doesn't deal with—"

"—terrorists?" Melissa asked.

"Extortionists."

"We're not asking for money," Zack assured him. "We just need a minute of their time."

At Melissa's command, Stitch dissolved Whistler's tempic shackles. He only had a moment to caress his sore wrists before Melissa dropped a handphone into his lap.

"You need to send a message to your people."

Whistler shook his head. "They change their numbers every week."

"Don't waste our time," Zack said. "You still know how to reach them. Tell them we have you and we're willing to hand you over. But we want to meet face-to-face with their . . ." He shot a quizzical look at Melissa. "How did we agree on saying it?"

"Their special people."

"Their special people," Zack echoed. "You know the five I'm talking about. The ones who aren't from around these parts. The ones who do strange things with time."

Whistler's eyebrow rose at the reference. As Evan had correctly attested, the man knew all about the Violets of London.

He took a nervous look at Stitch. "You're just like them, aren't you?"

She coated her hand in a mass of writhing tempis. "What makes you say that?"

"They're our people," Zack said. "We came a long way to find them. And we have information they desperately need."

"So send the text already," said Melissa. "Unless you'd rather wait for the South Africans."

"No, no." Whistler picked up the phone. "I know a good turn when I see one."

He entered a phone number into the device, then passed it back to Melissa. "There you are. Just say what you want to say. The message will reach them."

Melissa typed the missive herself and fired it off to the Sabre.

"Now what?" Stitch asked.

"Now we wait," Evan told her through the radio.

"You've seen what happens?"

"Seen it, lived it, bought the soundtrack." Evan kicked his feet up on the desk. "Trust me. This is the easy part."

The Milligan Cinema was the eyesore of Dunwoodie, a squat brick ruin covered in vandalized plywood, standing all alone on the outskirts of town on a half-acre plot of thistle. An out-of-town entrepreneur had built it in the summer of 1980, in the hope that his theater could compete with the local pubs.

It didn't. The cinema closed within a year, and no one had the cash to buy the property. So, like Ceannaideach, the building was left to the ravages of time. It enjoyed a brief second life as a teenage love den until the interior was overrun with beer bottles and condoms.

Nobody had dared to break in since, not until a quarter past noon, when Melissa claimed the Milligan as a temporary field base.

Luckily for them, Zack had worked his temporal magic on the interior. Ten minutes of solid, focused reversal had restored the place to its halcyon days. No trash, no filth, no creepy-crawly insects. There was even a film cued up in the projector, a 1981 British political thriller that was more propaganda than art.

Amanda paced behind the projection screen, her feet weaving deftly around eleven hog-tied hostages. As much as she was loath to admit it, Evan had planned a good siege of Ceannaideach—quick, quiet, and completely nonlethal. Aside from some bruises and electrical burns, the government operatives were fine. Four of them had already regained consciousness and were cursing at Amanda through their cloth gags.

"Calm down," she said. She'd already assured them they'd be reversed and released. They wouldn't even remember this.

Amanda stepped back into the audience chamber and took a casual look around. None of her teammates had moved in the last fifteen minutes. Mercy rested with her brother and Caleb in the front row, while Shade, Sweep, Shroud, and Sky played a quiet game of cards in the back. Mother cradled See in the middle of the aisle, stroking her hair and singing old Haitian folk songs. The poor girl was still wrecked from her ordeal in London, a ferociously rough reversal that had come with numerous side effects. Her skin burned with fever, her ears rang with tinnitus, and a migraine left her whimpering in pain.

Worse, just as Zack feared, See couldn't move or feel her legs. It was too soon to tell if the paralysis was permanent. All Amanda knew was that she needed serious medical attention, and she probably wouldn't get it until she returned to the States.

Evan sneered at Amanda from his eye-in-the-sky workstation at the edge of the screenstage. He'd switched half his monitors to European news sites, still chock-full of headlines about the mysterious Angel of London.

"Hoo boy," he teased. "You really stepped in it this time, sister."

Amanda scanned the monitors before looking away. "Glad you're enjoying it."

"What, you think I like seeing your face everywhere? That's my personal nightmare."

"Well, good. At least there's one upside."

Evan zoomed in on the home page of *The New Zealand Dispatch*, which had found a whole different photo of Amanda in flight. Her heart jumped at the clarity of the image, from the notches in her wings to the dimple on her chin. She'd never be able to step out in public again. Not here, not at home, not anywhere.

"Ironic, isn't it?" Evan said. "Hannah's the one who always wanted to be a celebrity. You just wanted to be a mom. Now she's pregnant, you're famous. It's like the universe went all *Freaky Friday* on you."

Amanda stormed across the stage and pointed a sharp white finger at him. "I don't ever want to hear her name out of your mouth, you understand me?"

Evan raised his hands. "Hey, no worries. I've got a dozen other names for her. Boopsie, Bambi, Tits McGee . . ."

"I'm *warning* you."

"Oh right. I forgot I can't mention her boobs anymore. People get *so* mad."

Evan shuddered at the new sensation on his skin, a pins-and-needle tingle that covered him from head to toe. He looked to the aisle and saw Mercy charging toward him, her right hand extended, her fingers outstretched.

He stared at his hands, dumbstruck. "What did you do to me?" he asked Mercy.

"Sapped your power for a good ten minutes."

"What? *Why?*"

Mercy rolled up her sleeves. "Because I'm gonna beat the shit out of you and I don't want you jumping back in time."

Everyone in the theater stopped what they were doing to watch the drama in progress. Evan pressed his temples and closed his eyes before looking at Mercy in horror.

"You *idiot!* I can't send or receive!"

Mercy chuckled with amazement. "Wow. You're just a scared little boy without your powers."

"Don't push me, bitch."

Caleb sped toward Evan in a blur and grabbed him by the collar. "What did you call her?"

"Look—"

"What did you just call the *mother of my child*?"

"The mission's not over! I need my powers—"

"I don't care," said Caleb. "I'm done with you and your incel bullshit. If the next word out of your mouth isn't an apology, you're going to see my darkest side."

No one in the room had any reason to doubt him. The "rabbi" had more than a hundred pounds on Evan. Even Mercy took pause at the rage on Caleb's face. "Babe . . ."

Amanda saw the fear in Evan's eyes and knew in an instant that Mercy was right about him. Without the power to escape the consequences of his actions, he was nothing but a paper tiger—the mugger with a plastic gun, the Internet troll who'd just lost his anonymity. She wished she could enjoy this vengeful moment, but one of the British prisoners was gasping for air and only Amanda was close enough to hear him.

She hurried back behind the screen and looked around at the captives. Strangely, all of them seemed to be breathing just fine. So who did that wheezing come from?

"Hello, Amanda."

His voice sent a shudder up the skin of her back, a smooth and silky haughtiness that she'd heard a thousand times before in a different accent.

"You."

It'd been more than a year since she last saw Semerjean, yet when she turned her head in the direction of his voice, there was nothing but dust and shadows.

"I'm not really there," he said. "Just a voice in the wind come to greet an old friend."

"Friend." Amanda had to fight to suppress a rash of stress tempis. "You were never my friend for a single moment. What are you doing here?"

"I told you—"

"What's your *voice in the wind* doing here?"

The sound of his chuckle traveled east along the wall, as if his invisible spirit was wandering. "If you want me to show myself, I will. But I doubt it'll help your mood."

"It won't," Amanda said. "Just tell me what you want. And God help me, if it's about babies—"

"No, no." Semerjean heaved a tired sigh. "That'd be a waste of time for both of us."

Amanda suddenly caught the conscious prisoners watching her with the same look of fear and confusion. Apparently she was the only one who could hear Semerjean. The others probably thought she was having a schizoid breakdown.

She lowered her voice to a self-conscious mutter. "Just say what you want to say already."

She could practically hear the smile in Semerjean's voice, the priggish little grin that had been quintessential David. "Funny," he said. "I was just about to praise you for your patience. The fact that you haven't killed Evan by now—"

"That's my business."

"Indeed. We've washed our hands of that pathetic man-child. His fate, like yours, is no longer our concern."

"Yet here you are," Amanda fired back. "Using stupid trick noises to get me alone."

"Yes, well, something interesting happened to you yesterday that presents us both with a new opportunity."

"If you're talking about that whole 'Angel of London' business—"

"No. I mean your meeting with Ioni Deschane."

Amanda stopped pacing, her heart thumping wildly. "What makes you think—"

"Amanda, please. The sooner we get through this, the sooner you'll be free of me."

"Fine," she admitted. "I met her. What of it?"

"She's always been a nuisance to us," said Semerjean. "But in recent weeks she's become a full-on threat. Our mission, our plans, everything we've worked for is in jeopardy."

Amanda chuckled bitterly. "Am I supposed to feel bad about that?"

"If you were smart, you'd be worried. The more she gets in our way, the more she pushes us toward . . . unpleasant solutions. Things we'd rather avoid."

Amanda's mind reeled at the dark possibilities. The Pelletiers were fine with genocide. What could possibly turn their stomachs?

"Unfortunately," said Semerjean, "she's proven quite elusive. But now that she's taken an interest in you, you're in a position to help us find her."

"And kill her," Amanda guessed.

"We'll handle that part ourselves."

Amanda shook her head, incredulous. "Our one last hope of saving the world and you want me to give her up."

"She's no savior, Amanda. If I told you the things we knew about her—"

"—I still wouldn't believe you. Try to guess why."

Semerjean's sigh seemed to come from everywhere, as if he'd expanded to fill the room. "I've no doubt earned your skepticism."

"Skepticism?"

"But what has Ioni done to earn your trust?" asked Semerjean. "This is the woman, after all, who provoked a needless war between your people and the Gothams. She betrayed poor Mia with harmful lies. Through Theo, she has you running around the world, chasing false leads and endangering yourselves. Now, thanks to her, the whole world knows your face. That's only a fraction of the damage she's done."

"Look—"

"Amanda, she caused both your miscarriages."

Amanda's thoughts went white and blank. Her hands balled into fists. "You're lying."

"We spent days trying to solve the mystery of their deaths," Semerjean told her. "By all accounts, those embryos had been healthy. But then I took a closer look at everything you'd consumed and there it was both times: a chemical abortifacient, teleported into your drink when you weren't looking. The formula was so potent that Ioni only needed a nanogram."

Amanda tensely shook her head. "Why would she even—"

"Because she's made it her business to hinder our plans. And you know what we want more than anything."

Amanda felt her headache coming back. She'd spent the night on the floor of a cramped Integrity safehouse, and had been so wound up by her bad time in London that she'd barely caught a wink of sleep. "I can't deal with this."

"I'm afraid you'll have to, because Ioni will come to you again in the near future. When that happens, just send us a signal: a tempic cross on the small of your back. That's all it'll take to fulfill your end of the bargain."

"Bargain?"

An unnerving chuckle filled her ears. "Did you think we'd ask for help without offering something in return? If you play your part, we'll be all too happy to compensate you. I believe one sister should cover the bill."

Amanda turned her wide gaze in the direction of his voice. "You expect me to believe that you won't take Hannah?"

"Oh, we'll take her," Semerjean said. "Keep her safe and comfortable until the child's born. But her fate after that?"

His voice turned as hard and sharp as knives. "That's entirely in your hands."

Amanda suddenly lost all sense of continuity, as if her life had been nothing but a long, dramatic movie and she suddenly just noticed the cameras. All the other concerns of the moment—Caleb and Evan, Zack and the Violets, the health of See, the "Angel of London," none of them mattered one bit. Her entire universe had contracted into a tight little sphere: just two sisters, a devil, and the deal he was offering.

"You don't have to answer now," Semerjean said. "Think it over for a couple of days and—"

"No."

"Excuse me?"

Amanda narrowed her eyes at the specter of Semerjean as if she could see every pore on his face. "I don't need to think it over. The answer's no."

Semerjean clucked his tongue. "You're letting your emotions cloud your judgment."

"Don't tell me what I'm thinking. I know my own mind. And for such a supposedly clever man, you don't seem to understand how credibility works. Let me spell it out for you: you have none. You broke my faith and trust in you, and you're never getting it back."

The room fell into testy silence. Amanda could just imagine the wrath in his cool blue eyes.

"So you'll work with a man like Evan," said Semerjean, "but you won't work with me."

"That's right," said Amanda. "He's the scum of the earth and he doesn't bother hiding it, but you keep wearing masks. The saddest part is that you still think you're the good guy after all the shit you've done. All the people you betrayed. All the innocent lives you destroyed. You're a plague on every world I've known. You and your twisted family."

She turned around and moved back toward the audience chamber. "So take your stupid voice in the wind and get the hell out of here."

Amanda had made it all the way back to the edge of the projection screen when she caught a new shadow out of the corner of her eye. She turned around and saw Semerjean standing five feet behind her, as youthful and lovely as he'd ever been. Amanda was so distracted by the hatred in his eyes that it took her an extra moment to notice that he was translucent.

"You've always been the most predictable of the Silvers," he said. "Though I was hoping you'd learned from your . . ." He flicked a hand at her tempic arms. ". . . mistakes."

Amanda struggled to maintain a level expression. Seeing him, even in his ghostly form, was so much harder than hearing him.

"I learned plenty that day," she said in a low tone.

"Not the right lessons."

He muttered something under his breath, in the arcane tongue of his people.

Amanda cocked her head at him. "What was that?"

"A taste," he said, "of things to come."

A shriek rose up from the other side of the screen. Amanda hurried back into the seating chamber and saw See thrashing violently in Mother's arms.

"We have to go!" the young augur cried. "We have to get out of here!"

Mother fought to keep her still. "What are you seeing, love? What—"

"They're coming!"

Shade looked up, then gasped in sudden horror. "Oh my God . . ."

A black mass spread across the ceiling like ink, dissolving everything in its path. Light fixtures crashed onto the seats and aisles as sunlight broke between withering planks of wood.

"It's mortis!" Shade yelled. "We're under attack!"

Oh no, Amanda thought. *He wouldn't.*

Mercy fired a blast of solis at the ceiling, an invisible cone of counter-energy that obliterated every last trace of mortis.

The orphans and Gothams shielded their eyes as the darkness gave way to bright summer daylight. Amanda peeked through tight fingers and saw a ring of strangers floating just above the hole in the roof, each one of them decked out in familiar green armor.

The Jades, she thought with bittersweet relief. She'd been expecting an attack from Azral and company, but instead they sent their minions.

Still, just one of them had nearly killed Zack and Melissa. Now there were eight.

Evan blanched at the floating sight of them. "No, no, no, no. Not them. Not now."

Amanda, Shade, and Mercy raised their arms in attack, but Mother beat them all to the quick. The sky above the cinema exploded with new radiance, a hundred-foot sphere of shimmering light that devoured every last shadow in Dunwoodie. By the time the white glow subsided, the entire upper half of the theater was gone, along with all eight Jades.

Caleb looked to Mother through the spots in his eyes. "Where did you—"

"London," she said in an unsteady voice. "I . . . didn't have time to strategize."

"Well, it worked," Sweep said.

"No it didn't," said See.

"They're coming back," Evan replied. "They have travelers too."

The others watched him, expressionless, as he gathered up his scant belongings.

"You're leaving?" Sky asked.

"Of course I am. I'm not going to die here with you idiots."

"You keep telling us what a great strategist you are," said Caleb. "So help us find a way to beat them."

"How?" Evan jerked his head at Mercy. "She plugged up my timehole with kryptonite! I can't do shit about anything!"

"You have memories," Caleb told him. "You must have seen us beat them in other timelines."

"I've seen them *kill* you in other timelines." Evan zipped up his bookbag and slung it over his shoulder. "Have fun with that."

"Hey!" Mercy blocked him in the aisle. "Be a man for once."

"Forget him," Amanda said. "He's right. He can't help."

She clutched Sky's arm. "Make your platform and get as many people out of here as you can. Sweep, keep her shifted. Shroud—"

"I can't hide them in daylight," the young lumic insisted.

"Try." Amanda gestured to Caleb. "Get Mother to the castle, *fast*. We still have three people there and they'll need a quick exit."

"What are you going to do?"

"I'll hold off the Jades when they get here," she said. "They're mostly after me, anyway."

"How do you know that?"

Amanda's expression turned grim. "Long story."

She noticed Evan still lingering by the exit. He stumbled back down the aisle and aimed his befuddled expression at Amanda. "I think I know how to beat them."

"I told you—"

"I heard your plan. It's shit. If you want to stop these guys, I have a way. But you have to do everything I tell you *when* I tell you, no questions asked. You hear me?"

He saw the deep hesitance in Amanda's eyes. "You have to trust me. It's our only way out of this."

Amanda could hear her sister in her head, reminding her of every horrible thing he'd done. How in God's name was Amanda ever supposed to trust him, especially now that his powers were jammed and he only had hunches to work with?

She took a nervous look at her fellow orphans, then nodded her head at Evan. "What do you need me to do?"

FOURTEEN

Zack checked the clock on his handphone screen and cursed the Scarlet Sabre again. Of all the reasons to bemoan a group of terrorists, "tardiness" seemed rather trivial. But he'd been pacing around Ceannaideach for twenty-two minutes without a clue as to what the Sabres were planning. Would they come in good faith? Would they charge in, guns blazing? Or would they skip the whole meeting out of caution? All Zack knew was that they had to decide fast. It was just a matter of time before the British checked in on their missing agents.

He peeked through a crack in the eastern wall. "I don't think they're coming."

"They'll be here," Melissa said.

"We should have brought doughnuts. No one says no to doughnuts."

"Just be patient." Melissa crouched on the grass and rummaged through her shoulder bag. "We have something they want more than pastries."

Whistler smiled at Zack from the other side of the room. "She's right. I'm one of the Sabres' brightest stars. People join up just to fight alongside me."

Zack sneered at him. "Humble bastard, aren't you?"

"Just stating the facts." Whistler covetously watched Melissa as she lit up a hand-rolled cigarette. "Got an extra one for me, love?"

"I'm not your 'love.' Go buy your own."

"Well, that's just mean."

"No meaner than the rift bomb you left in Southampton," she reminded him. "The one that killed thirteen children and maimed another six."

Zack grimaced at the man. "You sick fuck."

Whistler smirked. "If you're looking to shame me, you're wasting your breath. I'm a choirboy compared to the tea-drinkers."

"So it's okay to murder kids because the British are even worse."

"You don't win wars by being nice, Jack."

"It's *Zack*. And that's bullshit. It's what sociopaths say to excuse themselves."

Whistler waved him off. "Ah, what do you know? You're American. You don't even know what combat looks like."

"*I* do," said Zack.

"He does," Melissa agreed. "He's lived through conflicts you can't even imagine."

Whistler studied Zack skeptically. "You may have scars and a clockwork hand, but I know soft eyes when I see them." He jerked his head at Melissa. "*She's* killed people. That skinny girl in the other room's killed people. But you? You're a virgin. The eyes never lie, *Jack*."

"Uh-huh." Zack exited the room through the southern arch. He'd had quite enough of Whistler and his Robert Shaw impression. If anyone here was going to call him a milquetoast, he'd rather it be Stitch.

She stood in the light of the seaside window, her arms crossed in a knot. Her shoulders had become flecked with small white dots, a rash of stress tempis that Zack had seen a hundred times before on Amanda.

"This is all just a *balagan* waiting to happen," she said without looking at him.

"I'm guessing that's Hebrew for 'clusterfuck.'"

"It's Yiddish, but yes. We should call in the others."

Zack shook his head. "Too many people will scare off the Sabres."

"So Evan says. Have you heard from him lately?"

Now that Stitch mentioned it, the smug little prick had been surprisingly quiet. Zack had taken it as a blessing but now he was starting to wonder.

He reached for his transmitter, then froze at an anomaly behind Stitch. There was a faint but noticeable glimmer in the window, a barely perceptible ripple in the shape of a person.

"Get down!" Zack yelled. Stitch jumped out of the way, allowing Zack to fire a burst of temporis. Every dangling strand of ivy near the window aged six months in an instant.

Melissa rushed in through the archway, pistol raised. "What happened?"

"There was something in the window," Zack said. "But he was cloaked. I barely saw him."

Stitch climbed back to her feet and studied Zack's damage, a perfect ring of brown and withered flora. "Shit, man. You could have—"

A torrent of blood suddenly sprayed from her shoulder. She arched her head back and screamed. Both Zack and Melissa could see the spectral figure behind her, a shimmering blur in the sunlight.

Melissa fired a bullet into the air behind Stitch, only to watch it ricochet off invisible armor. The impact briefly disabled the lumiflage, enough for Melissa and Zack to get a glimpse of shiny jade plating.

"Shit," Zack muttered.

Of all the people he was expecting to fight today, the Jades were low on the list. And though her face was obscured by her ornate helmet, Zack could guess from her build that it was the same woman he'd encountered in Mexico, the one who'd rifted his hand into a little black nub and stabbed Melissa through the chest with a tempic blade.

Now here she was in the Highlands in Scotland, back for more trouble, despite the fact that Peter had killed her. Theo had already warned that her story wasn't over. He'd even managed to divine her name, though Zack was too rattled to remember it.

"Joelle," Melissa shouted. "We know who you are. Show yourself!"

"And let Stitch go," Zack pleaded. "She's just a kid."

Joelle deactivated her lumic cloak and shot a skeptical look at Zack. "This 'kid' has killed more people than I have."

Zack couldn't tell what creeped him out more: the lime-green eyes behind her mask or the electronic distortion in her voice, as if she were speaking through an old radio.

"What are you doing here?" Zack asked. "Why are you attacking us?"

"Ask your wife."

"What?"

"It doesn't matter," said Melissa. She tossed her gun into the next room and raised her hands in surrender. "Whatever you want, we can negotiate."

Zack had never seen Melissa fold so quickly, and he didn't think for a moment that it was genuine. She was hatching a plan, which meant he had to stall for time.

"What does any of this have to do with Amanda?" he asked Joelle.

"She made one of my fathers angry."

"Your fathers," Zack repeated with seething resentment. "If you're talking about Azral and Semerjean—"

"Shut your mouth," Joelle hissed. "You're not fit to speak their names!"

"They destroyed our world!" Zack yelled. "Everyone we knew and loved. Did they happen to mention that part to you?"

"They told me everything," said Joelle. "They *showed* me everything. I've flown through the skies of their beautiful world and it's greater than anything you can imagine. It's the only Earth worth saving."

"Holy shit."

"You doubt me, Trillinger?"

In point of fact, he very much doubted her, but that wasn't what he was reacting to. It only just now occurred to him what Melissa did with her pistol.

A gunshot rang out from the next room over, sending a bullet through a hole in the wall. Melissa had taken a big risk tossing her weapon to Whistler, but he ended up doing exactly what she hoped he would.

Well, *almost* exactly. Though the man was an accomplished killer, eight months of imprisonment at the hands of the British had left him malnourished and shaky. Instead of putting a bullet through Joelle's eye, he nicked the flesh of her earlobe.

Joelle stumbled backward with a shout of surprise. Her blade retracted from Stitch's shoulder. As the young tempic fell crumbling to the weeds, Zack fired a second blast of temporis at Joelle.

But even in shock, the woman was quick. She fled to the east in a speedy streak and disappeared around the corner.

Whistler stumbled into the room, hang-jawed. "What the bloody hell was that?"

Melissa took her pistol back from him. "Don't ask."

"Christ almighty! I'm getting out of here before she comes back."

"No you're not." Melissa pointed her gun at him. "You're staying with us."

She tossed a quick look at Zack. "How is she?"

He knelt at Stitch's side and examined her shoulder. "Not good. I won't be able to heal her."

"Why not?"

"Look at her."

Melissa peeked as best she could while keeping her gun on Whistler. The skin around Stitch's wound had turned black and patchy, the telltale sign of a temporal rift. If the damage was only surface-level, she'd probably survive with a scar. Otherwise, she was a goner.

Stitch clutched Zack's arm, frantic. "Don't let me die here."

"Stitch . . ."

"Please. My family needs me."

Zack squeezed her hand, heartbroken. For all their many differences, there were times like this when he could look deep inside the soul of the girl and see himself looking back. They were both driven by a need to belong—a need for a *purpose*, especially after the universe had gone out of its way to flaunt its senseless nature. They were both crazy and strong in all the same flavors. Siblings of the fractured spirit.

"You're not dying," Zack promised her. "Not today."

"Makes two of us," said Whistler. "So either come up with a plan or let me go."

"Shut up." Melissa stashed her transmitter. "I can't reach Caleb or anyone else."

Zack's stomach clenched. If Amanda really did piss off the Pelletiers, then she and the others were in trouble. But there was nothing that he or Melissa could do for them. Not while Joelle was still out there.

"I have an idea," he said. "But we'll have to keep close and move real—"

A hot gust suddenly blew through the room, knocking Zack flat on his back. His senses went dull for a fraction of a second. By the time he came around, he was completely disoriented. Whistler paced the floor in a hot new panic while Melissa tore a strip off her jacket.

"What . . . what happened?"

"She cut you," Melissa told Zack. "Stay still."

Zack suddenly registered a pain in his left arm, the last good one he had. Thankfully, the limb was still complete and attached, but it had a long new gash along the back of the wrist, from the base of Zack's hand to the crook of his elbow.

"Oh God . . ."

"Let me dress it," Melissa said.

"No." Zack knew the game Joelle was playing. She was toying with her prey, prolonging their torment. That gave Zack a little more time to get the upper hand.

He clambered to his feet, then extended his arms to the sides. Radiant cones of temporis emerged from his flesh and metal hands.

"What are you doing?" Melissa asked him.

"Aging the air," Zack said. "If she comes at us in either direction—"

"—she'll get rifted," Melissa realized. She peeked through the southern exit. "Clever."

Mostly, Zack thought. He didn't have the finesse to make a panoramic shield, so his trick only worked in tight spaces. If they crossed into a larger room or tried to leave the castle, it'd be open season all over again.

Melissa looked to Whistler. "We're moving. Pick up the girl and stay close to us."

"What do I look like, an ambulance?"

She threatened him with the gun. Whistler rolled his eyes. "I was safer with the limeys."

As soon as he had Stitch secure in his arms, Melissa led the group south. They moved in a cluster down the narrow stone corridor, with Zack providing cover from both sides. His temporal energies wreaked havoc on the plant life. Crabgrass died in even waves while his blood trail dried immediately in his wake.

Melissa checked his wound, then the color of his skin. His face was turning paler by the second. "Zack . . ."

"I'm fine," he insisted. "You want something to worry about, worry about that."

Melissa followed his gaze to the chamber ahead, the old great hall in the center of the castle.

"Terrific," she said. "Suggestions?"

Zack was starting to feel the strain of his blood loss, a queasy lightheadedness that made his legs buckle. "We stick to the wall till we get to the stairs."

"Stairs?" Whistler asked. "Stairs to where?"

"The undercroft," said Melissa.

Zack could easily hear the doubt in her voice and fought the urge to remind her of her own recent gambit. She'd tossed her gun at a terrorist on the dark horse chance that he'd do the right thing with it, and he did.

Still, Zack was going to have to think up a new trick and fast, because he was the only one in the group who had even the slightest hope of stopping Joelle.

As they inched along the edge of the great hall, Melissa activated the flashlight on her handphone. The stairs to the cellar had been almost completely reclaimed by nature, a slick green ramp of moss and weeds sloping down into the dark unknown.

"Hope you're right about this," Melissa said to Zack.

"Hope I am too."

Zack's knowledge of castles could barely fill a pamphlet, and had been twisted by years of romanticized media. He'd been expecting a maze of crypts and candelabras but the basement of Ceannaideach was just an overgrown cave, carpeted in lichen and garnished by foul-smelling fungal patches. Worse, Zack couldn't see any other exits. He'd steered them all into a hopeless mess. A *balagan*, as Stitch had called it.

Zack only had half a moment to hear rapid footsteps before Joelle came back in a shifted streak and weaved deftly around his temporal shield. By the time she finished cutting him, his prosthetic hand lay in pieces. Only the wires remained dangling from his broken stump. The rest was just wreckage at the base of his foot.

Melissa shined her light on him. "Zack!"

"Goddamn it!" Zack fell to his knees, then yelled into the darkness. "Did they teach you to be cruel or did you learn that yourself?"

Melissa clutched his shoulder. "Look—"

"Stay behind me!" Contrary to appearances, he actually had a plan, and part of it involved looking pathetic. Admittedly, it was a Method act. He felt sick enough to puke and mad enough to cry, and his addled mind kept plaguing him with images of Amanda's murder.

"What were you before all this?" he shouted at his unseen enemy. "A teacher? A nurse? A cartoonist?"

His question earned him nothing but silence. Clearly Joelle was done talking. "That's okay," Zack said. "You don't have to answer. Your voice creeps me out anyway."

He turned off his protective temporis. "Just get it over with, you green-eyed freak. Earn a Milk-Bone from your masters."

Whistler cocked his head, gobsmacked. "*That's* your plan? I could have—"

Melissa shushed him, to Zack's relief. She could see that he needed concentration. The lumics had lumis and the tempics had tempis, but the turners and swifters both worked with the same magic. If Zack put his mind to it, and if luck prevailed, he could sense the timeshifted aura of a swifter in motion and know exactly which direction she was coming from.

You have one shot at this, he warned himself. *Don't miss.*

Soon he felt her temporal energy like a hissing wind. Joelle was looping around at him from the east-northeast but was throwing her sound to confuse him. She must have seen right through his fake surrender and was prepared for a last-second trick.

But are you ready for this? Zack thought as he raised his stumpy hand in her direction. He fired every last bit of power he had, a geyser blast of accelerated temporis that hit Joelle square in the chest. Everything within five feet of her was aggressively aged, a year and a half's worth of natural decay condensed into a fraction of a second. By the end of Zack's move, there was no one left to attack him, just a bleached white skeleton in a tarnished jade suit, with nothing to hold the pieces together.

Whistler gasped as dozens of bones and armor pieces came rolling into Melissa's light field. "Holy Christ!"

Melissa clutched Zack's shoulder. "You did it."

"I did it," he feebly replied. A part of him wanted to howl in triumph, to grab Whistler by the collar and gloat in his face. *How do my eyes look* now, Jack? *They still seem soft to you?*

But even in victory, he couldn't shake the fact that his first true kill was an orphan. There was one less survivor from his world today.

Except hadn't they seen her die before?

Melissa looked to the jawless skull on the floor and suddenly shared Zack's concern. "I don't think she's coming back from that."

Zack narrowed his eyes at Joelle's empty sockets. "She better not."

By half past three, nearly everyone in Dunwoodie had stepped outside their cottages to enjoy the summer weather. It was the most beautiful Saturday they'd had in weeks, with coastal winds that were as warm as a kiss and a clear blue view of the sea. While the children played their dizzy games, the grown-ups sat on their patio chairs and basked in the pleasant breeze. Some mingled with their next-door neighbors. Some brought their busywork outside. Some simply read the local paper while nursing a pint of lager.

Only a few people noticed a peculiar occurrence at the northern edge of town: eight green and vaguely human shapes hovering motionless above the old cinema. The sight was hardly cause for alarm these days, with flying *whosits* and mechanical *whatsits* bounding all about the kingdom. Even here in the backwoods of Aberdeenshire, UFOs were a daily occurrence.

But then at 3:32, an explosion of light enveloped the invaders, a spherical white flare that burned spots in the eyes of all the townsfolk. Everyone shrieked and threw themselves to the ground, but the blast merely removed the floating green strangers, along with a chunk of the cinema's roof.

The locals of Dunwoodie blinked at each other dazedly, as if their spouses or cousins could explain what just happened. *Oh, that? Dinnae worry. It was just a Haitian woman from an alternate Earth teleporting her enemies to London.*

They barely had a minute to speak among themselves before a brand-new spectacle appeared in its place: a hovering disc of fiery light, fifty feet from top to bottom and thin as a paper plate. Eight figures emerged from the whiteness in unison, the same flying green oddities that had just been whisked away. Their angry eyes were aimed straight downward at the ruins of the Milligan Cinema.

"Be careful," Semerjean warned the Jades, a spectral whisper in their ears. "They've had time to prepare a defense."

The theater was impenetrably dark on the inside, despite the sun shining down through the missing roof. One of the Jades cast a cone of solis at the darkness, dispelling Shroud's illusion and exposing every inch of the interior. There were no orphans or Gothams to be seen inside, just eleven British captives and a fresh new hole in the floor of the lobby. It seemed the girl named Shade had used her mortis to burn an underground escape tunnel.

"Don't follow them," Semerjean told the Jades. "They're trying to limit your mobility. Stay together and keep to the sky. You have everything you need to find them."

He was right. All it took was a bit of concentration to sense Amanda's presence, a powerful aura of tempis and aeris moving east beneath the surface. Her progress was awkward and almost embarrassingly slow. The woman made a far better bird than a gopher.

Six of the Jades fired tempis into the ground, sending a dozen writhing tendrils in pursuit of her. They moved like needles through the earth, breaking every rock and water pipe in their path. Within moments, they'd latched on to Amanda and yanked her frame upward. The poor thing wasn't even a gopher now. Just a wriggling fish on their lines.

It wasn't until the Jades caught their first glimpse of their victim that they realized the trick that had been played on them. The woman in their tendrils wasn't Amanda at all, but a solid mass of aeris in her shape. Sky had taken a page out of Heath's playbook and fashioned her own living decoy.

"Behind you!" Semerjean yelled from his remote refuge, though his warning came a moment too late.

Amanda's great white fist barreled down from the west, knocking all eight Jades to the ground. She'd been hiding just beneath the surface of the grass, withholding every ounce of her power to avoid detection. Now her arms were back, her wings were spread, and she didn't stick around for an encore. The only goal now was to get the Jades to follow her, away from her people and toward the coastal bluffs.

And then what? Amanda asked herself. Evan hadn't had time to explain the next step. All he told her was to keep the pricks occupied.

The locals hurried en masse toward the eastern side of the village, all scrambling to get a better look as Amanda flew toward the sea. After two straight minutes of inexplicable chaos, they'd finally caught a glimpse of something familiar. It was her—*her!*—the Angel of London, the woman everyone in the world was talking about.

She dipped and teetered awkwardly while the eight blokes she'd clobbered recovered themselves. Within seconds they were back in the sky, shooting after her like missiles.

"There they go," said Caleb.

Here they come, thought Amanda. Evan had warned her that they'd catch up to her quickly. They were faster than her by multitudes, but she still had a hidden advantage.

Amanda had barely made it past the lip of the cliff when the Jades boxed her in from all sides. She came to a floating stop and took a quick peek down below. It was at least a one-hundred-yard drop to the shore of the North Sea, with a hostile beach that was all rocks and breaking waves. Amanda wouldn't survive the fall, not even with tempic armor.

She faced the Jades with outstretched wings, her teeth gritted tight in defiance. "Okay. Now what?"

From the looks on their faces, they didn't know either. There was a reason Amanda was flying so clumsily, and they only just realized why. She'd been carrying a passenger the entire time, a woman who presented . . . complications.

Mercy narrowed her eyes at her floating foes. "Yeah, that's right. *Try* something."

By herself, the young Gotham meant nothing to the Pelletiers. But the blossoming fetus in her womb—the passenger inside the passenger—was significantly important.

A spectral sigh filled Amanda's ears. "You really think this'll stop them?" asked Semerjean.

"Seems to be working so far." She glanced around at the surrounding Jades, with their eerie green irises and networks of black veins. "These were normal people once."

"So were you," said Semerjean. "Now look at you."

"You turned them into slaves."

"Don't be facile. They're not even servants."

"Then what are they?"

"Progeny," Semerjean indignantly insisted. "We consider them part of the family."

"The part that kills on your command."

"Funny you should mention that, because there are a dozen ways for them to end you right now, without harming a hair on Mercy's head. I'm not sure you thought this plan through."

Semerjean chuckled at the twitch in Amanda's eyes. "But then it wasn't your plan, was it?"

Unfortunately, it was Evan's, and now Amanda saw the punchline. He had bought enough time to make his own escape while throwing Amanda and Mercy to the wolves.

"You keep putting your faith in the wrong people," Semerjean said, "while continually shunning the right ones. I'm going to give you one more opportunity, Amanda. Your very last chance to save yourself and your sister."

Amanda's voice dropped a cold octave. "You want me to give you Ioni."

"That was the old offer. The terms have changed. Now the price of your life is Ioni and a child. Guess you'll be spending more time with Peter again."

Amanda's tempis turned coarse and jagged, enough to chafe at Mercy's skin.

"You okay?" she asked Amanda. "What's happening?"

"Nothing."

"Liar," Semerjean teased. "What happens next is in your hands. I can order my children to kill you, or I can order them to retreat. What'll it be?"

Amanda looked up the coast at the ruins of Ceannaideach, where Zack and Melissa still waited. She didn't think for a moment that they'd been spared from Semerjean's wrath. If there wasn't a Jade attacking them, then it was probably Azral and Esis.

This was pretty much inevitable, her inner Zack told her. *We've been on a crash course with the Pelletiers for two years. It was always going to end like this.*

Semerjean clucked his tongue impatiently. "Amanda . . ."

The Zack in her head smiled fiendishly. *But you can really piss them off before they kill you.*

"Amanda, what do I tell my children?"

She looked away from Ceannaideach and shot a contemptuous sneer at the Jades. "Tell them they need better parents."

"Now!" Evan yelled.

He stood in a tunnel in the middle of the cliff, hidden from view by a veil of Shroud's darkness. Ten feet to his left, Mother stood snugly between two swifters. While Sweep enveloped her in his temporal field, Caleb accelerated them both in a larger time bubble. The Gothams called it a "piggyback-shift," a maneuver as strong as it was dangerous. At roughly 150x speed, Mother had minutes to plan her next portal attack. This time, she hit the Jades individually.

This time, she only teleported their heads.

Amanda flinched at the gruesome chain of destruction, a rapid-fire string of decapitations that played out over a half-second. Though the eighth and final Jade was quick enough to dodge Mother's portal, Mercy hit him with a solic blast and stripped him of all his aeris. He fell through the sky with his headless brethren and crashed against the rocky shore.

Mercy looked down, wide-eyed, at the carnage on the beach. "Holy fuck. We did it."

Amanda's muscles remained locked in anticipation, just waiting for Semerjean's next move. She scanned the area for new signs of trouble, but all she could see was the crowd on the cliffs: hundreds of hapless bystanders, all slack-faced and hopelessly baffled.

Caleb beckoned her from the mouth of the tunnel. "Come on!"

Amanda swooped down toward the others. Mercy barely had a moment to reconnect with terra firma before her brother and Caleb hugged her.

Mother stumbled toward Amanda, a trickle of blood oozing out of each nostril.

"You okay?" Amanda asked her.

"I could very easily vomit."

Amanda weakly nodded. "Same."

Sky peeked down over the edge of the tunnel, at the mangled, bloody corpses of the Jades. "Wow. I can't believe that worked. I . . ."

One by one, the others turned to Evan, the mastermind behind their victory. Every single part of the plan, from the tunnels to the decoy to the double-shifted traveler, came from his warped brain, without a shred of help from the future. He'd put the whole thing together in less than a minute and he'd gotten it all right in one take.

Amanda would have expected him to be smarmy under the circumstances. Instead he met her gaze with heavy eyes, an expression so raw and uncharacteristic that she barely recognized him.

"There, uh . . ." Evan cleared the choke in his throat. "There are gonna be consequences for what we just did."

"I know," Amanda said with a sigh. She looked to the north, where Ceannaideach stood just out of view. "Will someone with a radio please call my husband?"

By the time Zack climbed back into the sunlight, Melissa could see his dire state. His skin had lost all semblance of color and his breaths were short and labored. If he lost much more blood, he'd fall into hypovolemic shock, and that would be the end of him.

Melissa helped him up the last few steps, then guided him to the nearest wall. "Sit down. Keep your arm raised."

Zack shook his head, his eyelids fluttering chaotically. "Gotta help Amanda."

"You know as well as I do that she can handle herself."

Whistler carried Stitch up the steps and indelicately placed her next to Zack. "How many freaks like these are out there?"

Melissa tore bandage strips from her windbreaker jacket. "One of them just saved your life."

"Yeah, by stripping a woman to her bones."

"You're the last person to—"

"Shhh!" Whistler looked to his left, wide-eyed. "Someone's coming."

Melissa readied her gun. She'd heard it too, the faint sounds of footsteps and rustling cloth. There were multiple people moving through the corridors, but who were they with? The British? The South Africans? *The Pelletiers?* Or maybe . . .

The intruders stormed in through every arch and doorway: three dozen strangers armed with pistols and assault rifles. They were dressed in a motley assortment of gear, from cheap and functional sweatsuits to custom-made combat armor. The only thing they had in common were the bandanas around their lower faces, each one dyed an infernal shade of red.

Melissa dropped her gun and raised her hands in surrender. It seemed the Scarlet Sabre had finally arrived, and they didn't look all too happy.

Whistler laughed with loud relief, his arms stretched wide in triumph. "Lord almighty, am I happy to see you bastards. You have no idea what—"

A loud and sudden gunshot made Melissa jump. She felt a warm spray of wetness on her cheek. She feared for a moment that she got hit, until Whistler fell dead to the grass. One of his very own people had fired a clean shot between his eyes.

Melissa registered Whistler's frozen expression of horror before looking up at his killer. "I thought you were here to liberate him."

"And so I did," said the Sabre, a bald and muscular Scotsman in aviator sunglasses.

"Fine way to treat your friend."

"He was more than that. He was a brother. But then the British got into that thick head of his and turned him into their lackey."

Melissa struggled to catch up to the twist in Whistler's story. "It was a setup," she said. "They *wanted* you to rescue him."

The head Sabre nodded wistfully. "And take him back into our fold like a poison pill."

Melissa knew the British could be ruthless at times, but to sacrifice eleven of its own operatives, just to get a turncoat spy into the Sabres? Even for them, that was monstrous.

"If you knew it was a trap, then why did you come?" she asked the leader.

"Because we wanted them to know in very clear terms that we don't approve of their tactics." He gestured at Melissa, Zack, and Stitch. "But then you lot came and made a right mess of things."

He aimed his smoking rifle at her head. "Now before we put you all in the ground, you're gonna answer some questions."

Zack followed the conversation as best as he could from his wavering state of consciousness. Were the Violets here? Did they already announce themselves?

Stitch muttered something at his side. He turned his head toward her. "What?"

"A tempic." She raised a weak and quivering hand at the Sabres. "Over there. I feel her."

"Who *are* you?" the leader asked Melissa. "Don't lie to me, 'cause—"

"Monty Python!" Zack yelled.

Every Sabre in the hall paused in matching confusion. Zack pushed himself up to a standing position. "Princess Di."

The leader looked at Zack askance. "What in the bloody—"

"Come on. You know what I'm talking about. Harry Potter. Benny Hill. Terry Pratchett. Doctor Who."

The head Sabre pointed his rifle at Zack. "Enough of this—"

"Wait!" cried a voice in the back.

A figure moved across the hall in a streaking blur and stopped in front of Zack—a tall and slender woman in camo fatigues. She took off her shades and fixed her tense brown eyes on him.

"Doesn't prove a thing," she said in an elegant British accent. "You could have picked up those names from any one of my people."

"So quiz me," Zack said. "Ask me anything."

"Name one prime minis—"

"Margaret Thatcher."

"Holy shit."

Four more Sabres stepped forward from the pack: three young women of various creeds and a towering hulk of a white man.

At long last, the Violets of London were found.

Zack smiled at their stupefied expressions. "Been a while since you've met one of us, I take it."

"A long while," said the swifter. "How did you find us?"

"It took some doing," Melissa said. "We need your help on a very important matter."

"We already have our own fight to deal with."

"This one's bigger," Zack insisted. "And way more urgent."

"How big?" asked the one male Violet. "And how urgent?"

Zack was briefly thrown by the large man's dialect, as familiar as it was surprising. He'd expected all five Violets to be British by pedigree, but this one was as American as him.

"Nine and a half weeks," Zack told him.

"Is that another cultural reference?"

"It's how much time we have to stop this world from dying the same way ours did."

The Violets fell into a stunned silence. The swifter pulled down her bandana mask. "What's your name?"

"Zack."

"I'm Yasmeen." She swept her hand at the other four Violets. "That's Bobby and Zuri and Jia and Fang. And if what you say is true . . ."

Yasmeen lowered her head in dark rumination before looking at Zack again. "Then I guess we have something to talk about."

FIFTEEN

There was a forty-year period of Altamerican history that had been scrutinized, canonized, and dramatized more than any other. The textbooks referred to it as the Post-Cataclysm era. Among scientists, it was called the Pre-Temporal Age. But to scholars of American geopolitics, the years 1912 to 1952 were almost universally known as the Great Compression, and for good reason. The destruction of New York had prompted the United States to seal its borders and shed its external provinces. Hawaii, Alaska, the Philippines, Puerto Rico—all the annexed territories outside the mainland were cast aside as vulnerabilities and sold to the highest bidder. By the time the map settled, the U.S. had reverted to a single continuous land mass. One nation: unified, fortified, and truly indivisible.

But within a decade, the United States found itself in a precarious position. The temporal revolution of the 1950s had abruptly turned nickel, a crucial component of timebending devices, into a precious commodity. The U.S. had already exhausted its own supply, forcing it to supplicate itself to fair-weather friends like Australia and Brazil. The only way for the nation to secure an independent future was to buy a nickel-rich island in the northern Caribbean and mine it for everything it was worth.

The name of that island was Cuba, and it wasn't the first time the U.S. had seized control of it. But after fifteen years as a British Crown dependency and another ten years under Mexico's thumb, the Cuban government was all too happy to give the United States another chance. Their only condition was full American statehood. They refused to be an asterisk on another country's flag, and they had the leverage to get what they wanted.

And so in November of 1969, Cuba officially became part of the American Union, its only disjointed territory.

To say the transition had been difficult was an understatement at best. The nation's dyed-in-the-wool conservatives refused to accept the Cubans as citizens, while the Cubans had a hard time adapting to America's carnivorous capitalism. Developers swarmed upon the island like locusts, razing everything in their path to make room for new hotels. The more destitute locals were forced into tent camps, where they were schooled in mandatory English and trained to serve the new white overclass.

To this day, Cuba remained America's Home Away From Home™, a tropical island theme park that offered an exotic getaway without the risk of foreign travel. While vacationers of every income could build a trip to suit their budget, the wealthiest tourists flocked to Havana's legendary Sapphire Coast, where all the hotels had Spanish names and the rooms cost more than motorcycles.

Ofelia wandered the lobby of the Ciudad del Plata, her nose crinkled in aversion. The five-star family beach resort, part of the Silver City franchise of luxurious American hotels, was the most egregious attempt she'd ever seen to bottle up Cuba and sell it. Everything in this awful place, from the fake palm fronds to the whitewashed Latin "music," had been committee-designed by marketers who barely knew the first thing about Cuban culture. They'd Disneyfied an entire nation, and Ofelia never felt more disgusted.

A concierge with a pencil-thin mustache noticed Ofelia and approached her. "Is there something I can help you with, *señora*?"

Señora, Ofelia thought with a scoff. The man was as Latin as mayonnaise dip, and he only wanted to help her to the exit. She was practically a vagrant in her five-and-dime tank top, the cheap pair of jeans that Integrity had bought in bulk for the orphans.

She gave the concierge a genteel smile. "Just looking around. I was born in Havana. It's my first time back in years."

"How nice," he said without an audible trace of sincerity. "I hope your visit brings back pleasant memories."

Ofelia stifled a black laugh. There was nothing here to remind her of the Havana she knew, but that was probably a blessing in disguise. Her father had turned her childhood into hell on Earth, a twelve-year string of perpetual abuse that had scarred her on every level. If it hadn't been for the strength of her dear brother Jury, she would have never left Cuba alive.

She proceeded to scan the ground-floor amenities until she found the Bacuranao Room, an ornate and spacious conference hall that hosted everything from bar mitzvahs to corporate retreats. In twenty-six hours, it would be the site of Merlin McGee's press conference, which was the only reason she was here. Theo was convinced that someone would try to kill Merlin in this room, a prognostication that Merlin himself refuted. Ofelia wasn't sure which augur to believe: the one she knew or the one *everyone* knew.

She entered the massive, sunlit chamber and found her teammate in a marble alcove. Eden paced between the doors of the men's and women's restrooms, embroiled in what appeared to be an extremely tense phone call.

"Don't put this on me. I *asked* you not to tell him. Now all the—"

Eden closed her eyes impatiently. "Noah. *Noah*. I know he's your dad, but he's also a clan elder. Now all your people are going to find out, which means all *my* people will."

She spotted Ofelia out of the corner of her eye and did a nervous double-take. "I have to go."

Eden closed her handphone. "How much of that did you hear?"

"It's not my business."

"How much?"

"I heard enough," Ofelia admitted. "If you're talking to your boyfriend and if you're talking about secrets—"

"Look—"

"—then I can only assume you're pregnant."

Eden pulled Ofelia into the ladies' room and addressed her in hurried Spanish. "I don't want anyone to know, okay? You see all the fuss they're making about Hannah."

"I won't say a word," Ofelia assured her in kind. "I told you it's not my business."

"Thank you." Eden rubbed her brow with metal fingers. "Amanda warned me this would happen if I dated a Gotham."

"I assume you were careful."

"*Extra* careful, every time. This is the last thing we wanted."

Ofelia chewed her lip in thought. "Maybe the Pelletiers messed with your protection."

"There's no maybe about it," Eden said. "I'm six weeks in. The doctors confirmed it."

She met her own gaze in a full-length mirror and vented a bitter laugh. "I just liked Noah and I wanted to be with him. I figured we'd all be dead in two years anyway."

Eden turned away from herself, her voice cracked and trembling. "Stupid, stupid, stupid."

Ofelia wished she knew the right thing to say, but glad-handing was never her strong suit. If anything, she was the kind of person to tell someone just how screwed they were.

And she believed Eden was very, very screwed.

"Anyway." Eden straightened her blouse, then seamlessly reverted to English. "We still have a job to do."

Ofelia followed her back into the Bacuranao Room, her phone camera primed and ready. In truth, she had no idea what to look for, but Eden certainly did. In less than two minutes, she managed to identify a dozen security weaknesses—every bomb-size nook, every sniper-friendly window.

"How do you know this stuff?" Ofelia asked her.

"I never told you what I did on the old world?"

"No. What were you?"

"A cop."

Ofelia was as surprised as she was unnerved. Her brother had been a policeman in San Diego. Now somehow here in another world's Cuba, her memories of him felt fresher. The pain of his loss cut deeper. Why the hell did she ever volunteer for this mission?

"You never told me what you were," Eden said. "On the old world."

Ofelia looked up at the pyramid skylight, then snapped a photo of it just to look busy.

"Nothing," she replied in a dark and somber monotone. "I was pretty much nothing."

Thirty years ago, in the grassy plains of southern Ireland, there had lived a tight-knit clan of cattle ranchers who'd been harboring a secret for decades. Some of them could see the future in its branching variations. Some could alter the flow of time. Some cast light from the tips of their fingers and some cast something harder.

None of the ranchers had particularly wanted their talents, a hereditary curse of their forebears. They'd all had at least two parents or grandparents who'd been conceived in New York around the time of the Cataclysm and had been genetically altered *in utero*. Those first timebenders might have eventually joined the Gothams if their families hadn't been caught in the immigrant purge of the 1910s.

Deported to the land of their ancestors, the Irish chronokinetics eventually found each other and formed a clandestine community of their own. They settled into the farmlands of County Kerry, where they lived discreetly among the normal folk for two generations.

But time and technology had given the British sharp eyes, enough for them to catch a tempic mishap by satellite. In April of 1984, after several weeks of covert surveillance, the Ministry of Defence sent a squad of armored soldiers after the Irish timebenders, killing twenty of their number and capturing another eight.

Only two young cousins managed to escape the siege: Michael Bellew, a ten-year-old augur, and Peter Maginnis, a twelve-year-old traveler. With nothing more than a portal and the clothes on their backs, they fled a hundred and fifty miles across the countryside and disappeared into the slums of Dublin.

By the time Peter and Michael were stumbled upon by a family of traveling Gothams, they'd been living on their own for three years—a pair of hardened, filthy street urchins who'd become wary of smiling strangers.

But these Americans weren't ordinary strangers, and they were all too happy to prove it.

"We have all the same blessings," said the Gotham Olga Varnov, a kindly-looking woman who'd healed a sickly cat right in front of them. "Come back with us to America and live safely among your own."

So in October of 1987, the two young cousins left Ireland forever and became the first adopted wards of the Gothams. Though they were welcomed as sons into Olga's family, they chose to remain an independent entity: a two-member house with a self-chosen name.

From that point on, they were Peter and Michael Pendergen. And they were no longer cousins but brothers.

Ironically, it was Peter, the one who'd initially been more skeptical of the Gothams, who embraced his new life in Quarter Hill. Michael never truly found his place with the clan, with all their arcane rituals and heteronormative mandates. He left them behind five years ago and never looked back, only forward.

Now the whole world knew him as Merlin McGee, humanity's first indisputable prophet. The man was practically an American superhero. To a couple million of his biggest fans, he was the next best thing to—

"Jesus." Peter wandered through his brother's beachside mansion, one of the plushest and prettiest homes in Havana. Every window in the house flaunted paradise from a different angle—*true* paradise, not the beauty-in-a-can that came with the underland. The furnishings were elegant without being ostentatious, and every aspect of the interior, from the skylights to the cloud chairs to the meditative music, instilled a natural sense of tranquility.

Merlin watched him from the corner of the living room, an eyebrow arched in suspicion. "Is that a good 'Jesus' or a bad 'Jesus'?"

"You ever hear me use 'Jesus' the bad way?"

"All the bloody time. Was that a trick question?"

Hannah sat between Theo and Heath on a sofa, her hands clasped nervously around theirs. She knew that Peter and Merlin's rapport had gone sour in recent years, but she didn't know the extent of it until she watched them reunite. Their hug couldn't have possibly been more grudging, like two celebrity athletes trying to prove that their feud was behind them.

But when it came to his nephew, Merlin was nothing but sunshine. He drank in Liam with an awestruck grin. "Sweet mercy, boy. I can't get over how big you are. What are you, fifteen?"

"Sixteen."

"Sixteen! Next thing I know, you're gonna tell me you have a girlfriend."

Liam smiled patiently, as if his uncle hadn't foreseen the news. "I have a girlfriend."

"Well, I'll be chugged. Who's the lucky lass?"

"Sovereign Tam."

"What, she's het now?"

"She was always hetero. You're thinking of her sister."

"Ah, yes. Regal. Poor girl." He tossed a dark look at the orphans. "The clan has a bug up their arse about same-sexers. If you won't make them babies, you might as well be dead."

Hannah responded with a cynical snort. She knew a few other people like that. "Is that why you left?"

"More or less," said Merlin. "They wanted to make me into something I'm not. I had to be true to myself."

Peter scoffed under his breath. Merlin looked at him through slitted eyes. "You think I should have stayed and married someone?"

"Of course not."

"So you're hissing about the other stuff then."

"I'm just confused," Peter said. "You're an introvert. You hate attention. Now you're a stage-name popshot giving national press conferences. You call that being true to yourself?"

Merlin shrugged uncomfortably. "I did what I had to do."

"For who?"

Theo stood up from the sofa and joined Peter in his restless pacing. On the surface, there was little to dislike about Merlin, one of the most down-to-earth celebrities a person could ever meet. He looked like a hippie with his long paisley shirt, messy blond hair, and beachcomber's beard. And there was a kindness behind his deep blue eyes that was way too strong to be artifice.

But his recent history told a whole different story, a tale of selfishness and betrayal, plus an apathy toward the world that bordered on criminal. Theo shared every ounce of Peter's frustration, and did an equally bad job hiding it.

He sighed at Merlin. "Look—"

"Don't you start on me now."

"I wasn't going to criticize you."

"No. You're just gonna tell me to cancel my press conference."

"Someone *will* try to kill you tomorrow," Theo insisted. "How do you not see that?"

"The only thing I can't see is a reason for you to care."

"What do you mean?"

Merlin motioned to Peter and Liam. "They're my kin. They're entitled to worry. But you barely know me from Adam."

Theo finally understood what he was getting at. There was no point lying about it. "I'm not trying to save you for sentimental reasons. I think you have information we need."

"Like what?" Merlin challenged.

"If I knew that, I wouldn't need you. I just know you're in contact with Ioni."

"It's been more than a year since I heard from her."

"But she's told you things she hasn't told me," Theo said. "If it's something we can use—"

Merlin laughed. "You think I'm sitting on the answers to all the world's problems?"

"Are you?" Peter asked.

Merlin eyed him woundedly. "You've known me my whole life."

"I have," said Peter. "I also know that you put the entire clan at risk when you went public."

"I covered my tracks," Merlin insisted. "Built a brand-new past with airtight paperwork."

"And what about the future?" asked Theo. "You know what's coming better than anyone. But when Peter asked you for help—"

"Stop." Hannah rose to her feet. "You've been here five minutes and you're already ganging up on him. For God's sake, Peter, he's your brother. You haven't seen him in ages." She turned to Theo. "And *you*. You're the other most powerful augur in the world. Do you really think this is the best approach?"

Theo and Peter looked away from her, chastened but still annoyed.

"Also, I smell food in the kitchen," Hannah noted. "It smells *amazing*. What is that?"

"Bunch of stuff," Merlin idly replied. "My cooking's shite so I ordered from three places."

Heath shot up from the couch like a rocket. "I want to eat."

Liam raised his hand. "I second that."

"Thirded," said Hannah. "So we're all going to sit down and have a nice lunch. And when everyone's sufficiently fed and well-rested, we'll talk about the future and who wants to kill who."

· · ·

As Hannah had hoped, the conversation remained cordial. Merlin presided over the meal like a talk show host, throwing questions great and small at his guests. After mercilessly grilling Liam about Sovereign, he pressed Hannah for details on the culture of her Earth. How did people get by without temporis? How did the world treat folks who were openly nonhetero? He questioned Heath at length about the musical catalogue of the Beatles, a topic of fascination ever since the orphans made one of their songs famous. Merlin then steered the discussion onto the biggest news of the weekend: the white-winged London oddity that billions of people knew, but only a few hundred knew as Amanda.

"Don't worry," Merlin assured Hannah. "She only has one more day in the headlines."

"Yeah?" Peter asked. "Then what?"

"And then me," Merlin said. "By the time I'm done tomorrow, they won't be talking about angels anymore."

That was all the cue Theo needed to broach the thorny matter of the press conference. He opened his mouth to speak but Liam cut him off.

"You ever think about Mother Olga?" he asked his uncle out of the blue.

A heavy silence filled the room. In addition to being the clan's best healer, Olga Varnov had practically raised Peter and Michael. She was brutally killed last year on Red Sunday, during the Integrity massacre in the village. Liam had been right beneath her when she took her last breath. Her final act of selflessness was to shield him from the soldiers' bullets.

Merlin eyed Liam tensely. "Of course I think about her. What kind of question is that?"

"He's skirting around the bigger question," Peter said.

"That being?"

"Did you know what Integrity would do to us that day?" Liam asked. "I mean you see earthquakes and wildfires. Why didn't you see that?"

Merlin pushed away his lunch plate with a dull and morbid expression. "Because God's more predictable than us mere mortals."

"He's right," Theo told Liam. "Any future that's shaped by human decisions is loaded with extra variables. It's always changing on the fly, as fast as we change our minds."

"Do you see the end of the world?" Heath innocently asked Merlin.

"That's a human disaster," the prophet replied. "Assuming the Pelletiers are even human. But yes, I see it. And though there are folks at this table who refuse to believe it, I've been doing my bit to help."

"I want to believe you," Peter said. "It'd square up with everything I used to know about you. But whenever I ask for specifics—"

"Phone."

"What?"

Merlin jerked his head at Theo. "His phone's about to buzz."

Theo felt a vibration in his pocket and pulled out his handphone. The screen was alight with a new text from Cedric Cain.

Just heard from Melissa. The Violets have been found. The Opals are on their way to join them. Mission was a complete success. Rander came through.

Grinning, Theo read the message aloud. While Peter and Liam rejoiced at the news, Heath and Hannah remained reserved. Theo assumed they were caught on the part about Evan. It was indeed hard to picture him doing the right thing.

Merlin studied his guests' expressions. "So what does it all mean?"

"We only have one more orphan group to find," Theo said.

"And then?"

"I was hoping you'd tell me."

Merlin chuckled bleakly. "I don't see as much as you think I do."

"But you do see tomorrow."

Hannah batted Theo's arm. "I told you to save it for later."

"It *is* later." Theo shook a stern finger at Merlin. "Someone's going to kill you at that press conference. You know it as well as I do."

"Oh, do I now?"

"You think I'm wrong?"

"I think you're stuck on one future," Merlin said. "A splinter possibility that's been haunting me for a year and a half."

"What are you talking about?" Peter asked.

"Do you know what it's like to be a world-famous augur? Everyone wants a piece of me. Governments are itching to study my brain. Criminals are scheming to make me their pet oracle. There are a thousand folks right here in Havana who'd club me for next week's lottery numbers. Every time I leave the house, I see my potential death. It's just part and parcel of being Merlin McGee. I know the risks and I live with them."

"Why?" Liam asked. "What do you get out of all this?"

Merlin slouched in his chair and sighed. "I don't have the colors to paint that picture for you. But by sundown tomorrow, I will."

Peter eyed him dubiously. "What on earth are you planning, Michael?"

"You're just gonna have to trust me."

"I'm trying, but you don't make it easy."

"Then try harder," Merlin snapped. "'Cause if there's anyone on this world who owes me faith, it's you, Peter Maginnis."

Peter swapped a look with his son, an expression so pained and complicated that Theo barely knew how to process it. Zack was the closest thing he'd ever had to a brother, and that bond only ran two years deep. What Peter and Merlin had stretched all the way back to their childhood, to a tribe that no longer existed. They were the last two survivors of their own mini-apocalypse, which made them more orphan than Gotham.

"All right," Peter told his brother. "But we're still gonna keep an eye on your press conference. If we see even one—"

"Phone," said Merlin.

"What?"

This time it was Hannah who got the text message. Ofelia and Eden had finished their reconnaissance and wanted to know where to meet up.

Merlin graciously invited the team to stay at his house, as he had plenty of room for all of them. Though Hannah cringed at the thought of more family drama, the rest of the day was a pleasure. She soaked in a hot tub with Ofelia, took a walk on the beach with Theo, sang old-world duets with Heath in the living room, and then played billiards with Eden. At sunset, she gorged on an exotic take-out dinner: a Cuban/Chinese fusion dish that tasted better than anything she'd ever had on this world. Unfortunately, the spiced meat didn't agree with her pregnancy, and she went to bed early with nausea.

By the time Hannah woke up at a quarter to midnight, her companions had retired to their rooms. She could hear Peter snoring through one of the doors, and felt a sudden nostalgia for their time together. In a more daring state of mind, she might have crept into his bed and spooned him, but their arrangement was over. The baby was made. Any ancillary affection would just complicate things.

As Hannah walked down the plush carpet stairs, she heard Merlin's voice in the kitchen. He spoke entirely in monologue, in words she couldn't make out until she was halfway down to the living room.

"—this next part will be the hardest. But I've seen the string with my own eyes and I know how the story ends. We win."

As Hannah drew closer, Merlin shuffled in his seat. "Hannah's here. Gotta go."

She stepped into the light of the kitchen and found him sitting alone at the table, his handphone facedown in front of him.

"I'm sorry," said Hannah. "I didn't mean to interrupt you."

"No worries, love. I was already done." Merlin motioned to the chair across from him. "Have a seat."

Hannah blinked at the tall glass of orange juice he'd already poured for her, the very thing she'd come downstairs to get.

She sat in the chair, astounded. "Damn, you're good. You make Theo look like an amateur."

"I've had the sight my whole life. He's only had it two years."

"True."

"He does wear me down though," Merlin confessed. "Forgive me for saying."

Hannah smirked. "He can get intense."

"Yeah, just like my brother. All hammers and nails."

"What?"

"Something Mother Olga used to say. 'When it comes to fixing problems, men are all hammers and nails. It's women who know how to do the soft mending.'"

Hannah laughed. "I like that."

"Yeah." Merlin's smile went flat. "But Peter carried me through some rough years in Dublin. His strength kept me alive."

"I'm sure your foresight kept him alive too."

"More than once, but still . . ." His phone buzzed with a media call. He switched it into silent mode and stashed it in his pocket. "It hurts the way he looks at me now, like I'm nothing but a disappointment to him."

Hannah nodded sympathetically. "I used to get that look from my sister all the time. Drove me nuts."

"But it got better?"

"Oh my God, a thousand times better. It hasn't been an issue for ages."

"What did it take to fix it?" Merlin asked.

A dark laugh escaped her. "The end of the world."

"Lovely." Merlin fetched a beer from the refrigerator and popped the cap. "So far, the apocalypse has only driven us apart."

"She put you up to it, didn't she?"

"Who?"

"Ioni. This whole Merlin McGee thing was her idea."

Merlin took a long swig of beer before responding. "We hashed it out together."

"Why?"

"I can't tell you until after the press conference." He shrugged at Hannah's visible chagrin. "The future's a fragile construct, love. I speak too soon, and it all comes crumbling."

Hannah sipped her orange juice. "I used to think it was just a Theo thing."

"Afraid not. It's a lonely life we augurs live."

"You don't have anyone?"

Merlin scoffed. "If folks knew I was gay, it'd be the end of my run. I need every bit of credibility I have."

Hannah shook her head bitterly. "This world really sucks sometimes."

"True," said Merlin. "But it's the only one we got."

He downed the rest of his beer and dropped the empty bottle into the zilcher. "Did Peter ever tell you how we chose the name Pendergen?"

"He told Mia," Hannah said. "Some literary thing."

"It's an Irish variation of Pendragon," Merlin explained. "As in Arthur, as in King."

"You liked those stories, huh?"

Merlin laughed. "Dear Lord, we were obsessed. Talked about it day and night. He always preferred the sword-and-shield types. I always liked the wizards."

Hannah nodded at the late but obvious realization. "Merlin."

"There you go."

"You have a dry and nerdy sense of humor. Zack would like you."

"I'm sorry I didn't get to meet him or your sister," said Merlin. "And I would have loved to meet Mia. The way Peter talks about her, it feels like I have a niece out there."

He studied Hannah with a canny smirk. "I'm sensing you and he have a different kind of—"

"Don't."

"Just saying what you both already know. It's nice."

Hannah scrambled to change the subject. "Can I ask you a loaded question?"

"Yes."

"Did you mean it when you said—"

"Yes," he repeated. "I don't have information that can help you, but I know plenty of stuff that can hurt. It's better to keep those bits to myself."

Hannah looked at Merlin anxiously. "You said 'we win.'"

"What?"

"Right before I came in here, I heard you say that you know how the story ends. 'We win.'"

Merlin stroked his beard in thought before replying. "I'm ninety percent sure this world will be saved."

Hannah was thrown by his optimism. "What makes you say that?"

"Because ninety percent of the job's gonna fall on Ioni's shoulders," Merlin said. "And I'm a hundred percent sure she's up to it."

"So what's the bad news, then?"

Merlin wandered over to the kitchen island. Hannah turned her chair to face him.

"You know my future," she said. "You saw it the minute you met me. My road ends with the Pelletiers, and there's nothing anyone can do about it."

Merlin shook his head uneasily. "I reckon there isn't."

"So tell me," said Hannah. "Give me the bad news and let me decide what to do with it."

Merlin paced the island's wooden edge, conflicted. He opened and closed his mouth three times before speaking.

"This world will be saved," he reiterated. "But it won't ever be the same. When all the dust settles in nine weeks and change, there won't be a place for people like us."

"Like us."

"Orphans, Gothams, Majee, Pelletiers, anyone who can do anything with time. Doesn't matter who we are or where we are. We're the cost of Ioni's cure."

While Hannah struggled to process that, Merlin moved behind her, clutched her shoulders, and breathed a gentle whisper into her ear.

"The road ends soon for all of us," he told her. "Do with that what you will."

SIXTEEN

By five P.M. on Sunday, while the other hotels on the Sapphire Coast prepared for the early dinner crowd, the Ciudad del Plata had been overtaken by newspeople: forty-two print journalists from the mainland states, twenty-nine radio reporters, three dozen lumivision news crews, and their *equipment* . . . Christ. Theo had never seen so many camera drones. They flew around each other at the front of the Bacuranao Room, a chaotic swarm of glass and metal orbs, each one the size of a basketball. For Theo, a two-time victim of government war drones, the sight was enough to revive old traumas. He imagined the cameras all going feral at once, sprouting gun barrels or chain-saw teeth before slaughtering everyone in the room.

A large and meaty hand gripped Theo's shoulder. "Sir?"

He turned around to a bald white man in a hotel uniform, one of Ciudad del Plata's many security guards. "Hi."

"This is a closed event," said the guard. "If you're not with the press—"

"I'm with Merlin." Theo rummaged through his pockets and retrieved a laminated card with his photo. "I'm a guest."

The guard studied the pass, expressionless, then radioed the main office. Theo supposed it was good that the guy was thorough. The more people looking out for Merlin, the better.

After confirming Theo's legitimacy, the guard returned his credentials. "Keep that pass where we can see it. And stick to the perimeter."

"Sure thing. Hey." Theo threw a quick look around the room. "You haven't seen anyone suspicious here, have you?"

"Besides you?"

"Besides me."

"Not yet. Is there something you know that we don't?"

Theo suddenly saw trouble in the guard's near future, a gray and creeping sickness that cut all his strings down to nubs. The man was riddled with cancer and almost certainly knew it. He had weeks to live at most.

"Just watching out for Merlin," Theo replied. "He says I worry too much."

The guard shrugged indifferently before resuming his patrol. "He's the augur. You're not."

Sadly, Theo was starting to agree. His foresight was all thumbs today, a jumble of inscrutable hints and hunches that either contradicted each other or made no sense. *The trouble will be coming from inside the room. No, outside! But the assassin will be a white man for sure, unless it's a Black man or a Black woman. If it's the woman, she'll be younger and she'll have a knife to Heath's throat. If it's the man, he'll be older and he'll take you to Japan.*

Confounded, Theo retreated to the back of the room and found Hannah standing alone by a generator. Like Theo and everyone else on the team, she was dressed in classy businesswear to help her blend in among the news professionals. She'd even tied her hair into a ponytail, a style that was so aggressively unlike her that Theo barely recognized her from a distance.

"You have really small ears," he noticed.

Hannah looked at him, blank-faced. "Is that what you came to tell me?"

"I was going to ask you to keep an eye on Heath."

"Why?"

"I had a vision of a woman threatening him."

"In here?"

"No. There were trees."

Hannah looked beyond the gaggle of reporters and saw Heath brandishing his guest pass to a guard. "That doesn't sound like a 'today' kind of problem."

"Probably not." Theo studied her tense, rigid jaw. "Are you okay?"

"I'm fine. Why?"

"I don't know. I've been getting weird vibes off of you and Eden."

"Yeah, well, I'm five weeks pregnant and I have small ears. Not sure what her deal is."

A press agent motioned to the security guards. They began to close every door to the room. The reporters stopped chattering and sat down in their chairs.

"It's starting," Theo said with a nervous breath. He felt like he was flying blind, and he hated every second of it. "I'm going to walk around a little more."

Hannah opened her mouth to say something, then stopped herself.

"What?" Theo asked her.

She looked to him with wavering resolve. "You saw the string with your own eyes, right? The one where we all win."

"Briefly. Why?"

"Who exactly did you see?"

"Melissa," said Theo. "As a very old woman."

"But you didn't see the rest of us."

"No." Theo eyed her suspiciously. "Hannah, what's going on? Did Merlin say something?"

The chamber fell into an overwhelming silence as the back doors opened and nine well-dressed people stepped into the camera lights. Theo had met Merlin's entourage an hour ago: his publicists, his managers, his lawyer, his physician, and a platinum blonde of no title at all, whose only job was to spark rumors that Merlin had a girlfriend. They filed into their chairs on a raised wooden dais while guards escorted the star of the show to the podium.

Merlin couldn't have looked less prepared for a press conference. Though he'd made some effort to tame his hair and beard, he'd come dressed as usual in his workaday clothes: a flowery short-sleeve button-down, baggy jeans, and a pair of black leather sandals that looked ready for the afterlife. His rough, unpolished touches only served to increase his credibility. To the American people, he was the anti-celebrity prophet, a welcome relief from the slick-talking, suit-wearing, fortune-cookie grifters who had previously dominated the augur trade.

The reporters wasted no time drowning Merlin in a cacophony of questions. "What can you tell us—" "What do you think—" "What do you know about the—" "—Angel of London—" "that Angel of London—" "—the mysterious 'angel' that was photographed in London?"

"People." Merlin raised his hands. "People, *please*. We're never gonna finish if you don't let me start."

He caught a quick glimpse of Peter and Liam, then anxiously looked away. "As I've said before a dozen times, I know nothing about that woman in London. She's as baffling to me as she is to you. But we have more important things to talk about. A new disaster's about to hit North California, the worst I've ever seen."

That was enough to silence the crowd. A hundred and thirty people stared at him intently, every living soul at the conference except one.

Heath stood in the rear corner of the Bacuranao Room, his tense eyes fixed on a utility door. Somewhere beyond it, at least thirty yards away, a solid mass of tempis walked around in the shape of a man. Heath could feel every molecule of its form, but sensed nothing of its creator. An unknown tempic was aping his gimmick, but who?

Merlin smiled at his docile audience. "Yeah. I thought that'd get your attention."

His quip only sparked a few chuckles. "Before I get into specifics," he said, "let me just say something. I've been doing this for a while now—eighteen months, but it feels like years. I don't like seeing the things I see. I don't like the thought of being wrong or, worse, being right and having no one listen to me."

Hannah and Theo were so caught up in what Merlin was saying that they didn't notice Heath leave the room. Even Ofelia and Eden, who'd been standing ten feet away from him, paid no mind to the boy as he tested the utility door. Its lock had been disabled, its hinges oiled silent. All it took was one touch for the door to swing open. Heath peered down the length of a concrete corridor and caught a glimpse of the tempic man before it ducked around a corner.

"Well, this time I've never been more sure that I'm right," Merlin told the press. "And I hope more than ever that you'll listen. On the fourth of October, nine and a half weeks from today, a catastrophe will strike the city of San Francisco—"

Three different reporters interrupted him with questions but Merlin waved them off. "The entire city and its outlying regions. Alcatraz. Daly City. Everything within five miles of Twin Peaks."

A young male reporter stood up in the front row. "Mr. McGee!"

"I'm talking *four million people* at risk."

"At risk of what?" the reporter asked Merlin. "If you're seeing an earthquake—"

"It's not an earthquake."

"Then *what*?"

Merlin steeled himself with a heavy breath. "A Cataclysm."

Theo and Hannah looked to each other, slack-jawed, as the whole room erupted in chaos.

Heath crept like a prowler down the long, narrow hallway, an army of Jonathans nestled ready inside his fingertips. Everything about this place felt suspiciously wrong, as if he'd stepped off the world of the normal-abnormal and stumbled into an even stranger realm.

You're walking into a trap, said a voice in Heath's head, the ever-present specter of the original Jonathan Christie. *Come on, buddy. You're smarter than this.*

He was no doubt right, but then Jonathan knew him better than anyone, enough to recite the First Law of Heath's Universe. When a burning mystery presented itself, Heath *had* to get to the bottom of it. Even if the answer was a Pelletier ambush, at least he'd be free of the question.

Heath rounded the corner of the L-shaped corridor and followed it forty yards to the exit. The door swung open as easily as the last one, revealing a courtyard arboretum that was almost off-putting in its manufactured beauty.

Corporate-pretty, Heath's mom would have called it. *Not people-pretty.*

There wasn't a soul to be seen among the trees and benches, just a large tempic man standing silently near a fountain. The creature crossed its arms expectantly, its blank eyes locked on Heath.

"So here we are," said a chipper female voice. "Thanks for coming."

Heath still had a firm enough grasp of reality to know that it wasn't the golem speaking. There was a woman behind a nearby tree, a young one from the sound of her.

"Who are you?" Heath asked. "What do you want?"

"I'm Meredith Graham and I'll tell you what I *don't* want."

She stepped out into view with her hands raised peacefully. "A fight."

Heath looked her up and down, unnerved. She was a tall and skinny twentysomething in a black leather longcoat and slacks—a wealthy woman from the looks of her, though she exuded enough goofiness to keep her from being corporate-pretty. Despite the fact that she was a fellow tempic, Heath didn't get the sense that she was an orphan. She couldn't have possibly been a Gotham either, as her skin was at least two shades darker than his.

Heath glanced back at the blank tempic man. "You made him."

"Yes. That's one thing we have in common." Meredith unsummoned her creature with a flick of the hand. "We both like telling white men what to do."

Her smile went flat at Heath's unamused reaction. "You always this uptight, kid?"

"I don't trust you."

"Probably wise," said Meredith. "And yet you came here all by yourself. Very brave. Not entirely smart."

A swifter looped around Heath in a blur and de-shifted right behind him, the cool, hard blade of a bowie knife pressed menacingly against his throat.

"Don't move," said the swifter. "If I see even a hint of tempis, I'll kill you."

Meredith sighed with guilt. "What my sister really means to say is 'Hi, I'm Charlene and I'm sorry to do this.'"

Charlene made no effort to play along. "We don't have time to be nice."

"You can at least try," said Meredith. "I mean *look* at him. He's adorable."

Heath struggled to keep his Jonathans inside of him as they scratched at the walls of his consciousness. Though they'd been walking and moving like men for a year, they were all still wolves at heart.

"You're here to kill Merlin," he said.

Meredith shook her head. "We couldn't care less about that walking sideshow. Our only business is with Theo."

Charlene pushed the knife against Heath's neck, a deft ounce of pressure that only barely broke the skin. "You better hope he gets here soon."

From the moment Merlin first uttered the word "Cataclysm," his press conference became the only show on lumivision. Soon every broadcast station in the United States had cut live to the Ciudad del Plata, decorating Merlin's screen image with alarmist banner graphics. ANOTHER CATACLYSM COMING! yelled the chyron of National-3. MILLIONS OF AMERICANS IN DANGER, said the overlay on Washington-10. The award-winning news team of San Francisco–5, who had more reason than most to be rattled by Merlin's announcement, took a denialist approach with their caption: AUGUR SPARKS PANIC OVER IMAGES IN HIS HEAD.

Merlin needed a full minute just to restore order in the room. *"Please,"* he implored the press. "One question at a time."

"How do you know it's a Cataclysm?" asked a print journalist.

"I saw a dome of light envelop the city and leave nothing but ash behind. Call it whatever the hell you want. Just don't be there when it happens."

"The last Cataclysm happened a century ago," a radio reporter reminded him. "Why now? Why San Francisco?"

"My visions don't come with explainers," Merlin testily replied. "I just know what I saw."

"What time will it strike?"

"It'll happen under the light of the sun. I'm guessing nine A.M. at the earliest."

A haggard old columnist in the front row eyed him cynically. "When you say four million people will die—"

"I said four million lives are at *stake*," Merlin stressed. "That's the one part of the future we control. If we all work together and clear out the city, we can see to it that no one dies."

The reporters once again fell into a shouting cross-match. "How do you expect to evacuate a whole—"

"Aren't you afraid that the panic will—"

"What do you foresee of the economic impact—"

"What if you're wrong about all of this?"

Theo turned his back on the bedlam. "Shit."

Hannah watched him guardedly. "You see any of the stuff he's talking about?"

"I see an empty city," Theo said. "But no—"

He suddenly glimpsed a repeat premonition: a vision of Heath with a knife at his throat. The image was so clear and proximate that he wasn't even sure it was the future anymore.

"Oh no. Heath . . ."

Hannah scanned the crowd for signs of him, her eyes getting wider by the second. "Shit."

By the time they circled around to the other side of the room, their teammates had noticed Heath's absence. The six of them converged at the restroom alcove, their collective gaze fixed on the utility corridor.

"You sure he went that way?" Ofelia asked Theo.

"Positive."

"Could be a diversion," Peter warned. "To draw us away from Michael."

Eden looked over her shoulder at Merlin. "It'd be a smart play."

Hannah stroked her wrist in thought before turning to Peter and Eden. "Stay here with Liam. We'll go after Heath."

"Good plan." Peter gripped Ofelia's arm. "Make a portal if you need me. I'll feel it."

As the Pendergens and Eden resumed their watch on Merlin, Theo hurried down the hallway with Hannah and Ofelia. Though he was far too rattled to form a clear picture, Heath's future felt as strong as it ever did. Whoever was holding him had no intention of killing him, so why were the hairs on Theo's arms standing up? Why couldn't he shake the dreadful sense that someone was about to die?

By the time the three orphans reached the courtyard arboretum, nearly a dozen men and women stood clustered behind Heath, a motley group if Theo ever saw one. Some were big, some were small, some were young, and some looked downright ancient. But they were all Black and extremely well-dressed. From the steely glints in their eyes, they were primed and ready for trouble.

Hannah froze at the sight of the knife at Heath's throat. "Let him go!"

"It's all right," said Theo. "He'll be okay."

Ofelia scanned the strangers through a wary squint. "They have travelers. I feel them."

"And swifters," said Hannah.

Meredith smiled patiently. "And tempics and turners and freezers and burners. Let's take it on faith that we're all kind of special."

"Who are you?" Hannah asked.

"Isn't it obvious?"

Theo nodded his head distractedly. He'd known about the Majee for more than a year, the African American timebenders who'd long parted ways with the Gothams. They'd fared just fine as a clan of their own, earning billions of dollars on investments. They had their own corporate plaza in downtown Atlanta and offices all over the world. And unlike the Gothams, they'd never been exposed through urban myths and rumors. To the public at large, they were just the wealthy scions of an international holding company.

Theo raised his hands in appeasement. "Look, we don't want trouble any more than you do. But we'll feel a lot better if you put down the knife."

Heath moaned in distress as Charlene tightened her grip. "We prefer it where it is."

Hannah stepped forward, red-faced. "I'm *warning* you—"

Meredith looked to her sister. "*Kare wo hanashite, neechan.*"

"*Yokunai,*" Charlene fired back.

"Do it anyway," said a tall old man in a business suit, the only Majee who Theo recognized. He'd been profiled in countless business magazines—Auberon Graham: CEO of Majee Enterprises and one of America's most renowned investors. *Fortune* had recently dubbed him "the Merlin McGee of the tech industry." Theo knew exactly what that meant.

As Charlene grudgingly lowered the knife, Auberon took a hobbling step forward on an ivory cane. "I apologize for the brusque introduction. It was my decision to hold the boy."

"Why?" Hannah asked.

He pointed a shaky finger at Theo. "We had to give your friend a reason to come here. We have very important business that I'm afraid can't wait."

Theo glared at him reproachfully. "That's a shitty way to get my attention."

"We don't need you to like us," said Auberon. "We just need you to listen. My name is—"

"I know your name," Theo snapped. "I've been leaving you voicemails for months."

Meredith rolled her eyes. "We know. I had to listen to them."

"Why didn't you talk to me?"

"Because we did our research on you," Auberon said. "And we judged you by the company you keep."

Theo cursed, exasperated. He didn't have time for this bullshit. "Whatever your problems are with the Gothams—"

"We don't care about the Gothams," Charlene said. "He's talking about Integrity."

Auberon nodded. "If you knew their history of cruelty and oppression—"

"I *know* their history," Theo said. "But I also see the future. If you're an augur like me—"

"I'm not like you," Auberon matter-of-factly replied. "I'm not an augur at all."

"But you know what's coming," Hannah said.

"We *all* know," Meredith said. "That's why we're here."

Auberon took off his glasses and cleaned the lenses with a silk cloth. "We've been looking for our own solution, and we do believe we found one." He tossed a quick, dark look at Meredith and Charlene. "But it doesn't save everyone, as my granddaughters keep reminding me. They want to hear your plan in detail so we can judge it for ourselves."

Theo threw a nervous glance over his shoulder. "You couldn't have picked a worse time."

"There's nothing more you can do for Merlin."

"How do you know? You're not an augur."

"The future speaks to me in a different way," Auberon said. "Come with us, Theo. This is your last, best chance to convince us."

Meredith nodded. "If things work out, you'll have a whole new army of timebenders on your side. Fifty-five of us."

"And nine of your own," Auberon pointedly added.

Theo looked at him askance. "What are you talking about?"

"You don't see it in the strings?"

The orphans and Majee all watched Theo closely as he struggled to clear the fog from his foresight. He could suddenly see them as clear as sunshine: the treasure on the other side of the world.

His angry expression gave way to stupefaction. "Holy shit."

Auberon grinned. "There it is."

"What's he talking about?" Hannah asked Theo.

He looked to her with wide, nervous eyes. "I have to go with them."

"Where? Atlanta?"

"No." Theo chuckled grimly. The Majee had abandoned their American headquarters the minute Integrity started spying on it. Their new home was farther east. Much farther.

"Why do this?" Ofelia asked Theo. "These people have given you no reason to trust them."

Charlotte snorted cynically. "'These people.'"

"It's not a racial thing. It's a 'holding a knife to Heath' thing."

"I don't have a choice," Theo told her. "They have them."

"Have who?"

"The Rubies of Osaka. The last missing orphans."

"Oh my God," said Hannah. "You sure it's not a trick?"

Theo shook his head. "They're there. I have to do this."

The Majee muttered among themselves before one of them waved a portal into the air.

Charlene released Heath. "You're free, boy. Run along."

"No!" Heath ran to Theo and clutched at his shirt. "You can't go alone! It's not safe!"

"I'll be okay."

"I'm coming with you!"

"Heath—"

"Bring him," Meredith said. "We'll treat him better than the Gothams ever did."

Ofelia sneered at her. "Right. Because you've already been so good to him."

"Calm down, gorgeous. We were never going to hurt him."

Auberon checked his watch impatiently. "It's your choice, Theo, but choose quickly."

"All right." Theo turned to Hannah. "We'll be okay, I promise. You'll see me and Heath in a couple of days."

"Will I?"

He caught the gist of her question and took another scan of the future. From what he could see, Hannah would still be there when he returned.

"This isn't goodbye," Theo promised her. "Not yet."

He gave her shoulder an affectionate squeeze, then followed Heath back to the Majee.

Hannah and Ofelia watched from a distance as, two by two, the strangers stepped into the portal. Hannah couldn't help but seethe as Meredith took Heath's hand and escorted him away. The woman had clearly taken a shine to him, but was it sisterly affection or something more sinister?

Soon, only Theo and Auberon remained of the exodus. Theo threw Hannah one last look of assurance, then jerked his head to the west. His implication was obvious. *Go help Peter.*

The portal shrank away in a swirl of mist, leaving Hannah and Ofelia alone in the arboretum.

"Hope he knows what he's doing," Ofelia said.

"He does." Hannah heard the distant chaos of the Bacuranao Room, then turned toward the exit. "Let's go."

By a quarter past five, more than a hundred million people across the United States had tuned in by radio, lumivision, or Eaglenet to hear Merlin McGee speak. The transmission relays in San Francisco were so inundated with phone calls that the network crashed for six minutes. Panic had spread like embers across the nation, and the press conference wasn't even finished.

Merlin rolled his head exhaustedly, his brow dabbled with sweat. "I've answered that question three times already. I'm running out of ways to say it. The Cataclysm cannot be prevented, but its death toll can be. We have nine weeks and change to evacuate the city. That's more than enough time."

As the reporters barked their endless questions, Eden leaned toward Peter and muttered under her breath. "There's a guy over there—"

"I see him," Peter said. "I know who you mean."

He'd been vexing Peter for several minutes, a heavyset man at the back of the press pool, the only reporter in the room who hadn't spoken yet. He merely watched Merlin through dark, baggy eyes, his right hand tucked inside his jacket.

"If he tries anything, I can freeze him," Eden whispered. "They won't even know it was me."

Peter shook his head. He'd already pointed out the man to security guards and had them double-check him. He was indeed a credentialed journalist. And like every other soul in the Bacuranao Room, he'd been thoroughly scanned for weapons.

But what continued to trouble Peter, now more than ever, was the way Merlin kept looking at him out of the corner of his eye—a nervous glance here and there, as if he knew the man was up to no good.

Peter's heart skipped a beat when the journalist in question finally rose from his chair, his deep voice thundering above the others. "Mr. McGee!"

Eden clenched her fist in readiness, but Peter held her back. It seemed the object the man had been hiding in his jacket was merely a digital recorder.

Merlin sighed from the podium. "Well, now. You've been quiet."

"Just waiting for my moment, sir."

"Indeed." Merlin chuckled at his audience. "As most of you know, Mr. Angenette is a staple of my press conferences. His queries have become, dare I say, predictable."

Angenette shrugged. "My question seems more relevant now than ever."

"Then go ahead and ask it."

"Why should we believe you?"

Peter exhaled in soft relief. It seemed the Angenette fellow wasn't a threat to his brother, just a longtime annoyance.

Merlin tossed up his hands. "You've been following me around for a year and a half. Have you ever known me to be wrong with a forecast?"

"I'm not questioning your accuracy, sir. Just your honesty. You've gone to great lengths to hide aspects of your past—"

"That's called privacy," Merlin snarled. "I don't want the people I love getting harassed just for knowing me."

"Especially if they're Gothams," said Angenette.

The other reporters chattered among themselves. Merlin glared at Angenette. "You know, for such a rational skeptic, it's strange to hear you dredging up old myths."

"It *is* strange," Angenette admitted. "But then we find ourselves in strange times, sir, with women with wings flying over London and bizarre fights happening in Scotland. And right here in America—"

"I've indulged this enough."

"*Right here in America* we have a bona fide prophet," said Angenette. "A man with tenuous connections to Quarter Hill, New York, the town long rumored to be the home of the Gothams."

Liam grabbed Peter's arm. "Dad . . ."

"I know." There was nothing Peter could do without making the situation worse. He'd just have to trust his brother.

Merlin clucked his tongue at Angenette. "If you were reaching any farther, you'd be touching the moon."

"I could be wrong about your origins, sir, but it doesn't change the fact that you're hiding something. Given the stakes of your latest pronouncement, the unprecedented disruption it would cause the American people, I'm forced to ask the question again."

"Oh, come on already . . ."

"Why should we believe you, Mr. McGee?"

"Come on!"

Peter suddenly caught new movement behind Merlin: a bald and burly security guard, the same man who had approached Theo earlier. He took a few steps toward Merlin at the podium, then reached inside his blazer.

"No!" If Peter's view of the scene hadn't been obscured, he would have portal-dropped the gunman through the floor or teleported his brother to safety. He could have even lived with the consequences of his actions, the first portal to be witnessed by millions. It seemed a small price to pay to save the life of a loved one. It was a far better future than the one that was coming.

The guard shot Merlin through the small of his back, sending a spray of blood onto the reporters and throwing everyone else into a panic.

By the time Hannah and Ofelia returned to the scene, it looked like the end of the world all over again. A hundred floating cameras buzzed furiously around the front of the room, half of them crashing into each other as they struggled to get a view of the carnage. The assassin lay flat in a pool of blood, shot dead by his fellow security guards.

Just ten feet away, at the foot of the podium, the great Merlin McGee stared quietly at the lights and cameras. Soon a shadow eclipsed his field of view, a man he recognized even by silhouette. As the nearest bystanders continued to shout, Merlin took a feeble grip of Peter's wrist and gave his brother a flickering grin.

"I did it," said the prophet. "It's done."

Hannah pressed her hands flat against the terra-cotta tile and let the shower douse all the fires inside of her. She'd been fighting the urge to cry for hours, ever since Merlin was pronounced dead at the hotel. But time and hot water had dulled her anguish. By the time she dried off and threw on a robe, she could even see an upside to this terrible day: the fact that no one was talking about Amanda. The Angel of London had been bumped from the news, just as Merlin had ably predicted.

She crossed back into the living room of her rental suite, a charming little space in a three-star coastal inn. She and Ofelia would have loved nothing more than to hop the first redeye out of Cuba, but the other three members of their dwindled team, the ones who'd watched Merlin's death at close range, were in no condition to travel. Hannah could hear Eden through the balcony curtain, pacing back and forth in the warm night air as she argued on the phone with her boyfriend.

"She's not doing well, is she?" Hannah asked.

Ofelia reclined on an easy chair, a computer tablet in her hands and a distant gloom in her eyes. "She was a cop."

"So?"

"Cops take it hard when they fail to protect someone."

"What could she have done? Burn the guy on live TV?"

"That's what I said." Ofelia resumed reading the newsportals. "Says here that the gunman worked twenty years at the hotel. Family man. No criminal record."

"Doesn't make sense." Hannah heard Eden's loud voice from the balcony. "Wow. She's really tearing into Noah. What did he do to her?"

Ofelia shifted in her seat uncomfortably. "No idea."

Hannah sat down on the edge of the sofa and checked the screen on her handphone. Still no word from Theo or Heath, just a quick text from Mia: **Can't reach Peter. How is he?**

Sighing, Hannah keyed a quick reply: **About to go check.**

Don't let him do his tough guy thing, Mia insisted. **He can't just walk this off.**

It'd been so long that Hannah had almost forgotten about Mia's four dead brothers. The girl knew Peter's grief all too well, just like Zack, Ofelia, and everyone else who'd lost a sibling. Hannah selfishly thanked the universe that she wasn't part of that club and prayed she never would be.

She tied her robe tight and made for the door. "I'll be back in a bit," she told Ofelia.

"Sure."

There was something in her tone that made Hannah stop and turn around. "You okay?"

"Yeah, I just . . ." Ofelia stumbled on her words, deliberating. "I don't know. I'm just wondering how you all manage it."

"Manage what?"

"This constant feeling that we're in over our heads."

"Oh." Hannah mulled it over a moment before shrugging. "I don't know."

She crossed the hall to Peter's door and only had to knock once before he opened it. At last, he'd changed out of his blood-splattered clothes and into a T-shirt and sweatpants. Liam slept facedown on the second king bed, his head half-buried in pillows.

"How's he doing?" Hannah quietly asked.

"You don't have to whisper. I gave him a sedative."

"That bad, huh?"

Peter nodded. "His grandmother died on top of him. His uncle died in front of him. He's still just a boy, for God's sake."

"Not after that."

"Maybe," Peter said. "But he's still just a boy to me."

He snatched his handphone from the edge of the dresser and passed it to Hannah.

"What's this?" she asked.

"Michael bitmailed me something in the middle of the night. Time-released. I just got it twenty minutes ago."

Hannah sat down on Peter's bed and played the embedded video. Merlin had filmed himself from the comfort of his kitchen, an enigmatic look on his face. Between his somber eyes and his Mona Lisa smile, Hannah could barely draw a bead on his mood.

"So, a funny thing happened a few years back," he said to the camera. "I was minding my business in an Arizona coffeehouse when a strange young woman approached me. She had two different watches on her wrist and a notable talent for prophecy. And when I say 'notable,' I mean 'Holy Christ.' This girl was an oracle."

Hannah looked to Peter, astonished. "He recorded this last night. I walked in on him."

"Keep watching."

Merlin continued: "After a fair amount of small talk, she got down to business. She said, 'I got a job for you, Michael. A very important one.' I told her I wasn't looking for work but she said, 'Too bad, 'cause you're the only one who can help me. Two years from now, on the fourth of October, I'm gonna need San Francisco to be empty.' I said, 'Why on earth would you need a whole city emptied?' She said, 'Because this world has problems. They started with one Cataclysm, and they'll end with another.'"

Merlin feigned a look of surprise. "As you can imagine, dear brother, I had questions for her, and she only had a couple of answers. When I asked her how she expected a nobody like me to convince four million people to abandon their homes . . . well, you already know the answer. I had to become the world's first celebrity augur. I had to be Merlin McGee."

He looked away from the camera distractedly. "I couldn't tell anyone about my reasons for doing it, not even you. *Especially* not you. You're a crucial actor in this drama, Peter. You and your orphan friends. If I told you my secrets, your decisions would change the future. Even your best intentions would have destroyed everything I was working for."

Hannah checked on Peter's reaction, but he kept his back to her.

"That was the hardest part of the last eighteen months," Merlin said. "Not the cameras or the questions or the insincere people. It was you. That ever-present look of hurt in your eyes, like I personally betrayed you. I really wish you'd extended some faith in me, brother. Lord knows I put faith in you when you ran off with a group of alien strangers and abandoned your son for months."

Hannah shook her head in objection. "That's not fair."

"That's not entirely fair," Merlin realized on his own. "I guess we've been angry at each other for a while. And in hindsight, I don't blame you. You couldn't have possibly known why I was doing all this. I was looking forward to finally telling you but then . . ."

He shrugged with frustration. "Turns out people are hopelessly stubborn, and I began to see a kink in the strings. It'll start with a journalist at my press conference tomorrow, a willful disbeliever who asks, 'Why should we trust you?' Then, day by day, it'll spread to another, and then another, then a hundred thousand others. Soon, before we know it, only three million people will leave the city when they need to. Or maybe two million. Or maybe it'll be just a couple hundred thousand. I can't live with those numbers."

Hannah's stomach twisted with dread. She didn't like where this was going.

"It's a no-win situation," said Merlin. "Challenging their doubts will only make them doubt me more. Running from their questions will only make them question me more. The only way to save the whole four million . . ." He threw his hands up. "Well, if you're seeing this, then you already know that Theo was right. Someone's coming to kill me tomorrow: a man with just weeks to live. He was looking for a way to provide for his family, long after the cancer takes him."

Merlin turned back to the camera with a guilty expression. "I gave him one."

Hannah's mouth went slack at his revelation. Merlin had hired his own assassin.

"I'm sorry you'll have to see it, Peter, and I'm doubly sorry for Liam. The whole thing seems unconscionably cruel. But the future sometimes demands a sacrifice, as you'll eventually learn yourself. You were always so much stronger than me, and always more ambitious. You're fighting to save all life on Earth, while I'm happy just to save a piece of it."

Merlin opened his mouth to say something, then stopped himself. Hannah had a pretty good idea what he was censoring, some very bad news about the future of the world's timebenders. *The road ends soon for all of us.*

"I hope you'll come to forgive me, Peter, because I'll be dead in sixteen hours and I don't know what's next." He laughed in amazement. "I suppose that's a new experience for me, the whole not-knowing thing. A part of me kind of likes it. The rest of me's scared silly."

His smile dissolved. He looked at the camera somberly. "Stay strong, brother. Don't lose hope. This next part will be the hardest. But I've seen the string with my own eyes, and I know how the story ends. We win."

He looked to his left and then reached for the phone. "Hannah's here. Gotta go."

The screen went black. Hannah dropped the phone on the bed. "Oh my God."

"I can't tell the others," Peter said in a low, creaky tone. "If it gets out—"

"Peter."

"—he'll have died for nothing."

"Peter." Hannah gripped his shoulders. "Look at me."

He turned to face her, his eyes red and cracked. He must have wept while Hannah watched the video. No wonder he'd turned his back on her.

"There's no shame in crying," she told him.

"I'm not ashamed of that. I'm ashamed of the anger I still feel."

Hannah flipped her wrists over and showed him her scars. "I tried to kill myself when I was thirteen. It took Amanda a decade to forgive me. And I didn't even do it for four million people."

"Neither did he."

"Peter—"

"He was a leaf in the wind his whole damn life. He never fit in anywhere. Between that and the constant visions in his head, I think he finally just . . ."

Peter closed his eyes in misery. "He was just tired."

Hannah wrapped her arms around him and held him tight.

"What are you doing?" Peter asked.

"Not me. *We.*"

"Hannah—"

"We're not making babies," she insisted. "We're not doing anything in front of your son. We're just going to lie down and hold each other."

Peter turned to face her and brushed his fingers along her cheekbone. "I'm not as tough as Michael says. I don't have the strength to lose anyone else."

"Listen—"

"I don't have the strength to lose you."

"Peter." She kissed him on the lips just to change the subject. She was tired of people worrying about her, tired of them looking at her like she had one foot in the grave. All she wanted tonight, before leaving Cuba forever, was to live like a normal woman and forget about the perils of the future.

They turned off all the lights and retreated under the covers, with Hannah opening her robe just enough to let Peter feel her skin. There was nothing even remotely lascivious about it. Just two weary soldiers in a never-ending war, providing comfort and affection before the next bombshell dropped.

As she held Peter in the darkness and felt his heartbeat against hers, Hannah suddenly found the answer to the question Ofelia had asked her, mere minutes ago.

This is how we manage, Hannah thought. *Right here. Just like this.*

SEVENTEEN

In September 1995, after their most vicious exchange of hostilities to date, the British Empire came to a gentleman's agreement with its enemies in the Scarlet Sabre. They called it the Minimum Decency Accord and they limited it to one provision: *Stop burning down our hospitals, and we'll stop blowing up your friends.*

All told, it was a generous offer. The Sabre had settlement camps scattered all across Europe, each one filled with noncombatant allies. The thought of sparing them all from missile attacks was too good for the insurgents to pass up, even if the agreement proved temporary. Both sides assumed that it was just a matter of time before the other went back on its word.

But to everyone's surprise, the accord endured. To this day, the Sabre refrained from attacking British hospitals and was rewarded in good faith by the government.

Emboldened by their new security, the rebel aid camps gradually stopped wandering and took permanent root in the wilderness. While most remained small enough to hold a few dozen people, some grew as large as villages and provided sanctuary for thousands.

The greatest of these settlements was Børnehjem, a sprawling metropolis of shack-tents and shanties in the remote northern grasslands of Denmark. The place was five times the size of the underland, with its own provincial mini-government, a field hospital, a plumbing network, and a school system. More than a third of the camp's population were children—nearly a thousand young refugees who'd lost their homes and families in the guerrilla wars. Børnehjem literally meant "orphanage" in Danish.

Amanda walked down an avenue of kitchens and mess tents, her thoughts split with cognitive dissonance. She'd been a guest of the Sabre for nearly a day and she still couldn't figure them out. Were they the Paul Reveres of the British Dominion or just a bunch of secular terrorists? To hear the Violets tell it, they were very much the former, though the crimes Melissa had ascribed to them had made Amanda physically sick.

No one raised a word of objection as Amanda walked into a cafeteria and loaded ten trays of food for her people. If anything, the locals were merely puzzled by her unseasonable attire. There was barely an inch of her visible in her camouflage fatigues, her long leather gloves and sunglasses. Her lower face was hidden behind a bandana mask while every strand of her long red hair was tucked away beneath a military cap.

As Amanda returned to the residential zone, a little girl eyed her curiously. *"Er du syg?"*

Amanda stopped to look at her—a filthy, blue-eyed beauty with a burn-scarred stump for a right arm. *Another casualty of war,* Amanda silently lamented. *And probably a future soldier.*

"Du ser så sjov ud," the girl said to Amanda. *"Er du syg?"*

"I'm sorry. I don't, uh . . ."

The girl seamlessly switched to English. "Your face is all covered. Are you sick?"

"No." Amanda smirked behind her scarlet bandana. "Just famous."

It was high noon on Sunday in her part of the world, her fortieth hour of infamy. If she knew what Merlin McGee was planning—the press conference in Cuba that was still ten hours away from happening—she would have finally seen relief on the horizon. But at the moment, the world remained hopelessly stuck on her. Some online stores were even selling T-shirts with her likeness.

Amanda ducked into a spacious tent, the temporary home of the Coppers. The Sabre had been nice enough to give her people a secluded section of Børnehjem, plus ample care for their wounded. Doctors had labored all night on Stitch's rifted shoulder, cutting away the rotted skin while pumping her with antibiotics. As for See, Amanda had no idea what the medics did, but the girl looked ten times better. She was even able to stand for a few seconds at a time, though walking remained an elusive chore.

Amanda handed out lunch trays to her fellow orphans, pulled down her mask, then sat at Mother's bedside. "You're looking better."

"I'm fine," Mother said. "I keep telling everyone."

The others were right to worry. Yesterday afternoon, while crossing the North Sea on a Scarlet Sabre aership, she'd collapsed to the floor in a seizure. Though the doctors lacked the equipment to diagnose her, Mercy had seen those symptoms before in her people: the cracked red eyes and bloody nose, the crippling tension headache.

"It's just power strain," she'd assured Mother. "You'll be fine in a few days as long as you lay off the portals."

But Amanda could hardly forget about her sister's strain, a malady she never recovered from. Hannah still couldn't swift without risking a fatal stroke. Was Mother now in a similar bind?

She placed a tray on Mother's table. "You should eat something."

"I'm not hungry." Mother gestured at See and Stitch. "I just want to go home and get the girls to a real doctor."

"Soon." Amanda squeezed her arm. "You've been absolutely amazing these past few days. We'd all be dead if it wasn't for you."

Mother dismissed her with a wave. "You could say the same about any of us. Even Evan."

Amanda preferred not to think about that. "You're a lot more of a hero than he is."

"Hero." Mother gestured at her fellow Coppers. "Everything I do, I do for them. If it hadn't been their lives at risk, I would have left you all to die."

Amanda sighed. It was talk like that that made people distrust Mother. It also reminded Amanda why their conversations were always short.

She stood up and took the last three lunch trays. "Let me know if there's anything you need."

Amanda proceeded into the neighboring tent, then stopped in surprise. "What are you doing? You're supposed to be resting."

Zack looked at her through the reflection of a shaving mirror, his face half-covered in foam. "I *am* resting. I'm just doing it vertically."

Amanda had been fussing over him since yesterday, when she stitched up his lacerated arm. Though the Børnehjem doctors had replenished his lost blood, he still looked pale and feeble. It didn't help that he was trying to shave with his untrained left hand, for lack of a better option. His prosthetic still lay in pieces in the basement of a Scottish castle.

Amanda turned him around. "Well, at least let me help you before you cut up your face."

"It's a safety razor."

"Not the way you're using it."

She took off her glove and morphed one of her fingers into a blade. Zack's eyes bulged at the sight of it. "*That's* your safe alternative?"

"Just trust me."

Amanda held him still with a tempic clamp and sheared the last bits of stubble from his face. She used to shave her first husband with a straight razor before his medical conferences so he wouldn't have to stress about shadow. She was amazed to think back on the worries of her old life, all the piddling trivialities that constituted a crisis: a bad Yelp review for the oncology practice, a sarcastic barb from her sister, a subpar house cleaner, a speeding ticket—so much drama that amounted to nothing. How did she ever let it bother her?

She flicked the foam from her hand, then passed Zack a towel. "All better."

He cleaned his face and reexamined his reflection. "Wow. Good job. I was expecting a lot more blood and screaming."

"You think I'd ever hurt you?"

"Of course not." He eyed the stitches on his arm. "I'm just not a big fan of tempic blades."

Amanda cupped the side of his face. "I'm sorry you had to deal with that woman again. If I hadn't pissed off Semerjean—"

"It's not your fault."

"I could have strung him along. Pretended to take his offer."

Zack shook his head. "He would have seen right through it."

"I don't know," Amanda said. "Behind all that smugness, he seemed a little desperate."

"Well, good. Maybe the future's finally turning against them."

Amanda wanted to believe it, but she couldn't seem to muster the optimism. Even her faith was at a low ebb today, after nearly losing Zack for the umpteenth time. *I wish you could just make it easy for once*, she thought to her Lord. *I'd even settle for "manageable."*

The tent flap opened, and the Violet named Bobby peeked inside. "Is this a bad time?"

"Not at all. Come in." Amanda gestured at the food trays. "Did you have lunch yet?"

"As a matter of fact, I haven't eaten all day. But that's not the reason I'm here."

"Our friends from the Netherlands," Zack guessed.

Bobby nodded. "They're landing soon. I figured you'd want to meet them."

He was one of the largest men Amanda had ever seen: six foot four and built like a tank. But behind his intimidating bulk was a quaint and doe-eyed boyishness, as if he'd never uttered a curse in his life.

She insisted that Bobby eat with them for a few minutes, if only to get some nourishment into Zack. Bobby sat down at the snack table and, with a wave of his hand, reversed his meal to steaming hot freshness.

"I didn't know you were a turner," Amanda noted.

"What's a turner?"

"The kind of people that do what we do," Zack said as he reversed the other two lunch trays.

Bobby watched him with chuckling awe. "I spent two years thinking I was the only one like me. But there's a name for us and everything. That's crazy."

Amanda studied him, perplexed. There was a curious familiarity to his face, especially in the eyes and nose. She would have certainly remembered if she'd met him before. So why did he set off her *déjà vu*?

"I've been meaning to ask you how you ended up in the British group," she said to Bobby. "Were you in London the whole time, or—"

"Kabul."

"Afghanistan?" Amanda's eyebrows rose. "You're an army guy."

"Yes, ma'am. Fourth Brigade, Eighty-Second Airborne. I'd been there three years when the shit came down. Next thing I knew, I was in some windowless room in the middle of God-Knows-Where. Took two whole months before anyone told me it was London."

Zack cut at his eggplant with a dour expression. "Let me guess. They were all pasty white physicists who pretended to be your friends, but were really working for the Pelletiers."

Bobby shook his head morosely. "They never pretended to be our friends."

Amanda swapped a heavy look with Zack. It seemed like only the Silvers had gotten the white glove treatment from Azral's scientist minions. But then the other groups didn't have Semerjean hiding among them.

"Those first six months were just a blur," Bobby said. "They put something in our food that kept us all docile. We never tried to escape and we did everything they asked. Gave them all the stupid samples they wanted."

He draped a napkin over his lunch tray. "After a few months, they started . . . experimenting on us. Pills and injections and other stuff they didn't explain. Some of it made us crazy. Some of it made us sick. And some of it . . ."

Bobby's expression turned cold. "We started out with fifteen people and ended up with five."

Zack clenched his jaw. "Motherfuckers."

Bobby nodded. "Yeah. You won't find much love for the Pelletiers here."

"How'd you break out?" Amanda asked him.

"We didn't. The scientists just disappeared one day. Took all their stuff and left the doors wide open. We were all clueless out in the world. We barely even knew we had powers."

Bobby looked to Zack and Amanda again. "If it wasn't for Yasmeen, we would have never survived. That woman adapts like nobody's business. Within a couple of days, she had the lay of the land. She knew who to talk to and who to avoid, how to get money, how to blend in."

"Wow," Zack said. "Is she military too?"

"She was a schoolteacher!" Bobby said with a laugh. "Taught history in Pakistan. I don't know when or how she got the way she is, but I'm glad she did. She's unstoppable."

Amanda eyed him uneasily. "You don't have to answer this, but—"

"You want to know how we ended up with the Sabres," Bobby said with a smirk. "Yasmeen again. She's hated the British her whole life, but on this world . . . well, you've seen how they are."

Zack nodded wearily. "About a year away from building a Death Star."

"Exactly!" Bobby laughed again. "It may be simplistic. It may even be self-serving. But after all the shit I've been through . . . I don't know. It felt like I was exactly where I needed to be, doing exactly what I needed to be doing. And I'll tell you what I told that other woman—"

"Melissa."

"Yeah. Her. I told her I only kill soldiers. To me, that's the difference between a freedom fighter and a terrorist. Most of us here are on the right side of the line."

"Including your people?" Amanda asked.

Bobby sighed at the ground. "I may not agree with everything Yasmeen does, but I understand her. She fights for what she believes in and she never gives up. And now that she knows the whole world's dying . . ."

He cast a troubled look at his two fellow orphans. "Why does this keep happening?"

Zack stood behind Amanda and clasped her shoulder. "Three reasons. You met them."

Bobby closed his eyes, sickened. "They took everyone I knew and loved on the old world. There's no way in hell I'm letting them do that again."

"Just don't underestimate them," Zack cautioned. "They're a hundred times more powerful than us."

"And a hundred steps ahead," Amanda added. "I've seen them take out a whole army."

"An army of our kind?"

"No," she admitted.

"Well, there you go," Bobby said. "If you have as many timebenders as you say you do, then we have enough power to take them down."

Amanda stroked Zack's fingers with an absent expression. Bobby had been battling British soldiers for so long that he forgot what a real enemy looked like. He would learn. God help him, he would learn.

Bobby checked his watch, then stood to full looming height. "Come on. Let's go meet the Dutch crew."

. . .

Their ship touched down at the southern end of Børnehjem: a hulking German Eisenfalke that looked like a whale with windows. It crushed the grass beneath its struts, then vented a hiss of steam.

Zack waited at the edge of the landing zone, his hand clasped tightly around Amanda's. Though it was always exhilarating to meet survivors from his world, his elation was tainted by cynicism. What if all these people had been turned by the Pelletiers, a subtle squad of orphan slaves, sent to infiltrate the enemy and take them down from the inside?

Amanda felt the tension in his grip. "You okay?"

He nodded at her and kept his thoughts to himself. If it had just been the two of them, he would have admitted that he was still suffering some trauma. But the Violets were standing directly to his left, next to Melissa and Caleb.

Yasmeen looked to Zack and her other new acquaintances. "Don't stare too hard at Lars when you see him. He's a little self-conscious."

"About what?" Caleb asked her.

"You'll see."

The side hatch of the Eisenfalke slid open with a *whoosh*. One by one, eight passengers disembarked.

At long last, the Opals of Rotterdam had arrived.

Zack looked them all over with stoic gray eyes, his mind dancing with random observations. The Dutch orphans were certainly an eclectic group, with half of them as young as the youngest of the Coppers and two on the cusp of middle age. One of the men looked gorgeous enough to be a model, while another one . . .

Well, that must have been Lars.

The man shared Zack's height and reedy build, but his skin was wrapped in bandages. His eyes lay hidden behind a pair of black sunglasses, and he wore the thick, heavy clothes of a skier. Zack couldn't help but think of Claude Rains in *The Invisible Man*, albeit a slightly more stylish version. Why go through the trouble of hiding himself? Was he scarred? Was he ugly? Was he as famous as Amanda?

"He's a lumic," Bobby explained. "Took a bullet to the head in a firefight and hasn't been able to turn his powers off since. He glows like a lamp, even when he's sleeping."

"Wow," said Zack. "Don't you have any solics on the team?"

"What's a solic?"

"Guess not."

The young Violet named Jia squealed with delight and wrapped her arms around the handsome male Opal. They fell kissing into a floating portal, then disappeared from view.

Caleb batted Zack's arm. "How come you never greet me like that?"

"We're not there yet. Don't rush it."

Bobby smiled. "Marc and Jia have been together for a while. Well, not *together* together, but they try to meet up as much as they can."

"Why didn't you just merge groups?" asked Amanda.

He shrugged. "They're dead set on liberating the Netherlands. We've got our eyes on the bigger fight."

"You do *now*," Melissa said. "The empire can wait."

"Yeah." Bobby watched Yasmeen as she addressed the Opals in Dutch. "That's just what she's telling them."

All Yasmeen had said to them over the phone was that they had to come quickly. It was a matter of life and death. Now the Opals were learning that it wasn't an understatement. The apocalypse was coming for everyone again, and this time no one would be spared.

Though Zack didn't speak a word of their language, he could easily read the expressions on their faces—the same volatile medley of denial and despair that he'd experienced two Octobers ago, in the living room of Peter's Brooklyn brownstone. One of the Opals looked ready to vomit. Another one walked away in a huff. Two of them hugged and two of them cried. It was only Lars who kept his reaction under wraps, so to speak.

He slowly approached Zack and Amanda, then addressed them in a heavy accent. "Is it true what Yasmeen says, that this world only has nine weeks to live?"

"We have nine weeks to stop it," Zack said. "If we don't, we'll have a couple more years before the end."

"How do you know this?"

"Because we have augurs."

Lars cocked his head in puzzlement. "My English is not good. What—"

"People who can see the future," Amanda explained. "They all see the same thing coming."

Lars took off his shades and rubbed his radiant blue eyes. If anything, Bobby had undersold the man's problem. Even his lashes glowed like neon.

"We had someone like that once," Lars said. "He killed himself. I guess now I know why."

He put his glasses back on, then shook his head in misery. "I still have nightmares about what happened to our world. I can't live through that again."

Amanda nodded sympathetically. "You'll find a way to handle it. You just have to give it time."

"Time." Lars chuckled blackly. "That's funny. I'll remember that."

The pilot of the Eisenfalke, a squat and hairy Englishman in a grease-stained yellow jumpsuit, poked his head out the cockpit window. "Oi! Where's my rider?"

Yasmeen tilted her head in confusion. "What rider?"

"I'm s'posed to be taking some bloke to Copenhagen."

"Yo! Right here!"

Evan hurried onto the landing field, a duffel bag slung over his shoulder. He gave a mock salute to Melissa and the others as he continued toward the aership. "Hasta la pasta, suckers."

Zack followed him to the Eisenfalke, baffled. No one had seen much of him since they first got to Børnehjem, but then none of them had spent much time looking. His teammates all figured he was amusing himself, probably at some stranger's expense.

"You're going to Copenhagen?" Zack asked him. "Why?"

"Because I've never been there, and I'm all about new experiences."

"I thought saving the world was your new experience."

Evan chuckled derisively. "You wanted Violets and Opals, I gave you Violets and Opals. I never said I was in it for the long haul." He shot a wary look at Melissa. "You'll hold up your end of the deal, right?"

"Yes," she promised. "As soon I get back, it's done."

"What's done?" asked Amanda.

"She's erasing my file from the criminal database," Evan said. "No more looking over my shoulder. No more wearing sticky disguises."

"Just in Europe," Melissa stressed. "Not America."

"Yeah, no worries. I've ridden that short bus long enough."

"Come on," Zack said. "You saw the difference you can make. If you keep helping us, we can win. You won't have to relive the same four and a half years."

Evan rolled his eyes. "Even if I bought into your bullshit, what do you think will happen the minute I set foot in the underland? If Hannah doesn't kill me, then Jury's hot sister will."

"Ofelia," Amanda said.

"I know her name. I also know how the Pelletiers work. They're gearing up for the mother of all smackdowns. I'd rather not be there when it happens."

"We beat them," Zack reminded him.

"We beat their *babies*," Evan stressed. "You think you have a chance against the Big Three?"

Caleb scoffed at him. "Coward."

"Oh, stuff it, dillweed." Evan looked to Zack again. "I'm not going back to their mirror room. Not now. Not ever."

Try as he might, Zack couldn't forget. The Pelletiers had only tormented him for a day, but they'd made it feel like decades. He could still barely look at his reflection without shuddering.

"So now what?" Amanda inquired of Evan.

"If you're asking about—"

"You *know* what I'm asking."

"Don't worry," said Evan. "I'm not coming after Hannah or anyone else. I'm done."

"That's just what you said to Mia," Amanda reminded him. "Right before you killed Jonathan."

"Yeah, well, this time I mean it."

The pilot tapped his watch impatiently. Evan nodded at him, then climbed aboard the ship. He leaned out the door and looked at Amanda in a way that Zack had never seen before, an evincible lack of disregard that came dangerously close to fondness.

"Guess I promised you a way to save your sister from the Pelletiers."

Amanda crossed her arms. "Don't bother. I knew you were lying."

"Mostly," he confessed. "But not entirely."

"What do you mean?"

"Semerjean," said Evan. "He's a vain son of a bitch and he still cares what you people think about him. He really wants you to believe that he's a straight-up, righteous dude."

Amanda shook her head. "That won't ever happen."

"No," Evan agreed. "But if Hannah's smart, she can use that to her advantage."

He crinkled his brow in contemplation, then let out a mocking laugh. "But come on, when has she ever been smart?"

Zack checked the cold expressions of Amanda and Caleb, disheartened.

Evan had to go squander what little goodwill he'd earned. It was like a compulsion with the guy. A sickness.

As the Eisenfalke engine started up with a *whirr*, Evan's cocky smile leveled out. He looked at Amanda earnestly. "I know you won't believe me but I truly . . ."

He forcibly swallowed the rest of his thought. Amanda eyed him cynically. "You truly what?"

"Never mind." He retreated into the aership. "Well, compadres, it's been a gas. Enjoy what little remains of your lives. I'll see you in Round 56."

With a creaky lurch and a loud puff of air, the Eisenfalke floated back into the sky. Zack and Amanda watched it disappear into the clouds before holding hands again.

"Hannah won't be happy," Amanda said. "She really wanted me to kill him."

"And what do you want?" Zack asked her.

She looked at Melissa and the European orphans, all currently embroiled in their own tense discussion. "I just want to go home."

That was exactly what the others were talking about. Zack and Amanda rejoined the group and listened to Yasmeen's plan.

"There's an aid ship leaving from Kristiansand at sundown," she told Melissa. "Goes all the way to Nova Scotia. I know the captain. I *trust* him. He'll get us there with no hassle."

"Will there be enough room?" Melissa asked. "There are twenty-six of us now, including three wounded."

"It's a big boat. It'll fit all of us."

Caleb's eyes widened. "Boat? As in the 'takes a full week to cross the Atlantic' kind?"

"It's an engine boat and it's shifted. We'll be in Canada by tomorrow night." Yasmeen looked to Melissa again. "I assume you'll have a way of getting us into the States."

"Don't worry about that," Melissa said. "You just make sure your people are ready."

"Can do." Yasmeen patted Bobby on the back. "Smile, Farisi. You're going back to America."

"Back?" Bobby chuckled. "I've seen the vids. That's not *my* America."

He paused as he noticed the strange new looks around him. Zack, Amanda, Melissa, and Caleb all stared at him with surprise. "What?"

"Did she just call you Farisi?" Zack asked.

"Uh, yeah. Why?"

"Your last name's *Farisi*."

"Yes." Bobby took a step back. "You're freaking me out. What—"

"You're from La Presa," Amanda said. "Just south of San Diego."

Bobby's mouth fell open. Yasmeen narrowed her eyes with suspicion. "How did you know that?"

"From his little sister Mia," Zack said.

Bobby bounced his bulging gaze between Amanda and Zack. "You knew Mia?"

"My God." Melissa studied him in astonishment. "I thought there was something familiar about you."

"What the hell's going on?" Bobby yelled. "How did you know my sister?"

Zack approached him in short, cautious steps, a dumbstruck grin on his face. "Bobby, listen to me. You're gonna want to sit down."

EIGHTEEN

Mia jogged through the underland's perimeter park, her mood growing bleaker by the minute. Instead of listening to her usual exercise music, she'd tuned her earbuds to the national news and the unprecedented bedlam that Merlin had caused. His final and most alarming prophecy had thrown the whole United States into a panic. The stock market crashed within an hour of opening, while arguments between the skeptics and believers had erupted into violence all over the country.

And that was all just a sideshow to what was happening in San Francisco. The city had descended into near total anarchy, with half the businesses shuttering and the other half scrambling to fight off looters. A man shot his landlord for not letting him out of his apartment lease. A woman was mauled by a lion after freeing it from the zoo.

Mia cursed beneath her breath. If that was how people reacted to one city, just imagine how they'd handle the big doom. Would there be anyone left when the apocalypse arrived, or would the sky come down on a planet of smoke and corpses?

Mia pulled her vibrating handphone from her pocket and saw a new text from Hannah.

About to board the plane. Any word from Amanda?

Nothing yet, Mia typed back. **How about Theo?**

Not much, wrote Hannah. **I'm fine. Heath's fine. Just got to Japan.**

Mia's face went slack. **Japan?!**

I know, right? We're really racking up the miles.

Speak for yourself, Mia thought. While the rest of her people were out seeing the world, she was grounded at home for her "anger issues." The most exotic trip she had to look forward to was a midday drive to Connecticut.

Fuming, Mia turned off the news and resumed her morning run in silence. She'd only managed to get half a block before she spotted curious activity up ahead: dozens of people in a picnic garden; half of them standing, the other half sitting at tables.

Mia teleported to the roof of the nearest building and peeked down over the ledge. The Gothams were having some kind of breakfast social with her people—four Pearls, five Irons, six Platinums: nearly every orphan left in the underland. They sat scattered among the cozy little tables, each one chatting with a Gotham of the opposite gender while the patriarchs and matriarchs of the clan watched from the sidelines.

"Holy shit." Mia suddenly realized what they were doing. She portal-jumped down to the park. "Are you guys insane?"

The conversations all came to a halt. Ben Hopkins stood up from his table. "Mia—"

"Were you the one who arranged this whole fuck party?"

"Don't be crude," a young Gotham snarled at Mia. "You know why we're doing this."

"Yeah, so you can all make babies for the Pelletiers."

"We're just hedging our bets," Ben said. "Even Theo admits that saving the world's a long shot. What do you want us to do?"

Mia mentally cursed out Semerjean, that ever-accomplished con man. Somehow, despite his history of lies, he got all these dopes to believe that there was a safe new home for them in the future, a paradisiacal wonderland beneath the mountains of Brazil. Eternal salvation was waiting for them. All they had to do was play ball.

Priora Kohl, a longtime elder of the Gotham clan, approached Mia from the edge of the crowd. "We gave this a lot of thought. We agonized over it. But in the end, we realized that making a few babies is a small price to pay for what the Pelletiers are offering."

"A *small* price?" Mia gestured at the seated couples. "You're pimping out your sons and sacrificing your daughters!"

Kohl shook her head indignantly. "No one's being forced into it. These are all volunteers."

"Right." Mia gestured at Rosario Navarette, the seventeen-year-old Pearl who barely spoke a word of English. "What bullshit did you use on her?"

Kohl looked to Rosario. *"Dila lo que me acabas de decir."*

The girl dipped her head and spoke in a glum tone. *"Esto nos salvará a todos."*

"'This will save us all,'" Kohl translated for Mia. "I didn't tell her that. She told me. She's an augur. She knows."

"Well, she's wrong." Mia took a sweeping look at the crowd. "You're all idiots if you think you can trust the Pelletiers!"

"Are Peter and Hannah idiots?" Ben asked her. "Because they were the first to make a deal."

"Yeah, and how do you think that'll work out for them?"

"I don't know, but I'm willing to take the same risk."

"Risk?" Mia scoffed at Ben. "You're not the one getting knocked up."

"Neither are you," said a voice behind her.

She turned around and flinched at the sight of Regal Tam: her ex-girlfriend, a *lesbian.* Now there she was with the orphan Matt Hamblin, sharing bacon and waffles in advance of their coupling. Mia could only guess that her parents had guilted her into it, as payment for years of embarrassment. From the look on Regal's face, she was thoroughly committed to the cause. All her fury was reserved for Mia.

"No one asked you to participate," said Regal. "And no one asked for your opinion."

"Regal, listen to me, please. I know the Pelletiers."

"Are you kidding me? You lived with one of them for months and you had no clue. You were *in love* with him and you had no clue. You're the biggest fool they've ever known and you have the nerve to call *us* idiots? Just shut up and go away. We don't need your hypocrisy."

Half the people around Regal broke out in applause. Mia's face burned red.

"Fuck you all," she said through gritted teeth. "I never had anyone warn me about Semerjean. You assholes have no excuse."

She turned around and stormed away, her stomach searing with acid. Even worse than her humiliation and rage was the fact that Regal was right. How many hints had she missed with David? How many warnings had she deliberately ignored?

She was so wrapped up in her own smoldering thoughts that she didn't notice the skinny young blonde standing nearby in a gazebo. "That went well."

Mia stopped with a gasp. She'd become a seasoned pro at avoiding Carrie Bloom, but now she'd practically walked right into her. "What are you doing here?"

"Relax. I'm not stalking you. I only came by to check out the baby brunch."

"You're not seriously—"

"Oh God, no. I'm way too young for that. Even if I wasn't, I'm not helping the Pelletiers. Not after the shit they've done."

Mia was stunned to see how much Carrie had matured in recent months. Her braces were gone. Her hair was long and straight again. Her voice had regained its precocious edge. With each new day, she was growing back into the girl that Mia had known and loved. That made her all the more painful to look at.

"And for what it's worth, you're right," Carrie said. She flicked a finger at Regal and all the other brunchers. "They *are* idiots."

Mia nervously checked her watch. "I have to go."

"Wow. You can't even look at me. I must have done a real number on you."

"It's not like that."

"Really? I've been trying to talk to you for months, but you keep ducking me."

"It's not what you think it is, okay?"

"Then what is it? Because I don't remember."

"Look—"

"You *know* what happened to me," Carrie said. "Have you ever been reversed two years?"

Mia meekly shook her head. "No."

"Oh, it's a barrel of fun, let me tell you. One minute I'm sitting at home with my parents. The next, everything's changed. My mom's dead and buried. My dad's drunk and mopey. There are government goons in the underland and everyone's talking about doomsday. I see pictures of myself from the last two years but I don't remember a thing about them."

Mia forced herself into eye contact and buckled under the weight of old memories. Unlike Carrie, she hadn't forgotten a moment of their time together. Every walk. Every laugh. Every sweet and tender kiss.

"I've been asking everyone I know to help fill in the blanks," Carrie said. "It was actually easy until late last spring, when a group of alien breachers started living with us. And from what everyone tells me—and I mean *everyone*—I got really close to one of them. 'Oh, you and Mia? You were the *best* of friends. You were inseparable. My goodness.'"

Mia opened her mouth to say something, but Carrie cut her off. "So just imagine my surprise, after everything I heard, that you don't want anything to do with me. You hate me and you won't even say why."

"I don't hate you!" Mia yelled. "I hate *him*."

"Him?"

"Semerjean! The man who timewiped you. He only did that because of me!"

"Why?"

"Because I fired a gun at his crazy wife's head."

"So why did he take it out on me?"

"Because that's how he works," said Mia. "He never hits his enemies directly. He goes after the people they love."

"Love," Carrie echoed. "So you admit we were close."

"Of course we were. I never denied it."

"But you never said the words until now." Carrie laughed, exasperated. "That's the part that really gets me, because I've heard all about your girlie flings."

"Carrie—"

"I'm gay too, but you already knew that. And I can't help thinking that we were more than friends. But if it was just a casual thing—"

"It was more." Mia could feel the levees breaking inside of her. She squeezed her fists to keep from crying. "A lot more."

Carrie threw her hands up. "Why keep that from me? Why hide from me at all?"

"I have to."

"*Why?*"

"Because of *him*," Mia said. "That's what I keep telling you! I'm going to see him again at some point soon. And when that happens, I'll do everything in my power to kill him. If I miss this time, he won't fuck around. He'll kill the people I love most."

Mia took deep breaths until her voice stopped quivering. "I keep my distance to *protect* you, Carrie. I don't ever want him hurting you again."

"Then forget about him."

"What?"

"You don't have to fight him," Carrie said. "He's got you outgunned anyway. Just let him be and live your life."

Mia chuckled bleakly. "I can't do that."

"Why? Because he hurt your pride?"

"Because he destroyed my world," Mia said. "My dad. My brothers. He took everything."

Carrie eyed her woundedly. "I'm still here."

"You're missing the point."

"No, I think you are. Semerjean could have ended my life, but he only took two years of it. Why do you think he did that?"

Mia nodded bitterly. "So I'd always be reminded of the girl I lost."

"So you'd always be reminded of the girl you *gave up*," Carrie said. "We could have started over together, but you turned your tail and ran. That wasn't his choice. That was yours."

Mia shook her head derisively. "You're not as smart as the Carrie I knew."

"And you're not as nice as the Mia I've heard about," Carrie said. "I'm looking at you now with your hateful eyes and I'm wondering how any version of me could have fallen for you."

"Fuck you."

"Fuck *you*. I've wasted enough time on this bullshit."

"Good, then move on already! I have."

"No problem." Carrie opened her mouth to say one more thing, but she abruptly walked away. She was ten steps along the jogging path when she took a photo out of her jacket and dropped it to the ground.

"What is that?" Mia asked her.

Carrie kept walking, her voice cracked with sorrow. "Just something I found in the wreckage, before they built that Orphanage of yours."

"A photo of us?"

"I thought so." Carrie shot a hurt and angry look over her shoulder. "But apparently it's a picture of two other girls."

She disappeared down the looping path. Mia drew a small portal beneath the photograph and dropped it into her hands. Amanda had taken the picture last June, in the bygone days of Freak Street. The old Carrie Bloom sat on the porch swing of her cottage, flashing a bright, daffy grin as she draped her arm around an adolescent orphan. Mia reeled at the sight of her younger self: brown-haired, apple-cheeked, a little bit doughy and achingly naïve. Even a full year after the apocalypse, she'd still been such a child.

Mia's handphone buzzed with a new text message from Felicity. **We're leaving in 30. You better be ready.**

Dismayed, Mia took one last look at the snapshot before dropping it. She had all the painful memories she needed. And Carrie was right. The photo had nothing to do with either of them. It was just a picture of two other girls.

Hartford was seventy-eight miles northeast of the underland, a thirty-minute trip by skyway. But because half of Connecticut was engorged in a lightning storm, and because nature loved using aeromobiles as target practice, most commuters had wisely decided to take the land roads. The Quinnipiac Freeway was packed with grounded aeros, making every mile a slog.

Mia slouched in the seat of Felicity's Cupid, her sullen gaze aimed out the window. Of course it would rain on her rare day out. Why enjoy the sunshine when she could stock up on gloom and humidity?

Felicity peeked at Mia from the driver's seat. "Well, if it's any consolation, you look nice."

Mia snorted cynically. She had only changed into a black T-shirt and slacks, the nicest she was willing to dress for this "mission." Felicity must have been referring to her restrained eye makeup, at least a quarter of the amount she usually wore.

"Could use a bit less rage in the facial area," Felicity teased.

"How would you feel if you were forced into therapy?"

"Nostalgic," said Felicity. "But for the record, she isn't really a—"

"I know."

Cedric had set Mia up with an old friend of his, the press secretary of some U.S. senator. Mia had no idea how this woman was supposed to help her. A wiser man might have sent her to someone a little more qualified, and a little more not-in-Connecticut.

A forked bolt of lightning split the sky to the east, then sent a rumbling shudder through the aeromobile. "Look, who knows?" Felicity said. "You might get something out of it."

The only thing Mia wanted was to get back on the active roster. If Cedric had let her go to London, maybe Amanda wouldn't be famous. If he'd let her go to Cuba, maybe Merlin wouldn't be dead.

At a quarter past one, they finally reached Hartford: the capital of Connecticut and one of the nation's first umbrella cities. Mia craned her neck to look at the famous tempic canopy: six square miles of retractable cover, projected from a network of a million flying lenses. In addition to keeping Hartford dry, the umbrella was sloped to steer rainwater into a reservoir. Even Mia, in her bitter mood, was amazed by humanity's ingenuity. They'd harnessed the power of a Cataclysm to create an age of pure wonder.

Felicity parked in the heart of the government district, then pointed Mia to a marble-domed complex. "There it is. You know who to ask for."

"You're not coming with me?"

"I have company business. I'll come get you in a couple of hours."

"Hours?" Mia asked. "What if I finish early?"

Felicity popped the lock on the passenger door. "Then enjoy Hartford."

Mia spent a small eternity in the lobby of the Capitol Building, stewing from the edge of a wooden bench as she played puzzle games on her handphone. Every ten minutes, an intern popped out of a door like a spring-loaded cuckoo and gave Mia a shrugging apology. "Sorry. Daphne's still running late." "So sorry. Daphne just got caught on a call." "Hang in there. Daphne's almost done."

By 2:30, Mia was ready to kill someone. She closed out of her phone game and started a new text to Felicity. **This is bullshit. I'm not waiting one more m**

"Well, you must be Mira."

Mia nearly fell off the bench in surprise. While everyone else walked with loud, clacking footsteps, the woman named Daphne moved in silence. Her antigravity wheelchair was like something out of *Star Wars*: a sleek black marvel full of complicated gadgetry. In addition to her network of floating screens and cameras, she had at least three dozen controls within reach of her right hand.

"Sorry to keep you waiting," said Daphne. "You picked a hell of a day to come here."

She was a plump woman in her fifties, with the same platinum blond hair color as Mia's. They probably used the same brand of dye, though Mia couldn't imagine that Daphne applied it herself. From the withered look of her legs and left arm, she only had one limb at her command.

"Oh, uh . . ." Mia blinked dazedly. "Yeah. I've been following the news. It's not good."

"Not good?" Daphne laughed. "Our economy's wrecked and the whole country's panicking. I'd say we're well past the point of 'not good.'"

A bitmail popped up on her screen. She dismissed it with a voice command, then sighed. "Look, I know you came a long way to be here, but if there's any way we can postpone—"

"I'll do you one better," Mia said. "Just tell Cedric we had a nice talk and you won't have to see me at all."

Daphne narrowed her eyes at Mia. "I've known that man for twenty-five years and he's only ever asked for three favors. The first two were matters of national importance. The third one is you."

"Mia."

"What?"

"You called me Mira before. My name's Mia."

Daphne nodded contritely. "Well, Mia, you must be pretty special to have the head of Integrity worried about you."

Mia shrugged. She was under orders not to reveal classified information, another impediment to her "counseling." How could she possibly talk about Semerjean in the abstract?

"All right," said Daphne. "I just need to get a few more things in order, then we'll chat. If you're tired of sitting around, I can put you to work."

Mia spent the next hour delivering pamphlets around the Capitol, a four-page guide on how to discuss the Second Cataclysm. The rules were just as scattered and clueless as Mia expected. *Don't take the destruction of San Francisco as a given but don't make light of the prophecy. Don't promise our constituents that everything will be okay but don't lend credence to any apocalyptic talk. This is* not *the end of the world.*

By 3:30, Mia was drained. She'd almost forgotten how arduous her life had been before portals, all that tedious walking around. She could have finished her task in a tenth of the time if she'd been allowed to use her powers in mixed company.

Her work completed, she returned to Daphne's office and sank into the couch. "We done?"

Daphne smiled at her. "I'm sensing you don't have a passion for politics."

"No."

"What do you want to be when you're older?"

Alive, Mia morbidly thought. "I don't know. Probably a novelist."

"Oh, you poor thing. Describe your favorite sandwich."

Mia looked at her confusedly. "Uh, roast beef on rye with extra mustard and cheddar?"

"Now you're talking." Daphne typed up a bitmail with impressive speed, then buzzed her assistant on her headset. "Hold the fort, David. I'm going out."

Mia scoffed at the name of her intern. It seemed the universe was all middle fingers today.

As Daphne led her outside the Capitol Building, Mia glanced around at the ambling locals and took a small amount of pleasure in the fact that none of them looked back. She would have expected at least a few rude souls to gawk at Daphne's wonder-chair—a unique sight, even for Altamerica.

Daphne smirked at Mia's sideways glance. "You like this thing? I had it custom-made twenty years ago and I've been upgrading it ever since. It's amazing, the ability to go anywhere."

Mia quietly agreed. "Must have cost a fortune."

"Yes, well, I have one," Daphne said with a humble grin. "I'm the only nut here who works for the fun of it."

She led Mia into Government Square, a four-acre parcel of manicured lawns and straight-edged shrubs, with enough kinetic sculptures to keep the view interesting. Mia figured the place would be pretty on a regular day, but under the fluorescent haze of the great tempic canopy, the park was just depressing, like a plastic simulation in an oversized warehouse. It would have actually looked better in the rain.

The vendor at the nearest sandwich cart, a burly young man who reminded Mia of Caleb, immediately greeted Daphne with her meal order: two wrapped sandwiches with chips and bottled water.

Mia unfurled her roast beef with extra cheddar. "Wow. You really have your shit together."

Daphne laughed. "Interesting expression. Are all the kids saying that now?"

"Not really."

Daphne motioned for Mia to sit on a bench, then swiveled her chair to face her. "What did Cedric tell you about me?"

"Not much," Mia admitted. "He said that in a better world, you'd be president."

Daphne chuckled. "I can't think of a job I'd want less, except maybe his."

"What did he tell you about me?" Mia asked.

"That you were an extraordinary girl who'd been betrayed by someone she trusted. He said the anger's put you on a self-destructive path and he was hoping I could turn you around."

Mia bristled at Cain's assessment, even if she couldn't dispute it. How many bridges did she burn in the underland this morning? How many ways did she screw up with Carrie?

She looked at Daphne timidly. "Can I ask you a slightly rude question?"

"How did I get stuck in this big, ugly chair?"

"What made him think you can help me?"

"Same answer to both," said Daphne. "Does the name Charles Novik ring a bell?"

Amazingly enough, it did, though Mia couldn't remember where she'd heard it. "Who is he?"

"He was a renowned Canadian doctor and engineer," Daphne said. "Almost single-handedly invented the medical reviver. He's saved more lives with temporis than the Cataclysm ever took. Nearly fifty million people around the world, at last count."

"Wow."

Daphne took a bite of her chicken salad griller, a distant sorrow in her eyes. "When I was thirteen, he married my mother and came to America to live with us. At the time, it felt like I'd won the stepdad lottery. He was gracious and funny and ridiculously kind, and he never lorded his fame over anyone. He just kept working on his beloved revivers, trying to make them even safer for the folks who needed them."

Mia felt a pang of dread. She didn't like where this was going.

"He got concerned one day when I started slurring my speech," said Daphne. "I'd been having trouble for a couple of weeks—headaches, nausea, chronic fatigue. I'd wake up feeling like I hadn't slept a wink, even though the whole night was a blur. But the slurred speech thing? That was new. Charles was worried that it was a sign of an aneurysm, and he was right. Two days after my sixteenth birthday, I had a massive stroke that all but paralyzed me."

Mia cocked her head. "Couldn't they, uh . . ."

"Reverse me? No. This was still back in the early days. The machine didn't do a thing for people with brain damage, except kill them."

A message light flashed on Daphne's console. She waved it away.

"Anyway, I'd been laid up a year when a housekeeper came crying to me. While cleaning Charles's office, she'd accidentally opened a secret compartment. Inside were hundreds of horrific photographs. Pictures of Charles doing all kinds of . . ."

Daphne paused, her eyes closed tight. "He'd been abusing me for months in the basement of our house, on the bed of the reviver he kept tinkering with. Every time he finished, he'd reverse me a couple of hours. All my bruises, all my memories, wiped away like they never happened. Until I saw those pictures, I had no idea. I certainly didn't know that he was the one who maimed me. You can't reverse someone that many times without wrecking their nervous system. Charles knew that better than anyone."

Mia covered her mouth. She remembered reading about Charles Novik last year. His crime had become a national scandal, one of the biggest news stories of 1980. "Oh my God."

"Yeah. That was an awful time for all of us. The stress killed my mom within a year."

"But they got him."

"Oh, they got him," Daphne said. "Those photos did him in."

"Hope they put him away for life."

"Life?" Daphne chortled. "For a man of his stature and worldly contributions? That's not the way it works, my dear. That's not the way it ever worked."

"So how many—"

"Nine."

"Nine years?"

"And I had to fight to make sure he even served that," Daphne said. "I wheeled myself to every parole hearing and yelled my bloody head off. 'You can't let him out! You can't ever let him out! He's a monster!'"

Mia nodded fervently. "He *is* a monster."

"And yet for four long years, I mistook him for a saint. That was half the source of my rage right there. That I could have been so stupid, so *blind*, as to not see his true nature."

At last, Mia realized why Cedric had sent her to Daphne. They had much more in common than she'd realized.

"I can see the anger in you," Daphne said to Mia. "You're a lovely girl on the outside and a fire demon on the inside, just like I was. And please don't think I'm judging you. That fire kept me going for years. You know why?"

It was hardly a puzzle to Mia. "Because he had to pay for what he did."

"He *had* to pay," Daphne echoed. "Nine years wasn't enough. A bullet to the head wasn't enough. I needed to find someone who could really make his murder messy. Drag it out for weeks, even months."

Mia sighed with preemptive disappointment. If Novik had truly died by torture, as he deserved, there's no way Daphne would confess it.

"But you never found a hit man," Mia guessed.

Daphne smiled wistfully. "No, just Cedric. He'd heard me making waves in the criminal world, and he took it upon himself to intervene. Good thing, too, because it wouldn't have ended well for me. These things rarely do."

A loud snap of thunder brought a hush to the park. There must have been a hell of a bolt beyond the tempis.

"So what happened to him?" Mia asked. "Is he still alive?"

"Charles? No. He died last year at a ripe old age." Daphne smirked. "Now ask what happened to me."

Mia eyed her strangely. "I'm looking right at you."

"Look harder. What's missing from the picture?"

Mia peered uncomfortably into Daphne's eyes. "The rage is gone."

"Dead and buried," said Daphne. "But not because of anything Charles did. Five years after his parole, he mustered up the nerve to come see me. He was a little older, a little thinner, not nearly as broken as I'd hoped. His good name was forever tarnished, but he still had money and friends."

She chuckled grimly. "He apologized for everything that happened to me, as if another Charles Novik had done it. And then he expressed his frustration that I went to the cops instead of keeping it inside the family. 'It caused a lot of grief to your mother,' he said. 'And it set back my work for decades. But I understand why you did it, and I forgive you.'"

Mia's mouth dropped open. A heat rose up in her cheeks. "Are you *kidding* me?"

"Wish I was."

"Holy shit. I would have killed him right there. What did you do?"

"The most surprising thing I ever did in my life," Daphne said. "I forgave him."

Mia gawked at her with disbelief. "You forgave him."

"From the bottom of my heart and for every last bit of it. Even his awful apology."

"I don't get it. *How?*"

"Mia—"

"After everything he did to you—"

"Mia, *look* at me."

Daphne moved her chair closer until her face was just a few feet from Mia's.

"I'd been carrying the fire inside me for years," she said. "That hatred burned everything I had left—my spirit, my intellect, my compassion for others. I'd thought the anger would make me strong. It didn't. It crippled me more than Charles ever did."

Mia looked away with a tortured grimace. "I don't want to hear this."

"You wanted to know what happened to me. *That's* what happened. The day I forgave him was the day I broke free. It was the day he stopped having power over me."

"You don't know what you're talking about!"

"I know my life, Mia."

"But you don't know *mine.*" Mia jumped to her feet, spilling the remains of her lunch. "You don't know what he did to me!"

"I don't even know who *he* is," Daphne confessed. "And according to Cedric, you're not allowed to tell me."

Mia was tempted to throw caution to the wind and share the whole ugly story. But what did Semerjean do to make her so mad, anyway? Destroy her world? He did that to every orphan. Betray her trust? He did that to every Silver. And yet somehow Mia was the only one who'd become obsessed with him. She was the only one who burned on the inside.

It's because he took Carrie from me! Mia insisted to herself.

He didn't take me anywhere, her inner Carrie replied. *It was you who closed the door on us.*

Mia fell back onto the bench, her face drenched in tears. All this hatred, all this fury, all for reasons that every living soul in the underland knew.

You were in love with him, sang the chorus of her peers. *And you had no clue.*

As Mia hunched over and wept into her hands, Daphne parked next to her and stroked her back. "Sweetheart . . ."

"Don't."

"I never said it'd be easy."

"It's not," Mia cried. "All I want to do is kill him."

"And that won't go away," Daphne warned. "Not on your own. Not even with help. Forgiveness—and I mean the honest-to-God, soul-cleansing kind—doesn't ever come on demand. You just have to wait for the moment to find you. And when it does, you can't fight it. You have to let it in or you'll never be free."

Mia looked up at her. "I don't *want* to forgive him. He doesn't deserve it!"

"It's not about what *he* deserves. It's about you. You're a beautiful young woman, just brimming with intelligence. And you still have decades left to you."

A jagged laugh escaped Mia's throat before she could stop it. "Don't be too sure."

"What do you mean?"

She looked beyond Daphne and saw someone approaching, a person she recognized, even from a distance. There weren't too many six-foot-one women in neon yellow pantsuits. Felicity must have tracked her to the park.

Daphne turned her chair around and grinned at her. "Now, who's this tall ray of sunshine?"

Mia would have expected that to elicit a smile from Felicity, or at least a pithy quip. Instead she looked to Mia with uncharacteristic urgency.

"We have to go."

Mia wiped her eyes. "Everything okay?"

"More or less," Felicity said with a nervous glance at Daphne. "I apologize but—"

"I'm not authorized to hear it," Daphne guessed. "Never be sorry for doing your job. I need to get back to mine anyway."

She squeezed Mia's wrist. "Cedric has all my contact information. You need me, you call."

Mia sniffled. "Thank you. I'm sorry I yelled at you. You're a good person."

"And you're a *strong* person," Daphne said. "I saw it from the moment I laid eyes on you. You'll find your way back to the light."

As she floated her chair back toward the Capitol, she turned around one last time and bounced a nervous look between Mia and Felicity. "I can't shake the feeling that the world's falling apart. Is there anything you can tell me that'll help me think otherwise?"

Daphne sighed at their matching expressions of gloom. "Yeah. That's what I was afraid of."

As Daphne drifted out of earshot, Felicity kneeled in front of Mia. "You okay?"

"Yeah, it was, uh . . ." Mia chuckled in amazement. "Cedric knew what he was doing."

"Listen, I just heard from Melissa. She and the others are riding a boat into Halifax. We're gonna go up there and meet them."

"Isn't that in Canada?"

"Yes."

"How will we get past—"

"I'm Integrity. I can get us anywhere." Felicity motioned to the bench. "Before we go, you need to sit down. Melissa had some news for me to give you."

"Oh God." Mia dropped back to her seat. "Who died?"

"Mia—"

"Just tell me who died!"

"Nobody died! Everyone's fine! In fact . . ." Felicity sighed as she struggled for words. "They found your brother Bobby in Europe. He's on the boat with them now and he's very much alive."

Mia turned to her in a dazed little stupor, her eyes neither moving nor blinking. "What?"

Her hands had barely stopped trembling all the way to Nova Scotia. Throughout every step of her five-hour journey—the car ride to Boston, the shuttle to Montréal, the customs check, the charter plane rental—Mia existed in a state of soporific denial, as if she'd stumbled out of reality and into a sublime dream. She'd seen doomsdays and aerstraunts and tempic wolves by the dozen, but somehow the existence of Bobby Farisi was a bridge too far. Nobody ever came back from the dead. Even this world was clear on the rule.

By the time Mia reached her final destination, an old commercial seaport in the South End district of Halifax, she was convinced that she was in for a gut punch. Maybe Melissa had made a mistake. Maybe this "Bobby" was an impostor. Or maybe the Pelletiers were setting her up for the mother of all tragedies.

That bullet you fired will return one day, Esis had warned Mia. *You won't like where it goes.*

"There they are," said Felicity.

Mia peered out at dark and distant waters, where a large ship approached at fast speed. At this time of night, there was little to see but its lumic hull: a glowing green aura with neon yellow trimmings, the maritime standard for humanitarian aid ships.

It de-shifted fifty yards from port, then docked gracefully at a wooden pier. Mia's whole body quaked with anticipation and fear as a tempic ramp extended from the starboard side of the ship and connected to the pier with a *clack*. There was already a crowd of people waiting to disembark, a mob of indistinguishable silhouettes.

"He's not there," Mia said. "I don't see him."

Felicity gripped her shoulder. "Patience."

"If he was there, I'd see him. He's huge."

"Mia—"

"Are you sure that's the right boat?"

As the passengers stepped into the light of the pier, Felicity's face lit up in a grin. "Yup."

Mia gasped at the sight of all the familiar faces approaching: Melissa and Caleb, Mercy and Sage, the Coppers of Seattle, plus the oldest two siblings of her Silver clan. Amanda was so wrapped up in casual concealments that Mia barely recognized her. But who else would be clutching Zack's hand like that? Who else would smile so brightly at Mia?

Beaming, Mia ran to Amanda and threw her arms around her. "I'm so glad you're okay."

Amanda stroked her hair. "I missed you."

Mia reached for Zack's right hand, only to notice that it was gone again.

"I'm all right," he said, though there was a weariness in his eyes that troubled her. Zack jerked his head at the crowd behind him. "Go on. He's been chomping at the bit to see you."

Mia looked to the many strangers in the pack, all the prodigal orphans of Europe. Their bracelets, like hers, had been long removed. She couldn't tell the Violets from the Opals. All she knew was that none of them were Bobby. Where the hell—

"Is she here?"

A hulking man came charging down the walkway, his wide gaze swiveling in all directions. Even in the dim light, the sight of her oldest brother sent Mia into a state of complete lockdown. Her mind, her heart, her limbs, her lungs, nothing seemed to work anymore. All she could do was stand there and blink as Bobby rushed past her.

He looked to Zack and Amanda and threw his hands up. "You'd said she'd be here."

"You walked right by her," Zack insisted.

"What?"

"Turn. Around."

At long last, Mia got her voice to work. She stammered at her brother's back. "Bobby."

He spun a one-eighty and scanned the area around Mia, as if his little baby sister was somehow hiding behind that blonde.

"Bobby, it's me."

"What?" He focused directly on Mia, bewildered. "I don't understand . . . I . . ."

He kneeled down in front of her and examined her up close. For all of Mia's thoughts and wild speculations, it had never once occurred to her that her brother wouldn't recognize her. But then he'd barely seen her since she was twelve, and she'd done a fair bit of changing since then.

"Holy mother of God." Bobby reached out with a quivering hand but stopped just short of touching her. "How . . . how many years have you been here?"

Warm, fresh tears ran down Mia's cheeks. She gave him a wavering smile. "Just two."

"That can't be right. You're all grown up. I mean . . ."

Bobby drank her in with wet-eyed awe. "You're a woman."

Mia hugged him tight. "Hi, Bobby."

Nearly two dozen orphans watched in quiet joy as they wept over each other's shoulders. Reunions like this were exceedingly rare, especially among their kind. There was no other way to look at it but as a victory. Two siblings had found their way back to each other, despite all the machinations of gods and demons.

There was one particular devil on Mia's mind as she embraced Bobby. Semerjean had once told her that she was the very last Farisi, and she'd been foolish enough to believe him. Now she could only curse his name as another one of his lies fell exposed.

You tried to keep my brother from me, Mia hissed in her thoughts. *You failed.*

She narrowed her eyes over Bobby's shoulder and cast her vengeful gaze at the darkness. *You failed.*

NINETEEN

The 1950s were an awful time for Japan. From the day their beloved prime minister died, the nation was plagued by a decade of bad fortune—a civil war, a Chinese coup, a flu pandemic, a volcano eruption, an earthquake, a flood, and a six-year economic depression that brought the entire country to a standstill.

As humanity came roaring into the Temporal Age, Japan's top scientists lacked the funding to compete with other nations. They could only watch helplessly as, one by one, their rivals rocked the planet with incredible new inventions: the shifter (Korea), the juve (Germany), the medical reviver (Canada), the tempic barrier (the United States).

What's left for us? asked the Japanese newspapers. *How do we reclaim our place as the world's greatest innovator?*

Their luck finally changed in 1960 when a young American businessman presented a prototype device to Omata Electronics, a state-owned conglomerate of Japan. The machine used a newly discovered form of temporis to channel and repurpose the light of the past, creating all kinds of visual wonders: holograms, screen displays, aerial projections, plus a virtually unlimited palette of tools to bring color and light to the world.

"This lumis will redefine life as we know it," the American promised Omata. "It'll put Japan at the front of a brand-new industry. How much is that worth to you?"

The businessman's name was Auberon Graham, and he was harboring a bit of a secret. He was a chronokinetic of the Majee clan, a traveler who received gifts from his future selves. One of those gifts contained a schematic for Omata's lumic projector, a machine they were still two years away from inventing. Graham had stolen their idea before they could have it, then sold it to them at a premium.

A dirty trick? Sure. But it worked out well for the buyers. The lumic technology took the planet by storm and brought Japan into a new age of prosperity. To this day, the country remained an economic powerhouse, the world's leading innovator of lumis.

Japan was also, as Theo discovered on Monday night, the world's greatest *abuser* of lumis. Nearly every inch of downtown Yokohama was lit in garish neon colors and infested with animated holograms. Even the street signs looked like advertisements, and the advertisements looked like nightmares. Motion detectors fired pop-ups out of a cannon, accosting Theo at every turn with bright and bewildering offers. A cartoon pig flew a circle around his head, peddling candy or bacon or possibly candied bacon. A hat store sent a creepy little mermaid to show him a picture of what he'd look like in a fedora. And God only knew what a holographic geisha was selling him. She kept waving him in through a bright red door, giggling with a suggestive smile. After ten minutes of sensory assault, Theo was ready to strangle someone. It didn't help that he was still jet-lagged from his flight, still fuming about the death of Merlin McGee.

"You all right?" asked his Majee guide, the affable young tempic named Meredith Graham. "I can still get you some blockers."

Theo looked to Heath and his bulky new glasses, which used wavelength filters to screen out the lumis. They even came with a pair of fur-lined earmuffs to keep the nonstop clamor to a minimum. As much as Theo coveted relief, he wasn't feeling secure enough to look that silly.

"I'm fine," he said. "I'm already getting used to it."

Meredith laughed. "You think this is bad, try Tokyo. Their Ginza district will make your eyes bleed."

"You know Japan pretty well."

"It's been our company's main market for fifty years."

Theo couldn't help but be impressed by his new timebender acquaintances. While the Gothams were merely a coterie of families, the Majee were a multinational corporation. Instead of elders, they were ruled by a board of directors, and every adult in the clan had an executive role. Meredith had spent half the flight from Cuba making business calls in Japanese.

Which prompted a sudden new query from Theo. "I thought American companies were discouraged from working abroad."

"Discouraged?" Meredith scoffed. "We're scrutinized, stigmatized, and taxed into oblivion."

"So why do it, then?"

Her expression turned cold. "You ever deal with American businessmen?"

"No."

"They're racist, sexist, corrupt, and myopic. They'd kill their own mother if it bumped up their quarterlies."

"But not the Japanese."

"They're sexist," said Meredith. "But they have long-term vision and they negotiate with honor."

"And how are they with, uh . . ."

"Black people?" Meredith grinned. "They're good to the ones who make them money. That's all I can tell you for sure."

Her sister, Charlene, walked ten yards ahead, only occasionally looking back to check on the others. Though she and Meredith were identical twins, Theo was in no danger of confusing them. Meredith was soft and friendly-looking, while Charlene seemed to be made entirely of sharp edges. If she was harboring some kindness beneath her gruff exterior, Theo had yet to see it. But then maybe he was biased from his bad first impression. He wasn't fond of anyone who held a knife to Heath's throat.

Meredith read his hard expression. "Don't judge her too harshly. She's under a lot of stress."

"We all are," Theo said. "I've been trying for months to work with you guys."

"We choose our partners carefully."

"And you apparently have your own plan to stop what's coming."

"We have a plan to *survive*," Meredith said. "But if there's a way to save everyone, as you seem to believe, then we're willing to hear you out."

"How generous of you."

"Hey." Meredith moved in front of Theo and stopped him on the sidewalk. "I know you're still mad—"

"Of course I'm mad. If you guys hadn't pulled me away—"

"You couldn't have saved Merlin."

"How do you know?"

"Because he wanted to die," said Meredith. "And he was a better augur than you."

Theo had heard the rumors on the flight to Japan, a conspiracy theory that Merlin had hired his own assassin. But the only evidence anyone had was the fact that his final words were "Come on." He'd yelled it twice, like he was urging the killer to pull the trigger on him. Theo flatly rejected the notion, even as his prescient instincts told him not to die on that hill. *You might want to prepare for the possibility*, they warned. *Just saying.*

An animated bee brushed by Theo's head and flashed him an ad for spiced honey chips. He swatted it away as if it were tangible. "Your timing still sucks."

"Maybe," said Meredith. "But if you're smart—and I think you are—then you'll stop complaining about it, especially around Auberon. He's the one you need to convince, and he doesn't have patience for whiners."

Whiners, Theo grumbled in his thoughts. The world's greatest prophet had just been killed, but that didn't make Meredith wrong. Theo needed the Majee and their nine orphan Rubies. He wasn't going to win by antagonizing them.

"You're right," he told Meredith. "It's ironic, actually."

"That I'm right?"

"That I'm being emotional instead of pragmatic," Theo said. "I usually have the opposite problem."

"Being pragmatic is never a problem."

"I let fifty strangers die last week because it was the only way to get the future I wanted."

"Did it work?"

Theo thought about the Opals and Violets, all currently en route to the underland. They would have never been found without Evan's help, and he would have never popped out of his spider hole if that accident in New Jersey hadn't happened.

"Yeah," Theo admitted. "I guess it did."

"Then you have nothing to be ashamed of," said Meredith. "My grandfather would admire you for making the hard call."

Theo wasn't sure how to feel about that, as Auberon was still an enigma to him. Though his motives seemed benevolent, there was a cold front in the old man's future that threatened all of Theo's plans.

"Any more advice on how to deal with him?" he asked Meredith.

"That entirely depends on how sure you are."

"About what?"

"Your plan to save the world."

"Oh." Theo stared down at the lumic walkway, which splashed with colors at every step. "It's not my plan and I'm not sure at all."

Meredith studied him with a hard look, enough to finally make her resemble her sister. "Well, there's my next advice right there. Don't tell Auberon any of that."

The Majees' Yokohama office stood at the edge of the marina district, a six-story tower that reminded Theo of a glass cigar. Like everything else in this flamboyant city, the exterior was covered in radiant animations. But instead of inflicting their corporate brand on bystanders, the Majee lit up their structure in a swirling array of colors, from the warm end of the spectrum to the cool end and then all the way back again.

Luckily for Theo and his beleaguered eyes, the interior was far more restrained. The only hologram in the lobby was a woman in a kimono who smiled and bowed whenever the front doors opened. Everything else was tastefully done, from the subtle underlighting of a cherry blossom tree to the glowing blue waters of a fountain.

Heath took off his blockers and studied the walls, each one filled with a faint but ghostly visage. "What is this?"

Meredith smiled at him. "Majikkuraito."

"What?"

"It's a Japanese design philosophy, a way to harmonize your home through the spirits of the past." She gestured at the wall of faces. "These are the founders of our clan."

Theo remembered reading about majikkuraito. The whole trend had been started by the lumis industry as a way to sell more projection panels. "It means 'magic light,' right?"

"Yes. Very good."

"Is that where you got the name 'Majee'?"

"No." Meredith pointed at the portrait of a strong-jawed woman, one who could have been a triplet to her and Charlene. "That was our great-grandmother, Marjorie Graham. Everyone called her Majee."

Theo studied her spectral image. "First generation."

Meredith nodded. "A child of the Cataclysm."

"Did you know her, or, uh . . ."

"No," said Meredith. "She was before my time."

"And died well before *her* time," said a baritone voice from the elevator bank. "Those of us who knew her still feel her loss every day."

Auberon walked across the lobby on his ivory cane, looking as dapper as ever in his crisp beige suit. Theo had learned some of his secret story on the flight to Japan. He was the planet's oldest living traveler, yet he'd never once teleported under his own power. A childhood illness had stunted his abilities, preventing him from drawing doors through the present.

But his skill with time portals was apparently unparalleled, and he certainly made them work for him. Unlike Mia, who'd gotten nothing but grief from her elder selves, Auberon had thousands of friends in the future. They sent him all the intel he needed to keep his corporation profitable: stock tips, earnings reports, newspaper clippings, even a few revolutionary gadgets that had yet to be invented. And though he was under no obligation to return the favor, Auberon regularly sent gifts of equal value to his counterparts in the past.

He shook Theo's hand. "Good to see you again. How's the hotel?"

"It's beautiful. Thank you."

"I'm sorry you couldn't rest more."

Theo swallowed the urge to criticize Auberon's timing. "It's all right. I know what we're up against."

The old man turned to Charlene and Meredith. "Why don't you take Heath upstairs and get him a snack?"

Heath took a firm hold of Theo's arm. "Not without him."

"You'll be fine," Charlene said.

Theo smiled at her. "He knows that. He's just looking out for me."

"That's so sweet," Meredith cooed. "I *love* this kid."

"It's all right," Theo told Heath. "I'll see you in a few minutes."

Once the sisters and Heath disappeared into an elevator, Auberon led Theo to a nook of couches by the fountain. "He's a real trooper, that boy."

Theo sat down on a sofa. "That's an understatement."

"If I may be so bold as to ask—"

"I don't know," Theo said with a shrug. "Could be autism. Could be trauma. Could be both or neither. He doesn't talk about it, and we don't ask. Heath is Heath. That's all that matters."

"Fair enough." Auberon sat down with a groan of discomfort. "I'm sorry for everything you people have been through. The nonstop threats and upheaval."

"Guess you heard all about it from the Rubies."

Auberon nodded. "They're fine young men."

"Men?"

"Yes. All of them. You didn't know?"

"No." Theo supposed he shouldn't be surprised. If the Mexican orphans could be a unisex group, then so could the Japanese. "How long have you had them?"

"They've been our friends and guests for eight months," Auberon said with a hint of defensiveness, enough to make Theo wish he'd phrased his question more delicately.

"Thank you for taking care of them."

Auberon eyed him guardedly. "They're important to you."

"You're all important to me," Theo said. "We need every timebender we can get."

"To save the world, you mean."

"Yes."

"How?"

Theo hesitated a bit before responding. "Let's save it for the meeting."

Auberon chuckled. "You remind me of me when I first became clan leader."

"How so?"

"You're clearly in over your head," Auberon replied. "But you know when to admit it and when to hide it, and I respect that."

Theo felt more patronized than praised. He once again looked to the image of Majee Graham.

"It never made sense to me what the Gothams did," Theo noted. "They have Indians, Asians, Hispanics, and Jews. But they drew a hard line at Black people."

Auberon laughed. "Is that what they told you?"

"It was implied."

"These stories have a way of getting simplified over time," said Auberon. "The split was never about race. Just differing philosophies."

"Philosophies?"

"You know how the Gothams are about breeding."

Theo nodded. "No outsiders. Just timebenders."

"Precisely. They want each generation to be stronger than the last. From an evolutionary standpoint, it makes perfect sense."

Auberon gestured at Majee Graham's likeness. "But my mother believed that people should be free to follow their hearts. She said that any society that puts restrictions on love is fundamentally broken at its core."

Theo thought about Merlin and his past troubles with the Gothams. "Wise woman."

"Indeed. She couldn't convince the majority, but she had pull with the other Black timebenders. When she left, they followed, and we've been upholding her principles ever since."

Theo stroked his chin, intrigued. "Your clan must have done a lot of, uh . . ."

"Crossbreeding," said Auberon. "Yes. And the results were exactly what the Gothams had feared. There are four hundred and thirty of us in the clan, but only fifty-five timebenders."

"No partials?" Theo asked. "Like a half-powered tempic or a—"

Auberon shook his head. "Either you have the magic or you don't. My granddaughters have it. My grandsons don't."

"Wow." Theo knew at least a dozen Integrity scientists who would kill for that information. "Doesn't that create a split society?"

Auberon gave him a testy shrug. "Show me one that isn't."

Theo could see that he didn't want to talk about it anymore. "You've done a good job," he told Auberon. "With the clan and the corporation. My people and I would be lucky to have you as friends."

The old man didn't look as pleased as Theo had hoped. "Did Meredith tell you how my mother died?"

"No."

"Integrity," he said. "They didn't even know she was chronokinetic. She was just trying to save some strangers from their abuses and they shot her in the street like an animal."

Sadly, Theo had no trouble envisioning it. "I'm sorry."

"Their horrors are well-documented. You had to have known about some of them."

"Of course I did. I've *seen* some of them."

"So why work with them?"

"Because we need all the help we can get," Theo said. "There's too much at stake to hold on to grudges."

Auberon snorted cynically. "I've been a venture capitalist for fifty-four years. I know how to work with bad people."

"Then why does this feel like an uphill battle?" Theo asked. "We both know the future and we both want to change it. Yet here I am, auditioning for you—"

"It's not an audition. I don't need a song and dance."

"Then what do you need? Tell me."

At long last, Auberon smiled again, a soft and cryptic grin that Theo couldn't read for the life of him.

"I stopped doing press interviews some years ago," said Auberon. "Because I got tired of answering the same question. 'You're an American investor, Mr. Graham. Why aren't you investing in America?'"

"What did you tell them?"

"I said my family *is* my nation," Auberon replied. "I'll go wherever I need to go, do whatever I need to do, to give them the best possible future."

"Isn't saving the world the best possible future?" Theo asked.

"Possible? Yes. But by your very own admission, it isn't very probable."

"When did I say that?"

"Twenty minutes from now," Auberon told him. "I already have a full transcript of the meeting. It came by portal last night."

Theo stood up, flustered. "Then why am I even here?"

"Because my people have two different plans on the table, and I promised my granddaughters that I'd look at both fairly."

"What exactly *is* your plan?"

"I never said it was my plan."

"Then who—"

Theo suddenly felt a shudder in the strings, as if a cold wind had blown across the future. Not even Semerjean had that effect. Only one man did.

Theo turned to Auberon, wide-eyed. "Are you insane?"

"I thought you already knew he was coming."

"How?"

"You're an augur, Theo. How could you not see?"

A strong light quickly turned their heads, a bright new portal in the elevator bank.

Auberon rose from his chair. "I told you I know how to work with bad people."

A tall, pale man stepped out of the portal and graced his host with a grin. "Hello, Auberon. Good to see you, as always."

Azral turned his attention to the Silver in the lobby, his smile now wide and mocking. "Theo."

TWENTY

The conference room on the fifteenth floor was designed in the majikkuraito style, full of artful lumic touches that honored the spirits of the dead. This particular space seemed dedicated to four Majee: an elderly man, a middle-aged woman, a teenage boy, and a preadolescent girl. Theo guessed from their contemporary hairstyles that they'd all been alive rather recently. And they all shared the same vacant expression on their faces, a thousand-yard stare that seemed to penetrate time itself.

"Our prophets," Meredith had said. "I probably don't need to tell you how they died."

Theo shook his head. The Gothams had lost most of their augurs to suicide over the last two years, and the few that remained were just pill-popping husks of their former selves. These weren't the best days to have a front-row view of the future.

Now the man who had mortally wounded this world was standing right by the doorway, making casual small talk with Auberon. Theo had no idea why Azral, the reigning charm vacuum of the Pelletiers, had volunteered to do the glad-handing. None of the other Majee seemed particularly beguiled. Meredith and Charlene could barely stand to look at him.

But it was Heath's reaction that worried Theo the most. The boy sat next to him at the long end of the conference table, his fingers hooked tightly into his thighs. Theo could practically hear the discord in his head, all the angry wolves and Jonathans that were howling for revenge.

Meredith leaned toward Theo and whispered into his ear. "Is he okay?"

"No," Theo said. "But he won't be a problem, and neither will I."

"Good," said Meredith. "You may not believe it, but my sister and I are pulling for you."

"Why?"

She glared at Azral through slitted eyes. "We know his type."

Theo assumed she was talking about cold white oligarchs, the kind who'd been molding and bleeding the world since the first Roman Empire. Though Azral certainly fit the look with his towering height, his shock-white hair, his opaline eyes, and haughty scowl, the man stood alone in his own class of bastard. He was callous on a cosmic scale, like a great black hole or a supernova.

Yet Theo noticed a change in the way Azral carried himself. His posture was less stiff than usual, more human. He even blinked at the rate of a normal person. Had he finally adjusted to life among the primitives or was it all just an act for the Majee?

At last, Auberon and Azral finished their parley, then joined the sisters and orphans at the table. Six middle-aged executives rounded out the meeting: the board of directors of Majee Enterprises and the leaders of the secret clan. But for all their sway and stately airs, Theo knew who was really calling the shots. Auberon was the first and last word on all important matters, and there was nothing more important than this.

"Thank you all for coming," the old man began. "Especially those who traveled a long way to be here."

He'd aimed his praise at both Azral and Theo, as if a portal jump and a ten-hour flight were equally arduous journeys.

Auberon nodded at Theo and Heath. "I'd also like to thank our two young guests for their extraordinary graciousness. I know they have a . . . fractured history with our associate, Mr. Pelletier. But they've put it aside for the greater good and I couldn't be more appreciative."

Theo had to fight to keep his composure. He'd traveled halfway around the world, and for what? Auberon had all but admitted that he'd decided to work with Azral. This whole dumb meeting was just a puppet show for his granddaughters, an illusion of a fair debate.

Theo pointed at the miniature camera drones that captured the room from every angle. "May I ask who else is watching?"

"We're broadcasting live to our entire clan," Meredith said.

"And the orphans?" Theo asked.

Auberon hesitated a moment before answering. "They're also watching."

"I'd like to see them, if you don't mind. I've been waiting a long time to meet them."

"Of course."

On her grandfather's request, Charlene keyed up a circular viewscreen above the table, a live image of nine Japanese strangers. At long last, Theo could see the Rubies of Osaka. Auberon had called them young men earlier, but none of them looked much older than Heath. Just a bunch of gawky boys in sweatsuits.

"You can talk to them," Meredith told Theo. "My cousin's translating."

Theo tossed a cordial nod at the Rubies. "Hi. I'm Theo Maranan, a Filipino American and a survivor from your world. By my count, there are sixty-nine of us left. My friends and I have traveled the globe, gone through all kinds of hell, to bring us all together. You're the very last group on our list. If you want to save this world from dying like ours, then we have to work together as one people. It's our only chance to survive."

He paused in thought before continuing. "I know the Majee have been good to you, and I thank them for it. I'm hoping I can convince them to join us as well. But whatever happens tonight, whatever they decide, I just want you to know that you'll always have a place in New York with my people. *Our* people."

While Meredith gave him an approving nod, Auberon shifted in his seat uneasily. Theo didn't have to guess why he was nervous. If he was casting his lot with Azral, then the Rubies were crucial to the survival of his clan.

"Well said," Auberon replied, almost convincingly. He motioned for Charlene to close the transmission before speaking to Theo again. "My people already know the particulars of Mr. Pelletier's proposal, but for your sake—"

"I know it," Theo said. "It's the same deal they offered us. Give them some babies and they'll bring you back to their era. They have a nice little time-share in Brazil."

Azral smiled wryly. "That's not the plan."

"We rejected that offer," Auberon told Theo. "There were too many variables and uncertainties for our comfort. We'd much rather stay on the Earth we know."

Theo tilted his head, baffled. "The Earth you know is going away."

"Not entirely." Auberon looked to Azral. "Did you bring the, uh . . ."

"Of course."

Azral reached inside his suit and placed a trinket on the table: a bracelet unlike any Theo had ever seen. It was only half as thick as the ones the orphans had been given, with two red bands on the outer edge. The material itself defied classification, a shiny black substance with swirling clouds of gray.

Auberon gestured at Meredith. "If you don't mind."

"Yeah." She stood up and approached the ominous-looking bracelet, then tossed a guarded look at Azral. "I assume it's been . . . safety-tested."

"Thoroughly," he assured her.

"On who? Prisoners?"

Auberon sighed at her. "Meredith."

"Okay, okay."

The bracelet expanded in Meredith's grip, enough for her to slide it over her hand. The loop gently enclosed around the skin of her wrist, then covered her in a sheath of yellow light. Theo's eyes bulged at the familiar sight of the energy: the very same stuff that had saved him from apocalypse, the same power that coursed inside Ofelia's bracelet.

"I call it aegis," said Azral. "My own invention. It's impervious to all forms of damage, from blunt force trauma to particle radiation. But it also repels its sister energies. No temporal force can penetrate it. Not even solis."

Auberon touched the edge of Meredith's barrier. "Amazing."

"How much air do I have?" Meredith asked Azral.

"As much as you need. The aegis generates its own oxygen."

"But how do I—" Meredith didn't have a chance to finish her question before the forcefield vanished in a blink.

"It only deactivates when you want it to," Azral said. "Not a moment before."

Charlene wasn't nearly as impressed as the others. "But we can't fight while we're inside those bubbles," she said to Azral. "Like if I needed to rift someone . . ."

Azral shook his head. "It's a bidirectional barrier. No temporis gets in or out."

"That's not an issue," Auberon said. "We don't need it for combat."

"What *do* you need it for?" Theo skeptically inquired. "You're going to wear those things when the sky comes down? Float around in your big white void?"

Auberon grinned patiently, as if Theo were missing the obvious. "If the aegis can withstand a temporal apocalypse, what else do you think it can survive?"

The answer hit Theo like a tight, closed fist. "Time travel." He turned to Azral, dumbstruck. "That's how you and your family got here."

Azral nodded. "Without aegis, the journey would have killed us all."

If only, Theo thought. "Are you the first time travelers of your era?"

"The first to survive," Azral clarified.

"But not the last," said Auberon. He looked to Theo. "Using Azral's technology, we plan to bring our whole clan back to 1912."

Theo scoffed at him. "Why not 1812? Or 1712? I hear things were great for minorities."

"They want to retain their temporal abilities," Azral explained. "Chronokinesis was impossible before the Cataclysm."

Theo was sorely tempted to ask about that, but he had more pressing questions for Auberon. "You think running away to the past will help you?"

"Between our knowledge, our talents, and our ample supply of gold, we'll have everything we need," said Auberon. "We'll make immediate improvements to the twentieth century. Better technology. More equality."

"Until everyone dies again," Theo grumbled.

Auberon shrugged. "We'll have a hundred years to find a solution. And if we don't, we'll simply jump to the past again. In either case, our children will have a chance to live full lives."

Theo wasn't sure if he'd laugh or scream. They were all signing up for a carousel hell, a grand-scale version of Evan's five-year loop.

"But the price is the same," he cynically mused. "Your women have to make a whole lot of kids with the Rubies."

Auberon checked the expressions of his granddaughters before leveling a cool look at Theo. "Nothing in this world is free."

"No," Theo agreed. "But you're going to lose a lot more than you bargained for."

"We only want the progeny," Azral insisted. "None of the parents will be harmed."

"You're lying!" Heath yelled.

Auberon shot him a stern look. "We're all here in good faith. Let's try to stay civil."

"Civil?" Theo pointed at Azral. "He's the reason that Heath and I are orphans!"

"I'm well aware," said Auberon. "Yet I seem to recall you telling me that there's too much at stake to hold on to grudges."

"There's too much at stake because of what he did," Theo said. "One world's dead and another one's dying, all because of *that* guy."

The Majee in the room swapped uncomfortable looks, though Auberon remained as calm as ever. "Listen—"

"Theo's right," said Azral. "I won't deny my culpability."

"How did you do it?" asked Charlene.

"*Why* did you do it?" Meredith demanded to know.

Azral let out a wistful sigh before answering. "I tampered with nature in unprecedented ways, which led to unprecedented consequences."

"You mean your travels back in time," Auberon said.

Azral shook his head. "Those trips are harmless, especially with aegis. But the lateral migration from Theo's world to this one proved . . . detrimental to the health of both. If I'd had decades more to perfect the technology, I would have found a way to prevent the damage. But given the progression of my mother's illness, the illness that all my people share, I didn't have the luxury of waiting."

"But you knew what would happen," Theo said. "As both an augur and a scientist. You charged ahead knowing full well that your trip would kill billions."

"I did."

"How?" asked Meredith. "How can you possibly justify that?"

Auberon clutched her arm. "Dear—"

"It's all right," said Azral. "She asks a fair question, but I'm afraid the answer won't suffice. As Theo said, I'm a scientist, more swayed by equations than I am by emotions. When I saw a path to saving hundreds of trillions of people—all of my people, across multiple timelines—I forged ahead despite the consequences. Numerically, it was just two Earths out of a centillion, a cost the universe would barely notice. If all it took to save this world was the death of two strangers from a distant past, would you kill them? Some people would and some people wouldn't. I am now, and forever will be, one of the people who would."

As furious as he was, Theo had to admire the sheer brilliance of the Pelletiers. He knew now why they didn't send Semerjean to deliver this sales pitch. Auberon was the one they needed to convince, and he didn't want to hear from their marketing guy. He wanted to meet the genius behind the company and see how his clever mind worked.

And now Auberon knew beyond the shadow of a doubt that Azral was *his* kind of genius—data-driven, logical, and unflinchingly committed to the greater good.

Theo's handphone buzzed in his pocket. He checked the screen and saw a text message from an unfamiliar number.

> **I know you're mad but you have to play it smart. My grandpa doesn't want to hear why he shouldn't work with Azral. He needs to know why he should work with you.**

Theo had assumed that the note came from Meredith, but she only had a water glass in her grip. It was Charlene who watched him expectantly, her hands hidden beneath the table.

Auberon looked to Azral. "Though I obviously lament the fallout of your actions, I do appreciate your candor. If you *do* find a way to fix the world's damage—"

"There isn't one," Azral curtly replied. "If there were, I would have found it and resolved it. This temporal fold's an obstacle to your work and mine. There's no benefit to having it remain."

"There's a way to fix it," Theo insisted.

Everyone in the room turned their attention to him as he mulled his next words carefully. His reflexive instinct was to keep hammering away at Azral's credibility. Theo had more than enough dirt to impugn the whole family. He could even tell them about the physicists at the Pelletier Group who'd gone out of their way to help Azral two years ago and were slaughtered en masse for their trouble. Did the Majee really want to end up like that?

But Charlene was right. Auberon didn't want to hear it. Theo's only chance was to sell him on Ioni's plan . . . what little he knew of it, anyway.

"I've seen it," he attested. "A future where we all manage to stop what's coming."

"How?" asked a board member.

"I don't have the exact details. I just know we need all the timebenders of the world to be in San Francisco on October fourth."

"October fourth," said Auberon. "The same day the city's supposed to explode."

Theo nodded. "There's something about that Cataclysm that's going to set everything right again. But it can't happen unless we're there. All of us."

Charlene's eyebrows rose. "You realize what you're saying."

"I know it sounds bad."

"Bad?" Auberon chuckled incredulously. "You're giving us nine weeks to live."

"No, I . . ." Theo looked to Heath and saw that even he was disconcerted. This would have been so much easier if Ioni had bothered to tell Theo everything, instead of leaving him with little scraps.

"It's not set in stone that we'll die in that Cataclysm," Theo insisted. "We could be teleported away, or *shielded*. I don't know."

"There's a lot you don't seem to know," Auberon noted. "We were led to believe that you were some kind of messiah."

Theo shook his head. "I never said I was. That was something that one of my Gotham friends started, out of wishful thinking more than anything else."

"You've only been an augur for two years, correct?"

Theo chuckled darkly. He didn't have to guess where Auberon was going with this. "Less, actually. I was out of commission that first month."

"Out of commission?"

"I was in detox."

Meredith and Charlene winced in sync. A short-haired Majee in a salmon-pink suit blinked at Theo through her bifocals. "Detoxification. As in drugs."

"Alcohol," said Theo. "I was a raging drunk for five years."

"*Five* years? But you're so young."

"I started young."

While the board members muttered among themselves, Azral leaned back in his chair with a magnanimous little grin.

"He's painting an unflattering portrait of himself," he informed the Majee. "In truth, he was a child prodigy, the kind of genius that comes along once in a generation."

Theo's heart lurched as Azral waved a hologram into the air, a flipbook montage of old graduation photos.

"He finished high school at the age of twelve," Azral said. "The valedictorian in a class of five hundred. Earned his undergraduate degree from Stanford at the age of fourteen—*magna cum laude,* if I recall. The following year, he became the youngest person in history to enroll in Stanford's law school. From all accounts, he was the pride of his community."

Theo laughed. "Go on," he urged Azral. "Tell them how I squandered it. Tell them how you found me drunk in a bus station—"

"That's true," Azral admitted. "And I pitied you enough that I almost left you to die. But I still saw a spark of potential in you, and I have to say that you've exceeded my expectations. You're more impressive now than you ever were on your homeworld."

Theo drank him in with slack-faced stupor, unsure if his praise was genuine or just the setup for a sucker punch.

Even Auberon was thrown by Azral's new tack. "When you say 'impressive'—"

"Can you not see it?" Azral gestured at the holomontages of the four dead Majee. "While nearly every other augur has crumpled under the weight of the future, Theo's persevered. He's been a guiding light to the people who need him. And despite all the pressure that's been put on him, he has yet to relapse into alcoholism. That's more than impressive. It's extraordinary."

Azral nodded at Theo approvingly. "You're a truly extraordinary man."

Son of a bitch. The whole world came to a quick and silent stop as Theo willed himself into the God's Eye. He couldn't take one more second of whatever the hell Azral was doing: a strategic mindfuck, a *torture session.*

He split away from his corporeal body and then wandered around the conference room. It was a perfect facsimile of the original environment, except for a faint sheen of light around the people. If Theo looked at them close enough, he could see the branching strings of their futures—*all* their futures, maybe even Azral's. Theo was tempted to take a peek, but what if that was exactly what Azral wanted him to do? What if it was all just a trap?

"What is this shit?" he asked the frozen form of Azral. "Seriously. What are you doing?"

"I'm not enjoying it much either."

Theo jumped at the presence on the other side of the room: a ghostly duplicate of Azral. He stood behind the chair of Theo's real-world counterpart and shrugged with sullen apathy. "I'm merely doing what needs to be done to resume my work. I don't have time for this nonsense."

Now *there* was the Azral that Theo remembered: the stern and snotty robot god who hovered contemptuously above everyone. His unblinking gaze was back in full force, along with his ubiquitous look of contempt.

Theo shook a finger at him. "I knew you were faking it!"

"Does that make you feel better?"

"A little, actually."

"Curious," Azral replied. "My father said the praise would upset you. Is your self-esteem truly so low?"

"Not as low as it was a minute ago," said Theo. "I didn't think I had a chance with Auberon."

"You don't."

"Then why are you playing these bullshit games?"

"Why are you?"

"What are you talking about?"

"Ioni Anata T'llari Deschane," said Azral. "Everything you do is at her bidding, yet you'd rather talk about your alcoholism than mention her to the Majee."

Theo crossed his arms. "I have my reasons."

"And they're good ones," Azral said. "Should you broach that particular topic, you'll be forced to answer uncomfortable questions. How can you trust someone who's been avoiding you for months, a woman who's betrayed you multiple times?"

"At least she's not a genocidal killer."

"Further proof that you don't know her."

"What do you mean?"

"The Cataclysm of 1912," said Azral. "That was all her doing. She didn't tell you?"

Theo shook his head, chuckling. "Bullshit. Even if that's true, you're in no position to judge."

"Of course I am," Azral insisted. "I did what I did for a higher cause. She destroyed half of New York just to see what would happen."

"I don't believe you."

"I don't expect you to." Azral moved to the window with a heavy expression. "But the question remains: How can you trust her after seeing what happened to her other helpers?"

He summoned the ghosts of two dead men, a pair of Gotham augurs that Theo had known all too well.

Azral moved behind the larger of the two. "Rebel Rosen. Ioni's first lackey. She enlisted him on a crusade to kill all orphans—a fraudulent war that cost him everything: his family, his dignity, and ultimately his life. He didn't benefit from their association."

He proceeded to the second prophet. "Michael Pendergen, also known as Merlin McGee. Ioni compelled him to become a celebrity prophet, despite his misgivings. The fame made him miserable for months on end. His reward for his troubles? A public assassination. He did not benefit from his association with Ioni."

Azral conjured an image of Theo himself, a dull-eyed distortion of the real thing. "And then there's you, her last remaining horseman. What fate does she have in store for you, I wonder. I'm sure if you look hard enough—"

"I have looked," Theo said. "I see you and your family getting increasingly desperate."

Azral waved away his spectral images. "And I see you all dead in San Francisco. Is that truly a future you want?"

"If it saves the world, then I'm okay with it."

"So you'll lay down your life for seven billion people," said Azral. "Yet when I offer you the chance to save *trillions*, you refuse."

Theo nodded with a seething glare. "That's right."

"You spite me to avenge your fallen world."

"No. Just Hannah."

Azral turned from the window and studied Theo curiously. "You are aware—"

"I know she's alive," Theo said. "But there isn't a single future left where you don't end up killing her. Believe me, I've looked."

He joined Azral at the window and peered out at the city. In still-frame, the onslaught of lumis was almost tolerable. Pretty, even.

"You swore to the Majee that the parents won't be harmed, but that was a lie. Admit it. There's no one but us here. I can't record this."

Azral focused his attention on the distant skyline and studied the holograms on the building tops. At least ten seconds passed before he spoke again.

"My mother is . . . deteriorating. Her terminus has progressed faster than we expected. In five years, she'll only have a fraction of her faculties. In ten years, she'll be dead."

He stuffed his hands into his ethereal pockets and sighed. "To watch a mind like hers crumble is one of the greatest pains of my life. A travesty. She was an unparalleled genius of her time, a neurogeneticist beyond compare."

Theo peeked at him out of the corner of his eye and was immediately thrown by his expression: the most sincere and human look he'd ever seen from Azral. He didn't believe it was a ruse. Even Semerjean wasn't that good of an actor.

"Now here we are at the end stage of our mission," Azral continued. "We're so close to triumph that we can smell it in the strings. She was right. My mother had been the first to see the cure for our disease. And soon she'll be the first to benefit from it. It's only fitting, don't you think?"

Theo couldn't have disagreed more. The only fitting future for Esis involved a straitjacket. "So what exactly are you saying?"

"I don't care about your concern for Hannah. I don't care about her well-being. I don't care about your notions of right and wrong, as childish as they are. I've dedicated my life to my mother's cause, and I will see it through to the very end, even if I have to tear you all down to your barest carbon elements."

Azral turned around and walked back toward the table. "That's what I'm saying."

If Theo had a heart in his avatar, it'd be pounding like a jackhammer. He looked at Azral with the coolest expression he could muster. "Well, I guess that answers that."

"Indeed." Azral once again paused behind the frozen form of Theo, the one who sat at the far end of the conference table. "And I can't help but wonder what you'll do with that knowledge. Will you still support a woman who manipulates you at every—"

"Yes."

Azral closed his eyes, exasperated. "Always determined to take the self-destructive path. The one tragic constant of your life."

Theo shrugged. "Maybe that's what keeps me going where other augurs fall. I'm used to a train-wreck future."

"Perhaps," said Azral. "But it was easier to be self-destructive when you only had yourself to worry about. Now you have friends and dependents, a lover, and a handful of people whom you consider siblings. They'll all follow you down the same dark road. Are you strong enough to handle the consequences?"

Theo kept a calm façade as his mind gave life to his very worst fears. "Guess I'll have to be."

"Oh, Theo. You fail to see how easy it is."

"To do what?"

Azral stepped behind Heath and raised his right hand to chest level. A sharp tooth of light popped out of his fist like a switchblade. "To break your resolve."

Theo's eyes went wide as Azral raised the blade. "No, wait!"

"This is the future you've chosen."

"No!"

Azral drove the blade down into the top of Heath's skull, and the whole world exploded into cold white light.

[Click.]

He lounged on a couch in an executive breakroom, his fingers curled around a quarkstick. The pen-size lumic projector, another groundbreaking invention of Omata Electronics, allowed anyone to draw a glowing line onto any surface, even from a distance. Though the light only lasted a couple of seconds, the quarkstick came in handy during business presentations. It also drove cats crazy and gave distraction to traumatized augurs.

[Click.]

With each press of the nub, the color of the light beam changed—one click for red, two for blue, three for white with a drop shadow. Theo couldn't decide which one he liked better, so he kept alternating between them.

[Click, click, click.]

Heath watched him closely from the facing recliner, a quarkstick of his own in his grip. Unlike Theo, whose hands had been shaking for ten minutes straight, the boy managed to draw in clean, shapely lines. His blue wall sketches, as simple as they were, actually looked like something other than seizures.

"You feeling better?" Heath asked.

Theo wasn't sure how to answer that. He felt *calmer* than he did ten minutes ago, when he thought Azral had murdered a loved one. But he was still humiliated by the trick. The bastard had set Theo up like a golf ball on a tee, then smacked him into another state.

He drew a jagged red squiggle on the ceiling, then waited for the glow to fade. "I just want to get out of here," he said to Heath. "There's no point hanging around."

"We can't go. They're still deciding."

"Deciding?" Theo laughed. "Come on, man. You were there."

To say Theo had reacted poorly to Azral's prank was an understatement at best. He'd thrown every drinking glass on the table at him, shouting vile obscenities until the Majee had to restrain him. To those who hadn't been privy to their conversation in the God's Eye, Theo's sudden change in behavior seemed utterly psychotic. The last thing Azral did to him, as far as anyone knew, was call him an extraordinary man.

But of course that was the point of the ruse, wasn't it? To make him look like a nut to the Majee. Even Auberon, who'd received a prescient transcript of the meeting, was shocked by Theo's behavior. Between that and his hatred of Integrity, the odds of him becoming an ally just got whittled down to zero.

Heath tried one last ceiling sketch with the quarkstick before dropping it onto a coffee table. "You can't let Azral do that to you again."

"Do what?"

"Upset you like that."

Theo lifted his head and eyed him hotly. "I thought he *killed* you."

"You can't let that stop you," Heath insisted. "You have a whole world to save. One person doesn't matter."

Theo shook his head. "That's a slippery slope. First you say one person doesn't matter, then it's two people, then fifty. Next thing you know, you're convincing yourself that two worlds don't matter."

He raised his quarkstick and whipped a bright red path across the ceiling. "Where do you draw the line?"

Heath slouched in his chair dejectedly. "I don't want to be the reason you fail."

"You're not," Theo assured him. "I've been failing on my own since I was your age."

He sat up at the sound of approaching footsteps, at least two different pairs of clopping high heels. Theo didn't need his foresight to know who was coming or what they had to say.

The Great Sisters Graham stepped into the breakroom and stood side by side in the doorway. While Charlene only appeared a little more morose than usual, Meredith had clearly been crying. She looked to Theo with dark, puffy eyes before looking down at her feet.

"They voted unanimously for Azral's plan," she told him. "But then I guess you knew that."

[Click.]

Theo changed the color of the quarkstick once again and waved a dizzy blue spiral onto the wall. "So I guess that's that, huh."

"What happened back there?" Charlene asked him.

Theo shrugged. "I screwed up."

"Yeah, no kidding."

Meredith glared at her exhaustedly. "Char."

"You want to tell him or should I?"

Theo sat up on the couch. "What, there's more?"

"Not from them," said Meredith. "From us."

"What do you mean?"

The sisters swapped a nervous look before Meredith answered his question. "We told the board, in very stark terms, that we can't support their decision. Our great-grandmother would spin in her grave if she saw us making babies at gunpoint. She wouldn't want us fleeing to 1912 when we have a chance to save everyone in the present."

Charlene nodded in fervent agreement. "And she wouldn't want us working with that sick piece of shit who did all the harm in the first place."

Theo suddenly realized why Auberon had looked so sad in the lobby. His future self must have warned him that his decision would cost him his granddaughters. Now here they were, two powerful free agents.

"Come back with us," Theo urged. "We'd be thrilled to have you."

Meredith chuckled. "We were debating that very notion." She looked to Heath. "What do you think, love? Would we be making a mistake?"

"What do you mean?"

"She's asking how they treat you," Theo said. "As a Black person."

"As *any* person," Meredith stressed. "Do you believe in the people you're with?"

"Oh." Heath drummed a beat on his thigh before responding. "Yeah. We're going to save the world."

Meredith traded a heavy look with her sister. "What else needs to be said?"

Charlene sat next to Theo and gripped his arm. "Just *promise* us that if we die, it'll be for something."

He nodded solemnly. "I promise if we die, that it'll be for everything."

Charlene took him in with an inscrutable expression before standing up again. "There's a dart to New York at noon tomorrow. I can get us all a cabin. That work for everyone?"

If it were up to Theo, he would leave right now. But he figured Meredith and Charlene needed time to settle their affairs. God knew he and Heath could use some rest. They'd barely caught a wink since Cuba.

By midnight, Heath was sound asleep on his hotel bed, but Theo couldn't seem to join him in slumber. He tossed and turned in the darkness, his head spinning with paradoxical thoughts. Everything and nothing was going according to plan, and he had everything and nothing to look forward to. The people he loved were utterly doomed and they would all live happily ever after.

At one A.M., a strange new light on the ceiling distracted him: a scribble of glowing blue letters, as if someone were writing with a quarkstick.

Hang in there.

Theo blinked at the message three times, then suddenly checked on Heath. The boy was still snoring from the other bed. So then who the hell—

His eyes went wide in realization. "You've got to be shitting me."

The old words faded and a new message came to life in its place. **Sorry, sweets. I still have to keep my distance.**

"Keep your distance?" Theo looked at Heath self-consciously, then lowered his voice to a mutter. "It's been more than a year."

I know, Ioni replied in glowing scribble. Shit happens.

Theo rolled his eyes. "I could have used your help a few hours ago."

You did fine.

"Fine? I blew our one shot at getting sixty-four timebenders. We're only going home with two."

It's all right, Ioni told him. You got the two we need.

"What are you talking about? I thought you needed everyone."

Just hang in there, Theo. Don't lose hope. The string is stronger than ever.

Theo wasn't assuaged. "One of these days, you're going to tell me everything."

Yes. Soon.

"When?"

;)

The smile faded, leaving Theo in the dark once more. He turned onto his side, struggling to make sense of Ioni's words. He wasn't sure how she could be content with just two Majee, but then causality worked in strange ways. If a butterfly could flap its wings and create a storm on the other side of the planet, then maybe Meredith and Charlene could prevent one. It certainly wouldn't be the first time two strong-hearted sisters had changed the landscape of the future. Theo had seen it before with a certain pair of Givens, and he had good faith he'd see it again.

PART THREE

OPEN WAR

TWENTY-ONE

July went out with a sigh of relief from the world. With August came the anxious hope that the new month would bring back a semblance of sanity. No angels in London. No cataclysmic omens. No prophets getting assassinated on live national lumivision.

"Let's all just dial it back a little," a comedienne told her audience. "This shit's getting way too biblical."

For the denizens of the underland, who had inside knowledge of the coming end times, August arrived on a cloud of uncertainty. All the remaining orphan groups had finally been located, and the ones who agreed to join the fight had been brought into the fold. With no more quests on the mission board, everyone had to wonder: *What now?*

As usual, the question was asked of Theo, and as usual, his answer came with a shrug. "I don't know," he said. "I'm pretty sure the next move is Ioni's."

And so they waited, day by day, though not everyone in the village remained idle. The Baby Brunchers, as Carrie Bloom called them, continued to enlist young orphans and Gothams into procreating for the Pelletiers. By the middle of August, fourteen women joined Hannah, Mercy, and Eden in pregnancy, an eclectic assortment of volunteers that included a teenage lesbian, a unilingual Mexican, a swifter with a history of mental problems, and a blind young tempic who navigated with tendrils.

If the Pelletiers were pleased by the many new offerings, they didn't say a word. The only time they made their presence known was when Eden, the sole woman in the group to conceive accidentally, scheduled an abortion at a Quarter Hill clinic. She barely had a chance to hang up the phone before a ten-pound object apparated into her kitchen: her own severed head, freshly lopped off the neck of a future Eden and sent back through time on a serving plate.

The message was received in the spirit in which it was intended, enough to drive Eden into a frenzy. She trashed her apartment and barricaded herself inside, refusing to eat or speak to anyone. While many feared she'd harm herself, the people who knew and loved her most had every confidence that she'd bounce back. She was the toughest of the Irons, an urchin from the streets of San Nicolás who became a decorated Texas policewoman. She'd been battling giants her whole damn life, and the end of her world had only made her stronger.

Indeed, after seventy-two hours, Eden emerged from her apartment with dry eyes and a new resolve. Not only would she keep her baby, she'd live each day to its fullest potential while she still had control over her life. She went hiking in the morning and dancing at night, and spent a chunk of her boyfriend's trust fund money on luxurious self-indulgences. Once she finally got tired of all the Manhattan spas and restaurants, she proceeded to the next item on her bucket list.

Amanda marveled at the sparkly new ornament on Eden's finger, a diamond and white-gold engagement ring that had been custom-fitted for her mechanical prosthetic. "You're kidding."

"Nope." Eden tilted her hand and admired the diamonds. "I asked Noah. He said yes. It's all happening this weekend."

"Wow. I didn't realize you guys were so serious."

"Serious?" Eden laughed. "I'm not even sure I like him anymore."

"So why get married?"

Eden lowered her head with a doleful expression, the same look that had become a fixture on Hannah's face. "Because I like weddings."

Though she'd been hoping for a small and casual service, she was marrying into the Gotham clan, and the Gothams didn't do anything casually. On

Sunday afternoon, August 19, nearly eleven hundred people filed into the underland's amphitheater: a thousand and nine Gothams, fifty orphans, sixty-six Integrity agents, and two Majee. Even Cedric Cain had shuttled in from Washington to catch his first transdimensional wedding, and he wasn't disappointed. Eden had insisted on infusing some Mexican Catholic traditions into the ceremony, like the gift of thirteen golden coins and the draping of the rosary lasso. The end result was both beautiful and fascinating, a union of two star-crossed cultures from distant sibling Earths.

Amanda wished she could have enjoyed the occasion, but the shadow of the Pelletiers cast a gloom over all of it. When Noah promised to honor Eden's memory, Amanda found herself tearing up for all the wrong reasons. It was the only tacit admission of what was coming. The rest was just a lovely sham.

The ceremony ended at a quarter to three, and the audience split among factions. The Integrity agents went back to work. The Gothams held a banquet in the village square. The orphans returned to their own domain for an intimate little after party—*la tornaboda*, as the Mexicans called it. Traditionally, it was held after the reception, but Eden insisted on having it concurrently.

"I'll need a place to hide from the big Gotham party," she'd told Amanda and Hannah. "Can you set it up?"

The sisters did, though not without difficulties. Heath was feuding with his band on a Beatles-related matter, so Hannah enlisted him to play DJ with old recordings. There were almost no drinks left in the commissary, thanks to Eden's bachelorette party, so Amanda had Zack and Mia raid all the apartment fridges. Most frustrating of all, at least sixty young Gothams had crashed the shindig. The commissary became so ridiculously crowded that Amanda had to open the clubhouse. Soon she had a hundred and twenty people reveling inside the two buildings, with only tap water and condiments to serve them.

Luckily, Meredith Graham had a devious solution. She returned to the commissary with twelve tempic men, each one carrying food and drinks from the Gotham banquet.

Amanda laughed at all the sumptuous new goodies. "Oh my God. You're a genius. Did anyone give you trouble?"

Meredith waved her off. "One of the elders made a fuss. I said it was official bride business."

Amanda smiled as she helped her set up the food tins. Of all the underland's newest residents, she'd come to like Meredith the most. The woman was brilliant, funny, and naturally kind, and her tempic aura was so relaxed that Amanda felt calm by proximity. Her sister Charlene wasn't nearly as affable, but Amanda couldn't blame her for being testy. She'd left the Majee to help save the world, only to learn that there was nothing to do . . . at least not yet, anyway. The waiting was driving her crazy. It was driving *everyone* crazy.

Once the last of the food was placed on the table, Meredith willed her white minions away. "Have you ever heard of a flat future?" she asked Amanda out of the blue.

"A what?"

Meredith motioned to the other side of the room, where See sat with Heath at his DJ station. "I noticed she was looking pretty nervous at the wedding. And when an augur gets nervous, *I* get nervous. So I asked her if there was anything we should be worried about. And she said the future looks fine, just flat."

Amanda's brow creased in puzzlement. "Like a pancake?"

"No idea," Meredith said. "I couldn't get her to explain. I was hoping you'd know."

Amanda studied See from a distance. The poor girl had never recovered from her chronoregression in London, and was still hobbling around on elbow crutches. The doctors had confirmed See's darkest prediction: that she'd need help walking for the rest of her life.

But all that talk of a flat future was new to Amanda. "I don't know," she told Meredith. "That's way outside my wheelhouse."

"Yeah, mine too. I'll ask Theo when I see him."

A shoving match broke out between two large men: the orphan Ben Hopkins and the Gotham Eli Rubinek. Amanda had no idea what it was about, but she could tell from the way they wobbled that they weren't entirely sober.

"It's all right," Meredith told Amanda. "I'll handle it."

"No, no, no. You've done more than enough."

"*You've* done enough. Take a rest, Red."

Amanda shook her head with awe. "You keep this up and the next wedding will be ours."

Meredith laughed. "You might want to check with Zack first."

Amanda retreated to the back of the commissary, where Hannah and Peter had sequestered themselves. They sat shoulder to shoulder at the far end of a dining booth, their arms angled rather tellingly. Amanda knew they'd resumed their casual affections, but this was the first time she'd seen them holding hands under the table.

"You guys doing all right?"

"We're lovely," Peter said with an acerbic grin. "We just need a funeral to lighten things up."

"Yeah." Amanda looked around at all the heavy faces. "I feel bad for Eden. I think she just wanted everyone to have a fun distraction."

"It's not working," Hannah grumbled.

"No." Amanda checked on Meredith as she broke up the squabble on the other side of the room. "Doesn't seem to be."

Peter rose to his feet. "You seen Liam around?"

Amanda shook her head. "Not since the ceremony."

"He's probably at the big bash. I think I'll go embarrass him."

He disappeared through a wall portal. Amanda took his place at Hannah's side. "So."

"Don't start."

"For such a professed non-couple—"

"We're *not* a couple."

"Then what are you?"

Hannah swirled the water in her glass, her dark eyes locked on the ripples. "We're just there for each other, that's all."

"Well, whatever it is, I think it's great."

"'Great.'" Hannah chuckled. "You say it the same way you did when I got my nose pierced."

"It was a septum ring. Those hurt to look at."

"Does it hurt to look at me and Peter?"

Amanda fidgeted with the sleeve of her minidress. "It hurts to know the reason you got together."

Hannah's expression softened. She held her sister's hand. "You know what one of the happiest days of my life was?"

"This wedding?" Amanda joked.

"*Your* wedding. Seeing you and Zack on the dance floor, smiling for the first time in months. That was magic for me. That was worth doing."

Instead of taking comfort in that, Amanda fell into a recent bad memory. "I blew my chance to save you back."

"You had to," Hannah said. "If you gave them Ioni, you would have screwed over everyone."

"So why do I keep thinking there's still a way to save you?"

"There isn't," said Hannah. "But you can still save Peter."

"Hannah—"

"I know what you said. I heard you. But I'm *telling* you that Evan's not done. Even when I'm dead and gone, he'll want to kill Peter just for having me."

Amanda sighed. Hannah was still mad at her for not killing Evan, despite Ioni's stern warning against it, and despite the fact that Evan had actually helped them. More than that, he'd seemed . . . different somehow. Not reformed. Just different.

The last time Amanda tried to explain it to Hannah, they ended up having a shouting match. Hannah simply didn't want to hear it, and Amanda wasn't about to start another fight over it. She felt dirty enough defending Evan.

"I hope you're wrong," she told Hannah. "You probably aren't. In any case, you don't have to worry. I'll kill him before I let him hurt any of us ever again. I promise."

Hannah nodded approvingly, though she still wore that look of grim resolve that broke Amanda's heart every time she saw it.

"I'm counting on you to get them all through this," Hannah said. "All the people we love."

"Don't."

"They have to live."

"Hannah, *please.*"

Amanda clenched her jaw. If she started crying now, she'd never stop. Worse, it might set off other people around her. Nearly everyone was dangling by a thread today, and Amanda didn't think it was just the wedding that was eating at them. There was something in the periphery of her animal instincts, a prescient sense of danger. While See glimpsed nothing but a flat and placid future, Amanda felt trouble coming at a hundred miles an hour.

The music player came to a stop. Heath popped out the spool and replaced it with another: a quality recording of the Great Remains at Amanda and Zack's wedding.

Hannah smiled at the sound of her own voice, a soprano version of "At Last" by Etta James.

"Hey, I know this one."

"You sure do," said Amanda. "You were on fire that day. Every song, every note. You were just . . ."

Amanda could feel the floodgates open again. She had to summon every last quantum of willpower to keep her tears inside her.

"You were just perfect."

The mood in the clubhouse was considerably lighter. From the moment Amanda unlocked the door, fifty orphans and Gothams claimed the place as their own and established the new world order. There'd be none of that somber shit that was going on in the commissary. The clubhouse was a place for jokes and games. You want to be broody? Take it outside.

Zack sat on the edge of the tempic bandstage, a dozen people watching him as he tapped his chin in thought. He'd just invented a party game that was proving to be a hit, a customized spin on Two Truths and a Lie that could only be played among this crowd.

"Okay," he said to the Gothams around him. "An African American president, a singer named Engelbert Humperdinck, or a movie called *Help, My Mom's a Banana*. Which one never existed on my world?"

The British orphan named Jia scoffed at him. "Too easy."

"Shhh. This is for the natives."

Harold Herrick eyed Zack suspiciously. The plump young blond was one of the Gothams' most talented lumics, though no one would mistake him for a well-adjusted kid. His best friend was still a figment of his imagination, a talking blue tiger that everyone could see.

"I'd say you're making up the banana movie," Harold guessed. "But then I was wrong about the killer tomatoes one."

Zack smiled slyly. "You also botched it on *Honey, I Blew Up the Kid*."

The tiger, Bo, narrowed his bright yellow eyes at Zack. "I still don't think that was real."

"It was real," said Ofelia. Unlike most people, she got a kick out of addressing the big cat directly. "My parents made me watch it when I was fourteen."

"Is that why you ran away?" Zack asked her.

"It's one of the reasons."

Regal Tam leaned forward in her folding chair, a rare look of confidence on her face. "The banana movie's not real."

"What makes you so sure?" Zack asked her.

"Because I already—" She was interrupted by cheers from the other side of the room, a sporting event that was even sillier than Zack's game. "Because I already knew about your country's Black president. And the name Engelbrett Humperjack, or whatever you called him, is just too weird to be fake."

Zack shook a finger at her. "The smart girl wins again."

Regal chuckled jadedly. "If I was smart, I wouldn't be pregnant."

Zack cringed at her gallows humor. At sixteen, she was the youngest of the baby bunch, way too young to play incubator for the Pelletiers. Zack could have strangled her parents for pressuring her into it. Who the hell would do that to their kid?

He clapped his flesh and metal hands together, then looked to his audience. "All right. One last round before we—"

More cheers rose up from the eastern side of the clubhouse. Mia raised her arms in triumph, then pointed vengefully at her brother. "In your face!"

"Never mind," Zack said to the crowd. "I'm taking a break."

He hopped off the stage and moved toward the action, yet another competition between Mia and Bobby Farisi. The two of them had been inseparable these past few weeks, enough for them to move beyond their gobsmacked awe and into a more natural coexistence. They bickered, they teased, they roughhoused a little. Zack figured they were resuming a lifelong dynamic, but Bobby insisted that it was all brand-new.

"My brothers and I used to treat her like glass," he'd told Zack. "She was our little baby sister, you know? If we didn't protect her, who would?"

But now Bobby had become acclimated to this world's Mia—a foul-mouthed, battle-scarred, teleporting asskicker who'd seen more combat than half of his old army buddies. He'd cursed up a storm when he learned about the David/Semerjean saga, and had been downright floored by Mia's response to it.

"Don't worry," she'd promised Bobby. "I'll kill him before I ever let him hurt you."

Zack weaved his way into the circle of spectators and watched the two siblings as they continued their tournament. Their current game, just the latest of many contests and dares, involved a baseball, a ramp, and five empty beer pitchers. As far as Zack could see, they'd reinvented Skee-Ball.

"Congratulations," Bobby told Mia. "You finally caught up to me."

"Caught up? I'm a full game ahead of you, chump."

"I gave you that win as a birthday gift."

"Yeah, right."

Zack turned to Mia, surprised. "Wait. It's your birthday?"

"Uh-huh."

"Again?"

"What do you mean 'again'? It's been a year." She tapped the tiara on her head, a faux diamond trinket that she'd borrowed from a Gotham. "Why do you think I'm wearing this?"

"I don't know. I figured you lost a bet."

Everyone around them snickered as Mia flipped Zack off. Bobby grinned at him. "It's weird, right? She was never into the sparkly stuff. Her big thing as a kid—"

"No," Mia yelled.

"What?"

"You're not talking about that."

"Oh come on," said Bobby.

"Yeah," Zack said. "I'm running out of things to tease you about. Think of *my* needs."

Mia pointed a stern finger at her brother. "You say one word and I'll tell everyone here about that time at Disneyland. You know the one I'm—"

"Yes." Bobby shrugged at Zack defeatedly. "Sorry, man. She's got me over a barrel."

"Just *throw*," Mia said.

As the two of them continued their game of Not-Exactly-Skee-Ball, Ofelia joined Zack's side. "They're sweet together, aren't they?"

"Yeah, in a loud, Italian kind of way."

"Oh stop. You love it."

"I do," Zack said. "I haven't seen her smile like that in ages."

Ofelia rested her chin on his shoulder and sighed. "It hurts a little. Selfishly."

"It does," Zack admitted.

Like Mia, they each had a brother who'd survived the apocalypse, but hadn't been as lucky as Bobby. They'd never had a chance to reunite on this world.

Ofelia felt the tension in Zack's shoulder. She moved away from him. "I'm sorry. I forgot the rules about brooding in here."

"It's all right," he said. "I won't rat you out."

"That's what I admire about you. You never get dark. No matter how much stuff gets thrown at you, you always find a way to stay funny."

Zack shrugged. "It's just the way I cope."

"Was your brother like that?"

"Josh? God no. He was a brooder and a shouter and a hurler of large objects."

Ofelia smiled. "Sounds like Jury. Total alpha male. There are times I wanted to strangle him, but now I wish I was more like him. He was always the strong one."

"Oh, come on," Zack said. "You're one of the strongest people I know."

"Are you kidding? I'm two years behind the rest of you."

"That's my point. You only have . . . what, eight weeks of conscious experience here?"

Ofelia nodded. "Something like that."

"You should have seen me and my friends at eight weeks," he said. "We were practically tripping over each other. But *you*, you've leveled up like crazy."

"Leveled up?"

"It's a nerd term," Zack attested. "The point is, you adapt like a freaking champion. You're one of the few people here I don't worry about."

Expressionless, Ofelia took a final sip of her drink and then tossed the cup into a portal. "I should go."

"I'm sorry. Did I offend you? I wasn't trying—"

"You didn't offend me at all," she said. "I've just had too much to drink, I'm in a weird mood, and I don't want to like you more than I should."

"Oh." Zack blinked at her, dumbstruck. "If it helps, I can say something repugnant."

Ofelia smiled uneasily, then moved toward the exit. "You're a good man, Zack."

He watched her leave, distracted. The day had already felt a little off-kilter. But now that he'd accidentally charmed a beautiful woman, things were starting to become surreal.

Everyone in the clubhouse turned to look as a new portal opened and a bride in a lovely white dress emerged from the light. A dozen onlookers applauded Eden as she returned once again from the main reception.

She acknowledged their cheers with a half-hearted wave, then cut a quick path toward Zack. "Holy shit. I thought I'd never get out of there."

"What'd you do, fake a seizure?"

"No. I just saw Peter and begged him to make a portal." She peeked out the window at the party in the commissary. "Have you seen Caleb or Mercy?"

"Not since breakfast," Zack said. "Why?"

"There's a rumor going around that Mercy's dad died."

"*What?*"

"None of the Lees were at the ceremony," Eden said. "No one can reach them, and I can't reach Caleb."

"Shit." Zack pulled his phone out of his pocket and shot a quick text to Mercy. "That's the last thing they need."

"If you don't hear in ten minutes—"

"I'll go up to their house," Zack promised. "I got this. Don't worry."

Eden looked over her shoulder and saw Stitch and Shade smoking cigarettes by the restroom. Though the two young Coppers looked gorgeous in their taffeta dresses, their expressions were as grim as they ever were.

"I was hoping the mood would pick up here," said Eden. "This whole thing was a bad idea."

"Hey." Zack held her by the shoulders. "It was a beautiful ceremony."

"Yours was better."

"Well, you married a good man," Zack offered. "You can't say that about me."

Eden rolled her eyes. "At least you were smart enough to marry one of your own. All this Gotham bullshit's going to kill me."

"It's not their bullshit you're angry about."

"No," Eden said with a sigh. "It's not."

"And Noah—"

"I know. He's a good man. He's a *very* good man. I might even love him. I don't know."

Zack had no idea why he found that so funny. Even a moment of thought exposed the tragedy of the sentiment, and yet hearing it from the bride on the day of her wedding was so droll and unorthodox, so very *Eden*, that Zack could only bellow with laughter.

Eden struggled not to laugh with him. "Don't tell anyone I said that."

As he settled down to simmering chuckles, Zack took her metal hand in his. "Oh no. I wouldn't dare. But you have to see it from my—"

A harsh white light suddenly overtook his vision, as bright as it was fleeting. In his blindness, he suffered a quick series of puzzling sensations: an arctic chill, a whistling breeze, a painful tug on his prosthetic.

"Zack!" Mia ran to his side. "Where did she go?"

"What?" Zack looked around through the spots in his eyes, but he couldn't see Eden anywhere. He barely had a moment to process her absence before a second burst of light erupted near the bandstage. The chair that Regal Tam had been sitting on suddenly fell onto its side, empty.

Zack suddenly realized what was happening. "Oh no."

Mia blanched at the sight of Regal's fallen chair. "They took her. They took them both."

Zack looked at his mechanical hand and saw fresh new scrapes on the surface. Eden must have been holding on to him for dear life while the Pelletiers grabbed her. It must have all happened at shifted speed.

Bobby shot to his feet, wide-eyed. "What the hell's going on?"

"They're taking all the . . ." Mia grabbed Zack's arm. "Oh no. Hannah!"

Amanda had been getting a drink for her sister when the abductions began in the commissary. The lightbursts came and went so quickly that she thought someone was snapping flash photographs. But then a Pearl yelled Rosario's name. A Platinum shouted for Sarah Brehm. Amanda only needed half a second to remember what the two girls had in common.

"No!"

She dropped her drink and ran for Hannah, her thoughts all tangled in a scream. If the Pelletiers had approached her right at that moment, she would have given them anything they wanted—her legs, her womb, her soul, her *future*. She would have handed them Ioni on a silver platter. Screw the world. *Just leave Hannah,* Amanda begged. *Please!*

Hannah looked to Amanda with tense, wet eyes. "Oh God. It's happening."

"No!"

"I'm not ready."

"Hannah!"

"Just remember what I told you. You have to see the others through this!"

Panicked, Heath sent a Jonathan scrambling from the DJ station, just as Amanda stretched her arms toward Hannah. But neither of them had a chance to reach her in time. A sharp white glow lit Hannah from behind, silhouetting her for just a splinter of a second before enveloping her body.

By the time Amanda could see again, the dining booth was empty, and her sister was gone from the underland.

TWENTY-TWO

"I hate to say it, boss, but I don't think she's coming back."

Melissa muttered a string of curses. High above the eastern village, eight yards beyond the ceiling dome, a turbine air recirculator had died with a sputtering wheeze. Felicity had sent a repair drone to fix it, only to have the blasted thing suffer a system malfunction halfway into the duct. Now two expensive pieces of technology lay dormant behind the illusive sky, out of sight and out of reach.

"Lovely," said Melissa. "And to think we volunteered for this."

Felicity shrugged. "Still beats the other job."

That was true. They'd only offered to fix the turbine because they didn't want to chaperone the orphan party on the other side of town. Still, neither one of them was keen on crawling through an air vent, especially in their expensive dresses.

"You know, Amanda could easily get that drone back," Felicity mused. "And Zack could reverse the fan back to health."

Melissa shook her head. "Let them enjoy the party."

"I don't mean now. It doesn't even have to be today. We still have twenty-one working circulators. More than enough air for all of us."

Melissa wagged her finger at Felicity. "You're a bad influence on me."

"Praise indeed."

"Still, let's give the drone one last try."

Sighing, Felicity fiddled with the sliders of her command tablet. "Yes, boss."

Melissa returned to the stoop of the travelers' guildhouse, where her employer and partner conversed. While Cain was still dressed in his wedding suit, Theo had gone home and changed into a hoodie and shorts. A new adornment dangled from a chain on his neck: the mysterious silver bracelet that he'd liberated from Ofelia. He insisted on keeping it near him at all times, as if its purpose could reveal itself at any moment.

"Everything all right?" Melissa asked the two men.

"We're dandy," Cain said. "I'm still filling him in on all the latest bullshit."

Melissa had already gotten the spiel from Cedric, and it wasn't just bullshit, it was worrisome. The economic crash continued to leave the country in turmoil, especially the U.S. government. Even Integrity was under the budgetary microscope, and Cain was still spending money like it was the end of the world.

"Congress is getting suspicious," he told Theo. "I can't trust them with the truth, but I can't keep fooling them forever. There's already talk of replacing me."

Cain cued up a photograph on his handphone screen, a square-jawed blond who looked like Semerjean on steroids. "This is the front-runner for my chair. A star of the radical right. If he gets in, he'll drag the agency back into the dark ages. He certainly won't be a friend to you folks."

Theo swapped a tense look with Melissa. "I assume you have a contingency plan."

"I do," said Cain. "But it's tricky. I'll need your divine guidance."

Theo shrugged helplessly. "The future's been quiet since I got back from Japan. I'm not seeing any trouble on the horizon."

Cain raised an eyebrow, perplexed. "Isn't that a good thing?"

Melissa knew exactly what Theo wasn't telling him. While the visions in his head were comforting to look at, there was something slightly off about them—a two-dimensionality, as if he were seeing flat-screen images of the future instead of the real thing. Theo assumed it was just a quirk of the brain, still ornery from mescaline withdrawal. Melissa hoped there wasn't a more sinister reason behind it.

"Guys." Felicity beckoned them from the intersection, her wide eyes fixed to the west. "Something's happening."

Theo could suddenly hear the panic from the center of town. Dozens of Gothams shrieked and fled as quick bursts of light overtook the wedding reception. From a distance, it looked like a hypnagogic dream: a ground-level lightning storm, or an attack of feral flash cameras.

"Shit." Cain switched his phone to transceiver mode and opened an emergency channel to the command center. "Leticia, what's going on in the square?"

Leticia Gutiérrez, the director of underland operations, wasted no time replying. "I don't know, sir. You told us to keep our distance."

Yes, and Melissa knew why. The last thing the Gothams needed today were government soldiers in the village square. It would have been an unwelcome reminder of the massacre that had claimed nearly two hundred of their people last June.

"On camera, it just looks like a flare-up," said Leticia. "Maybe one of their lumics got a little too drunk, or . . ."

Her voice was drowned out by a mess of loud cross talk.

"What's happening?" Cain asked.

"It's just not light," said Leticia. "People are disappearing."

"Disappearing?"

"Oh my God." Felicity nearly dropped her drone console. "The Pelletiers."

Melissa spoke into Cain's transceiver. "Leticia, what do you see of the Orphanage?"

"Same deal. Same lights. Folks are just . . . oh my God. It's chaos."

Panicked, Theo ran for home. Melissa chased after him. "Wait!"

"They're taking Hannah!"

"And how do you plan on stopping them?"

"I don't know!"

"Theo, you *can't*."

He spun around to face her, furious. "What if it was Amanda?"

Melissa eyed him woundedly. "You think I don't care about Hannah? You think I haven't been dreading this day?"

A sharp new glow lit the village from above. Hundreds of people craned their necks just in time to see humanoid figures floating high in the air. Nine of them.

Zack and Amanda stumbled out of the commissary, their hands clasped, their faces pale and sweaty. They both had to brush the tears from their eyes to recognize the strangers high above: the assembled Jades of Calgary.

Mother watched them with disbelief. "No, no, no. I killed them."

Though the enemy orphans were dressed in their formidable stone armor, none of them wore helmets. Even from ground view, it was easy to spot their leader, Joelle—the woman that Peter had shot dead in Mexico, the one that Zack had rotted to a skeleton in Scotland.

Cain raised his transceiver. "Leticia—"

"I see them, sir."

"Good. Now see them out."

Integrity was nothing if not proactive. From the moment they took control of the underland, they installed contingency measures for nearly every kind of calamity, natural and otherwise.

The Pelletiers and their minions rode the top of the "otherwise" list.

Cain himself had overseen the installation of the village's defense network, an unprecedented assemblage of high-tech ordnance designed specifically to take down gods. The system had even been automated and randomized to confound the predictions of augurs. Would they get the solic cannon first? The dragonette drones? The guided missiles? Only the computer knew for sure. All Integrity had to do was set the targets and turn the key.

But by Pelletier standards, the system was archaic, all mindless ones and zeroes that could be disrupted at any point in the chain.

Cain looked to the roof of the Integrity field office, where the gun turrets rose but didn't fire. "What's happening?"

"It's not working," Leticia said. "Any of it."

Cain turned to the Integrity science lab at the north end of Guildhouse Row. "Terminal B?"

"Same problem," said a male voice on the radio. "Let me try something."

The Jades clenched their fists in unison, their attention split in two directions. Both the Integrity main office and the science lab began to glow with the same white radiance, one anyone on this world could recognize.

"The buildings," Melissa said. "They're reversing them!"

Cain's eyes bulged. "Leticia, get out of there! Get everyone out of there!"

It was too late. By the time Cain had yelled her name, both buildings had been regressed to their skeletal girders. Within moments, the structures were erased and replaced with their most recent predecessors: a two-story gymnasium where the field office used to be, a creaky old playground on the site of the science lab.

All the people inside the buildings were gone, zilched from existence forever.

"No . . ." Melissa looked at the Jades in terror. They'd just murdered more than a hundred agents, while the flashbulb abductions still plagued the village square, at least two dozen of them in the last twenty seconds. Somewhere in the back of Melissa's shrieking thoughts, she remembered that there had only been seventeen pregnant women.

Who the hell else are they taking? she wondered.

Two hundred yards to the west, just outside the commissary, Mia asked herself the same question. Harold Herrick had been standing just ten feet away from her when he and his tiger vanished. A half-second later, a young Opal named Julian disappeared in a glowing blip.

Mia fumbled for her brother's arm. "Bobby, stay close to me."

Amanda kept her hard gaze up at the Jades, her tempic fists curled tight. Her wings tore out of the back of her dress and expanded to full span.

"No!" Zack said. "Don't!"

"Someone has to!"

"Even if you kill them, they'll just come back!"

"So what do we do?"

"We have to get out of here," said Mia. "All of us."

Shade pointed up at the floating Jades. "Wait! They're leaving!"

Though no one on the ground could see it, the young Copper felt her signature energy on all the Jades' hands: concentrated mortis, corrosive enough to melt through steel. The invaders ascended to the crest of the dome, then burrowed nine tunnels into the framework.

Before anyone could utter a word, the Jades had vanished beyond the projected sky.

Melissa looked to Theo unblinkingly. "Are they doing what I think they're doing?"

"I'm not sure."

"*Can* they?"

Theo nodded tensely. There were billions of tons of bedrock above them, just looking for a reason to fall. The Jades had mortis and gravity on their side. Their victims had nothing but minutes at best.

"My God." Melissa pulled her handphone out of her thigh holster. "I'm calling it."

She punched a twelve-digit number into the keypad, setting off every alarm klaxon in town. The celestial projection changed from sunny blue sky to a blood-red canopy, one marked with giant white letters.

CODE T.

Melissa had created four different kinds of evacuation plans for the underland, from a calm and orderly stairwell exodus to a coordinated run for the elevators. Code T was the most urgent and desperate of all of them. It was a cue for every traveler to make a portal to the surface and get as many people out as they could.

Five seconds after the Jades disappeared through the roof, the ceiling panels began to splinter and fall in pieces. Some of the fragments were as small as books. Others were the size of surfboards. A twenty-pound piece of fibercore missed Theo by inches and hit the pavement hard enough to chip it.

Melissa pulled Theo under the overhang of the nearest guildhouse, then waved for Cain and Felicity. "We have to get to a traveler," she said. "The square's closer than the Orphanage."

Theo shook his head. "We won't make it to either one."

"We have no choice."

He took her hand in his. "Melissa . . ."

"I'm *not* giving up."

Neither was Theo. He had a plan to survive the next couple of minutes, but his foresight had little to say on the matter. He was still being teased with flat and happy visions: a pleasant walk with Hannah, a funny conversation with Zack, a gratifying epiphany in the middle of the night.

But now at the cusp of a fierce and local apocalypse, Theo knew exactly who'd messed with his foresight. This was the day the Pelletiers had been waiting for, the day they took every orphan and Gotham they wanted, and declared open war on the rest.

Not everyone had stayed for the wedding reception. By the time the great banquet began in the square, more than two hundred Gothams had retreated to their surface homes. Some were tired. Some were sick. Some were merely feeling antisocial. And some had no interest in celebrating what they believed to be an ill-advised union. Sure, they went to the ceremony. It was mandated by clan law. But they refused to raise a glass to Noah Rall and his bride, a pregnant alien breacher who wasn't long for this world anyway.

Only four Gothams and an orphan had skipped the wedding entirely. Six hours earlier, as his family ate breakfast in the downstairs parlor, the augur Jun Lee had died just the way everyone had expected him to: deep asleep on his canopy bed, with nothing in his stomach but sedatives. Ever since the apocalypse had first appeared on the strings, the poor man had been plagued by constant visions of it. His only respite, besides prescription barbiturates, had been the power-blocking talent of his daughter. Mercy's solis had been both a solace and a mercy.

Now, at last, her father was at peace.

Caleb leaned against the wall of the Lees' master bedroom, keeping a quiet, awkward vigil while Mercy and Sage wept at Jun's side. Their mother had been sitting on the news of his death for hours, chatting idly with her children as if nothing had happened. It wasn't until the others had changed to go to

Eden's wedding that she finally told them, in a perfectly flat monotone, that their father had passed away.

Mercy glared at her mother through hot, wet eyes. "You're the strongest augur in the clan. How did you not see it coming?"

Prudent Lee dipped her head, her hair bun barely bobbing. Her voice trickled out in the slow and muddled way that made Caleb want to shake her like a ketchup bottle. "It's . . . difficult to see what one doesn't wish to see."

Mercy pointed at her mother's prescription tranquilizers, a bedside collection that was as formidable as Jun's. "If that was true, you wouldn't need the horse pills."

"Darling—"

"How are you so *fucking calm*?"

Caleb sighed at her. "Hon."

"I'm sorry. I'm just . . . I don't even know how to deal with this."

Caleb had only defended Prudent on principle. Secretly, he couldn't stand her. For such a soft-spoken woman, she threw her words around like wrecking balls. She could bring Mercy to tears with a cutting observation, or darken Caleb's day with a prescient hint of doom. She'd all but ruined Zack and Amanda's wedding for him when she shared a grim forecast of their future.

"They'll never see their first anniversary," she'd muttered to him. "One will fall and the other will crumble."

Sage stretched out on the empty side of the bed and closed his fluttering eyes. The boy had been inconsolable an hour ago. Now he looked ready to sleep for a month.

"Uh, Prudent?" Caleb took a cautious step toward him. "I think your son—"

"He'll be fine," Prudent said. "I mixed a few pills into his food."

"You *drugged* him?" Mercy looked to her brother, wide-eyed. "*Why?*"

"He's been through so much, darling. I didn't want him to see."

"See *what*?" asked Mercy. "Mom, what are you not telling us?"

Prudent cupped her face, her voice finally cracked with emotion. "My angel . . ."

Caleb's heart sank in realization. *Oh, no. No, no, no.*

Mercy backed away from her, stammering. "Oh, shit. It's me. You're talking about me."

"I love you so much."

"Mom, tell me this isn't happening."

"No!" Caleb leapt from the wall, panicked. "Mercy, use your solis! Block them!"

"Don't be a fool," Prudent snapped. "Just tell her how you feel. Quickly!"

Caleb was far too rattled to think or speak. All he could do was jump into blueshift. At maximum speed, there might be a way to help Mercy, or at least inflict some harm on the bastards that were coming for her.

Sadly, all his velocity afforded him was a slow-motion view of Mercy's abduction. A seven-foot portal, blazing bright, suddenly sprang to life behind her. Four thick tempic tendrils popped through the surface. Even in Caleb's accelerated perceptions, they cut through the air with jarring speed. They snaked themselves around Mercy's limbs before tightening into coils.

Caleb ran toward her as fast as he could, but the Pelletiers were faster. They yanked her body through the portal and then immediately closed the breach.

"Mercy!" Caleb de-shifted and turned to Prudent. "You knew! You knew they'd take her!"

"Be quiet," she growled. "Their attack has only just begun, and I need you to save my boy."

"What are you talking about?"

"The Pelletiers are destroying the underland. This town will fall with it."

"What?"

Prudent motioned to Sage. "Take him as fast as you can to the eastern gate. Don't stop for anyone, even if they beg."

"But—"

"You'll be safe beyond the gate," she said. "Do you understand what I'm telling you?"

Caleb looked to the pale, gaunt corpse of Jun Lee and suddenly understood more than he wanted to. *She did it,* he thought. *She euthanized him.*

"What about my people?" he asked Prudent. "They're all down below."

"I . . . don't know. Our kind is often too hard to kill. I imagine a number of us will survive."

"Mercy?"

Prudent looked away. "You won't ever see her again."

A violent quake suddenly rocked the house, cracking every window. Caleb braced himself against the wall to keep from toppling over.

"It's begun," said Prudent. "Take Sage and go. Quickly! Please!"

"What about you?"

"I'm exactly where I need to be. Go!"

Caleb slung Sage over his shoulder and fled the house at shifted speed. The moment he reached the Lees' front stoop, he could see nearly all of Quarter Hill wavering, from the nearby mansions to the distant water towers. At 70x speed, it all looked like a bad acid trip. Roofs shed their shingles one by one, as if they were casually rotting. Trees and light posts dipped in all directions. Strange new shadows bloomed on every street and driveway like ink blots. It took Caleb a moment to realize that they were fissures. Hundreds of them.

Good lord. Prudent was right. The whole town was crumbling. And if it looked like the end of the world up here, then Caleb shuddered to think of the hell down below.

The underland had been built to withstand a Sigma-class earthquake, the kind that had destroyed San Francisco in 1906. The key to its stability lay hidden between the dome's two shells—an interlocked lattice of rubber, steel, and tempis that combined strength with flexibility. The dome was shockproof, steadfast, and virtually impervious to nature. The weight of the world only served to make it stronger.

But it wasn't immune to saboteur timebenders. The Jades only had to dissolve the extensive tempic plating to make the framework vulnerable to pressure. After that, it was just a matter of altering the landscape above it. With enough mortis at their disposal, a team of powerful orphans could turn hundreds of feet of bedrock into six billion tons of loose, angry rubble.

From there, gravity did the rest of the work.

The shift in weight caused the weakened dome to bend, cracking hundreds of insulated ceiling panels and sending them down onto the village. By the time the tempics were able to form their umbrella shields, more than a hundred people had been fatally struck by fragments.

Thirteen people had died in the Orphanage before Amanda finished her barrier. It was one of the largest constructs she'd ever made, a mushroom shield that stretched a hundred and sixty feet from edge to edge, protecting the clubhouse, the commissary, and half the main courtyard.

But a barrier was only as strong as its wielder, and Amanda could feel every impact on the tempis. She wouldn't have lasted another five seconds if Heath hadn't melded a dozen Jonathans into the shield, sharing her burden and absorbing half her pain.

Within moments, all the nearby tempics joined in to help. Stitch formed a panoramic catchnet to keep bouncing debris away from them. Meredith sent a pair of tempic giants to bolster the shield at its edges. They shouldered the canopy on their kneeling frames, like matching white statues of Atlas.

Amanda looked to her right at the unprotected parts of the Orphanage: the six apartment towers and the stand-alone structure that housed Melissa's team. The fibercore hail had shattered all the windows, but the structures still held, at least for now. Mother had enlisted Ben Hopkins and three of her Coppers on a mission to save any trapped orphans. Ben still had two friends in the towers, while Mother was intent on finding and saving Shroud. Amanda hoped to God they got back soon before—

The great dome once again creaked with strain, a piercing metallic screech that turned everyone's skin to gooseflesh. Amanda didn't have to be a structural engineer to know what was coming. The ceiling panels were just the opening wave. Soon it'd be raining rocks and girders.

"I can't take it," cried a trembling young tempic, the Gotham named Suzanne Rosen. "I have to get out of here!"

"You can't," Amanda told her. "We need every tempic we have."

"Please. I just lost my brother."

Stitch jerked her head at Amanda. "She lost her sister. You don't hear her whining."

Amanda closed her eyes. There was still a wide, dark hole in the universe where Hannah used to be. If Amanda looked at it too hard, she'd fall in and lose herself.

"We're all getting out of here," she promised Suzanne. "We just have to hold tight."

Twenty yards to their left, a pair of young travelers provided quick escape to the surface. The Gotham Shauna Ryder formed an exit on the outer wall of the commissary, while Mia waved a line of evacuees through a floating door by the clubhouse.

A panicked young lumic cut ahead of the line, brushing his shoulder against the edge of Mia's portal. He fell hollering into the spatial breach, leaving a fat, wet chunk of flesh behind.

"Goddamn it!" Mia yelled at the others. "Single file! Don't push!"

Unfortunately, there were more people arriving under the tempic umbrella than leaving. Ofelia and Jia, the traveler of the Violets, had two open portals to the village square, where hundreds of Gothams remained trapped in the center of the rock storm.

Mia could feel Peter's presence on the portal network. He was somewhere near the municipal building, ushering his own line of people to safety. From the fear and grief at the front of his thoughts, it was pure bloody carnage out there.

Come back to us, Mia mentally pleaded to Peter. *You'll be safer here.*

The travelers of the underland were connected to each other in ways they couldn't explain. Some were spatially attuned. Some were linked through dreams. Some, like Mia and Peter, could telepathically communicate while they both had open portals.

Peter's response flittered into her mind like a whisper. *Can't. Not till I find Liam.*

Mia cursed. He'd pulled the same shit on Red Sunday, and nearly died for his efforts.

So find him, she demanded. *Then get back here. I don't want to lose you!*

His deep-seated dread reverberated through her senses. *Hannah? Did they—*

Yeah. Mia fought back tears. *They took her.*

She could feel all of Peter's howling rage, a mere echo of the hatred inside her. A very wise woman had recently advised her to forgive Semerjean, for the sake of her own sanity, and Mia had actually come close to considering it. But now that door was closed forever. There'd be no forgiveness, no armistice, no "live and let live." Even saving the world became a secondary task to killing every last Jade and Pelletier.

As more and more Gothams flooded into the Orphanage, Priora Kohl, elder of the clan, cupped her hands around her mouth and shouted at the new arrivals. "If you are a tempic, please help with the shield! If you're a traveler, please help make an exit! Everyone else, *calmly* proceed to Shauna's and Mia's portals. We'll all survive if we just—"

Everyone around her screamed as she disappeared in a flash of light. The Pelletiers hadn't stopped their abductions for a moment, and there didn't seem to be any strategy to their choice of victims anymore—man or woman, orphan or Gotham, old or young, it didn't matter. If there was a common thread among the taken, Mia was far too rattled to figure it out.

Meredith looked to the space where Elder Kohl had been standing, her face drenched in sweat. "This is a nightmare."

Amanda could see Meredith's tempic giants faltering. For all her wonderful qualities, the woman wasn't battle-tested. She'd never seen war outside the corporate boardroom.

"Stay strong," Amanda urged her. "We need you."

"I-I don't see my sister. I keep looking for her, but I don't—"

"Meredith—"

"*Where's Charlene?*"

"Meredith, stop!" Amanda had to bite her lip to keep from crying. Dozens of people were already dead, and she was starting to fear the worst about her missing loved ones. "You *have* to hold it together."

"Charlene's alive," See said.

Meredith turned to her. "How do you know? Did you have a vision?"

See nodded. "The future's not flat and fake anymore. I can see again."

"What about Theo?" Heath asked her. "Melissa?"

"Theo's alive," See replied. "Not sure about Melissa."

Amanda's tempis rippled with strain. She gritted her teeth and rechanneled her energy. "No more prophecies. It's hurting my focus."

See nodded contritely. "Sorry."

A middle-aged Gotham got struck by debris just a moment before escaping the village square. He fell through Ofelia's portal in a bloody heap, only to be trampled by the evacuees behind him.

"Stop! Stop!" Ofelia frantically looked to her left. "Zack!"

Zack and Bobby rushed over to the wounded man and carried him into the clubhouse. The turners had converted the place into an infirmary, though it was starting to look more like a morgue. Nine people had died before anyone could heal them. Another one perished during the reversal process. Two more had disappeared in a flashburst.

Bobby kept checking on Mia every few seconds to confirm that she hadn't been kidnapped. Zack found himself doing the same with Amanda. He knew how important she was to the Pelletiers. It was a miracle they hadn't snatched her already.

Noah Rall watched his fellow turners from the bandstage, his tuxedo splattered with other people's blood. Zack could see the trauma in his big blue eyes. It had barely been an hour since he exchanged vows with Eden. Now his wife was gone, his best man was dead, and he was living through a horror show that made Red Sunday look quaint by comparison.

Zack moved to Noah's side and gestured at Mia's portal. "Look, why don't you get out of here? Bobby and I can handle this."

"Where would I go?" Noah bleakly inquired. "Where can any of us go?"

"Noah—"

"It's over, Zack. We lost. There's nothing to do but accept it."

Zack palmed his face, exasperated. There were eight confirmed deaths among the orphans alone. His people. His *family.* As much as he sympathized with Noah, he didn't have the strength to handle his grief. "Listen to me—"

He was blinded yet again by a momentary portal, a lightning-quick abduction just three feet away from him. And just like that, Noah was gone forever.

"Motherfuckers!" Zack thought he'd seen the worst of the Pelletiers' cruelty, but he had no idea. They'd been holding back. They'd been holding back this whole time.

Bobby rushed to Zack and held him by the shoulders. "You okay?"

"They took them right in front of me. The bride and groom. *Right in front of me!*"

"Look—" Bobby froze in the sudden silence. "It stopped."

He was right. After eighty seconds of relentless bombardment, the last ceiling panel had finally fallen.

The tempics beneath the great white canopy shared a loud sigh of relief. "Keep that shield up," Amanda warned them. "We don't know what's coming."

One girl did. See stood up on her elbow crutches and looked to Ofelia and Jia in terror. "Oh my God. Close your portals! Close your portals!"

"What?"

The ceiling girders broke in four different places, dropping hundreds of boulders onto the village. The central stretch of Guildhouse Row was demolished in an instant—the turners' hall, the travelers' hall, even the tunnels beneath the street had been pulverized.

The eastern half of the Orphanage received its own share of the wrath. A dozen huge rocks came down on the apartment towers, tearing the façade off one of the buildings and sending another one crumbling to the ground.

But the biggest hit came to the center of town, in the four-acre parcel of gardens and benches that had once served as the village square. The bedrock fell in house-size stones, battering every corner of the area. By the time the onslaught ended, two seconds later, the square and the buildings around them had been reduced to debris.

The impacts were loud enough to shatter half the remaining windows, and powerful enough to kill the lumic-electric grid for good. The survivors in the Orphanage could hardly see in the darkness. Only the glow of Mia's and Shauna's portals provided a semblance of illumination.

Amanda struggled to get back onto her feet. "Light! We need light!"

A dozen handphone flashlights came to life, while seven lumics set their fists aglow like lanterns. While most of the bystanders stared at the wrecked apartment towers, Meredith gasped at the new piles of rubble that had found their way beneath the tempic shield. They'd spilled through Jia's and Ofelia's portals, and then onto the travelers themselves.

"Oh no." Amanda blanched at the sight of Ofelia's limp arm. "Zack!"

Zack and Bobby led the effort to free Ofelia and Jia, though one of them was clearly beyond saving. Bobby gazed into the frozen eyes of his fellow Violet, a woman who'd become such a surrogate little sister to him that he'd sometimes accidentally called her Mia.

"Oh shit. Oh God." He pulled Jia out of the rock pile and carried her into the clubhouse, while Zack checked Ofelia's vitals.

"She's alive," he said. "I feel a pulse."

"*¡Ayúdenla!*" yelled Jackie Paredes, one of the last four Pearls who hadn't been killed or abducted. "Please!"

Zack didn't need a translator to know what she was asking. Unfortunately, there were issues that kept him from healing Ofelia on the spot. If her injuries weren't immediately life-threatening, then it was safer to stabilize her before reversing her. But how badly was she hurt?

"Don't heal her yet," See warned Zack. "She won't survive it."

Ofelia groaned in Zack's arms. He cast a nervous look at See. "You sure?"

"Just trust me!"

"Shit." While Zack carried Ofelia into the clubhouse, Amanda looked to the ruins of Orphan Tower 2. She could only assume that Mother and her team had been in one of the surviving buildings. Otherwise, See would be screaming.

Everyone in the safe zone turned their heads as Mia's high shriek split the air. She clutched her head and fell to her knees. Her portal disappeared in a blink.

Bobby hurried back to her. "Mia! What happened? Are you hurt?"

"It's Peter." She clutched Bobby's wrists, her eyes wide with panic. "I can't feel him anymore."

TWENTY-THREE

Theo bumbled along a path of red-leafed trees, unsure where he was or even *if* he was. He'd been running for his life just a minute before, dodging heavy chunks of ceiling as they shattered onto Guildhouse Row. He and his companions had been just forty feet from shelter when Melissa shouted Theo's name. An unholy force slammed into him like a meteor. A flash of pain. A cut to black.

And then suddenly he was somewhere else.

Theo struggled to make sense of his new surroundings: a lush and grassy city park underneath a twilight sky. The benches and light posts all looked like antiques with their black iron frames, their ornate and curvy frills. Theo peeked beyond the nearest fence and saw a row of squalid tenement houses, the kind that only seemed to exist in historical photographs. He couldn't tell if it was dusk or dawn. All he could guess, from the rusty color of the trees, was that it was autumn. Had he stumbled into a dream or something more prophetic? And if he *was* seeing the future, then why did it look so much like the past?

"Come on," Theo urged his brain. He didn't have time for this. If he was still alive in the reality he knew, then he needed to get back.

And if he *wasn't* alive . . .

Shit. He didn't even want to finish the thought. All that buildup, all that pomp, just to die like a third-tier character in a Hollywood disaster flick. It seemed patently unfair, but when did the universe ever care about fairness? Theo's whole native Earth had been filled with unfinished stories. What made him think he'd be treated any differently?

He followed the path to a concrete pavilion and found a wooden sign that had been neatly hand-painted.

PLEASE KEEP THIS AREA CLEAN.
CURB YOUR REFUSE. DESTROY NO SHRUBS.

SINCERELY,
THE WINTHROP PARK VOLUNTEER SOCIETY

Winthrop Park. Theo rolled the name around in his thoughts. Why did it sound so familiar?

He caught a sharp new glow out of the corner of his eye, as if someone had turned on a flashlight. There was a tree to his left that, unlike the others, had refused to change color with the season. Hovering in the air near one of the lower branches was an anomalous orb of radiance, as small as a baseball and as bright as a full moon. The sight of it set off every alarm in Theo's head. While his lizard brain told him to run, his foresight compelled him the other way.

Hold the light! an inner voice shouted. *Hold the light!*

Theo rushed toward the sphere, his other concerns all forgotten. If the underland was crumbling, he no longer cared. If the whole world was dying, it no longer mattered. He'd fallen deep into dream logic. And in *this* dream, he had to keep the light from expanding. It was the linchpin of his entire existence, the reason he was born and the manner in which he'd die.

Hold the light, Theo! Hold the—

The sphere exploded in a silent conflagration, throwing Theo's whole consciousness into chaos. By the time his senses came sputtering back in fragments, he was flat on his back in a dimly lit room. His head throbbed. His scalp bled. His left arm stung as if it had been stabbed. He looked at himself through hazy spots, and saw his limb wrapped in a sling that had once been his hoodie.

Theo tried to sit up, but that only aggravated his arm. The sharp knife pain suddenly turned into a chain saw. "Ow! Shit!"

"Careful." Melissa crouched at his side. "Your arm's broken."

Theo glanced around the room and recognized all its elements, from the reflective metal wall panels to the great mahogany conference table.

"The war room," he said. "We made it."

It had been Theo's idea to take cover in Integrity's secret conference chamber, the only structure in the underland that had been fortified with tempis. But to get there, they had to run through eighty feet of deathly hail. If Theo had been conscious for the last half of the journey, he didn't remember it.

He examined Melissa and saw her hands covered in blood. "You're hurt."

"It's not my blood. I was treating Cedric and Felicity."

"Are they—"

"We're here," Cain said from the other side of the room. Theo couldn't see him beyond the large conference table.

"What happened?" Theo asked Melissa. "Was I hit?"

"Hit? You were nearly crushed from above."

"So how am I still alive?"

Melissa jerked her thumb to the right. "You can thank them for that."

Theo turned his head and saw a pair of unexpected faces: Yasmeen Ghazali of the Violets and Charlene Graham of the Majee. The two of them had become friends over the past few weeks, thanks to their shared circumstances. They were both swifters, both misanthropes, both painfully new to the underland. And they were both increasingly frustrated with Theo's submissive idleness. Rarely a day went by when they didn't pester him about the world's looming crisis. "Forget Ioni," they'd told him again and again. "We need our own plan *now*."

Luckily for Theo, neither one of them were big on wedding parties. They'd been jogging through the village when the dome started collapsing, just a quick sprint away from Melissa and the others. Charlene was the one who'd saved Theo's life, though her high-speed tackle hadn't been gentle on either of them.

Theo noticed the makeshift sling around her right arm. "It is broken?"

"Dislocated," she said. "Melissa popped it back in. I'm surprised you didn't—"

A hellish rumble shook the room. The emergency lights flickered.

"This is a mess," Yasmeen said. She pointed at Melissa. "I warned you three weeks ago that we're all sitting ducks here."

Melissa eyed her wearily. "Every place we go is vulnerable to the Pelletiers."

"Well, now we're trapped and cut off from the others."

"If they're even still alive," Charlene said. "My sister—"

"Meredith's fine," Theo assured her. "If we had time to hide in here, then the tempics had time to make a shield."

Melissa nodded in agreement. "And unlike us, they have travelers to get them out."

Theo looked to her, confused. "Wait. Can't we just—"

"We already tried calling Mia," she told him. "And Peter and Ofelia and Mother. It's no use. We can't get a signal in here. Felicity's working on it."

Theo looked to Felicity at the end of the table, her left thigh wrapped in a bloody cloth bandage. Her attention was fixed on a pair of open handphones. From what Theo could guess, she was trying to use one to boost the signal strength of the other.

"How much time do you—"

"Shhh!" Felicity waved him away. "I need to focus."

Theo turned to Melissa. "Can't one of the swifters speed her up?"

She shook her head. "Not without frying the processor."

"Don't worry," Cain told Theo. "Felicity's been building phones since she was a kid. If anyone can get a call out, it's her."

Theo looked beyond the table and saw Cain on the floor, his head propped up on his blazer. From the way blood seeped from his stopgap compress, he'd taken a mighty blow to the skull. "Oh no . . ."

Cain smiled weakly. "Looks worse than it is."

Theo didn't believe it. His foresight was starting to come back through the pain, enough to see the end of Cain's strings.

"Cedric—" The building shook again. Theo braced Melissa for support. "Shit."

She hurried to an open wall panel and checked the readout on the generator. "The tempic shield won't hold much longer. Once that goes, we're in trouble."

"Goddamn it." Theo closed his eyes. "I should've seen this coming."

"I agree," said Yasmeen. "So why didn't you?"

Melissa kneeled at Cain's side and tended to his wound. "The Pelletiers must have tampered with his foresight."

Theo shook his head distractedly. "No. This was different."

"What do you mean?" asked Charlene.

"I don't think they got in my head. I think they changed the look of the whole future."

Yasmeen cocked her head. "How?"

"I don't know," said Theo. "I don't even know why they're doing this. It feels like a shift in strategy."

Cain scoffed at him from the floor. "You think murdering people is new to them?"

"I think murdering orphans is."

A rock slammed into the neighboring guildhouse, sending shockwaves through the war room. By the time the overhead lights stopped sputtering, there was a fresh new crack in the floor.

"Son of a *bitch*," Felicity yelled. "I can't do this without a steady table!"

"Keep trying," said Theo. "You're our last hope."

Charlene grimaced at the floor. "I should have never come here."

"It's not over," Theo said. "We still have a chance."

Yasmeen glared at him. "I hope you don't mean Ioni."

"Don't start with that."

"That savior of yours just let you down *again*."

Charlene nodded. "If she's as good as you say she is, then there's no way she could have missed this. So why didn't she warn us? I thought she needed us."

Theo checked on Melissa and saw her looking back at him in contemplation. He could only guess she was thinking the same thing as him: that the Pelletiers had either tricked Ioni or they had taken her out of the picture. In either case, it spelled bad news for the future.

"I have no idea," Theo told Charlene and Yasmeen. "All I know is that we need to get out of here."

By the time the dust settled on the ruins of the square, more than half of the village had been leveled. Only twenty-one buildings remained standing in full or part. All of the less fortunate structures, from the clinic to the library to the great Gotham amphitheater, had been crushed to the ground in a cannonade of boulders.

The heavier rocks hadn't stopped at the floor. They punched straight down through the streets of the village to the labyrinth of tunnels that spanned the width of the underland. Mia had tried numerous times to forge a spatial link with the subcellar, but all her jump points were too wrecked to connect with. Every failed attempt sparked a pain in her frontal lobe, the traveler's equivalent of an "out of service" signal.

But on her ninth try, she got it: a strong, clear portal to the center of the warrens, just sixteen feet beneath the remains of the municipal building.

Mia stepped out into a T-shaped intersection and took a sweeping scan with her phonelight. Only the southern corridor offered any hope of passage. The eastern tunnel, the one she needed, was clogged with debris from the clock tower. Mia spied a dozen huge gears among the wreckage. The minute hand of a clockface jutted out from the rubble like a tongue.

Zack and Bobby followed her out of the portal and coughed in the dusty air.

"You sure about this?" Zack asked her.

Mia wasn't sure about anything except that Peter was still alive. She could feel his flickering presence on the network—a six-inch portal, opening and closing in a deliberate sequence, like a Morse code *SOS*.

She closed her disc behind her, then pointed her phonelight to the east. "Yeah. He's not far that way. We'll have to loop around."

Bobby eyed her awkwardly. "Can't you just teleport there?"

"I can only jump to places I know," she said. "And I don't know that part of the tunnels."

"How do you even know this one?"

Mia swapped a heavy look with Zack. He'd been with her in the warrens toward the end of Red Sunday, when Mia had foolishly tried to kill Esis. It had been right over there in a storage room, just forty feet away, that Semerjean punished her in the cruelest way he could, by turning the girl she loved into a stranger.

A nearby corridor collapsed in a clacking rumble, sending new clouds of dust into the junction. Bobby shot a nervous look at Zack. "We should've listened to your wife."

Amanda had nearly pitched a fit when she'd heard about Zack and Mia's plan. To go fumbling through the tunnels while the rocks were still falling was absolute lunacy, a suicide mission. But then how many times had Peter jumped into fire for them? He was part of the nuclear family, and he wouldn't have signaled Mia if it had been only his life at stake. There must be other people with him who needed help.

Mia led Zack and Bobby around a corner, then stopped in place with a gasp. The tunnel abruptly ended in an impenetrable pile of wreckage, and some of the remains were human. Eleven limbs protruded from the impasse, all clad in fancy suit sleeves or garnished with expensive jewelry. Mia reeled to think how many Gothams had died in the village square . . . *again.*

Only one of the victims of the cave-in had managed to die with his head exposed. Zack shined his phonelight onto him and recognized him immediately.

"Sunder," Zack said. "Shit."

"Who?" asked Bobby.

Mia sighed at the man's bloody face. "Irwin Sunder. One of the clan elders. He was a prick."

"He was a *tempic,*" Zack said. "A strong one. The rocks must have come down right through his shield."

Mia could see the worry on his face. He was no doubt picturing Amanda at the bottom of a similar rock pile. "Zack . . ."

"I'm okay. Let's just go."

Bobby looked to the blockage of the northern tunnel. "Can't go this way. We'll have to double back."

Zack shook his head. "No time."

Mia eyed him anxiously as he raised his metal hand. "Wait. Are you—"

"Yup." Zack readied himself with a deep, anxious breath. "Stand back."

The corridor lit up in a gossamer glow, then quickly regressed through time. Rocks and corpses ascended through the air before blinking out of existence. A thousand broken pieces of the tunnel neatly snapped back to their original places.

Bobby watched in astonishment as the ceiling cracks mended before his eyes. "Okay. Wow. You're better at that than I am."

Zack shrugged. "I had some good teachers."

"Don't burn yourself out," Mia warned him. "We still have to heal Peter."

As she hurried down the corridor, Bobby watched her in marvel. "She really loves that guy."

"It's mutual," Zack said. "He'd kill or die for her."

"It's weird to see the way she looks at you guys, like you've been her family her whole life."

Zack's expression turned morbid. "You know what war does to people."

Mia turned around and beckoned them. "Come on!"

After two more turns, they reached a dead end with a vault door: a thick metal hatch that was only eight inches ajar. Mia peeked through the opening and saw army cots and ration boxes. It must have been one of the Gothams' old bomb shelters, the ones they'd built during the nuclear scare of the nineties.

"Hello?" Mia pulled at the door, but ceiling damage kept it stuck. "Peter, are you in there?"

"Mia?" Liam peeked through the opening, his face covered in dust. "Oh my God, it worked!"

He looked over his shoulder at people Mia couldn't see. "It's Mia! She's here!"

Mia heard sounds of relief from behind the door, a cacophony of sighs and sobs.

"Dad knew you'd find us," Liam said to Mia. "Did you bring a turner?"

"I brought two. How bad is he hurt?"

"Real bad." Liam waved her in. "Hurry!"

Though Mia was small enough to squeeze through the opening, there was no way Zack and Bobby would fit. She waved a new portal onto each side of the door.

Six young Gothams hailed her like a hero as she crossed into the shelter. She recognized them all from the thermics' guild, Liam's teenage friends and girlfriend.

Sovereign hugged Mia. "Oh God. I'm so glad you're here. You have to get us out!"

Mia could see from the half-empty liquor bottles that the thermics had been here a while. They must have skipped the wedding reception to have their own little party. Lucky for them that they chose a reinforced bomb shelter. It had probably saved their lives.

Except the place hadn't entirely withstood the devastation. The whole left side of the room had collapsed, leaving a dead young thermic and a very injured traveler.

Mia ran over to him. "Peter!"

He lay faceup in a puddle of blood, his ankles crushed beneath a slab of stone. Trickles of blood dribbled out of his mouth and his breath came out in quick, shallow wheezes.

"Oh my God." Mia squeezed his hand. "Hang on. We're gonna get you out."

He shook his head, his voice strained and creaky. "Just take the kids and go."

Zack crouched at Peter's other side and checked his carotid pulse. "Bobby and I can handle him," he told Mia. "Get the others out."

"Wait!" Bobby looked to Liam and his friends. "Any tempics among you?"

Sovereign shook her head. "We're all thermics."

"Great." He studied the pile of rocks atop Peter, a sloppy cairn of large and small stones. "This won't be quick or easy."

Mia opened a new portal to the Bear Mountain Nature Preserve, six miles to the north. God only knew what the Pelletiers were doing to Quarter Hill, if anything. It seemed a safer bet to avoid the town entirely.

She waved the young thermics into the exit. "Let's go. Quick. Single file!"

As they lined up for the portal, Sovereign looked to Mia. "Did you see my family up there?"

"I saw Regal. She, uh . . ."

"Oh no. Is she dead?"

Mia shook her head. "The Pelletiers took her."

Sovereign stared at her with tense dilemma, as if she couldn't decide if Mia's news was the world's biggest or smallest surprise. "And my parents?"

"I didn't see them. I'm sorry."

Liam fidgeted at Mia's other side. "Listen, there's something you should know. She was with us in here when the trouble started. She'd been drinking more than she should have."

"Who are you talking about?"

"Carrie," said Sovereign.

Mia's heart jumped. She'd been out of Carrie's life so long that she forgot that she was part of the thermic clique. "*What?* Is she okay?"

"We don't know," said Liam. He pointed at the vault door. "When the ceiling came down, she panicked and ran. We have no idea where she is."

"Son of a bitch." Mia paced the floor in frantic thought. She couldn't just let Carrie die, but if she left to go look for her, she'd be endangering Peter, Zack, and Bobby. The three most cherished men in her life would be trapped in this crumbling vault.

Mia shook her head. "I-I can't. I can't help her."

"We get it," said Liam. "We just thought you should know."

As the last of the other thermics escaped, Liam led Sovereign to the portal. "Your turn."

"You're not coming with us?"

"Not without my dad."

"No!" Peter struggled to face him. "You have to go!"

Zack held him down before he could aggravate his injuries. "Peter, stop. Stop!"

Sovereign held Liam's hands. "If you're staying, I'm staying."

A shuddering impact in the village square brought deep new cracks to the ceiling. Bobby mended them all with a regressive blast of temporis. "We don't have long."

"Go!" Liam yelled at Sovereign. "Please!"

Once Sovereign fled for safety, Mia closed the portal and threw a tense look at Zack. "Just heal him already!"

"I can't. Not while his legs are pinned. I'll only end up rifting him."

"So let's get him out!"

"We tried," said Bobby. "The rocks are too heavy, even for me."

Peter clutched Zack's wrist. "Just take my son and go. I'm begging you."

"We're not just leaving you!" Liam yelled. He turned to Zack with shaky inspiration. "What about an area reversal?"

"No," said Zack.

"No," said Mia. Area reversals were dangerous on the living, and had virtually no chance of succeeding. If Zack undershot by even a fraction of a second, then Peter would suffer his injuries all over again, along with a case of reversal sickness. If Zack overshot, the consequences would be worse. Peter would get zilched out of existence.

"There's only one way to save him," Zack said to Mia. "You have to cut him free."

"Cut him free?"

Zack traced a finger path across Peter's wounded legs, just below the base of his knees. "With a big enough portal, you can make it quick and clean."

Mia eyed him hotly. "Are you crazy?"

"He'll bleed out before we can patch him," Bobby warned Zack.

"Not if Liam cauterizes the wounds."

The boy gaped at Zack. "You want me to burn my own dad?"

"Just part of him."

Peter chuckled from the floor. "I knew you didn't like me."

"I actually do," said Zack. "That's why I want to keep you."

"It won't keep all of me."

"No," Zack admitted. That was Mia's other objection. Everyone knew the limits of reversal. It couldn't bring the dead back to life and it couldn't restore missing limbs. The replacements would be inferior duplicates, with spongy flesh, brittle bones, and a ninety percent chance of blood poisoning. There'd be no saving Peter's legs.

However . . .

"You'll still have options," Zack told Peter. He brandished his mechanical hand. "Trust me."

Peter scoffed. "I think the body shop's closed after today."

A loud, metallic shriek filled the shelter from above. The framework of the ceiling was coming undone. And once that happened, it was Armageddon.

Mia punched her palm, her mind haunting her with the faces of the missing and the damned: Theo and Hannah, Melissa and Felicity, Regal, Eden, Cedric, *Carrie*. There were so many friends beyond her reach, but Peter was right there in front of her. She wasn't going to let the Pelletiers take the father of her heart. Not on her fucking birthday.

She clutched Peter's hand, then aimed her resolute gaze at the others. "All right. Get ready. I'm cutting him on the count of three."

Time passed strangely in a crisis. For those who were trapped in the underland, it felt like the roof had been collapsing for hours. Amanda could have been struggling under her shield for days. Melissa might have been stuck in the war room for weeks. By the time Peter passed out from the pain of his cauterizations, he barely knew any other life than the one beneath the rock pile. All temporal perspective had been skewed to infinity, and there wasn't a soul in the village who would have believed that they were only halfway into a six-minute catastrophe.

For the Gothams on the surface, the pendulum swung the other way. The destruction of Quarter Hill played out over thirty-eight seconds, from the first ground tremor to the last fatal casualty, but the time had passed like lightning in the minds of the afflicted. There had been no warnings, no harbingers, no reason to believe that a great new void had been carved into the earth below their feet. Most of the victims mistook the tremors for an earthquake and were hiding beneath their doorframes when the ground gave way beneath them. Some had made it as far as their garages when their houses fell crumbling into the sinkhole.

Only Prudent Lee knew the hell that was coming, and only because Semerjean had told her. He'd appeared on her balcony the night before, his first visit to the house in months. And for the first time that Prudent had ever seen, there wasn't any smugness on his face. By the time he'd finished describing the future, she almost believed that he felt bad about it.

"It shouldn't have come to this," said Semerjean. "I tried to steer you all in a better direction, but all I got for my efforts were a mere seventeen pregnancies. *Seventeen*, Prudent. Do you know how foolish I look to my son?"

He'd glanced out at the homes of the lower village, all the prefabricated mini-mansions of Quarter Hill's lesser barons. "So now we do it Azral's way, the short and bloody road to a better tomorrow. It's a shame that we have to kill half of you to get the other half to take us seriously, but you know how stubborn young minds can be."

As always, Prudent held her tongue out of fear and desperation. God only knew what Semerjean would do to her son this time if she ever made him truly angry.

"You were good to me," Semerjean had told her. "You never revealed my secrets, and always helped me whenever you could. If you wish to leave town with Jun and Sage—"

"No." Prudent knew that her husband would never survive the grief. And after all the times she'd betrayed her own people, she didn't deserve to outlive them.

So at 3:25 on Sunday afternoon, as the whole town crumbled and the walls of her bedroom cracked, Prudent nestled on her mattress with the body of her husband, then shared her very last prophecy with him.

"Our son will survive," she said in a choked-up whisper. "He'll live."

At that moment, a half-mile east, Caleb didn't share her optimism. Though he was shifted at sixty times the speed of a normal person, the impediments of his situation slowed him down to a maddening crawl. He had a hundred fifty pounds of unconscious Gotham slung over his shoulder, and his dress shoes had little to no traction. The ground kept splintering ahead of him, forcing him to make circuitous zigzags through the streets. Worse, he had to be careful about every step he made. The last time he'd tripped at 60x speed, he ended up breaking two wrists and a shinbone. If he fell now, he and Sage were both dead.

Most worrisome of all was Caleb's despair, a sinkhole that threatened to consume him from the inside. He couldn't stop replaying his final image of Mercy, the terror in her eyes as she was rope-dragged to Hell. No doubt Eden and Hannah had been stolen away with her, and Caleb could just imagine what was happening to his friends down below. Even if some of them managed to survive the cave-in, there wouldn't be enough timebenders left to stop doomsday from happening. It was over. Finished.

No. Mercy would haunt his sorry ass if he gave up now, especially with her brother's life in his hands. The least he could do was get the kid to safety before waving the white flag.

His calves burned with strain as he carried Sage toward the town's eastern gate. At his accelerated pace, the sounds of destruction were like something out of a fever dream, a slow demon groan that was getting fiercer by the moment. Closer.

Caleb looked over his shoulder and gasped at the devastation behind him. The entire Heaven's Gate district of Quarter Hill, the elevated enclave where all the Gothams lived, had sunken into the ground in a funnel. From Caleb's view, it looked as if the whole world was deflating. Half of the mansions, like the great Tam house, had already collapsed under the strain. The properties in the center were disappearing in slow motion, dropping inch by inch into a black and growing chasm.

"Holy . . ." Caleb suddenly flashed back to his childhood, all the bad dreams he'd suffered after studying the *Bereshit*. The God of the Hebrew Book of Genesis hadn't been shy about expressing his vengeance, and what was happening to Quarter Hill looked a lot more like His wrath than the apocalypse ever had. Caleb could only recall the lesson that Lot had learned while fleeing the destruction of Sodom: *run like hell and don't look back.*

He turned and ran as fast as he could, his thoughts a howling void. It wasn't until he saw the half-frozen frame of a nearby jogger—a middle-aged brunette he'd never met before—that his mind suddenly fell into conflict.

Don't stop for anyone, Prudent had warned him. *Even if they beg.*

No. Caleb may have lost his faith in God, but he still believed in humanity. Without that tether, he'd be a miserable nihilist, a wretch no better than Evan Rander. He'd never be able to live with himself if he didn't at least try to save that woman.

He ran to the jogger, de-shifted in front of her, then encased her in an expanded time bubble. "Hang on to me and stay as close as you can. I'll get you out, but you have to keep up!"

The jogger reeled at her altered surroundings, the sluggish blue haze that had become a second home to swifters. Caleb had hoped that the woman was a Gotham he hadn't recognized, but she was just an everyday suburbanite who'd picked the wrong town to live in.

"*What's happening?*" she cried.

"No time to explain," Caleb said. "Just come with me. Please. It's your only chance."

The jogger shook her head in terror before fleeing. "Get away from me!"

"No, *wait!*"

The moment she stepped out of his temporal bubble, the front half of her body was rifted. She fell to the grass in a shuddering heap, her face a discolored horror, like old, spoiled meat.

"No!" Caleb contracted his acceleration field, then continued his dash to the east. His vision became blurred with what he thought was his own sweat, until he realized that he was crying.

Oh God, he thought. *I can't do this. I can't do it anymore.*

A deep new fissure suddenly opened up in front of him, bisecting the street in a jagged line. By the time he managed to stop in place, the concrete on the other side of the crevice had risen two feet.

"Shit." It was too high a step for Caleb's wobbly legs to climb. He had to go another way. But the pavement was rising on three different sides of him.

He suddenly realized—too little, too late—that the concrete around him wasn't rising. His whole piece of the street was falling into the sinkhole. The slow, groaning demon had finally caught up to him, all because he'd stopped and failed to save a stranger.

Caleb closed his eyes and held Sage tight, his thoughts falling back on Mercy. *I'm sorry, hon. I tried. I tried.*

A cool, hard force enveloped him and Sage, and for a moment he feared they were being crushed. When Caleb finally dared to open his eyes, he saw tempis all around him. Someone had encased him and Sage in a giant hand and pulled them out of the abyss.

Caleb traced the tendril upward to a large, bearded man, a Gotham he easily recognized. It was Stan Bloom: the primarch of the tempics, the father of Carrie, and one of the best wing-flyers in the clan. Caleb had seen him swooping around the underland on dozens of occasions.

"Hold tight," Stan yelled down at him. "We're gonna regroup about a mile outside town."

We? Caleb looked to his left and saw a slew of other Gothams in their wake: thirteen winged aerics, each one with a handful of survivors in their grip. Behind them flew a quintet of aeromobiles, all the swifters and their loved ones who'd managed to get to their vehicles in time. There must have been at least sixty timebenders in the convoy, maybe more.

Our kind is often hard to kill, Prudent had just told Caleb.

She was right, but a bird's-eye view of the sinkhole made it painfully clear that the dead outnumbered the living. There must have been hundreds of victims in the great yawning pit, and that didn't even include the people down below.

"We have to check the underland," Caleb yelled at Stan. "There might still be—"

"I know." Even in the rushing wind, Caleb could hear the tears in Stan's voice. "My daughter's still down there."

By the time the convoy reached the edge of town, the news media had arrived in force. Only six of the camera drones had bothered to film the sinkhole. The rest of them chased after the real story of the day: the flock of flying angels over the ruins of the town.

Caleb turned his head and saw two of the drones following him in pace, watching him unblinkingly like a pair of gobsmacked eyes. After forty-one years of rumors and myths, and on the very worst day of their lives, the secret timebenders of Quarter Hill had been formally exposed to the world.

TWENTY-FOUR

Melissa didn't need a prophet to know what was coming. The future announced itself through the walls of the war room: the tortured squeal of distressed girders, the dying moans of a dome shell. The very last bones of the underland were breaking. And when they fell, that was it. Every single person who remained in the village would be flattened in a hail of bedrock.

She caught Theo's eye from the other side of the room and saw every bit of his misery. Unlike Melissa, he *could* see the future, especially the parts that were (and she hated herself for thinking the expression) set in stone. The destruction of the village had become a fixed event in the strings, a given. There was only one question left.

How long? Melissa mouthed to Theo.

He tossed a furtive glance around the room before flashing a trident of fingers.

Three minutes, Melissa thought. *Dear God.*

The solic generator died with a plaintive *click*. The light panels flickered before going dark forever. Only four phones and a penlight provided the room's illumination. Most of them were fixed on Felicity as she continued her efforts to boost the signal strength of Theo's phone.

"So that's it for the tempic shield," Yasmeen said.

Melissa nodded. "It's gone."

Cain beckoned her from his spot on the floor, his voice a windy rasp. "Hey . . ."

She crouched beside him and examined him under the penlight. He must have aggravated his head wound since the last time she checked on him. The folded jacket beneath his skull had become drenched with blood.

"Hold still," said Melissa. "I have to adjust your compress."

"Don't bother," he said. "Just hand me my cigarette case. It's on the floor to my left."

He smirked at her dubious expression. "I'm not going to smoke. Just trust me."

Melissa found the silver case by his hip, then pressed it into his hand. The moment his index finger touched the monogram engraving, a one-inch springsleeve popped out of the base. In the middle of the sleeve was a dime-size disc of crystal and palladium: a micro data-spool.

"My contingency plan," Cain told Melissa. "I've been squirreling away resources in case I lost control of the agency. Money, armor, weapons, drones, that disc will lead you to all of it. There are also incriminating files against some folks who might get in your way, up to and including the president."

Melissa studied the spool, dumbstruck. "Cedric—"

"Don't tell me I'm getting out of here, because I'm not. And don't tell me you're not up to the job, because you are. You're the most brilliant and ethical person I know. You're everything Integrity should have been."

Melissa teared up before she could stop herself. Cain was pressing an old sore spot, and reminding her again what a rarity he was. With his shrewd intellect, he could have easily become a billionaire. Yet he'd dedicated himself to government service, the *good* kind of service that valued life over power. The agency wasn't ready to lose him, and neither was Melissa.

"When that portal comes, you'll get the others out," Cain told her. "And then you'll find all the scattered survivors. It doesn't matter if they're orphans or Gothams or federal agents. You're one people now, and you have one job."

Cain squeezed her hand. "Finish it."

Melissa closed her eyes, her thoughts drifting off into the future. Even if there were hundreds of survivors left, there was no place on Earth where the Pelletiers couldn't find them and slaughter them all over again.

"I got it!" Felicity held up her conjoined handphones. "A signal!"

"Send it!" Theo yelled. "Fast!"

Felicity fired off a text to one of Theo's contacts. There were only four travelers who'd been inside the war room, and the destructive nature of Mother's portals ruled her out as an option. Only Mia, Peter, or Ofelia could save them, though Theo's foresight insisted that none of them would be reachable.

But Heath was an entirely different matter. Of all the people Theo knew, he was the most likely to still have his phone with him, the most likely to check it in the middle of chaos. If anyone could get word to the nearest available traveler, it was him.

The phone signal died a moment after the text went out. "Holy crap," said Felicity. "I got it right under the wire."

Theo exhaled in hot relief. "Good work."

"Hope the kid's still alive," Yasmeen said.

"He is," said Theo.

"He is," Charlene agreed. "He's a strange one, but he's got fight in him."

Theo peeked over at Melissa and Cain. "Oh no . . ."

Felicity limped around the table, then covered her mouth in horror. "Oh God! Is he—"

"Afraid so."

Melissa closed Cain's eyes, her jaw clenched tight in suppression. She couldn't afford to fall into despair. Not with two minutes left to escape. All she could do was pocket Cain's disc and cast the tattered remains of her hope onto Heath.

By the halfway point of the underland's collapse, the Orphanage was in shambles. The last apartment tower had crashed into Melissa's building, killing two orphans and a Gotham with flying debris and sending a vengeful cloud of dust beneath the tempic shield.

Choking, half-blind, the survivors retreated into the clubhouse. While Stitch used her tempis to seal the broken doors and windows, Amanda coordinated the other tempics into forming a new shield through the roof.

They mobbed together in the center of the room, their tendrils wrapped around each other like the roots of a great white tree. Infused among the vines were the half-melted forms of Heath and Meredith's tempic men, a scattered array of wriggling limbs that unnerved everyone who looked at it. Between the corpses in the room and the piercing cry of girders, they already had all the proof they needed that they were trapped in Hell.

"Keep that light up!" Amanda yelled at Matt Hamblin. The kid had been beaned by a bouncing chunk of concrete and almost certainly had a concussion.

But if he went to sleep now, like he very clearly wanted to, he'd probably never wake up again. Even worse, he'd leave them all in darkness. He was their last surviving lumic. Without him, they were blind.

Amanda turned her attention to the upper stage, where Ashley Nielsen tended to the wounded. "How's Ofelia?"

"She's conscious," said the freckled young Integrity agent. "But in a lot of pain."

"Is she well enough to—"

"No."

"No," Ofelia weakly insisted. "I already told you."

"Shit." In all the chaos, Amanda had forgotten about her limits. A traveler was only as good as their memory, and Ofelia barely had any outside the underland. The only places she knew well enough to jump to were in Havana, well outside her teleport range.

Amanda cursed, helpless. The Pelletiers had abducted their other traveler, Shauna Ryder, leaving twenty-three people stranded in the Orphanage. All they could do was wait for Mia or Mother to come back from their rescue missions. If they were both hurt, or worse—

No. The thought of Mia lying crushed in the tunnels was enough to make Amanda's knees buckle. She had to stay strong for the sake of the others, especially the tempics who were linked to her. The battering of the shield had pummeled their minds, painting their eyes with cracked red vessels and filling their heads with agony. From the fluctuating pulses in Heath's tempic aura, the boy was on the verge of a nervous breakdown.

"Hey." Amanda tried to get a clear line of sight on him, but the tempics between them kept shuffling. "I know it hurts, but you have to hang in there. We need you."

Heath looked to the west side of the clubhouse, where the dead had been placed in a long, messy row. The body count had swelled to a staggering eighteen, including Mateo McGraw and Joey Fehrenbach, the two orphan bandmates whom Heath had recently been feuding with.

But they weren't the ones he was staring at. He pointed at the corpse at the end of the row. "He's glowing."

"What?" Amanda turned her head and saw exactly what he was talking about: Lars Van Handel, the poor, bandaged Opal who couldn't turn off his lumis. The flying debris that had killed him had knocked his shades clean off his head. Now his unblinking eyes were lit in a faint, eerie green. The overall effect was . . . unpleasant.

"Oh God." Amanda looked away, sickened. If the glow wasn't a postmortem reflex, then the Pelletiers were taunting the survivors. "Can someone *please* cover Lars?"

Her white arms rippled with strain, distracting all the other tempics.

"Keep it together," Meredith pleaded. "You're the linchpin here."

Amanda refocused her tempis, even as her thoughts slid back into hostile territory. It had seemed like forever since Zack and Mia left to save Peter. Were they even still alive?

The floor tiles by the foot of the stage turned black with mortis, then dissolved in a steamy mist. Before Amanda could turn her head to look, a brand-new tunnel had been forged from below. A quartet of orphans climbed out of the warrens, their clothes half-shredded and covered in dust.

See gasped with relief at the sight of her four fellow Coppers. "You made it!"

They'd burrowed their way to the apartment towers to search for one of their own, and had miraculously survived the destruction. But they all seemed desolate now. Shade, Sky, and Sweep were crying, while Mother looked to the ground with dark, hollow eyes.

Stitch studied the tunnel expectantly. "Where's Shroud?"

"Gone," said Mother.

"They took him," Sky cried. "The Pelletiers took him right in front of us!"

See teetered on her crutches, her eyes filled with tears. "Oh no. No . . ."

"What about Ben?" Amanda asked.

Mother shook her head. "He didn't make it out."

Amanda's throat tightened at an awful realization. Between the deaths and the kidnappings, the Irons were all gone. Wiped out. Extinct.

"Come," Mother said to Stitch and See. "We're leaving."

"Wait!" said Amanda. "You can't go yet. We still have people out there."

"There's nothing left," Shade insisted. "Everyone else is dead."

"You don't know that."

"I don't care," said Mother. Amanda could hear the cracks in her voice. She was barely holding herself together. "I won't lose any more children."

Amanda jerked her head at the cracked drywall. "If you leave now, you'll take down half the building!"

"Then you better come with us."

"Just give Zack and Mia one more minute," Amanda begged. "Please!"

"We don't *have* another minute." Mother glanced around at the other survivors. "You leave with us or you die."

"No!"

Eight tempics cried in turmoil as Heath's wrath overtook their creation. The shield support column wriggled with distress, expanding the hole of the clubhouse ceiling and raining tiny chunks of plaster on the others. A dozen wolf heads bloomed from the tempis, each one snarling in a silent growl.

"Oh no." Amanda could feel Heath's rage through their construct, a whirlwind that had been brewing from the moment that Hannah vanished. Since then, it had been fueled by one trauma after another, from the nonstop pain of the rock barrage to the glowing green eyes of Lars's corpse.

Amanda suddenly realized the real breaking point: Shroud. The boy had been the bassist of Heath's cover band. But now he was gone, leaving Heath the last of the Great Remains. For the kid who'd outlived everyone—his family, his friends, his fellow Golds—it was too much. It was too much loss for a young mind to handle.

See screamed as the wolves began wriggling out of the tempis in a furious bid for freedom.

"Heath, no!" Amanda extricated herself from the cluster of tempics, then raised her white hands high. "Please. I know it hurts. I know how much it hurts."

Heath crouched on the floor with his wrists over his ears. "No! No! No!"

He was drowned out by the noise from high above, the ceiling girders screeching with strain. Though even the augurs didn't know it for sure, the one-minute countdown had begun.

Mother frantically waved to her fellow Coppers. "Gather around me. Hurry!"

"No!" There was something on the strings that stood bright and clear in See's vision, a thin ray of hope that connected directly to the present.

She limped toward Heath, her face drenched in tears. "It's Theo! He's alive!"

The wolves stopped in place. Heath matched their blank expression. "What?"

"Check your phone. He texted you!"

Heath pulled his handphone out of his blazer pocket and read the message onscreen. "Oh my God."

"Portal's coming," Theo said. "Get ready."

Melissa's mood had only worsened since Cain passed away. Without a phone signal, she had no idea if Heath had gotten their message, or if help was coming anytime soon. All she could do was look to Theo and wait for good news from the future.

Now apparently he'd found it. "Who is it?" Melissa asked him. "Mia? Peter?"

"Ofelia, but . . ." Theo closed his eyes in concentration, his mind struggling to make sense of his visions. "Shit. She must be hurt."

"What does that mean?" Felicity nervously inquired.

"The portal won't last long," Theo said. "Three seconds at most."

He bounced his gaze between Charlene and Yasmeen. "You'll each have to shift and bring someone with you. One of you take Felicity and one of you take Melissa."

"No," said Melissa. "You're injured. I'm not. I can move faster than you."

"Look—"

"This isn't a sacrifice," she insisted to Theo. "It's the smarter play, and you know it."

"She's right," said Yasmeen. "Don't be sexist."

"*Sexist?* I want her to live!"

"I will," Melissa assured him. "I have every intention of making it through that portal."

Theo closed his eyes in tense dilemma before shaking a finger at Melissa. "I've seen you in the future as a very old woman. Don't you dare make a liar out of me."

She gave his arm an affectionate squeeze. "I'll be right behind you."

The ceiling cried the one-minute warning. As the others lined up for their quick escape, Melissa slipped Cain's data disc into Theo's back pocket. If all went well, she'd take it back from him shortly. And if not, then he and Felicity would figure out what to do with it.

The portal opened on the north side of the chamber, a weak and flickering disc of light that looked as dodgy as a frayed rope bridge. Though Ofelia had a strong recollection of the war room, one of the weirdest places she'd ever been, the pain of her injuries left her willpower in tatters. Even holding the portal open for three seconds was agonizing, like lifting a barbell made of broken glass.

As Ofelia wailed with pain from the back of the clubhouse, four people burst in through the portal in a pair of windy gusts.

Meredith rushed toward her sister. "Charlene!"

Theo was still shifted in Charlene's grip when he turned around to look at the portal. The surface remained blank for what felt like forever before he saw the first hints of Melissa. He had seconds to update his biggest fear, from never seeing her again to seeing her cut in half.

Mercifully, Charlene de-shifted him, allowing him to watch the rest of Melissa's escape in real time. She made it through the portal with just a half-inch to spare when the disc blinked away like a popped balloon.

Amanda caught Melissa on a flat sheet of aeris. "Oh thank God. Thank God."

Melissa flipped over and checked her lower limbs. "Am I all here?"

"You're all here," Amanda assured her. "I'm so glad you're okay."

"For now." Melissa sat up and looked to Theo. "How much time?"

"Seconds." He took a cursory scan of the clubhouse and did a double-take at Heath. The kid looked even worse than he did last June, when he first learned that Jonathan died. "Hang in there, buddy. We're almost out."

Heath sniffled and brushed his runny nose. "They took Hannah."

"I know." He looked to Mother. "You're our only way out. You've got to make it big."

"I'm ready."

"Not yet!" yelled Amanda.

"Not yet," said Theo. He pointed at the Gothams near the edge of the bandstage. "Portal's coming. Move!"

The group cleared out just in time for a new travel door to open, a much larger and stronger portal than Ofelia's.

Zack and Bobby burst through the surface with Peter in their grip. Everything below his knees was missing, and the stumps had been so freshly cauterized that the skin still smoldered with wisps of smoke. His only mercy was that he wasn't conscious enough to feel his infirmities.

"Oh no." Amanda coated his legs in tempis to keep him from going into shock. "I got him."

Mia rushed out of the portal with Liam in tow, then closed the disc behind her. She only took a moment to register Mother and Theo before opening a new door.

"Don't wait for me," she told Theo. "I'll find you."

Bobby turned to her. "Wait. What are you—"

She disappeared through the portal, then closed it before her brother could follow her. "What the hell is she doing?"

"Oh my God," said Liam. "She's going back for Carrie."

"What?"

The framework of the underland let out its final roar. The clock had run out, the ceiling had shattered, and no amount of tempis could save them from what was coming. The next rock to hit would be a worldkiller.

And it was already on its way.

"Now!" Theo cried.

With a frenzied cry, Mother raised her fist above her head, then enveloped the clubhouse in blazing light.

Her portal left a great round void in the Orphanage, a vacuum strong enough to inhale all the nearby dust. The vortex only lasted a tenth of a second before the world above came rushing down to fill the empty spaces: every pocket of air, every delicate construct, every human corpse or corpse-to-be.

By the time all the wreckage settled into place—the bedrock, the girders, and the broken remains of Quarter Hill—there wasn't a single recognizable facet of the underland. The whole village was just a smear on the floor of creation, a dirty little secret that the Earth would take to its grave.

TWENTY-FIVE

Zack woke up on the floor in a muddled daze, his wedding suit flecked with plaster dust. The portal jump had been one of Mother's roughest, like being stuffed in a metal barrel and rolled down the side of a mountain. Zack had blacked out somewhere along the way, but his body remained dazed and afflicted. His head throbbed, his muscles ached, his stomach threatened violence of one sort or another. Worst of all was his vertigo, a spin so bad that he wouldn't have been surprised to see the clubhouse still in transit. Maybe it hadn't finished twirling through the folds of space, like Dorothy's house on the twister ride to Oz.

Grimacing, he looked up through the hole in the ceiling and saw clear blue sky in a morning shade, in defiance of his inner clock. He caught a brief white glimmer in the sky, like light reflecting off glass. The glint came back after sixteen seconds, and then another sixteen seconds after that.

Zack sat up and examined all the bodies around him: Amanda, Theo, Melissa, Heath, nearly everyone he knew and cared about. The portal hadn't been any gentler on them, but mercifully they all showed signs of life. Even Peter and Ofelia, the most injured of the lot, twitched in place like restless dreamers.

"Wow." For all his aches and queasiness, Zack had to give Mother her due. She'd moved the whole damn clubhouse out of the underland, saving half the world's remaining orphans from a cruel and senseless death.

But then of course there was the other half to think about.

"Goddamn it!" Stitch cried from twenty feet away. "God *fucking* damn it!"

Zack looked to his left and saw five Coppers—all the teenagers in the group except for Shroud—kneeling in a circle by the bandstage. Unlike the others, their bodies had long acclimated to Mother's wrenching teleports. For them, it was barely a slap.

But they still looked miserable, worse than Zack had ever seen them. While Stitch cursed and railed, the rest of them wept hysterically.

Zack stood up on watery legs and made a slow, fumbling path toward the stage. After fifteen feet, he was able to peek over Sky's shoulder and see exactly what they were crying about.

"Oh no . . ."

Mother lay faceup on the tile, her eyes wide open and a trail of blood dribbling from each nostril. She'd suffered a bad case of power strain while fighting the Jades in Scotland, but that had been three weeks ago, more than enough time for her injured brain to heal.

Yet a fruitless search for a carotid pulse confirmed Zack's worst fear. She was gone.

"Oh God," he said. "I'm so sorry."

"She's still warm," See said. "Maybe you can reverse her."

"See—"

"You don't know her like we do! She's a fighter."

"Can't hurt to try," Sweep said to Zack. "Please."

With a sigh of resignation, Zack cleared a space around Mother and reversed her ten minutes. Her blood retracted into her nose, the scrapes evaporated from her skin, and her torn dress cleaned and mended itself. But she was no more alive than she'd been a moment ago. Despite all the myths and media hoaxes, there hadn't been a single proven case of temporal resurrection. For the spiritualists, it was all the proof they needed that the human soul was real. For the scientists, it was just more evidence of the brain's mysterious complexity.

"I'm sorry," Zack said to See and the others. "If I could bring her back, I would."

The image of Mia suddenly hit him like a fist as he remembered that she hadn't come with them. The thought of her dying alone in those tunnels was . . . no. He refused to believe it. The girl could jump a hundred miles in a blink. She had to have gotten out.

A large piece of ceiling collapsed in the corner, startling all the conscious survivors. Zack looked to the Coppers with new urgency. "Look, I know you're upset, but this place isn't stable. We have to carry everyone out of here. Now."

"Fuck you," growled Stitch. "Do it yourself."

He grabbed her wrist and spoke through gritted teeth. "You think you're the only one who lost someone today? *Everyone* has."

"I don't care!"

"Then congratulations," said Zack. "You're playing right into their hands."

"Who?"

"Who do you think?"

Stitch shook her head skeptically. "They were trying to kill us, not break us."

"If they wanted us all dead, we'd be dead," Zack told her. "They could have zilched the whole village, or flooded it with seawater. But they picked a messy cave-in, knowing full well that some of us would survive. Why do you think that is?"

Sky nodded in dark agreement. "Because they still need us."

"And they'll keep trying to break us." Zack jerked his head at Stitch. "Until we all give up, like her."

"Fuck you!" Stitch jumped to her feet. "I never said I was giving up."

"Then *help* us." Zack studied the ceiling. "I have an idea."

On Zack's request, Shade used her mortis to dissolve the remains of the roof, while Stitch knocked down the walls that threatened to topple inward. It was quicker and safer than moving the wounded, and it allowed them to keep using what was left of the clubhouse.

While Shade and Stitch secured the building, Zack sent Sky and Sweep on a flying reconnaissance of the area. There seemed to be nothing but grasslands in all directions, a vast and verdant sea of hills with squat blue mountains on the horizon. If there was a place like this within teleport range of the underland, Zack didn't know about it. It certainly didn't *feel* like the tri-state area. The weather was too dry and cool for August, and the sky was utterly devoid of vehicles. Even the hickelsticks of Scotland had a semblance of aer traffic, but this land was as quiet as an undiscovered planet.

Yet there was one sign of civilization. Fifty yards east of the clubhouse remains, silhouetted in the light of the rising sun, was an iron-walled compound the size of a shopping mall—a military base from the looks of it. The buildings were made of a drab gray metal, rusted around the edges and overgrown with weeds. The satellite dish that stood atop the largest structure had become little more than a hanging vine garden. Zack couldn't imagine that the place was inhabited. By best guess, it had been abandoned for decades.

Melissa and Theo joined Zack on the grass, their bleary eyes fixed on the army base. They had both woken up within moments of each other, and were still scrambling to adjust to their new reality.

"We're either in China or Mongolia," Melissa guessed. "The morning sun puts us at least fifteen time zones east of New York, and the climate suggests a central northern latitude."

In a better mood, Zack might have uttered a quip, or at least a sarcastic "Indeed." But his only urge now was to tear his hair out. None of this made sense. None of it.

"Mother couldn't jump more than five or ten miles," he reminded her.

Melissa shrugged. "I can't even begin to explain it." She pointed up at the sky. "Or that."

By now, every waking soul in the clubhouse had seen the exact same oddity that Zack first spotted: the reflective shimmer in the lower atmosphere that appeared every sixteen seconds, like clockwork.

"Your foresight isn't telling you anything?" Zack asked Theo.

He shook his head. "I've blacked out twice in the last ten minutes. I barely know my name."

Felicity shambled out of the clubhouse, then froze at the sight of the military base. "Oh no . . ."

"You know that place?" Melissa asked her.

"Of course I do. It's Sergelen."

"Sergelen?" Melissa looked to the compound in horror. "Oh dear God."

Zack swapped a baffled glance with Theo. "What the hell is Sergelen?"

Felicity tried to explain it as best as she could in her groggy state. In 1990, at the height of their cold war against the British, the Chinese government built a state-of-the-art research facility on the steppes of eastern Mongolia. Their goal was to create a low-yield, long-range nuclear missile, a "clean bomb" that could irradiate a city without leveling a single building.

But on August 7, 1992, a test went wrong and killed every last soul at Sergelen. Worse, it irradiated everything within eight miles of the base. By most estimations, the area would stay toxic until the end of the twenty-first century. The region was cordoned off behind a concrete wall nearly two hundred miles in circumference. The name Sergelen had become so notorious around the world that it was practically a synonym for scientific hubris.

Zack blinked at Felicity in a stupor. "So you're saying we're all gonna die."

"You'd think so, but . . ."

She pointed to a pair of white-tailed rabbits that foraged in the nearby grass. They were just a sampling of the wildlife Zack had already noticed, all the sprightly birds and insects that fluttered about without a hint of illness.

"I don't know what's happening," Zack said. "I don't know how we got here. I just know we have a bunch of dead and missing people."

"And we still have a Pelletier problem," Theo added.

Melissa checked her handphone. "Even if we could get a signal out here, Integrity will be in turmoil. I'm not sure we can trust them to help us."

"Terrific." Zack looked over his shoulder. "I'm gonna check on Amanda."

Liam accosted him the moment he stepped back into the clubhouse. "You've got to help my dad. Please!"

Zack crouched at Peter's side and examined him. His pulse was weak and his breathing was labored, but there wasn't a lot Zack could do. Reversing him would only afflict him with a bigger problem: a flawed new pair of feet and ankles that the rest of his body would reject. He'd die of septic shock within hours.

"I can't do it," Zack told Liam. "Our best hope is to get him to a hospital."

"How? We don't even know where we are."

Zack would have gladly corrected him if he thought it would help his mood. "Just keep him wrapped in that blanket. When Theo wakes up more, he'll figure out something."

"That's not a good answer."

"No," Zack admitted. "It's not."

He looked to the north and saw two figures disappear over a distant embankment. One of them had been large enough for Zack to recognize. "That's Bobby. What's he doing?"

Liam followed his gaze. "He thinks Mia's alive on the other side of that hill."

"What? *How*?"

"Says a voice in his head told him."

"A voice in his head."

Liam shrugged. "He's stressed about Mia. I think he might be, uh . . ."

"Yeah." The chance of one traveler coming here was crazy enough, but two was ridiculous. Either Bobby had stumbled onto a divine and holy miracle, or his mind had gone to the Big Rock Candy Mountains. "Who's with him?"

"His swifter friend," Liam said. "That bossy woman."

"Yasmeen," Zack said. That was good. She might talk some sense into Bobby, or at least keep him out of trouble.

Zack checked on Amanda and saw Charlene dabbing her forehead with a wet cloth. "Thanks for doing that."

"No problem," she said. "She looked like she needed it."

Meredith lay shoulder to shoulder with Amanda, still down for the count with no sign of waking up soon. The tempics more than anyone had been put through the wringer. Mother's portal had been the capstone of a long and arduous ordeal.

Zack noticed one tempic missing from the pack. "Where's Heath?"

Charlene jerked her head to the left. "Over there. He's not doing well."

Zack scrambled to the other side of the clubhouse and found Heath sitting cross-legged on a table. See stood at his side, but the boy wasn't paying her any mind. He merely sat in the light of the morning sun, his calm gaze fixed on a pair of waddling pheasants.

"*Please* talk to me," See begged him. "Even if you want me to leave you alone, I'll understand. Just say something. Anything."

"Ah, shit," Zack grumbled. "See."

She hobbled toward Zack, her eyes filled with tears. "He's not talking!"

"It's okay."

"It's not okay! You weren't here when he had his breakdown."

"Look . . ." Zack led her away to the restroom area, then lowered his voice to a mutter. "You know his mind works differently. When things get bad—I mean *really* bad—he has to shut down for a while and go inside his head. It's a coping mechanism."

See wiped her eyes. "What if he never comes out?"

"He will," Zack promised. "I won't let him stay in there, and neither will—"

He froze in the middle of his sentence, horrified. See clucked her tongue with sympathy. "You were going to say 'Hannah.'"

In his battered mind, she'd been right there in the clubhouse, just waiting to wake up with the others. But then reality came flooding back to him, and he finally had a moment to process it.

Zack clutched See's shoulder with a quivering hand. "I, uh . . . I have to . . ."

He retreated into the men's room and closed the door behind him, despite its absent roof and two missing walls. It didn't matter. He just needed a place to collect himself, for all the good it did him. He was stuck on the thorn of a memory, something Hannah had said to him last April, a few days after he'd been freed from the Pelletiers' mirror room.

"I couldn't stand it," she'd told him. "That whole time they had you, I was a mess. I put on a brave face for Amanda, but I couldn't stop thinking about what they were doing to you."

Zack suddenly knew that feeling, just as he knew that Hannah was suffering right now. Even if the Pelletiers kept her in good health and comfort, she was suffering. And there wasn't a thing on Earth he could do about it.

He dried his eyes in the bathroom mirror before absently turning the sink knob. *There's no plumbing*, his brain sharply reminded him. *It's dead and crushed on the other side of the world, just like half your people.*

"Zack." Melissa's urgent voice hit him from the other side of the sink wall. "Get out here."

He stepped back out into clubhouse proper and followed everyone's gaze to the new guest: a large, curly-haired man standing mournfully by the corpses. Like everyone else, he was dressed in tattered wedding attire. Except this man hadn't gone to the wedding. He hadn't even been in the underland when all the shit came down.

Zack drank him in, bewildered. *"Caleb?"*

Caleb kept his gaze on the bodies of two Platinums. "I'm gonna kill them," he said in a croaking rasp. "Every last Jade and Pelletier."

"How the hell are you here?" Felicity asked him.

"I was hoping you'd tell me," said Caleb. "We had to jump through a portal to escape the news media. Next thing we know—"

"Back up," said Melissa. "News media?"

Caleb looked around the room, slack-faced. "Holy shit. You guys don't even know."

He filled them in on the events on the surface, from the abduction of Mercy, to the destruction of Quarter Hill, to the live national exposure of the Gothams. The eyes of the world had become fixed on the town . . . what remained of it, anyway. By the media's best guess, more than two thousand people had perished.

"Holy shit." Zack wanted to cry all over again. Most of the victims were just innocent neighbors, people who wouldn't know a Gotham from a Freemason. But the hole had swallowed them anyway, because what did the Pelletiers care? To them, this Earth was as dead as the last one, a graveyard waiting to happen.

The only silver lining to Caleb's news was that there were nearly a hundred surviving Gothams just a quarter-mile west of the clubhouse: all the swifters and aerics and quick-thinking travelers who'd managed to escape Quarter Hill. They'd converged in a clearing outside town. When the newsdrones came, they had no choice but to flee through portals.

"Even the travelers don't know where we are," Caleb said. "They thought they were jumping to Connecticut, but they obviously missed."

Melissa chuckled bleakly. "We're most definitely not in Connecticut."

"A couple of us swifters volunteered to scout the area," Caleb told her. "When I saw this place, I thought I'd gone nuts. I still haven't ruled it out."

He looked to the corpses on the floor again, grieving. "There are so many people I want to ask about, but I don't think I can handle the answers."

"They're not all dead," Zack assured him. "We got a lot of them out before we left."

Liam raised his head with new hope. "Sovereign! She and my friends got away through Mia's portal. You think they're here too?"

Zack shrugged. "I still don't know how this is possible."

"Someone must have rerouted all the travelers," Charlene said. "If my grandfather's quick enough, he can redirect someone else's portal."

"To Mongolia?" Melissa asked.

"No," she admitted. "That obviously takes a lot more power."

"That's what I'm afraid of," Caleb said. "If this is just Phase Two of their final solution—"

"It wasn't the Pelletiers," Theo said.

"How do you know?"

"Because the person who did it is standing right there."

The others followed his pointed finger to the front door of the clubhouse, where a young woman stood waiting. She'd arrived on the scene so quietly that only Theo had noticed her.

Ioni looked around at the weary survivors, her expression as grim as everyone else's. "Hi."

She'd been meddling in their lives for nearly two years, this spry and cryptic pixie who seemed curiously attached to the Silvers. The sisters and Mia had each encountered her at various intervals, while she'd practically become the burning bush of Theo's prophetic career.

Yet somehow Ioni had never crossed paths with Zack, which made her sudden appearance even more surprising. The fragments of his mind snapped together like magnets and began churning out random observations. She was blonde. She was small. She wore a cute white sundress. Her watches looked old and jarringly clunky. She had the perfect little teeth of a catalogue model.

And Zack didn't like her one bit.

He wasn't entirely sure why his instincts were growling, but he could certainly hazard a guess. Like everyone else in the clubhouse, he was wondering how this powerful oracle—a woman who desperately needed them all—could let the Pelletiers ravage them so thoroughly. Either she was coldly indifferent or grossly incompetent. Zack couldn't decide which was worse.

Ioni opened her mouth to say something, but Theo cut her off. "I thought you were dead."

"Theo—"

"That's the only reason I could think of why you didn't warn us."

"Theo!" Ioni raised her palms. "I'll explain what happened. I promise. Just give me a minute to take care of some business."

"Business," Melissa cynically echoed.

Ioni looked at her with heavy eyes. "Hi, Melissa. I'm—"

"I know who you are."

"I was just going to say I'm a very big fan, even if the feelings aren't mutual. Anyway . . ."

Ioni flicked her hand upward, causing a new light to shine down from the sky. Zack and the others craned their necks and saw a glowing white arrow pointing straight down at the clubhouse. The hologram was large enough and bright enough to be seen from miles away.

"It's a beacon for the rest of you," Ioni explained. "I spread you guys out so you wouldn't teleport into each other."

Felicity eyed the arrow nervously. "The Chinese have lots of satellite cameras."

"They won't see us," Ioni promised. "You might have noticed that shimmer in the sky."

"Yeah. What is that?"

"I'll get to it in a minute. Item Two . . ."

She opened her fist to reveal four beads of light, then blew them through the air like spores. The others watched blankly as the orbs fluttered across the room in resolute paths. Within moments, they disappeared inside the mouths of their sleeping targets: Peter, Ofelia, Meredith, and Matt Hamblin.

Liam gasped as his father's skin began to glow. "Please tell me you're healing him."

"I'm healing all of them," Ioni said. "No one else is dying today."

Stitch motioned to Mother's corpse. "But you couldn't save her?"

Ioni shook her head. "She was out of my reach when she died. I'm sorry."

Charlene cradled Meredith as her body started to shudder. "How bad was she hurt?"

"She took a real beating with the tempic shield," Ioni said. "It gave her a subdural hematoma that would have killed her by nightfall."

Charlene's eyes bulged. "But she's okay now."

"She will be," said Ioni. "At least as okay as the rest of us."

Zack was tempted to ask about Amanda's health, but he let the urge pass. There was a nasty storm brewing inside his head. If he opened his mouth now, he'd say something he'd regret.

Liam watched his father guardedly as the charred remains of his ankles healed into clean stumps. "His feet aren't—"

"No," said Ioni. "I'll have something for that later."

She looked back to Theo and his freshly broken arm. "I'm afraid that'll have to heal the old-fashioned way. I have a limited supply of menders, and I want to save them for—"

"I don't care," he said. "All I want right now are answers."

"I'm almost done. Just one last thing."

The clubhouse suddenly went freakishly quiet, as if Zack had gone deaf in both ears. If anyone else was having the same problem, they didn't show it. No one else moved at all. They stood completely frozen in still-frame.

"What . . . ?"

"A temporal trick," Ioni explained. "You have a couple of yards to move around, but it's probably best you stay put."

Zack wasn't quite thrilled to be the focus of her attention. "So I'm your last bit of business."

"My last? No. But I've been eager to meet you for a very long time."

She detached from her corporeal self like a spirit, her translucent image drifting across the floor tile. "I'm Ioni Anata T'llari Deschane, and I'm a big admirer of your work."

Zack blinked at her, confounded. "My work."

"I'm from your distant future," she said. "A string of time that never got cut by the Pelletiers. On that world, you grew older and wiser, and you found your true calling. Your political cartoons were absolutely inspired—hilarious and brutal, always poignant, always gorgeous. The historians of my era still talk about you."

Zack let out a jagged chuckle. "You picked the wrong day to drop that on me."

"I know," she said. "I'm sorry. I'm sorry for so many things, Zack. I see the way you're looking at me, and it hurts even worse than Melissa."

At close range, Zack could register new aspects of her countenance, some notable differences between the Ioni who'd been described to him and the one who was standing in front of him. She wasn't as white as Amanda had made her out to be. Her features hinted at a blend of different races: some Asian, some Mediterranean, maybe even a few ethnicities that didn't exist yet. And she wasn't as young as she first appeared. When viewed as a whole through an artist's eyes, she looked older. Much older.

But the most jarring realization was why he despised her—a simple and painfully obvious truth that he hadn't been able to grasp until now. It all came back to a single old grievance, the one loss in his life that he couldn't blame on the Pelletiers.

"My brother," he said. "You killed him."

"Listen—"

"Before you say that Rebel did it—"

"*I* did it," Ioni attested. "I convinced Rebel that you orphans had to die. I created the conflict that cost lives on both sides."

"Why?"

"Because if I hadn't, a lot more people would be dead today. People I need."

Zack gestured at the frozen image of Heath. "Tell it to him. The Golds were his family."

"I'll tell him when he's ready to hear it. Right now I'm focused on you."

"Why?"

"Because we're officially in the endgame, Zack, and I know who the crucial actors are. I need you alive and on my side. Otherwise, we might as well pack it in."

Zack glanced around the room and became lost in the negative space, all the people he loved who hadn't made it here.

But he suddenly realized that there was still hope for one of them.

"Mia," he said. "You were the voice in Bobby's head who told him where she is."

Ioni nodded. "He already found her. She's hurt but she'll live."

"And Carrie?"

"Same."

Zack laughed with overwhelming emotion, a paradoxical mixture of relief and incredulity. "Those tunnels were huge. How did Mia find her so fast?"

Ioni smiled humbly. "I may have guided her portal a little."

"So you *were* able to save people."

"I was able to save two," Ioni said. "If I could have saved more, I would have. But despite what Theo told you, I'm not all-powerful and I'm not all-seeing."

She looked at the corpses on the other side of the clubhouse. "And I'm very truly sorry for the ones I couldn't help."

Zack was too caught up in the memory of Hannah to focus on the dead in the room.

"They did it," he said in low and doleful mumble. "They broke us."

Ioni shook her head. "It's not over."

"You still think you can stop what's coming?"

"I do," Ioni said. "But not alone. And not while the Pelletiers are still breathing."

Zack peered out at the distant grass, his eyes slitted with resentment. "I may not be your biggest fan, but I do like your priorities."

Ioni grinned softly. "I thought you would."

She looked to Amanda. "Your wife will be awake in fifty-eight seconds, and she'll need you more than ever. You have to hold her together, Zack, because she's very important to my plans."

Zack scoffed at her. "I thought Hannah was important to your plans."

"She was."

Ioni floated back toward her physical self, then disappeared inside her own skin. The clock of the world started up again, bringing noise and movement back to the clubhouse.

Theo resumed his antsy stance. "Well?" he asked Ioni.

"Well what?"

"You said you had a last bit of business."

"It's done. I just took care it."

She sat on the edge of a broken table and toyed with the bands of her watches. "Before I tell you all how I horribly failed you, would anyone like a drink?"

By the time Amanda fumbled her way back to consciousness, the clubhouse smelled like coffee and antiseptics. Ioni had summoned a whole mess of goodies onto the bandstage: food and drinks, bandages and painkillers, six working sinks, and enough soapsheets to clean off every bit of blood and dust.

While the survivors washed up, Amanda rested against Zack in a cushioned recliner, yet another amenity that had been abracadabra'ed out of thin air. Her mind and body were too weak to make tempis, forcing her to rely on Zack to be her arms. As he fed her ice-cold water from a paper cup, he gave her the latest on the people they cared about, from the good news (Mia, Peter, Ofelia) to the bad news (Mother) to the wait-and-see developments (Heath).

But of course Zack didn't mention the one person she needed to hear about, which meant he hadn't gotten any news about Hannah. Amanda had hoped there'd be at least some hope for her in the strings, but from the way Ioni avoided eye contact with her, it seemed the future had become as grim as the present.

Theo grudgingly waited for the last person to sit down before putting Ioni on the spot. "How did they do it? How did they take all the augurs by surprise?"

Ioni slouched in her chair and took a long sip of coffee. "The third eye's a lot like the other two," she said. "It can be tricked into seeing things that aren't there, or not seeing things that are right in front of you. What the Pelletiers did was . . . advanced stuff. Time-consuming. It must have taken months to prepare their trick."

"Their 'trick,'" Caleb repeated with venom. "Thousands of people died."

Ioni sighed. "I'm not talking about the consequences. I'm just explaining the how."

"Is it the kind of trick they can do again?" Felicity asked.

"No." Ioni shook her head emphatically. "They played their hand, and it was a mean one. I won't underestimate them again."

Amanda didn't have the strength to say what she was thinking, and prayed that someone in the room would say it for her.

As ever, Melissa didn't disappoint. "They destroy worlds," she sternly reminded Ioni. "Typically not the kind of adversary a person would underestimate."

Ioni acknowledged her with a grudging nod. "You're certainly right, but you have to understand something. The era I come from makes the world of the Pelletiers look like the Wild West. I've been running circles around them for two years."

Charlene was thrown by that. "You're from their future?"

"A different future," Ioni said. "My tools are alien to them, but Azral's a fast learner and he's way ahead of his time. He could probably go toe-to-toe with the geniuses of my era."

See curled on her chair with her arms around her knees. "I thought they needed us."

"The Pelletiers never needed all of you," Ioni said. "But like all good scientists, they wanted spares and redundancies, especially as your kind was about to become extinct."

Disgusting, Amanda thought.

Shade finished her cherry vim, then disintegrated the can with mortis. "They took Shroud," she said to Ioni. "Him and a whole lot of other people. What's going to happen to them?"

Amanda's heart thundered as Ioni mulled her response.

"I don't know," Ioni confessed. "They're out of my sightline and out of my reach. All I can tell you is that the pregnant women are still alive. The others, uh . . ."

"Just say it," Stitch snarled. "They're dead."

Ioni obliged her with a somber nod. "In all likelihood."

A heavy air filled the room as See and Shade cried again. Amanda looked out to the distant hills and did a double-take at the tiny people in the distance.

She opened her mouth to say something, but her voice was still all wind and wheezes. Luckily, Zack was able to see what she was looking at.

"There are people coming," he said. "A bunch of them."

Caleb scrutinized the shambling crowd. "They're not the ones I came with."

"They're Gothams," Ioni said. "The ones Peter and the other travelers got out of the village square. They'll be the first to follow the arrow here, but a lot more are coming."

"And where exactly are we all going to live?" Theo asked. "Sergelen?"

Ioni nodded. "I've spent the last few weeks cleaning up the place. It won't be the Ritz, but there are enough beds for everyone. You'll have food, clothes, medical supplies."

"Cancer," Felicity grumbled.

Ioni chuckled. "I fixed the radiation problem. This is the cleanest air you've ever breathed."

Melissa looked up at the sky in time to catch the next perennial shimmer. "And this energy field you've created. What exactly does it protect us from?"

"Everyone," Ioni said. "We're completely invisible and undetectable. Even the Pelletiers won't be able to find us."

"Unless you're underestimating them again."

Ioni shrugged. "I won't discount it, but I wouldn't bet on it. They needed months of work to fool us last time. They'll only have seven weeks to fool us here."

"Why?" Charlene asked. "What happens in . . ."

She remembered the answer before she could finish the question. "San Francisco. Right."

"So that's still happening," Theo said. "Even after today."

"The string's not broken," Ioni replied. "It's weaker than it's ever been, but we still have a chance to save this world. All of us."

A large aeric platform abruptly touched down on the grass, fifteen feet from the clubhouse. Sky and Sweep had returned from their reconnaissance, and they'd found a whole lot more than they'd expected. Amanda counted seven teenage Gothams on the platform with them, only one of whom she knew by name.

Liam leapt to his feet. "Sovereign!"

"Oh my God!" The girl nearly knocked down Sky in her rush to get to Liam. Everyone watched quietly as two young lovers came together in a hug. Until recently, they'd been the scourge of the underland—the gropiest, kissiest, "Jesus, get a room"-iest couple in the village. But here in the dark and smoldering aftermath, their embrace was more than welcome, it was beautiful.

Their reunion was just the first of many over the next several minutes, as all the scattered survivors came bumbling toward the clubhouse, hundreds of them. All the Gothams who'd dodged the Quarter Hill sinkhole. All the time-benders and Integrity agents who'd managed to escape the underland. They'd all been whisked to the other side of the planet, to an infamous patch of no-man's-land that the world still considered toxic.

Amanda stood with Zack near the southern wall of Sergelen, her eyes darting eagerly along the green and grassy hilltops. After a maddening wait, she finally saw them in the distance: Bobby Farisi and Yasmeen Ghazali, two of the last three Violets. A dazed young blonde rode Yasmeen's back, while another girl dangled limply in Bobby's arms. Amanda's heart lurched in dread, until she saw the maniacal look of relief on Bobby's face.

Mia was alive and back among her people.

Zack squeezed Amanda's shoulder and breathed a heavy sigh. "There she is. Thank God."

Try as she might, Amanda couldn't find the strength for gratitude, only fury. She broke away from Zack and stumbled toward Ioni.

"Hey!" At long last, Amanda's voice had returned, and it was strong enough to get Ioni's attention. "*Look* at them."

Amanda's tempic arms weren't thicker than garden hoses, but she still managed to sweep one at the survivors. For every two people who embraced in teary reunion, there were six more who wandered the crowd alone, sobbing as they searched for their missing loved ones.

"How much longer will you tease them?" Amanda asked Ioni.

"Amanda—"

"How long will you let them hope?"

Zack quickly caught up to her. "Hon."

"No!" Amanda kept her wrathful gaze on Ioni. "You see clearer than anyone. You know who survived and who didn't."

Ioni nodded meekly. "I do."

"Then *show* us," Amanda insisted. Her voice wavered with strain. Her lips trembled. "Show us the names of the people we lost, so we can stop wondering and start grieving."

Ioni cast a nervous look at Theo and Melissa, as if it were them, not her, who were calling the shots.

"As you wish."

With a flick of her finger, a new spectacle filled the sky: a giant tableau of names above the clubhouse, a final tally of the dead and abducted.

One by one, the survivors stopped what they were doing and cast their attention upward. Ioni had split the list into three major factions, each one teeming with losses. For Integrity, the death count almost read like an employee directory. More than ninety percent of the agents in the underland had lost their lives in the cave-in. The majority of them had died before the first rock fell, when the Jades reversed their buildings out of existence.

Melissa scanned the tally, thunderstruck. Cedric Cain was just the seventeenth name in a list of two hundred and nine. "My God."

The Gothams had it even worse. Their casualty count spanned a full eight columns: six hundred and seven kinsmen, nearly five times the toll of Red Sunday. Entire families had been either wiped out or abducted in the attack—the Ballads, the Byers, the Chisholms, the Fords. They'd been sitting at Eden and Noah's wedding, and now they were all gone.

Amanda cringed at the anguish she'd triggered, the sound of hundreds of Gothams in grief. She peeked at Zack out of the corner of her eye, half-expecting him to be livid. *Why did you make her do that, Amanda? You could have at least let them get settled.*

But his rapt attention was fixed on the list, specifically the column that had been reserved for the orphans. There had been fifty of them in the underland this morning, more than half the surviving population of their Earth. Now they'd been whittled back down to twenty-eight. Mother and Shroud, Eden and Ben, old friends, new friends, every last Iron. People they'd crossed the globe to recruit. Gone.

Smack dab in the middle of the column was the cruelest cut of all, the one that made Amanda drop to her knees. She'd been praying with every fiber of her being that Ioni would make an exception for her. But no, her name was right there with the rest of the fallen, just another indelible casualty of war.

Hannah Given.

NUL'HASSA E'NUL

TWENTY-SIX

If she didn't know better, she would have thought her captors liked her. Her prison was a virtual paradise: a sleek and glassy cottage on the sands of a tropical beach. She had a Jacuzzi on the front deck, a swimming pool in the back, a cathedral roof, three window walls, and the furnishings of a five-star island resort. The place could have been ripped from her childhood fantasies, when she had her dream life planned to the last perfect detail.

Of course, the dream didn't involve being someone's pregnant hostage, a fact that no amount of splendor could hide. Hannah only had to walk fifty yards in any direction before her path was blocked by a translucent wall of light. The Pelletiers had trapped her in a giant box of illusions, just her and her Malibu dreamhouse.

Is this it? Hannah wondered to herself. *Is this where I'll be the rest of my life?*

She conducted a more thorough inspection of the cottage and found an out-of-place object in the kitchen: a waist-high Roman pedestal made entirely of silvery metal. Touching the surface triggered a holographic menu screen that was gesture-controlled and filled with endless food options—breakfasts and lunches and multicourse dinners, hot and cold drinks, even a few enigmatic categories. Hannah waved the menu open for "Extinct Foods," half-expecting to find dodo eggs and mammoth steaks. Instead, she discovered a treasure trove of old-world junk, from Oreos to Slim Jims to the menu line of Burger King.

"Holy shit." Hannah zeroed in on the thumbnail image of a bag of Hershey's chocolate eggs, the little candy-coated delicacies that had only been available around Easter time, and only when they could be found. The stores couldn't stock them for more than an hour before customers depleted their supply.

Hannah only had to point at the menu to make the candies appear like magic on the pedestal: dozens of chocolates in a decorative glass bowl, in all the pastel colors she remembered.

She picked up an egg and studied it before taking a cautious nibble. Her eyes rolled back in nostalgic bliss. "Oh my God."

The food synthesizer was just one of several household wish-bringers. The genie in the bedroom conjured brand-new clothes of every style, while the one in the bathroom offered health and beauty items. The front deck console gave her godlike control over her environment, from the color of her furniture to the size of the moon. She could swap her beach house for one of a hundred other modules: a cabin in the Alps, a yacht on the Caribbean, a posh urban penthouse, even a gingerbread cottage. The sky was the limit, although technically it wasn't. Hannah found a nested submenu for spaceships and lunar bases.

Overwhelmed, she stuck with the default setting, then moved on to the genie in the living room, the one that provided entertainment. Like its sibling in the kitchen, the pedestal was a conduit to her late, great Earth: every book, every movie, every recorded song in history, all digitized and catalogued for her personal enjoyment. It was as if the Pelletiers had taken the soul of her world and stuffed it inside a jukebox.

"Christ." Hannah's heart pounded as she scrolled through the images of old movie posters: *Mary Poppins*, *Singin' in the Rain*, *My Fair Lady*, all the musical classics of her formative years, the films that had inspired her to become a stage performer. To see them offered up like snack treats, by the Pelletiers of all people, made her nauseous. They were feeding her the soul of the planet they'd killed, completely unaware of the ghoulishness. They might as well have offered the skull of her mother to use as a bookend or paperweight.

Hannah huddled inside a closet, then cried in the darkness for hours. There was no household genie that would let her see her people again, or have any meaningful control over her life. She was living at the mercy of sociopaths who could keep her as a broodmare for decades.

By the time the illusory sun went down, Hannah was too hungry to ignore the food offerings. She wished a steak and lobster dinner out of the kitchen genie, then ate it on the beachside patio. The food was delicious, *crazy* delicious, enough to embolden her to try the other amenities. Within minutes, she was relaxing in the Jacuzzi, eating chocolate eggs by the handful while the long-lost songs of Sarah McLachlan filled the air through invisible speakers.

Careful, said the Zack in her head. *The cozier you get, the more you play into their hands.*

Her inner Amanda disagreed. *You do what you need to get through this.*

Hannah hated to think about the mood in the underland, after losing seventeen women so abruptly. Amanda and Heath were probably sedated in their apartments, while Mia vented her rage in the gym. Peter and Zack would be their usual stubborn selves, and would try to rile up the troops for a rescue mission.

And Theo? He was probably blaming himself, as always. The thought of him made Hannah so sad that she nearly broke down in tears again.

She turned her anguish into fury, and vented it at the sky. "So that's it, huh? You're gonna keep me locked in here until I'm ready to pop? At least let me talk to Eden!"

If her jailers were listening, they didn't let on. Hannah stepped out of the hot tub, wrapped herself in a towel, then tested her temporis on a ceiling fan. Just as she feared, her powers were gone. Time was a weapon the Pelletiers couldn't afford to leave her. She might rift her own heart with an angry thought, or use her broken speed power to trigger a fatal hemorrhage. Who knew how desperate their prisoners would get, especially without human contact?

The next two days passed in manic discomfort as Hannah battled her gloom with idle distractions. She summoned a closetful of clothing out of the wardrobe genie—T-shirts and tank tops and cozy pajama bottoms, all made of a fabric that put the smoothest silk to shame. She used the environmental genie to turn her prison into a madwoman's paradise: a floating glass palace in the middle of the Caribbean, with a subaquatic viewing cellar, an infinity pool on the roof, and a gravity-defying sundeck that could only be reached by monkey bars. The living room had a karaoke station, the bedroom had a soda dispenser, and the basement had a massage chair that could have qualified as a boyfriend.

By her third night, Hannah came dangerously close to finding her new existence tolerable.

"I still hate you," she yelled up at the Pelletiers. "If I don't see Eden or Mercy soon, I'll get stressed. And you know what stress does to a pregnancy."

The next morning, as Hannah decorated the sky with colorful new planets, a tall white portal bloomed to life at the edge of her wooden sundeck. She waited ten seconds for someone to emerge before realizing the disc was an exit, not an entrance. The Pelletiers were letting her out of her cage, but why?

Hannah stepped through the portal and into a whole new environment, a large and sunny sofa lounge that could have come from the world's nicest airport. A great glass dome enclosed the space, and the view from every side was breathtaking: miles and miles of lush green hills, with snow-capped mountains in the backdrop. All it needed was a young Julie Andrews to twirl around on the grass and sing.

More than a dozen young women came stumbling into the lounge through portals, all the orphans and Gothams who, like Hannah, had volunteered their wombs in the hopes of saving their loved ones. But where was Mercy? Where was—

"Hannah!"

She barely had a chance to turn around before Eden yanked her into a hug. "Oh my God. I'm so glad to see you."

"You too." Hannah pulled back to look at her. Like everyone else, she was dressed in the sleek silk garments of the wardrobe genie. But where the others were content to wear pajamas and sweatsuits, Eden had wished up a glittery, strapless party dress. Between her makeup, clothes, and jewelry, she looked ready for a night at the opera.

"Wow," Hannah said. "You're, uh . . ."

Eden peeked down at herself, then shrugged. "I was just playing dress-up to pass the time. I've been cooped up alone for a week."

"A *week*?" Hannah blinked in bafflement. "This is only my fourth day."

"What? When did they take you?"

"Right after the wedding."

"Me too." Eden eyed her diamond ring with misery. "Of all the fucking days."

Hannah squeezed her arm. "I'm sorry."

"I only stopped crying an hour ago," Eden said. "I guess they gave us each the time we needed to calm down."

Hannah felt awful for her. Unlike the others, Eden had never signed up for this nightmare. The pregnancy had been forced on her by circumstance and malice.

"Whatever you do, just play it cool," Hannah warned her. "I'm not telling you to give in—"

"I get it," said Eden. "I was the only Latina cop in my unit. I know how to pick my battles."

"I know you do." Hannah pressed her forehead to Eden's. "I'm sorry you're here, but I'm so relieved too."

Eden stroked her back. "Let's make sure they don't split us up again."

"We won't," someone said from the front of the lounge.

Every woman turned their head to see Semerjean relaxing on a plush recliner. He looked like a model in the artificial sunlight, his Henley shirt unbuttoned to the sternum. Hannah couldn't tell if he was trying to beguile his prisoners or intimidate them into compliance. But there was something different about his appearance now, a subtle adjustment that she couldn't quite pinpoint.

His bright blue eyes lingered on her for a moment before surveying the others. "If you would all be kind enough to have a seat, we can begin your orientation. It won't take more than a couple of minutes. I'm sure you all have questions."

He motioned to the many sofas, all curved in a semicircle. "Please."

As the prisoners hesitantly gathered around him, Hannah finally recognized the change in Semerjean's expression: a sweet and boyish kindness that she hadn't seen in ages.

It's David, she thought with a sharp pang of dread. *He's wearing his David face again.*

He stared out at the mountains for a drawn-out moment, as if he was carefully deliberating his words. But it all reeked of acting to the Silvers in the room, who'd spent months at his side and knew all his dramatic flourishes. Hannah would have been flat-out stunned if he hadn't already perfected his spiel, right down to the thoughtful pauses.

"I can only imagine how difficult this is," Semerjean began. "You're far from home in a foreign environment, in the care of a people you see as an enemy. Though your future's not as grim as you think it is, I won't mince words about your situation. You are not free women. This facility's hidden deep beneath the Antarctic tundra. Your friends won't find you. Your temporal gifts have been suppressed. You have no rights but the ones we give you. And anyone who insists on causing trouble will find their stay here to be most unpleasant."

As his audience chattered and shifted in their seats, Hannah glared at Semerjean. She would have expected more sunshine and rainbows in his opener. There must be a hell of a "but" coming.

"But," he continued, "our demands are quite simple. We only want your children to have a healthy, natural development. It's in our best interest to keep you as comfortable as possible, physically and emotionally. If all goes well, these next several months will be easier than you ever imagined. And you *will* go home again. I can promise that to each and every one of you, as long as you cooperate."

As he spoke, Eden translated every word for the young Mexican orphan named Rosario Navarette. "You don't have to do that," Semerjean told her. "She understands English now."

Rosario nodded at Eden in nervous confirmation. *"Le entiendo. Cada palabra."*

"What?" Eden threw her confused look at Semerjean. *"How?"*

"The human brain's just an organic computer," he explained. "With the right technology, we can install vast amounts of knowledge into it."

"I, uh . . ." Rosario stumbled on her words before looking at Semerjean helplessly. *"¡No sirve!"*

"Don't rush it," he told her. "Your tongue needs time to adapt to the new language. A few weeks of practice and you'll be speaking fluently."

Eden gave him a dubious look. "Did you force this on her or—"

Rosario shook her head. *"Está bien. Se lo pedí."*

"She asked for help learning English," Semerjean said. "And we had just the remedy. I would have just as gladly implanted Spanish in the rest of you, but she preferred to do it this way."

Hannah studied Rosario, a petite young beauty who was barely a year older than Mia. Ofelia had come to love her like a sister, and had repeatedly insisted that she was wise beyond her years. But how wise could she be to get knocked up and sent here?

Semerjean proceeded to explain the new rules of order, a surprisingly short and simple list. The prisoners could spend their time however they wished, either in their own domains or in the large common area, which boasted some unique diversions. The closet chambers in the back of the room were all sensory experience simulators that were indistinguishable from reality and packed with a million different thrills, from swimming with dolphins to flying with eagles. It had virtual games, historical tours, even a few "adult" modules that Semerjean mercifully didn't elaborate upon.

The only schedule commitment that the Pelletiers demanded was a daily health examination, which would be conducted in private by either Azral or Esis. Semerjean promised that the tests would be quick and noninvasive. There wouldn't even be any skin contact.

"What about our diets?" asked Thalia Ballad, a plump blond swifter who looked strangely excited to be there. "I saw foods in the dispenser that are really bad for babies."

The other Gothams traded uncomfortable looks, for reasons Hannah could guess. Thalia had been a paranoid schizophrenic for most of her life, and had done a litany of awful things to herself. Her face and arms were marked with knife scars—deep and symmetrical, like tiger stripes. From what Hannah was told, she'd been relatively stable these past few years, thanks to a potent combination of antipsychotics. But then Hannah had also heard a rumor that she'd gone off her meds for the pregnancy.

If that worried Semerjean, he certainly hid it well. He smiled at Thalia. "I appreciate your vigilance, but you don't have to worry. All the foods here are made of the same plant-based gel, which can be molded to mimic anything. If you want ice cream for dinner instead of a salad, then by all means, have it. They're nutritionally identical."

While Hannah quietly made plans to eat her own weight in chocolate eggs, she suddenly realized why "David" had always gagged at the smell of cooked meat. The people of his era must have moved so far beyond animal flesh that they didn't even pretend to consume it anymore.

Regal Tam meekly raised her hand until Semerjean called on her. "Will we be able to talk with our families, just to let them know we're okay?"

He shook his head. "I'm afraid the nature of this facility makes outside communication impossible. We're in a hyper-accelerated continuum."

"How hyper?" Thalia asked him.

"For every month we spend in here, only an hour passes in the outside world."

"Holy fuck," Eden exclaimed. "Is that even safe?"

"We've made it safe," Semerjean insisted. "If everything goes according to plan, you should be home in time for your wedding night."

"My wedding night." Eden laughed venomously. "You lying-ass motherfucker."

Hannah held her wrist. "Eden—"

She jerked her arm away, her vengeful gaze locked on Semerjean. "You killed my world. You ruined my life. You sent me my own head on a platter. Now you expect me to believe that you'll just let me go, out of the goodness of your heart."

"Not goodness," Semerjean said. "Strategy."

"What are you talking about?"

He sighed at Hannah. "Will you please explain it?"

Somehow he knew that she'd figured it out, a borderline psychic deduction. A part of her wanted to play dumb in defiance, but what would be the point?

"They want more babies," she glumly informed Eden. "If they send us back, alive and well, it'll convince more of our people to sign up."

Semerjean nodded. "Especially once they hear how well you were treated."

There was something in his tone that bothered Hannah, a whispering hint of insincerity that made her question the whole scenario. Maybe Semerjean was back to slinging his bullshit. Or maybe it was all true. Hannah didn't have the strength to untangle the matter. Her thoughts were still flailing around Mercy's ominous absence.

"Our interests are aligned," Semerjean told Eden. "If you work with us, then everyone benefits."

"What about our babies?"

The question came from a woman at the edge of the audience, a willowy young Gotham whom Hannah had only seen on a few occasions. Mischa Varnov—or Moon, as everyone called her—almost never came down to the underland. The acoustics of the place set her teeth on edge, and the preponderance of tempics threw her senses into a tizzy. She needed those senses to get around, as she'd been blind since birth.

Hannah had always noticed Moon when she visited the lower village. She was a uniquely lovely woman, a long-haired albino with delicate features and a mesmerizing grace to her movements. Even the tempic tendrils she used to navigate had a beautifully hypnotic rhythm to them.

Semerjean puffed a heavy breath before answering Moon's question. "Keeping your children was never part of the arrangement. We were clear on that from the start."

"I know we won't keep them," Moon calmly replied. "I just want to know what you'll do with them."

Semerjean looked to Hannah once again, and for a moment she feared he'd ask her to chime in. This time, she had no idea of the answer. She wasn't even sure she wanted to know.

"They'll be archived," Semerjean told Moon. "Converted into a temporal state that'll allow us to make infinite copies."

Eden's eyes bulged in horror. "Alive?"

"Not in any sentient capacity. They'll be vegetative bodies, suitable only for study. But we'll be able to run certain tests and experiments that we wouldn't be able to do otherwise."

An anxious silence filled the room, until Regal asked the obvious. "What about the originals?"

Semerjean shook his head. "I'm afraid archiving is a permanent process. Irreversible, even for us. But they won't be conscious and they won't feel pain. They'll essentially be frozen in time."

Eden turned her head in disgust. "You're monsters."

"I could have lied to you."

"I wish you had," said Hannah.

"You of all people know why we're doing this," Semerjean said. "We have a world to save, just like you—fourteen trillion people who are marked for death by nature. Only a monster would pass up the chance to cure them. All the sacrifices we're making—"

"*We?*" Eden challenged. "I don't see a bulge in your belly."

Semerjean's expression hardened. "You have no idea what my family and I have given up."

"I don't care."

"And luckily you don't need to," he said. "But you do have to carry your child to term, and you have to fully cooperate. Do you need me to detail the 'otherwise' part, or can we keep it unspoken between us?"

"Don't bother," Eden said. "I know what you can do to me."

"This doesn't have to be hard for anyone," said Semerjean, his David face back in full bloom. "I *want* you all to be comfortable here. I *want* you to go home to your families. What else can I say—"

"Mercy," Hannah interjected. "What have you done with her?"

Semerjean looked wounded by the question, as if it were an insult to their long and trusting friendship. "We had to isolate her due to some . . . complications to her pregnancy."

"Complications," Thalia echoed.

"She's much further along than the rest of you," said Semerjean. "And she didn't take the best care of herself. Now she has gestational hypertension, among other issues. We had no choice but to keep her bedridden."

"Can I see her?" asked Hannah.

Semerjean tapped his arm in thought before answering. "Last I heard, she wasn't in a mood for visitors, but I imagine she'll make an exception for you. Let me ask her."

He disappeared in a flash of light, leaving nothing behind but a gaggle of nervous women.

"Oh my God," Eden said. "We're all gonna die here."

Rosario shook her head. *"Eso no lo sabes."*

"I *do* know. He's full of shit. They have no intention of letting us go."

Hannah touched her shoulder. "Eden—"

"I will *not* let them archive me."

"Eden, stop!" Hannah took a furtive glance around the room. For all she knew, Semerjean had never left. He could be standing right behind them, as invisible as the wind. "I'm not saying you're wrong, but we have to be smart about this."

"So what do you suggest?"

Hannah wished she could give her a helpful answer, but the Pelletiers had all the advantages. They could see every move, hear every word, predict every act of sedition. And despite all of Semerjean's rosy assurances, Hannah knew where she and the others fit on the food chain. They were living, breathing incubators, just counting the months until they became expendable.

"I don't know," Hannah said to Eden. "Just keep your eyes open. Learn everything you can. And don't give them a reason to worry about you."

A portal opened ten feet in front of them. Semerjean stepped out of the disc, then motioned for Hannah. "Mercy's ready to see you."

She followed him into a stark white hallway, a narrow lane of tempis that seemed to stretch on to infinity. The air was cool enough to give Hannah goosebumps, with a deep humming noise that she could feel in her teeth.

There were no doors or windows anywhere. There was certainly no sight of Mercy.

"Where are we?" Hannah asked Semerjean.

"The eastern wing of Lárnach."

"Lárnach?"

"The name of this facility," said Semerjean. "It means 'central base of operations' in my native—"

"I don't care. Where's Mercy?"

Semerjean gestured up the hallway. "About fifty meters."

"You couldn't just take me there?"

"It's our first chance to speak alone," he said. "I wanted to see if you were all right."

"All right?"

"Look—"

"You snatched us away without warning!"

"What choice did we have?" Semerjean asked. "If we'd given you notice, do you think Peter would have handled it gracefully? Amanda? Heath?"

"You're afraid of them hurting you?"

"We were avoiding the need to hurt them."

"That's bullshit," Hannah growled. "You're hiding something, as usual."

Semerjean closed his eyes, exasperated. "Hannah, you and I will be spending a lot of time together . . ."

"Yeah. I'm not happy about that either."

"Would you prefer I have Azral take my place? Perhaps you'd rather deal with my wife."

"I just want the *truth.*"

"I told you the truth about your child's future," Semerjean insisted. "And I told you the truth about yours. But if you'd like to change that fate for the worse, then keep doing what you're doing. Keep scheming with Eden."

Hannah studied him carefully as he started up the corridor again. There was an uneasiness in his expression that she hadn't seen since his David days, a genuine anxiety this time. Was his family running out of time on the baby-making mission, or were they seeing new problems in the future?

She rushed to catch up with him. "You know Thalia's schizophrenic, right? If she's off her meds—"

"She's free of her illness," Semerjean replied. "Esis cured her with a simple procedure."

"Okay. What about Moon?"

"What about her?"

"She can't see. She needs her tempis to get around."

"And she has it," said Semerjean. "We left her just enough power to navigate."

"Oh." Hannah suddenly felt silly for second-guessing the Pelletiers. They'd never been anything less than a dozen moves ahead. "Why didn't you just cure her blindness?"

"We offered. She declined. She has a system that works for her. It's admirable, really." He looked to Hannah with softer eyes. "And it's admirable that you're concerned about two Gothams you barely know."

Hannah turned away from him. "I don't need your flattery."

"I'm not offering flattery. I'm offering you an opportunity."

"What are you talking about?"

"We'll discuss it later." He stopped, then waved his hand at a wall. The tempis parted, revealing a perfectly round doorway. Hannah couldn't see anything but whiteness beyond the entry, but she could hear the sounds of anguish—a woman's cries, peppered with curses. From Mercy's strained and winded voice, Hannah could easily guess the nature of her pain.

"Oh my God. Is she—"

"Yes," said Semerjean. "Her water broke an hour ago."

Hannah processed his news, flummoxed. Last she saw Mercy, she was just beginning her third trimester. "It's way too early."

"Actually, she's right on time."

"What?"

"It'll all make sense in a moment," Semerjean promised. "Come on."

The moment he put his hand on her back, Hannah spun a one-eighty and pointed a finger in his face. "Don't. Don't *ever* touch me."

Semerjean stepped back. "I'm sorry. I thought—"

"What? That I forgave you?"

"No. But I was hoping you'd at least be more mature about it than Mia."

"Mature." Hannah laughed bitterly. "I loved you like a brother, you lying shit. You broke my heart."

"I kept you alive."

"So we could all make babies for you to 'archive,'" Hannah fired back. "Don't pretend you did it for us."

"Hannah—"

"And fuck you for that Mia crack. You killed every last bit of kid she had in her."

Hannah brushed past Semerjean, then froze in the expanse of Mercy's prison. "Whoa."

The place was as big as an industrial warehouse, a vast and empty cube with bare tempic walls. It must have been what Hannah's cell looked like without the illusory glamour. The sight of it shook her on an existential level, like stepping into an unfinished part of creation.

Mercy's living quarters took up a tiny fraction of the space, just a bed and a couple of amenities on a forty-foot carpet square, plus a bare-bones art studio that had clearly been put to use. Dozens of oil paintings hung on floating easels, each one an elaborate and angry abstraction.

Oh my God, Hannah thought. *She's been here for months.*

Mercy lay upright in her adjustable bed, wearing a two-piece gown that exposed her pregnant stomach. Nestled among her abdominal tattoos were a dozen metal discs of cryptic purpose—some of them as large as silver dollars, others as small as shirt buttons. The Pelletiers must have been managing Mercy's health remotely. But for all their fancy gadgetry, they weren't doing a thing to ease her pain.

"Why aren't you helping her?" Hannah asked Semerjean. "I thought—"

She turned around to face him, but he was nowhere to be found. "What the fuck?"

Mercy looked at her in delirious disbelief. "Hannah?"

"I'm here." Hannah hurried to her bedside and gave her a thorough once-over. She almost looked like a different person without her cosmetics, the black cherry lipstick and heavy goth eyeliner that had defined her appearance for ages. She seemed younger now, sweeter, but no less doleful than the woman Hannah knew. To be here all alone these past few months, just her and the Pelletiers . . . Christ. The days must have passed like long, bitter seasons.

"You don't have to be here," Mercy said to Hannah. "You don't owe me anything."

Admittedly, the two of them had never been close. They made for a fiercely discordant pair, like punk rock and showtunes. And Hannah had never fully forgiven her for the harm she'd caused as Rebel's foot soldier.

But in this place, they were sisters, except Mercy was seven months ahead of her. *Is this how I'm going to be at the end?* Hannah selfishly wondered. *Writhing alone in a bare white room?*

Mercy reached out to Hannah and touched the barely existent folds of her stomach. "Holy fuck. You still aren't showing. How long's it been?"

"I'm at eight weeks."

"Still?"

"They're doing weird shit with time," Hannah said. "I've only been here a few days."

"Oh God." Mercy grimaced. "It's only just starting for you."

Hannah struggled to ignore the stress pain in her stomach. "Did they hurt you?"

"Hurt me? No. They treated me like a queen. Locked me up in my own little paradise. But the illusions get old and painful fast. And the *nights* . . . fuck. The nights were the worst. I just wanted to die and get it over with."

Mercy chuckled grimly. "Guess I'll finally get my wish."

A sharp new contraction made her sit up and cry. Hannah frantically looked around for a call button. "I'll get help."

"No! I don't want them here!"

"But—"

"They did something to our people," Mercy told Hannah. "Something bad."

Hannah's heart hammered. "What are you talking about?"

Mercy's eyes welled with tears. "The day they took me, my dad died. I thought it was an accident, but I've had months to think about it. My mom killed him. She gave him an overdose."

Hannah clutched Mercy's arm. "Oh my God."

"She's the best augur we have. She must have seen something coming. And for her to do that, it must have been awful. Even worse than Red Sunday."

"No, no, no." The only thing holding Hannah together was the comfort that her loved ones were alive and well. If she lost that, she was done. There'd be nothing left of her to kill.

"They wouldn't hurt our people," Hannah insisted. "They *need* them."

Mercy sniffed and wiped her eyes. "I don't know. I hope I'm wrong. If anyone will tell you, it's Esis. She doesn't lie like Fuckface and son. You get her mad enough and she'll forget the cover story."

She arched her head back and shrieked with pain. Hannah held her arm. "Mercy!"

A portal opened on the other side of the bed, bright enough to make Hannah shield her eyes. She peeked through her fingers and saw two hazy figures step out of the light.

"No!" Mercy yelled. "Get away from me!"

"Ha'ttun e-la," said a stern female voice. "R'mana agrés."

The portal subsided, giving Hannah a blurry glimpse of Esis and Azral. They were each covered from head to toe in a suit of glimmering blue fabric, like a million tiny sapphires stitched together. Only their faces were visible behind a transparent forcefield.

Surgical scrubs, Hannah thought. *Holy shit. Are they . . . ?*

Mercy looked at her in horror. "They're gonna kill me, Hannah! Don't let them kill me! Please!"

Esis waved her hand over Mercy's face, a brusque little gesture that immediately put her to sleep. A thick tempic ooze bled out of the mattress and immobilized Mercy's body.

"What are you doing?" Hannah asked. "Stop it!"

Azral cast his weary blue gaze at something beyond Hannah. "Sehfarr."

A strong hand gripped her shoulder from behind, while another one covered her eyes.

"It's all right," Semerjean whispered into her ear. "Rest."

His fingers glowed with a pulsing yellow light, one bright enough to fill Hannah's entire being, before sending her into a deep and dreamless slumber.

She woke up on a poster bed, her thoughts packed in cotton and her senses torn asunder. Her inner clock was so muddled that she could have been anywhere in time. Maybe her mother would come in to check on her, or her old college roommate, or Jonathan, or—

"Semerjean?"

Hannah regained her temporal bearings and took in her surroundings. She was back in her dungeon of sunshine and lies, in that stupid glass palace she'd built out of custom settings. From the soft pink hue of the make-believe sky, it seemed dusk was fast approaching. Semerjean must have knocked her out for hours, maybe days. But what did that mean for Mercy?

Hannah hurried down the steps to her wooden dock lounge, but the portal to the common area was gone.

"Hey!" She waved at the sky as if she were flagging down a rescue plane. "I know you can hear me, Semerjean! We have to talk!"

No response. Hannah knew what that meant: *Let's wait until you're calmer.*

"Fine." Hannah treated herself to a strawberry parfait, and then took a skinny-dip in the sea. Though the waters of the Caribbean caressed her like a lover, the experience was marred by a hint of surreality. There was something slightly off about the seawater—a thinner consistency, a faintly gelatinous texture.

Hannah opened her mouth to taste the ocean, then immediately discovered the problem.

I can still breathe, she realized. *The fuckers don't want me drowning myself.*

She returned to her house to dry off and change, then spent the next hour pacing her sundeck.

"You're avoiding me," she snarled at Semerjean. "Which can only mean that Mercy was right. You assholes did something to Amanda and the others. Did you . . ."

Hannah fought back tears. "Oh my God. Did you kill them?"

"Of course not."

She turned around to find Semerjean on the other side of the deck, sitting impatiently at the table as if she were the tardy one.

"Prove it," Hannah demanded. "Show me they're still alive."

Semerjean chuckled. "You know how good I am with illusions. I could bring you face-to-face with your sister right now, and you still wouldn't believe it."

He gestured at the empty chair. "If you would just sit down—"

"Fuck you. You know what Mercy told me."

"And you know her state of mind."

"Don't gaslight me!"

"Hannah, why on earth would we attack the underland?"

"Because you're out of patience," she said. "Out of time."

"We're low on one, but we have plenty of the other." Semerjean looked out at the pretty horizon. "And if you don't believe me, then at least trust your own instincts."

"My instincts."

"All chronokinetics are a little bit prescient," he told her. "It's hardwired into our senses. Even now, in your bleak mood, there's a tiny bead of light in your consciousness. You can't see it, but you can feel it, the *possibility* that you'll be reunited with your people. That's not just wishful thinking. It's a genuine glimmer in the strings."

As much as Hannah was loath to admit it, he was right. There was a stubborn little part of her that insisted that Amanda and the others were still alive. Yet the very same part of her was also convinced that Semerjean was playing her for a chump.

She took the seat across from him and crossed her arms defensively. "I'm going to believe you, not because you deserve it—"

"—but because you need to," he said. "I understand."

"If you understood us, you would have treated us better."

"Better? If it wasn't for me, you would have never seen a day of freedom on this world. You would have been trapped right here in Lárnach, forced to copulate with Gothams under threat of death. Would you prefer that?"

"I'd prefer you assholes out of our lives."

"All the more reason to give us a child," said Semerjean. "As soon as we find one with the right mutation, we'll have no more reason to stay."

He waved a finger, prompting a silver dolphin to leap out of the ocean. Hannah watched it drop back into the rippling waters before facing Semerjean again. "How's Mercy?" she asked him. "Did she give birth?"

"She gave birth," he said with a tired sigh. "Her child . . . doesn't suit our needs."

"I don't care about your needs. How is *she*?"

Semerjean contemplated his response before answering. "You remember the day we arrived in New York?"

"Just answer my question!"

"I'm answering," he said. "You remember it. The Gothams lured us into an abandoned office building. They'd tricked us so thoroughly that even I didn't see it coming."

Hannah wound her finger impatiently. "And you're bringing this up because . . . ?"

"Mercy took part in that ambush, as you recall. Nearly killed you and Amanda."

"I remember," Hannah said. "I forgave her."

"That's nice of you, but it wasn't her only transgression. She hit Esis with a lucky blast of solis, leaving her defenseless against Rebel's brutality. He shattered her teeth, broke her nose, cracked her jaw in three places. My wife, who'd never so much as suffered a scrape, had been subjected to pains and indignities that our people hadn't felt in centuries."

Hannah didn't like where this was going. "That was Rebel. You got him back."

"Yes, but he couldn't have done it without Mercy's help. We never forgot." His voice turned cold and venomous. "We never forgave."

Hannah felt a sharp lurch in the pit of her stomach. "You killed her."

"We archived her," said Semerjean. "Which is functionally the same as death."

"Oh my God." Hannah tried to stand up from her chair, but her pants were suddenly as rigid as iron. They held her in her seat, immobilizing her from the waist down. "Let go of me!"

"Hannah—"

"Let go!"

Semerjean looped around the table and kneeled at her side. "Hannah, *listen* to me. I could have just as easily lied to you, but I decided to trust you."

"Why?"

"Because you're strong enough to handle the facts."

"Fuck you!"

"Mercy was a special case. We bear no grudge against you or the others."

"Bullshit!"

Sighing, Semerjean reclaimed his seat and muttered a foreign word. Hannah's sweatpants reverted to fine, pliant silk, allowing her to move again. She leapt to her feet, ran away from Semerjean, then turned around to face him from the edge of the deck.

"Put yourself in my shoes," she said. "If you were me, would you believe the shit you're hearing? After all the murders and all the lies, would you buy a single word of it?"

"I'd be skeptical," Semerjean admitted. "But in a calmer state of mind, I'd see how limited my options were, and I'd follow the only path to survival."

"You mean play nice and be a good breeder."

"Not just a breeder," Semerjean said. "A *leader.* That's the opportunity I was talking about earlier. You're a natural empath and a well-respected peer. You can comfort these women in ways that I can't."

"Until you archive us."

"That's a fate we'll reserve for the difficult subjects," he replied. "The ones who make it their business to impede us."

Hannah didn't have to wonder who he was talking about. "Eden."

Semerjean nodded. "We've seen her string, and we know how it ends, but it's not too late to save her. You have the power to bring them all home. And if one of you, just *one* of you, gives us the right kind of child . . ."

He threw his hands up in the air. "That's the end of your Pelletier problem."

Hannah leaned against the railing and eyed Semerjean balefully. Once upon a time, in his own native era, he'd been a celebrated stage performer . . . or so he'd told Mia, anyway. It was the one thing about him that Hannah believed, aside from the fact that he was evil.

He'll never let you go, said the Mia in her head. *It's not in his nature.*

But he's also a cocky bastard, said Peter. *There's a loose bar somewhere in that cage of yours, and he doesn't expect you to find it.*

Her inner Theo nodded in agreement. *You had the right instinct from the start. Play along and keep your eyes open. In the meantime—*

Act, said Amanda. *He's not the only one with theater experience.*

Hannah clenched her hands around the balcony rail, then fixed her dark eyes on her captor. "They can't find out about Mercy," she told him. "They'll need a cover story."

Semerjean smiled, then pointed at the empty chair. "Let's work it out. Are you hungry?"

The thought of dining with him made her physically sick, but that wasn't the thing to tell him. She paused just long enough to sell her reluctance, then consciously relaxed her posture. "I could eat."

TWENTY-SEVEN

The music was loud enough to shake the whole theater. Every bass note from the orchestra sent a thrill up Hannah's back, while the vibrato of the mezzo-sopranos gave her all the right kinds of goosebumps. It had been ages since she last saw *Les Misérables*, and that had just been a shoestring community production. This was the illustrious London premiere, presented by the Royal Shakespeare Company and performed three years before Hannah was born.

As the holographic actors gathered onstage for the finale, Hannah squeezed the arm of the woman next to her, the only other member of the audience. "This is the closing song."

"Shhhh!"

Moon couldn't see a blessed thing, but that didn't matter. She followed every beat of the plot through the lyrics, and let the music take her mood to delirious extremes. Hannah had caught her crying behind her sunglasses on at least six occasions, none more so than a minute ago, when Fantine and Éponine came back as singing spirits and welcomed Jean Valjean into the afterlife.

After a rousing refrain of the main musical number, in which the peasants sang of hope and liberation, the show came to an end. The orchestra settled into a placid outro, and the performers took a synchronous bow. Hannah almost felt rude for not applauding, but what did it matter? They were just more ghosts in the Pelletiers' machine, an echo of a long-dead culture.

"Clear stage," she said.

The cast and set disappeared with a ripple, while the house lights snapped awake above the audience chamber. Hannah had swapped out all the seats for a simple plush sofa and ottoman. She hardly needed more, as none of the other prisoners gave a crap about her ghost productions, only Moon. The sweet young Gotham was the best theater date Hannah could have hoped for. She had an insatiable love for musicals, and her first-time reactions to alien classics made every old show feel new again.

Moon brushed the dribbling tears from her eyes, then nestled herself against Hannah. They'd become experts at the fine art of cuddling without putting undue pressure on their babies. While Moon was a few weeks behind Hannah, her twins had already given her a watermelon belly at five and a half months.

"God, that was intense," Moon said to Hannah. "You didn't tell me I'd be crying my eyes out."

"It's *Les Mis*. What did you expect?"

"I didn't know the story."

"You never read the book?"

"How would I? It's French."

Hannah rolled her eyes. Score another one for the Altamerican school system.

Moon felt Hannah's face with her fingers. "Look at you. You didn't cry once."

Hannah shrugged. "Guess I've seen it one too many times."

"Was it one of the shows you acted in?"

"No. I always wanted to play Éponine, though."

"You still can."

True enough. Semerjean had given Hannah the theater on her hundredth day of captivity as a gift for her continued assistance. In addition to having access to a thousand stage productions, she had the power to freeze a show at any moment and swap herself in for an actor. It was the ultimate karaoke machine, though Hannah didn't much relish the thought of singing with dead people. She certainly couldn't dance with them at this stage of her pregnancy, unless one counted waddling as dancing.

Moon sat up with a creaky moan. "Well, now that I've sobbed myself silly, I say we go to your place and listen to some music."

"Can't," said Hannah. "I have my checkup in a few minutes."

"Oh crap. You should have warned me." Moon raised her wrist and spoke into her traveler's bracelet, the same thin metal bauble that all the inmates wore. "Portal. Home."

A round white gateway swirled open near the stage, and Moon wasted no time navigating toward it. Hannah had hoped that the ability to not see Azral and Esis would make them less terrifying, but Moon dreaded their presence more than anyone. Their voices chilled her to the bone, while their tempic auras continually pushed her to the edge of panic.

"Like standing under a giant boot," she'd told Hannah. "Just waiting for it to squish me."

Sighing, Hannah helped her halfway into the portal, then held her by the hands. "I'll come find you after dinner."

"Why not before?"

"I promised Regal I'd eat with her. She's been really down."

Moon smiled. "You're so good, the way you take care of us. The way you care for *me*."

"Oh, stop," said Hannah. "You make me sound like your therapist."

"You're not?"

Hannah laughed. "The meter's off when I'm with you. You're my fun time."

"Oh, I like that," Moon said. "I'm glad I make things easier. I just wish there was more I could do about . . . you know."

"Yeah." Hannah dipped her head. Over the past four months, she'd become everything that Semerjean wanted her to be: a leader, a counselor, a strong-hearted advocate. To the Pelletiers, she was the voice of the prisoners. And to the prisoners . . . well, most of them appreciated having Hannah as a buffer, though some took a less charitable view of her new authority. To hear Eden tell it, Hannah was selling out her people for a few special perks, a vile accusation that had all but killed their friendship.

Luckily, there were others to fill the void. Hannah pressed her forehead against Moon's. "I'll be okay. Just keep spending time with me."

"Oh, hon." Moon hugged her. "I'm here for you whenever you need me. But next time we take in a show, please, for the love of God . . ."

Hannah smiled. "Make it a comedy."

"Make it a comedy."

A large black object suddenly materialized onto the stage, a cross between a dentist's chair and a living room recliner. Hannah never thought she'd see the day when she'd prefer Azral's company over anyone's, but the black chair meant his mother was coming, and she was the absolute worst.

"You better go," Hannah warned Moon. "Fast."

By the time Esis arrived on the theater stage, Hannah was already in the exam chair. It was never wise to keep the woman waiting, as she had no qualms about abusing her captives. She'd stabbed Rosario's arm with a tempic quill, sprained Eden's wrist, bloodied Regal's nose, all for being late to their health screening. Anyone who talked back to her had their vocal cords disabled, and those who cried excessively usually found themselves paralyzed for a couple of hours or more.

Not that Esis needed a reason to hurt someone. She'd once smacked Hannah across the face without any provocation whatsoever. Semerjean's best guess was that she got angry about something she saw in the strings, or perhaps in a parallel timeline.

But for all her cruel and irascible ways, Esis was the easiest Pelletier to read. Hannah could tell from the moment she stepped out of the portal that she was in uniquely good spirits. She came dressed in a breezy white summer wrap, one that flattered her slender figure. Her hair was down and expertly teased, and she wore a little more makeup than usual. If she was stepping out for a social occasion, it must have been one she looked forward to. Her red lips were curled in a crooked grin, the first Hannah had seen in weeks.

Esis waved a small scanner over Hannah's stomach, her dark eyes smiling with amusement. "I see you and the blind girl continue to coil. What's that term the Gothams use?"

Hannah suppressed every hint of her annoyance. "Prison gay."

"No. The other one."

"Pen pals."

"Pen pals." Esis chuckled. "As I recall, that had a different meaning on your Earth."

"Yes." Hannah found it appropriate that she was on a theater stage, as all she ever did around Esis was act. At the moment, she was acting like someone who didn't want to kill the bitch, who laughed at the slang of a world she'd helped murder.

"You're awfully restrained for a pair of young lovers," Esis noted. "You should explore your desires. Enjoy them."

Hannah faked a bashful smile, even as she seethed on the inside. Everyone assumed that she and Moon had become "pen pals," a misconception that neither of them bothered to correct. In reality, they were just two affectionate friends who were drowning in anguish and proxy love. Through each other, they were touching all the people they missed: Moon's mother, Hannah's sister, every cherished friend whose company had been stolen from them.

"There's no shame in your attraction," Esis said. "Where I come from, unisexuality's considered a minor impairment, like being blind in one eye."

Hannah's thoughts straddled the fence between curious and doubtful. "You're saying Semerjean got it on with other guys."

"Got it on." Esis chuckled at the term. "When I first met my husband, he was in a polyamorous union with several men and women. Did he not tell you?"

"No."

"Our love is quaint by modern standards," Esis said. "But the moment we met, our strings entwined to infinity. We were bound together for the rest of time, to the exclusion of all others."

That was the mushiest thing Hannah had ever heard from Esis, not that there was much competition. "I don't want to pry, but, uh . . ."

"Just ask," Esis snapped. "You stammer less than the other girls. It's one of the few things I like about you."

"When you first met Semerjean, how much of the future did you see? I mean—"

"You ask if we saw Azral."

"Yes."

"Of course we did," Esis said. "He's the culmination of human potential. The universe all but demanded we make him."

Hannah looked away, her thoughts grumbling curses. *Thanks, universe.*

Esis smirked at her barely masked disdain. "You dislike him."

Hannah knew better than to lie about it. Even the fake, obliging version of herself couldn't credibly answer in the positive. "I don't like any of you."

"A fair reaction," said Esis. "Yet it was Azral who'd compelled us, many years ago, to rescue you and your sister from a disfiguring road accident."

"Disfiguring?" Hannah fell back into a childhood memory: the exploding oil truck that would have killed her whole family were it not for the Pelletiers. "I thought you were saving our lives."

Esis shook her head. "You would have survived with pain, and some unappealing scars."

Hannah closed her eyes, disgusted. Even as kids, the sisters had been marked as future breeders. Azral had only intervened to keep Hannah and Amanda attractive to potential mates. "How long were you on our world?"

"Many years," Esis replied. "It was a wretched place, reeking of petrol. But those pollutants mutated some of your brains in just the way we needed."

Hannah snorted at the unflattering revelation. The Gothams and Majee were all made by the Cataclysm, while the orphans apparently got their powers through gas fumes.

"So you spent all those years looking for people like me and Amanda."

Esis nodded. "A difficult prospect. The lack of temporis on your world made you indistinguishable from the common folk."

"But you sniffed us out," Hannah said. "All ninety-nine of us."

"Oh, we found more than that."

"Really? How many?"

"Thousands."

"Thousands?"

"Your mutation was rare," Esis said. "But not exceedingly rare. We have an embarrassment of riches in our facility."

Hannah's eyes bulged. "You're saying there are thousands of orphans right here."

"Yes. In our archives."

Hannah felt the urge to vomit. Every time she thought she'd plumbed the depths of the Pelletiers' depravity, they revealed a whole new basement of horrors.

Esis checked the readout on her scanner, then shot Hannah a disapproving look. "Your serotonin levels are lower than they should be. You need more sleep."

"I get plenty of sleep."

"Your son disagrees."

Hannah froze in place, dumbstruck. Her voice stuttered out in a whisper. "I-I told you . . ."

"What?"

"I told you not to tell me."

"Tell you *what*, child? Speak."

"I told you not to tell me his gender!"

Esis stared at her in outrage, her hands balled into fists. *You did it now*, a meek inner voice told Hannah. *Nice knowing you.*

But then Esis abruptly relaxed her posture and forced a contrite expression. "I had forgotten about your . . . stipulation. It wasn't my intent to distress you."

"Look—"

"I can reverse you thirty seconds, if you choose. You can unlearn everything I just—"

"No," Hannah said. "Forget it. I'll just deal."

"As you wish."

Esis dropped her scanner into a portal, then willed away her tempic gloves. "If you need a sleep aid, I can provide one, though natural remedies are preferable. I'll have my husband speak to you about cognitive meditation. He knows several techniques."

Right, Hannah thought. *Because there's nothing more relaxing than alone time with Semerjean.*

"One last matter," said Esis. She formed a hard band of tempis around Hannah's neck, choking her. "You may have authority over the little creatures here, but I am not one of them. You don't make demands of me. You don't raise your voice at me. Are we clear on this?"

Hannah clawed at the tempis, nodding, crying.

"Semerjean insists that you're the only Silver with sense," Esis said. "Prove it."

The tempis disappeared from Hannah's neck. She sat up and hacked a cough. By the time she brushed the tears from her eyes, Esis had departed.

Hannah remained all alone in her personal theater, just her and the haunting voice in her head.

Your son, it played on a continuous loop. *Your son.*

The calendar was a meaningless item at Lárnach, thanks to the facility's accelerated tempo. For every twenty-four hours spent inside the continuum, only two minutes passed for the rest of the world. It blew Hannah's mind to think that the people she loved were still crawling through the tangle of August 19, just a few hours past her abduction. They were so far back in her rearview mirror that she feared she'd never find them again.

Despite the temporal discrepancy, and to the consternation of her fellow inmates, the young Gotham named Thalia kept an oversized calendar in the common lounge and marked each day as if it had officially passed. On Day 13, she'd flipped the page to September and made a cake for her twenty-sixth birthday. On Day 74—October 5, by her count—she'd lit a commemorative candle for the victims of the New York Cataclysm. She'd dressed as a cat for Halloween, and held a huge turkey feast for Thanksgiving. When anyone tried to convince her that it was still technically August, Thalia dismissed them with a smile. "Not for us!"

On Day 126, just seventy-two hours before the next big holiday, the other Gothams pulled Hannah aside for a secret, urgent meeting.

"You have to stop Thalia," said Artemis Rosen, a muscular tempic and niece of the late Rebel Rosen. "Please. We don't want to have Christmas here."

"Not without our families," said Katie Rubinek, the former wing-flying aeric who everyone still called Sparrow. "It'll break us. I mean *really* break us."

Determined to find a workable solution, Hannah invited Thalia back to her private domain, then offered her a compromise. "Look, you can still do Christmas. Just make it, you know, optional."

Thalia leaned back in her chair and stroked her jaw in thought. Unlike Hannah and all the other prisoners, she had only gotten thinner with pregnancy: fifty pounds of weight shed in four short months, without doing a hint of exercise. Her only trick was to stop taking the antipsychotics that had warped her metabolism.

She shot Hannah a dubious look. "You mean have Christmas in my private domain, where no one else will come."

"*I'll* come."

"Wow." Thalia laughed in scorn. "I knew I wasn't popular, but I didn't think they hated me."

"No one hates you."

"But they do think I'm crazy."

Sadly, that was true, but not for the reasons Thalia thought. The Pelletiers had cured her of her schizophrenia, and her gratitude had grown into an almost religious devotion. She rarely passed up the chance to sing their praises, and even scolded the inmates who badmouthed them. That made her quite difficult to be around. Even Hannah wanted to smack her sometimes.

"It's not a matter of crazy or sane," Hannah said. "We just don't see eye to eye about the Pelletiers."

Thalia looked down at her half-finished dinner, a barely seasoned chicken breast with boiled cabbage and rice. She still ate by old nutritional rules, as if they hadn't become as moot as the calendar. "Do you know what it's like to be mentally ill?"

Hannah showed her the scars on the undersides of her wrists. "I've had issues."

"But you never had mine." Thalia rolled up her sleeves and brandished her own scars, dozens of them along the skin of her arms. "For three years, I filled a jar with my blood. Every night, like clockwork. If I didn't, I thought scaly red demons would come to my house and rape me. My own brain made me fear that, as much as you fear the Pelletiers."

Hannah nodded with sympathy. "I understand."

"No you don't. And you don't know what it's like to be on neuroleptics. Those stupid pills made me fat, sick, and dull. I could barely hold a thought together."

"Thalia—"

"I am *happy* for the first time in my life," she said. "I owe the Pelletiers everything. As soon as I give them one child, I'm going to go home, get pregnant, and do it all again."

Hannah had to fight to keep from throttling her. The poor girl had swapped one set of delusions for another. There had to be more than gratitude at play. Maybe Thalia had come down with a bad case of Stockholm syndrome. Or maybe the Gothams had been so shitty to her that she latched on to the first people who treated her with value.

Despite all her empathy, Hannah stuck to her guns on the holiday matter, until Thalia finally relented. She removed her calendar from the lounge on Christmas Eve and disappeared to her domain without a word.

"Great," Moon grumbled. "Now I feel guilty."

Hannah nestled with her on the sofa and breathed a heavy sigh. "It was a bad idea that would have hurt a lot of people. I'm glad she listened to me."

"Is Christmas a big day for you?"

"No," said Hannah. "But it's big with Amanda. I just . . ."

Moon stroked her hand. "You miss her."

"Yeah." Hannah reeled at the irony of the situation. There was a time in her life, long ago, when she would have faked her own death to avoid her sister. Now every day without her was torture. Even Moon, bless her soul, couldn't fill the yawning void.

The next day was a hard one for the prisoners of Lárnach. Even without Thalia and her godforsaken calendar, the dark specter of Christmas cast a pall. All the Gothams retreated to their own domains, either sleeping or crying or losing themselves in old movies. Hannah had invited Moon to her theater for some musical comedy, but even she preferred to wallow in solitude.

Desperate for distraction, Hannah ventured to the northern end of the common lounge, where her three fellow orphans typically congregated. Sarah Brehm, ever the bookworm, had amassed quite a library of old-world novels, along with the most comfortable-looking reading chair that Hannah had ever seen. Rosario had her cherished babel box, a forty-third-century learning device that allowed her to explore foreign languages as if they were spatial constructs. Hannah had sampled the experience for herself, and found the whole thing weird and disorienting. But for Rosario, whose sudden mastery of English had sparked a passion for linguistics, the machine was her own little slice of heaven.

Oddly, neither she nor Sarah were at their usual stations, leaving Eden all alone in the alcove. Her diversion of choice was an elaborate woodshop, complete with drill press, belt sander, and three different kinds of power saws. Why Eden asked the Pelletiers for that, Hannah didn't know. She had no evident talent for woodwork, or even a desire to learn it. Her hundredth cedar duck looked just as bad as the first one, like a ten-pound petrified dog turd.

Eden briefly looked up to register Hannah before resuming her work on her latest mallard. "Look who's back."

Hannah leaned against the wall, stone-faced. "I never left."

"Well, you certainly haven't come to our hood in a while."

That was true. While Hannah's problems with Eden were too civil to be called a feud, they still kept her at a distance. The orphans hardly needed mothering, anyway. After two long years on an alien Earth, they were used to displacement and turmoil.

"Where are the others?" Hannah asked.

"Sarah's got a case of the knockup trots, and Rosario's resting up before her health test." Eden looked beyond Hannah to the empty lounge. "Where's your white shadow?"

"Homesick," Hannah said of Moon. "And she's not my shadow. I'm hers."

"Can't say I blame you. She's gorgeous."

"I'm having a son."

Eden froze in the middle of her sandpaper path and lifted her goggles at Hannah. "I thought you didn't want to know."

"I didn't."

"Guess that explains your tiff with Esis."

"You heard about that?"

"Everyone heard," Eden said. "She told Sarah that she smacked you."

"Choked me, actually."

"Why?"

"For raising my voice at her."

"You?"

Hannah flashed her a seething look. "Are we starting this again?"

"I'm just saying you've been a model prisoner."

"That's a nicer term than what you called me before. What was it again?"

Eden sighed and blew the sawdust off her duck. "That was six weeks ago."

"*Sonderkommando*," Hannah replied on her behalf. "The death camp Jews who helped out the Nazis."

"Look—"

"You know, I took college history, too," said Hannah. "None of them did it for the perks. They were forced into it."

"I was angry, okay?"

"You *hurt* me."

"You hurt *me*," Eden said. "I thought we were in this together."

"When were we not?"

"When you lied to me about Mercy!"

Sadly, Eden had her dead to rights. While Hannah had convinced the others that Mercy was safe at home, Eden had seen right through the charade.

Even if Hannah could have explained her strategy (and it was getting harder and harder to explain it to herself), there was no safe place to talk about it. The Pelletiers were always listening. Always.

Hannah crossed her arms, sulking. "I don't want to get into this again."

"Me neither," Eden said. "Because you're just going to deflect and piss me off."

"Do you think I like spending time with Semerjean?"

"No."

"Do you think I'm just looking out for myself?"

"Of course not."

"If I was selfish, I wouldn't even be here."

"I know what you did for Amanda," Eden said. "I respect it. I respect *you*. That's why I've been so confused."

"By what?"

"Hannah, do you honestly believe they'll let us go?"

Hannah clenched her teeth, livid. If Eden had asked her four months ago, she would have said, "No. Of course not." But she'd been acting like someone who believed for so long that the lie had overtaken her reality. There were some moments—especially at night, when she didn't have Moon to comfort her—that she swallowed every bite of Semerjean's logic. It *would* make sense to send the prisoners home. It would serve their interests perfectly. Why add more bodies to the virtual archives when you could use the old mothers to recruit new ones?

Yet they archived Mercy all the same, an inner voice reminded Hannah. *They put their own petty grudge ahead of the mission.*

"What would you have me do?" Hannah asked. "Curse at them? Piss them off? How's that been working out for you?"

"Shittily," Eden admitted. "But you get to go places the rest of us don't. You *see* things. Things that might help us."

"Help us." Hannah snorted derisively, then approached the band saw. "Let me tell you something you already know."

She flipped on the power switch and moved her wrist toward the pulsing blade.

"What are you doing?" Eden asked.

As soon as Hannah's skin came within an inch of the teeth, the entire blade vanished in a blink. It didn't come back until she pulled out of harm's way.

"They've covered all the bases," Hannah flatly informed Eden. "They know all our moves before we do. It isn't even an effort for them." She gestured at the safety saw. "That was probably an automatic response."

Eden closed her eyes. "So just give up and give in. Is that what you're saying?"

"I'm saying the only hope we have—"

Eden's eyes bulged at a sight beyond Hannah. "Holy shit."

Hannah turned around and goggled at Thalia Ballad, the Pelletiers' happiest prisoner. Her hair was six inches longer than it had been yesterday, and her skin bore a new, healthy tan. More jarring still, she'd become as thin as Amanda. Even her belly was flat.

Thalia beamed with excitement at Hannah and Eden, as if Santa Claus himself had brought a miracle to her doorstep.

"I gave birth," she said. "I'm going home."

Einstein said that time was relative, but the Pelletiers lived it as a credo. When Thalia asked them if she could finish her pregnancy in solitude, they doubled the size of her personal domain and accelerated it to a speed that Hannah could barely process: 140 times faster than the rest of Lárnach, which was already shifted at 720x. That was more than a hundred thousand times the speed of reality, or seventy days for each passing moment. Thalia could have run through her pregnancy in 3.86 seconds. She could have lived her whole life in the time it took for a person to make a sandwich.

If the aggressive speed had adversely affected her, it certainly didn't show. Thalia hugged Hannah with a warrior's strength and smiled with perfect teeth.

"You were the only one who was nice to me," she said. "I won't forget it. Is there anything you want me to tell your people?"

Hannah labored to come up with a cogent response, her thoughts torn between doubt and envy. "Just, uh . . . just tell them I love them. Please."

The news had spread fast among the other captives, a flurry of activity on the text relays. Within minutes, every orphan and Gotham had come running back to the lounge through portals.

Moon clutched Hannah's arm, slack-jawed. "Is it true? Did she really have her baby?"

"Sure looks that way."

"Where is she?"

By that time, Azral had already taken Thalia to another wing of the facility, while Semerjean teleported into the lounge. Fifteen women clustered together in taut anxiety as he showed them a live screen image of Thalia's release.

"Azral's opening a portal," Hannah explained to Moon. "Thalia's looking a little nervous."

"I don't blame her," said Rosario. Her English had become so fluent that she barely had an accent, though the language in her head was almost proper to a fault. "I'd be very suspicious, were I her."

Semerjean smiled at her. "She'll be fine. Just watch."

As he spoke to Rosario, his spectral voice drifted into Hannah's ears like a whisper. *We'll need to talk after this. Just stay calm and keep an open mind.*

Hannah shot him a tense look. What the hell did that mean?

"You're quiet," Moon said. "What's happening? Is Thalia okay?"

"She's stepping through the portal," Hannah replied. "The picture's changing to . . . oh. Wow."

Half the prisoners around her gasped at the familiar backdrop. It had been seventeen weeks since any of them had seen their beloved secret refuge. Now it was looming right in front of them, and it never looked more wonderful.

"It's the underland," Hannah said in an overwrought voice. "She's home."

Azral's portal had opened in the heart of the village square, where a huge mob of people had gathered. Hannah's heart pounded wildly as she scanned the faces of the crowd. Semerjean had maddeningly chosen a wide-angle view, making it hard to identify anyone.

Eden narrowed her eyes at Semerjean. "Every time I think you can't get crueler . . ."

"Be quiet," he said. "This is a special moment for the others."

"It's *bullshit*. You're probably archiving Thalia right n—"

A portal opened behind Eden, and she was yanked out of the room by tempic tendrils. Though some of the prisoners flinched at her violent exit, they all recovered quickly. It was Eden's dozenth "time out" by anyone's guess, a deceptively mild punishment. She'd merely be locked in her domain for a few days, with her communication privileges revoked.

Regal cut to the front of the cluster, her pleading eyes fixed on Semerjean. "Zoom in. Please! I want to see my family!"

"Me too!" said Sparrow.

"Mine too!" yelled Trinity Ryder, the one-time traveler of the group.

"In a minute," Semerjean promised. "This is Thalia's moment. She earned it."

Hannah continued to describe the scene to Moon as the Ballads reunited with Thalia. Most of them looked baffled to see her, as she'd barely been gone half a day. Yet there she was: nine months older, fifty pounds lighter, and more lucid than she'd ever been. If everything that Hannah was seeing was real—

(*Real?* said the Eden in her head. *For fuck's sake, Hannah. It's Semerjean.*)

—then her course was clear for the rest of her pregnancy: behave, comply, and keep the other women in line. That was the only way out of here.

Regal scanned the sea of faces behind Thalia, then pointed at the screen with a gasp. "There's my sister! That's Sovereign! I see her!"

Sarah beamed at the sight of her fellow Platinums. "There's Joey and Matt and Caleb and . . ." Her eyes went wide. "Oh. Wow. Hannah was right."

"I see her," Rosario said. She looked at Hannah contritely. "I'm sorry I ever doubted you."

Hannah blinked at her, bewildered. "What?"

"Right there." Rosario pointed at the woman next to Caleb, one of the easiest Gothams to recognize. While her people were dressed in their usual suburban finery, she wore a ratty leather jacket over a miniskirt and combat boots.

"Who are you guys looking at?" Moon asked.

Hannah suppressed every hint of her inner turmoil, her furious gaze locked on Semerjean.

"It's Mercy," Hannah said. "We're all looking at Mercy."

TWENTY-EIGHT

She'd long grown tired of pretty illusions. After four long months of panoramic grandeur, she'd stripped all the scenery from her domain and settled for a house on a soundstage. It felt a lot more grounded than her silly fake beaches, but it wasn't as glum as a prison cell. On the contrary, Hannah drew inspiration from the metatextual setting, a clever reframing of her predicament. She wasn't a captive, she was an actress in a difficult production. The only way through it, as any actress knew, was to stay strong, be smart, and manage the worst egos.

But the script had changed two minutes ago, and she hated herself for even being surprised. Of *course* that scene with Thalia had been faked. Of *course* Semerjean had been playing her.

She kicked over a folding chair outside her house, then hollered into the outlying darkness. "You lying piece of shit!"

Semerjean stepped out of the shadows, grim-faced. "Hannah—"

"You promised you wouldn't kill the rest of us!"

"We didn't kill Thalia."

"No. You archived her. Same difference."

"We *released* her, Hannah, just as I said we would. She's back with her people as we speak."

"Bullshit." Hannah shook her head in disgust. "You just can't stop playing me."

"I'm telling the truth."

"That live show you gave us—"

"That was fabricated," Semerjean admitted. "We never sent Thalia back to the underland."

"Right. Because you're a lying prick."

"Because none of your people are there anymore."

Hannah stopped in place and turned to him. "What?"

"Have a seat and I'll explain."

"Fuck you."

The folding chair righted itself by telekinesis and then brushed up against her thigh. Hannah grudgingly sat down, her arms crossed in a rigid hitch. "What do you mean, they're not there?"

Semerjean conjured a second chair out of nothingness, then sat a few feet across from her. He scratched his chin, flummoxed, as if he were about to explain chess to a monkey.

"For context, you should know that we've slowed our progression. The facility's shifted at a tenth of its former speed."

"Why?"

"The temporal strain was causing harm to one of the pregnancies."

"Whose pregnancy?"

"Moon's," said Semerjean. "It's nothing to worry about. She and her twins will be fine."

"What does any of that have to do with—"

"I'm getting to that," he said. "As a result of our deceleration, the outside world's had a chance to advance. Three days have passed since your people last saw you. Suffice it to say that things have changed."

Hannah felt her baby twitch, as if he were processing every word of the conversation. "Changed how?"

"Ioni," said Semerjean. "She came back into their lives and offered them a new home, a much safer one than the underland."

"Safe from you, you mean."

"Yes. Our . . . acquisition of you and the others has left them feeling vulnerable."

"Where did they go?"

Semerjean shrugged. "I'd tell you if I knew, but Ioni delivered on her promise. We can't see them in our scans or feel them in the strings. We can't even figure out how she's hiding them. Her technology's alien to us."

Hannah rubbed her belly in a futile attempt to calm her son. If Semerjean was faking his frustration, then it was an Oscar-worthy performance. "But Amanda and the others—"

"We assume they're okay," said Semerjean. "Ioni's betrayed them more than once, but she's always had a purpose. Killing them now would be senseless."

Hannah bristled at his judgmental tone. He was the last man to criticize anyone for betrayal.

"So the underland's empty," she said. "They just packed up and moved on her say-so."

"I'm guessing they did it on Theo's say-so, but yes."

"And you expect me to believe Thalia's with them."

"You can believe it or refute it," Semerjean replied. "But that's exactly where she is."

"How could you send her back to them if you don't know where they are?"

"We were counting on them to know where she is," said Semerjean. "And they did. I can show you, if you wish."

"Show me what?"

"What really happened to Thalia."

Hannah mulled his offer before tossing him a wary nod. "Go on. Lie some more."

Semerjean conjured a projection in the air, a flat-screen image of Thalia in a vast and sunny grassland. She hugged herself with thin white arms, disoriented and unnerved.

"Where is that?" Hannah asked Semerjean.

"The Gansu province of China."

"China?"

"We have a hunch that your people are somewhere in Asia," he said. "Not that it matters. We could have put Thalia anywhere on Earth and Ioni would find her."

"Except here," Hannah grumbled.

"Except here," Semerjean said with a smirk. "We're not entirely outmatched."

Hannah flinched at the sudden glow on the screen, a twelve-foot dome of light that completely enveloped Thalia. By the time the flare subsided, she had disappeared, along with all the grass around her.

"Wait. Was she—"

"Teleported," Semerjean said. "In a manner that we can't trace. Ioni even disabled our tracking devices. The woman's sharp. I'll give her that."

Hannah eyed him hotly. "You put tracking devices on Thalia."

"On her and in her."

"Seriously?"

Semerjean waved the spectral image away. "We didn't start this war with Ioni. She's made it her mission to fight us. And if you think that makes her a friend to you, just wait to see what she's planning. She's a threat to every chronokinetic on Earth."

"Shut up." Hannah rose back to her feet. "I'm so tired of your shit."

"I've been honest with you from the start."

"About what?"

"About our plans for your child. About Mercy. About Thalia."

"You *lied* about Thalia."

"I lied to the others," Semerjean stressed. "I warned you in advance not to trust what I was showing them."

"If she really is alive, then why fake that scene? Why not show them the truth?"

"Because most of the women here are Gothams," Semerjean reminded her. "They practically grew up in the underland. If they learned that their home had been abandoned like that—"

"It would stress them out," Hannah said with a sigh.

"And their pregnancies would suffer for it."

Hannah closed her eyes, stymied. She desperately wanted to believe what Semerjean was telling her, but his motive for manipulating her was just too strong. The hope of release was the only carrot he had to dangle. Without it, his prisoners would be unmanageable.

"I don't believe you," Hannah told him. "I think you're stringing me along, just like you did when you were David."

"Look—"

"More than that, I think you *need* to con people, just to preserve your fragile ego. Because without that, what do you have? Nothing. You're just smoke and mirrors."

Semerjean waved his hand bemusedly. "By all means, keep venting."

"You're not even good at lying," Hannah continued. "That stupid city you offered us, the one beneath the mountains—"

"Novo Belém."

"Yeah. Whatever. That was some serious bullshit. I've seen more convincing spam mail."

"It exists," said Semerjean. "The offer was genuine."

Hannah laughed. "Fourteen trillion people on your Earth, and there are empty cities just lying around."

"We have dozens of them," Semerjean attested. "This planet can hold a hundred trillion people if you use the space properly."

"Uh-huh."

Semerjean conjured a brand-new hologram: a six-foot sphere of reflective metal panels.

Hannah cocked her head. "What is that?"

"That's the Earth of my era."

"That's a disco ball."

Semerjean magnified the image until it filled up half the soundstage. Up close, Hannah could see the gaps between the mirrors, teeming with sunlight and clouds. Every panel had millions of nubs on the surface that looked like complex machinery.

"We call it the 'skorup'ka,'" Semerjean said. "The shell of the world, nearly five centuries old. It gives us control over the terrestrial environment, and provides power to all our technology. Best of all, it collects passing matter from the universe and converts it into infinite resources. There's no material poverty in my age. No wars over dwindling assets."

Hannah wasn't impressed. "So the whole world's like the underland. Fake sky, AC, and fruity tropical air fresheners."

Semerjean scoffed. "Our 'fake' skies are healthier than natural sunlight. We removed the harmful effects and enhanced all the benefits. Our air is pure. Our rains are clean."

"But your people are still assholes."

Semerjean ignored that. "You'll want to sit down for this next part."

"Blow me."

"Suit yourself."

His illusion expanded even more, until he and Hannah were swallowed by it. Dizzied, Hannah fell back into her seat. "Shit!"

She could only assume from the bright new surroundings that Semerjean had taken her inside the skorup'ka. The panels were just faint shadows in the heavens, a twilight sky so fiery red and gorgeous that Hannah could only marvel at it. It seemed that humans would eventually beat God at His own shtick and send Him shuttling off to Florida with a plaque and a pension.

"Whoa." Hannah looked around the thermosphere, filled with an endless assortment of giant, floating orbs. They practically glowed with swirls of color, like stained glass marbles. If they hadn't been placed in such an even array, Hannah might have taken them for tiny planets.

"What are those?" she asked.

Semerjean smiled proudly. "Our highest cantons."

"Cantons?"

"City-states," he explained. "Each one twice the size of Manhattan. They have their own skies, their own weather, even their own gravity."

"Their own *gravity*?"

Semerjean willed away the shell of the nearest canton, revealing an odd round construct that looked like a silver blowfish. On closer examination, each spike was a tall glass skyscraper. The towers stretched all across the surface of the sphere.

"Holy shit." Hannah struggled to process the mind-blowing construct. Apparently the cantons *were* tiny planets. The Earth had become its own pocket galaxy.

"Only the aerial cities are spherical," said Semerjean. "The ones on the ground and water—"

"You have cities on the water?"

"Oh yes. We've built entirely new continents for ourselves, and colonized the ocean floor. And that doesn't even count our underground cities, which are slowly being abandoned in favor of orbitals."

"Orbitals," Hannah echoed.

"Artificial moons, a relatively new development."

"Oh my God." Hannah suddenly realized how trillions of people could fit on the planet. They'd turned almost every inch of it into living space. "You still have animals?"

"Of course. Thirty percent of our land mass has been converted into natural preserves."

"What about space travel? Like deep space."

Semerjean shrugged indifferently, as if she'd asked about the future of cat litter. "We have the technology, just not the desire."

"Why?"

"Because the farther we move away from Earth, the less temporis works."

"Wow." Hannah had to give Semerjean credit for the distraction. Her rage had become eclipsed by her dazzled curiosity.

"Show me one of your flying cities," she said. "I want to see it from the inside."

Semerjean hemmed, grimacing. "That's . . . not a good idea."

"Why not?"

"Imagine taking a woman from ancient Rome and dropping her in the middle of Times Square. I don't think she'd enjoy the view. She certainly wouldn't understand it."

Hannah pursed her lips indignantly. "What, you think I'm going to shit in my hand and throw it at you?"

"I'm just trying to avoid distressing you."

"Are you kidding? That's *all* you do."

"Fine."

He dispelled the image and replaced it with a new one: a clean but busy thoroughfare in what appeared to be a corporate plaza. At first, Hannah thought Semerjean had been worried for nothing. The place had dozens of recognizable elements, from the benches to the shrubs to the polished marble floor. Hundreds of people walked to and fro, and God knew their outfits were strange. But it was nothing worse than San Diego in the middle of Comic-Con.

Hannah studied the locals as they passed her by. "It's interesting. Everyone's really young and pretty. It's like being at UCLA."

"We have almost infinite control of our appearances," Semerjean told her. "Age, height, shape, bone structure. In fact, uh . . ."

Hannah eyed him warily. "What?"

"I may be censoring some of the more extreme cosmetic choices."

"Just show me!"

"As you wish."

Semerjean adjusted the illusion for accuracy, causing most of the locals to mutate. Hannah gasped at the new and updated crowd, a thoroughly alien lot. There were now strangers of every color: purple, orange, ruby, jade, even a few mineral textures. One woman looked like she was carved out of emerald. Another had a skin of pure reflective metal, like quicksilver poured into a business suit. Some people had been stretched into spindly giants, while others sported bestial features. Hannah gasped at a two-legged leopard man in a suit made entirely of mirrors. He walked and laughed with a bi-gender companion who'd been altered to resemble glass.

"That's just . . ." Hannah threw her blinking eyes back on Semerjean. "I thought they all looked like you."

He shook his head, chuckling. "I used to look like them."

Hannah wasn't amused by that, as she could easily guess why he'd changed. He couldn't have played David as an Australian half-jaguar, or a twelve-foot metal androgyne.

"At least the environment's sane," she said.

Semerjean gave her a sheepish look. "Well . . ."

"What? You censored that too?"

"We have the capacity to process large amounts of information, from hundreds of sources at once. A person of your era might find it—"

"Just shut up and show me."

With a hesitant sigh, he adjusted the view again. The entire plaza became filled with millions of animated holograms. They filled every inch of the common space, some as small as fortune cookie slips, others as large as blimps. The written words looked like alien hieroglyphs, while the images could have come from a bad acid trip.

Hannah stumbled backward, overwhelmed. She was finally starting to feel like the Roman in Times Square. "God."

"It can be a little much," Semerjean admitted. "Even for us."

She crossed her arms in stubborn defiance. "Anything else you're holding back on?"

"Oh yes. The powers. The sounds. The directional ambiguity."

"Directional ambiguity."

"This is the rotating core of a canton," Semerjean said. "There's more than one vertical axis."

"Just give me five seconds of the uncensored view."

"It'll make you sick."

"So what? So do you."

Semerjean sighed defeatedly. "You used to be the less stubborn Given."

He raised his hand in preparation. "If you have to vomit, do it away from me."

At long last, he took off all the safeties, and the scene changed once again. The sounds of the plaza became as oppressive as the images, like a thousand foreign radio stations that were cranked up to noxious volume. The high frequencies hit Hannah like weaponized tinnitus, while the low notes shook her hard enough to make her baby kick in protest.

Hannah looked around the plaza through one flinching eye and saw what Semerjean meant by the powers. Nearly everyone was either shifting or teleporting, which made the whole crowd look like a computer glitch.

She craned her neck for sanity's sake, but the view above had changed. The paneled ceiling had been replaced by another floor of people: upside down and flittering around and buried in their own sea of holograms. For a moment Hannah thought it was a mirror image until she saw the whole floor moving. The core of the canton was actually several cores, and they all turned slowly on their own gravitational poles. The whole effect was nauseating, like being trapped in an animated Escher sketch while spinning in a giant clothes dryer.

"Oh my God." Hannah fell back into her chair, but the queasiness had already taken hold of her. She pressed her hands over her eyes. "Take it away!"

"I already did."

Hannah peeked through one eye just to confirm that the illusions were gone. They were back on her soundstage, and Semerjean was once again facing her from a simple folding chair.

"You all right?" he asked.

"Fuck you. Your whole world's a nightmare."

"It just takes some adjustment," Semerjean insisted. "Once the senses adapt, there's beauty to be found everywhere."

"Bullshit." Hannah rubbed her aching eyes. "If the future's all that and people like Esis—"

"Careful."

"—then what the hell are we fighting for?"

"I know exactly what *I'm* fighting for," Semerjean said. "May I show you?"

"No!"

"No scenery. Just one person."

"Who?"

"No one you know or ever will know."

"Fine," said Hannah. "Make it quick, then get the hell out of here."

Semerjean summoned the image of a child, a brown-skinned girl in a long silver dress. She was beautiful in a quirky kind of way, with abnormally high cheekbones that made her look like an alien. She stood under an ethereal spotlight and sang an *a capella* aria like nothing Hannah had ever heard, a song as beautiful as it was bizarre.

"Wow . . ."

Hannah kept listening, enraptured. Though the language was foreign and the time signature was erratic, the notes were lovely enough to give her chills. The girl had a voice that put angels to shame, and the meter of the song kept growing on Hannah. It shouldn't have worked by any reasonable logic, like a story with five endings or a house made entirely of closets. But somehow it rose above its own baffling structure and became stronger for it. Gorgeous.

Semerjean smiled at Hannah's gobsmacked awe. "Brilliant, isn't it? She wrote it herself."

"That *kid*?"

"She's no child. She just chose a child's body because it gave her the best voice."

"Who is she?"

"Kitara L'enoïa," Semerjean said. "She's been dead for nearly a hundred years, forgotten by most of humanity. But she was a legend of the Australian cantons of my youth."

He paused Kitara in still-frame and eyed her specter wistfully. "She'd contracted terminus early in life. Much too early. Barely a day goes by where I don't wonder about the songs she would have written if she'd been given more time. She could have redefined the nature of music itself."

Semerjean looked to Hannah again, his voice now cool and bitter. "Instead she spent her last years in a hospice, losing everything that made her extraordinary, piece by piece."

Hannah's sympathy died as soon as she smelled the sales pitch. "Why not just reverse her?"

"Temporis only exacerbates terminus," said Semerjean. "The only way to survive it, theoretically, is to transfer one's consciousness into a body that's naturally immune."

"But you don't have that," Hannah guessed.

"That's exactly what we're trying to create." He pointed at Hannah's belly bulge. "Your child might be the first-ever cure, our deliverance from the cruel yoke of time."

"So, what? You're all gonna jump into one kid?"

"Of course not. With one, we can make trillions, and make them infinitely customizable. We'd all be the people we were before. Whatever we lose in temporal ability can be made up with implants and augments."

He noticed Hannah's cynical sneer. "What?"

"Why do you even care?" she asked him.

"About my people?"

"About what I think of you," said Hannah. "Azral and Esis don't give a shit. Why do you?"

"Well—"

"You destroyed my world and now you're destroying this one. You'll never have my forgiveness or respect. You have to be smart enough to see that."

Semerjean pondered her words, expressionless, before nodding. "You're right. It's a fool's errand."

"So why do you keep trying?"

He tossed up his hands. "To hear my wife and son say it, I have a soft spot for the Silvers. I guess I bonded with you more than I realized."

Hannah closed her eyes and swallowed her rage. There was no point cursing him out. She had to get strategic again, which meant throwing him the occasional bone.

"We still miss David," she admitted. "All of us. Even Mia."

Semerjean looked away in absent thought. "I have no doubt the feelings are mutual."

He waved away his image of Kitara L'enoïa, then opened an exit portal. "I've taken enough of your time. I'll let you get some rest."

Semerjean looked around the soundstage with a furrowed brow. "This place is depressing. You should find a nicer setting."

He disappeared into the spatial fold. Hannah watched the portal shrink away, her dark eyes narrowed to slits.

"I plan to."

Five weeks after Thalia's release—or Groundhog Day, as her calendar would have marked it—Semerjean called the prisoners to the lounge and addressed them with enough cheer to make them nervous.

"The last of you has entered her third trimester," he proclaimed. "The final phase, and also the hardest. Your hormones will be in overproduction and your moods will shift erratically. Just make sure you get the rest you need. Talk to Hannah or me if you need anything. And take comfort in the fact that you're nearly done here. Before you know it, you'll be back in Quarter Hill, among the people you love."

Hannah waited for Eden to call bullshit on him, but she wisely kept her thoughts to herself. She'd become a lot more cooperative in recent weeks, for reasons Hannah could only guess at.

Semerjean proceeded to his second bit of news, which nearly made Hannah spit out her drink. It seemed two of her fellow prisoners, Sarah Brehm and Regal Tam, had decided to follow Thalia's lead and take the accelerated path out of Lárnach. But instead of spending their last few months in solitude, they would finish their pregnancies together.

To everyone who knew them, it was a baffling decision, as the pair made unlikely roommates. Sarah was an orphan from another world's Florida, a former assistant professor of literature who was happier around books than around people. Regal was a daughter of the Gotham clan, a bouncy teenage chatterbox with a love for loud music and the attention span of a mosquito.

Yet Lárnach had a way of making strange bedfellows, as Hannah herself had learned. Immediately after Semerjean's announcement, he escorted Sarah and Regal into their own private continuum and then turned up the speed dial to maximum.

A day and a half later, they returned to the lounge: three months older, several pounds thinner, and all too ready to leave. If their joint isolation had caused any friction, they did a masterful job of hiding it.

"Sarah's amazing," Regal told Hannah. "She gave me all these books on self-identity that were just . . . oh my God. I can't believe I ever felt bad about being gay. I thought I deserved all the shit I got from my parents, but I didn't. They're just assholes."

Sarah was equally effusive about her young Gotham friend. Regal's warmth and compassion had held her together, especially during those tough final weeks.

"It gets bad," Sarah warned the others. "For those first eight months, it was like carrying a stranger. But that last month . . ."

She closed her eyes in misery, her voice a quavering wisp. "They wouldn't even let me see my baby. I didn't have to hold her. I just wanted to see her."

After saying their goodbyes to the remaining inmates, Sarah and Regal followed Azral to the exit portal, while Semerjean broadcast their release in real time.

Hannah watched his projection from the back of the lounge, her face a stone mask. Only she knew for sure what the other women feared: that the show was a sham. Semerjean's fake rendition of the underland was flawless, from the light refractions to the particles in the air. All the background players looked exactly the way they were supposed to look, without a single red flag of discrepancy.

Hannah's heart sank at the sight of Mercy and Thalia, standing front and center of the welcoming crowd. *That's all I'll be when they're done with me,* she thought. *Just a face in their propaganda films.*

Later that night, Semerjean visited Hannah in her soundstage house to assure her, once again, that her darkest suspicions were wrong.

"Regal and Sarah are fine," he said. "They spent twenty-one seconds in a Chinese field before Ioni brought them back to her hideout."

Hannah rocked in her new floating recliner, a forty-first-century hyperchair that soothed every aching joint in her body. "Okay."

"You still don't believe me."

"I know your track record," Hannah said. "But I'm praying to every god there is that you're telling the truth this time."

He chuckled in the way she hated most: a soft little snicker that walked the fine line between genial and condescending. "We did away with gods a long time ago," he said. "Our discoveries have all but disproved them."

"How do you prove the lack of God?"

"By ghosting the milestones of history," he replied. "We've retroactively witnessed the creation of every religious text, from the Kesh Temple Hymn of Ancient Sumer to the American Book of Mormon. In each case, it was always the same. The generous term would be 'speculation.'"

Hannah scoffed. "If we had proof, then we wouldn't need faith."

"I'd expect that from your sister, not you."

"Amanda's the reason I'm defending it," Hannah said. "She's the strongest person I know."

"And you credit her faith for that?"

"It's a big part of it. Yeah."

"So where was that faith last January?" he asked. "When she attempted a messy suicide."

Hannah shot him a thorny look. "She talked about it. She never tried anything."

"She went out of her way to pick a fight with Esis."

"That was anger!"

"It was strategy," said Semerjean. "Her Catholic laws forbid self-harm, so she found what she thought was a loophole."

He shrugged at Hannah's seething expression. "I'm just saying that faith is tenuous."

"So why do you have it?" she asked.

"What do you mean?"

"Your Holy Grail cure for terminus," Hannah said. "You don't have proof that it exists, but you keep chasing after it anyway."

Semerjean smiled patiently. "Our 'faith' is supported by scientific data. We've seen our success in the strings."

"But you still haven't found it," Hannah reminded him. "Even with all your high-tech whosits and mutagenetic whatsits, you still can't get the kind of kid you need."

"That's a rather simplistic—"

"Maybe you've been wrong this whole time."

"Hannah . . ."

"Maybe you came all this way for nothing."

"Enough." Semerjean rose to his feet in smoldering ire, the most gratifying reaction she could have hoped for.

He saw the smile in her eyes and defused himself with a chuckle. "Well played. That was very well played."

"Am I next?"

"Next for what?"

"Next to go," said Hannah. "I'm at least a month ahead of the others."

"You were," Semerjean said. "Now you're a week behind."

"What?" Hannah sat forward, hang-jawed. "How?"

"We've been decelerating your continuum every time you go to sleep."

"*Why?*"

Semerjean chuckled as if the answer were obvious. "We need you, Hannah. You keep the other women in line."

He opened a portal, then stepped halfway into it. "Don't worry. You may be the last one to leave this place, but you're still going home at the end of it."

Semerjean shot her a wry little grin before exiting. "Have faith."

Hannah woke up the next morning with the faint recollection of a dream, something about angels and Cataclysms. A lovely, winged woman (who kind of looked like Amanda, but also a little like Moon) had guided Hannah down a city street, toward a portal in an empty intersection. With terror in her bright blue eyes, she'd urged Hannah to escape as fast as she could. *Just go, go, go, before the city falls!*

But where will it take me? the dream-Hannah had asked of the portal. *What if it goes to someplace worse?*

The Amanda/Moon angel had said something profound in reply, but Hannah couldn't remember it. By the time she took care of her howling bladder crisis, the dream had become mist in her thoughts.

After a long, hot shower and a fresh change of gowns, Hannah touched the edge of her traveler's bracelet and spoke into the silver band. "Portal. Moon."

Hannah waited for the shortcut to Moon's domain, but the bracelet flashed red in refusal. For all she knew, it had forgotten Moon's nickname and had taken Hannah's request literally.

She raised the bracelet to her lips again. "Portal. *Mischa.*"

Another pulsing red "no." What the hell was going on? Did the Pelletiers put Hannah in time-out? Was it because she had the nerve to talk back to—

"Morning."

Hannah jumped at the sight of Semerjean sitting cross-legged on the edge of her bed. To her surprise, he didn't look the slightest bit peeved with her. His expression was almost shockingly demure, as if he were eager to stay on her good side.

"There was a small crisis a few hours ago," he informed her. "She's okay, but—"

"Who?"

"Moon."

"Moon?" Hannah sat down on the ottoman, wide-eyed. "What happened?"

Semerjean shrugged exhaustedly. "Her body's ill-suited to carry one child, much less two. We've tried to manage her health proactively, but every time we averted one problem, another one took its place. Yesterday, she developed a pulmonary embolism that threatened to kill her and her babies."

"Oh my God."

"It's okay," said Semerjean. "Esis operated on her immediately. She and the twins are fine."

Hannah could just imagine poor Moon's trauma. To be woken up by Pelletiers and then hauled away for surgery . . . Christ. Knowing Esis, she would have found the cruelest and most byzantine way to explain the situation, if she even bothered to explain it at all.

"Where is Moon now?" Hannah asked.

"Back in her domain. Recovering."

"I just tried to go there."

"I know," said Semerjean. "I wanted to talk to you before you saw her. Prepare you."

"For *what*? What are you not telling me?"

Semerjean's handsome face shifted from discomfort to sympathy. "Her pregnancy's over. She's done."

"What?"

"Listen—"

"You said the twins were okay!"

"They're okay because we removed them," Semerjean said. "They're in our incubators. It's not the ideal solution for our purposes, but it was safer than leaving them in the womb."

Hannah's heart froze. "Does that mean—"

"Yes," said Semerjean. "She's the next to go."

He sneered at Hannah's unmasked fright. "Imagine how much better you'd feel if you trusted me."

"Don't you dare kill her."

"We have no intention of—"

"Don't *archive* her. I mean it."

"We're not doing that either. We're releasing her back to her people."

Semerjean stood up with a tired sigh. "The door to Moon's domain is open. You have one hour to say goodbye."

Hannah wasted no time teleporting to Moon's country house. Unlike most of the other prisoners, who changed their virtual environments on a whim, Moon had stuck with a simple rural cottage from her very first day at Lárnach. The setting provided all the best perks for a sightless woman: an intuitive layout, the smell of fresh lilacs, a babbling brook that could be heard from the bedroom, and the ever-present chirp of crickets.

Moon curled on her mattress in a fetal position, her hands pressed tight against her stomach. The surgery had been so thoroughly advanced that her body barely needed to recover—no weakness, no soreness, not even a scar.

But the lingering effects on her mind and soul were plain for Hannah to see.

"It feels so strange," Moon said in a broken voice. "Like they took out all my insides. You'd think I'd enjoy being light again, but it doesn't feel good. I just feel . . . hollow."

Hannah lay with her for the next fifty minutes, holding her as she wept. Such an abrupt and anticlimactic ending to her six-and-a-half-month struggle, as cruel as a double stillbirth, and quite possibly worse. For once, Hannah hated Semerjean for being overly truthful. He should have never said a word about those cursed archives. He should have convinced them that the babies would grow up on a farm somewhere—happy, healthy, and loved.

At the moment, Hannah was much more worried about the fate of the twins' mother. "I'm going to buy you some time," she said to Moon. "Find you another way out of here."

Moon shook her head, sniffling. "If you fight them now, you're going to lose everything. They'll kill us both."

"There are things I haven't told you."

"About what? Mercy?"

"Yeah."

"She's gone," Moon said. "I know. I hear it in your voice whenever you talk about her. But you don't sound like that with Thalia, Sarah, and Regal. There's a part of you that believes they're okay."

Hannah sighed over Moon's shoulder. "Only a little part."

"That's good enough," Moon said. "Better than our odds of escaping."

"If Semerjean's lying—"

"—then I'm dead," said Moon. "But if he's telling the truth, then I get to go home."

She turned around on the bed and cupped the side of Hannah's face. "I miss my family. I need them more than ever. If this is my chance to get back to them, I'll take it."

Five minutes later, the Pelletiers arrived to begin the parole ritual once again. While the other prisoners watched remotely from the lounge, Hannah was allowed to accompany Moon all the way to the final exit.

The release room was barely the size of a kitchen, a hollow cube of tempis at the end of a long corridor. The only visible furnishing was a thin metal stand in the front left corner. Its top plane was tilted at sixty degrees, as if it were meant to hold sheet music for an exceedingly tall conductor.

Hannah held Moon tight as Azral took his place behind the stand. The surface lit up at his approach: a holographic keypad that was as red as Mars and as strange as a Venutian alphabet.

"He's opening the portal," Hannah told Moon. "I can still ask for time."

Moon squeezed her hand. "Just point me in the right direction."

Azral pressed a button on the console, creating a portal along a wall. The sight of it immediately threw Hannah into a dilemma. If the gateway led to a Chinese field, as Semerjean claimed, then Hannah was just four yards away from freedom. She could make a desperate break for it, and pray that Ioni snatched her before the Pelletiers did.

You'd never make it, said a dark inner voice. *It's all bullshit, anyway. The only thing waiting on the other side of that door is Esis and her archive machine.*

Azral gestured at the portal impatiently. "Go on," he said to Hannah. "Take her."

Reluctantly, Hannah led Moon to the portal's edge. "Listen—"

"Don't," said Moon. "Just hope for the best and hug me. That's all I need from you. Please."

Hannah held her close, her thoughts desperately fleeing to the sunny side of the "maybe." She imagined Moon getting teleported to Ioni's hidden base, where all of her loved ones were waiting for her and she never had to worry about the Pelletiers.

"I'll see you soon," Hannah said.

"You better," Moon replied. "Because after everything we've been through, we're sisters for life. And there are musicals we still haven't seen."

She let go of Hannah, straightened her shirt, then followed her tempic feelers through the portal. Hannah barely had a chance to watch her leave before Azral closed the disc behind her.

"Return to the others."

Hannah wiped the tears from her face, her voice a sandy rasp. "If you hurt her, I'll kill you. I swear to God."

Azral met her gaze with an irritable sneer, as if she were just a yapping little dog at his feet. "Go."

TWENTY-NINE

If behavior alone was the measure of a man, then Azral would have been a popular warden. He wasn't a manipulative deceiver like Semerjean or a serial abuser like Esis. On the contrary, every woman who lay on his examination bed was treated with the utmost professionalism. He ran his scanner above his subjects' clothes, rarely uttering a word unless it was a health directive. "You need to eat on a regular schedule." "Remember to sleep on your side." "Try working more exercise into your day." "You're not adequately managing your stress."

Yet despite his disciplined—some might even say decent—conduct, Azral never stopped scaring the daylights out of his captives, for reasons none of them could adequately pinpoint. Was it the height? The voice? The cold blue eyes that never seemed to blink? Or was it merely the air of brutal indifference that emanated from his pores like pheromones?

For Hannah, who'd had more run-ins with Azral than the rest of her peers, her revulsion was based purely on experience. The man was responsible for some of her life's greatest miseries, as well as her very worst trauma. She couldn't look him in the eye without reliving the morning when he slapped a silver bracelet on her wrist and made her watch the sky come down on San Diego. In Hannah's mind, Azral *was* the apocalypse more than anyone else. That alone made her perpetually ill in his presence.

On her hundred and seventy-fourth morning in Lárnach, six days after Moon's departure, Azral apparated into Hannah's living room to conduct her daily health check. Unlike Esis, who made her patients sit back in a dentist-style recliner, Azral preferred them to lie propped on their side on a floating gurney. That worked out fine for Hannah's purposes. The bed was more comfortable than Esis's chair, and the position allowed her to get through most of the exam without having to see Azral's face.

She studied the buttons of his pressed white shirt as he waved his scanner above her. Even here in the comfort of his secret lair, he wore the same outfit every day: a sharp gray suit without a tie, the blazer completely unbuttoned. As far as Hannah knew, he'd been dressing that way his entire life, even back on his flashy homeworld. He probably sneered at the whole concept of personal flair—a brainless diversion, like cats playing with tinsel.

"Your health is atrocious," Azral sharply informed her. "You're not taking care of yourself."

No shit, Hannah thought. She hadn't had a good night's sleep in nearly a week, and not just because of Moon. The six-pound boy inside of her had become a natural force in his own right: a bucking little bronco who continually sought to remind her, as if she could hardly forget, that he was the son of a stubborn Irishman. *Are you even gonna try to save me?* his tiny voice yelled in a brogue. *Or will you just let them put me in their computers? It hardly seems a proper fate for a wee little lad like me.*

"Do you hear me?" Azral asked.

Hannah looked up with a baleful glare. "I heard you."

"You need to get more restful sleep."

"Right," said Hannah. "I'll just think of all the good things I have going for me."

"If you want a natural calmative—"

"I want to know what happened to Moon."

Azral heaved a nasal sigh, his own little version of an eye roll. "How many times must we assure you?"

"I don't need to be assured. I need to be convinced."

"There's no measure of proof that will satisfy you."

"You haven't even tried! You just—"

"Stïl'zin."

He pressed his fingers to the base of her neck, as if he were merely checking her pulse. But his touch came with a harsh vibration that paralyzed her vocal cords.

Azral crouched down to eye level, his white brow furrowed in pique. "We teleported your young friend to China, where she was quickly acquired by Ioni. You can accept the truth or you can torment yourself, but you will no longer torment me. Are we clear?"

Hannah nodded, terrified. Even worse than the total theft of her voice was the sight of his eyes at close range. Her reflection looked shockingly small in his pupils—insignificant, like she was nothing but a microbe on one of his glass slides. Worse, she caught a fresh new glimpse of the void behind his eyes: a cold black absence of something fundamental, something that even sociopaths had.

Azral released his hold on Hannah, then rose back up to full height. "Get more sleep or we'll confine you to bed."

Hannah stroked her throat, her voice a croaking rasp. "I don't believe you about Moon."

Azral willed an exit portal and shot a cold look over his shoulder. "I don't care."

With awful sleep came awful dreams, virtually the same one every night. Though the ancillary details changed each time, the constants were clear and disturbing. There was always a lovely woman with wings, always a portal, always a desperate need to flee before something terrible happened.

You have to go! the angel repeatedly begged Hannah. *Please! Think of your child!*

After four more nights, Hannah's subconscious finally switched things up. In the new dream, she was back in old-world San Diego, walking arm in arm with her sister on the beach. With a deep breath and a pang of trepidation, she asked Amanda if it was okay if she named her child Robert.

From the way Amanda stopped in place, Hannah feared she'd made a grave error. Robert wasn't just the name of their long-dead father, it was the name of the son that Amanda never got to have: the one who'd died in his third trimester, a loss that had derailed Amanda's career and first marriage.

Yet none of that seemed to bother the dream-Amanda. She looked at her sister in the best kind of shock, her green eyes glistening with joy.

"It's perfect," she said. "It's beautiful."

Unfortunately for Hannah, the dream bled into her waking thoughts, staining them a different color. She suddenly couldn't think of her doomed little boy without thinking of him by name.

"Fuck!"

Hannah sank to the floor of her shower stall and wept in a huddled mass. She might have had a chance at handling this shit if Moon had still been with her. But now that she was far away—

(*Not that far*, said a cynical voice in Hannah's head.)

That was the other thing that was killing her: the ambiguity of Moon's fate. Hannah had been able to accept it with Thalia, Regal, and Sarah, but not Moon. No. She was way too large in Hannah's heart to settle for a shrug and a "maybe."

The Pelletiers are dangling a hope over your head, said her inner Peter, a man she missed more and more each day. *They're controlling you with it.*

Break their lie, said the Mia in her thoughts, *and you break their chains.*

Hannah dried herself off, threw on a robe, then opened a portal to her theater. She had no interest in watching a musical, but the dark environment and broody lights made the stage a good place to strategize. She would never get the truth out of the Pelletiers unless she discovered a weakness to exploit. But *what*?

She suddenly remembered Mercy's comment about Esis, one of the last things she'd said about anything: *She doesn't lie like Fuckface and son. You get her mad enough and she'll forget the cover story.*

Even in Hannah's fractured state, it seemed a horrible idea to enrage Esis. But were the consequences any worse than the ones that were coming?

Of course not, said Zack, who'd done his own hard time in the Pelletentiary. *They're already walking you to the slaughterhouse. The least you can do is kick some fences.*

"Okay," Hannah muttered to herself. "I'll do it. Right here. Today."

Unfortunately, she had to wait another three days before Esis became her examiner again. She apparated into Hannah's theater and took a disapproving look around the stage. "I thought you were done with this dreadful place."

Hannah sat down in the examination chair. "I still like it."

Esis scrutinized Hannah's updated appearance: her chic white sandals, her fine silk blouse, her deft little touches of makeup. "You seem more . . . collected than usual."

And you're a freaking mess, Hannah thought. Her advanced-stage terminus was eating away at her faculties, and on days like this, it showed. There was a noticeable shudder to her head and arm movements, and she seemed to react at half her usual speed. Her deterioration must have been a constant stress to the Pelletiers, a thought so nice that Hannah nearly smiled.

"You doing all right?" Hannah pointedly asked her. "You look a little, uh—"

"I'm fine," Esis snapped. She moved her scanner over Hannah's baby bump. "Worry less about my health and more about yours."

"Hey, I'm great. My kid's got the moves like Jagger."

"He's not moving at all at the moment."

"Oh, he never moves when you're around. He really hates you."

Esis's dark eyes narrowed to slits. "I can't tell if you're being rude or just dim."

"Can't it be both?"

"If you won't speak maturely, then don't speak at all."

Esis continued her work in silence, until she caught Hannah studying her intently. "What are you doing?"

"Just trying to figure out how old you are."

"Excuse me?"

"I mean, I know how old you look," Hannah said. "But you've obviously lived longer than fifty."

"Fifty?"

"No fifty-year-old has a white-haired son."

"I am not fifty," Esis snapped. "My physical form is thirty-five. It has been for decades."

"Really? How many?"

Esis fought to hide her exasperation. "It's considered crass to keep a tally of one's experiential age."

"Semerjean does it," Hannah reminded her. "He told Mia last year that he's three hundred and something."

"He's an actor," Esis grumbled. "They have fewer stigmas than doctors."

"You're a doctor?"

"Don't be obtuse. You knew that already."

"I didn't," Hannah lied. "I figured you were just some kind of dog breeder, but with people."

Esis closed her eyes and took a deep, calming breath, a reaction so lovely that Hannah wished she could film it.

"I'm a neurogeneticist," Esis replied with forced patience. "The best of my kind. My work has redefined the nature of cerebral engineering. Everyone in my field knows my name and accomplishments."

"Wow," Hannah said with exaggerated awe. "I had no idea you were such a big deal."

Esis smiled. "At last, she sees in proper light."

"Of course, to me, you're just the bitch who cut my sister's arms off."

Esis lowered her scanner, aghast. "What on earth are you playing at, child?"

"Who said I'm playing at anything?"

"You're clearly trying to enrage me."

"Maybe I'm just sick of your bullshit."

Hannah swung her legs off the side of the chair and clambered awkwardly back to her feet. For a brief, tense moment, she feared she'd listened to the wrong voices. Maybe this was nothing but a kamikaze flameout: suicide-by-Esis, like Amanda had tried last winter.

Esis arrived at a more accurate guess. "You're still in a froth about the blind girl, aren't you?"

"Still?"

"We told you—"

"You *lied*. And fuck you with your reductive terms. Her name was Mischa Varnov."

Hannah wasn't entirely sure when her plan had collapsed, but it was backfiring on her horribly. The angrier she got, the calmer her opponent became.

"I fear your hormones have made you irrational," Esis said. "For your sake, I'll leave and pretend this never happened."

"Just admit that you assholes lied about Moon!"

"Nonsense. She's safe at home with her family, as we've told you many times."

"Home?" Hannah laughed. "You mean Quarter Hill?"

"No. I meant—"

"Because that's the story the others got," Hannah said. "I was told a different lie."

Esis's voice dropped a cold octave. "I'm well aware of what you were told."

"So you admit it's all bullshit."

"Of course not," said Esis. "Don't think you can get the better of me, girl. I may be a wisp of my former self, but I'm still smarter than you."

"Probably," Hannah replied. "But I'm already a better mother than you ever were."

Hannah didn't have to wonder if that punch landed. Esis froze at her in pale-faced shock. "Ho'ëto a-sha'et."

"I *a-sha'et* you not," said Hannah. "Theo told me about the chat he and Azral had in Japan. He said you raised him from birth to be a part of your crusade, the whole 'cure for terminus' thing. That's all he's ever known. He's had no other plans, no dreams or ambitions. He's probably never even had a lover. And the craziest part, at least to me, is that you never once noticed the irony. You brought your only son onto the 'eternal life' bandwagon, and yet he's never actually lived a day."

Somewhere deep in the back of Hannah's mind, she knew that she'd jumped off a cliff. She didn't care. She'd fired her last rocket when she'd dreamed up a name for her son. She was shattered, gone, and there was no turning back.

"The rest of us see it every time we look at Azral," Hannah said. "The great big nothing in his eyes. You're the one who put it there. What the hell kind of mother—"

She felt a sudden new pressure on the top of her head: a hard pincer grip that was strong enough to lift her. Hannah feared she'd fallen prey to Esis and her tempis, but the woman stood fully in view, arms crossed, without a single white tendril to show for herself. Someone else must have grabbed Hannah from behind.

A low male voice oozed into her ear, as cold and sharp as an arctic wind. "No more talk," Azral said. "We've heard enough."

Hannah shrieked in all-new agony, a fierce and constrictive seizure that left her paralyzed from head to toe, as if every inch of her skin had been turned into concrete.

"Your body has been locked in a state of calm stasis," Azral explained. "Disconnected from the strain in your thoughts. Scream all you want inside your head. The stress won't affect your child. I see no need to punish the boy for the crimes of his foolish mother."

If there was a quantum of calmness anywhere inside of Hannah, she couldn't feel it. Her consciousness was buried miles inside of her in a tight little coffin of stone.

Azral spun her around to face him. "Look into my eyes. Do you still see a void? Or do you merely see a man out of patience?"

The harsh white flash of a portal briefly filled the theater. Hannah heard a familiar voice behind her.

"Azral, stop!" yelled Semerjean. "She's been helpful to us!"

"Ma'tta gein-tzé!" Esis bitterly replied. "Tu k'alla-la ho-kiesse!"

"Regah'la n'ien," Semerjean snapped back.

Azral glared at Hannah. "My parents quarrel over you yet again. I've grown tired of hearing it. You Silvers were our most arduous effort, but what do we have to show for it? One infant—*one*—as dull and unpromising as the others. All those times we saved your lives, all the nonsense we've put up with. We should have let you all die at Rebel's hands."

Fuck you, Hannah yelled inside her head. *Go ahead and kill me. I don't care. At least I'll be done with you.*

Azral snorted amusedly, as if he could hear her every thought. "You think this is the end. I'm afraid not. Your child still has a semblance of value, and we'd prefer to see him birthed naturally. But now that he's safe from your unhinged emotions, and because you've been so curious, I think it's time we . . . I forget the colloquial idiom. Is it 'clear the air'? I believe it is."

He turned Hannah around again. She barely had a moment to process the folds in the theater curtain before a flat lumic image appeared right in front of her: an aerial view of a suburban town that had been devastated by a giant sinkhole.

"Those are the remains of Quarter Hill," Azral explained. "Destroyed on the day we took you. All it needed was a small tectonic adjustment to bring one village down on the other."

While her physical self remained inert and reactionless, her thoughts shrieked in horror. *No, no, no. You wouldn't. You wouldn't fucking dare.*

"Obviously it was worse for those in the underland," Azral teased. "We weren't able to obtain a great many images, but the ones we have . . ."

Hannah's whole mind reeled at the next picture in his slideshow: a shot of the village square in ruins. She could see dozens of dead Gothams among the dust and rubble, all dressed for a wedding that had become ancient history to her. *Oh my God . . .*

"Terrible," said Azral. "Even worse than I anticipated. Had you and your people been more cooperative, we might have avoided that tragedy."

The presentation advanced to a close-up image of a man in a tuxedo, sprawled flat on the floor of a musty bomb shelter, his lower legs pinned beneath a pile of rocks. The poor guy looked so wretched that Hannah didn't recognize him at first. But then she looked beyond the blood and dust on his face and saw the father of her child.

Peter, she thought. *Oh no.*

"He survived," Azral admitted. "But I'm afraid you won't ever see him again, for reasons you'll understand shortly."

Azral progressed through a dozen more images, going slow enough for Hannah to process each one. Her thoughts cried out at the familiar faces in strain: Amanda struggling beneath a tempic shield, Theo dawdling with a broken arm, Ofelia lying battered and bruised, Heath clutching his head in hysterical grief.

No more, Hannah thought. *Please. I'm begging you.*

"Stop!" Semerjean broke away from Esis and crossed into Hannah's view. "Listen to me. You spoke out of turn, but it's not too late to fix this. All you have to do—"

"We're far beyond apologies," Esis said. "And as always, our son has a perfect solution. Let's lift the veil of her ignorance and give her all the truth that she craves."

She cleared Azral's lumic projection in favor of her own: a short silver console, not unlike Hannah's pedestal genies. But instead of displaying a holographic menu, it projected a three-dimensional image of a young, naked man—a Gotham that Hannah recognized.

"You know this fellow," Esis said to Hannah. "I forget his name."

Noah, Hannah thought.

"Noah Rall," Semerjean grudgingly informed Esis. "The one Eden married."

"Ah, yes," said Esis. "His name's a slippery thing in my mind, but I most certainly remember his amygdala. The construction of it is marvelous. I could study it for days."

Though Noah's eyes were wide open, Hannah didn't think for a moment that he was conscious. He looked like a corpse on a vertical slab.

Archived, Hannah realized in horror. *That's what it looks like. Oh God.*

"He was just one of dozens we liberated that day," Esis informed her. "Young chronokinetics with such interesting brains. It would have been a shame to let them perish without study."

With a flick of her finger, she displayed the next casualty: a familiar teenage orphan. Poor Shroud had been the bassist of Heath and Hannah's band, a strong-willed boy with a healthy sense of pride. He would have never wanted anyone to see him like that: naked and helpless and splayed out for science.

Please, Hannah thought. *Please stop.*

Esis continued to scroll through her archives, flipping each victim's image like a page in a pop-up book. No matter how fast they passed through Hannah's vision, she recognized their faces. Ben Hopkins, Harold Herrick, César Osario, Elena Josef. Orphans and Gothams, grown-ups and children, old friends, new friends, people Hannah couldn't name. There were so many people who'd been snatched away to Lárnach. And unlike Hannah and the rest of her pregnant inmates, these poor souls never had the chance to wake up.

By the fortieth image, Esis became impatient. "No, no, no. These aren't right. There's one in particular I seek."

Hannah's mind froze in dread. Which victim was Esis dying to show her? Heath? Mia? Zack? *Amanda?*

No, Hannah cried in her mind. *Don't you dare!*

Esis paused at the image of a young, tattooed Gotham, a woman who'd been haunting Hannah's thoughts for months.

"Mercurial Lee," Azral said with a scoff. "A most unpleasant child."

Esis nodded bitterly. "She received a better ending than she deserved, but she's still not the one I'm looking for."

"Enough," said Semerjean. "You made your point. Now you're just being petty."

"Petty?" Esis gestured at Hannah in outrage. "Did you hear what she said about my mothering skills? What she said about our *son*?"

"And do you think she'll be respectful now, after showing her what we've done?"

"We don't need her respect," Azral told his father. "We need her to understand."

He took control of the archive interface and scrolled ahead through four more victims. Though Hannah had spent weeks preparing for the worst, it still shattered her to see the nightmare come to life. Thalia Ballad. Regal Tam. Sarah Brehm.

Moon.

Azral eclipsed Hannah's view and gave her a vindictive smile. There was no more void behind his eyes. They were filled with something awful now. Something a lot like malice.

"We're done making bargains," he calmly informed Hannah. "We are no longer in the business of coddling soft minds. We came to this world on an imperative mission, and we're done letting fools impede us. Now, at last, you know the truth."

He shuffled to the side, giving Hannah one last view of Moon's archived specter. "Now you know your future."

. . .

There had been a number of times in Hannah's life when she felt like she understood the cruel and senseless nature of the universe. When her best friend in high school was killed by a drunk driver. When her father lost his fight against cancer. When a college professor harassed her and easily got away with it. When Jonathan fell through the world.

In each case, the epiphany had taken her by surprise, as if it had been hiding in plain sight all along. Indeed, all she'd had to do was look at nature in action to see the truth in its purest form. It was all just one thing killing another—predators and prey, victors and victims. No one had built the system by design. It had created itself through the absence of structure, like air rushing into a void.

Hannah had hours to think about that as she lay awake in her bed. Azral had brought her back to her domain without lifting his paralytic curse on her. He'd merely posed her like a doll in a resting position, then propped her on her side between a pair of body pillows.

If it was a comfortable stance, Hannah didn't know. She still couldn't feel anything outside her mind, and there was plenty enough to feel on the inside. But even in her grief and rage, she understood why Azral chose to keep her in stasis. Had her stressful thoughts been allowed to travel, they would have shocked poor Robert in the womb, maybe even enough to kill him. Even worse: Hannah might have let it happen out of spite. It would save him from a worse fate anyway.

After three long hours on her left side, a spindly tempic limb popped out of Hannah's mattress and gently turned her over. It suddenly dawned on her that her paralysis might be permanent. She might spend the rest of her pregnancy as an inanimate object, a human plant in the Pelletier garden.

She stared helplessly at the wall for another two hours, until Semerjean arrived by portal. He sat down in her field of view and addressed her in a somber tone.

"Though Rosario doesn't remember it," he began, "she's been our guest before. She and Ofelia and the rest of the Pearls spent a good long time here at Lárnach. Well, not a *good* time, as such. We kept them all in a prolonged state of severance, just as you are now."

Hannah reeled at the lack of guilt in his voice, as if he'd merely inconvenienced them instead of putting them through hell.

"It made them easy to manage," Semerjean admitted. "But it wasn't as beneficial for their children as we'd hoped. It certainly wasn't good for the mothers. By the time we released them, they were functionally insane. The experience broke their minds. All of them."

He gazed down at the floor with a compunctious shrug. "That's why we erased their memories."

Hannah continued to watch from the well of her consciousness as Semerjean continued his monologue.

"For this round of pregnancies, we wanted to try a different approach, but we weren't quite sure what. My wife and son's ideas were . . . extreme, to say the least. You would have not been very comfortable here."

The laugh in Hannah's head was so loud and venomous, she was amazed that Semerjean couldn't hear it.

"So I took the lead again," he said. "A gentler plan that favored deception over oppression. Now that you've had a taste of the alternative, can you truly blame me?"

Semerjean looked deep into her eyes. "I guess you can, and I suppose I deserve it. I knew that I couldn't manage these women on my own. I needed your insight and empathy, and you delivered. You made life easier for everyone here. I just wish it could have continued."

A long and brooding moment passed before he spoke again. "I don't know what possessed you to insult my wife and son like that. You had to have known the consequences."

Hannah could guess from his tone and body language that he was becoming increasingly frustrated with the one-sided nature of the conversation.

"I'm going to free you from your stasis," he said. "But before I do, I need you to think very carefully. If you try to harm me or yourself, I'll have no choice but to put you back into severance. Do you understand me?"

Hannah didn't know what he expected her to do. She couldn't even nod her head.

"All right." Semerjean moved toward the bed and removed something from Hannah's hair, a two-inch disc of polished silver that had been affixed to the top of her skull like a magnet. The moment Semerjean peeled it away, Hannah sat up in bed with a gasp. She felt like she'd been dug out of a shallow grave. But the open air only inflamed her emotions. They suddenly had all the room in the world to burn.

She threw a pillow at Semerjean, her eyes wet with rage. "You motherfucker!"

"Look—"

"You twisted, evil piece of shit! You're the worst of them!"

"Hannah—"

"You're the fucking worst."

She leaned back against the headboard and wept into her hands, her eyes basking in the darkness. If only she could have covered them back in the theater. Then she wouldn't keep seeing those poor, naked victims in her head, all the orphans and Gothams who'd been converted into templates. And that didn't even factor in the other half of the equation, the loved ones she *didn't* see in the archives. Were they even alive, or did they die in the underland?

Semerjean dropped the pillow back onto Hannah's bed. "Azral told you the truth about Peter surviving. He's safe right now in Ioni's care, along with Amanda, Theo, Mia, Zack—"

"Bullshit."

"—Heath."

"Bullshit!" Hannah yelled. "You lie about everything! *Everything!*"

Semerjean shook his head despondently. "Only when there's a good reason."

"Now you're lying to yourself. You're sick in the head!"

"Not sick," he insisted. "Just out of my depth. My wife and son are both brilliant scientists. I'm just an old stage performer. So when I see a chance to use my talents, I take it. It's the least I can do for the people I love."

Hannah shot him a hateful look. "The people you love are monsters."

"You're back to insulting them? Haven't you learned—"

"I don't care," Hannah said. "It doesn't even matter. You're the one I hate the most. I hate you more than I've ever hated anyone."

Semerjean chuckled. "That's not true. I can even prove it."

"What are you talking about?"

He waved a new portal on the far side of the room. "I have a very special gift for you," Semerjean said. "You'll have to come with me to see it."

"You've got to be shitting me."

"I know it won't buy your allegiance," said Semerjean, "and it certainly won't buy your trust. But it'll make your final weeks here a little less painful. It'll also balance the scales on an old injustice. I've been waiting a long time to give you this opportunity."

"I'm not going anywhere," Hannah insisted. "So take your 'gift' and get the fuck out."

Semerjean stood up and shrugged. "The door will remain if you change your mind."

He exited through a second portal, leaving Hannah alone in her misery. Her teleport bracelet had been fully disabled, along with her communication relays. The Pelletiers couldn't have her stressing out the other prisoners, which was probably just as well. Hannah was in no hurry to tell Eden about the fate of her husband, and would have rather eaten glass than break the news about the underland.

She spent the next two days in a doleful languor, suppressing her thoughts through dreamless sleep and nonstop creature comforts: every junk food treat she could stuff into her gullet, every musical comedy from her late, great Earth.

By her third morning of solitude, there was no escaping her despair. It had become impervious to her household distractions, except one.

Furious, she opened the door of her kitchen pantry to the portal that Semerjean had left for her. She'd had to rearrange her whole house to keep the damn thing out of sight, but its presence continued to vex her. Was it really a gift or just another false hope? What if it was a trap?

"Fuck it," she muttered to herself. "What more can they do to me?"

She stepped through the disc and into a stark white chamber, an eerie twin of the release room where she'd last seen Moon. Near the right wall stood a simple wooden workbench, its surface covered in a neat assortment of hand tools.

No, not tools. Weapons.

Hannah warily approached the arsenal, her eyes growing wider by the second. The bench boasted some of the most painful-looking implements she'd ever seen: bludgeons and blades, torches and tasers, a whip, a chain, a set of spiked knuckles, even an oversize corkscrew that could have come from a medieval torture room.

Oh no, Hannah thought.

Panicked, she turned around for the portal, then jumped at the sight of Semerjean. He stood mere inches behind her, his face lit up in a preening grin.

"No!" Hannah tried to get around him, but he caught her by the shoulders.

"It's all right," he said. "Those weapons are there for your usage, not your suffering."

Hannah backed away from him. "What are you talking about?"

"You said you hated me more than anyone," Semerjean reminded her. "That's not true. There's someone you hate more."

He pointed at the farthest wall, which immediately began to retract into the ceiling. Hannah could start to see the hints of a shallow alcove, a pair of wriggling legs in blue jeans.

"That man in there has caused you great pain," Semerjean told Hannah. "It's well past time that you returned the favor."

The last of the sliding wall disappeared, revealing the newest prisoner of Lárnach. He hung against a great white *X*, his wrists and ankles bound in tempis.

Evan squinted in the light of the torture room, then fixed his nervous eyes on Hannah. "Oh shit."

THIRTY

He'd been working his way down the French Riviera, wreaking havoc in a manner that had become part and parcel of his nonlinear existence. The casinos of Monte Carlo were still recovering from his visit, the smug little American who kept horsewhipping them at their own table games. He'd wagered like a man who knew exactly how the dice would land, and seemed to know the roulette ball better than it knew itself.

After winning a fortune in British pound sterling, Evan had proceeded along the coast to Saint-Laurent, where he'd settled into a seaside inn and bought the affections of a lovely young lounge singer—or rented them, anyway. She'd crept out of his room in the middle of the night, along with all his money. Disappointed, but hardly surprised, Evan turned back the clock of his life six hours and jabbed a syringe full of bleach into her heart.

From there, he'd moved west to the village of Éze and became smitten with a young Spanish archeologist. Though it had taken thirty-one rewinds and a crash course in medieval metallurgy, he'd managed to charm her into dinner at a cozy little lodge in the mountains. Yet despite all of Evan's best efforts and temporal re-efforts, he couldn't jump-start a romance between them. Even offering to fund her research for a year only earned him a drink in his face. "I'm not a whore," she'd yelled at him. "And you're not the man you pretended to be."

Dejected, Evan sent his consciousness back in time fifty-eight hours, then loosened the bolts of her balcony railing. The archeologist plummeted to her death, having never known Evan or his hatred for her.

By the time Semerjean found him in the city of Nice, Evan had left a trail of bodies across the Riviera: a waiter who'd been rude to him, a masseuse who'd been rough with him, a man who'd made fun of his pidgin French. He'd arranged an electrical "accident" for a verbally abusive father, then poisoned the drink of a Welsh brunette for reasons Semerjean could only guess at.

"She did bear an uncanny resemblance to you," he noted to Hannah. "Guess that was enough to seal her fate."

Hannah had only been half listening as he described Evan's latest acts of malice—his *final* acts, by all reckoning. Unless Semerjean was planning another surprise, then that poor Welsh girl had been Evan's last victim.

Evan looked at Hannah in fright and resentment, as if it were her, not Semerjean, who had engineered his downfall. He looked ten years younger without his abrasive arrogance, and so utterly pitiful that Hannah had to wonder how she ever feared him.

Her attention was caught by Evan's new adornment: four small silver discs that had been infused onto the back of his left hand. "They keep his basic needs satisfied," Semerjean explained. "We don't want him dying of hunger or thirst."

He smiled at Hannah. "Unless, of course, you do. His life and death are now entirely in your hands."

Evan blanched at the very notion. "Look, come on. I've been helpful to you. You need me!"

"Need you?" Semerjean chuckled. "Your long life makes you an interesting study, as least as far as my wife is concerned. But now that you've cast your lot with Ioni—"

"I haven't!"

"So that wasn't you who killed eight of our Jades in Scotland?"

"That was all Mother. I didn't do a thing!"

"Now you're just insulting me."

"Okay, then let me go and I'll undo it," Evan promised. "I'll make it like it never happened!"

"Pathetic." Semerjean looked to Hannah. "After all his circular travels in time, he still doesn't understand how it works."

Hannah kept her gaze on Evan, her voice a low growl. "Get out."

Semerjean cocked his head. "I assume you mean me."

"Yes. *You*. I can't handle both you assholes at once."

"You do have the power to kill one of us," Semerjean reminded her.

"Can I choose which?"

"No."

"Then get the hell out," Hannah snarled. "I'm not doing anything until you leave."

"As you wish."

Semerjean opened a portal next to Hannah's, then grinned at Evan. "As you can see, she's not in the best mood. I don't envy you."

"Just go!" Hannah yelled.

As Semerjean left and closed the disc, Evan spoke in a frantic whisper. "Listen to me—"

"Shut up."

"—we're both in the same jam."

"I said *shut the fuck up*." Hannah snatched the electric gun from the table and pointed it at him. "This looks like the same thing you used on my sister. Two years ago, in Battery Park. You remember?"

"Look—"

"She had a broken leg, but you didn't care. You just kept on zapping her while she screamed."

"I did," said Evan. "I also saved her life in Scotland."

"You just told Semerjean you didn't do a thing."

"You know he's playing you, right? You're never getting out of h—"

Hannah fired the gun, sending an invisible bolt of electricity into his chest. His body shuddered in its restraints and he screeched like a creature out of a dark fairy tale—an imp or a gremlin or a little baby wraith. For a brief spell, Hannah forgot all her troubles and enjoyed the sweet taste of justice. How many times had she fantasized about this moment? How many nights had she hoped and dreamed for the chance to avenge Jonathan?

Yet something about the experience felt jarringly hollow, as if she were still just an actress on Semerjean's stage. She could picture all her loved ones watching her from the audience, not a single one of them enjoying the show. Even Mia, the silver queen of vengeance herself, shook her head in lament. *Oh, Hannah . . .*

Trembling, queasy, Hannah lowered her gun. "Son of a bitch."

Evan sniffled from his hanging perch. "Please. I'm sorry."

"Oh, fuck you. You're only sorry that I'm hurting you."

"Probably," he admitted. "But if I had a chance to do it all over—"

"You've had *every* chance to do things over, and you just keep killing people!"

"They come back."

"Bullshit!"

"Nothing I do is permanent. It all gets undone in the end."

Hannah drank him in with slack-faced horror. "Holy shit. He's right. You don't know how time works. You don't get how *consequence* works. You think the whole world's your video game."

Evan opened his mouth to object, then flinched at the sight of her stun gun. Hannah threw it back onto the table. "Fuck. This is pointless."

"You want to hurt someone? Hurt *him*."

"Him."

"Semerjean. The guy who's keeping you here. The guy's who been pulling your strings from Day One!"

"Oh my God." Hannah vented a bitter laugh. "You both think I'm just a mindless little hate beam that you can point at each other. Let me explain something real simple."

Hannah glared at the ceiling, at whatever hidden camera that Semerjean was watching her through. "I don't give a shit about anything anymore. And I have more than enough hatred for both of you."

She turned around and made for the exit portal. "Wait," said Evan. "Where are you going?"

"Back to my cell."

"That's it? You're done with me?"

Hannah laughed again. By Pelletier estimates, she was seven and a half months along in her pregnancy, which meant that she had six more weeks to live. That gave her ample time to settle old scores, but she wasn't going to do it with a weapon. No, she would break Evan in her own special way, and she'd love every goddamn minute of it.

His dungeon was remodeled to Hannah's specifications, a handwritten list of forty-six notes that had been forwarded to Semerjean by portal. To Hannah's surprise, he'd indulged every one of her requests without a single objection, not even an "Are you sure?"

Evan was released from his shackles, freed of his feeding discs, and detained in a cell like a normal prisoner. He was given a cot, a chair, a toilet stall, a metal sink with hot and cold water, and a food genie with limited options.

In the southern half of the room, beyond a two-inch wall of sound-conductive glass, was Hannah's new visiting station, complete with her own little kitchen and bathroom amenities, plus the queen of all cushioned recliners. She figured she might as well get comfortable here. Evan was about to become her new personal theater.

If her captive was pleased with the new accommodations, he certainly didn't look it. Evan paced the length of his oblong cell, his nervous eyes dawdling around the console on Hannah's lap. The machine was the centerpiece of her devious brainstorm, a high-tech replacement for the table of torture tools. Every function on the holographic display had been specially requested by her: a button to shock Evan, a button to mute him, a button to hold him in place. Hannah had six new ways to humiliate him, and ten psychological torments. There was also a little black button that she was saving for the end, though she didn't tell Evan what it did.

She motioned to his folding chair. "Have a seat."

Evan snorted derisively and continued his anxious loop. "So we're doing *Silence of the Lambs* now?"

"Evan . . ."

"Just because I can't rewind—"

Sighing, Hannah pressed a button on her console, prompting tempic tendrils to pop out of the wall and force Evan down onto the seat.

"Ow! Fuck!"

"Rule Number One," Hannah told him, "you do what I say when I say it. I won't ask anything twice."

Evan struggled in the tempic ropes. "So this is what gets you off, huh?"

Hannah shocked him with the *Zap* button. "Rule Two: you don't insult me or anyone I love. That's a shortcut to a very bad day."

Evan gritted his teeth. "I know what you're doing."

"Oh yeah? What am I doing?"

"You're trying to have your cake and eat it too. The moral torture."

"Moral torture?"

"You don't want to admit what you really are."

Hannah smiled, then pressed another button on her console. The entire wall behind her became a giant silver mirror. "I think you're the one who needs to take a look at yourself."

Evan shrank away from his reflection, just as Hannah had expected. The last time he'd been a prisoner of Lárnach, the Pelletiers had kept him in a fully mirrored cell. Hannah hardly would have considered that a torture by itself, yet Zack had suffered the very same treatment and still flinched whenever he passed a looking glass.

"It's hard to explain," Zack had admitted to Hannah. "All I can tell you is that I never got used to it. It just kept getting worse."

Evan focused on Hannah to avoid his own image. "So that's the game, huh? You're gonna wear me down till I confess all my crimes?"

"I don't want to know all your crimes."

"No, you just want me to feel bad about them." He did a double take at her shirt. "God almighty."

"What?"

"If I told you, you'd zap me."

"Is it about my breasts?"

"No."

"You're looking right at them."

"How can I not? They're like balloons now."

Hannah shocked him until he squealed. "Do I need to explain Rule Two again?"

"It was a compliment!"

Hannah shocked him once more. "Rule Three: no bullshit. You knew exactly what you were doing."

"Okay, okay!"

"The next time you say *anything* about my body—"

"I won't!" Evan struggled in his restraints. "Can you please, uh . . ."

She released him from the tempic ropes and eyed him with naked revulsion. "All this hell you put me through, just because you like my tits."

"You really think it's that simple?"

"I know you're creepily obsessed with me."

"That door swings both ways, sister."

"Oh, please," said Hannah. "I never killed anyone just for looking like you."

"I never did that either."

"Semerjean—"

"I know what he said." Evan slouched in his chair, exasperated. "That Welsh girl didn't look a thing like you. And I didn't kill her."

"He said you poisoned her."

"Yeah. With a laxative."

"What?"

"I just gave her the runs," Evan insisted. "Unless she crapped on a land mine, I'm pretty sure she lived."

"Why did you do it?"

"What does it matter?"

Hannah held her finger threateningly above the *Zap* button until Evan acquiesced. "I just wanted to know where the train station was."

"And she didn't tell you?"

"She told me with attitude."

"Attitude."

Evan mimicked a haughty sneer. "That 'Why are you talking to me?' look, like I wasn't attractive enough to be speaking to her."

Hannah gaped at him with dark astonishment. "Holy shit. You have issues."

"Don't act like that's not a thing."

"She could have been having a bad day," Hannah mused. "Or maybe she just had good instincts about you."

"I know what I saw."

"And you're always right about everything."

Evan cackled. "If that was true, I wouldn't need an undo button."

"So you've been wrong about people before."

"Sure."

"Who?"

"You," Evan said. "There was a time in my life when I thought you were awesome."

Hannah considered jolting him again, but he'd just broached an interesting topic. "Let's talk about that."

"Why?"

"Because you've been mad at me for fifty-five lifetimes," she said. "Over some vague shit that another Hannah did."

"It was still you," Evan coldly insisted. "All you."

"I broke your heart."

"You broke my *faith*."

"Because I didn't want you back," Hannah said. "I made the mistake of being nice to you, and you thought that entitled you to me."

"Wrong." Evan crossed his arms. "Yet another oversimplification."

"So tell me what really happened."

"Why?"

"Because we'll both be dead soon," Hannah said. "And we have nothing else to do."

Evan sat up in his chair, his tense eyes locked on Hannah's console. "You know, I've seen those things around before. They're all connected to the Pelletiers' neural net. I hope you like being on their psychic Wi-Fi."

"The more you dodge, the more I know I'm right."

"I never thought you owed me anything!" Evan snapped. "And I wasn't just some horny guy, okay? I was a fucking wreck those first few months. I wasn't thinking with either head."

"So what did I do? Give you attitude?"

Evan glumly shook his head. "You and Zack were the only ones who were good to me."

"Oh come on. I can't imagine Theo and Mia—"

"They mostly kept their distance. And Amanda was a real b—" Evan stopped himself before Hannah could zap him. "Let's just say she wasn't friendly."

Hannah chuckled. As usual, her sister was sharper than her. She must have smelled Evan's shit from the start. "But I was nice."

"You were more than nice," Evan admitted with discomfort. "I . . . wasn't my best self in those early days, which I guess made me hard to be around. But you never looked down your nose at me, or treated me like a charity case. To get that from a woman like you . . ."

Hannah raised a skeptical eyebrow. "A woman like me."

"Don't play dumb. You know how you look."

"What does that have to do with anything?"

"Women like you don't have to be nice," Evan told her. "You can just wear a tight shirt, bat your eyes, and get whatever you want."

Hannah's mind reeled at the magnitude of his dysfunction. He'd been alive for hundreds of years, yet he was still nothing more than a clueless adolescent.

"So a good-looking woman suddenly shows you some kindness—"

Evan rolled his eyes. "It wasn't just about looks."

"That's all you keep talking about!"

"You had other qualities I appreciated."

"Like?"

"Look at you, fishing for compliments."

Hannah held a threatening finger over a punishment button. Evan threw up his hands. "You were *smart*, okay? You were smart, you were nice, you were funny, and you were interesting. I got good at my powers just so I could have more talks with you."

"What, like redone conversations?"

Evan nodded. "I'd jump back, change the topic, and then spend a whole new hour chatting with you. I didn't even have to look at you. We'd just lay on the patio and stare at the sky. It was . . ."

He dipped his head in anguish. For once, he actually looked disgusted with himself. "It was just what I needed at the time."

Hannah struggled to suppress her surprise. She would have never thought in a million years that the prick had a romantic side. It only made his actions even more horrific in retrospect.

"But then came Jury," Hannah said. "This hot Cuban guy who had all his shit together."

Evan's laugh was sharp enough to prick her through the glass. "Shows how little you knew him."

"That's only because you keep killing him," Hannah growled. "All because we were . . . What? Lovers? Partners?"

Evan scoffed. "Even 'fuck buddies' gives it more depth than it had."

"Excuse me if I don't take your word for it," said Hannah. "Whatever we had, it was enough to drive you nuts."

"It's not that simple."

"Sure it is." Hannah pressed a button on her console, summoning a still-frame hologram of Jury Curado. He looked handsome enough in his license photo, but in life-size and living color, he was an absolute Adonis. Yet despite all his strong and masculine features, Hannah could count at least a dozen ways that he resembled his sister, especially in the eyes. They both had the same dark, complicated gaze that teased a whole universe inside them.

Evan yelped as Hannah zapped him twice. "Ow! Fuck! Why'd you do that?"

"For Ofelia," she said. "You killed the only family she had left."

"Yeah? And why did that happen?"

"Because you were jealous! Is that a trick question?"

"I mean why did the Pelletiers *let* me kill him?"

Hannah caught his gist. "Oh, fuck you."

Evan pointed at her baby bump. "They saw the strings and they knew he'd be an obstacle. If you'd just kept your legs closed, he'd still be alive."

Hannah pressed the button that closed off Evan's airway, then calmly observed him as he fell to the floor. "Bet you wish you could unsay that."

Evan clutched his throat and looked up at Hannah pleadingly.

"Not so easy, is it?" she said. "To be stuck in one timeline with the messes you made. All your victims and all your victims' sisters. We're still here no matter where you go. You never undo a thing."

Hannah released him from the choke hold and left him gasping on the floor. "Jury's death is all on you. Take some fucking responsibility for yourself."

She cleared away Jury's ghost, then waited for Evan to catch his breath.

"Get back in the chair," she ordered him. "Or I'll do it myself."

Weakly, Evan climbed back onto the seat, his red face filled with loathing. "This must be fucking Heaven for you."

"Just a slightly better Hell," Hannah replied. "Did I lead you on?"

"What?"

"Did I do *anything* to make you think you had a chance with me?"

"No." Evan looked away from her. "You even gave me the speech. You know the one."

Hannah nodded. "The 'I'm not looking for a boyfriend' speech."

"Or lover," Evan added. "You said you couldn't even think about it with all the shit going on. But that was a lie."

"So you hate me for trying to let you down easy."

"I hate you for being like every other woman," Evan croaked. "I thought you were better than that."

Hannah closed her eyes, sickened. "You know, I used to think it was the end of the world that broke you. But now I see you were always like this."

"Like what, a realist?"

"Like a woman-hating fuckwad."

Evan shrugged. "I'd rather be a sexist than a sexist cliché."

"What, *me*?"

"Hannah, what do you think happened when I took Jury out of the picture?"

She didn't have to wonder. She avoided his gaze, incensed. "I hooked up with Theo."

"You hooked up with Theo," Evan repeated. "You barely gave him a second glance when Jury was around. But as soon as he was gone, *boom*. You moved right on over to Bachelor Number Two."

Evan chuckled as she reached for the console. "You want to choke me, go ahead. You know it's all true."

"Fuck you!" Hannah stood up and paced the room. *Why are you even doing this?* she asked herself. *You suffered enough. Just kill him.*

Evan smiled sardonically. "Hey, look, I get it. Sex feels great."

"Shut up."

"But you took that need to a whole new level. A rather sad one, if you ask m—"

Hannah smacked a button on her machine, bringing the tempic tendrils back out of the wall. They wrapped around Evan like rope cords, binding him to his chair, gagging him.

"This is old news," she told him. "You've said that shit before. 'Hannah Banana, always needs a man-a.' You remember that? Because I do."

Evan writhed in his restraints, shooting daggers from his eyes.

Hannah continued. "You're so caught up in your own selfish needs that it never even occurred to you that maybe *I* was a wreck back then. Maybe *I* needed something to hold me together."

She paced along the barrier, her baby boy thrashing angrily inside her. "And let's not kid ourselves about why you're really mad. It's not because I wanted intimacy from those guys. It's because I never wanted it from you. You can start over and try a million more times. It'll never, ever be you."

Evan cursed at her through his tempic gag, his eyes welling with tears.

"I'm gonna go to my cell and wash the stink of you off me," Hannah said. "I'll be back in a few hours. I'm not done talking about Jury Curado, and I haven't even started on Jonathan."

She stepped to the side to allow Evan to view his reflection. "While you sit there staring at the prick in the mirror, think about this: there are men out there who look just like you who are getting all the love that they want. It's not the shallowness of women that keeps you alone. Just the opposite. We all see the sickness inside you. You're the deepest and worst kind of ugly."

Hannah raised her traveler's bracelet. "Portal. Home."

As the exit disc opened, Hannah took a last bitter look at Evan. "I know," she said. "Life's not fair, especially here in Pelletier Land."

She shined him a cruel little smile from the portal's edge. "You'll get used to it."

. . .

The next four days passed miserably for both of them as Hannah continued to try Evan for his sins and atrocities—or tried to try him anyway. He seemed to prefer electric shocks to any semblance of introspection, and he insisted with all the zeal of a martyr that he was completely blameless. The people he'd killed deserved to die, and the ones who didn't were going to die anyway. And it was all fucking moot, to hear Evan tell it, since his victims would be back in the next round. Also, Hannah had some nerve wagging the finger at him after the horrible things she'd done in other timelines.

Furious, Hannah took a day off from Evan's company, but left a medley of showtunes to play in his cell at full volume: songs from *Kiss Me, Kate*, *The Pajama Game*, and other Broadway musicals of the fifties. She even included some numbers that tested her own will to live, like the finale of *Paint Your Wagon*.

The torment worked so ridiculously well that Hannah wished she'd thought of it sooner. By the time she visited Evan the following morning, he looked ready to confess to anything.

"What do you *want* from me?" he cried. "You want me to say I'm sorry? Fine! I'm sorry! I'm sorry! I'm a very bad man and I'm sorry, okay?"

Hannah eyed him glibly from her easy chair. "I don't know. Just doesn't seem sincere."

"Fuck you!"

"See, that was sincere, but it wasn't contrite."

"Oh my God." Evan buried his face in his hands. "And you wonder why I hate you."

"No I don't," said Hannah. "I figured that out two years ago. The only real question is how you live with yourself."

"You should know by now. You're practically her again."

"Who?"

"Second-Half Hannah," Evan said. "The one who survives the war of San Francisco—"

"Stop."

"—and finally realizes that there's no point to anything."

"I said *stop*." Hannah hovered her finger over the *Zap* button. "I told you I don't want to hear about those other timelines."

"I'm talking about *you*," Evan said. "I'm looking at you now, and I see that same black cloud in your eyes. You don't believe in anything anymore. It's all just a big fat cosmic joke, except now you're finally in on it."

Hannah sneered at his prognosis. "So I might as well kill people, because why not?"

"You mock, but yeah, that's Second-Half Hannah in a nutshell. She has nothing left to do but settle old scores, and I'm always at the top of her list. She chases me halfway around the world. Stalks me wherever I go. It was flattering at first, but I can't lie. It's getting a little creepy."

"Are you still in love with me?"

"What?" Evan chuckled defensively. "How did you get that from—"

"Because you're obsessed with the notion that we're both alike," Hannah said. "Two sick peas in a twisted pod."

"All I'm saying—"

"I know what you're saying, and you're right about one thing. I've lost all hope for the future. But the difference between us—and this is not a small difference—is that I don't kill innocent people."

"Not yet, but—"

"And I'm not paying you back for some pissant thing you did in another timeline. You murdered Jonathan right in front of me, right in this very string!"

"So kill me!" Evan fired back. "Use that neural network box and wipe me off the planet. Just stop trying to get me to see things your way. And stop pretending you're better than me."

"Oh my God." Hannah stood up and dropped her console onto the chair. "How the hell did she ever think you changed?"

"Who?"

"Amanda."

Evan's brow rose in surprise. "She said that?"

"Yeah. Can you believe it?"

"Not really. She's always been Shrilly McJudge-a-Lot."

"You don't know shit about her."

"I'm starting to think you're right."

Hannah froze in place. "What?"

"She seems different this time," Evan said. "A lot less screechy and a lot more together. Either she's changed too, or I've been getting her all wrong."

He laughed at Hannah's gobsmacked expression. "Did I just blow your mind?"

"No, but I'm starting to think I broke yours."

"Oh, I still hate her," Evan insisted. "She ruins Zack in every string, and she always finds a way to annoy me. But that's mostly Second-Half Amanda. This one's not so bad."

Hannah looped behind her chair and leaned against the headrest. "So you've seen her survive San Francisco."

"More than once," Evan said. "For all the good it does her."

"Shut up."

"What? You said you lost all hope."

"Yeah, and it pisses me off," Hannah said. "I really thought the world had a chance."

Evan shrugged. "I'm not happy about it either, but I know what I've seen. You guys never even come close."

"So why did you help us?" Hannah asked. "You didn't have to go to Europe."

"I wish I hadn't."

"Then *why*?"

"I don't know!" Evan flicked a lazy hand. "It was just something new to pass the time."

"You're either lying to me or fooling yourself."

"So you're the expert on me now?"

"Yes," said Hannah. "You're a cancer in my life, and I've had a long time to think about you."

Evan clasped his hands and cooed. "Awww. That's the sweetest thing you ever said. I feel like we're finally connecting."

"Uh-huh." Hannah summoned an exit portal. "I'll come back tomorrow and ask you again."

Evan's eyes went round as she fiddled with her console. "Do not play that fucking—"

With the press of a button, the room once again shook with the music of Broadway, the opening number of *Guys and Dolls.*

"Enjoy!" Hannah said.

She returned the next morning to find Evan on the floor, his body curled in a fetal position. Hannah turned off the music and laughed at his catatonic expression. "Wow. You *really* don't like showtunes."

She settled into her recliner, then eyed him skeptically. "All right. You made your point. If you can get through the day without being a prick, I'll give you a break from the music."

Evan still didn't move or acknowledge her. Hannah looked him over, baffled. Was this a strange new ruse or just a committed tantrum?

"Evan, if you don't move in the next three seconds, I'm gonna light your ass up like a Christmas tree. Don't test me on this."

She counted to three and then pressed the *Zap* button, but she might as well have been shocking a corpse. Whatever was happening to Evan, it wasn't a feint. If he hadn't sporadically blinked his eyes, she would have wondered if he'd actually died.

Unless . . .

"Oh no." Hannah had to yell Semerjean's name six times before he arrived by portal. He checked on Evan through the glass, then clucked his tongue in pity. "Unfortunate."

"What happened?" Hannah asked. "I thought you took his powers away."

"We did."

"So how did he escape?"

"Escape? He's right there."

"I mean his mind," Hannah said. "Zack saw the same thing happen in London. He said Evan's brain goes blank whenever he jumps back in time."

Semerjean chuckled cynically, as if Hannah had just read him his horoscope. "That's not even remotely true. Zack's out of his depth on the matter."

"So what the hell's going on?"

Semerjean motioned to his portal. "Walk with me. I'll explain."

"Can't you just tell me here?"

"I have work to do. Either come with me or we'll talk later."

"Fine." Hannah suspected that he was manipulating her, trying to ease them back into a friendly dynamic. Then again, he looked more agitated than usual. Was there a new problem behind the scenes?

She followed Semerjean through the portal, into a narrow white corridor that, like all the hidden pockets of Lárnach, was completely indistinguishable from all the others. Hannah could only guess that she was near the heart of the facility because she could hear the hum of the energy reactor. From what Semerjean had told her, it was five times as large as the underland, and strong enough to power a nation.

He kept his cool eyes forward as Hannah followed him down the hall. "Evan should recover in an hour or so, but his overall condition will worsen."

"What condition?"

"He has terminus."

"*Terminus?*" Hannah nearly tripped over herself. "I thought only your people got that."

Semerjean shook his head. "Anyone who lives to their third or fourth century is eventually struck by the illness. The fact that it took Evan this long to contract it is remarkable. Your people have a natural resistance that mine have lost over the years."

Hannah was still stuck on Evan's long life, the clearest proof she'd ever seen that age doesn't guarantee wisdom. "How much time does he have?"

"Just what I was about to ask you," said Semerjean. "I assumed he'd be dead by now."

Hannah fumed at his rebuke. "I'm not done with him yet."

"From what I can see, you're only torturing yourself."

"You didn't answer my question."

"He has roughly a year left," Semerjean guessed. "If you were hoping for nature to do what you can't, then I'm afraid you'll be disappointed."

"Fuck you," Hannah growled. "It may be easy for *you* to kill a helpless man—"

"Is that why you hesitate?"

"I don't know."

"Because I can arrange a more sporting execution."

Hannah stepped back, repulsed. "Do you even hear yourself sometimes?"

"There are victims who dream of the opportunity I've given you," said Semerjean. "It pains me to see you squander it."

He melted a door in the tempic wall, then smiled at a young woman who was waiting on the other side. "Shi'pátma. Datsch'e mo-wic'ha."

Joelle returned his grin with doting affection. "No-sare'k ohöi."

Hannah followed Semerjean into the room, but kept a nervous distance from Joelle. She'd only seen the Jades around Lárnach on a handful of occasions and was always unnerved by the sight of them. Whether this Joelle was a clone or the original, Hannah didn't know or care. She'd been refashioned beyond any hint of humanity, an alien race both advanced and subservient.

Joelle only gave Hannah the briefest of looks before taking her place at the wall.

"What's going on?" Hannah asked Semerjean.

"Some materials are easier to purchase than synthesize," he replied. "So I'm sending Joelle on a shopping trip."

Hannah studied her foreign embellishments, all the dark veins and subdermal protrusions that made her stand out like a *Star Trek* villain. "She's going out like that?"

"Of course not," said Semerjean.

"No," Joelle confirmed. She aimed her sneer at Semerjean. "Sei-un pandar'a."

Hannah didn't have to speak Pelletese to know when someone was calling her a dumbass. She might have responded if she hadn't been distracted by Joelle's sudden transformation. With a twist of her wristband, her jade armor turned into a verdant summer dress. Her skin gave way to a clean and healthy complexion. She almost looked pretty in her incognito form. But the green in her eyes was still distractingly bright, and she still had the stare of a zombie.

Semerjean moved to a control stand and waved a holographic keyboard onto its surface. "She was teasing me," he said to Hannah. "Not you."

Hannah snorted cynically. "Oh, so you're the pandar'a?"

"It's not a noun. It's a verb. It's means 'educate' in Ory'an."

"Ory'an?"

"The language of my people," said Semerjean. "Did I never tell you its name?"

"No."

"Well, that just proves Joelle's point. I've done a poor job teaching you."

Hannah couldn't have been less interested in the topic. Her attention was focused on Semerjean's console. It was a near-perfect twin of the one she used on Evan, except mounted on a stand and decked with different functions. While Hannah's buttons were all in English and lit in cool blue, Semerjean's were red and marked with complex alien symbols. Clearly one of them was Ory'an for "make a new portal."

Semerjean keyed in the coordinates for Joelle's destination. "Once we evolved into a multidimensional species, all our existing languages became obsolete," he explained to Hannah. "There's no simple way in English to describe my past misdeeds in an alternate future, or my future intentions for a string of the past. But Ory'an has seventy-two active verb tenses, and enough temporal conjugations to make any discussion easy. It's been our universal tongue for a thousand years. All the others are as dead as Latin."

He flicked his finger above the keypad, causing two of the buttons to glow. Hannah noticed that he didn't even have to specify which ones he wanted. They simply lit up at his whim, then summoned a portal on Joelle's side of the room.

"Stái'shia," Semerjean said to Joelle.

"Ish'bin a-ma," Joelle replied before disappearing into the portal.

"I just told her to call me in the past if she foresees trouble," Semerjean explained. "And in two words, she told me that she's never intentionally disappointed me, and will never disappoint me in the future. A simple suffix draws a clear contrast between past and future intent."

"Huh." Hannah eyed him bitterly. "Will there be any creepy, green-eyed versions of me in the future?"

Semerjean closed the portal. "That's a grim question."

"I'll take that as a yes."

"You will not," he assured her. "The Jades have been uniquely cultivated."

"So I'll just be another naked body in your archives."

"We can discuss it," said Semerjean. "Or you can indulge me and let me finish my point."

"You had a point with the whole language thing?"

"I still do."

Hannah leaned against the wall and swept her hand in surrender. "You're the captor."

Semerjean's face lit up in a reminiscent grin. "One of my first lead roles as an actor was Hamlet, a modern retelling performed entirely in Ory'an. Though the stagecraft was exquisite, the rest of it was . . . not good. For all the practical advantages of our language, it didn't lend itself well to Shakespeare. Every line proved inferior to the original text, with one notable exception."

He summoned the illusion of a theater stage, plus the ghost of a stately old actor. The monarch kneeled in terror before Semerjean as he was forced to drink wine from a poisoned goblet. "When Hamlet finally gets his revenge on Claudius, he says something slightly cumbrous in the original play. 'Here, thou incestuous, murderous, damnèd Dane. Drink off this potion. Is thy union here?'"

Semerjean froze the action and cast a side-eyed look at Hannah. "But in the Ory'an version, the line was changed into something much simpler: *Nul'hassa e'nul.*"

"Nul'hassa e'nul," Hannah curiously repeated. "What does it mean?"

"'Now I send you to the void, which is all you've ever known.' It's a paradoxical expression in English, but in Ory'an, it's pure poetry. With just two words, Claudius is reduced to his bare, pathetic essence—from his pointless birth to his ignoble death, and all the temporal variations in between. A trillion lifetimes encapsulated and spit upon, the most perfect expression of vengeance. I still get goose bumps thinking about it."

Hannah crossed her arms, unimpressed. "So that's your point?"

"I'm just saying—"

"I know what you're saying. You want me to kill Evan already."

"I want you to *enjoy* it," Semerjean stressed. "He's a pitiful wretch beyond any hope of redemption. Put him out of his misery. Put him out of yours. And when you finally rid the world of his stench, remember the phrase I told you."

Try as she might, Hannah couldn't forget it. "Nul'hassa e'nul."

Semerjean grinned as if all was right with the world again, as if she weren't imagining herself standing over his corpse, throwing his own hateful words right back at him.

Six hours after his neurological episode, Evan finally regained consciousness. He sat on his cot with his back against the wall, his eyes bloodshot and flecked with dark circles.

"Terminus, huh?" Evan chuckled bleakly. "Well, shit. I guess that explains the blackouts."

Hannah had given him his terminal diagnosis without sympathy or schadenfreude—just a flat, even tone, as if she were merely discussing the weather. From Evan's cool and inscrutable reaction to the news, he shared every bit of her detachment.

"I'd ask how long I have," he said. "But I guess—"

"One year," Hannah told him.

"—it doesn't matter." Evan gestured at her console. "I can see my death right there on your brain box. That little black button you never talk about."

Hannah sat back in her recliner, her heavy thoughts churning in conflict. Evan was an abomination from any angle, a misogynistic psychopath who murdered people for kicks. No fate was too cruel for a man like him. So why was she having such a hard time?

Evan picked at a frayed fingernail, a wistful grin on his lips. "One thing even you can admit: I was pretty good at surviving."

"You've lived longer than I can even wrap my head around," Hannah admitted. "You afraid of what's next?"

"You mean the death itself or the stuff that comes after?"

"The stuff that comes after."

"There is no after," Evan plainly attested. "Though if you want to think of me in Hell, being forced to listen to showtunes—"

Hannah laughed. "I don't hate the thought."

"But you don't believe in that Heaven/Hell crap any more than I do."

"I don't know." Hannah's smile went flat. "It doesn't even matter. I'm only getting archived."

Evan matched her somber look. "I wouldn't wish that on anyone."

"Not even your worst enemy?"

"You're not my worst," he told her. "You're not even in my top three here."

"Is that why you helped us in Europe?" she asked. "As a middle finger to them?"

Evan shrugged. "I don't know why I do half the things I do. I just know that mirror room sucked. It really got me pissed at them, in a not so healthy way."

For once, Hannah related. She couldn't stop fantasizing about killing the Pelletiers: a litany of vicious scenarios, from the gory to the sublime. She imagined pushing them into a portal to oblivion, then watching them scream in the void. *Nul'hassa e'nul, you twisted motherfuckers.*

After a brief silence, Evan snapped out of his thoughts and snickered. "I used to have this crazy notion. Way back in my first weeks here, when I didn't know shit about anything. I imagined all the people who'd died on our world were watching us from the great beyond, like we were all just characters on a movie screen. They'd root for some of us, boo some others, laugh at our jokes, and go 'Awww' at all our big romantic moments."

Hannah eyed him strangely. "And this was a *good* thought to you?"

"I loved it."

"Having all those people judge you."

"I've been judged my whole life," Evan said. "And not very kindly. If the afterlife worked the way I hoped it did, then all the motherfuckers who made my life hell would be forced to watch me on the big screen and admit that they got me wrong."

Hannah wasn't sure what she pitied more: his delusions about himself or his loneliness. He so desperately wanted to be loved and accepted, but he didn't know how, and he was too far gone to figure it out. Even if he'd somehow found a way, the looping nature of his life (or lives) made it impossible to form lasting connections. He merely fluttered alone across the strings of time—up and down, back and forth—between the death of one world and another.

"I suppose it's a good thing that I don't believe in that anymore," Evan added. "I've done some stuff that . . . Well, let's just say it wouldn't play well in the theaters."

Hannah kept silent. He seemed closer than ever to acknowledging his sins, and if she opened her mouth now, he'd backpedal.

"But I did good in Scotland," Evan insisted. "Came up with the plan that saved a whole bunch of people."

"How did it feel?" Hannah asked him. "To be the hero for once."

"At the time, it was nice." Evan gestured around his prison cell. "But look where it got me."

Another minute passed before he made eye contact with Hannah. "I know you don't owe me anything, but if you could do me one big favor before you kill me—"

"Evan . . ."

"Just play something nice," he pleaded. "A little David Bowie. Some classic Queen. Hell, I'd even go for some 'Weird Al' Yankovic."

"Evan, I'm not going to kill you."

He looked at her the same way Semerjean had, as if she'd taken full leave of her senses. "What?"

"I'll never forgive you," Hannah swore. "And I sure won't miss you when you die. But I don't want to be the one to pull the trigger. Not here. Not like this."

She narrowed her eyes at the stark white ceiling. *Not while we hate the same people,* she thought.

"So what now?" Evan asked.

"I don't know." Hannah studied the console on her lap, the mysterious tool of her enemies. Evan had called it lots of different things over the past week: a brain box, a thought machine, a psychic Wi-Fi terminal. For a device that caused him so much pain, she would have expected him to find harsher names for it. But he'd only referenced its ability to link to her thoughts, as well as to the Pelletier systems.

What if he's trying to tell me something? Hannah suddenly wondered. He'd been a prisoner of Lárnach more than once, and he knew the Pelletiers better than anyone. What if there was a way to use their own technology against them, and he'd been hinting at it all this time?

She looked up at Evan in sudden surprise. "What?" he asked.

Hannah shook her head tensely. She knew as well as he did that they couldn't discuss it, not with their enemies listening. But if Evan was half as clever as he pretended to be, then he could find a coded way to tell her what she needed to know.

"I want to hear more about your life on the old world," she said.

"Why?"

"Because there are things about you I still don't get," Hannah replied, her finger tapping intently against the edge of the console. "And I think it's time I learned."

Evan noticed her finger, and for a moment he seemed entirely different. There was a spark in his eyes that Hannah had never seen before: a hint of emotion that, in the right light, looked a hell of a lot like affinity.

"All right," Evan said. "Let's talk it out."

THIRTY-ONE

Thirty-one.

Thirty-one.

Thirty-one days.

Hannah had been rolling the number around in her head, but she still couldn't get a grip on it. The Pelletiers had always measured her pregnancy from the starting point, and always in the same unit of time: five months, six months, seven months along.

But then just that morning, at the end of her health check, Azral had flipped the temporal compass on Hannah and turned her calendar into a countdown. Thirty-one days until her due (and die) date.

Thirty-one days to escape.

From the way her son kept thrashing inside her, he was feeling the pressure as well. *We're running out of time*, he said in his chimerical brogue, like

Peter on helium, or a nervous leprechaun. *You gonna do something about it, mother of mine, or will we be measuring my lifetime in minutes?*

Hannah wasn't sure if it was normal to imagine her unborn child speaking to her or just the product of her crumbling mind. She'd been carrying him for so ridiculously long that she could barely remember being one person. Even more jarring was the way he'd expanded inside her consciousness, from a concept to a prospect to a certified Given.

Luckily, Hannah had a plan to save him . . . or a semblance of one anyway. It required the help of a certain orphan, and Hannah was still cut off from the other inmates.

Frustrated, she sat down at her Pelletier terminal and sent Semerjean a new text missive.

It's been nearly three weeks since I talked to Eden and the others. I'd really like to know how they're doing. If you won't let me see them, at lea

Her message-in-progress disappeared from the screen and was replaced by bold red text: **Your social privileges have been restored.**

Hannah read Semerjean's response three times, mystified. She didn't expect him to fold so quickly.

I won't tell them about the underland, Hannah promised. **If you're worried about that.**

A full minute passed before Semerjean responded. **Tell them whatever you want.**

Hannah showered and changed into a smock wrap dress before opening a portal to the common lounge. She barely had a chance to step inside before she was mobbed by seven Gothams.

"Hannah!"

"Oh my God!"

"Where *were* you? We were so worried!"

"We weren't even sure you were alive!"

"I'm fine. I'm fine." Hannah scanned the group. "Where are Meadow and Helene?"

"Home," said a short-haired blonde, the traveler named Trinity Ryder. "They took the fast track out."

Hannah's stomach sank. Two more bodies for the Pelletier archives. Ten women left.

She looked across the lounge and was relieved to see Eden and Rosario.

Aside from their larger bellies and the new dark circles under their eyes, they both looked relatively healthy.

Thank God, thought Hannah. She had half expected Eden to be dead or archived. And she needed Rosario for what she was planning.

The young Pearl cut through the cluster of Gothams and hugged Hannah tightly. "Holy shit. I was starting to think you died!"

Hannah returned the embrace, smiling. "Your slang's gotten better."

"Yeah. I've been learning. Are you okay?"

"I'm fine." Hannah locked eyes with Eden and could see that she wasn't buying it. She looked to the others. "I need to talk to Eden a minute. I'll come back and catch up with you."

The two of them retreated into Eden's private woodshop, which had become overrun with ugly cedar ducklings. Eden pushed one off a folding chair, then set the seat out for Hannah. "Sorry. I don't usually entertain here."

"It's all right," Hannah said. "I missed you."

"I missed you too. I was fearing the worst." Eden studied Hannah carefully as she sat down. "Wow. You really don't look good."

"Thank you."

"I'm just talking about your eyes."

Hannah smirked and pointed at Eden. "Well, if we're going by that . . ."

"Oh, I'm a mess," Eden admitted. She clutched her bulging stomach. "I finally stopped caring what happens to me, but I just started caring about her."

Hannah nodded grimly. "My baby talks to me in my head."

"Mine talks to me in my dreams," said Eden. "She really doesn't want to be archived."

She read every twitch in Hannah's reaction. "Ah, so that's what it is."

"What?"

"That look of yours," Eden said. "You finally realized that none of us are getting out of here."

"Eden—"

"Just tell me what you know!"

"I don't want to push you over the edge."

"What edge?" Eden swept her hand at all the power equipment. "This place is totally suicide-proof. You think I'd still be here if it wasn't?"

Hannah cast a furtive glance at the door. "You can't tell the others. It'll break them."

"Tell them what? That we're all getting archived?"

"It's worse than that."

"How can it possibly be worse?"

Hesitantly, and with as much delicacy as she could muster, Hannah spent the next five minutes sharing everything she'd learned, from the biblical destruction of the underland to the hundred new bodies in the archives—Gothams and orphans, friends and acquaintances, plus one particular victim who Eden knew all too well.

"Oh my God." Eden sank to the floor. For all her dark hunches, she'd never guessed that her husband was in Lárnach. He'd been right there with her from the start: the father of her child, trapped in a state of living death. "Oh my fucking God. Those monsters."

Hannah sat down next to her, her eyes wet with tears. "I'm so sorry."

"Who else got archived?" Eden asked. "César? Nick? Maria?"

Hannah could only shrug. She didn't recall seeing any of Eden's Brown Irons, but what did she know? Esis had scrolled through the casualties so quickly.

"Amanda?" Eden asked.

Hannah shook her head. "She wasn't there."

"So she might still be alive."

"Maybe," said Hannah. "Semerjean said she made it out, but you know what that's worth."

"Yeah." Eden wiped her eyes. "She's probably just as screwed as we are."

Hannah wished she could tell her about her budding escape plan, even though it was just a sliver of a fragment of a half-baked theory that she had worked out in code with a psychopath. In rational light, it looked like a pure fool's dream, a bad end waiting to happen.

Eden rested her head against the wall, her grief quickly hardening into rage. "Oh God, I'm so sick of this shit. I'm sick of being angry and helpless all the time."

"Me too." Hannah scoffed with self-resentment. "I thought I was being clever by playing along, but I ended up believing Semerjean's lies. I let him fool me again and again."

"You did what you had to do to hold yourself together," Eden said. "And then you used that strength to hold the rest of us together. That's nothing to be ashamed of. If Amanda was here, she'd be proud of you."

Hannah brushed away her tears and squeezed Eden's wrist. "I love you."

"I love you too, but I think I might need, uh . . ."

"You want time alone to process."

Eden nodded. "I've got an ugly cry coming, and that's not the kind of thing I like to share."

"I get it. Believe me." Hannah clambered to her feet and scanned the lounge. Rosario and the Gothams watched her from the distant sofas, all nervously intrigued. "Gonna have to make up a reason for crying."

Eden chuckled bleakly. "In this place? Are you kidding?"

"Yeah. Good point." Hannah stepped out of the alcove, then glanced back at Eden. "Come get me any time you need me."

"Yes. Of course. I . . ." Eden paused in thought before speaking. "I'm sorry for all the crap I gave you. No matter how angry I got, I never stopped caring about you and I never lost sight of who you are. You're a strong, kind woman, and you never let them change you."

Eden clenched her jaw, her face wet with tears. "They never broke you. You remember that at the end."

As touched as Hannah was, she couldn't help but note the finality in Eden's tone. She spoke as if she were saying goodbye, but where the hell could she go?

"Eden—"

"It's all right," she said in a cracked voice. "We'll talk again later."

Rattled, Hannah spent the next hour catching up with the other inmates, evading all their questions like a skillful politician. The tale of Evan alone kept them ably distracted. Hannah didn't even have to embellish the story.

By the time the illusive sun began to set, the Gothams went back to their diversions. Hannah led Rosario to a quiet corner of the lounge and made a little more small talk before getting down to business.

"Are you still using that language machine of yours?"

"The Babel box," Rosario said. "Not as much as I used to. Why?"

"How many languages does it teach?"

"As far as I know, all of them," Rosario said. "I've seen some that I never knew existed, like Bambara and Marshallese."

"What about Ory'an?"

"Ory'an?"

"The language of the Pelletiers," Hannah said. "Did you ever see that as an option?"

"Not that I remember." Rosario turned suspicious. "Is there a particular reason you're asking about it?"

"I just think it's fascinating," Hannah said with loaded truth. "Semerjean taught me some last week, and I can't stop thinking about it. Like, you know how the Inuit have fifty words for snow? Well, Ory'an has just as many words for portals and teleportation. Or so I'm guessing anyway."

"You don't know."

"No," said Hannah. "But it's the kind of thing I'd like to learn, and I'd rather ask you than Semerjean."

She could see from the sharp new look in Rosario's eyes that the girl was catching on. She was every bit as clever as Eden said she was, almost preternaturally intuitive for a seventeen-year-old.

"I'll check out this Ory'an," Rosario pointedly replied. "If you think it'll benefit me."

Her subtext was obvious. *Whatever you're planning, it better include me.*

"It will," Hannah assured her. "I'm hoping it's something we'll all find usef—"

Sparrow shrieked from the other side of the lounge, startling everyone. Though Hannah couldn't see what had triggered her reaction, she recognized the room that Sparrow was looking at: Eden's woodshop.

Oh no . . .

A portal opened next to Sparrow. Three Pelletiers burst out of the disc and hurried toward the woodshop together.

Rosario clutched Hannah's arm. "What's going on?"

"I don't know. Come on." They crossed the lounge as fast as their addled legs would let them. By the time they joined the pool of rubbernecking Gothams, the Pelletiers had retreated into the woodshop and sealed it behind a thick wall of tempis.

"What happened?" Hannah asked Sparrow. "What did you see?"

"There was blood on the floor. A lot of it."

Rosario covered her mouth. "Oh no."

The tempic barrier split open, and a human figure moved toward Hannah in a streaking blur. Esis de-shifted in front of her and clutched her by the throat.

"Were you aware of this?" she yelled. "Did the two of you conspire?"

"Esis!" Semerjean rushed to her side. "Let her go. She didn't know!"

"On-ma röc," Azral said to his mother in a low but strident tone that clearly signified agreement. "Ni'hi-a wied'zala."

Esis dropped Hannah to the carpet and shot a sweeping glare at the other captives. "Idiots! Ungrateful children! I should kill you all and be done with you!"

Red-faced, gasping, Hannah peeked into the woodshop and saw exactly what Esis was raging about. There on the floor, in a puddle of blood, lay the indomitable Eden Garza. She met Hannah's gaze with frozen eyes, her throat slit open in a wide, triumphant grin.

She'd never cared a bit about woodcraft. If amusement had been her only goal, she would have asked for a more engaging diversion: a jet fighter simulator, or a gun range with Pelletier targets. The act of shaving wooden blocks into colorless, duck-shaped paperweights had been every bit as boring as Eden made it look. Yet she'd labored in her workshop, day in and day out, forging mallards out of cedar as if her life depended on it.

It wasn't until the day she died that her true intentions were revealed. The shop had been nothing more than a means to an end. It had only been her death that depended on it.

Eden had been smart enough to know from the beginning that the Pelletiers wouldn't trust her with power tools, at least not without installing safety measures to protect her from her own ill intent. Even the most basic handsaws went soft against her skin, as if the teeth had turned into foam rubber.

But while her woodworking tools were useless against flesh, they had no qualms about harming her mechanical hands. It wasn't like she'd die of circuitry loss, or develop a fatal infection in her servos. And if she was clumsy enough to cut off a metal finger, that was her problem and no one else's.

But Eden was smarter than the Pelletiers expected, and a hell of a lot more patient. Twice a day, while buffing her ducks, she'd pressed the pad of her thumb against her belt sander—just one Mississippi every time, as if she'd simply made a careless mistake. Her movements never raised a bit of suspicion, or a change in her biometric readings. And over the course of two hundred and thirty-one health examinations, neither Azral nor Esis had noticed for a moment that her right thumb was getting thinner.

By the time Hannah disappeared under ominous circumstances, Eden had finished her project. Her thumb had become so flat and sharp that she'd had to hide it in a wrap of electrical tape. At long last, she'd acquired a functional blade, one that wouldn't go soft at the thought of cutting her.

Of course, having it and using it were two different things, especially for a pregnant young Catholic. The rules were clear on suicide and infanticide, and a stubborn little part of Eden's mind kept insisting that there was a better way to avoid being archived.

But then Hannah came back and shattered her last illusion. There was no getting out of Lárnach, no home left to go to. Eden's last and only hope of escape was the one her blade offered. Even if the good Lord damned her to Hell, her daughter would get a clean start on the next world. It was better than having her soul trapped on this one, just a string of mindless ones and zeroes spinning endlessly in the Pelletiers' computers.

She'd also figured her death would piss off the fuckers, and she was proven right again.

While Esis raged around the lounge, and while Semerjean fought to subdue her, Azral scrutinized Eden's body with an unprecedented hint of emotion. From Hannah's low and slanted angle, it almost looked like he was grieving.

She struggled to a standing position, then looked to Eden again. "What about her baby?" she asked in a quavering voice.

Azral's expression hardened into its usual mask of stone. "Return to your domain."

"You can't even save her kid?"

He swept his hand at Hannah and the other prisoners, creating a floating portal behind each of them.

"Return to your domains," he snarled. "You're all sequestered until further notice."

Though the rest of the captives were forced to mourn Eden in solitude, Hannah still had one option for company. She teleported to Evan's prison cell, then sat silently in her recliner.

Evan watched her from the other side of the glass, perplexed. "Are you, uh . . ."

"Don't," said Hannah. "Just don't."

"I was only going to ask if you're okay," he said. "Guess it's a stupid question."

Hannah opened her mouth to respond, but her voice suddenly quit on her. Something had become wedged in the base of her throat: a dense ball of grief that she couldn't suppress or release, no matter what she did. Even the thought of Eden lying dead on the floor, her throat cut open in a bloody gash, wasn't enough to dislodge her emotions.

Evan read Hannah's face with clinical detachment. "Someone died."

She raised her head. "What?"

"You look like someone close to you died, and I doubt it's one of the Gothams. That leaves Eden and Rosario. I'm guessing Eden."

Hannah drank him in through wet red eyes, then pulled her console onto her lap. "How about I just kill you?"

"Hey, come on. I was only trying to—"

"*What?* What were you trying to do?"

"I was just trying to save you the trouble of telling me," Evan said. "I thought I was being nice."

"Nice." Hannah shook her head in dark wonder. "You can't even find your way back to 'human.' Why am I keeping you alive?"

"You know why," Evan calmly replied. "And I'm sorry."

"For what?"

"For Eden. She was your friend and she was a badass. I'm sorry that she's gone."

"Oh my God." Hannah wept into her hands. As if the universe hadn't gone crazy enough, Evan was suddenly offering his sympathies over a devastating loss.

"It was my fault," Hannah said through tears. "I pushed her."

Evan shook his head, clueless. "I don't—"

"You were right, okay? Eden's dead. She slit her own throat because I told her everything."

"Ah." Evan slouched in his chair with a wistful sigh. "You couldn't have known she'd kill herself. I didn't even think it was possible here."

Hannah wiped her nose. "She found a way."

"I told you she was a badass."

"*Badass?* Her baby was due in three weeks."

"Her baby was *doomed* in three weeks," Evan countered. "She knew the deal, and she did the ballsy thing."

"She should have cut *their* throats."

Evan pursed his lips in skepticism. "How do you think that would have ended?"

"Same way, probably."

"Worse," Evan said. "They'd do something far worse than kill her, and she knew it."

Hannah retreated into her mini-bathroom and washed her face in the sink. By the time she dried off and returned to her seat, Evan was huddled on the end of his cot. He wrapped his arms around his knees and stared at the distant wall.

"My mom killed herself when I was nine," he said. "Never left a note or anything. Just cut her wrists with a piece of glass, and then let us all deal with the fallout."

He checked Hannah's expression. "Now, you may think that's the secret origin of Evan Rander: Woman-Hater, but I didn't take it personally. She'd been depressed her whole life. Been in and out of hospitals since I was a kid."

Hannah listened to him with rapt attention. She was getting more from Evan now than she had gotten in fifty lifetimes.

"She was actually in a hospital when she killed herself," Evan told Hannah. "On suicide watch and everything. Despite all their cameras and safety measures, she still found a way to beat the system."

Hannah didn't know if the story was true. She was too busy processing the subtext. Evan had proven to be deft at the art of coded conversation, enough for Hannah to read between the lines. He was making a point through allegory, and it was a damn good one.

The Pelletiers never saw Eden's death coming. She hadn't just fooled their security systems, she'd slipped through every crack in their foresight.

"How?" Hannah sharply asked Evan. "The doctors at that hospital should have been ten steps ahead of your mom."

"You'd think so, yeah. It was a top-notch place. But even the world's smartest pricks can step on a rake, especially when they're losing their shit."

Hannah struggled to keep an even expression. She thought she'd been imagining the Pelletiers' strain, but even Azral looked tense and unrested. "You're saying the doctors were in trouble."

Evan mulled his words carefully before responding. "That hospital was on the verge of shutting down. From what I recall, it did."

"Why?"

Evan shrugged. "Who knows? Maybe it was just a case of bad luck. Maybe they bit off more than they could chew. Or maybe their whole mission statement was flawed. All I know is that those last weeks there were . . . not a good place to be."

Hannah's thoughts spun wildly in all directions. She'd lived so long in the shadow of evil gods that she'd almost lost sight of their weaknesses. The

Pelletiers had staked everything they had on a scientific theory, and had convinced themselves that victory was a given. But nature apparently had other ideas, and now it was setting them straight.

No wonder the bastards were coming undone. Decades, even centuries of their lives, all wasted on a wild-goose chase. The more they grappled with that realization, the more unhinged they'd become.

Hannah was suddenly in danger of laughing herself silly. Only the bleak thought of Eden kept her wild emotions grounded.

You should have held out just a little bit longer, Hannah thought. *We might have been able to save you.*

"How's Rosario?" Evan suddenly inquired. "She and Eden were tight. She must be all kinds of sad."

Hannah knew what he was really asking about: the status of the escape plan. It now depended entirely on a seventeen-year-old orphan and her ability to learn Ory'an.

"She'll manage," Hannah told Evan. "That language machine of hers really helps her cope."

From his look of relief, Evan caught her true meaning. They had their third conspirator, and she was ready to get to work.

Hannah couldn't have picked a better accomplice in Rosario Navarette. The girl had grown up in the slums of Guadalajara and had been surviving on her wits since she was ten. The black market smugglers used to pay her top dollar for her preternatural skills at subterfuge. She could prowl through any restricted area, cross any checkpoint, deliver any package without a hint of suspicion. And when her employers needed a strategic distraction, Rosario was always there to save the day. She was a prodigy at improvisational acting, able to use her small stature and innocent face to lower people's expectations.

Even Semerjean didn't detect her performance when she came crying to him in the wake of Eden's death.

"I'm a wreck," she said, the truest lie she'd ever told. "I just keep seeing her on the floor like that. I can't get it out of my head."

Semerjean nodded sympathetically. "You've done better than most to distract yourself. Are you sure you can't—"

"I'm tired of that stupid Babel box. All the languages are the same."

"Are you looking for a different diversion?"

"I'm looking for a different language," Rosario said. "Hannah told me about yours. Orcan."

"Ory'an," Semerjean said with a chuckle, though Rosario knew full well what it was called. "That's not an easy tongue to learn, especially for someone of your age."

"My age."

"Your era," Semerjean clarified. "You don't have the temporal perceptions to become fluent."

"I'm not trying to become fluent," Rosario insisted. "I'm trying to be distracted."

Semerjean muttered at the floor, his expression tense and perturbed. "Ic'sal a-na késhen."

"What?"

"My wife's upset and summoning me. I have to go."

"I need something to focus on. Please!"

Semerjean mulled over her request a moment. "If you want to try Ory'an, I'll install it on your console. But I imagine you'll find it more frustrating than gratifying."

If anything, he'd undersold the problem. While the Babel box made the study of languages fascinating, like walking through the house of an eccentric stranger, Ory'an proved to be an utterly baffling ordeal, like being trapped in an alien maze. Rosario needed a week just to get her linguistic bearings, and then another five days to form a toddler's grasp of the grammar.

"It's crazy," she told Hannah. "There are forty different words for 'teleport,' and at least fifty conjugations of each. I don't even get half the stupid verb tenses. I get a headache just thinking about them."

Hannah nodded with feigned apathy, as if it were all just chitchat instead of a matter of survival. Her baby was due in eighteen days, and she was still behind most of the others. A few of the Gothams were already in the golden zone. They could pop at any moment.

Rosario saw the stress behind Hannah's calm façade. "I think I might be reaching my limit with Ory'an, unless there's some interesting part I haven't discovered yet."

Hannah could easily translate her comment: *What the hell am I looking for, and why?*

"Those portal words sound pretty interesting," Hannah said. "I'd love to hear as many of them as you can remember."

"Now?"

"No." Hannah peeked at the other women in the lounge, then fidgeted with the hem of her blouse. "Soon."

Though she'd never seen the Pelletiers more distraught and disorganized, Hannah refused to underestimate them. She knew she couldn't try anything until all three of them were distracted, which limited her to one tragic option. She had to wait for an inmate to go into labor, a sacrificial lamb for the others. Hannah felt so sick and guilty about it that she could barely keep a meal down.

"You can't save everyone," Evan told her. He'd been talking about his stint as an Altamerican firefighter, but his real point was obvious enough. "Sometimes you find yourself in a tricky situation where it's now or never, us or no one. It sucks, but what can you do?"

Hannah shot him a skeptical look through the glass. "Easy for you to say. You don't give a shit about anyone."

"Oh, come on. I thought we moved past that."

"What, you think we're friends now?"

"No. I just thought that maybe you understood me better."

"I do," Hannah admitted. "But I feel like I've sunken down to your level instead of bringing you up to mine."

Evan laughed and shook his head. "Wow. Okay."

"What?"

"You think you're Joan of Arc because you got knocked up for your sister?"

"It's one more sacrifice than you ever made."

"So you'd lay down your life for any woman here."

"Any woman who isn't Esis."

"So there you go," Evan said. "Your moral ass is covered."

"What do you mean?"

"Consistency," he explained. "I won't be a martyr for anyone, and I don't expect them to be a martyr for me. But if you're willing to take that proverbial bullet, then it's okay to expect one of the women here to take the same kind of bullet for you."

Hannah finally understood his point, and it only made her feel worse. Only a loveless son of a bitch like Evan would view sacrifice as a transactional balance. But he was right about one thing: there was no saving everyone from the Pelletiers. That ship had sailed with Mercy Lee, and it had flat-out sunk with Eden.

Hannah was thirteen days from her projected due date when nature chose its next victim. Moira MacDougal was a good-natured lumic, the only second-time mother in Lárnach. She'd had a child at sixteen with a young local outsider, a scandal that had rocked the Gotham clan and forced her to give up the baby for adoption. She had only volunteered for the Pelletier "mission" to save her broken reputation. Hannah found it ironic, in an infuriating kind of way, that Moira had to use one out-of-wedlock pregnancy to absolve the so-called sins of the other.

Moira was knitting a scarf in the common lounge when she hunched forward in her chair and hollered in pain. Her water had broken five days ahead of schedule, making her the first prisoner of Lárnach to take the slow road to the finish line.

Right on cue, the Pelletiers teleported into the lounge and spirited poor Moira away. Their portal had barely finished closing before Hannah tossed a resolute nod at Rosario. *It's time.*

Hannah spoke into her traveler's bracelet. "Portal. Evan."

The remaining six Gothams watched Hannah intently as she addressed them from the edge of the gateway. "I think it's time you guys met Evan Rander."

The others reacted with surprise and revulsion, as if she'd just offered them a plate of her stool samples. Hannah hadn't told any of them about her crazy escape plan, even in coded talk. It would have only jeopardized the effort, as none of them had Rosario's discretion.

"Why would we do that?" Trinity asked Hannah. "You said he was awful."

"Yeah, well, I've been beating him down for a couple weeks, and I finally made a breakthrough. You really need to see it for yourselves. All of you."

"I don't want to," said Sparrow. "I'd rather wait to hear how Moira's doing."

Rosario tugged Hannah's arm. "Come on. Let's just go."

"No!" Hannah felt bad enough leaving Moira to her fate. She refused to abandon the others. "I've bent over backwards for you guys, and I've never asked for anything in return. Well, now I'm asking you to come with me. *Please.* It's really important."

After another minute of begging and cajoling, Hannah finally got the Gothams to agree.

Evan's mouth fell open in a comical gape as eight pregnant women stepped out of the portal, then crowded into Hannah's side of the cell. "Holy shit. You brought the whole Mormon Tabernacle."

Not all of them, Hannah thought with remorse.

"You realize you just—"

"Yes." Hannah was more than aware of how suspicious it looked, and what it did to their time frame. They'd be lucky if they had more than a minute or two before Semerjean came barging in. "Ladies, this is the prick I told you about. Prick, meet the ladies."

Evan smiled and spoke through gritted teeth. "You just killed us all, Given."

"Shut up." Hannah sat down in her easy chair and pulled the control console onto her lap. "Why don't you show them some of the charm I taught you?"

Artemis Rosen, the tallest and burliest prisoner of the bunch, looked down at Evan in bewilderment. "*This* is the man who caused you so much trouble? He's barely even a nugget."

Evan turned to the others in mock confusion. "Can someone translate what she's saying? I don't speak Bear."

"He doesn't seem particularly reformed," Sparrow noted to Hannah.

"Hey, I know you," Evan said to her. "You're that bird girl. Titmouse."

"*Sparrow.* And I never met you before in my life."

"Not this life, no, but I definitely remember you. You were the easiest lay in the wing squad."

The Gothams gasped with collective outrage. Artemis thumped her fist against the glass. "You're lucky I can't get to you, you shit-mouthed little bastard!"

"I'm sorry. I still don't understand you. Do you want salmon? I don't have any."

Rosario whispered into Hannah's ear. "What the hell's going on?"

"He's creating a distraction," Hannah whispered back. "Tell me some of the words you learned."

Rosario looked to Hannah's console. "Wait. Is that—"

"Just tell me! Quick!"

Even if Hannah had more time, she would have been loath to explain it. When spoken out loud, the plan seemed even crazier: to mentally hack into Lárnach's neural network and unlock the teleport functions. If Evan was right, then it was entirely doable. The Pelletiers wouldn't bother to protect their system from Hannah, in the same way they wouldn't hide their passwords from the family dog. What harm could Hannah possibly cause? She didn't even speak the language.

"Bish'tel-ma," Rosario muttered to her. "Means 'teleport me.'"

Hannah cupped her hands around the edges of her console, her eyes closed tight in concentration. *Bish'tel-ma.*

She peeked down at her keypad and saw its usual configuration. Of course it wouldn't be that easy. "Next one."

"Bish'tel-a'ma," Rosario said. "Same thing, more immediate."

Bish'tel-a'ma, Hannah thought, to a similar lack of result.

Evan checked on Hannah nervously before forcing a smile at Sparrow. "Hey, I'm not insulting you. I'm totally on board the 'free love' wagon. But from the rumors I heard, you and your brother Nuthatch—"

"His name's *Finch,*" Sparrow yelled. "And don't you dare—"

"I'm just saying I heard you both give a flying fuck, if you know what I mean."

"Oh my God." Trinity looked to Hannah. "Open the portal. I'm not spending another minute with this creep."

Artemis noticed Hannah and Rosario in tense collaboration. "What are you guys doing?"

"Hey, hey, hey," Evan said. "Let's focus on me here."

"Fa'sir-u ciet'a," Rosario told Hannah. "'Make an exit now.'"

Fa'sir-u ciet'a, Hannah thought. *Please let this work.*

Nothing. Artemis studied Hannah's console with amazement. "Holy crap. I've seen that thing. That's what Azral uses to send people home."

Trinity looked to Hannah. "Are you trying to—"

"Shhh!" Evan said. "For fuck's sake, show some sense!"

"You're in on it," Sparrow openly realized. "You're working with her."

"Oh my God." Evan shook his head at Hannah. "Pack it in. We're done here."

"No!" Hannah turned to Rosario. "Give me another!"

"We've already tried the ones I know!"

"That's it?" Evan cynically asked her. "Two weeks of study and that's all you got?"

Rosario shot him a seething glare. "Fuck you. It's complicated."

"I thought you were smart."

"And I knew you weren't," Rosario replied. "I learned everything I need to know about you from Ofelia."

"She hasn't even met me yet."

"No, but she knows you," said Rosario. She motioned to the other women in the room. "We all know men like you."

Evan chuckled bitterly at Hannah. "Thanks again for bringing the whole hen squad. You just killed our only chance to—"

"Shut up." Hannah kept her eyes closed and her head bowed. "Everyone just be quiet."

She felt stupid for ever thinking she could escape this way. The Pelletiers were the smartest and most prescient beings on the planet, centuries ahead of everyone else. They were probably laughing at her from another room while she fumbled and flailed about.

That's bullshit, said a voice in her head, an echo of the late Eden Garza. *You saw them after I killed myself. Did you notice any of them laughing?*

How did you do it? Hannah had to ask. *How did you know it would work?*

Eden's chuckle echoed throughout Hannah's consciousness. *I didn't,* she said. *I just thought about my baby. And then I got mad.*

Yes. The thought of Robert's little body in the Pelletier archives was enough to make Hannah want a bladed thumb. Except she wouldn't use it on herself like Eden had. She'd hunt down her captors with a madwoman's fury and make them all pay for their sins. And as the last spark of life dissolved from the eyes, she'd curse their whole existence in their own native tongue: *Nul'hassa e'nul.*

Rosario did a double take at the console. "Holy shit! Hannah!"

Hannah opened her eyes. "What?"

"Your keypad! It just went red for a second!"

Evan nodded his head, wide-eyed. "I saw it too. What'd you do?"

"Oh my God." Hannah could have smacked herself. She'd been throwing empty words at the Pelletier system, when all it needed was a phrase that she understood. And thanks to Semerjean, she knew "Nul'hassa e'nul" all the way down to its deepest meaning.

Now I send you to the void, which is all you've ever known.

Hannah watched in amazement as the keypad changed right in front of her, from blue English buttons to red Ory'an glyphs.

"You did it!" Artemis shouted. "Which one makes the portal?"

Hannah was pretty sure that they all did. The controls were entirely contextual and catered to her immediate desires. The buttons were just for precise coordinates, but Hannah didn't think it mattered. Wherever they went on the face of the planet, Ioni would be able to find them. If all went well, she'd snatch them up before the Pelletiers could pull them back.

"Hannah." Evan threw her a pleading look from the other side of the glass, his finger pointed at the edge of the barrier. "If you put the portal right there in the middle, there'll be enough room for all of us to get out."

"Forget him," Rosario said to Hannah. "He doesn't deserve it."

"It was my plan," Evan insisted. "I deserve half a portal at least."

"Enough," said Hannah. The clock was ticking. She gripped the console and aimed her thoughts at the wall. *Give me seventy percent of the portal on my side of the glass,* she commanded. Evan could squeeze his way out if he was careful.

A ten-foot portal opened up on the eastern wall, but something went wrong in translation. At least sixty percent of the disc fell on Evan's side of the glass. The women only had a curved and narrow piece of exit: twenty-four inches at its thickest width, and sharp as a blade around the edges.

"Shit!" Hannah waved her companions toward the portal. "Go! Go! Hurry!"

The next ninety-nine seconds were some of the longest of Hannah's life as her people staged their one and only chance at escape. They lined up single file with their backs against the glass, their hands pressed tight against their swollen bellies while they attempted to squeeze through the portal.

Artemis shook her head at Hannah, crying. "I can't do this. I won't fit."

"You'll make it," Hannah said.

"I'm six foot one and nine months pregnant!"

"I can help you," said Trinity. "I've gotten bigger things through smaller portals."

Hannah looked to Rosario at the end of the line and saw her bouncing on her feet in a panic. She was no doubt thinking what Hannah was thinking. *This is going too slow. We're not all going to make it.*

"Hannah."

She looked beyond the glass and was shocked to see Evan still there. He had all the room in the world to leave, yet he lingered behind with a look on his face that Hannah had never seen before. If she hadn't been so frightened, she might have recognized it as concern.

As she approached the glass at the far end of the cell, he joined her at the other side. "Cut the line," he told her. He jerked his head at the portal. "You made this happen. You earned your spot."

"What do you care?"

Evan watched Sparrow depart, then looked back to Hannah. "I may not share your moral code, but I know what's fair. If you get stuck here—"

"Evan—"

"Just cut the line!"

"Evan, *listen* to me." Hannah pressed against the glass, her face just inches from his. "It doesn't matter to you if I get out. Your way is clear. You're going to go back to the people I love, and you're going to help them win in San Francisco. I don't care how many rewinds it takes. I don't even care if it kills you. You're going to see all of them through to the finish line, and stop this shit for good."

Evan shook his head. "Hannah—"

"You'll *do* this," Hannah stressed, "not because I told you to, but because this is the very last year of your life. The terminus will get you no matter where you run. So take this one last chance you have, and do something good with your power. You hear me?"

Evan peeked at the portal nervously. "I don't have a choice," he said. "Without Ioni's protection, my ass will be right back here."

"Then *earn* it," Hannah urged him. "Go!"

Evan hurried to the portal, then looked at Hannah one last time. "Cut the line."

By the time he fled through his share of the exit, four Gothams had wriggled their way through the portal, and Trinity was helping Artemis escape. Hannah cringed with guilt at the sight of Rosario: the young girl stuck behind the older one. She wanted to shout at Trinity for not letting her go first.

"Hurry up!" Rosario yelled. "We're almost out of time!"

To her credit, Trinity delivered on her promise to help Artemis out, and the young traveler was every bit as small as Rosario. They'd both only need a fraction of the time that Artemis took to get through.

Maybe this'll work out, Hannah thought. *Maybe we'll all—*

A tempic tendril suddenly burst out of a ceiling portal and snaked around Trinity's waist. Hannah barely had a chance to look at her before she was yanked away.

"Oh no!" Rosario rushed for the exit, but a new disc opened up beneath her feet and swallowed her whole, like a whale's mouth.

"Rosario!" Hannah watched her disappear, her face a ghostly white sheet. "No!"

All three portals closed in synch, leaving Hannah alone in the prison cell. Except she could see the hint of a man's reflection in the glass, one of the handsomest faces she'd ever come to loathe.

Semerjean stood behind her easy chair, her console clutched at his side. As it crumbled to ash in his mortic grip, he kept his stern blue eyes on Hannah.

"Why?" he asked her.

If she hadn't been so furious, she might have wept at the tragedy of the situation. There were now just three prisoners left in Lárnach, and Hannah had the misfortune of being one of them.

She walked toward Semerjean in an even keel, her dark eyes narrowed to slits. "Nul'hassa e'n—"

He struck her hard across the face, enough to drive her down to the floor.

"You're saying it out of context," he calmly informed her. "And you didn't answer my question, so let me rephrase."

He grabbed Hannah by the hair and dragged her across the floor, until her face was pressed against the glass of Evan's cell.

"He was your *enemy*," Semerjean hissed. "A man completely undeserving of clemency. Yet you let him go at the cost of your own freedom. *Why?*"

Hannah mumbled something into the glass, prompting Semerjean to release his grip on her. "What?"

"Because you were wrong," Hannah repeated. She shot a cold dagger stare at Semerjean, her bloody lip curled in a sneer. "I hate you more."

THIRTY-TWO

Her last days at Lárnach were almost shockingly quiet. No howling castigations from her jailers. No paralytic torments. She merely puttered around her dungeon in a contemplative silence, like a cloistered monk in a remote Himalayan temple. The Pelletiers had stripped her cell down to its barest vital elements: a cot, a couch, a bathroom in a box. Everything else was just flat white tempis as far as the eye could see. Hannah's domain looked so vast without its illusions that she could barely tell the walls from the ceiling. Her living space had been placed right in the middle, just a few paint daubs on an otherwise blank canvas.

Though her punishment seemed mild in light of her crimes, Hannah didn't think for a moment that she was forgiven. Her stark-white environment was a constant middle finger, as if the Pelletiers had brought her all the way back to the scene of their first apocalypse. *This is all that remains of your homeworld,* said the void. *This is all that remains of your life.*

If there was an upside to the Pelletiers' anger, it was that she didn't have to suffer their company. The health checks had been suspended indefinitely, while Semerjean stopped his visits. The only time they even acknowledged her existence was when they delivered her manna by portal: food and drinks, a fresh change of clothes, even a few creature comforts. They included a bag of her favorite chocolate eggs, as if to insist they were civilized oppressors.

Civilized, her child said with a scoff. *No one can do what they do to babies and still pretend to be good. I'm minus five days old and even I know that.*

Hannah could feel Robert's notional wrath turn her way. *Not that you're any better. You had a chance to get me out and you blew it.*

"I know," Hannah somberly replied.

You screwed us both, Ma.

Hannah wandered the expanse of her prison cell, her finger brushing against the tempic wall. She'd had little to do these past eight days but amble and nurse her regrets. If she had just left Evan to his well-deserved fate, she could have used the whole portal for her girlfriends. They would have all escaped with time to spare, and Hannah would be back with her people.

Don't forget Rosario and Trinity, Robert said. *You doomed them and their babies too.*

Sighing, Hannah returned to her cot and settled in for another bad spell. The nights in her dungeon (if they could even be called that) were the worst. The fluorescent glow of the tempic walls penetrated her eyelids, making meaningful sleep a chore. Worse, the light cast horrible shadows in her mind, drawing arrows to thoughts that were best left buried.

Dad always loved Amanda better. He barely hid it.

I was never really that good at acting. I should have just been a singer.

I barely think about Jonathan at all these days. I think about Peter too much.

If the Pelletiers are our future, then fuck the world. Just end it.

I don't have any fight left in me.

Hannah woke up the next morning and found a strange new addition to her living space: a mirror twin of all her furnishings, planted right next to hers on an identical rug. From the sizable lump on the bedspread, it seemed Hannah wasn't alone anymore. But her cellmate was hidden entirely beneath a blanket.

She wasn't moving at all.

Oh no. Hannah crept toward the bed, her hands clenched tightly at her sides. For all she knew, the Pelletiers weren't done torturing her. Maybe she'd lift the cover to find Rosario's corpse, or Trinity's, or half of each fused together.

"Hey." Hannah poked the body through the blanket. "Hello?"

She flinched when the figure began to writhe. A young brunette poked her head out from the covers and looked around in a sleepy daze. "Hannah?"

"Rosario!" Hannah sat on the bed and hugged her. "Oh my God. Are you okay?"

"No." Rosario scanned the vast white cell. "Did you get moved or did I?"

"I don't know." Hannah pulled down the blanket to confirm that Rosario was still pregnant.

Of course she is, young Robert chided her. *You think she'd still be breathing otherwise?*

"Did you see Trinity?" Hannah asked her.

"Yeah. They put us together."

Hannah stopped herself before she could ask the next question. The hopeless look in Rosario's eyes told her everything she needed.

"She went into labor," Hannah guessed.

Rosario nodded grimly. "They came for her last night."

"Shit." Hannah fought back tears, even though Trinity had never been the most pleasant or enlightened Gotham. She'd still referred to the orphans as "breachers," and had pestered Hannah with ignorant questions about her native United States. *Did they really let foreigners into the country? How did you manage with all the crime and disease?*

Yet despite all her shortcomings, Trinity had sacrificed her place in the escape line—sacrificed *herself*—to help Artemis through the portal. That alone earned her a better fate than the one she got.

"I'm so sorry," Hannah said to Rosario. "It's my fault we didn't get out."

"We were mad," Rosario admitted. "Trinity especially had some not-so-nice words. But if it wasn't for you, we'd all still be here. It's a miracle you saved even five of us."

Six, Hannah thought, but she could understand why Rosario didn't count Evan. What did it matter, anyway? The two of them were still in dire straits, the very last pair to the gallows. The fact that they were allowed to spend their final days together was an unexpected kindness, one that Hannah wasn't entirely sure how to interpret. Was Semerjean trying to convince her of something, or was he only trying to convince himself?

Rosario brushed the tears from her eyes. "Guess we're all out of options, aren't we?"

Hannah nodded. "Yeah. Even if we had a way to get out, they'll be watching our every move."

"So what do we do?"

Hannah mulled it over, her finger tapping her thigh. Though she'd lost her will to fight the dark forces, she didn't take her existence for granted. Every moment of life was a precious gift. Every minute spent in the company of a loved one was a victory against the void.

"You told me you were a smuggler in Mexico," Hannah said.

"A smuggler's helper," Rosario corrected. "I was just a kid."

"Well, you must have been good if they were willing to pay you."

"Are you kidding? I was the best."

"Really." Hannah folded her legs up onto the bed, then held Rosario by the hands. "Tell me all about it."

The next four days passed like an eccentric theater production: two pregnant young women on a near-empty stage, discussing everything under the sun while they casually waited for death. Hannah would have never expected her life to resemble a Samuel Beckett play, but there it was: her new reality.

Stranger still, a part of her enjoyed it. She couldn't remember a time when her existence had been so simple. No schedules or demands, no choices or dilemmas. Even the pressing concerns of the outer world had been bleached away in the whiteness. There was just a Silver, a Pearl, and their doomed little passengers. With each new day, their worries drifted more and more inward, until their two babies dominated every thought and topic.

"I was going to name him Robert," Hannah confessed. "I guess I did. I'm still not sure it's the best pick."

Rosario lay on her side on the facing cot, her body propped on a half-dozen pillows. "Why not?"

"Because it was my dad's name, and we never . . ." Hannah shrugged and sighed. "I was always closer to my mom."

"Can't you boy up your mom's name and give it to him?"

"Boy up 'Melanie'?" Hannah laughed. "I'd have to call him 'Mel.' That ain't happening."

Rosario only grinned for a moment before turning solemn again. "I never knew my mother, so my choice is easy." She glanced down at her bulging stomach. "My girl's name is Eden, now and forever."

Hannah's eyes welled up at the thought. "That's beautiful."

"No it's not. It's tragic."

"It's both, okay? Just shut up and work with me."

Rosario chuckled. "I keep trying to convince myself that archiving is painless. That it's all just like a pleasant dream."

"I think it's more like another version of death."

"It's the one good thought I have. Don't ruin it."

"I'm not trying to ruin it," Hannah insisted. "There's a silver lining to my theory."

Rosario tilted her head, perplexed. The Pelletiers had uploaded English into her brain, but had left out the contemporary idioms.

"An upside," Hannah clarified. "If archiving is death, then our souls get to leave. Only our bodies will be trapped in their machines."

Her young cellmate eyed her skeptically. "I don't believe in that stuff."

"You don't have to," Hannah told her. "I'm not that religious myself."

"But you believe in the soul."

"I believe that death is just a transition to something we don't understand," Hannah said. "Something we *won't* understand until long after we get there."

Rosario chewed her lip in thought. "It sounds much less stupid that way."

"Thank you."

"I like the idea of both Edens getting a chance on another world."

"*We* did," Hannah reminded her. "We're living proof that—" She sucked a sharp breath and clutched her abdomen in pain.

"You okay?" Rosario asked her.

"I'm okay. Just a little cramp."

"Hannah . . ."

"I'm *fine*. I swear."

They'd both been experiencing the same sporadic spasms: a quick and painful tightening in the core of their bellies. The doctors on the old world had called them Braxton-Hicks contractions. The Gothams simply called them the Preludes. For Hannah and Rosario, they were the beginning of the end, a coin toss with no good outcome. One of them would be the next to go, while the other would become the last lonely victim.

Rosario helped Hannah to the couch, then propped her feet up on a folding chair. "Tell me about the afterworld," she said as a distraction. "I'd like to hear your theory."

"I don't think it's just one world," Hannah mused. "Not after everything we've seen. Maybe our souls split off into parallel versions, and we each go a trillion different ways."

Rosario sat down next to her. "You think we'll remember who we were?"

"I hope so, because there are a lot of people I'd love to catch up with." Hannah gazed off into the whiteness. "If it turns out my sister's already gone, then I'll know exactly who to visit fir—"

She hunched forward and cried again. Rosario gripped her arm. "Oh God. Please tell me it isn't happening."

Hannah would have leapt at the chance to deny it. She still had three days till her due date, and she'd had false alarms that felt worse than this. But from the frequency of the contractions, and the new, wet warmth between her legs, it seemed the dreaded moment had finally arrived. Her son was coming into the world, and the Pelletiers were coming for both of them.

They took her from one white room to another—a considerably smaller space than her prison cell, barely the size of a studio apartment. The only furnishing was a floating bed, tilted upward at one end to keep her head raised, and split at the feet to keep her legs apart. Hannah only had a limited range of motions, thanks to her creepy new gown. It moved across her body like sentient milk, constraining her limbs to a limited range of motions and projecting a floating screen above her stomach. Hannah figured that it was a window to her womb, though she could barely see it from her vantage.

"How is he?" she asked Azral and Esis. "Is he okay?"

They'd been buzzing around her bed for nearly an hour, dressed once again in their sapphire scrubs. Though she couldn't see their expressions behind their reflective face masks, she could tell from the petty way that they ignored her that they were still furious. Neither one of them bothered to speak to her or comfort her. They merely let her sweat and writhe as they muttered to each other in Ory'an.

"Well, fuck you too," Hannah said between shallow breaths. "You think I want to be here with you assholes? I'd sooner—"

A new and seemingly endless contraction made her yell out in pain. When it finally subsided, she turned her head away from the Pelletiers and wept.

Oh God, she thought. *This can't be it. This can't be the way I go.*

It is, said the voice of her son, as Irish as he'd ever sounded. *It's how we're both going. Best not to dwell on it.*

He made a fair point, and another one by inference. If these were her last conscious minutes of life, and if her imagination still worked for her, then she could ride out the clock around a better class of people than Azral and Esis. She could bring all her loved ones back for the grand finale.

It's all right, said the Amanda in her head. *We're here now.*

She envisioned Theo squeezing her shoulder. *We're staying right with you to the end.*

Hannah opened her tear-drenched eyes, then summoned her entire family: four Silvers, one Gold, a stubborn Irish Gotham, and all the women she'd loved at Lárnach but hadn't been able to save.

You got this, said Mercy, the first one to fall. *I know it hurts—*

"I don't care about the pain," Hannah weakly replied. "I just want him to live."

Of course you do, Moon said. *You're a mother now, and your love makes you stronger than ever.*

Eden jerked her head at a pair of shapeless blurs, which Hannah could only assume were Azral and Esis. *Stronger than* those *fuckers*, she said. *If you could see their faces right now, you'd know how much they're freaking out.*

Heath nodded in agreement. *All their plans are falling apart, and they're finally starting to see it.*

Hannah gritted her teeth at the pain of a fresh contraction. "It doesn't matter. My kid's still screwed."

Screwed? asked Peter, the father of her child. *There was a time we thought your sister was screwed. And then you came up with a plan.*

"It was our plan."

You talked me into it, remember? Now here we are at the tail end of things, and you've got a whole 'nother Given to save.

"So-bäishya," Esis snapped to Azral. "Gef'ha-meer no-kiena!"

Ignore them, Zack urged Hannah. *Think. There's no way out of this for you, but the door's not closed on Robert.*

And Rosario, Ofelia added. *You can save her and her child too.*

Hannah shook her head, grimacing. Even if she had something left to trade, there was no one left to trade with. She'd burned all her bridges with her captors.

Except the one who's not here, Mia bitterly reminded her. *The weakest one, too chickenshit to even face you.*

"No," said Hannah. Semerjean was by far the worst of the Pelletiers. He'd proved it more than once.

That may be, Melissa said. *But you still have a special history with him, and that history gives you power.*

Amanda agreed. *Use that power. Use your head.*

My whole life's depending on it, her little boy told her. *Please, Mother. Save me!*

Hannah sat up in the gurney, her face soaked in sweat. "Semerjean!"

Esis pushed her back down. "Be still, you fool!"

"Shut the fuck up." She fixed her resolute gaze on the ceiling. "I know you can hear me, Semerjean, so listen. I have a new proposal for you."

Azral scoffed at her hubris. "You have nothing more to offer us."

"I'm not *talking* to you!"

Azral reached for Hannah's neck with two extended fingers. "Stïl'zin."

"Wait!" yelled a voice from the periphery. "Let her speak."

Hannah turned her head and saw Semerjean standing near the wall. Like his wife and son, he'd come dressed in a shielded bodysuit, but the glass of his visor was nonreflective, giving Hannah a clear view of his face. She could tell from the unnerved look in his eyes that the voices in her head had been right. Whether he liked it or not, he still cared what she thought about him.

"Azral's not wrong," Semerjean cautioned Hannah. "At this late stage—"

"It's not too late," she insisted. "I'm only twenty-five. That still gives me time."

"Time for what?"

"Time to make you more babies," Hannah said. The contractions were coming in fast and hard, forcing her to speak through agonized wheezes. "I'll make you five in a row. All I ask is that you let Rosario go. Give her her baby. Give her mine."

The Pelletiers reacted with matching surprise, a slack-mouthed look that might have been comical under better circumstances.

Hannah kept her attention on Semerjean. "You already know I'm a woman of my word. I made you an offer a year ago, and I kept my end of the bargain. Now I'm promising you right here and now that I'll make you five babies however you want, and I won't cause trouble again. You can even archive me at the end of it. I don't care. Just let Rosario go. Give her her baby and give her mine."

Azral and Esis conferred in Ory'an. Hannah didn't have the strength of mind to decipher their tones. It was only Semerjean that mattered in this negotiation. Just her and him.

"You're a son of a bitch," Hannah said to him. "But you understand us in ways your wife and son don't. You played one of us for months. You *were* one of us. You know we hate death just as much as you do, and we'll do whatever it takes to save the people we love. All we want is for them to have more time. We want our *children* to have more time."

She felt a hard new pressure in the center of her being: a violent, wrenching upheaval, as if she were being turned inside out. She grunted and groaned and pushed with all her strength, then locked her crying eyes on Semerjean.

"I'm not asking for charity," she said between gasps. "I'll work for it. But you have to give me the one thing I ask. Let Rosario go. Give her her baby. Give her m—"

Azral waved his hand over her eyes. "Presz'pa."

Hannah felt her senses fall violently away from her, as if they'd been thrown out the door of an airplane. She tumbled helplessly through the folds of her fading consciousness, a twirling little object in space. She could have been falling for seconds or weeks. She had no idea. All she heard, as the liquid embrace of darkness overtook her, was a shrill little noise in the distance. It hit her like a cry from the heavens—a high and piercing wail, as if somewhere far away on another world, a child had taken his first breath.

She woke up on a bed in a sunny beach cottage, her body in disarray, as if someone had rewired all her muscles. She needed a full ten seconds to get her physical bearings, then another five to recognize her environment. The cathedral roof, the window walls, the pedestal genie in the corner. Someone had returned her to her prison cell and switched it back to the "Malibu dreamhouse" setting. The scene triggered such a strong sense of *déjà vu* that Hannah feared she'd been sent back in time. Maybe she was doomed to relive her pregnancy over and over. Maybe that was the true hell of the archives.

But a quick scan of her midsection was enough to correct her. While her belly was no longer a cumbersome sphere, it bore the fresh new marks of motherhood, from the loose white skin, to the distended navel, to the discolored line of skin up her abdomen: the linea nigra. And if she'd somehow managed to miss those clues, she'd apparently produced some milk in her sleep.

I'm still here, Hannah thought with astonishment. *Still alive.*

She washed up in the bathroom and changed her shirt, her mind frantically exploring the options. There was clearly a reason why the Pelletiers hadn't archived her yet, but she couldn't imagine that any of them were good. And what did they do with her son?

With slow, creaking torpor, she settled onto the settee of her seaside porch and watched the lapping waves. Whatever was happening, Semerjean would eventually come by to explain it. The best thing she could do for herself was wait and stay calm.

Sure enough, an hour later, she heard footsteps from inside the house. Her heart began pounding a timpani beat, and all the fears that she'd been holding back suddenly flooded her from a dozen directions.

He's gonna tell you that Robert—

Gonna tell you that Robert—

Gonna tell you your baby—

He's gonna tell you everything they did to your poor little baby, before they do it all again to you.

By the time Semerjean joined her on the settee, Hannah was already crying. She clenched her teeth and kept her eyes on the ocean, afraid to even look at his face for fear of confirmation.

"You've been out for three days," he informed her in a low and exhausted voice. "During that time, Rosario had her child. A six-pound girl in perfect health."

Hannah closed her eyes tight as the baby's name hit her like a slap. *Eden.*

"Your son was born at seven pounds, three ounces," Semerjean added. "Not as flawlessly healthy as Rosario's baby, but very close."

Hannah spoke in a small and distant tone, more breath than voice. "Don't."

"He has a microscopic defect in his occipital lobe that will eventually impair him in some fashion. Dyslexia, dysgraphia, maybe trouble with numbers. It's a mostly moot issue, since—"

"Please don't."

"Don't what?"

"Don't tell me he's gone," Hannah said. "I don't want to hear it. I can't."

Semerjean shook his head. "He's sleeping right now in our nursery."

Hannah finally turned to look at him, and saw the strain on his face. Though he was the youngest Pelletier by physical appearance—barely twenty years old, if a day—his eyes were noticeably cracked and weathered, enough to make them look middle-aged.

"It's been a dramatic few days for my family," Semerjean admitted. "We've had . . . many arguments. The only reason you're still here is because I won. At least for the time being."

Hannah narrowed her eyes suspiciously. "Rosario?"

"Nursing her child as we speak."

"Holy shit." Hannah's heart thundered all over again. "You're taking my deal."

"We're accepting the premise, not the terms."

"What do you mean?"

"You offered five pregnancies," Semerjean said. "My counteroffer is eight."

"Eight?"

"One for your child's freedom. Two for Rosario and her daughter. Five for the Gothams you took from us. Seems a fair enough trade, considering."

Hannah watched the waves a moment before answering. "Fine."

"These will be all *in vitro* fertilizations," Semerjean assured her. "With three months to rest between pregnancies."

"I don't care."

"You'll stay right here the entire time. We'll monitor your health remotely."

"I *said* I don't—" Hannah looked at Semerjean in surprise. "Remotely, as in no daily visits from Azral or Esis."

Semerjean nodded. "They would prefer that as much as you would."

A delirious chuckle escaped her. "Well, shit. You just made it easy."

"Easy." Semerjean scoffed. "There'll be no more bargains after this. No amnesty for you or any of your future children. If you get attached to the next one—"

"I won't," Hannah swore. "I thought I was prepared. I wasn't. I won't make that mistake again."

Even as she said it, she could hear the sharp objections from the chorus in her head: all the people she loved, united in their disbelief. *You can't! You won't! It'll happen again! You're just setting yourself up for more pain.*

I don't care, Hannah told them. *I'll do whatever it takes to save Robert.*

Semerjean studied her quietly, his eyes only showing a hint of turmoil. "You know you're not buying much for your sacrifice."

"What do you mean?"

"Your son," said Semerjean. "He'll die next week in San Francisco, just like everyone else you know."

Hannah struggled to keep her emotions in check. Among the other revelations of the day, it seemed that the outside world had progressed to the end of September. Nearly six weeks had passed during her seven months in Lárnach.

"You still want to go through with the deal?" Semerjean asked her.

"Of course I do. What's my alternative?"

"You can rest," he said. "Whatever you think of archiving, it's a lot gentler than eight more pregnancies. No one would think any less of you."

Hannah laughed derisively. "Holy shit. How were you ever an actor?"

"What do you mean?"

"You were supposed to understand us before playing one of us."

"I thought I did," Semerjean confessed. "The Silvers were a greater challenge than I expected, you most of all. Even now, you keep finding ways to surprise me."

Hannah wasn't sure if it was a compliment, an insult, or both. She didn't care. The weight of her new future—the sheer misery of it—was finally starting to sink in. Was she really going to spend eight more years in this awful place, just to buy Robert a week?

"I want to see my boy," she demanded. "I want to see them all before they go."

Semerjean nodded. "I figured you would. We'll leave in a minute."

"Look—"

"I'm sorry I struck you," he said out of the blue. "It was uncivilized and misdirected. It was only my negligence that allowed you to stage that escape. I'd underestimated you yet again."

Hannah didn't care a whit for his contrition and praise. She was more tripped up on his twisted sense of ethics. He'd never once apologized for helping to destroy her world. Not once.

"Can we please go now?"

"One more thing," Semerjean insisted. "A question that's been vexing me."

Hannah could already guess what it was. "You want to know why I let Evan go."

Semerjean nodded. "He'd done nothing I could see to earn your forgiveness. Yet you went out of your way to give him a piece of that portal, knowing full well the harm he could do. I've been pondering it for two weeks, and I still can't make sense of it. Why did you do it?"

Hannah took another long look at the ocean horizon before turning to Semerjean again. "You wouldn't understand."

"Try."

"I don't think so."

"Why not?"

"Because I only agreed to make you babies," Hannah said. "It's not my job to educate you."

She rose to her feet and shot him a thorny glare. "Now take me to my goddamn kid."

To call the place a "nursery" would be stretching the word to the snapping point. It was little more than a cozy lounge, a miniature clone of the common area that the Pelletiers had given their captives. Same couches. Same genies. Same fake mountain view. The room struck Hannah as an afterthought, and why wouldn't it be? The infants of Lárnach were only meant to be archived. Nurturing them was never part of the plan.

Still, the Pelletiers had made some effort to keep the two babies comfortable: a pair of bassinets, a baby tub, an assortment of clothes and linens. They provided a bed and chair for Rosario, the mother of one child and default nanny of the other.

She had just finished putting her daughter down for a nap when Hannah and Semerjean arrived by portal. She blinked at them in a hang-jawed stupor, her eyes red from strain.

"Holy shit." Rosario hugged Hannah. "I thought he was lying when he said you were alive."

"I'm okay. I, uh . . ." Hannah glimpsed the rim of her son's bassinet, then nervously refocused on Rosario. "How are you holding up?"

"I'm tired, I'm sore, and I'm very confused. Why haven't we been archived?"

Hannah looked to Semerjean. "You didn't tell her?"

He shrugged. "I was waiting for the deal to be finalized."

"What's he talking about?" Rosario asked. "What deal?"

"He'll explain it," Hannah said. She peeked at the bassinet again, then froze at the sight of a tiny, flailing arm. "Oh God."

Even seeing just a piece of her son was enough to send her thoughts into panic. A part of her wanted to run like hell and pretend she was never here.

Why bond with a child that she'd have to give up in minutes? Why even *look* at him?

Rosario clutched her shoulder. "I know what you're feeling. I went through the same thing. It's weird and it's scary, but you have to see him. He's yours."

All the sound in the room became white noise to Hannah as she took a full look at her child. At first glance, he was just a stranger again, a writhing little creature in a turquoise blanket and a white cotton cap. He could have been anyone's progeny. He could have been whipped up in a lab.

But then Robert opened his tiny eyes, and Hannah recognized them immediately.

"Oh my God." She covered her mouth with both hands, crying. "They're blue. His eyes are blue like Peter's."

Somewhere in the fringe of her awareness, she heard Semerjean say something about melanin. Some blue eyes change to brown over time, but his might not, et cetera, et cetera. Hannah barely listened. She was too busy scrutinizing Robert's face. He had his father's eyes, his mother's lips, and a nose that looked like a compromise. Hannah could even spy a few resemblances to his other living relatives, all the tiny little hints of Amanda and Liam that had worked their way onto the canvas. If there had been any doubt in Hannah's mind, it was utterly eradicated. The boy was a Given and a Pendergen, a Gotham and an orphan.

Half-orphan, Hannah darkly reminded herself. *He'll never know me after this.*

"You can hold him," Semerjean said. "If you wish."

Hannah shook her head in terror. Though her motherly instincts were still painfully new, she was aware enough to know the consequences. If she picked up her baby, she'd never let him go. If she smelled him even for a microsecond, she'd become one with him all over again. There'd be no way to remove him without killing her.

By the time Hannah forced herself away from the bassinet, Semerjean had explained the new deal to Rosario.

She looked at Hannah with teary rage. "You can't do this! It's not right!"

"Rosario . . ." Hannah held her by the shoulders. "It's okay. He still has family. You're going to take him to his father and aunt."

"I can't just leave you here!"

"I'll be all right." Hannah gestured at Robert. "Just knowing that I got him out will carry me through the rest of this."

Rosario turned her wet glare onto Semerjean. "Why can't you just let her go?"

"It was hard enough to secure *your* release," he said. "They're livid about it. In fact . . ." He cast a nervous glance at the door. "I suggest we act quickly, before one of them reconsiders."

He moved to the distant corner of the room and summoned a console out of the floor. Hannah had no trouble recognizing the make of the device. She'd recently used one just like it to liberate five friends and an enemy.

Semerjean punched teleport coordinates into the keypad. "Get the children," he told Rosario. "You won't have to carry them long before Ioni finds you."

Rosario looked to Hannah guiltily as she retrieved Robert and Eden from their bassinets. Her choking sobs were loud enough to make both babies cry. "I hate this."

"I know," said Hannah. "But it's the only way. You have to take it."

As soon as the portal appeared against the wall, Hannah instantly lost her bravada. She remembered parting with Moon under similar circumstances, and that had proven to be a tragically short trip.

She tossed a distrustful look at Semerjean. "Wait. How do we know—"

He secured Hannah's body in a tight tempic harness, then thrust her twenty feet through the portal. True to his word, there was freedom on the other side: a wide and sunny grassland with lush green mountains in the distance. Hannah assumed from her previous talks with Semerjean that she was somewhere in the wilds of China. Wherever it was, it was almost certainly no illusion. The air felt crisp in a way it never did in Lárnach, filled with scents too complex to be simulated. Hannah had almost forgotten how good the real world tasted, even from the end of a leash. It was her first breath of fresh air in seven months, and probably the last one she'd ever take.

Semerjean yanked her back through the portal, a hint of a sneer on his lip. "Satisfied?"

"Yes. Just get on with it."

Despite Rosario's vocal objections, she didn't waste any time getting out. The girl was a lifelong pragmatist, and she'd already learned the hard way not to tarry in the presence of an escape portal. She held the bundled infants close to her chest, then threw a teary glance over her shoulder at Hannah. "*Nos vemos en el próximo mundo.*"

Hannah furrowed her brow. "Something about the other world?"

"The next world," Rosario explained. "I'll see you there."

Hannah lowered her head and wept as Rosario carried the children away. The portal had silenced the sounds of their wailing, as if they'd been swept into the depths of a milky-white sea.

"Shit." Hannah brushed the tears from her eyes. "I forgot how much portals hurt the first time. He must be in so much pain."

Semerjean shook his head. "You teleported frequently while he was *in utero*. His body has already adjusted."

"Good." Hannah ran her finger along the lip of Robert's bassinet. "Guess I'm ready to go back to my cell."

Semerjean took in the portal with heavy blue eyes, one of the most woeful looks that Hannah had ever seen on him. "What is it?" she asked. "What's the problem?"

"You stayed true to your resolve to the very end," he said. "You didn't falter. You didn't even beg."

Hannah didn't like the grave tone of his voice, or what it suggested. "What are you saying, that this was only a test?"

"No test. Just me trying to understand you."

"So that whole thing about making more babies—"

"We're done with those," Semerjean said. "We've produced countless hybrids in multiple timelines, and not a single one of them has helped us."

"Then why am I still here?"

"I don't think you understand the gravity of our situation, Hannah."

"Yeah. I get it. You guys are fucked up the ass."

Semerjean scoffed with distaste. "I see why you don't write your own musicals."

"Am I wrong?"

"If you mean to say that our life's work is ruined, then no. You're not entirely wrong."

Hannah might have expressed her lack of sympathy if Semerjean hadn't left the portal open. Was it just an oversight, or was he building up to a—

No, she told herself. *There's no way this ends with you getting out of here.*

"You're right," she said to Semerjean. "I don't understand the gravity of your situation. I don't even know how it could have gone wrong. I thought you guys were the best augurs in the world."

"My wife and son are," Semerjean corrected. "My terminus has all but blinded me."

"But *they* saw a cure in the future."

"Yes." Semerjean looked to his feet with a doleful expression. "We've been chasing that string for nearly as long as I can remember, longer than Azral's been alive. But the future evolves in ways we can't always control. Old roads close. New ones open. Sometimes the whole landscape changes. And sometimes, when our desire's strong enough . . ."

He self-consciously lowered his voice, as if Azral and Esis were listening.

". . . we see things that were never there."

Hannah wished she could take pleasure in the Pelletiers' sorrow, but there were too many distractions in the way. Her motherly grief, her nebulous future, Semerjean's selective despair. Billions of people had died in their crusade, and he was moping over his family's crushed hopes.

"So what now?" she asked him. "You pack up and go home?"

Semerjean looked at her in rumination, as if he were deciding between the truth and a lie. "We have one last avenue to explore," he said. "Your people would call it a 'Hail Mary' play."

"Is that why you're keeping me?"

"No." Semerjean smirked with impenetrable humor. "You're not the proverbial Mary in this scenario."

"Then why am I here?"

"Because Azral and Esis hate you," Semerjean said, as if it were the most obvious fact in the world. "Have you forgotten the way that you insulted them, or robbed them of five pregnant Gothams? Because I assure you that they haven't."

Hannah was deathly afraid to ask her next question, but the words slipped out anyway. "What are they going to do to me?"

"You really want me to describe it?"

"If I'm dying today—"

"That would be a mercy," Semerjean said. "What they have in mind is worse. My wife wants to remove your arms and legs and leave you dangling in a cold room for months. My son, on the other hand, is far more practical in his vengeance. He simply wants to convert you into an asset."

"An asset," Hannah said. "Like the Jades."

"Yes. He thinks it'll be suitably ironic to send you to war against your own people."

Hannah blanched at the awful thought of it. "Which one did they decide on?"

"Decide?" Semerjean chuckled bitterly. "They have every intention of doing both."

Hannah's knees buckled. She teetered on her feet. "And what do *you* want?"

He fidgeted with his wedding ring, his heavy gaze fixed on a bassinet. "At this point, Hannah, I just want to rest. I'm tired of fighting. Tired of struggling. Tired of hating my enemies. And I'm tired of watching people die. I've seen more than enough of it for one lifetime."

Hannah nodded her head with vacant gloom. "You just explained it perfectly."

"Explained what?"

"Why I let Evan go."

Semerjean drank her in through cool blue eyes, his face an inscrutable wall. "Do you ever wonder how your life would be if my family had never come to your world?"

"All the time."

"And?"

Hannah shrugged. "I'd probably still be an actress in San Diego, with a crap-ton of debt and a shitty relationship with my sister."

"I met that Hannah years ago," Semerjean said. "You're superior to her in every way."

Hannah didn't smile at his compliment, as sincere as it sounded. "You think I owe you for making me stronger?"

"No. The credit is yours and yours alone."

"And you think I'll be 'superior' when your wife takes my arms and legs?"

"No." Semerjean shook his head ruefully. "That is not a fate I intend for you to suffer."

"What are you talking about?"

She took a nervous step back as his right fist encrusted with tempis. "Whoa. Wait a second . . ."

"There's another great expression in Ory'an," he said. "A complement to 'nul'hassa e'nul.'"

"Semerjean—"

"Kal'yanna la'mori."

"Don't do this."

"It means 'Die with the people you love.'"

"What?"

The last thing she saw before everything went black was Semerjean thrusting his hand at her. Everything after that was just a blur in her consciousness: a cold smack of tempis, a vengeful momentum, a twirling sense of disorientation, as if she were rolling blind down a steep and grassy hill.

By the time her body stopped moving and she recovered her tactile senses, she was flat on her back on an abrasive surface, all rocks and weeds from the feel of them. She opened her eyes and saw Heaven above her, a pristine canopy of blue sky and clouds, marred only by the familiar silhouette of a friend.

"Rosario?"

"Hannah!" Rosario crouched to the ground and held her. "What *happened*?"

"I don't know." Hannah sat up with Rosario's help, then took a bleary-eyed scan of her surroundings. She was back in the empty Chinese field, without a tether this time. The portal to Lárnach was nowhere to be seen, just a flat and empty expanse of nature, with two blanket-wrapped infants within reach.

Hannah took no relief from her new status quo. If she'd learned anything from Semerjean, it was to never trust the news at face value, especially if it was good. He was probably toying with her emotions out of pure spite and hatred. Why remove her arms and legs when he could take a chain saw to her soul?

Rosario looked just as skeptical. "I thought you were dead when you came flying out of the portal. I didn't think he'd just—"

"Free me," Hannah said. "No. I still don't believe it."

"What do we do now?"

"There's no point walking," Hannah said. "Someone will come get us."

"Someone," Rosario cynically repeated.

Hannah didn't have to spell it out for her. If Ioni, the good witch, was coming for them, then they'd be home free in minutes. But it was just as likely that Azral and Esis would get there first and drag them all back to Hell.

Robert cried from his resting place, as if his mind were stuck on the latter outcome. Hannah pulled him into her grip without thinking, her body moving on pure maternal reflex. There was a whole new switchboard of functions inside her that were completely alien to her. The buttons might as well have been labeled with Ory'an glyphs.

"Shhhh." Hannah held her son against her chest and fought the urge to tell him that he'd be okay. Why start their relationship on a possible lie?

"I'm here," she whispered to him. The words triggered an unexpected joy in the core of her being, enough to prompt her to keep talking. "I'm here, you're here, and neither of us are there. We're free and we're together, and it feels so nice. It feels like the whole world is right again."

As her little boy's anguish settled down to soft gurgles, Hannah experienced a curious epiphany. Maybe life was more than just a fight for survival. It was a nonstop quest for moments like this, all the little golden treasures hidden throughout the strings. A billion other Hannahs could have walked the same road without ever discovering this bliss. What an absolute gift from the powers of fate. What a perfect reward for her struggles.

Rosario clutched her daughter defensively, her nervous gaze aimed upward. "Hannah . . ."

She craned her neck and saw a new shimmer in the sky: a translucent membrane of . . . something. It surrounded Hannah and the others in a fifty-foot dome, like a soap bubble made of pure energy.

Rosario followed Hannah to her feet, wide-eyed. "Is this them?"

Even if Hannah had known which "them" Rosario was referring to, she couldn't have answered the question. "No idea."

A new portal bloomed to life in the near distance, a few yards inside the edge of the bubble. Hannah's heart pounded wildly against Robert's body as a willowy woman emerged as a silhouette. Though she was way too tall to be Ioni Deschane, she moved with a grace that had thoroughly eluded Esis. She was an entirely different player in the game, though not a new one by any stretch.

"Oh my God." Hannah let out a delirious laugh. Even before the woman became defined in the light of the sun, Hannah knew who she was looking at. Nearly anyone on Earth would have recognized her: the Angel of London, the flying wonder of Europe, the harbinger of strange days to come.

Amanda fixed her wet, smiling eyes on her sister, then beckoned her with a tempic hand. "Come on. We have to hurry."

Hannah and Rosario made a mad dash across the grass, their children bobbing against their torsos. On some deep level, among her last few embers of rational thought, Hannah knew the reason for Amanda's urgency. The shield would only deter Azral and Esis for so long. And if they managed to break through, it would be a disaster for everyone. They'd be able to trace a portal line all the way to Ioni's hideout.

Yet none of those concerns stopped Hannah from hooking her free arm around Amanda and pulling her into an embrace. "Oh God. I can't believe it."

"I know," Amanda said, her voice choked with tears. "It's all right. You're all right."

"Where are the others?"

"Just on the other side of the portal," Amanda replied. "Come on."

Despite her resolve, she pulled back from Hannah and studied her nephew in awe. "Oh my Lord. He's beautiful."

"Amanda . . ."

"I know. I know. Let's go."

Wisely, Rosario had already escaped with her daughter, leaving three Givens alone in the bubble. With a thundering heart and a head full of clouds, Hannah took a tight grip of her sister's hand, then smiled in the light of the portal. She was still riding high from one of her life's sweetest moments, and she could already see the edge of the next one.

PART FIVE

THE GIRL WITH TWO WATCHES

THIRTY-THREE

Sergelen had never been known for its looks. Even by the standards of the Chinese army, the world's leading innovator in utilitarian joylessness, the research base was a dismal sight: eight and a half acres of drab gray concrete with shoebox buildings stacked together like coffins, plus a thirty-foot rampart that blocked every view of nature. The empire had prisons that were nicer to look at, and twenty years of abandonment hadn't made Sergelen any prettier. Nearly every square inch of the exterior had been overrun with chickweed, rust, and bird droppings.

For the newest residents of Sergelen, the five hundred and twenty-one survivors of Quarter Hill, the place felt more like a punishment than a sanctuary. Zack had taken to calling it Sergatory. And like most of Zack's names, it stuck.

But an interesting change occurred every morning as the first light of dawn cracked above the mountains. For eighteen minutes, the sky cast a violet glow across the premises, adding luster to the concrete surfaces, while veiling their cracks and blemishes. When combined with the glimmer of Ioni's protective cloakshield, Sergelen could have almost been mistaken for a magical place: a training camp for sorcerers, or a college for elves and Hobbits.

Theo stood on the southern bulwark and took a sweeping look at the compound. The view alone was worth getting up for, but the silence made it a blessing. Sunrise was the sweet spot of calmness at Sergelen, the transitional respite between the night owls and the early birds. No one was awake to pester him with the usual questions: "What's going to happen in San Francisco?" "When does the Cataclysm start?" "Does [insert name of loved one] really have to fight there?" "Theo, are we all going to die?"

He felt an all-too-familiar twinge in his foresight, then turned his head to the left. There she was, right on schedule, standing next to him on top of the wall.

"Morning," Ioni said with a melodic yawn. She tore open a silver foil pouch, then offered a share of its contents. "Breakfast?"

"No thanks." After six straight weeks of military rations, Theo would have preferred a bowl of fingernails to those freeze-dried steak and eggs. "You're supposed to add water to that."

"Gross." Ioni munched on a piece of crystallized egg, her sleepy gaze fixed on the dorms. "So who are we worried about today?"

"Artemis Rosen. She—"

"I know her. She's Rebel's niece."

"And one of the Gothams that Hannah saved."

"Right," said Ioni. "What happens?"

"Nervous breakdown, sometime before noon."

"Violent?"

"She's a tempic."

"Shit." Ioni clicked her tongue in sympathy. Poor Artemis had escaped the Pelletiers, only to learn that her family had died in the underland. She had trauma and grief on top of postpartum depression, and there wasn't a single psychologist to help her.

"All right," Ioni said with a sigh. "Take her to Protection."

"I already plan to. There's just one problem."

"Her baby," Ioni guessed.

"Her baby," Theo confirmed.

"Double shit." Ioni rapped her knuckles on the railing, her hazel eyes dancing in thought. "Give him to Candy Ballad."

"Candy Ballad." Theo thought that Ioni was making a joke. The name sounded like a bus song for kindergarteners. "I don't know her."

"She lost her toddler in the massacre," Ioni said. "She's hanging on by a thread. A baby will force her to hold herself together. She'll make a good mother to him."

"Temporarily, you mean."

The grim new look on Ioni's face did not bode well for Artemis.

"Jesus," said Theo. "You're going to put her in the front lines."

"Like you said, she's a tempic."

"She won't be in any condition to fight."

"She'll have to be. Who's our next problem?"

Theo rubbed his upper left arm, which had suffered a clean but nasty break in the underland, and had been bound in a cast for six weeks. Though the bone had fully mended itself, it was still sore and testy from its long ordeal and throbbed with pain at the slightest disruption.

"Ofelia," he said. "She's still looking for Evan. If she finds him—"

"—she'll eviscerate him." Ioni cursed under her breath. "She needs to let it go already."

"He killed her brother."

"I killed Zack's. You don't see him gunning for me."

"You were trying to save the whole world's future," Theo reminded her. "Evan killed Jury just for fun, and he still has no regrets about it."

"Doesn't matter," Ioni said. "We need him."

"I can try talking to her again."

"No." Ioni chewed down another hard morsel of egg. "This is Evan's mess. Let him do the heavy lifting."

"You mean talk to her?"

"I mean hide from her. I'll handle it."

Ioni brushed the crumbs off her little white top, just one of a thousand cotton tees that she had purchased from a Beijing reseller. Though the shirts ran the gamut in size and color, they all had the same Chinese lettering across the front, the Mandarin slang for "Lucky Woman." It was all she could get in bulk on short notice, to the consternation of some of the men. Theo couldn't have cared less about wearing a misgendered shirt. He would have sung first chair in the Lucky Woman Choir if it actually brought good fortune.

Ioni shook the last of her breakfast into her mouth, then dissolved the bag with mortis. "Anyone else going to be a problem today?"

"Yeah," said Theo. "Me."

Ioni tossed her hands up. "This again?"

"I keep dreaming about Winthrop Park," he told her. "Something about holding a light."

"Theo . . ."

"I don't know what it means, but I know it's important." He toyed with Ofelia's silver bracelet, still dangling from a chain around his neck. "And I know it's connected to this."

"Theo, *listen* to me." Ioni gripped him by the shoulders. "I need you to focus on the immediate future. I can't have you jumping ahead."

"You're afraid of what I'll see there."

"I'm afraid of what we're not seeing here," she said. "Breakdowns, revenge killings, anything that cuts our number. We lose one more person—"

"I know."

"Then help me. *Please.*"

Theo broke out of her grip and paced the bulwark. His life had been so much easier when he had Melissa to keep him sane. But she'd gone ahead to San Francisco, in preparation for the final conflict. She'd never set foot in Sergelen again, the lucky woman.

Ioni leaned on the railing and looked down at the courtyard. The pretty violet sheen was already starting to fade, and the first early risers were stepping out of the dorms. "Theo . . ."

"No other issues for today," he reported. "At least not any life-or-death ones."

"And Hannah?"

Theo paused, grim-faced. "She won't be a problem."

"I'm asking how she's doing."

"How do you think? She's still catching up on who lived and who died, and the mood here's making her crazy. This wasn't . . ." Theo rejoined Ioni at the railing, his expression more dismal than ever. "This wasn't the reunion she was hoping for."

Ioni matched his dour look. "I heard how Heath reacted to her."

"Yeah. He thinks she's a Pelletier clone or something."

"She's not."

"Of course she isn't," said Theo. "But they still could have put something inside her. I have a hard time believing they'd just let her go."

Ioni shook her head. "They didn't give her her freedom. She took it from them. She weaved that string from her own pain and suffering."

Theo suddenly felt the strong urge to cry. "Please don't do it."

"Do what?"

"Don't put her on the front lines," he begged. "She's not ready."

"It doesn't matter where I put her. The war will find its way to her."

"You mean *they'll* find her."

"Yes," said Ioni. "She still has a chance of surviving it, but only if she's ready. You understand me?"

Theo understood perfectly, but he still didn't like it. One of the most cherished people in his life had just clawed her way back from Hell, with a head full of nightmares and a new baby son. Now she only had three days to recover and get back into shape for the most crucial fight of her life. Lucky woman.

She woke up in a concrete cellar, her body splayed diagonally across a pair of twin-size mattresses. The only light in the room came from a narrow sliver of window at the corner of the wall and ceiling, barely enough to let Hannah get oriented. From what Peter had told her, they were inhabiting the former office of a Chinese nuclear physicist, one of the first men to die in the great radioactive disaster. Not the nicest environment for a newborn child, though Peter had assured Hannah that they'd be out in a couple of days.

"And then what?" Hannah had asked him. "Where do we go after San Francisco?"

Peter had merely shrugged at her, as if she'd asked him when the sun would explode. His mind was hopelessly stuck in the tangible present, on the surprise new member of their family. He'd spent half the night studying Robert in awe, his expression as bewildered as the baby's.

But in the dim light of morning, both father and child were nowhere to be found.

"Shit." Hannah's scarred and ragged psyche took her to the worst places first. Maybe Peter had teleported Robert to God-Knows-Where in an act of desperate protectiveness. Or maybe the Pelletiers were attacking the base. They could have shrunken themselves down to atomic size and ridden Hannah like a Trojan horse into Sergelen.

Soon the door creaked open and Peter returned with their son. He sat down on his wheelchair with Robert in his lap, then deactivated his new feet and ankles.

"Sorry," said Peter. "The boy was getting ornery, and I wanted you to sleep. I took him for a walk around the commons."

Hannah was stunned to see Peter walking at all. His original legs ended just below the knees, with a strange metal cap on each stub, like sieves. On Peter's command, they produced tempic prosthetics: sturdy, responsive, and fully capable of sensation. To hear him tell it, he could feel the whole world through his soles.

Unfortunately, Ioni's technology worked better on her own people than on a man from Peter's era. His new feet required so much mental exertion that he could only walk for minutes at a time. He spent most of his day in a squeaky Chinese wheelchair and saved his tempis for when he needed it the most.

Hannah kneeled at Peter's side and ran her fingers through Robert's thin weave of hair. "Well, whatever you did, it worked."

"Oh, he's easy," Peter said with a smile. "He got all his mother's strength and goodness. You can see it from a mile away."

Hannah felt a new cry coming on. She must have sobbed a full bucket since coming to Sergelen, most of them happy tears. But there was a lot of bitter to take with the sweet: all the friends who'd died in the collapse in the underland, all the broken and grieving survivors. Hannah had wept when she saw Caleb—his scraggly beard and dead, haunted eyes. He'd asked Hannah if Mercy had suffered much, and she couldn't find the strength to lie to him.

Peter saw the gloom on her face. "You okay?"

"Yeah," she replied with a squeeze of his thigh. "Just processing."

Even in the low light of the cellar, Hannah could see the strain of recent events on Peter. He had new crow's-feet around his eyes, and a frailty to his movements that hadn't been there before. She knew it was more than his injuries at play. Something terrible had happened to Liam a few weeks back that no one wanted to talk about, least of all Peter. All Hannah could get out of anyone was that the boy was still alive.

Yet Peter was nothing but smiles around his other son. He lifted Robert high in his arms and studied him from below. "Lord, he is something, isn't he? I still can't get over it."

"Yeah, me neither," Hannah said. "I only met him ten minutes before I got here."

"Well, you've certainly taken to motherhood."

Hannah laughed in sharp dispute. "You saw when I tried to feed him."

"It's not your fault. He could have tongue-tie."

"Tongue-tie?"

"Just a minor thing some babies get," Peter said. "Makes it hard to form a latch."

Hannah shook her head, flustered. "Shit. I don't know any of this stuff. I'm not even remotely ready."

"Yeah you are." Peter caressed her hair. "You fought the devil himself to keep him alive, like any good mother would. That love right there is the main job requirement. The rest is just details."

Hannah squeezed his hand. "I missed you."

"I missed you too." He chuckled feebly. "When you think about the way we got together—"

"Forget that," Hannah said. "We're in this now, you and me."

"Hannah . . ."

"Even if we're not a traditional couple, we're both going to raise him together."

"Hannah, *listen* to me."

She stopped to hear him out, only to watch him stumble on his words. "You . . . remember the party we had back in July? When those corpses came out of that portal."

Hannah nodded darkly. "It's hard to forget."

"It was a time portal," Peter said. "I was talking to Ioni about it the other day—"

He paused midsentence, then looked to the door. "Your sister's here."

"What?"

Sure enough, a soft knock came. Hannah rose to her feet, rattled. She'd never seen Peter sense a tempic before. Apparently he was one of their kind now, at least from the knees down.

Amanda stood in the hallway in a worn pair of jeans and a shirt that had become all too familiar to Hannah. She'd already received her own paltry clothing allotment: two LUCKY WOMAN tees, one pair of pants, two shoes, four socks, and a pittance of ill-fitting underwear.

"Sorry to come by so early," Amanda said. She held up a device in her hand. "I just thought you'd want this as soon as possible."

On first glance, Hannah thought she was delivering a plastic air horn, until her groggy mind caught up. "A breast pump."

"You'll need it," said Amanda. "Especially if he's not latching." She looked beyond Hannah and smiled at Peter and Robert. "Aw, look at him. He already loves his dad."

"Feeling's mutual," Peter attested.

"You going to introduce him to Liam?"

Peter's grin went flat. "When the time's right."

"Peter . . ."

"When the time is right." He jerked his head at Hannah. "Why don't you give her a tour of the place? I'll watch the boy."

Though Hannah cringed at the thought of parting with Robert, she was eager to talk to Amanda. She washed up, changed, then followed her sister down the hallway. "Can you *please* tell me what happened to Liam?"

Amanda waited until they turned a corner, then spoke in a furtive mutter. "You remember his girlfriend, Sovereign?"

"Yeah." Hannah shuddered at the memory of her twin sister, Regal, one of the first to get archived at Lárnach. "Did she die in the underland?"

"She made it out," Amanda said. "But her family didn't, and she just couldn't take it. And being a thermic, like she was . . ."

Hannah covered her slack mouth. "Oh my God. She torched herself?"

"Not intentionally. At least we don't think so. You know what stress can do to our powers."

"Holy shit."

"Yeah. Poor Liam's been a wreck ever since she died. He's in Protection now."

"Protection."

"*Self*-protection," Amanda said. "We don't want to lose him the way we lost Sovereign."

Hannah suffered a sudden flashback to Eden, her throat slit open in the woodshop. "Why won't Peter visit him?"

Amanda lowered her head, disquieted. "There are things about Protection that don't sit well with some people."

"What things?"

"Ask Theo when you see him. It's his department."

Amanda cupped Hannah's face and smiled at her in wonder. "My God."

"What?"

"Your eyes," she said. "It's like you've become the older sister."

Hannah glumly shook her head. "I may have closed the gap a little—"

"I'm not talking about time. I'm talking about experience. The things you've been through."

Hannah was more stuck on all the things she'd missed: the collapse of the underland, the six weeks at Sergelen, the changes on everyone's faces. It felt like the world had moved on without her, and not to a better place. Even Amanda seemed different in a host of subtle ways. Hannah could see it whenever she looked closely: a serene kind of sadness, more like resignation than depression. Whatever was going on inside her, she wasn't in a hurry to share it.

Amanda showed her the cafeteria next, a vast gray chamber buried neck-deep in the ground—as joyless as the rest of the base, even with the sun gleaming down through skylights. Hannah peeked down over the mezzanine railing and saw dozens of people eating breakfast out of cans and packets. The Coppers sat clustered in a corner, a dismal bunch without Shroud and Mother. Even sweet little See looked like a back-alley criminal with her ratty hair and hateful expression.

"God," said Hannah. "It's like being in a Russian prison camp."

"Fewer beatings," Amanda feebly joked. "But the food's not as good."

"I thought Ioni was all-powerful."

Amanda shrugged. "Almost everything she has is being used on the shield. The rest is for San Francisco."

"How much do you know about that?"

"Very little," Amanda said unconvincingly. "The more Ioni talks about it, the more variables it adds to the future."

"That must really piss off Theo."

"And Zack," Amanda added. "There are times he wants to throttle her."

"How are you two doing?"

"Me and Zack?" Amanda laughed. "Our marriage only gets stronger in bad times, so it's close to perfect now." Her smile melted away. "He really held me together while you were gone."

Hannah clasped Amanda's hand and looked down at the cafeteria again. The Pearls dined a few tables away from the Coppers, yet another orphan group that had been cut down to five. While Ofelia ranted angrily to her dark-haired sisters, Rosario caught Hannah looking at her, then awkwardly turned away. Hannah didn't take it personally. They were both living reminders of the hell they'd endured, and poked each other's wounds by proximity. Hannah would have been happy enough to avoid all the survivors of Lárnach, one of them in particular.

"You see Evan around?" she asked Amanda.

"He mostly keeps to himself, but we spoke a few times. It's the strangest thing."

"What is?"

"The way he talks about you now," Amanda said. "Like he respects you."

Hannah couldn't have been less moved by that. "As long as he doesn't expect us to be friends."

"I think he's okay with 'not enemies.'"

A portal flashed in the lower cafeteria, then vanished as quickly as it had appeared. Hannah had no idea who conjured it until a pair of short, strong arms hooked around her from behind.

"Oof." She could easily guess who was hugging her. "Careful. You're gonna squeeze all the milk out of me."

"Eww." Mia stepped back, her nose crinkled in revulsion. "Can that really happen?"

Amanda laughed. "No."

"You never know," Hannah teased. She turned around and smiled at Mia, the only one in Sergelen who looked better than Hannah remembered. Her hair had reverted to its natural brown color and grown into a laid-back bob, and her lack of access to dark cosmetics let her natural beauty shine through. She sported a brand-new scar on the right side of her face that only added to her allure. It cut a thin line through the middle of her brow, then continued beneath the eye.

Hannah traced her finger down Mia's scar. "I assume you got that in the underland."

Mia nodded. "A piece of rock hit me as I got away. Another half inch and I would have lost the eye."

"She was the last one out," Amanda told Hannah. "We thought she was dead."

"God." Hannah clasped Mia's hand. "I can't even imagine what you guys went through."

"Us?" Mia laughed in amazement. "That was six minutes of hell. You spent *seven months* with Semerjean."

Someone called out to Amanda from the other side of the mezzanine. Hannah looked across the way and saw a stout, bearded Gotham frantically motioning for her sister.

"Wait. Is that—"

"Stan Bloom," Mia said. "Carrie's dad."

Amanda sighed at Mia. "I have to take care of this. Can you show Hannah around?"

"Sure."

"Take care of what?" Hannah asked her. "What does he want with you?"

"It's nothing," said Amanda. "I'll catch up with you."

The diners below barely gave Amanda a second glance as she levitated across the mess hall.

"What's going on with her?" Hannah asked Mia.

"Something with the flying tempics," Mia said. "They've been spending a lot of time together. I think Ioni has a special mission for them."

Hannah didn't like the sound of that. "What kind of mission?"

Mia shrugged. "I don't know. She won't talk about it, not even to Zack."

"Shit." Hannah was officially worried now. Amanda knew more about the future than she was letting on.

Mia waved a new portal into the air, then took Hannah by the hand. "Come on. I'll show you the one cool thing we have in this shithole."

They were halfway up the stairs to the rampart when a pitch-black anomaly streaked across the sky. Hannah froze on the steps, bug-eyed. Though the object had moved like a blur across her vision, it didn't look like anything that belonged in the air.

She turned to Mia, slack-jawed. "What was that?"

"A wraith," Mia said with a smile. "I got to try one out the other day. It's awesome."

"But what *is* it?"

"It's a war drone. I'll show you."

Hannah followed her to the parapet, then gawked in surprise at the view beyond the wall. There was an entire shantytown outside of Sergelen: all canvas tents and tempic huts, enough to fill two football fields. Hannah barely had a chance to look at the residents before the wraith buzzed her and Mia.

Hannah crouched to her knees. "What the hell?"

"Be careful!" Mia yelled down at the locals. "You know what those things do!"

A large, heavily tattooed man waved sheepishly from his control station. *"Ich lerne noch!"*

"Yeah, whatever." Mia helped Hannah back to her feet. "You okay?"

Hannah craned her neck and watched the wraith circle above. On closer scrutiny, it resembled a flying manta ray, a similar design to the stormbirds that Hannah and Amanda had used in Mexico. But while those drones had been cast in a black glossy metal, the wraith could have been forged out of shadows. It had no reflective surfaces, no light or dark areas. It was just a flying silhouette of itself, an ink smudge against the cloudscape.

"It's covered in mortis," Mia explained. "Dissolves anything it touches, and it's almost indestructible."

"Wow." Hannah kept a nervous eye on the wraith. "I didn't know they had the technology."

"Me neither," said Mia. "Cedric had a whole bunch of secret projects going on."

"Had?"

Mia's expression turned doleful. "He died in the underland."

"Oh my God. I forgot he was even there."

"Yeah. He was a good man. I gave him way more shit than he deserved."

Mia proceeded to tell Hannah about Cedric Cain's legacy, all the money and resources that he'd squirreled away, then passed off to Melissa. They had enough firepower now to take down a small country, and more high-tech armor suits than they could possibly fill.

Until recently, that is. A few weeks back, Bobby and Yasmeen traveled to England and enlisted a couple of hundred friends to help fight for them.

Hannah glanced down again at the denizens of the settlement, all gruff and seedy roughnecks who were no strangers to guerrilla combat. "Wait. So these guys are—"

"Scarlet Sabre."

"The *terrorists*?"

"Shhh!" Mia peeked at the nearest Sabres. "They don't like that word. And don't ever use it around Bobby. He knows these guys. He trusts them." She stuffed her hands into her pockets and breathed a heavy sigh. "We can use all the help we can get."

"I thought Integrity was on our side."

"They *were*," Mia said. "But the guy who replaced Cedric's a total prick, and he pulled all the agency's support. Now all we have are Melissa and Felicity. They've gone totally rogue."

"Huh." Hannah turned around and scanned the military base. "I haven't seen either of them yet. And whatever happened to what's-their-name? The sisters."

"Meredith and Charlene," Mia replied. "They went back to Japan to talk sense into the Majee. Melissa and Felicity are already in San Francisco."

Hannah watched with anxious ambivalence as a second wraith took to the sky. She couldn't imagine the Sabres would ever give up their new toys, and shuddered to think how they'd use them in Europe. "Well, I'm glad at least your brother's okay."

"Me too," Mia said. "I almost feel guilty."

"Why?"

"Because everyone here keeps losing people, while I keep getting them back. First Bobby, then Carrie, now you."

"Carrie?"

Mia smiled shyly. "I saved her life in the underland. We get along pretty well now."

"Really."

"Calm down. We're just friends."

"You think you could be more again?"

"Who the hell knows? I'm just glad she's alive."

Hannah smiled and stroked Mia's arm. "You're amazing."

"Oh, shut up."

"It's true. You're one of the strongest people I've ever known."

"Not as strong as you think." Mia looked away with flinching guilt. "I gave up on you before I should have. I convinced myself that you were dead."

"I don't blame you."

"I didn't think I could hate them more," Mia said. "But after what they did to you and the underland . . ."

"I know." Hannah squeezed her wrist. "I know that hatred. It kept me alive and almost killed me at the same time."

"How is it now?"

Hannah thought it over before shrugging her shoulders. "Muddled, like everything else in my head."

"Have you even tried your powers again?"

"No," Hannah said with a laugh of amazement. It had been months since she'd had access to them, enough to forget that they existed. "Guess I should at some point."

"Uh, yeah. You're gonna need them for the Pelletiers."

"What do you mean?"

"In San Francisco." Mia gestured at the flying wraiths. "Who do you think all this is for?"

Hannah blinked at her dazedly. "We're fighting the Pelletiers?"

"And about two thousand Jades." Mia studied Hannah in dead-eyed wonder, as if she'd just been thawed out of an ice block. "Wow. You're *really* out of the loop."

"Of course I am. No one's telling me anything!"

"I guess they're easing you into it," Mia said.

"Well, I want to know, so fill me in."

Mia stroked her chin in anxious thought. "When's the last time you saw the news?"

"The day I got taken."

"Holy shit." Mia opened a new portal. "I know where we're going next."

There was only one lumivision in Sergelen, but it was unlike any other. Ioni had jury-rigged the console to capture signals from all over the planet. Even low-watt newscasts from the backwoods of Chile could be plucked from the ether and reproduced in perfect quality, with homemade subtitles and contextual links to GlobalNet articles. It was the ultimate window to the outside world, though only a few had the stomach to look through it. The existential anguish that infected everyone at Sergelen had spread into a global pandemic.

By the time Mia and Hannah arrived in the lounge, a dozen timebenders had gathered in front of the lumivision. Zack saw his fellow Silvers by the door and waved them over. "Hey."

"He'll get you up to speed," Mia told Hannah. "I have to check on Bobby."

Hannah joined Zack on the sofa, her dark eyes fixed on Mia as she vanished into a portal. "I'm starting to feel like a hot potato."

"I'm surprised Amanda passed you off," Zack said. "She wanted to spend all day with you."

"She got pulled away on wing business."

"Again?" Zack rolled his eyes. "They've become a real clique, that bunch."

"Mia says they're going on some kind of mission."

Zack shrugged uncomfortably. "First rule of Flight Club—"

"Zack."

"I honestly don't know. I can't get Amanda to tell me. She says even talking about it will screw up the future."

Hannah let out a bleak chuckle. "That's a line I'd expect from Theo, not her."

"It's not Theo she's channeling."

"Ioni," Hannah muttered. Every dark thread in Sergelen seemed to trace back to her, and everyone but Hannah seemed used to it. "It doesn't bother you that she has Amanda keeping secrets?"

"Of course it does," Zack said. "But Ioni doesn't do anything for shits and giggles. She's playing the long game."

"With us as pawns." She caught Zack's heavy look. "What? Am I wrong?"

"You're not wrong."

"Merlin was one of her closest friends, and look what happened to him."

"Right now I'm more worried about you," Zack said.

"What do you mean?"

"The Pelletiers kept me for a day and a half," he reminded her. "And I'm still messed up from it. I can't even imagine what you're going through."

"What does that have to do with Ioni?"

"You're traumatized and you're rightfully pissed—"

"Zack, I'm *telling* you that things are wrong here!"

Hannah could feel the side-eyed stares of the other people in the room. She slumped in the couch and lowered her voice. "It all feels wrong."

Zack nodded his head obligingly. "Okay. Let's go somewhere quiet and talk."

Hannah bristled at his calming tone, as if she'd just hijacked a school bus. "Not yet. I want to see what's going on in the world."

After a few more minutes of Australian morning chatter, the lumivision jumped to the west. It was six P.M. in Washington, D.C., just in time for the start of *The National-1 News*.

Hannah watched the screen in a hang-jawed stupor as the anchor caught her up on the latest. The last six weeks had been a nonstop nightmare for the United States, especially in San Francisco. With three days left before the prophesized Cataclysm, the city had fallen into turmoil. Only ten percent of the population remained, while army reserve soldiers patrolled the streets in tanks, fighting looters and lunatics and every other anarchist.

The rest of the nation wasn't faring much better. An economic depression had wreaked havoc from coast to coast, throwing twenty percent of the populace out of work, and driving crime to a hundred-year high. Fistfights and riots had become a daily ordeal in every city, and there was a whole new breed of paranoid violence that the media had dubbed "Gotham Mania."

"What?" Hannah turned her stunned gaze onto Zack. "Are you *kidding* me?"

"We got outed," he said. "It's been a real mess."

Hannah was one of the last people on Earth to watch the infamous video that had been captured on August 19: fifteen aerics flying high in broad daylight while their hometown collapsed into a sinkhole. There was no more debate over whether Gothams existed, and barely an hour passed on any news channel without the same questions being asked. *Who are these people? What do they want? Were they responsible for Quarter Hill's destruction? How did they hide in plain sight for so long, and where are they hiding now?*

To hear the public tell it, the answer was "everywhere." Anyone even remotely offbeat was accused of being a Gotham, and the definition grew darker with each new conspiracy. By the end of September, half of America viewed the Gothams as an insidious menace, the secret cabal behind everything bad. That house that burned down in Schenectady? Gothams. That senator who died of a heart attack? Gothams. The impending fall of San Francisco? Oh, you better believe that's the Gothams.

"Oh my God." Hannah buried her face in her hands. Even in the best case, the timebenders would never get a moment of peace again. They'd have to look over their shoulders for the rest of their lives, their reward for saving the world.

At the twenty-minute mark, the news moved on to a puzzling tragedy, one that had been plaguing the planet for days. Aeromobiles were falling out of the sky for no clear reason: a flying coupe here, an aerovan there, even some commercial cruise ships. Nearly ten thousand people had plummeted to their deaths, without a single factor or pattern to link them. Any vehicle of any condition in any part of the world had become susceptible to sudden liftplate failure, as if God was smiting His victims at random. Naturally, the problem was blamed on Gothams.

"Wow." Hannah looked to Zack again. "What's that about?"

Zack fumbled with the knuckles of his mechanical hand, his voice low and edgy. "She doesn't have a choice."

"*She.*" Hannah eyed Zack intently. "You mean Ioni."

"Look—"

"You're saying Ioni killed those ten thousand people."

"There was no other way."

"No other way to *what*? How the hell is mass murder—"

A high, shrill cry pierced the air from outside, the unmistakable sound of a baby in distress.

Hannah was on her feet and halfway down the hall before she even knew what was happening. The thought of Robert in trouble was enough to send her mind and body into a state of animal reflex.

She followed the cries to a sun-drenched courtyard, where a crowd of familiar faces had gathered. Hannah only briefly registered Theo out of the corner of her eye before she finally laid eyes on the newborn. His chubby face and shock-red hair quickly marked him as someone else's baby. Hannah's higher functions returned to her, and she finally breathed again.

Caleb clutched the child in his meat-hook hands, looking like a half-crazed mountain main with his bushy, unkempt beard. He held the infant out to a reluctant young Gotham, a teary-eyed brunette whom Hannah recognized as Candy Ballad.

"I can't take him," Candy attested. "He's not mine."

"He doesn't have anyone else," said Caleb. He jerked his head to the left. "Look at his mom. You think she can handle him?"

Unnerved, Hannah turned her attention to Artemis, her fellow Lárnach escapee, lying disturbingly still on a floating tempic gurney. Hannah feared she was dead from her wide, empty eyes, but then relaxed when she finally blinked.

"It's all right," Theo assured Hannah. "She'll be okay."

She could barely hear him over the child's loud wails. She cut across the lot, until she faced Theo from the other side of Artemis's stretcher. "What are you doing? She's my friend."

"She was about to have a meltdown," said Stitch, the creator of the tempic gurney. "We're just getting her the help she needs."

"Help?" Hannah took a closer look at Artemis and saw a thin glass disc, the size of a quarter, placed securely in the middle of her forehead. "What did you do to her?"

Theo tossed a curt nod at Stitch. "Go on. I'll meet you there."

"Theo, *what did you do to Artemis*?"

He looked back at Hannah hesitantly. "It's Ioni's technology. It pacifies her."

"Pacifies? She looks brain-dead! And why are you giving her kid away?"

Theo held her by the arm. "Let's talk somewhere."

"No! Stop treating me like I'm the crazy one!"

"I'm not."

"You're giving weapons to terrorists and knocking people out of the sky!"

"Hannah, *stop*."

"Fuck you."

She broke away from Theo and followed Stitch into a dank and massive chamber, the most depressing part of Sergelen yet. The sun filtered in through a single moldy window, casting a broken yellow beam on the floor. At least three dozen beds had been placed against the walls, and in each bed lay a perfectly still patient. They stared up at the ceiling in a catatonic trance, their foreheads flecked with the same glass device that Theo had placed on Artemis.

This is Protection, Hannah realized. *Holy shit.*

By the time Theo and Zack caught up to her, she'd found Liam on a nearby army cot. At last she knew why Peter didn't want to see him like that—his firstborn son, reduced to a blinking mannequin.

"This is sick," Hannah said to Zack and Theo. "How can you be okay with it?"

"It's for their own good," Theo insisted. "It's saving their lives in ways you can't see."

"It looks like something the Pelletiers did to me," Hannah said. "When I pissed them off too much."

Theo shook his head. "It's not punishment. It's preservation. We can't afford to lose anyone else before Thursday."

"Is that all we are now?" Hannah asked him. "Just soldiers in Ioni's war?"

"Yes," said Theo. "Until this is over, that's exactly what we are."

Zack sighed at Theo's lack of tact. "What he's trying to say, poorly—"

"I don't care." Hannah made for the exit, then turned around in the doorway. "You're right, Zack. I *am* traumatized. Enough for me to wonder if this is actually happening. Maybe I'll wake up in my prison cell and find out it was all a trick."

Her voice cracked with emotion. "And a part of me will be relieved, because this isn't how I wanted to see any of you."

Stitch's shoulders broke out in small spikes of rage tempis. "You selfish bitch. You know how much they cried over you?"

"Don't," Zack said to her.

"They would have sold their souls to get you back."

"Enough," Theo snapped at Stitch. "You're not helping."

Hannah closed her eyes in sickened guilt, then fled back into the courtyard. Any urge she'd had to apologize was undermined by the hideousness all around her. She couldn't stay in Sergelen for one more second. She had to get out.

She bumbled through an open gate and took her first steps into the Mongolian wilderness. With the military base just a few feet behind her, the view was actually pretty: a rippling grass meadow that seemed to go on for miles, still vibrant from a healthy summer. It was calming enough that she was surprised that the Pelletiers didn't use it. It would have made a nice backdrop for their prisons.

"It's not as bad as you think," said a low voice behind her. Hannah turned around to see Caleb leaning against the outer fortification, a few feet from the edge of the gate. He must have successfully fobbed off the baby to Candy Ballad, because all he had in his hand was a lit cigarette. Hannah didn't even know that he smoked.

"What's not as bad?" she skeptically inquired. "This place?"

"Protection," Caleb said. "I was there for two weeks. So was Stitch. It kept us both from doing something stupid."

Hannah studied him skeptically. "How did being a vegetable help you?"

"Our minds were in the God's Eye," Caleb explained. "A nice, relaxing environment. Theo and Ioni visited us every day. Worked with us until we were finally ready."

"Ready to what? Embrace the beauty of life?"

Caleb gravely shook his head. "Ready to make our deaths count for something."

Hannah felt a smack of queasiness, and a strong urge to keep running. But then a better thought occurred to her. "Where does he go in the daytime?"

"Who?" Caleb suddenly realized who she was talking about. "Oh. Yeah. I'll show you."

The clubhouse was the last surviving piece of the underland, if one was loose with their definition of "surviving." The roof was gone, along with three of the walls, while the interior had become so marred with debris that it could have served as the set of a war movie. The clubhouse was what the end of the world should have looked like to Hannah—not a void of pure white nothingness, but the tattered remains of a cherished place that had once been filled with music.

Hannah hunkered down in a corner booth, the very place she'd been sitting when the Pelletiers snatched her away.

Full circle, she thought as she brushed her finger across the table.

She looked beyond the bandstage and saw Heath nestled quietly near a missing wall of the clubhouse, his large eyes fixed on a meadow. From what Caleb told Hannah, he sat there every day. In the evening, he did whatever anyone asked of him. He talked and trained and helped around the base. But the daylight hours were all about the clubhouse, and the others let him have it out of respect. The boy knew better than anyone how to heal himself. And according to Amanda, it was working.

"I can feel the tempis inside him," she'd said to Hannah. "It gets calmer every day."

Of course, Heath looked anything but calm at the moment as Hannah lingered at the edge of his awareness. He kept checking on her out of the corner of his eye, like a skittish little rabbit in the wild. Hannah figured he'd bolt if she moved any closer. But maybe if she talked to him from a distance . . .

"Don't."

Startled, Hannah turned in her seat to find Ioni sitting across from her, an arrival so quiet that she could have fluttered in with the wind. Stranger still, she'd managed to set the broken table without making a sound. Hannah looked down at her new breakfast bounty: a plate of rehydrated steak and eggs, with half a juvenated bagel and a bottle of warm orange juice.

"First off, eat," said Ioni. "Your body's still reeling from childbirth. It's screaming for protein."

Hannah opened her mouth to object, but Ioni cut her off. "Secondly, you don't want to talk to Cutie over there. The more you try to prove you're real, the more he'll think you aren't."

"So you're the expert in Heath now."

"I'm an expert in futures," Ioni evenly replied. "But then you already knew that."

Hannah studied her warily, her mind still reeling at her visual inconsistency. The woman had enough power to make the Pelletiers nervous, yet she looked as sweet and innocuous as a kindergarten teacher. Only the side-by-side watches on her skinny right wrist suggested any hint of abnormality.

Ioni took a sip of her water bottle, her eyes locked on Hannah the whole time. "My foresight isn't perfect, of course. Even I thought you were a goner when the Pelletiers took you. But you found a way back, and I'm still in awe. No one else could have pulled that off. Not even your sister."

"Is that why you made her miscarry?" Hannah asked.

"Yes," Ioni said without a trace of guilt. "They would have killed her in Lárnach."

•

"But I was expendable."

"That's not the way I see it."

"Just like Eden, Moon, and Mercy."

At last, Hannah saw remorse in Ioni's hazel eyes. "I had to let you all go," she said. "The Pelletiers were onto me. If I had lifted a finger to help you, that would have been the end of me."

"And everyone else," Hannah assumed by inference.

Ioni nodded. "I'm afraid I'm not expendable. Not until after Thursday."

The scent of breakfast wafted into Hannah's nostrils, causing her stomach to growl. She picked up the fork that Ioni had set for her, then took a cautious bite of egg. "I don't blame you for putting the world before me."

Ioni sighed down at her lap. "But you saw the news without proper context—"

"You crashed ten thousand cars to the ground!"

"I crashed ten thousand people," Ioni corrected. "By the time I'm done, it'll be closer to twenty thousand."

"Why?"

Ioni toyed with her analog watch, a clunky antique from the look of it. "There are roughly three hundred million people in the sky at any given moment on Earth. They love their aeric vehicles here, but it's about to become a one-sided affair."

"What do you mean?"

"There'll be a blast of energy on Thursday," Ioni said. "A shockwave this world has never seen. While it'll fix our little apocalypse problem, it'll screw up every temporal device on the planet. Everything in the air will fall like bricks. The damage will be . . . substantial."

Hannah struggled to follow along. "So by crashing cars now—"

"I've scared the bejeezus out of them," Ioni said. "Half the nations of the world have already grounded their aer traffic indefinitely. By Wednesday night, they all will."

Hannah nodded in revelation. "So when the big wave hits, there'll be no one in the sky."

"There'll be some," Ioni said with a shrug. "You always have your dopes and mavericks."

"So you're killing twenty thousand people—"

"—to save three hundred million." Ioni finally met Hannah's gaze again. "If there was a gentler way to do it, I would."

Hannah peeked out at the garden of stick-and-twine grave markers, just a few yards to the left. All the corpses of the clubhouse had been laid to rest in a mass burial, including Mother and two of Hannah's bandmates. Even more painful to look at were the ten bodyless markers that Caleb had added, one for each victim of Lárnach.

"I sacrificed someone for the greater good," Hannah confessed. "Moira MacDougal. Just left her to her fate while the rest of us tried to escape."

"It was the only way," Ioni insisted. "If you had tried to save everyone, you would have saved no one."

Hannah closed her eyes. "Doesn't make it any easier."

"No, it doesn't."

"It hurt to see Artemis like that," Hannah said. "I thought she was one of the lucky ones."

"She is," said Ioni. "She'll be back on her feet by Thursday."

"Just in time to die in San Francisco."

"Most likely," Ioni admitted. "But I see a few strings where she doesn't."

Hannah checked on Heath at the other side of the clubhouse. "Merlin said it was the end of the road for all of us."

"Merlin was brilliant," Ioni said. "I adored him, and I can never repay him for what he did. But the man had his blind spots, just like Theo."

Hannah wasn't appeased. "Why are the Pelletiers going to be in San Francisco?"

"Semerjean didn't tell you?"

"No," said Hannah. "He just said they had a Hail Mary plan."

Ioni sneered at the lingo. "I have lots of names, but Mary isn't one of them."

"You're their plan."

"I'm their last hope," said Ioni. "The people of my era are immune to terminus. None of us die until we choose to."

"So you're the cure they're looking for."

Ioni nodded. "They've been hunting me from the day they got here, and I've managed to stay a step ahead of them. But they know exactly where I'll be on Thursday at nine A.M. They'll come after me with everything they've got."

"Shit."

"The worst part is that I won't be able to defend myself," said Ioni. "I'll need all my concentration for the work I have ahead of me."

"Which is why you need us."

"All of you," Ioni stressed. "And the Sabre, and the Majee, and whoever else can help. They won't stop throwing Jades at us until we make them stop. And when the Big Three come . . ."

Ioni sighed at the many grave markers. "A lot of good people will die."

Hannah pushed away her breakfast. Her stomach wasn't clamoring for sustenance anymore.

She watched a butterfly hover above one of the grave markers, then froze it in the air with a thought. "Huh."

Ioni let out a soft grin at the spectacle. "Guess your powers are back."

"I'm still out of practice."

"Well, that's your second priority."

"What's my first?"

Ioni responded without moving her lips—a soothing voice in Hannah's head, as soft as a babbling brook. *Heath's still afraid that you're a Pelletier trick. But he's listening to every word we say, and his defenses are starting to crumble. Just sit with him for a while and don't say a word. By this time tomorrow, he'll find his way back to you.*

That was the best news Hannah had heard all day, enough to bring tears to her eyes. "Thank you."

"You were never expendable," Ioni said. "Not to me. Not to the people who love you. Not even to this world. You're a crucial player in this drama, and you will be to the very end."

Hannah was only briefly flattered before she thought about Amanda again. "What do you have my sister doing?"

Ioni's serene smile wavered. "Something important. That's all I can tell you."

"Will it kill her?"

The morbid look on Ioni's face was enough to crush Hannah's heart. "Oh my God."

"Don't read too much into it," Ioni warned her. "The future's still writing itself."

"I don't know how much more I can take."

"You won't have to." Ioni scrambled her way out of the booth. "One way or another, it all ends on Thursday."

Ioni caught Heath looking at her, and then gave him a pleasant smile. He turned back around to his front-facing view, as stoic as he ever was. Hannah cried a few more happy tears at the promising sight of that look. It was so very typical, so very *Heath*, that it was suddenly easy to feel optimistic about him.

He was clawing his way back from his own personal Lárnach, and he could already see home on the horizon.

Ioni disappeared without a flash or sound, leaving two orphans alone in the clubhouse. As the wind blew dust across the grassy plains, and a family of pheasants touched down outside the window, Hannah quietly took a seat in the booth next to Heath's, then joined him in his peaceful vigil.

THIRTY-FOUR

Thursday broke across the eastern world, bringing a cloud of apprehension with it. At long last, the fourth of October had arrived: the day that Merlin McGee had warned about. The great prophet had saved his darkest prediction for last, and even the skeptics were nervous. One didn't need a history degree to know what the last Cataclysm did to humanity. Years of chaos and social upheaval. New wars, new plights, even new rules of nature.

Now it was threatening to start all over again in just a matter of hours.

For the refugee residents of Sergelen—all the orphans, Gothams, and Scarlet Sabre fighters who had a front-row view of the conflict—Thursday rolled in like a boulder, then moved as slowly as a slug. Their little slice of Mongolia was fifteen hours ahead of San Francisco, which meant that they wouldn't be deploying until midnight. That gave them the whole day and evening to spend as they wished: training, sleeping, screwing, whatever.

By sunset, Mia was close to losing her mind. The day had already passed like a week and a half, and her brain practically had a charley horse from all the thinking she'd been doing. She would have gladly found distraction with someone she loved, but that was a small pond to fish from, and they were all busy doing their own things. Bobby was getting it on with some blond Dutch Sabre, while Amanda and Zack had hung the proverbial sock on their own doorknob. Hannah was nursing her kid. Theo was cruising the God's Eye. Peter was catching up with Liam, freshly sprung from Protection. No one knew what Heath was doing, which was par for the course these days. Mia figured he was deep inside his own quirky mind, shooting the shit with the wolves and Jonathans.

When Carrie knocked on her door at a quarter to nine, Mia hugged her in desperate relief. "Oh, thank God. I've been going crazy."

"Me too. You should have come get me."

"I figured your dad wanted to spend time with you."

"That's why I'm going crazy," Carrie said. "He's wearing me down with all the hugs and 'I love yous.' I mean I get it. He's nervous."

Mia nodded sympathetically. "We all are."

"Right. Exactly! Him being all moony isn't helping. I've already brown-buttered the toilet nine times."

She looked to Mia with cringing eyes. "Sorry. That was probably better left unsaid."

On the contrary, her lack of filter was like sunshine to Mia, one of the many things she'd loved about the old Carrie Bloom. Mia could barely tell the difference between the past and present versions after six weeks of hardship had aged Carrie into early womanhood. She'd earned a couple new scars while escaping the underland, and a few more from her rigorous power training. Her fingers had become so blistered from frostnip that she wore motorcycle gloves to hide them.

Carrie looked to the garments on Mia's bed, all the gray and leathery components of her combat gear. Ioni had provided a warsuit to every timebender in Sergelen: custom-fitted, with a slew of high-tech bells and whistles that no one fully understood yet. "You try yours on?"

"Yeah," Mia said with a sigh. "I look like I'm in a motorcycle gang."

Carrie laughed. "I look like a junior dominatrix."

"You can make them looser," Mia told her. "There's even a slider on the sleeve that changes the color."

"Really." Carrie gave her wrist a cursory scan. "I must have missed that part of the tutorial."

Mia noticed her tense new look. "You okay?"

"Okay? No. I feel like . . ." Carrie peeked at Mia through a nervous side-eye, then bounded toward the door. "You know what? Forget it. I shouldn't have come."

"No, no. Wait." Mia held her by the arm. "Just tell me. Please."

"I'm just scared," Carrie said. "It's embarrassing to admit it around people like you."

"Like me?"

"Come on. You've been fighting for your life since you got to this world. This is just another day for you."

"It's not," Mia assured her. "I'm just as scared as you."

"Well, you hide it better."

"That's just because I'm usually angry."

"Maybe." Carrie laughed with jittery tension. "I used to think that's all you were when I saw you around the underland—this cute, angry girl with a chip on her shoulder. I didn't understand it and I didn't see past it."

Mia dipped her head in guilt. "I didn't give you a reason to."

"None of that matters now," Carrie said. "You risked your life to save me, after all that shit I'd said to you."

Mia shook her head. "We both said stupid things that day. And there's nothing you can do that'll ever make me stop caring about you."

Carrie peeled off a glove and held Mia by the hand. "Sorry. I know my fingers are gross. I just wanted to touch you and feel it."

"They're fine." Mia brushed her thumb over Carrie's knuckles. "You're going to be okay."

"What makes you say that?"

"Well, for starters, you'll be with Ioni the whole time."

"Yeah, next to the enemy's main target." Carrie laughed. "Real safe place to be."

"You'll be shielded, is my point."

"Look, Mia, if I die—"

"Don't say that."

"*If* I die," Carrie continued, "I just want you to know that I see it now. I may not remember what we had, but I see exactly why I loved you." She chuckled at herself before Mia could react. "Great. Now I'm the one getting all moony. Forget I even—"

Before Mia could stop herself or even think, she pulled Carrie into her arms and kissed her. On hindsight, it seemed the only rational move. If Carrie died, if *Mia* died, if the whole world imploded in hours, then there was no better time to right an old wrong, and steal a quick taste of better days.

Carrie pulled back from Mia, thunderstruck. "Okay. Wow. That was . . . wow."

"I'm sorry I ever pushed you away," Mia said in a quavering voice. "I should have started over with you a long time ago."

"It doesn't matter." Carrie kissed her on the lips. "We have three hours."

"No, you don't," said a disembodied voice in their ears. *"I need Mia for a meeting. I'm sorry. It's important."*

Both girls grumbled at Ioni's spectral intrusion. The woman was nowhere when they needed her, and everywhere when she needed them.

"Crap." Carrie worked in one more kiss before dashing for the door. "Come find me when you're done. We have unfinished business."

Mia smiled. "I'll be there as soon as I can."

Carrie's strong voice reverberated from down the hall. "Ask her how to make those stupid suits looser!"

Mia sat on her bed and looked down at her trembling hands. She felt like she was nothing but chemical emotions, a volatile compound that was liable to explode at any moment.

"Mia . . ."

"I'm coming! I'm coming!"

She reached for her sneakers, then noticed something on the floor: a rolled-up scrap of notebook paper. Mia unfurled it in her fingers, thinking Carrie dropped a note for her, but the handwriting was all her own, albeit a rushed and sloppy version:

Let him go.

Mia's heart skipped a beat. The message must have come by portal during her catnap, her first temporal dispatch in sixteen months. She'd never expected to hear from Future Mia again, and was dismayed to find her as cryptic as ever. Even worse was the ominous inference of timing. Her other self was probably just a few hours older than her. Mia didn't have to wonder where she was.

Ioni answered her door before Mia could knock on it, yet she still somehow managed to look surprised. She clutched the towel wrap around her torso and blinked at her new guest dazedly. "What are you doing here?"

"You said we had a meeting."

"Yeah, at the Mother Rock. Not here."

"You didn't mention that part."

"I didn't?" Ioni furrowed her brow. "Shit. I hope I told the others."

She waved Mia into the room. "Come in. Come in."

Mia stepped through the door and took a cautious look around. Ioni had claimed the old base commander's quarters—an appropriate enough choice, all things considered. Her suite was ten times the size of Mia's concrete bunk, and a hell of a lot less depressing. But for all its hardwood charm and soothing earth tones, it barely sported any more furniture than the other rooms.

Mia did a double-take at the foot poking out from beneath Ioni's bedspread. "Uh . . ."

"Don't worry about him," said Ioni. "You'd need a tuba and a firehose to wake him up."

Her bedmate was so snug under the blankets and pillows that Mia could barely make him out, assuming he even was a man. His one visible arm was slim and dainty enough to leave Mia in a fog of uncertainty.

"I'm sorry to interrupt your moment with Carrie," Ioni said. "It looked really sweet."

"Yeah, thanks." Mia was still harboring some resentment toward Ioni, whose horrible advice had nearly gotten her and Carrie killed last June. The only reason Mia was speaking to her at all was the good turn she had done for them recently. Without Ioni's portal guidance, Mia would have never saved Carrie from the underland. Both girls would just be messy stains at the bottom of the Quarter Hill sinkhole.

Ioni disappeared into a closet. "I'm getting a weird vibe off of you. Did something—"

She poked her head back into the hallway, her wide eyes fixed on Mia. "Oh."

"Oh, what?"

"I thought you were done passing notes to yourself."

"*I* didn't do it. My future self did."

"I bet you don't miss talking like that."

Mia poutingly crossed her arms. "I don't."

She gasped to find Ioni standing right next to her, fully dressed in a T-shirt and jeans.

"Holy shit." Mia jumped back, startled. "You know we hate when you do that."

"Let me see the note."

"Why?"

"Because it's obviously distracting you." She snatched the message out of Mia's hand, then rolled her eyes. "Oh, for God's sake. Did you write this in a hurry?"

"It wasn't me!"

"You're all part of the same you." Ioni reread the note with marked skepticism. "'Let him go.' You probably mean Semerjean."

"Yeah. No shit."

"In any case, it's good advice."

"Why?"

"Because hatred is a distraction," Ioni said. "And I need you clear and focused."

Mia was starting to think that Ioni's latest mistake was anything but one. She wanted Mia to come to her room before the meeting.

"You still barely told me what I'll be doing in San Francisco," Mia complained. "Am I in the front lines, the back lines?"

"You'll be everywhere," Ioni said. "You'll be taking the Special Support team wherever they need to go."

"That team being?"

"You, your brother, Hannah, and—" Ioni jerked her head at her slumbering lover. "That schmuck."

The man turned on the mattress with a somnolent groan, then flopped his other arm on the bedspread. Mia's eyes bulged at the tattoo on the back of his hand: a branded *55* that she'd seen more than once.

"Oh my God." Mia looked to Ioni in horror and disgust. *"Him?"*

"Listen—"

"You slept with *Evan*?"

"Shhhhh!" Ioni held Mia by the shoulders. "Let's keep that between us."

"Why?"

"Because if Ofelia finds out where he's hiding—"

"No, I mean why sleep with him? Do you know what he's done?"

"I've done worse," Ioni insisted. "And when you've lived as long as I have, you start to see things differently."

"How?"

Ioni moved to the nightstand beside Evan and retrieved her two watches. "Inside every monster is a human being and a tragedy. It doesn't make us any less responsible for our sins. But sometimes, when the moment's right, you need to take a step back and look at the full map of a person. Sometimes the only way to tame a beast is to simply understand him."

She eyed Mia intently as she secured her twin timepieces. "That's actually the reason I called the meeting."

"What do you mean?"

"You'll see." Ioni opened a portal in the middle of the room, then took Mia by the hand. "Come on."

THIRTY-FIVE

A quarter-mile east of the military base, just inside the lip of Ioni's protective cloakshield, stood a six-foot natural granite formation that had become a holy site to Buddhists. They called it the Eej Khad, or Mother Rock, for the matronly shape it had developed over the millennia. Pilgrims had once traveled in flocks from all over Asia to seek its divine blessing. Though the mother was believed to grant all wishes, she specialized in prayers of fertility and the protection of little children.

But then the nuclear accident at Sergelen had made the entire area radioactive, sealing the Mother Rock away from its worshippers. Trapped in a cursed and toxic land, it endured on its own for twenty years, until Ioni healed the entire region and turned the base into a refuge for timebenders.

While she didn't put much stock in the Mother Rock's spiritual powers, Ioni admired the old gal for her resilience. She also found the site to be ideal for meetings, especially at night when the stars were at peak brilliance. She'd set a circle of chairs around an illusive bonfire that provided just enough heat to counter the evening winds.

By the time Mia and Ioni arrived on the scene, only Zack and Amanda were waiting for them. They sat hip to hip on a two-seat lounger, both prematurely dressed in their warsuits. While Zack had customized his outfit to be black and loose-fitting, Amanda stuck with the snug default gray. Her sleeves had been removed to let her tempic arms breathe, while a special mesh weave over her shoulder blades allowed her to form her aeric wings without shredding her gear.

Ioni smiled at the couple. "Look at you, all battle-ready."

"We were trying them on when you called us," Amanda said. "We didn't have time to change back."

Zack examined his warsuit with a mordant sneer. "It's never too early to dress like a low-budget superhero."

"Low-budget." Ioni scoffed. "Any army would pay a fortune for the tech you're wearing. It took me years just to gather the shield components."

"These things have shields?"

"Of course they do," Ioni said to Zack. "You think I made them just for looks?"

"I *hope* not."

"Shut up."

Ioni had just finished closing her portal when another one opened right behind it. Though Mia recognized Peter's energy signature, only Theo, Hannah, and a baby stroller emerged. The disc swirled shut behind them.

"Peter's not coming?" Mia asked.

Hannah parked Robert's stroller and tightened his blanket wrap. "He says he wasn't invited."

"That's a harsh way of looking at it," Ioni said. "I just wanted him to have time with Liam."

"What about Heath?" asked Theo.

Ioni grinned. "Heath's standing on the rampart with See at his side, listening to the music of the Sabre camp. There's a Belgian who's killed at least two dozen people playing classical guitar by a campfire. Heath doesn't know the man's history, or the song that he's playing. He just knows that it's beautiful. Between the music and the company, he's feeling better than he has in a long time. Who am I to ruin that?"

While the others were clearly touched by the notion, Mia seethed with quiet resentment. Ioni had no qualms about ruining her moment with Carrie. Why did Heath get special treatment?

Zack gestured at the last empty chair by the fire. "Uh . . ."

"One more coming," Ioni told him.

Mia was about to ask who when another portal opened and practically roared with the wrath of its creator. "Wow."

"Yeah," Ioni said with a sigh. "She's in a real shit mood."

Ofelia stormed out of the portal and waved it shut behind her. "What the hell is this stupid meeting about?"

Though pity was the last thing Ofelia wanted, Mia still felt sorry for her. She'd lost three of her Pearl sisters in the underland, and had been injured so badly that even Ioni couldn't entirely fix her. She wore a motorized brace to help work her left arm, and took a bevy of sedatives to sleep through her night pains. Even the miraculous return of Hannah and Rosario had only lifted her spirits a few notches.

"It won't take long," Ioni promised Ofelia.

"It better not. My girls need me. They're terrified."

Mia suddenly found it curious that Ioni would want Ofelia here. Not Peter, not Heath, and apparently not Bobby. Just six particular orphans with one trait in common.

Silvers, Mia thought. *She only invited the ones who got silver bracelets.*

Ioni took a long, pensive look at the Mother Rock before finally commencing the meeting. "Thank you for coming. I know your nerves are shot and you'd rather be resting but, like it or not, you're all generals in this war. The decisions you make will mean life or death for people. Maybe even *all* people. It's hard to say."

"It's hard to hear," Zack interjected. "I don't like having that power."

"I know."

"I was a cartoonist."

"I know," Ioni patiently replied. "Believe me, I'm just as scared as you are. That doubting voice in the back of your head is a full-scream blast inside mine. What if I make the wrong move in San Francisco? What if I made the wrong move a year ago and the consequences haven't hit us yet? Or . . ."

She cast a sweeping look at the others. "What if I make the right move and one of you gets in my way?"

Mia felt a sharp flutter in the pit of her stomach. *This is too much pressure*, she shrieked in her thoughts. *For fuck's sake, I'm only sixteen.*

"It's not your fault," Ioni assured them all. "I know I keep things close to the vest, and it drives you all crazy, especially . . ." She clicked her tongue and jerked a thumb at Theo.

Hannah clasped his hand with a wry little grin. "It's okay. He pulls the same shit on us."

"For the exact same reason," Ioni said. "The strings are never anything less than volatile. Even the tiniest ripples can become tidal waves. Experience has taught me to err on the side of caution, but I can see that my secrets have created a trust gap between us, and that's a problem I'd like to fix."

She sat forward in her chair. "So right here, right now, I'm going to take your questions and answer them with complete honesty. The only difficulty is that you can't ask me about the future. Everything else is fair game. *Capiche?*"

"Works for me," said Ofelia. She struck a match against its tinderbox, then lit up a hand-rolled cigarette. "Where are you hiding Evan?"

Ioni chuckled. "Let's try this again—"

"I'm not asking about the future. I'm asking where he is now."

"And if I told you, you'd kill him, and then the whole future changes."

"Yes," said Ofelia. "For the better."

Ioni shook her head. "If that were true, I'd let you have him."

"How does that psycho help your cause?"

"That's a future question."

Ofelia threw her hands up. "Then this is all for nothing, because I don't trust you."

Robert whimpered from his stroller. Hannah picked him up and cradled him in her arms. "Ofelia, listen to me. There's no one in the world who knows your anger more than I do."

Ofelia looked away. "Don't ask me to forgive him."

"I'd never ask that. God knows I haven't."

"But you still set him free."

"I did," Hannah said. "And I may end up regretting it. But in the here and now, it feels really nice, because he's not stinking up my thoughts anymore. He lost all his power to hurt me. I set *myself* free."

Mia shifted in her seat uneasily, her thoughts drifting back to Semerjean. Her future self hadn't been the only one to tell her to let him go. A senator's aide from Connecticut, one of the nicest and wisest women who Mia had ever met, gave her the exact same advice.

But it still felt painfully wrong to Mia, maybe even a little sexist. Why should the woman be shouldered with the burden of mercy, especially when the man had done nothing to deserve it? It should have been Evan's job to earn Ofelia's lack of hatred. It should have been Semerjean's job to earn Mia's.

From Ofelia's hard look, she fully agreed. "Would you be saying all these things if he'd killed Amanda?" she asked Hannah.

"Probably not."

"I didn't think so." Ofelia looked to Ioni again. "Just promise me he'll die in San Francisco. I don't need to be the one to kill him. I just need him gone."

"I can't promise you that," Ioni said. "All I can tell you is that he'll be dead within a year, and he has no one left to hurt but the Pelletiers."

"But—"

"And he *will* hurt them, Ofelia. In ways that only he can."

"Shit." Ofelia took another drag of her cigarette before looking at Hannah again. "I didn't mean to dismiss you like that. I'm sorry."

Hannah smiled at her. "It's okay."

"No, it's not. After everything you did for Rosario, you deserve nothing but my respect. You're an incredible woman and I'll always listen to what you have to say."

Ioni leaned back with a wan expression. "I'm continually touched by the faith you all have in each other. And jealous, really. I wish I could get some of that."

"What do you expect?" Amanda asked. "You've hurt us before. You killed my unborn babies."

"So ask me about it," Ioni challenged. "Ask me why."

Amanda shook her head. "I know why."

"We know you've been trying to save the world," Zack said to Ioni. "And we know it hasn't been easy. But for those of us who've been caught in your steamroll path, it's hard not to wonder if there were better ways."

Ioni nodded heavily. "You're talking about the war between you and the Gothams."

"I'm talking about *Rebel*," Zack snapped. "You're the one who set him against us, and look at what he did. He killed my brother, shot Mia in the chest."

"And nearly killed Zack twice," Amanda added. "I had to strong-arm Esis to get her to heal him. Was that all really part of your plan?"

Mia reeled at the memories of all those traumas—nearly a hundred years old from the feel of them, and brutally ironic on hindsight. To think there was a time when the Pelletiers fought to save the Silvers from Ioni's machinations.

Ioni peered into the blazing nonfire, her face looking older than ever. "I didn't choose the consequences, and I certainly didn't like them. I was just reverse-engineering the future I wanted, and that was the path it laid out for me."

She fixed her attention on Zack. "None of that absolves me of my crimes. I'd known Rebel since he was a kid. I *loved* him, and I destroyed his life. Even if I help save the world, I'll never forgive myself for what I did to him. Ever."

A muddled hush overtook the circle, until Mia broke the silence. "You told me to shoot Esis last year. 'Just pick up Rebel's gun and fire it at her head. The bullet will kill her. I promise.'"

Ioni bristled and cringed at the same time. "Those weren't my exact words."

"I just want to know what you were thinking," said Mia. "Did you lie to me or did you just get it wrong?"

Ioni glanced down at her kicking feet. "I lied."

Ofelia shook her head, mystified. "I don't think this meeting is helping you."

"Why did you do that?" Mia demanded to know. "What did it accomplish?"

"Nothing," Ioni said with lament. "At least not yet."

"What do you mean?"

"I can't answer that, Mia. It's a future question."

"Bullshit." Mia crossed her arms, livid. "Ofelia's right. I trust you less than ever now."

"Listen to me—"

"You could have warned us about David," Mia added. "You had every chance in the world!"

"And what do you think would have happened?" Ioni asked her. "You think he would have just melted into a puddle, like the Wicked Witch of the West?"

"He would have gone away," Mia said. "Like he did when we finally found out."

Ioni shook her head. "By that point, he was practically done with his job. There was nothing else to do but run. If I'd ratted him out sooner, he would have reversed all your memories until you forgot everything I told you. And if I blew his cover in a way he couldn't undo, then he would've taken you all back to Lárnach. You would have spent the rest of your days as breeding stock. Would you have preferred that?"

"No." Mia looked away, her voice a low mutter. "But I still hate the way it played out."

"So do I," Ioni said. "I'll sit here and take the heat for my sins, but I won't take heat for his."

Hannah placed Robert back into the stroller. "What about Jonathan and Heath?" she asked Ioni. "You were the one who told me how to find them. Did you have an ulterior motive, or—"

"No," Ioni's expression brightened. "I just saw an opportunity to tie two strings together in a way that benefitted everyone. Those don't come along very often."

"I think Jonathan might quibble with your definition of 'benefit,'" Zack grumbled.

"Maybe," said Ioni. "But he would have died within a week if you guys hadn't met him. Him and Heath both."

"I'm glad you did it," Theo told her. "For their sake and ours. Thank you."

Ioni turned to him in mock surprise. "He speaks! I was starting to think you drifted off."

"I've been here. Just listening."

"And scheming," Hannah said with a smirk. "He's trying to come up with a question that doesn't involve the future."

Theo snorted. "Am I that predictable?"

"Just consistent," Amanda said. "But we'd all be dead if you weren't the way you were."

Ioni marveled at the Silvers. "The Pelletiers didn't know what they were getting when they put you guys together. Even they couldn't have predicted how strong you'd make each other."

While Hannah and the others grinned at the praise, Theo looked to Ioni's wrist in revelation. "How did you get those watches?"

That was the last question Mia would have expected from Theo: Mr. All-Business, who could have worn a T-shirt that said *Cut to the Chase*. From Ioni's reaction, she was just as surprised, though there was a hint of grudging awe in her expression.

She shook a finger at Theo. "You sneaky bastard. Well played."

Zack tilted his head in puzzlement. "Is this an augur thing I'm missing?"

"Sort of," said Ioni. "Theo's been trying to get some information out of me, and he found a real clever way of doing it." She held up her watches for everyone to see. "There's no way I can talk about these without talking about the past and future."

Ioni stroked her thigh in contemplation before leveling a squint at Theo. "All right, buddy. You got what you wanted. Let's go down that rabbit hole."

Robert shrieked a high cry from his carriage, as if he were objecting to the direction of the conversation.

"Sorry," Hannah said. "I fed him before we got here. I think he's just restless."

"He is." Ioni smiled at Robert. "I'm not fluent in baby speak, but I'm guessing he wants a turn in Aunt Amanda's arms."

Amanda tensely shook her head. "My tempis isn't the most comfortable—"

"You'll be fine," said Hannah. She brought Robert over to her. "He likes you."

Amanda took him into her cool white hands, trying hard not to think about their power. She'd once destroyed an entire wing of an aerport with them. Now here they were on the most fragile of bodies: a nephew she'd never expected to meet, much less hold.

After five long seconds of fussing and writhing, Robert calmed down. He peeked up at Amanda with that glazed baby look that she loved, like he was trying to figure out where he knew her from.

Zack smiled over Amanda's shoulder. "Look at that. You're a natural."

"She was always great with kids," Hannah said. "She'll make an amazing mom someday."

Amanda cringed at the bittersweet compliment, and the fresh new tension in Zack's touch. Her future as a wife and a mother had become such a sore spot that he had raged about it right before the meeting. "I don't know what Ioni has you doing," Zack had said to Amanda. "But it scares the living shit out of me. Not just the secrets, the look in your eyes. It's like you're actually expecting to die."

Ioni studied Amanda from the other side of the fire. "Where I come from, she *was* an amazing mother. It's a documented fact."

Mia blinked at her confusedly. "What are you talking about?"

"You all know my deal by now," Ioni said. "I grew up on an untampered version of your world, one the Pelletiers never destroyed. In my string, you kept on living your normal lives. I have enough historical records to know how they turned out."

Ofelia's cigarette nearly fell out of her mouth. "Bullshit."

"It's true." Ioni pointed at Amanda. "She divorced her schmuck of a first husband, started a family with a better man, and then went back to medical school. Not only did she become a renowned oncologist, but her son and daughter followed in her footsteps."

"Oh my God." Hannah looked to Amanda in awe. "That's amazing."

Amanda narrowed her eyes at Ioni. "I thought the Pelletiers saved our lives when we were kids, me and Hannah. If they never showed up—"

"Neither of you died on that freeway," Ioni said. "You were just a little more banged up than Azral would have liked."

Only Hannah knew what she was talking about, and only because Esis had told her. *You would have survived with pain, and some unappealing scars.*

Hannah was quietly relieved to see her sister drop the matter. "Doesn't matter," Amanda said. "Another world, another woman."

Ioni shook her head. “You’re both facets of the same woman. Her triumphs are your triumphs, and your triumphs are hers.”

“My *triumphs*?”

“Sweetie, if that other Amanda could see you now, she’d be blown away at what you’ve become.”

“I’m afraid to ask what *I* became,” Ofelia said. “I probably ended up dead in an alley.”

“On the contrary,” said Ioni. “You stayed off drugs for the rest of your life, and helped hundreds of other junkies get straight. You married a nice man—”

“A *man*?”

“A nice one.”

“Am I not as gay as I think I am?”

Ioni laughed. “You love who you love. That’s the way it should be.”

“And my brother?”

Ioni’s smile faltered. “Killed in the line of duty at thirty-five.”

“Fuck.” Ofelia stomped her cigarette into the dirt. “Why does the universe hate him?”

“The universe doesn’t hate or love anyone,” Ioni said. “It just is.”

“What about me?” Mia asked. “Do I even want to know?”

“You became a highly regarded writer,” Ioni told her. “Nonfiction, mostly. Biographies. You got great reviews across the board, but your book sales were, uh—”

“I don’t want to hear it,” Mia said. “And I don’t want to hear about the nice man I married.”

“In point of fact, you married a great woman.”

“Really?” Mia shot a teasing look at Ofelia. “How about that?”

“Don’t be smug,” Ofelia retorted.

Ioni jerked her head at Zack. “I already told him what he became: a political cartoonist. Pulitzer-winning. Still talked about in my day.”

“You never mentioned the spousal situation,” Zack said.

“You were married,” Ioni hesitantly informed him. “Often.”

“Great.” Zack rolled his eyes. “I don’t need to hear any more.”

“And you can skip me,” Hannah told Ioni. “The way I was going, it couldn’t end well.”

“I beg to differ,” Ioni replied. “You never became famous, but you lived a good life. You started a musical theater in upstate New York that became a historical landmark.”

Hannah slumped in her chair dejectedly. "That was a real nice way of saying I died poor."

"Oh, don't be so negative. You did what you loved. And you were loved by many."

"Many husbands, you mean."

Ioni shook her head. "You had the same partner for forty-eight years, but you never got married and you never had kids."

"Well, shit." Hannah took a quick, nervous look at Amanda. "Did she and I ever, uh . . ."

"Afraid not," said Ioni. "You weren't estranged, but you were never close either. Not like you are now."

Amanda supposed she shouldn't have been surprised. Without an apocalyptic struggle to bind them together, their baggage would have only accumulated. How tragic for those other Givens. They'd missed out on something wonderful.

All eyes in the circle slowly gravitated toward Theo. He chortled with morbid humor. "Ioni already told me what happened. It won't surprise you one bit."

Amanda understood immediately. "Alcohol."

"Sadly," said Ioni. "He died in Mexico at twenty-three."

"*Twenty-three?*" Hannah turned to Theo. "You were twenty-three when we met you."

Theo nodded. "I was waiting for a bus to Tijuana when Azral found me. I had five hundred dollars in my pocket, and I knew exactly how I was going to spend it."

He snickered in the heavy silence. "Finally. A plan that worked."

None of the others were amused one bit. Even Robert bleated in disapproval.

"I only told Theo his fate for perspective," Ioni said. "A dead drunk on one world can be a savior on another."

"And what about you?" Mia sharply inquired. "You said you were going to tell us about yourself."

"And the watches," Ofelia added.

Ioni sighed at the crackling fire. "I can't explain any of it without explaining my era. It's a hell of a lot different than your world or this one."

"How so?" Theo asked.

"Well, for starters, we came about temporis naturally. No Cataclysms. No hand of God. Just a chain of scientific discoveries spread out over a couple of centuries. By the time we pierced the veil for good—"

"The veil," Hannah repeated.

"The Hawkridge-Belgrove Veil," Ioni explained. "The invisible wall of quantum energy that keeps temporis from flooding the planet. On your world, it was nice and strong until the Pelletiers showed up. On this world, it's been Swiss cheese since the Cataclysm."

"That's why we didn't get our powers till we got here," Ofelia guessed.

Ioni nodded. "And why your cars never flew for shit."

Amanda adjusted Robert's blanket to keep her tempic skin from chilling him. "So your people got temporis when they were good and ready."

"Oh, we got it," Ioni said. "But we still weren't ready. The timebenders of the era had declared themselves a master race. And when the non-chrons finally caught up with the technology, there was war. A lot of it."

She looked to Theo before he could ask. "No, I wasn't there for that. It was still way before my time."

"But things got better," he assumed.

Ioni nodded. "We started over with peace in mind. New laws. New values. New social protections. Thanks to genetic engineering, we were all chronokinetic. And we were all freaking brilliant. Within twelve hundred years, we were able to achieve what the Pelletiers couldn't."

Amanda's eyebrows rose. "You cured death?"

"It still existed," Ioni said. "But we tamed it to the point where it was entirely optional. Every time nature tried to throw us a new curveball, we threw it right back in her face."

She groaned as Ofelia lit up a new cigarette. "Really?"

"Would you rather I be angry?"

"I'd rather you live to see forty."

Ofelia vented a smoky laugh. "I'll be lucky if I live past tonight."

Zack anxiously fidgeted with his warsuit's wrist console. "I can't even imagine a deathless world. You must have been up to your ass in each other."

"Our population grew," Ioni confirmed. "And we had a few more wars over what to do about it. Eventually, we agreed on a trillion-person cap, plus a very strict enforcement policy. No one new comes into the world until someone old goes out. But with life on Earth being as cozy as it was, there weren't a lot of people who wanted to leave."

She chuckled in reminiscence. "By the time I was born, it had been three years since the last childbirth. And it was another seven and a half until the next one."

Mia's eyes went wide. "You were the only person born in your *decade*?"

"Legally," Ioni said. "There were still illegits popping out here and there."

"That must have been hell for the diaper industry," Zack quipped.

"It must have been hell on *families*," Amanda stressed. "When you practically outlaw parenthood—"

"It wasn't the problem you think it was," Ioni said. "Our sensibilities changed with the times. We didn't have a biological clock, or future generations to worry about. It was just us. And with artificial labor doing all the busywork, we had nothing but time on our hands."

"Sounds boring," said Mia. "Did everyone just screw around?"

"We had our share of hedonists," Ioni confessed. "But there were many, like me, who set their sights higher. Some lived for their art. Some lived for discovery. Some lived for the thrill of the hunt."

Ofelia looked at her askance. "The hunt for . . . ?"

"Anything. Fortune, fame, domination over others. There were still a fair share of pricks on my world."

"And what about you?" Zack asked.

"You're asking if I'm a prick?"

"I know you're a prick. I'm asking what your big thing was."

"History," Ioni said. "I was an unabashed scholar, obsessed with the past. I wanted to break new ground in pre-temporal studies, but we had so many people looking back on those years that there was barely any ground left to cover. So, like a hundred million other wannabes, I dove headfirst into the field of speculative history."

"Speculative history," Hannah repeated. "Like 'what if Hitler had been killed as a baby'?"

Ioni laughed. "A little more complex than that, but yeah. I loved it. I must have written a thousand works before I finally got tired of theorizing. I wanted to do something more hands-on."

Amanda could already see where this was going. "You mean time travel."

"Yes," said Ioni. "There's a very elite group in academia, just a couple hundred folks around the world. We call them 'alterants,' and they're the rock stars of the field. They don't just speculate. They go to the past and create new histories. I coveted that job more than anything I ever wanted. But the application process was rigorous, and the competition was fierce."

The conversation paused when Robert became surly. Amanda sent him around the circle on elongated arms, all the way back into his mother's care. "I take it you got the job."

"I got it," Ioni said. "My friends and lovers were all so jealous, but I didn't care. When you're an alterant, you don't just visit the past. You live there. You blend. You observe and report for decades at a stretch."

Amanda suddenly realized why Ioni seemed so . . . normal for a woman of her origin. She'd been living in the contemporary past for so long that it had overtaken her speech and mannerisms.

"So how does it work?" Hannah asked. "You flap a butterfly's wings and then follow the ripples?"

Ioni smiled. "Some play it subtle. Some don't. I was one of the ones who didn't. My focus of study was temporis and its transformative effects on society. I wanted to see what would happen if the world got it early. And to do *that*, I needed a—"

"Cataclysm," Theo said.

Ioni nodded grimly. "It was the only way to tear the veil."

Ofelia's cigarette fell out of her hanging mouth. "That was *you*?"

"Yes."

"You were behind the 1912—"

"Yes," Ioni said. "I killed two million people with clear mind and intent, and it wasn't my first time doing it."

Amanda was glad she wasn't holding Robert anymore. Her arms had turned craggy with stress. "You made more than one Cataclysm."

"Two," said Ioni. "In two different strings. My first one was in Paris in 1980. I didn't choose the time or place. My mentor did. It was more of a training session than anything."

"A practice genocide," Zack muttered with scorn.

Ioni fussed with the band of her digital watch, her vacant gaze fixed on the fire. "That's not the way my mentor saw it, and she warned me not to fall into that trap. She said, 'These people are long dead. They're not even ghosts. They're just temporal copies of ghosts. Just keep your perspective and don't get too close to them, or you'll never survive as an alterant.'"

Hannah turned her head in disgust. "Your people are just as bad as the Pelletiers."

"Actually, we're worse," Ioni said. "The Pelletiers are trying to cure their last fatal disease. We just stir shit up because we're curious."

"Your people still do this?" Theo asked.

"*They* do. I don't."

"How long did it take you to see the light?" Mia asked.

"Longer than it should have," Ioni said with a sigh. "It was a multistep epiphany that began with Genevieve Cassin."

"Who?"

"A seventeen-year-old Parisian girl," Ioni explained. "Deformed since birth. Her face was misshapen. Her right leg was withered. She was in constant pain from her skeletal defects, and her family was absolute shit to her."

She closed her eyes and took a deep breath through her nose. Amanda couldn't tell if she was thinking or just collecting herself.

"When the Cataclysm struck," Ioni continued, "they'd been walking through Saint-Mandé, right on the edge of the blast zone. As usual, they'd forced Genevieve to follow ten steps behind, since they hated being seen with her. But their cruelty ended up saving her life. The family was obliterated. Genevieve wasn't. On paper, she was one of the lucky ones."

The Silvers watched Ioni, expressionless, as her voice began to tremble.

"I don't know what made me visit her in the hospital. Guilt, perhaps. Masochism. Or maybe I was just trying to toughen myself up. In any case, I spoke with her a good long time, and wouldn't you know it? She was sweet. She believed that God had called her family to Heaven, but He refused to take her because she was too ugly. But she figured if she lived a good enough life, He'd have no choice but to accept her."

Ioni showed off her digital watch, an antiquated timepiece with blood red digits. "She gave me this as a goodwill gesture, the last treasured item she had. She didn't need it anymore, so—"

"Why didn't she need it?" Hannah asked.

Ioni's voice turned low and grim. "The flare of the Cataclysm had burned out her retinas. She was completely blind."

Amanda swapped a heavy look with Zack, and saw him in the exact same fix. Ioni was practically inviting the whole group to hate her, but why?

"What happened to her?" Mia asked Ioni.

"What happened to the *world*?" Theo asked. "To blow up a city in the middle of a cold war—"

"Like I said, I didn't choose the target," Ioni said. "I warned my mentor that it would end in a nuclear holocaust. She said, 'Yes, but how quickly?' It turns out the answer was six and a half weeks."

Ioni looked to Mia again. "That's what happened to Genevieve."

"*Mierda.*" Ofelia massaged her aching arm. "That wasn't enough to make you quit?"

"Afraid not," said Ioni. "I thought I could do things better next time, on my own terms. By choosing 1912, I didn't have to worry about nukes. If anything, I figured the Cataclysm would *prevent* a global conflict, and I was right. Without the forty million casualties of World War I—"

"You think that excuses it?" Mia asked.

"I'm just telling you my excuse at the time."

Amanda gestured at Ioni's analog watch, the most cumbersome-looking timepiece she'd ever seen. "Who did you get that from? Another survivor?"

Ioni slowly shook her head. "A victim."

"So you talked to him before it happened."

"Yes." Ioni rose to her feet. "I'm going to employ some visual aids for this part. Hope you don't mind. It—"

"I *do* mind," Hannah said. "If you're about to show us the Cataclysm—"

"I'm not," Ioni promised her. "Just bear with me."

With a flick of her hand, the entire scene changed. Only the chairs and bonfire remained. The rest had transformed into a green and spacious park in the middle of a tenement slum. The sky took on a soft violet hue that suggested either dusk or dawn.

One by one, the orphans stood up and took a cursory scan of the environment. If Ioni hadn't mentioned the setting in advance, Amanda would have thought it was Victorian London. The lampposts were all kerosene-lit. The street beyond the iron fence sported multiple piles of horse droppings, and there wasn't a motorized buggy in sight at that hour.

Hannah held Robert close as she looked around the park. "*This* is Ground Zero?" she asked Ioni. "Looks more like 1812."

"It's 1912," Ioni assured her. "October fifth, five fifty-two A.M."

"But where exactly—"

"Brooklyn," said Ioni. "Greenpoint. Just a half-mile from where you used to live with Peter."

"Not far from where I grew up," Zack added. He pointed at the shelter pavilion in the distance: a pair of squat stone structures that were connected by a wall of Roman columns. "I recognize that. It's from McGolrick Park."

"That's not its original name," Ioni said.

Zack nodded. "Right. They changed it in the forties. I forgot what it used to be called."

"Winthrop Park," Theo said in a faint voice.

"Winthrop Park," Ioni repeated. "A historical footnote on our world. A notorious landmark on this one. I believe a couple of you have seen the modern-day version."

"Yes," Amanda and Mia said in synch. Peter had taken them both on a tour of the place, not long after they'd settled into his brownstone. It didn't look anything like what Ioni was showing them. The park had been converted into a high-tech memorial garden. A digital wall let visitors scroll through six hundred thousand names of dead Brooklynites, while a holographic obelisk marked the exact epicenter of the Cataclysm.

But this version of Winthrop was clearly the "before" model, the one that two Earths shared in common. And if Ioni was right about the date and time, then it was just a few minutes away from changing.

Ofelia looked to Ioni impatiently. "What's the point of all this? Why—"

"There." Ioni motioned to a man on a nearby bench, the only living soul within view. He'd been sitting so still in the shadow of an elm tree that the Silvers hadn't noticed him until now.

Amanda struggled to process him in the low light of the park. He was a young Black man of extraordinary size, dressed in a threadbare coat and gray wool cap that practically made him a poster boy of the era. He clutched a suitcase to his chest as if his very life depended on it, his kindly face contorted in a dumbfounded look. Amanda couldn't tell if he was reeling from good or bad news. From the way his mouth hung, he didn't know either.

"Freedom Williams, Junior," Ioni told her companions. "Seventeen. Dropped out of school in the middle of eighth grade to take his late father's job at the iron foundry. Sixty hours a week of backbreaking labor, all to keep his mom and siblings fed."

"Wow," said Hannah. "Good guy."

"The best," said Ioni. "He was strong in a way I'd never seen before. Certainly not among my kind."

"Why does he look so freaked out?" Zack asked.

"He had a strange couple of minutes," Ioni explained. "A man even larger than him nearly killed him for his wristwatch, and then I showed up and got all superpowery."

"How?" Mia asked. "If that was before the Cataclysm, there wouldn't be any temporis."

Ioni smiled humbly. "There are ways to pierce the veil without ripping it."

Ofelia noticed Freedom's bare wrists. "Did he lose the watch? I don't see it."

"I took it," Ioni said. "Bought it, actually, for four hundred grand."

Amanda suddenly realized what the suitcase contained, and why Freedom was so utterly gobsmacked. In 1912, that was "set for life" money.

Zack looked to Ioni, confused. "So you saved his life, made him rich—"

"—and then killed him in a Cataclysm," Ofelia finished. "Why?"

Ioni sighed at the grass. "I saved him because I wanted to talk to him. I made him rich because I wanted his last few minutes to be happy."

"You could have teleported him and his whole family away."

"Yes," said Ioni. "And I could have stopped the whole Cataclysm with the flip of a switch."

"Why didn't you?" Hannah asked.

"Because I was still missing something that Freedom and Genevieve had," Ioni said. "Something that all my people lack. We'd lived so long as functional immortals that we couldn't even see what it cost us. When we stopped the clock, we killed the value of time. When we beat death, we lost all perspective on what makes life precious."

She gestured all around at her company. "Look at what the shadow of mortality has done to you guys. Look at how strong it's made you. I didn't have that. I didn't even have a frame of reference. Even walking through history couldn't open my eyes."

Ioni looked to Freedom again. "It wasn't until I was standing in the ashes of Brooklyn that the truth finally hit me. I'd thought the people of this world were just temporal abstractions, but they were all more alive than I'd ever been. It was *my* world that needed a cataclysmic shake-up. This one was just fine."

Amanda looked to her left and saw Theo standing alone. Though he was well within earshot of the conversation, he didn't look like he'd been listening to a word of it. He merely fixated on the smallest tree in a copse, the only one that hadn't changed color with the autumn.

As the other Silvers talked with Ioni, Amanda worked her way over to him. "You okay?"

"No." Theo chuckled. "She just can't stop playing us."

"What do you mean?"

"She pretended like I cornered her when I asked her about the watches, but she knew exactly what I was going to ask. She was counting on it."

"Why?"

Theo shook his head, his eyes still fixed on the sapling. "It doesn't matter."

"She said you wanted information from her."

"I got it," Theo said. "It's nothing any of you need to worry about."

Amanda had no idea what Theo was keeping from her, but she couldn't imagine that it was a small matter. All those stupid augur secrets. She'd never understood the need for them until Ioni gave her one of her own.

"It's a lonely life you people live," she said to Theo. "I'm sorry you had to go through that."

Theo smiled gently. "I've had more family on this world than I ever had on the old one."

Amanda peeked over her shoulder at Ioni. "Well, she's definitely walked a lonely road."

"No question," Theo said.

"I don't think this was just a strategy meeting," Amanda mused. "She wants us to understand her."

Theo looked back to the copse of trees, a nervous new twitch in his face. "Here it comes."

"What?"

A three-inch ball of light suddenly materialized in the exact place that he was looking at: five feet off the surface of the grass, under the lowest branch of the park's one green tree. The orb pulsed in the air in a quick, erratic rhythm.

Amanda was just about to call for Ioni when the anomaly suddenly froze in still-frame.

"It's all right," Ioni said. "I promised I wouldn't show you the destruction. That's as far as it'll get."

The other orphans gathered around Amanda and Theo, their stunned eyes locked on the orb.

"Holy shit," said Zack. "That's the Cataclysm."

"The start of it," Ioni replied. "Amazing, isn't it? Every single difference between your world and this one, it all hatched out of that egg."

"*Your* egg," Mia emphasized. "You made this world more than anyone."

"I changed it," said Ioni. "And I take full responsibility for all the bad things that happened. I've been here every day since 1912. I've watched events unfold in real time: the Gothams, the Majee, the new British Dominion, the Temporal

Revolution, all of it. Even the Pelletiers are a product of this string. I made them, and now they're unmaking everything."

Hannah eyed her suspiciously. "You never went home again?"

"This is my home," Ioni attested. "I'm bound to it forever. But to answer your question, I did go back a couple of times. Mostly to steal some technology."

"Like the shields," Theo mused.

"Most definitely the shields."

"But what have you been *doing* the last hundred years?" Ofelia asked her.

"Lots of things," Ioni attested. "Little things. I've gotten to know a bunch of good people. I tried to improve their lives whenever I could. And sometimes I went big."

"Big," Zack said.

Ioni smirked at him. "I've stopped a few baby Hitlers in the making."

She swept away the illusion of Winthrop Park, and brought the old scenery back. The Mother Rock watched from her eternal perch, her stoic face underlit by the bonfire.

"I love this Earth with all my heart," Ioni told the Silvers. "I won't let it suffer the same fate as yours, and I'll be damned if it ever becomes like mine."

She checked the time on her watches, then looked to her company again. "Any more questions?"

Amanda had several, and she was sure the others had their own, but nobody needed to hear more. Their hard drives were already filled to capacity, and they just wanted to rest before leaving for San Francisco.

All the same, Amanda felt the strong urge to say something to Ioni.

"I can't speak for anyone else here," she began. "But this is too big for me to judge. All I know for sure is that you didn't put this world in danger. The Pelletiers did. And you're the closest thing we have to a messiah."

Ioni opened her mouth to object, but Amanda cut her off. "We may be the generals, but you *are* the war. None of us can do it without you. And if all your schemes and hopes come to fruition, then . . ."

Amanda shrugged, stymied. But Theo knew what to say next.

"You can officially stop hating yourself," he told Ioni. "If we save this world, your slate is clean."

Ioni's eyes welled up with tears. "I hope you're right, but I'm not sure. I'll probably find out someday. No one is ever truly immortal. And if the system works like some of you think, then I'll have to account for myself one day."

She lowered her head and laughed with maudlin humor. "I only hope I get to go where the good people go, because I imagine you'll all be there."

Ioni glanced around at all the long and tired faces, then forced a flippant grin. "All right. I've taken enough of your time."

She blew at the bonfire and extinguished it with one breath. "Meeting adjourned."

At midnight, all the forces gathered in the great plain south of Sergelen: four hundred and ninety-one Gothams, two hundred and sixty-two Scarlet Sabres, twenty-eight orphans from a dead sister Earth, and seven newborn infants of transdimensional heritage. While the Sabres came dressed in tempic-plated speedsuits, the timebenders wore the battle gear that Ioni had provided them. Each suit had been tailored to the individual's talents. The swifters had armor to protect them from speed impacts. The tempics had shifters to help them move faster. The thermics' suits were girded with enough protective underplating to keep them from burning or freezing themselves. Ioni had already given everyone a quick orientation on the suits' other special features: from the comm link communicators to the energy shields that provided complete invulnerability . . . for a limited time, anyway.

"You each have ten seconds of shield power," Ioni had explained. "You can transfer the time to someone else, or you can use it all for yourself. But when you're out, that's it. I can't give you any more. I need the rest of the juice for the big shields."

Hannah looked down at the base of her wrist and saw a *12.5* in ominous red lumis. Theo had already portioned out his shield time between the sisters, Zack, and Mia, on the insistence that he wouldn't need it. "I'll be deep in the command center," he'd assured them. "And I'll have Melissa protecting me."

But with seconds to go before final deployment, he didn't look all that confident to Hannah. He stood off in the near distance and mumbled softly to Zack, his anxious eyes darting furtively between Amanda, Hannah, and Mia.

"You okay?" Mia asked Hannah.

She adjusted her son in her grip. "Not really. I feel like an understudy who doesn't know her lines."

Mia squeezed her wrist. "I'll be with you the whole time."

"So will I," said her brother Bobby, an intimidating figure in his big black warsuit. "With two Farisis, you can't lose."

Hannah smiled at him before checking on her own sibling. Amanda was deeply enmeshed in a tense-looking discussion with Caleb. They stopped talking the moment they saw her approach.

"You guys all right?"

Amanda gave her a shaky grin. "Just going over some last-minute stuff."

"I thought you were gonna be with the wing crew."

"I am," said Amanda. "We've each partnered up with a swifter."

Hannah shrugged. "I'd be your speedpack if I could. Just like in the old days."

"No," Amanda said, a little too tensely for Hannah's comfort. "Caleb and I are good."

Caleb smiled at the child in Hannah's arms. "Look at him. He's as pretty as his mom."

"That's what *I* keep saying," Hannah joked.

"He'll survive this," Amanda solemnly promised her. "He'll live to a ripe old age, and so will you."

Hannah felt hot tears prick the corners of her eyes. "I wish I had your confidence."

"Not confidence. Just faith." Amanda hugged her just enough to keep Robert snug between them. "You carried me all through this world. I would have never made it without you."

"Same to you, a hundred times over." Hannah pressed her forehead to Amanda's. "Those other-world Givens have nothing on us."

Amanda laughed. "We're closer."

"*And* cooler."

Caleb shook his head, befuddled. "What the hell are you two talking about?"

A sharp new hush fell over the crowd as Ioni appeared high above them. Her spectral form was so large and translucent that she almost looked like she was made of stars.

"I won't waste your time with speeches," she told the assembled forces. Despite her grand and majestic appearance, her voice sounded no different than it would have if she'd been standing right next to them. "I'll just say this: we only have one shot to stop what's coming. If we fail, that's it. There'll be no appeal. No escape. Everyone on this planet will die."

The people below her exchanged dark looks and mutters. Hannah frowned at the celestial Ioni. "Nice pep talk."

A half-moon portal sprang to life at the base of the field: four hundred feet wide at the base, and bright enough to light the area for miles.

"Go on through," Ioni said. Her specter had become invisible in the glow of the portal. She was nothing but a voice in their ears. "I'll see you on the other side."

Slowly, hesitantly, the many combatants proceeded into the breach. Hannah moved with the flow, her nervous gaze locked on the portal as it drew closer. The fluorescent haze turned the people in front of her into silhouettes before swallowing them one by one.

By the time Hannah reached the front of the queue, she was walking shoulder to shoulder with her family: Amanda and Mia, Theo and Zack, Peter and Heath, Ofelia and Caleb. Robert mewled anxiously in her arms. She quieted him with a kiss and a whisper. "It's all right, baby. It's all right."

She stopped at the shimmering base of the portal and sucked her last deep gulp of Mongolian air. "It'll all be over soon."

PART SIX

THE GREAT SISTERS GIVEN

THIRTY-SIX

As the sun finally broke over the American West, the collective gaze of the civilized world flittered anxiously to San Francisco. Newsdrones buzzed like flies around the city, which, after nine straight weeks of evacuation chaos, had been reduced to a plundered wasteland. Half the ground level windows had been shattered by looters, while the automobiles that had been caught in the riots lay ravaged in the middle of intersections. From the looks of it, the city had already suffered its apocalypse, yet the main event hadn't even started. More than three billion people from a hundred and eighty nations gathered in front of their lumivisions, even sacrificed sleep, to watch the spectacle unfold in real time: the very first Cataclysm of the broadcast age.

"Assuming it even happens," said the many news anchors, ever determined to hedge their bets. For all the dread and hysteria, there still wasn't a shred of empirical evidence that San Francisco was about to go belly-up in a temporal conflagration. Maybe Merlin McGee had finally botched a prediction. Or maybe he'd lied just to mess with people. In any case, he'd been vague about the timing of the calamity. All he'd said was that it would occur in the daylight.

For the beleaguered government of the United States, still twice-shy when it came to Cataclysms, it was better to be safe than sorry. They closed down

Alcatraz Aerport at six A.M., then recalled the last of the rescue shuttles at seven. The authorities made it starkly clear that anyone who remained in the danger zone after sunrise was officially on their own.

Indeed, once the last extraction crews departed, the stubborn and elusive holdouts came crawling out of their hiding spots: the skeptics, the misfits, the last-minute looters, the doomsday cults, the fetishists, and the people who just wanted to die. An unemployed actor strolled the Embarcadero, livecasting his last will and testament over the Eaglenet. A gray-haired guitarist took the stage at Golden Gate Park and played a farewell concert to an empty field. A haggard old woman—homeless, drunk, and rambling for as long as anyone could remember her—climbed to the top of Twin Peaks and lay faceup on the grass. As the media drones circled above her like buzzards, she held up a hand-scrawled sign that merely said *I EXISTED.*

One person the cameras didn't see was Melissa Masaad, to her continued amazement. Ioni had provided her with a hundred crystalline cubes that, when linked together and activated, cloaked her entire section of the city. Prior Circle flanked the western edge of Eureka Valley: a twelve-acre compound of trees and squat buildings that served as the headquarters for Prior Chronolectrics. Roughly a third of the nation's households had a Prior-brand rejuvenator in the kitchen, while the company's speed-cheesers and marinators had become a staple of American restaurants.

The news media had taken a special interest in Prior Circle, as it lay smack in the geographical center of San Francisco and would likely serve as the staging ground for whatever mayhem was coming. If the drones were quick or lucky enough, they might even catch a glimpse of something interesting before the explosion: an alien saucer, a portal from Hell, a terrorist from the twenty-fifth century. Who knew? Maybe God Himself would show up with a dynamite plunger. Anything seemed possible these days.

Thanks to Ioni's illusory magic, the public only saw what she wanted them to see: a hastily abandoned corporate campus, only slightly less trampled than the rest of the city. The newsdrones failed to register Melissa or any of the ordnance she'd brought to the central plaza: the auto-turrets, the missile launchers, the electromagnetic rail guns. And those were just the Integrity toys. Ioni had given her dozens of alien objects to install, all hatched from crystal eggs. Some of them sprouted into twenty-foot towers. Others formed impregnable shelters. Four of them converged into a diamantine platform that rose fifty feet into the air. Yet the drones flew past them without a second glance, as if they'd always been part of the scenery.

Melissa unwrapped a protein bar, then eyed it with soft revulsion. With the orphans and Gothams arriving in five minutes, her quiet time in Prior Circle was coming to an end. Her stomach was too nervous to crave any food. But the last thing she needed, today of all days, was a hypoglycemic headache. She forced a few bites down, then stashed the remains in her bag.

Felicity beckoned her from the northern edge of the plaza. "Boss, he's back."

Melissa joined her on the metal bench and scanned the image on her tablet. The cameras had picked up an intruder at the compound's main entrance, a doddering old man in a bathrobe and slippers who'd been tripping off the sensors since sunrise.

Felicity clicked her tongue, baffled, as he shook the iron gate. "What does he want in here?"

Melissa shrugged. "I don't think he's entirely lucid."

"Senile," Felicity said with a sigh. "I was afraid of that. Someone probably brought him in from out of town."

Unfortunately, Melissa couldn't rule out the possibility. A Cataclysm was a handy way to get rid of unwanted burdens, if one had ice for blood.

"Capture his image," Melissa said. "When this is over, I want to find whoever left him here."

"And do what, arrest them? Under whose authority?"

Loath as Melissa was to admit it, Felicity was right. Neither of them were government agents anymore. They weren't even technically Americans. The moment they went rogue, Integrity revoked their status as naturalized citizens and marked them both as terrorists. The shoe fit better than Melissa would have liked, having just planted the seeds of an American city's destruction.

Felicity shared her ambivalence. "That old man's a goner no matter what we do. And if the media's right, there are still at least two thousand people here."

"There could have been millions."

"There should have been none," Felicity countered. "I never agreed to mass murder."

Unlike Melissa, who'd come dressed for battle in one of Ioni's custom warsuits, Felicity simply wore the bright green coveralls of a utility worker.

Her main job was to keep the Integrity machines running. For that, she only needed her toolbelt and a lot of pockets.

Melissa squeezed her shoulder. "You know why we're doing it."

"Yeah, but why did it have to be *here*?"

Others had previously suggested to Ioni, as if the thought had somehow never occurred to her, that there were plenty of better places to blow up: an empty desert, a remote tundra, a lifeless patch of the stratosphere. But Ioni's machines didn't work in a vacuum. They needed to siphon the energy of at least two million solic generators, which only the densest cities offered in concentration. San Francisco made an ideal choice, as it was buffered by water on the north, east, and west, which minimized collateral damage. Alcatraz and Daly City would be the only neighbors to fall. The others—Oakland, Marin, even nearby Treasure Island—lay safely outside the blast radius.

"It's not my preference either," Melissa said to Felicity. "But given the alternative—"

"I know. I know. It just sucks." She switched her tablet to the local news, currently fixed on a pullback view of the skyline. "This was a one-of-a-kind city. The only one in the nation that welcomed weirdos like me."

Melissa couldn't dispute that. After the Cataclysm of 1912, half the surviving artists of New York fled to San Francisco and turned it into one of the most colorful and eclectic places on Earth—a haven for anyone who didn't fit the white-bread American paradigm. Even the architects flouted the rules of convention, with its tilted glass skyscrapers and Siamese towers that conjoined at the highest levels. The San Francisco skyline was a work of art in itself. And soon it would be gone forever.

Felicity switched off her tablet, then forced a weak smile. "I'll be okay, boss. You don't have to worry about me."

"I don't," Melissa assured her. "You've earned my faith a hundred times over."

A bright new fluorescence suddenly caught their attention. One of the nearest crystal formations, a seven-foot arch of thin, hard diamond, began to shine like moonlight along the inside edge. Within moments, the glow expanded into a sheet of rippling white energy that Melissa easily recognized. A portal.

Three limber figures came stumbling out of the light, as if they'd been pushed through the arch by bouncers. Like Melissa, they were dressed in Ioni's high-tech armor, their faces obscured by their reflective silver helmets.

They each pressed a button on their sleeves, prompting their headshields to retract into their suit collars. Though the lone man of the trio, a slender young Asian with unkempt hair, was a stranger to Melissa, she was well-acquainted with the sisters in his company.

"Christ." Meredith squinted in the sunlight. "I wasn't prepared for that."

Melissa could imagine. If they had teleported from Yokohama, as she suspected they did, then it was nearly one A.M. on the other side of the portal. "You all right?"

"No," said Charlene. "That hurt like a bastard."

Meredith checked on her male companion, who looked a hair's breadth away from vomiting. *"Mada ikiteru?"*

The man grumbled a few words in Japanese before hocking a gob of spit.

"One of the Rubies," Melissa guessed.

Meredith nodded. "Akio. Yeah. He doesn't speak a word of English. I also have to warn you. He's a bit of a—"

Felicity greeted him in his native tongue, only to get a brusque and sneering response. Charlene smacked the back of his head.

"Sorry," she told Felicity. "As my sister was about to say, he's a real charmer."

Melissa looked to Felicity. "Did he just insult you?"

"Tried to," she replied with a caustic smirk. "Nothing I haven't heard before."

Melissa shot a dubious look at the Grahams. "And you brought this man with you because . . . ?"

"We need him," said Charlene. "He's the only amp we have."

"Amp?"

"The opposite of a solic," Meredith explained. "He can supercharge anyone's temporal power. Make us gods for at least a minute or two."

"Goodness." Melissa checked the portal behind them, which had yet to produce more timebenders. "And the rest of your people?"

The sisters swapped an edgy look. "They're still debating if they should come," said Charlene.

Felicity threw her hands up. "*Debating?* What more do they need?"

"Ioni never even introduced herself to us," Meredith replied. "Now she wants us all to fight and die for her."

"Not for her," Melissa corrected. "For everyone."

"That's what we told our grandpa," Charlene said. "But he still has reservations."

Despite her annoyance, Melissa couldn't fault Auberon. Ioni had already let the Pelletiers kill half the orphans and Gothams. Why would she do any better for the Majee? Still, the old man was playing a dangerous game. If he waited too long to join the fight, he'd be dooming his clan to extinction.

Akio looked up with sudden confusion, then muttered something in Japanese.

"He says the air's gone heavy with energy," Felicity translated. "A kind he's never—"

The sky suddenly turned a lighter shade of blue, while the clouds became blurred by a gauzy new radiance. From the convex shape of the refraction, Melissa assumed that she was looking at Ioni's handiwork: a powerful new shield dome that enclosed all of Prior Circle.

At least Melissa *hoped* it was Ioni's dome, because otherwise—

"Look out!" Charlene cried. She tackled her sister to the ground as the air was rocked by lightning and thunder.

Melissa fell to her knees, her sight and hearing hobbled by the mayhem.

We're under electric attack, she thought. Yet aside from a static tickle on her skin, she didn't feel any worse for the wear.

The bombardment stopped as quickly as it started. Melissa looked around and saw smoldering corpses, *dozens* of them, scattered all around the central plaza. Her heart sank at the thought of the orphans and Gothams lying dead in some botched teleportation. But the hard stone ridges of their armor suits pegged them as soldiers of a different army.

Felicity approached the nearest cadaver and gave him a cautious once-over. "Holy cow. He's a Jade."

Charlene peeked over Felicity's shoulder. "What the hell's going on?"

"Not sure," said Melissa. "I thought the war wouldn't start until Ioni arrived, but I guess the Pelletiers are being proactive. These Jades must have been here for hours."

Felicity checked her temporal scanner. "We didn't catch the slightest whiff of them."

Melissa nodded uneasily. "Luckily, Ioni did. I only hope she got them all, because—"

"*Yaba! Miro!*" Akio yelled, his finger pointed to the east.

Melissa heard a shrill new whistling in her ears, like tea kettles, and caught the strong mixed scent of metal and petrichor. Those were the telltale signs of an impending portal, but from the enormous ripple in the air, it was shaping up to be a doozy.

Felicity gripped Melissa's arm as the plaza became drenched in a bright and moony glow. "Boss, please tell me—"

"Yes," Melissa assured her. With the shield dome raised and the hidden Jades purged, it was safe for Ioni's soldiers to arrive.

"Get ready," Melissa warned the others. "It's about to get crowded in here."

They came pouring out of the light by the dozens: a chaotic procession of silhouetted figures that moved more like children than soldiers. They stumbled. They clustered. They gawked at their surroundings. They held each other with tight, hooked fingers, as if one false step could send them plummeting off the edge of creation.

They're terrified, Melissa noted with no shortage of irony. They were the chronokinetics of Planet Earth, each one crackling with power. When assembled in the hundreds and united under one cause, they were a force unseen in human history.

But then the same could be said for the threat they were facing, which made a perfectly good reason to worry.

As a soft Mongolian breeze wafted through the portal, flush with the scent of dry needlegrass, Felicity studied the Scarlet Sabres in the mix. They were all decked out in tempic armor, and armed to the teeth with conventional weaponry. A third of them guided wraith-class war drones behind them, like black metal kites tied on strings of ones and zeroes.

"That's some serious tech they've got there," Felicity griped. "They could bring all kinds of hell to Europe."

Melissa had voiced the same concern to Ioni, only to get a cryptic and ominous reply. "Their toys won't work when this is over," she'd promised. "Not anywhere."

As the Sabres flocked to their battle stations and the timebenders loitered in clusters, Theo stood atop a bench and pressed a button on the collar of his warsuit. His voice filled the plaza with divine omnipresence, as if it were being broadcast through a thousand speakers.

"All right, guys, we only have a minute. If you're seeing white arrows, that means you're not where you're supposed to be. Follow the lights and get to your places. Ioni will be here soon."

A pair of flat white arrows, no larger than dimes, appeared in Hannah's visor. They moved like snakes across her vision, until they converged at the edge of a crystalline dome that looked large enough to hold twenty people.

Hannah proceeded to the door of the glimmering construct and was joined by six familiar women, all her fellow survivors from Lárnach. As they cradled their blanket-wrapped newborns in their arms, they all took turns peeking into the dome shelter: some futuristic nursery, judging by the seven crystal bassinets.

"I'll keep watch on your kids," Rosario assured the group. "I've got my foresight back and a whole lot of weapons. If trouble comes—"

"Trouble *is* coming," said Sparrow. "This igloo won't do shit against a Pelletier."

"Or a Cataclysm," Artemis grumbled. She peeked down at the chubby little boy in her grip. "We should have just left them at a convent or something."

Rosario clutched her daughter defensively. "I'm not giving Eden to a bunch of nuns."

"Would you rather she die?"

"She won't," Hannah insisted. "None of our babies are dying here."

She scanned the faces of her coterie and saw their matching skepticism. "Ioni planned this out to the very last detail." Hannah gestured at the dome. "For all we know, this thing is Cataclysm-proof. Or an escape pod. Or a teleporter. I can't say. I just know it's something that'll keep the kids safe."

She looked to Sparrow next. "As for the Pelletiers, they don't care about babies anymore. The only person they want is Ioni."

Though none of the others challenged her, their expressions remained conflicted.

"Look," said Hannah, "the only reason we're still alive is because we each took our chance when the moment came. Now here we are again with one chance—*one*—to do the right thing."

She raised Robert up to eye level. "I don't want him to just survive the day. I want him to grow old."

The women all nodded in maudlin agreement.

"So let's take it on faith that our kids will be okay," Hannah said. "We don't need any more distractions right now. We just need to do what we came here to do."

Amanda watched her through the bustling crowd, astonished. She thought she'd seen every iteration of Hannah on this world—a warrior, a fugitive, a savior, a mother—but she'd never recalled seeing her as a leader. Yet there she stood among the escapees of Lárnach, addressing them all with the grit and resolve of an army general. Amanda knew she'd missed a chunk of her sister's life, but the gap suddenly felt like decades.

Melissa joined Amanda and followed her gaze to Hannah. "I remember a time, not long ago, when she barely knew those women. Now they seem as close as—"

"Sisters," Amanda flatly interjected.

"A little stronger than the word I was thinking of."

"Well, sisters of a different sort," Amanda said. "After everything they've been through—"

"That's *bullshit*!" a young man shouted.

Melissa and Amanda looked toward a nearby fountain and saw Liam Pendergen in a tizzy. He paced an angry loop on the concrete, his skinny arm pointed at a throng of young tempics.

"Why can't I just go with them?" he asked his dad. "I *want* to fight."

"You have your job," Peter patiently replied. "Ioni needs all the thermics with her."

He was standing upright on his tempic feet, an effort that usually left him winded. But now he seemed as spry as ever. Melissa wondered if it had to do with the strange chrome loop that he wore around his skull like a headband, one of the least Peter-like adornments she'd ever seen on him. Clearly, it was Ioni's gadget, but what did it do?

Amanda was more focused on Liam. "Poor kid," she said to Melissa. "All that time in Protection, and it didn't help at all."

"He'll do as he's told," Melissa said. "If Peter doesn't see to it, then Ioni will."

Amanda looked beyond the Pendergens and saw Caleb waving for her. "I have to go," she said. "Stay strong, okay? Theo needs you to keep him focused."

Melissa smiled as nonchalantly as she could. "I won't let him get ahead of himself."

Amanda formed her aeric wings through the mesh of her warsuit, then aimed a tender look at Melissa. "You're mine, you know."

"Your what?"

"My sister of a different sort."

Melissa matched her plaintive grin. "I couldn't have asked for a better one."

Amanda spread her wings, then launched above the crowd with a graceful leap.

Melissa only had a moment to watch her scoop up Caleb before she heard a heavy breath over her shoulder. She didn't have to look to know who was standing behind her.

"I suppose it's time," she said to him.

Theo nodded distractedly, his heavy eyes fixed on Amanda. "We have to get to our station."

Four minutes after its creation, and two seconds after delivering its last passenger, Ioni's great white portal blinked out of existence, taking all its fluorescence with it. Though Hannah was relieved to finally stop squinting, she managed to catch a few details in the natural light that she hadn't noticed before: the rooftop gun turrets, the scattered Jade corpses, the ring of crystalline structures in the center of the plaza that resembled an alien Stonehenge. It all served to remind her of how woefully unprepared she was for the madness to come.

Unnerved, she followed Ioni's arrows up the fire escape of a three-story building that, until recently, had been the marketing nerve center of Prior Chronolectrics. But the place could have been anything from what she saw through the windows. The offices had been scavenged from top to bottom, right down to the last sticky note. Hannah couldn't tell if it was the work of thorough looters or just some frugal corporate bean counters. All she knew was that Merlin McGee was smiling from the great beyond.

Drink it in, she thought. *You gave your life to clear out this city, and it worked.*

Hannah climbed all the way to the stucco roof and found two siblings waiting for her. They leaned shoulder to shoulder against a solic generator (or shoulder to elbow, Hannah noted, as Bobby was at least eighteen inches taller than Mia), their tight gray warsuits a perfect match. The mere sight of them sent Hannah into a fit of mawkish sentiment, enough to make her want to hug them for hours.

Mia once again checked the gun in her side holster, as if it were in danger of floating away. "Sorry," she said to Hannah. "I would have 'ported you up here, but I couldn't find you."

"I'm fine," Hannah feebly attested.

Mia peeked down over the edge of the rooftop. At least a third of the timebenders were still scrambling into position, each one following the arrows that Ioni had put in their visors.

"She's moving us around like chess pieces," Mia grumbled. "Like pawns."

"That's nothing new," said Bobby. "It was like that in the army. It was like that in the Sabres. It's just the nature of war."

Hannah scanned the tempics and swifters in the crowd, all gathered in a ring around the inside edge of the forcefield. They were the front-line infantry, the first wave of defense against the Jades, once the shield fell. Hannah's heart broke to think of Heath down there, nestled in a mob of Gotham strangers.

Mia looked to the center of the plaza and saw Carrie looking back at her. She kissed the tips of her fingers and held her palm out to her.

"I don't care about orders," she told Hannah and Bobby. "If I see someone I love in trouble, I'm saving them first."

"That's the spirit," said a voice in the near distance.

The Farisis and Hannah turned their heads to see the final member of their team on the fire escape. Despite his arsenal of intimidating weapons—two hip-holstered sidearms, a sniper rifle on his back, a grenade belt filled with four different kinds of explosives—Evan still managed to look like a child in his baggy black battlesuit, a trick-or-treater going house to house as a mercenary. Hannah couldn't tell if the effect was intentional. The prick rarely missed a chance to mock a serious situation.

Evan's smile faded when he caught Hannah eyeing his pistols, the very same kind that had been used to kill Jonathan. "Are we going to have a problem?"

"Are you going to *be* a problem?"

"Only to the Jades and their three muppeteers."

"Then we'll be fine." A question suddenly occurred to Hannah. "How many times have—"

"None."

"What?"

"I haven't lived through any of this shit," Evan said. "This is my first run-through."

Mia didn't like hearing that. "Shouldn't you be more prepared?"

Evan shrugged uneasily. "It's not up to me. It's up to the Evans-to-come. You know as well as I do how our future selves can be."

"Maybe they're all dead," Bobby darkly suggested.

"You better hope not, big guy, because—"

A bright new portal lit the plaza from ground level, emitting a high, piercing squeal that was loud enough to kill every conversation.

The shrill noise faded, and a small young woman stepped out of the portal. Her conspicuous arrival was uncharacteristic—some might even say anathema—for Ioni Anata T'llari Deschane: the black cat queen of quiet entrances. But dire circumstances demanded drastic measures. She didn't have time to wait for everyone to notice her.

As the portal dissolved, she appeared on a dais of pure white crystal, a humble presence in her sleeveless white blouse and blue jeans. Hannah would have expected her to show up in the same fancy battlesuit she'd furnished for the timebenders, or perhaps something even more elaborate. Was she sending a message or merely making a stylistic choice?

"So here we are," Ioni began. She spoke at a conversational volume that somehow managed to reach every ear in the plaza without a hint of mechanical distortion. "I was hoping to do this without any bloodshed, but that's not the way you work. You've all but cemented this conflict in the strings. For three such shining champions of life, you really know how to feed the reaper."

Her audience quickly came to realize that the speech wasn't meant for them. Instead of rallying the troops, Ioni had opted to address the unseen enemy.

"I'm giving you one last chance to walk away," she continued. "Whatever victories you see in the future are an illusion, the very same kind that led to your failures at Lárnach. You can't win here today. You can only make us all lose."

Hannah checked the expressions of Evan and Mia and saw the exact same look of loathing. There was no doubt left about Evan's allegiance. In the end, all friends and enemies were united in their hatred of the Pelletiers. All Silvers were siblings again.

"All right." Ioni sighed as if Azral had already rebuffed her. "Have it your way."

Bobby turned to his companions, confused. "I didn't hear it. Did they say something back?"

Hannah shook her head. "I think she was just looking at the future."

Mia glanced up at the sky beyond the forcefield. "Not anymore."

By the time her companions craned their necks, the portal had opened to full width: a horizontal breach in the San Francisco air that matched the width of Ioni's shield dome. If there hadn't been so much light on the underside, it would have drowned the whole plaza in shadow. Instead it merely swapped sunlight for a sickly white glow, one that quickly became peppered with silhouettes.

Hannah clutched Mia's hand as the first of many enemies came storming down from above. "Here they come."

THIRTY-SEVEN

The airwaves of the world fell into a synchronous silence as the Jades rained down on the shield dome. All around the globe, all across the network spectrum, the narrating news anchors wore the same dumbstruck expression, their lips moving soundlessly as they struggled to form a response. There were barely any words in their language—*any* language—to describe the scene in Prior Circle, no talking-head experts to help them make sense of what the camera drones were showing them. It was as if the whole planet had plowed through the guardrails into a wild new reality that only their comic book writers had ever dared to imagine.

"I wish I could tell you what we're looking at," said the host of *Kingdom Now,* one of England's most sober and respectable news programs. "They pay me a ridiculous amount of money to speculate, but I fear there's nothing I can say that will be of any use."

The headline anchor of New York–1, more afraid of dead air than of being wrong, took a blind stab anyway. "Those people in green, whoever they are, seem to be trying to get inside that bubble of light, whatever it is. Whether they're looking to start or stop the Cataclysm that Merlin McGee predicted . . . it's too soon to tell. The only thing I can confidently say is that there are two forces at conflict in the heart of San Francisco."

"It's a war," said the radio host of *Dare to Pray.* "It's a flat-out war between God's holy angels and the legions of Satan. It doesn't get any simpler than that."

If Theo had heard him, he might have agreed, though the truth came with an asterisk, as usual. They were fighting to save billions of lives from an enemy who was hoping to save trillions. From that perspective, it was hard to tell who the assholes were.

Oh, cut the crap, he told himself. *Only one side's wiping whole Earths out of existence. So get your head in the game and do your job.*

Melissa had only needed a few hours on Wednesday to turn the Prior cafeteria into a state-of-the-art command center, and it had only taken that long because she'd wasted time installing an Integrity surveillance system. Those cameras were nothing, mere children's toys, compared to the futuristic wizardry that Ioni had given her. The liquid metal consoles had set themselves up in seconds, creating a forty-foot ring of lumic screens that provided more intel than Melissa or Theo knew what to do with. They had a full 3D view of the area, both inside and outside the barrier, plus another set of screens that provided a bevy of real-time data on the timebenders. Their health, their mood, their personal shield status, even their temporal power efficiency could be gauged through the link in their warsuits.

Theo wasn't encouraged or even remotely surprised by the dire red mood bars of his people. Within twenty seconds of their arrival, the Jades had swarmed the shield like locusts and covered every inch of the crest. Their bodies would have thrown the plaza into darkness if their hands hadn't become illuminated in a pulsing green iridescence.

All the chatter of the ground troops could be heard from the command center, the same nervous question asked in twenty different variants: *Why the hell are they glowing?*

Theo activated his comm and addressed everyone directly. "The Pelletiers are clever. They may not fully understand the tech behind Ioni's shield, but they looked to the strings and found the best way to weaken it. That way, apparently, is lumis."

He scanned the array of floating screens that measured the enemy's strength. There were more than three hundred Jades eating away at the forcefield, with at least two dozen more dropping out of the portal each second. The shield was already down to eighty-two percent. An ominous red countdown clock estimated the amount of time it would take before that number reached zero.

"We have a minute and forty-one seconds before that first barrier comes down," he announced. "And then things get messy. For those of you on the front lines, you'll have a hell of a fight on your hands. But you won't be alone. We have automated weapons. A lot of them."

His assurance did little to improve morale. He checked on Ioni through the dining hall window and found her exactly where she was when she left him: floating lotus-style in the middle of her own crystal circle, her eyes closed shut in exertion. She needed eighteen minutes, every thermic and lumic, and all of her concentration to jump-start her great engine, the one that would reverse the blight of the world and ensure a continuing future for everyone. Until then, she was out of commission. It was up to Theo and Melissa to play the twin generals and carry out the battle plan.

Melissa checked the other clock on the display board, the one in green digits that estimated Ioni's completion time.

"Don't lose sight of our main objective," she reminded the troops via comm link. "We have to keep the Jades away from Ioni while she does what she needs to do. Nothing else matters. Not our lives. Not theirs."

Upon seeing the critical red state of the mood bars, she quickly turned the thought around. "But consider this: if we win, we'll be wearing that crown for the rest of our lives. No matter where we go, no matter what kind of day we're having, we'll be able to look at the world all around us and know the role we played in its continued existence. I can't speak for the rest of you, but that to me is worth fighting for."

Theo turned off his mic and smirked at her. "You almost sounded like Peter there."

"I was trying to imagine what Cedric would say."

Twenty feet away, on the other side of the screen circle, See leaned forward on her crutches and studied the orphan telemetry readings. "Theo."

She beckoned him over and pointed out a new detail on Zack's status screen: a small square light with constantly shifting colors. The gauge had no label, unlike the others, and was completely unreadable to non-augurs. But somehow, through a technological magic that Theo couldn't comprehend, the dancing hues acted like a bar code in his foresight, enough to unpack and expand a brand-new view of the next few minutes.

"Shit."

"Is Zack in trouble?" Melissa asked him.

Theo shook his head. The warsuits had no barometer to measure a person's future health, just their future helpfulness. And from all indicators,

Zack was going to jeopardize Ioni's plans for his own noble but shortsighted reasons.

"Doesn't matter," Theo said, yet another truth with an asterisk. The problem with Zack—if it happened at all—was still at least three minutes away. That pushed it somewhere to the middle of Theo's list of worries.

As the invading Jade legion grew five hundred strong, Theo checked the shield strength onscreen. It was down to fifty percent and would be gone in sixty-eight seconds.

Melissa squeezed his hand. "Stay strong. We've got this."

Theo wished he could agree, but this was the part of the future he'd been dreading for months, the reason he'd kept his distance from his people. It was the part where he'd throw them all into fire, just to buy a little more time for Ioni.

Seeing the Jades onscreen was nothing compared to the naked-eye view from below. As the glowing horde pressed against the roof of the barrier, more than eight hundred pairs of eyes looked up at them—unblinking, unnerved. The Jades' oscillating lights created an eerie illusion, turning their perfectly still forms into a strange kinetic nightmare: a radioactive alien blob, or a cluster of angry green bees.

Even when processed empirically, the Pelletier minions were a disturbing sight. Just nine of them had taken down the underland. Now there was a whole army of them, with an endless stream of reinforcements dropping down from the sky.

Zack watched the swarm from his low perch: the flat gravel roof of a two-story office building. Though he wasn't nearly close enough to tell the Jades apart from each other, he figured there were at least a hundred Joelles in the mix. The Canadian orphan who'd nearly killed him twice had come back in multitudes to finish the job.

Ofelia crouched at his side, her right hand clutching the hilt of a throwing knife. "Stop looking at them. You're going to strain your neck and then you won't be any use to me."

Zack briefly met her stern brown gaze. "Thank you. I feel loved."

"You *are* loved," Ofelia said. "Just imagine the look on Amanda's face if I let anything happen to you."

Zack peeked at the squadron of allies in the near distance: fifteen aerics and fifteen swifters, all clustered together on a high crystal platform. Every time he looked their way, he found Amanda and Caleb standing shoulder to shoulder. When the time came to fight, they'd be fighting in pairs, just like the turners and travelers.

"You don't have to worry," Zack said to Ofelia. "I've become pretty good at not dying."

"Well, See just whispered in my radio and told me to keep an eye on you."

"What does she think I'll do? Run off and pick flowers?"

"You know exactly what she's worried about."

Zack did know, and he'd already gotten an earful about it. "You're going to see a lot of people hurting," Theo had warned him. "And you're going to want to help them all. You can't. Every second you spend away from the enemy is another second we lose."

On a pragmatic level, Zack understood the logic. They were all embroiled in an eighteen-minute war, with heavily lopsided numbers. Even Zack could see how killing the enemy was far more important than healing friends. Still, he found the augurs' strategy to be a little too cold for comfort. Even worse, he found it familiar.

He flicked a finger at the swirling mass of Jades. "So the key to winning is to be more like them."

"The key is to do what needs to be done," Ofelia said.

"Well, now you sound like a Pelletier."

"Listen—"

"What do you think a throwing knife is going to do against them, anyway?"

Ofelia dangled the knife from her fingertips. She had four more just like it in her thigh holster. "I don't know," she admitted. "I'm just better with these than I am with guns."

A second shield suddenly sprang to life beneath the first one, half its size and significantly less inclusive. Once the outer dome fell, all the major combatants would be trapped outside with the enemy.

Well, *nearly* all of them. Zack checked on Amanda and found her safely ensconced beneath the crown of the backup barrier, along with the rest of her team. Whatever Ioni had in mind for the wing squad, she was saving it for last.

Amanda noticed Zack through the shimmering light and held a tempic fist to her heart.

"I love you too," Zack muttered. He shuddered to think of the awful things he'd do to help ensure her survival. Betray some allies. Kill some innocents.

He might even throw a close friend into the wood chipper. The line stretched deep into the shadows of his soul, to a part that was better left unexplored.

You think you're above it, teased the Semerjean in his head. *But love makes monsters of us all.*

A hiss in his earpiece pulled him out of his thoughts. "Ten seconds," Theo announced over the radio. "Everyone get ready."

Zack stood up and activated his helmet. "I won't be a problem," he promised Ofelia. "Just stay sharp and don't get killed. A lot of us would miss your accent."

She rose to her feet, smirking. "Don't worry. I'm good at not dying too."

The outer shield perished with a fizzling pop, and nearly a thousand Jades fell like meteors toward the ground.

Not meteors, Zack realized. The Jades on the outside were all curving inward toward the newer and smaller shield dome, the next little obstacle in their furious path to Ioni.

"Now!"

The cry had come from inside the cafeteria, to no human being in particular. Felicity Yu had spent two days converting the north end of the dining hall into the mother of all weapons stations, and her hard work paid off. With the push of a button, all her automated ordnance around the perimeter of Prior Circle sprang to life and unleashed their fury on the invaders.

The tempics and swifters watched the carnage from ground level, their mouths drooped open as a hundred Jades were torn to shreds in seconds. Their stone armor suits might as well have been paper for all they fared against Felicity's .50-caliber rounds.

While the turrets took out the lower Jades, a pair of electromagnetic rail guns made short work of the soldiers above them. They barely had a chance to drop through the portal before high-velocity projectiles cut through them with ease. One of the spikes managed to impale three Jades before sending them back through the breach.

Even Theo was shocked by the ferocity of their own defense. The Integrity weapons were as crude and archaic as slingshots, at least as far as the Pelletiers were concerned. Yet somehow they let Felicity—a rogue, stateless agent in coveralls—mince half the troops to slurry before the first boots hit the ground.

Melissa followed the action onscreen, dubious. "They wouldn't make it this easy unless there's a trick coming."

Theo was inclined to agree, until he caught first sight of the surviving Jades. They descended on the shield dome as gently as butterflies, then began their lumic penetration. First ten, then twenty, then fifty of them.

"Shit." Theo opened a comm channel to his allies outside the shield. "Get them off that barrier! All of you! Hurry!"

He'd been so busy expecting sleight-of-hand deceptions that he'd never considered the obvious. The Pelletiers had infinite troops at their disposal, while Ioni most certainly didn't. Why waste time on complex maneuvers when you can overwhelm the enemy with numbers?

See bit her lip in apprehension as she watched the timebender infantry spring into action. "Can't Felicity take out those Jades?"

Melissa shook her head. "Not without friendly fire. And not without hurting the shield."

"I'm sorry," Theo said to See. "I don't want Heath there any more than you do."

See resumed her duties with a bitter scowl. She may have been in love with Heath, but she had two Copper sisters on the front lines too, without Mother to guide and protect them.

Nonetheless, her eyes kept darting back to Heath's telemetry readout, just to make sure the bars hadn't gone black.

Be careful, she thought. *Please.*

For all her mighty prescience, Ioni wasn't immune to the pitfalls and pratfalls that came with predicting other people's behavior, especially when those people were Pelletiers. In her many attempts to divine their plan of attack, she became stuck at the fork of two competing futures, without the manpower or resources to fully prepare for both.

So she positioned her infantry in anticipation of Battle Plan A: a ground assault of a thousand Jades, all cloaked from sight and shifted at deadly speed. She'd programmed every warsuit visor to filter out lumic illusions, then ordered the tempics and swifters to form a protective ring around the inside edge of Prior Circle.

But then, as a middle-finger gesture more than anything else, the Pelletiers changed their strategy at the last minute to Battle Plan B: a drop-attack from the sky. Ioni's soldiers at the circular front were forced to double back to the central plaza, only to immediately face a new obstacle.

Heath peered through the roof of the shield dome, where nearly two hundred Jades resumed their penetrative green glow. There was no good way to fight them from the ground. The Jonathans, for all their prowess, couldn't fly or climb energy walls any better than the average person.

Stitch cast a tempic tendril up the side of the barrier, but reached the end of her spool at thirty yards. "What the hell do they expect us to do?" she asked Shade, her longtime companion and sister in arms.

The teenage mortic shook her head. She had to yell to be heard above the noise of the gun turrets. "I can't reach them either. I can't even shoot them from here!"

The swifters in the mix were equally stymied. "This is ridiculous," Yasmeen said to Charlene. She pointed at Amanda on the high diamond platform. "We're down here. Our flyers are in there. Nobody's where they need to be!"

That wasn't entirely true. While the main troops idled at street level, Theo opened a radio channel to the rooftop fighters, all the special support timebenders and Scarlet Sabre guerrillas who had a clear line of sight on the enemy.

"Take them out however you can," Theo said. "Just be careful not to—"

A wraith-class drone plowed into a throng of Jades, killing twenty of them instantly with its mortic shell, though not without collateral damage.

Theo cursed as the barrier lost five seconds of life span. "Don't hit the shield! Do *not* hit the shield!"

The high-perched orphans had an easier go of it. Evan sniped at the Jades with his long-barreled rifle, looping through time to edit out all the missed headshots. Mia ripped a horizontal portal through a crowd of thirty minions, cutting each of them in half and sending their upper parts tumbling into San Francisco Bay. Both Hannah and Bobby cast time from their fingers like a deadly whip, rifting five or six Jades with each lash.

Three hundred feet away, on the southern side of the shield, Zack and Ofelia adopted the Farisis' attacks, but were somewhat less sanguine about it. It was clear that the numbers weren't going their way. For every Jade they snuffed from existence, two more took their place.

Ofelia looked up at the Pelletier portal. The cursed thing never stopped producing enemies, and Felicity's weapons only had so much ammo left. "We have to close it!"

Zack rifted another half-dozen Jades. "What are you going to do? Throw a knife at it?"

"Will you shut up about that?"

"Mercy was our last solic," Zack said. "Without her, we can't close that portal."

"Well, we can't hold out like this. They just keep coming."

Zack didn't want to know what the Pelletiers did to create so many expendable foot soldiers. They probably sapped every last bit of free will out of them to get them to serve as cannon fodder. He couldn't imagine any sales pitch that would inspire them to lay down their lives so readily. Then again, wasn't that the story behind every war? Generals throwing bodies at the problem of the day, with no shortage of volunteer suckers and very few questions asked.

"Zack!" Ofelia smacked his arm. "We need a new plan!"

"Like what?"

"I don't know! Maybe something that puts the rest of our people to use?"

Zack certainly agreed with that. There was a whole brigade of tempics and swifters going unused, just waiting down below like piranhas. There had to be a way to get them onto the shield . . . or knock the majority of Jades off of it.

Two stories below Zack, and fifty yards to the east, Meredith Graham was the first to see a solution. "Akio!"

She'd brought the young orphan all the way from Japan, the only timebender on Earth with the power to boost others. But she'd been so distracted by the noise and gore of the battlefield that she'd nearly forgotten about his unique power.

She gripped Akio with a trembling hand and spoke to him in Japanese. "I need you to amp up my tempis."

Akio eyed her skeptically, and not without a hint of disgust. She'd already thrown up twice at the sight of Jade blood, all the charred and mangled body parts that Felicity's guns were producing. All her combat experience was corporate in nature. She'd never even seen a dead body until the underland collapsed.

"You can't handle it," Akio told her in his native tongue. "Look at yourself. You're a mess."

"I'll be fine!"

"No you won't," Charlene replied in English. "Your tempis needs concentration, and you're all kinds of distracted."

Meredith was just about to protest when the booming blast of a Scarlet Sabre rocket made her gasp. "Shit."

Heath turned around at the barrier's edge and eyed the Grahams intently. "I can do it."

Charlene and Meredith blinked at him, baffled. If they had both known him just a little bit longer, they would have learned about his freakishly fine-tuned hearing, the kind that allowed him to reproduce note-perfect songs from memory, or to eavesdrop on people in the middle of an explosive skirmish.

Meredith approached him and held him by the hands. "Sweetheart, you don't know what you're signing up for."

"Yes I do." Heath gestured at Akio without making eye contact, as he'd decided quite early in their mutual acquaintance that he didn't like the man. "You told me two minutes ago that he can make you more powerful. Can't he do that with me?"

"He has a point," said Charlene.

Meredith glared at her. "He's a *boy*."

"A boy who's seen more war than both of us," her sister countered. "A boy who does exactly what you do, but better."

While Meredith hemmed, Charlene kneeled down in front of Heath. "Look, this isn't a painless process, okay? It comes with risks."

"Like what?" asked Heath. "I could die?"

"Yes," said Charlene.

"Yes!" yelled Meredith. "You're a sweet kid. I don't want anything to happen to you."

Rarely a day had passed in Heath's hectic life where the world didn't remind him that he was atypical. The looks he got from friends and strangers was more than enough to convince him that, despite whatever flowery words they used to describe his condition, he was missing a crucial circuit. He simply didn't make the mental connections that most other people formed with ease.

But then there were times, like now, when it seemed like the problem went the other way. For these women to worry about Heath's well-being in the middle of a fight for all life? That was *their* issue, not his. To Heath, the truth was as simple as two plus two. The world needed to live. He didn't.

He looked at the sisters with all the patience he could muster. "I can do this."

THIRTY-EIGHT

For the three dozen lumics and thermics in Prior Circle, the struggle hadn't changed from the start. They stood five feet apart from each other in an inward-facing ring, their eyes, their hands, their every thought aimed at a short crystal platform as they hit it with their powers at full blast.

The balance between thermics and subthermics was so skewed that Liam would have expected them all to be cooked alive, while there were enough lumics going nova around him that he wasn't even sure how he could see. The answer, no doubt, was floating lotus-style above the platform: Ioni Deschane, the star of the show. If she'd explained how she was keeping them all comfortable in this glowing white furnace, then Liam must have missed it. All he remembered from her orientation spiel was a bunch of unpalatable truths.

"We are not soldiers," Ioni had told them, mere minutes before. "Our only goal is to power up the machine that will give this world new life. Some of you may feel guilty, being tucked away in here while the people you love risk their lives to protect us. But I promise you that our job is just as crucial as theirs. Just keep your energies on the crystals and don't let up for a second. The quicker we finish, the better our odds."

Despite her plea, the commotions of battle nipped away at Liam's concentration: the *rat-a-tat-tat* of government turrets, the muffled shouts of comrades, the Jades falling to pieces right above him.

Most distracting of all was the sight of his own father, just a hundred feet away. He sat at the base of a tall diamond tower, his legs crossed beneath him, his eyes closed in serene contemplation. Anyone with even a passing knowledge of Peter knew how ill-suited he was to meditate, especially in the middle of war. So what the hell was he doing? Why wasn't he out there on the other side of the barrier with the rest of the fighting travelers?

Ten feet to Liam's right, Carrie watched his power falter while he ruminated.

"Liam," she hissed a loud whisper. *"Liam."*

Liam blinked three times and met Carrie's gaze. "Focus," she snapped.

He waved her off as if she'd only just imagined his lapse. "I'm fine."

Bullshit, said a woman's voice in his head. *You just put us behind by three seconds, which is three more than we may get.*

Though Ioni had yet to open her eyes, she was clearly alert and aware.

Liam certainly knew how it felt, after two weeks in the Protection ward, to have her puttering around in his mind.

What's my dad doing? he mentally inquired. *What's that thing around his head?*

You'll know soon enough, Ioni replied. *Keep your heat on the crystal.*

Liam felt a momentary gap in her concentration, like a record skip. *Ioni?*

The combatants to the east suddenly got a lot louder, just a few yards outside the shield dome. All Liam could hear from his safe vantage was a cacophony of shouts that fell somewhere in the nebulous space between terror and triumph. By the time he looked, he saw fifty allies cheering. One quick glance was enough to reveal the reason.

Liam's wide gaze rose toward the sky. "Oh my God."

Theo thought he'd witnessed Heath's wrath in every flavor, from his temperamental shrieking fits to his full-fledged power tantrums. He'd even seen him make the Pelletiers sweat at the business end of a giant wolf. But that beast had been twenty feet high at the most. This new tempic creation that Theo was looking at on the monitors—the King Kong of Jonathans—dwarfed the tallest building in Prior Circle by six or seven stories. The shield dome was just a curved round thing at its hip.

Felicity had to adjust her targeting systems to keep the turrets off their huge new ally. "How the hell is he doing that?" she yelled from her side of the cafeteria.

"He had help," Melissa surmised. "From that unpleasant Japanese man."

"Well, I sure as hell like him now!"

So did Melissa. Yet she reeled to think of the whole world's reaction as the camera drones circled Heath's Goliath. Indeed, more than a few news anchors *holy shitt*ed on live air. A dozen of them paused to pray for salvation, while one unclipped her microphone and quit her job midbroadcast.

Theo had more pressing concerns at the moment. He scanned the spiking bars of Heath's health display, then hailed him on the comm link. "Heath, if you can hear me—"

"He can't," See said, her voice choked with anguish. She enlarged him on the camera screen. The poor boy was practically catatonic except for the sporadic twitch. Meredith held him tightly in her arms while Charlene kept a bead on his vitals.

Theo cursed under his breath. Heath's dynamic with his golems had completely reversed itself. Instead of hosting them all inside his head, one of them was now hosting him.

The Jonathan swept a giant arm, knocking fifty Jades off the top of the shield and dropping them into hostile territory. The tempics and swifters swarmed over them all and eviscerated them within seconds.

Mia watched the carnage from a rooftop, unsure whether to be thrilled or suspicious. The Jades, for all their power, were barely raising a finger in their own defense. The few who'd managed to get back on their feet merely resumed their attempts to dissolve the shield before someone finally killed them.

Bobby stood at his sister's side, baffled. "They're like robots."

Mia nodded her head. "There's nothing human left in them. They're just stripped-down copies of copies."

As the Jonathan pushed another four dozen Jades onto the infantry, Hannah peered into its dead white eyes. When it came to the ghosts of long-dead orphans, the Jonathans weren't much better than the Jades. Even this behemoth was just a cold and silent copy of the man Hannah loved, an unpainted tribute that didn't even move like its namesake.

Still, for all its deficiencies, the looming sight of the Jonathan was enough to make Hannah miss him all over again. He should have been here at the final battle, dropping Jades by the dozen while surrounded by the people who loved him.

Instead, Hannah had to settle for the company of his murderer, a man standing two feet behind her.

"Uh . . ." Evan reached out to touch her shoulder, then wisely reconsidered. "We still have a critical influx of assholes. I think I know a way to help."

The moment he explained it, Hannah could have kicked herself for not coming up with the idea on her own. She didn't imagine her slowtime field would be of much use here, with its limited area of effect and minimal damage to the enemy. But then she didn't entirely think it through. It had been so long since she'd lived in San Diego that she forgot about the cascading nightmare of traffic jams.

She thrust her right hand toward the sky and created a ninety-foot sphere of temporal discordance, enough to slow several dozen Jades in mid-descent. Though her time bubble covered just a fraction of the reinforcements, the number of affected enemies kept increasing by the second. The Jades above the hindered Jades began to sink into the temporal amber, while the ones above them began to crash into their heads.

Evan smiled with triumph as the enemies at the bottom of Hannah's temporal field fell to Earth in real time as rifted corpses. "Well, look at that. It's like a timey-wimey meat grinder. I can't imagine Gandhi would approve, but it's not like he ever met—"

"Shut up," Hannah snapped. She still wasn't in the mood to get chummy with Evan, and she was starting to worry about Heath. Hannah's damage was nothing compared to the Jonathan's. How much longer would the Pelletiers allow it before they made Heath their top target?

Not far away, in the Prior cafeteria, Theo juggled the exact same concern with another. Whatever Akio did to Heath wasn't healthy, and the telemetry readouts confirmed it. The boy was lumbering his way toward a bad case of power strain, possibly even a fatal one.

See clutched Theo's arm, panicked. "We have to pull him out!"

"We can't," Theo said.

"It's too much for him!"

"We *can't*," Melissa emphasized. "He's buying us the time we need."

While Theo and See remained focused on Heath, Melissa kept tabs on the enemy numbers. The Jade count was finally shrinking for once, and the structural integrity of the second shield had remained all but steady since the Jonathan came to life. Heath was single-handedly tipping the war in their favor, and not a moment too soon. Ioni still needed twelve minutes and forty-nine seconds to start her great machine.

Unfortunately, it was becoming painfully clear, even to the non-augurs, that Heath wouldn't last that long. Blood began trickling out of his nostrils, and his twitches had turned into full-fledged seizures.

"Enough!" See hobbled toward Heath's data screen, her wet eyes locked on a command button. Ioni had given her strategists the ability to turn off anyone's power through their warsuit, a safety measure to keep the less stable timebenders from becoming a danger to their allies. Except Heath didn't even remotely qualify for that option. His Jonathan continued to fight like a champion, without any trouble distinguishing friend from foe.

Melissa grabbed See before she could deactivate Heath's tempis. "Stop!"

"No!" See struggled in her grip. "We can't let him die like Mother did! Not like that. Please!"

Melissa looked to Theo and saw the dilemma in his eyes. "If we fail here, we lose Heath anyway," she reminded both augurs. "We're all expendable in this fight."

Theo recalled something similar he'd been told, in the twentieth-floor breakroom of a Yokohama office building. "You have a whole world to save," Heath had sternly reminded him. "One person doesn't matter."

His stomach churned with sickness and dread as he fixed his wet eyes on See's. "I'm sorry."

"You're a monster!" she cried. "You're no better than Azral!"

"See . . ."

"Heath *loves* you!"

"I love him," Theo said in a cracked voice. "But you know what he would say if he was here now. You know what he'd want us to do."

A short distance away, at the southeast edge of the shield dome, Meredith had taken See's view on the matter.

She shook Heath by the shoulders. "Heath, wake up! You need to stop and come back *now*!"

At long last, the Jades turned their attention onto the Jonathan. The falling reinforcements who'd dodged Hannah's trap suddenly buzzed around the giant like mosquitos, melting small chunks away with their solic attacks. The Jonathan instantly grew back all the tempis they took, then swept sixty-one grunts off the shield.

Charlene slit a Jade's throat with a hunting knife before speeding back to her sister. "Mer, stop! We still need him!"

"I don't care!"

"You're being foolish," Akio said in Japanese. "That boy's winning the war for us!"

"That boy has a name," Meredith yelled back. "He'll be dead in a minute if we don't help."

"And if that minute decides the fight?" Akio challenged.

"That's not your choice to make."

"Or yours," Charlene said to Meredith. "I love you, sis, but you're letting emotions blind you. We're here for one reason, and that—"

A new portal opened directly behind Charlene. Zack emerged from the light, then turned his hard gaze on Meredith.

"Get back."

Meredith jumped back to her feet. "Are you—"

"Yes."

Ofelia followed Zack out of the portal, then waved the disc shut. They'd just finished having the same argument as the Grahams before Ofelia relented. Zack was going to do his thing with or without her. It would be safer for him to take the direct route.

The moment Meredith left Heath on the ground, Zack enveloped him in a fluorescent white sheen of reverse-time. Heath's blood trickles retracted like cables into his nose, while the cracked red vessels in his eyes disappeared. By the time Zack finished, five seconds later, Heath had been regressed seven minutes. Even the short journey back was enough to leave him ill. He retched onto the dirt, then toppled over in a semiconscious daze.

Zack pressed a small button on the wrist of Heath's warsuit and triggered a holographic projection of his vital signs.

"He's okay," Zack announced. "He'll recover."

Only Meredith showed any sign of relief. Everyone else in the vicinity remained focused on the space where the enormous Jonathan used to be. Their one big advantage had vanished into mist the moment Zack had started Heath's reversal. From the looks of the boy's condition, it wasn't coming back anytime soon.

"Dōshite?" Akio inquired.

Zack blinked at him distractedly. "What?"

"He asked you *why*," Charlene explained.

"Oh." Zack looked to Meredith for help on the answer, but she, like him, was fresh out of words. All he could do was glance around at his detractors before lazily shrugging his shoulders. "It's Heath."

Caleb sighed from the edge of a tall crystal platform as the Jades took advantage of Heath's absence. Ten by ten, they descended onto the shield and resumed their obsessive drilling.

"I don't mean to be a downer," Caleb said to his partner, "but I think your husband may have just lost the war for us."

Amanda pensively shook her head. "It's not over yet."

She wasn't sure why anyone was surprised by Zack's actions, at least anyone who claimed to know him. He'd never tried for a moment to hide his true nature. He was a short-game player, a natural-born healer, a moralist so steadfast and rigid that he made his wife's Catholicism look watery by comparison.

More crucial to Amanda, he was a man who cherished life. Not just the life in the near and distant future, the lives they were living right now. Even if it wasn't evident to the allies who despised him, the world needed people like Zack as much as they needed augurs.

Amanda saw him looking back at her with tense, conflicted eyes. She gave him a warm smile and held her fist to her heart. "I love you."

THIRTY-NINE

At 9:14 A.M., Pacific time, the war reached its quiet halfway mark. Ioni needed nine more minutes to start her benevolent engine, but the second of her three protective shields had been beaten down to half its original life span. The computer in the command center estimated that she'd be fully exposed to the Pelletier forces in five minutes and fifty-four seconds.

That was not a good outlook to Melissa Masaad. In fact, it was downright dire.

She retreated into her mind for a cigarette break—a desperate consolation, as she lacked the time and cigarettes to enjoy a real smoke. But even the rehashed memory of a nicotine rush was enough to release a few endorphins. Soon most of the shouting in her head had quelled to a murmur and she remembered how to think analytically.

She pored over the visual map of the timebenders, then opened a radio channel to the ground troops. "All right. Here's what we're going to do . . ."

Under the temporal acceleration of swifters, fifteen Gotham tempics worked together to create the most impressive group structure of their lives: a stairwell platform, massive in all dimensions, tall enough to put a squad of their best killers within reach of the Jades on the shield. Though some were initially hesitant to climb a construct of pure willpower, its builders assured them that it was safe. They had reinforcements ready to replace every exhausted tempic, plus a secondary team to catch anyone who happened to fall.

Eighty-two seconds after Melissa gave her order, the strike team was elevated and ready for combat. While Artemis Rosen used her giant tempic hands to sweep Jades off the shield, Stitch impaled them five at a time on thick, bladed tendrils. Nena Hall, a thirty-year-old swifter who was widely considered to be the Gothams' best marksman, fired round after round from her .357, scoring six to eight headshots per second.

Most lethal of all was Callista Williford, the young orphan from Vancouver whom everyone knew as Shade. Black mortis flew like lightning from her fingertips, burning fist-size tunnels through her enemies' chests before moving on to the next victim.

Meanwhile, Yasmeen recruited Charlene and three other swifters to help the Scarlet Sabres with their wraiths. At 60x speed, the remote drone pilots had all the time they needed to plan a careful attack that inflicted maximum casualties without jeopardizing the health of the shield. One wraith connected with Shade's mortis and dragged a rope of corrosive energy through the necks of thirty Jades.

"Fantastic," Melissa said to the squadron. Their coordinated attacks were improving the odds, but it still wasn't enough to ensure a safe victory. Even a minute of vulnerability for Ioni would be catastrophic. Melissa had watched Azral and Esis take down a fleet of Integrity warships in less than forty seconds.

She checked on Theo at the other side of the screen ring and found him staring at Heath's telemetry readout.

"Snap out of it," she chided him. "What's done is done."

While he'd certainly been out of sorts since the whole Heath incident—a whirlwind of conflicting emotions that left him furious at Zack and furious at himself for not siding with Zack—his attention was focused where it belonged: on the next eight minutes of the future.

"It's going to get worse," Theo said. "The Jades are ignoring us for the shield, but—"

"—it won't last," See cautioned. Her tears had dried since Zack saved Heath, and she was back at the top of her game. "The Pelletiers are about to change their tactics."

"How?" Melissa asked.

Neither augur had a definitive answer, but Melissa could see how nervous they were getting. Even Rosario had joined the chorus of foreboding. She radioed Melissa from the fortified crystal nursery and urged her to get everyone's shields ready.

Evan was the first to get a glimpse of the problem to come. A mere half-second after his future self overtook him, he hailed Theo and Melissa on the network. "Witchsticks!"

"What?"

Only Melissa knew what he was talking about, but it still made little sense. The Pelletiers had never relied on contemporary weapons before. If it was true—

She opened the emergency comm channel. "Everyone get your suit shields ready. Do *not* turn them on until I tell you to."

Every warsuit came equipped with its own personal forcefield, but it only had ten seconds of power. Using it too early could be just as fatal as using it too late.

Unfortunately, Melissa's warning had already prompted Meredith and forty other combatants to activate their shields right away. The borders of their health screens lit up in white, and their meager little countdowns began.

"Not yet!" Melissa yelled. "Not yet!"

Theo noticed that the fighters on the high tempic stairwell were having the opposite problem. They were so engrossed in their attack on the Jades that they hadn't heard Melissa at all.

He opened a voice link to as many of them as he could. "Listen to me—"

"No!" See cried.

Melissa didn't have to wonder anymore when the attack was coming. A rather awful future had just kicked down the door to the present.

"Shields up!" Theo shouted to everyone on the comms. "Shields up now!"

The aerics and swifters of Amanda's squad had a panoramic view of the destruction. It began as a fireball explosion to the north, one large enough to level a small building. Amanda barely had a chance to think the word "bomb" before a second explosion erupted right next to the first one. And then another next to that. Then another. What began as one blast became a clockwork chain of conflagrations that looped all around the edge of the shield dome—twenty-five of them in total, though no one in the area had the time or mind to count. All Amanda could tell with any degree of certainty was that it had happened over the span of mere seconds.

Theo's heart sank with dread as the status screens of a hundred and fifteen timebenders went dark at the same time. "Oh no."

The Pelletiers hadn't brought any weapons from their era, as there were barely any left to be found. The wars of their people, as rare as they were, had evolved into purely financial and informational conflicts. Murder had become an impractical chore in the age of cloning and instant healing. The whole idea of explosive munitions was as quaint and outdated as cholera.

Luckily for Azral and his family, this ugly little patch of humanity's past offered plenty of access to such weapons. A portal jump to an old British armory gave them everything they needed to commit a good old-fashioned slaughter: seventy-five Denisov shoulder-launched needle rockets, more colloquially known as "witchsticks" for their resemblance to flying brooms.

If the Pelletiers were ashamed or embarrassed to be resorting to such archaic tactics, it barely came up in conversation. All Semerjean said was "A'nagha Röm-al" ("When in Rome . . .").

Mia cursed his name from the roof of the marketing building, one of the last surviving structures in the blast zone . . . but only barely. The front wall had collapsed into rubble. Had Mia and Hannah been standing three feet closer, they would have tumbled to the ground with it.

The noise had knocked Mia off her feet and left her ears ringing. She feared she'd lost her hearing too, until she heard Evan yell at her.

"Turn off your shield!"

She'd been so rattled by the explosions that she forgot about her time limit. She switched off her barrier with one second of power left.

Fuck, she thought. *That won't be enough to save me next time.*

"Stay close to me," her brother said. "I still have seven seconds on mine."

It suddenly occurred to Mia why she'd thought she'd gone deaf. The witchsticks had killed all the previous clamor: Felicity's turrets and rail guns, the Scarlet Sabre rockets—even the solic-electric *whirr* of the wraiths had fallen silent. The Pelletiers had just destroyed all their enemies' heavy ordnance.

Hannah climbed to her feet and peeked over the crumbling edge of the roof. The smoke and dust had yet to clear at street level. "I can't see anyone."

"Be careful," Evan cautioned.

"Zack and Heath are down there. I don't know if they're—"

"Hannah, the roof isn't stable!"

Though she wanted to smack Evan for yelling at her, her rage was tempered by the fact that he'd just saved her life with his bubble shield. Her attention had been focused on slowing the Jades, enough to keep her from activating her own barrier. The fact that Evan had held her tightly from behind only made her want to forget the incident more.

"Oh no." Without Felicity's weapons to cut down the Jades, their numbers had swelled in short order. The portal kept spitting them out by the dozen, and now they were free to eat away at the barrier without a hint of resistance. No wonder they'd been so slow to fight back. They knew from the start that they wouldn't have to.

Hannah retreated to a more stable part of the roof and readied her temporis again.

Evan raised a cautioning hand at her. "Wait."

"We have to do something."

"You don't understand—"

"There's no one left on defense!"

A fierce metal squeal froze them all where they stood. The rooftop cracked in five places.

Bobby looked to his companions in alarm. "I think we have a problem."

Evan threw his hands up. "That's what I've been trying to—"

Another chunk of building suddenly crumbled to the pavement, taking a quarter of the roof with it. Huge, angry fissures snaked toward Hannah and the others.

"Shit." Mia threw a quick glance at the space behind Bobby, then filled it with a floating portal. "Run!"

The next five seconds were a jumbled blur to Hannah as she scrambled to flee to safety. Had she been the first one through the portal? The third? The fourth? Did she escape at the last second, Hollywood-style, or were there a few moments left on the clock? Her memory, like the marketing building of Prior Chronolectrics, had crumbled in a cloud of dust. All she knew for sure was that she and her team had gotten away.

But to where? Hannah's first steps out of the portal sent her stumbling onto a wobbly surface that felt like an overfilled waterbed. Her baffled legs lost their sense of balance and she toppled onto her hands and knees.

Hannah took her first look at the invisible ground and saw a platform full of allies staring back at her from below. She immediately recognized one of them as her sister.

She threw her wide gaze at Mia. "The shield? You teleported us onto the *shield*?"

Mia shrugged. "I only had time for a line-of-sight jump. There was nowhere else to go."

As Bobby helped Hannah back to her feet, Evan and Mia studied the Jades all around them—dozens of clones in every direction, with even more fluttering down from above. Though most of them remained committed to dissolving the barrier, a few stopped what they were doing to register the new enemy in their midst.

"Shit." Evan reached for his sidearm. "Now you know why I never come to this war."

Nearly one full minute after the missile strike ended, the dust finally settled onto the ruins. At long last, the survivors on the ground could see again, though the smoke from all the flattened buildings made breathing an uncomfortable chore.

Zack had to remind every coughing ally around him that their helmets had their own oxygen supply—at least twenty minutes' worth, if he recalled from his orientation. But then who the hell knew? Ioni had rushed through their warsuit training like an auctioneer, and the explosions had only muddled their memories. Zack had to run a mental roll call of everyone he loved to remember who'd been caught inside the blast zone and who was safe beneath the shield.

He walked along the barrier's edge, his hand clasped tightly around Heath's. He'd already lost tabs on Ofelia during the bedlam. He wasn't about to let the boy wander away, especially in his condition. Zack's reversal had left Heath in a sick and sleepy languor, as if he'd just come out of surgery. The explosions would have killed him if Zack hadn't shielded them both.

"Where are we going?" Heath asked, seemingly unaware that the question had been asked and answered thirty seconds earlier.

"We're looking for Ofelia," Zack patiently repeated. "And anyone who needs healing."

Sadly, there was no middle ground in the aftermath of the attack. Those who'd activated their shields in time were as healthy as they ever were.

Those who hadn't . . .

Zack flinched at the sight of another corpse patch: at least fifteen bodies, all charred beyond recognition. Their warsuits had been so thoroughly shredded that their electronic ID tags were useless. Zack couldn't glean their names through the data screen in his visor. He could only pray with selfish desperation that none of the victims were friends of his.

Heath turned away from the cadavers, queasy. "Where's Hannah?"

"She's fine," Zack said, unsure if he was lying or not.

"What about Meredith and Charlene?"

"Uh . . ." Zack wasn't sure how to answer that. Charlene had gone off to help the Sabres who, from the sheer lack of noise from their weapons, had likely been wiped off the map. As for Meredith, Zack couldn't guess. He had yet to see any corpses with her distinct red color of warsuit.

A teenage girl knelt just a few yards ahead of Zack, her black suit pierced by angry spikes of tempis. Zack didn't need his visor to tell him who he was looking at. There was only one tempic he knew who wore her moods so conspicuously.

"Stitch!" Zack hurried over to her, then paused at the sight of the body she was kneeling over. Unlike all the other victims in the area, Shade hadn't perished in flames. She merely lay with her frozen blue eyes on the sky, her neck bent at an ungodly angle.

"We were up on the platform," Stitch said in a tear-choked voice. "They told us it was safe."

Zack closed his eyes in sorrow as he pieced together the rest of the story. The huge tempic stairs had only been as strong as the people who made it. When the missiles hit, it must have popped away like a mirage. Those blackened bodies he saw earlier were probably the tempics in question.

Scattered across the broken pavement, just a few yards past Stitch, lay a number of unsullied corpses like Shade's: Nena Hall, Artemis Rosen, everyone else who'd plummeted to the ground when the platform disappeared. Stitch had apparently been the only one of them to survive. Whether she'd saved herself through tempis or a last-second use of her suit barrier, Zack didn't know. He supposed it didn't matter.

"Are you hurt?" he asked. "I can—"

"Fuck you!" Stitch punched him in the head with a hard tempic fist, a blow that would have killed him if he hadn't been wearing a helmet. He flew five feet back into the wall of the shield dome, then fell to the ground in a heap.

Stitch followed him to his landing spot, her fists growing larger and rougher. "We wouldn't have been up there if you had let Heath do his thing!"

"No!" Heath tried to sic a Jonathan on her, but was too sick to summon his tempis. "Stop!"

Stitch ignored him. "You're worse than a coward," she snarled at Zack. "You're a traitor!"

"Enough!" Ofelia popped onto the scene by portal, then opened a plate-size disc by Stitch's neck. "You make one more move, I'll cut your head off. Don't test me, girl."

Stitch retracted her helmet into her suit, her dark eyes drenched in tears. "He killed Shade!"

"That's bullshit and you know it," Ofelia said. "Now walk away."

"You don't—"

"Walk. Away."

Furious, Stitch backed away from Ofelia's portal and pushed through a throng of survivors.

"Zack." Ofelia crouched at his side. "You okay?"

Zack groaned from his crumpled position on the concrete. Even with his helmet protection, Stitch had done a real number on him. There was blood in his mouth, his head throbbed like murder, and he couldn't make sense of anything his left eye was showing him. It was all a kaleidoscopic blur.

He willed his helmet back into his collar, then took in Ofelia through his one functioning eye. "Where were you?"

"Out looking for you." Ofelia opened Zack's eye and grimaced at all the broken new blood vessels. "Oh, man. She got you good."

"Yeah." He looked to the body of Artemis Rosen, a woman who'd survived seven months at Lárnach, only to die a week later in a senseless act of slaughter. "She's not wrong about Shade. When I saved Heath, I, uh . . ."

"Zack . . ."

"I didn't think about the consequences."

"Zack, *stop*." Ofelia draped his arm around her shoulders and helped him back to his feet. "Meredith needs your help."

"What do you mean? What happened to her?"

Ofelia jerked her head at the smoldering ruins. "What do you think?"

Zack was wrong. There was some middle ground between the victims and survivors. Whether it was through their powers or dumb luck or a combination of both, a handful of timebenders had managed to withstand the missile attack without the use of their shields. A young Gotham named Portia Chisholm had taken quick refuge in a dumpster and managed to avoid death with just a smattering of burns. Monty Melford, one of Caleb's last surviving Platinums, had forgotten how to use his personal shield but remembered how to cover himself in tempis. Unfortunately, he'd exposed his eyes in a last-second fit of claustrophobia, and then immediately lost both in the heatburst.

Last but not least, there was Meredith Graham, who'd activated her forcefield ten seconds too early, and had none of it left for the witchsticks. But the same quick panic that had squandered her shield had conjured three tempic minions to defend her with their bodies.

Between the tempis in front of her, the shield wall behind her, and the meager bits of protection that her warsuit offered, Meredith managed to survive the explosion . . . at a cost. Her eardrums were ruptured, the left side of her face had been singed, and a flying piece of masonry—no larger than a pebble—had made an unholy mess of her right eye.

Most worrisome was the injury that Zack couldn't see, except as a readout in his visor. If her warsuit was right, then a broken rib had ruptured her spleen. That was a serious problem.

Meredith sat against a scorched half-wall, her breath coming out in wheezes. "So stupid," she said in an overloud voice. "I used the shield too early. I used it too early."

"Calm down," Zack said, for all the good it did. Her hearing had gone the way of her right eye.

Akio looked Meredith over, then snapped something churlish at Zack.

"I think that's Japanese for 'fix her already,'" Ofelia dryly mused.

Zack didn't see the humor in that. "It's not that simple."

"Why not?" asked Heath. "You healed me."

"That was before I . . ."

Zack looked to him in stammering frustration before finally coming to grips with the problem. "I'm pretty sure I have a concussion," he admitted. "I can barely see straight. If I try to reverse her now, it'll probably kill her."

"How much time do you think she has?" Ofelia asked.

"Enough to find another healer," Zack guessed. "There are still at least twelve of us. Or at least there were."

Meredith scanned the people around her through her one working eye. "I'm not sure what any of you are saying, but I know it can't be good."

"Meredith—"

"It's okay." She clutched Zack's arm. "If you want to make things better, go find my sister. She's worth ten of me. I know she's still alive."

Ofelia was just about to say something when Theo's stressed and weary voice reached everyone through the comm link.

"There's another attack coming," he warned. "If you don't have any shield time left, then find someone who does. If you *do* have shields, look for other people to help. You can easily fit someone else in your barrier. Two, if you squeeze. Look . . ."

Zack knew Theo well enough to feel an apology coming and cringed in anticipation. That was the last thing anyone needed to hear right now.

Fortunately, Theo took a sharp left turn from his own nature. "We're working on a way to stop them."

The mood in the command center—if Theo even dared to call it that anymore—had become bleak. More than twenty percent of their army had been killed: six orphans, fifty-one Gothams, and nearly all the Scarlet Sabres who'd traveled halfway across the planet to fight for them. If there was a strategic benefit to having these people come and die here, Theo couldn't see it. That was apparently just for Ioni to know, and she was still incommunicado.

Help us, goddamn it, Theo hissed in his thoughts. *Give us* something *we can use!*

"Here it comes," See said, her voice a sandy wisp. She'd choked back a cry when she'd learned of Shade's death, and was still putting her grief on layaway.

"Shields up," Theo told his allies on the ground. "Now."

The second wave of the Pelletier attack hit exactly the same as the first: a staccato barrage of witchstick explosions that started due north and moved clockwise around the barrier. The last standing structures finally toppled to the asphalt, while half the rubble and debris from the previous attack went flying in all new directions. Onscreen, it almost looked like gravity had gone haywire. Theo might have even found it captivating, in his own warped way, if his mind wasn't lost in the consequences.

By the time the salvo ended, another eighty-one timebenders were gone, along with most of the survivors' shield time. There was barely anyone left on the battlefield with more than two seconds of power remaining.

Melissa swallowed all her howling expletives as she scanned the gruesome data figures. "The Pelletiers knew our limits," she said. "They gauged every bit of our shield capacity, then methodically chipped away at it."

"Not methodically," Theo said. "This was overkill, even for them. They're being spiteful now. *Emotional.*"

Melissa followed his train of thought. "Like they already know they can't get what they want and they're taking it out on us."

See looked at them both as if they'd gone mad. "Who the hell cares? They're slaughtering us!"

Theo sighed at her. "We're just trying to—"

"You're not doing *anything*. That next wave of rockets is gonna finish everyone out there!"

"Rockets?" Felicity absently inquired.

With all of her automated weapons gone, she had little to do but join Melissa and the others. But there was something she'd noticed—an *absence* of something—that no one else had caught.

"Rockets come with rocket trails," she reminded them. "I didn't see any."

Melissa eyed her quizzically. "You think we were hit by something else?"

"No. I know what witchsticks look like when they explode. That was definitely them. But these ones didn't have any trails, and that means—"

"Portals," Theo interjected, his mouth slack in revelation. A bright new door in the future just opened, but barely enough to see inside. "They're firing the rockets through portals."

Melissa tapped her chin in thought. The past fifteen months had been a nonstop feast for her scientific curiosity, and she hadn't been shy about pestering the Gothams for knowledge. Her number one target was Peter Pendergen, perhaps the world's greatest expert on portals. Though he'd initially been hesitant to share his clan's secrets, Melissa had gradually squeezed enough information out of him to fill an entire dissertation.

She turned to the others, wide-eyed. "If a traveler is quick and strong enough—"

"—they can close someone else's portal," Theo said.

He wasn't sure if he was sharing her idea or stealing it from the future. Either way, it was still a draft in progress and it still had glaring issues.

Felicity didn't hide her skepticism. "You want one of our travelers to go head-to-head against the Pelletiers."

Melissa pointed at Akio on the positional map. "I want an *augmented* traveler to go head-to-head against the Pelletiers."

Theo checked the map for himself. With Peter stuck inside the shield and Mia busy on top of it, they would need another candidate, and fast. Sadly, the only traveler in Akio's vicinity was their least experienced one by far.

But with the Pelletiers just one move away from destroying all futures, Theo was fresh out of options. He had to put his faith in Ofelia. The rest would be up to her.

FORTY

Somewhere deep in the back of Mia's thoughts, behind a great black storm of fear and exhaustion, she found the space to note the irony of her predicament. She was fighting for her life on top of a shield dome, with open air for miles in every direction. Yet her options for movement had become so limited that she might as well have been locked in a cage. She was trapped—*her!*—the girl who could rip a door into anything, the teenage queen of quick escapes.

But she had barriers, literal and otherwise, that were sealing off all exit paths and holding her smack dab in the middle of an unwinnable situation.

With a guttural grunt, she waved a horizontal portal into the air: an eight-foot disc that cut through the chests of three Jades. She barely had a chance to catch her breath before she was forced to throw a plate-size wormhole in front of Hannah and swallow the flying shard of tempis that had been fired at her head.

That was Problem Number One: no fucking time to plot a safe exit. While most of the Jades around them remained focused on disabling Ioni's forcefield, at least ten percent of them had been given a counterorder to take out Mia and her teammates. Dozens of large and aggressive brutes (it only just now occurred to Mia that they were all clones of the same Jade) tried to rush them or pierce them with tempic projectiles. Even with Hannah impeding them in the mother of all slowtime fields—a hundred feet from edge to edge, with a doughnut hole of real time in the center—the attackers were still moving too fast for comfort. Bobby rifted the Jades to the north and east while Mia cut up the ones on the other side.

"Watch your six," Evan said to Mia. He'd run out of ammo twenty seconds ago, and his elder selves, if there were even any left at this point, had wisely given up on him. He had no more prescient intel to offer. Just two wide eyes and a lot of bad suggestions.

"What about there?" Evan asked Mia, his finger pointed at a patch of ground that lay just outside the barrier.

"I told you," Mia shouted back. "I can't jump through the shield."

"It's not *inside* the shield. It's right on the other side."

But Mia could only see it *through* the shield, which prevented her from getting a spatial lock on it. She'd explained it already, their Problem Number Two. Ioni's portal-proof barrier was screwing up her senses.

Bobby zilched three tempic bolts from existence before they could impale Hannah. Whether it was wartime strategy or just a Pelletier vendetta, the Jades seemed determined to kill her first.

"What if we move closer to one side?" Bobby asked. "Give you a better view of the ground."

"No," said Hannah.

"No," said Evan. "This stupid shield is like walking on Jell-O. If one of us trips, we're dead."

"And it'll pop any minute now," Mia reminded Bobby. "If we're somewhere else, who's going to catch us?"

Amanda had already taken care of Problem Number Three: the fleeting nature of the floor they were standing on. She kept an unblinking watch on them from twenty feet below, her tempis primed and ready to rescue them as soon as the barrier disappeared. Gravity was one less thing to worry about, but only while the group stayed close to Amanda.

Evan found a spare bullet in his warsuit pocket and loaded it into his .38. "Then I guess we're fucked."

He closed one eye and fired his last shot. It tore through the neck of a large green aggressor before hitting the eye of another.

"Well, that's a wrap, folks. See you all next time."

"Don't you dare rewind!" Hannah yelled.

Evan shrugged. "What do you want from me? We lost. It's over."

"You have terminus," she told him, as if he needed reminding. "You barely have a year. What are you going to do with it?"

"Not die here, for starters."

"We're not dead yet," Hannah insisted. "I've been in worse spots than this. *Recently.* We both have."

Evan was about to respond with a cynical jab when he saw a tempic spike sailing toward Hannah. His eyes went round. "Mia!"

Mia caught the bolt in portal and sent it flying into the chest of another Jade. Even more surprising than her own ninja move was the fact that Evan had just shown genuine concern for Hannah's well-being. The irony levels were starting to get toxic.

She was abruptly thrown by a flutter in her senses, an odd new distraction from the edge of the portal network. Someone had crashed onto the psychic scene like Godzilla, making earthquakes with every step. Mia had never felt anything like it, even when Ioni had drawn a great white door between Sergelen and San Francisco.

More shocking still, Mia recognized the aura of the new power player. *"Ofelia?"*

Hannah looked at her, confused. "What?"

Mia opened a portal inside a Jade and sent half his organs to Alcatraz. Whatever was happening with her friend and fellow traveler, she didn't have time to ponder it. She could only hope that Ofelia did something good with her upgrade.

Make it count, Mia implored her. *Make it hurt.*

When she first heard the plan, she thought Theo had gone nuts. She only had ten weeks of portal-making under her belt, barely enough to fill a high school semester. Now suddenly she was being asked to use her knowledge against the Pelletiers, to beat them at a form of mental jujitsu that they'd been practicing for decades, if not centuries.

"We don't have a choice," Theo had told her over the comm link. "If they get in one more hit with their rockets, it's over."

Ofelia already knew that part. That second round of explosions would have killed her, Zack, and everyone else around them if they hadn't tripled up beneath their last remaining bubble shields. Now their defenses were depleted. They had nothing to save them from the fire next time.

"It's now or never," Theo had told Ofelia. "Please."

Felicity had briefed Akio on the new game plan via radio. He'd looked at Ofelia skeptically, then grumbled something in Japanese.

"He says he's never amped up a traveler before," Felicity told Ofelia through her earpiece. "He doesn't know how it'll affect you. But he can see that you're a strong woman and he feels good about your chances."

Ofelia snorted cynically. "You made up that last part."

"Okay, he might have said the opposite," Felicity admitted. "But he doesn't know you like we do."

For the first few moments of her augmented state, Ofelia didn't feel much different. No pains or spasms. No adrenaline rush. No crackling energy between her fingertips.

She did, however, have a stronger sense of the portals in the vicinity, particularly the big, floating Pelletier disc that kept crapping out Jades by the bowlful. It pressed against her thoughts like a cold metal plate, and left an ethereal trail of residue that stretched all the way to Earth's southern pole. If Ofelia had any influence over the portal, she couldn't find it. There wasn't a trace of human consciousness behind the breach. For all she knew, it had been made by machine.

This is hopeless, Ofelia thought. *How am I supposed to take them on if I can't feel them?*

She tried to replay her training sessions with Peter, all the long-winded prattle about portal networks and intertraveler mind melds. At the time, she'd dismissed it as Jedi crap, and let it all pass by like the wind.

Should've listened to him, Ofelia chided herself. *Now everyone's fucked.*

She suddenly detected more portal activity near the top of the shield dome: a nonstop barrage of small spatial wormholes, popping in and out of existence. They were all being formed by the same desperate mind, one Ofelia had no trouble identifying.

Oh no. Mia.

Even from a distance, Ofelia could hear her young friend's thoughts, and experience them as if they were her own. Poor Mia had been fighting nonstop since the first rockets hit the plaza, and was well past the point of fatigue. But Mia knew that if she let down her guard, even for a moment, her brother and Hannah would die.

That was not an outcome that Mia could live with. Dying before she got to confront Semerjean was not an outcome she could live with.

Ofelia caressed her psyche from the inside. *Oh,* manita. *You have it worse at sixteen than I ever did. And my life was shit.*

She wasn't sure when she'd stopped thinking about Mia and started looking at her, but somehow she'd made the transition. Ofelia could see everything that was happening on the shield dome with a clarity that exceeded mere vision. The entire scene had been slowed to a near freeze-frame while a flood of new data entered her through senses she had yet to discover. All the friends and foes on top of the barrier carried the residue of their recent portal jumps, and those flecks of psychic energy had their own little stories to tell. Apparently Bobby was in serious pain, and was dead set on hiding the fact. He also feared that he was going to Hell for the victims he'd claimed as a

Scarlet Sabre: men, women, even a few teenagers who'd been labeled as enemies for reasons Bobby never questioned. He'd carry the guilt for the rest of his life without speaking a word of it to anyone.

Hannah, on the other hand, didn't believe in Hell, even though she'd been there for months. Her trauma from her time with the Pelletiers bled down to the very core of her, reshaping every part of her inner world. Between that and the strains of motherhood, Ofelia didn't know how Hannah kept functioning. Yet she fought like a heroine anyway, despite her own pains and discomforts. Without her temporal field to slow down the Jades, she and her team would have been killed six times over.

Incredible woman, Ofelia marveled. *I won't let you die here.*

She fixed her spectral gaze on the last member of the group, the vicious little imp who'd murdered her brother.

"Evan," Ofelia muttered, loud enough for Zack to hear. While her consciousness fluttered a hundred feet above, her body leaned casually against a scorched brick wall, her arms crossed and her eyes gently closed, as if she were just listening to music. Zack checked her warsuit's health readings to confirm what his own eyes were showing him: aside from her elevated stress levels, she was doing just fine. Akio's power boost was apparently much gentler on travelers than it was on tempics.

Ofelia circled around Evan's frozen countenance, examining him from every angle. On some morbid level, she hoped her Super X-Ray Traveler Vision would reveal something new about him, some mitigating factor that helped explain his twisted nature.

But a deep scan only confirmed her worst assumptions. The man was black as tar on the inside, a creature functionally incapable of empathy. Even more repulsive than his endless bad will was the warped sense of justice behind it. He didn't bear a shred of guilt for his victims. In his mind, they'd all done something to deserve their fate, most especially Jury Curado.

Monster, Ofelia thought. *I should kill you right now.*

Wait. *Could* she? She didn't need her body to draw a portal, just her mind and her spatial awareness. An ounce of thought in the right direction could slice the little bastard in half.

But for all she knew, Evan's creepy time power was keeping Hannah and the others alive. She wouldn't sacrifice three good people on the altar of her vengeance.

Besides, she still had a job to do.

She felt a strange new chill at the back of her senses, like a splash of cold water in her hair. Ofelia turned her ethereal head and saw a smokelike trail of energy approaching. It had popped up over the southern horizon and was heading her way like a comet.

No, not a comet, Ofelia thought. *A rocket.*

Except it wasn't exactly a rocket either, just the portal that was about to deliver it. The Pelletiers' third and most lethal attack was coming, and Ofelia still had no idea how to stop it.

"Mia!"

Ofelia wasn't even sure she was audible in her current state. She was operating on an entirely different plane of existence, at an entirely different speed, using a language that—if anything—merely pecked away at the edge of Mia's consciousness through the nebulous rapport that all travelers shared. Even if Ofelia *could* reach her, she was afraid to distract the poor girl while she was fighting the Jades.

But with hundreds of people about to die, Ofelia had no other choice.

"I'm sorry to do this," she said to Mia. "But Peter's in the dead zone down below. I can't reach him. I just . . ."

Ofelia palmed her face, a movement that was mimicked by her physical form. "I need you to teach me what he taught you about closing other people's portals. And I kind of need it fast."

She checked back on the Pelletiers' progress and saw the energy trail closer than ever. Worse, it now had seven siblings in tow, with at least six more breaking over the horizon.

"Mia—"

"What does it even matter?" Mia fired back.

Ofelia studied her in a dead-faced stupor. Mia had responded without moving her lips, and spoke in a faint and muffled voice that made her sound like she was talking through a bath towel.

"What do you mean?" Ofelia asked her.

"What are you talking about?" asked an unseen man in a familiar Irish brogue. "Of course it matters. They're the Pelletiers."

"That's my point," Mia told Peter. "If they want to open a fucking door, how do you expect me to close it?"

It's a memory, Ofelia realized. *She's giving it to me.*

Soon, Ofelia could see the vignette in question: Peter and Mia, nearly one year ago, standing side by side beneath the fake morning sky of the underland. They had teleported to the roof of Orphan Tower 5, but clearly Mia was in no mood for a training session. She'd just lost her virginity to the Copper named Sweep and had all sorts of complicated—

"No." Ofelia waved away the intimate detail, lest she fall into the memory of a memory. This was the moment she needed to see.

Peter shook his head at Mia. "The Pelletiers aren't gods."

"No, they're demons."

"They're people," Peter insisted. "With human flaws and weaknesses."

Mia eyed him cynically. "Yeah? Like what?"

"Well, for starters, they *think* they're gods, at least compared to the rest of us. That's an exploitable weakness right there."

Ofelia's thoughts lit up with inspiration. The Pelletiers had already launched two successful attacks against their enemies. The last thing they'd expect is for the greenest and weakest traveler among them to mount a fierce resistance. That at least put surprise on Ofelia's side.

The Peter of last year continued: "Secondly, the portals don't play off strength like tempis does. It's not an arm-wrestling match. It's more like . . ." He cocked his head at Mia. "You ever play slap-hands, or is that just a boy thing?"

Mia rolled her eyes. "I had four brothers. Of course I played."

"And I bet you even won sometimes, despite them being stronger than you."

"More than sometimes," Mia said. "I won a lot."

"Because you were quicker on the draw and you knew how to anticipate them."

Mia smiled fiercely. "My brothers weren't subtle."

"Neither are the Pelletiers," Peter insisted. "If you ever end up playing slap-hands with their portals, I'd already put good money on you."

"Holy shit," said Ofelia. While she knew the fight wouldn't be as easy as Peter promised, he'd just given her a better perspective on it.

And in this mad realm of human existence, perspective had a power all to itself.

Ofelia focused her attention on the nearest approaching portal and was almost relieved to feel the alien thoughts behind it. Unlike the big Jade disc that loomed above, these rocket doors were forged by human mind—a *woman's* mind, filled with chaos and contempt and a palpable amount of sickness.

Esis, Ofelia guessed. *She still doesn't know I'm coming, which gives me one free shot.*

She willed the totality of her consciousness into the shape of an open hand, then took a fierce swipe at the nearest portal trail. Her giant palm connected with such abrupt force that she could practically feel the impact from the real world.

A startled shriek from Esis. A shockwave across the network. The next thing that Ofelia saw, when she finally dared to look again, were clear blue skies all across the psychic firmament. One hard slap at the portals' creator was enough to slam all her doors shut.

Though she full well knew that there'd be hell to pay, Ofelia flashed a savage grin at the specter of her enemy. "Surprise."

Theo paced the cafeteria floor, his mind swiveling like a spotlight across the strings. Whatever Ofelia was doing was happening well beyond view of the cameras. Aside from checking her health on the telemetry screen, there was little he could do but press his ear to the future and listen for the sounds of explosions.

"Theo."

Melissa drew his attention to the close-up view of Ofelia's face, an ever-shifting tableau of expressions that ran the gamut from hope to despair. But sometime in the past few seconds, her reaction had changed into something altogether new: a nasty little smile, like the proverbial cat who'd caught the canary.

Felicity peeked over Theo's shoulder and studied Ofelia's countenance. "What does that mean? Does that mean she's winning?"

Theo grimly shook his head. "It's not over yet."

"What on earth are you playing at, child?"

Ofelia was a lot happier before Esis started talking, though "talk" seemed a generous term for it. Her voice hit Ofelia like a megaphone in the ear, at the peak of her very worst hangover. And each syllable came loaded with telepathic undertones that broadcast every ounce of her disdain. In Esis's eyes, Ofelia was nothing more than a coarse and matted street rat, not even useful to science. Worse, Esis's haughty amusement at Ofelia's "attack" was enough to deflate all sense of accomplishment. Ofelia had only won at slap-hands because Esis didn't know they were playing.

But now her opponent was fully aware, and was itching for her turn to slap back.

"Do you think you stopped anything?" Esis pointedly inquired. "You closed one door without even locking it. Did you expect that to keep me out?"

In point of fact, Ofelia did not. She could already get a whiff of the woman's next move: a stealth attack with a rocket portal, one that could instantly pop up anywhere.

"Fascinating," Esis said, with enough encoded derision to make Ofelia queasy. "Of all the travelers they could have enlisted, they chose their feeblest amateur."

Ofelia felt a telling swirl in the air, just a few yards south of the shield dome. She rushed to the nascent portal and smacked it shut just before it could launch a witchstick.

"Though perhaps not the dimmest," Esis said. "For all your limits, you do learn quickly."

"Shut your fucking mouth," Ofelia snapped. "I just met you and already I can't stand you."

"That's not true."

"You think I don't hate you?"

Two new portals began to form on opposite sides of the dome. Ofelia had to shatter her physical sense of herself to slap them both shut at the same time. The effort caused her bodily pain, like having both arms twisted and stretched.

"I don't question your feelings," Esis replied. "Only your grasp of history. You say you just met me when we've known each other for years."

A harsh psychic grin cut into Ofelia like a blade. "Perhaps this will refresh your memory."

Her mind was suddenly overcome by a multisensory hallucination: a cold white dungeon made entirely of tempis, overlit from all sides with a sickly white fluorescence.

In the center of the cube lay eight dark-haired women whom Ofelia easily recognized: all the Pearls of Guadalajara, including herself. They floated side by side in horizontal positions, as if they'd all been tucked into invisible beds. Their skin had been draped in silky white slips of fabric that were long enough to touch the floor and loose enough to leave their bellies exposed.

Their very pregnant bellies, Ofelia noticed.

Even more disturbing than the Pearls' matching stillness were the many tubes and wires that ran in and out of their bodies. The poor girls looked like nothing more than components of a great machine: a hybrid baby factory.

A cold, black dread rushed through Ofelia. *Oh no . . .*

Like the rest of the Pearls, she'd been stripped of all memory of her time as a Pelletier captive. But now she was getting a glimpse of what she'd missed through the eyes of her jailer.

It was worse than she could have possibly imagined. So much worse.

"You were our guest at Lárnach for five and a half years," Esis told her. "Accelerated time, naturally, though not from your perspective. The way we kept you and your dull little sisters, I imagine the moments passed like weeks."

Against Ofelia's will, the view closed in on the prisoner at the end of the floating chain—her own suffering self, locked in a state of paralysis except for her wide, round eyes. They fluttered back and forth helplessly, crying, before focusing on something in the near distance.

"You were looking at me," Esis explained. "Begging me to kill you, again and again. Thankfully, we'd severed your brainstem connection so your stress didn't affect your pregnancies. But I'm afraid the experience left your mind in shambles, each and every time."

Esis heaved an exaggerated sigh. "You were always the first Pearl to crumble."

Ofelia had to summon every ounce of her willpower to keep from screaming. When Semerjean had visited her in a dream, he'd painted a much brighter picture of her captivity: a gorgeous beachside mansion, with buffets and puppies and every other indulgence. But that had been nothing but a lie, a smokescreen to hide the true horrors.

Mia had been right all along. The Pelletiers weren't human. They were demons. Pure, vicious hellspawn.

Ofelia had been so lost in torment that she didn't even feel the slap coming. A twelve-inch portal opened northwest of the dome and sent a rocket into a large crowd of timebenders.

By the time the witchstick hit the floor of its target—the area's third bombing in two and a half minutes—there was little of it left to destroy. Just a former corporate shuttle bay that had been reduced to fragments of fragments.

Esis couldn't have cared less about the history of the place, or its strategic value to her enemies. Her only metric for choosing it was the large number of people who'd gathered there: sixty-two Gothams and three hapless orphans, none of whom had any shield left.

"Oh no . . ." Ofelia looked away from the slow-motion carnage, for all the good it did. Sight was just one of a dozen senses she had available to her on the travelers' plane, and most of them were still so new that she didn't even know how to block them. Ofelia could taste every bit of the victims' pain through the portal residue on their skin: an intense burst of heat and bone-breaking force that stretched their final milliseconds into a small and torturous eternity.

One of the casualties, a sixteen-year-old teleporter named Wendell "Split" Whitten, had managed to air his dying grievances through his travelers' rapport with Ofelia. *What was the point of all that training?* the young Gotham wondered. *What was the point of anything?*

Crying, Ofelia focused her consciousness on the architect of Split's demise. "You!"

"Don't be childish," Esis said. "You wanted to fight above your station, to test your mettle against an experienced opponent."

A new wisp of energy appeared to the south, nestled right in the middle of another mob of timebenders. Ofelia was so distracted by the familiar faces in the group—Zack, Heath, Meredith, and Akio—that she nearly forgot that her own physical self was standing right there with them.

Esis shined another psychic grin. "You should have anticipated the consequences."

"No!" By the time Ofelia caught wind of the coming portal, it had already opened a crack. She was too late to close it, but if she fought hard enough, she could keep it from opening wider.

Esis forced the portal's jamb from the other side, her thoughts half-curled in a sneer.

"If only you'd listened to my husband," she said. "He warned you that Maranan would lead you to ruin. Now here you are at Theo's behest: a sacrificial lamb, a momentary hindrance. You gave up your life to delay the inevitable by one or two seconds at most."

Ofelia struggled to keep her grip on the portal. She and Esis were apparently done playing slap-hands. Now they were locked in a telepathic arm wrestle. But while Esis had the stronger mind, her thoughts were still muddled with sickness. Ofelia could almost count the black spots on her consciousness, the blight that was claiming her, thought by thought.

"You want to talk inevitable?" Ofelia said. "Look at yourself. You're dying. And all the little babies you made from us haven't done shit to help you."

Esis's psyche turned a hot shade of red. "My death remains a speck in the distance. Shall we measure yours?"

Ofelia reeled in compounding pain. Her struggle was becoming an agony, like pressing down a window from a cracked and jagged edge.

"Every one of your big ideas has failed," Ofelia said with a grunt. "Now you think Ioni's the answer. You're gonna be disappointed again."

Esis scoffed. "Pathetic. You're as clumsy as you are transparent."

Ofelia owned that one. It was a weak attempt at distraction. But her only hope was to find something to use against the woman, a psychological Achilles' heel that would wreck her concentration.

Esis flooded Ofelia's mind with scornful, mocking laughter, as if she could follow every beat of her plan. "Oh, you poor, desperate child."

"Shut up."

"You're playing with forces you barely comprehend."

"Shut up!"

"Don't take it to heart," Esis teased. "It's not your fault you're so inexperienced."

As her hold on the portal continued to weaken, Ofelia felt her consciousness slide down a greasy slope of despair. Her thoughts tormented her with the horrors of Lárnach, her wide eyes helplessly pleading for death while the Pelletiers used her as an incubator.

What was the point? What was the point of anything?

"No!"

Ofelia channeled every spark of her wrath until she was finally able to visualize Esis. She locked her dark eyes onto hers, furious.

"You want experience?"

She tore open the floodgates of her very own memory, to one of her thousand worst nights in Havana.

"My father abused me for years," Ofelia said. "Even worse, he convinced me that I deserved it. He said I was born under a bad moon and was cursed to bring out the worst in people. That was all the excuse he needed to rape me, night after night. And every time he finished, leaving me crying and bleeding, he stood in the light of my bedroom door and said the same fucking thing. '*Es lo que es.*' 'It is what it is.'"

She felt Esis recoil at the visceral details of the memory, an earthshaking trauma that the woman had never once imagined, much less suffered. Though Ofelia had inflicted it on her without a hint of strategy, she was starting to see the advantage. Maybe the Achilles' heel she was looking for was in her own mind, not Esis's.

"You want experience?" Ofelia jumped ahead to her teenage years in the slums of Miami: a runaway junkie, perpetually ill, bouncing like a pinball between bad and worse lovers. "Even after I left my father behind, he followed in my head and told me what I deserved. I ate out of garbage cans, filled my veins with poison, gave myself to any man or woman who could keep me high for another day. And if they should happen to cut me or smack me around . . ." Ofelia shrugged. *"Es lo que es."*

Her brother Jury suddenly barged into her memories, as he'd done so many times in real life: her savior, her healer, her crusading avenger. Ofelia had to flush him out of her thoughts to keep Esis from getting a reprieve. Let her wallow in the taste of a stale and moldy chicken wing. Let her feel the hard slap of a drug pusher.

Sickened, Esis tried to open a second portal in the same vicinity as the first. Ofelia kicked it into vapor, then grabbed her enemy by the spectral throat.

"Oh, I'm not done, bitch. I've barely even started. You want to know what it feels like to get a knife between the ribs?"

Ofelia brought her back to a wretched night in the Gaslamp Quarter of San Diego, just six months before the sky came down.

"This was after I got clean," she told Esis. "I didn't seek this man out for abuse. I didn't even want him to talk to me. But he decided that stabbing me was a perfectly good way to handle rejection."

While Esis hollered with phantom pain, Ofelia pelted her mind with the worst agonies she could recall: her first broken rib, her second heroin withdrawal, her third abortion, her fourth suicide attempt. She brought Esis back to the collapse of the underland and showed her just how it felt to get crushed by rocks. She had the Pelletiers themselves to thank for that one.

And speaking of appropriate memories . . .

"You want experience?" Ofelia asked Esis one last time. She rolled her life back ten and a half weeks, to the day that Melissa had sat her down and told her the fate of her planet. Everyone that Ofelia knew and loved, all killed in a manmade apocalypse.

"*That's* how it feels to lose your world."

Esis retreated from the travelers' plane without a parting thought or sensation. All that remained was the sliver of her portal, a jagged little rift in the fabric of space that Ofelia had inherited full control over. She slapped it shut before the witchstick could emerge, and only sampled a tiny taste of its wrath as it exploded on the Lárnach side of the portal.

"Fuck."

Under better circumstances, Ofelia might have been jubilant. But she knew that her victory was temporary. One of the other Pelletiers could come crashing in at any moment to finish the job that Esis started. Or maybe the Bitch Queen herself would bounce back after a breather. In either case, there was little Ofelia could do to stop them. Her mind was teetering on the edge of collapse, like a rickety wooden scaffold.

Worse, whatever temporal spinach that Akio had fed her was starting to wear off.

"*Mierda.*" In all the chaos, she forgot about her promise to help Mia and Hannah.

She launched herself back to the top of the shield and connected to Mia through their travelers' link. Though the girl subconsciously resisted all attempts to manipulate her, Ofelia soothed her concern.

"It's all right," she told her. "I got you. Just let me help."

Once Mia relaxed, Ofelia was able to reorient her spatial senses and guide her portal to a safe place on the ground. *Well, not exactly safe*, Ofelia thought. *But safer than where you were.*

At long last, Ofelia's upgrade expired, and her consciousness fell crashing back into her body. The sensation was so rough and painfully disorienting that she felt like she'd been forced out of the womb all over again. Her thoughts and limbs stopped functioning in unison. She collapsed to the shattered pavement.

"Ofelia!" Zack dropped to her side. "Are you okay?"

Even if she'd remembered how to get her mouth working, she wouldn't know what to say. Her thoughts and recollections, even her sense of time, had become a chaotic muddle, a maelstrom that sent her twirling all around her personal chronology. All the pain and abuse, all the bad decisions, all the traumas that had hit her point-blank in the face.

What was the point? a soft voice echoed. *What was the point of any of it?*

Like the proverbial newborn, there was little she could do but cry. Even as her body slowly began to recover and her memories flew back to their proper place on the shelves, Ofelia found herself weeping over tragedies old and new.

"It's all right," Zack said. "You did it. You saved us."

She struggled to speak through trembling lips. "Not all of us."

Zack stroked her arm. "I heard the explosion. There was only just one. Whatever you did, you saved the rest of us."

It suddenly dawned on her that, among all of her other recent bad moves, she may have just inadvertently saved the life of Evan Rander. Sixty-eight people had perished on her watch, yet she let her brother's killer escape the justice he was begging for.

Es lo que es, Evan teased in her thoughts. *It is what it is.*

She lifted her head and weakly looked around. The portal she'd helped draw for Mia should have been here already. "Hannah and the others. Did they—"

"They're here," Heath said. He gestured at the group in the nearby wreckage, fresh from the top of the shield dome. They'd spilled out of Mia's portal as silhouettes and tumbled to the ground in a collective heap.

"Oh." Ofelia lowered her head, puzzled. The portal had opened just twenty feet away from her, yet she hadn't felt a trace of it. It was just the first sign of an ugly truth that would gradually unfold over the next few minutes. Her power had become a casualty of war. Her short but brilliant career as a traveler had already come to an end.

Theo sat down for the first time in minutes, his mind scrambling to keep up with the data. Nearly half their army had perished in the rocket attacks, but Ofelia had stopped it from becoming a total massacre. Better still, all the futures and augurs available to him agreed that the Pelletiers were done launching witchsticks.

But the good news was just a thin strip of wallpaper that barely obscured the grim numbers. The Jades were raining down on them faster than ever, and the shell-shocked timebenders that remained weren't nearly enough to defeat them. Though Theo refused to say it out loud, he knew exactly why the Pelletiers had stopped their missile strikes: they didn't need them anymore. The futures were still calling victory for them. All Ofelia bought for her pain and suffering was a little more time on the game board.

Twenty-nine seconds after the last loud explosion, a warning light came to ife on the shield console. They were about to enter the final defense stage, at east a minute and a half before they were supposed to. That didn't bode well for the rest of the war, but the Jades didn't leave Theo much choice.

"Here we go," he said as he flipped a small switch on the console. Their hird and final shield dome was only sixty feet wide in diameter and thirty eet tall at the crest, just enough to protect Ioni and her thirty-six assistants as hey continued to power her engine. Everyone else, from the strategists in the ommand center to the children in the crystal shelters, would officially become part of the battle zone once the outer shield crumbled for good.

Theo exchanged a grim look with Melissa before addressing the surviving roops. "All right, folks. We're pretty much at the endgame. The second barier will break in about thirty seconds, and Ioni still needs five and a half ninutes to do what she needs to do. I know that seems, uh . . ."

He had to swallow a fatalistic sentiment before it escaped and spread loom everywhere. "I know you're exhausted. Your ears are still ringing. And ve're all mourning the friends we just lost. But we still have a job to do, each nd every one of us. We have to keep those Jades off the last shield."

Theo scanned the remaining mood bars with lament. He wished he had ven a fraction of Zack's and Hannah's talent for galvanizing.

"This war isn't over," he insisted to everyone. "The future's still up for rabs. Anyone who still has some fight left in them—please—do whatever ou can to buy time."

He watched Melissa hurry to the weapons rack and procure two Integrity ssault rifles.

"We'll be out there fighting with you," Theo said in closing.

Melissa stopped Felicity before she could grab a gun. "Not you. We still eed eyes in here. Keep watch on the screens and keep your radio open."

"But, boss—"

Melissa clutched Felicity's shoulder. "You're the most brilliant friend and lly I could have hoped for. But I need your brilliance here. Not there." She hrew a quick look at See before muttering in Felicity's ear. "Keep her safe."

Melissa passed her second rifle to Theo as he followed her out of the cafeeria. "I hope you're right about our chances."

"I said the future's still open," Theo replied. "I didn't mention our chances."

"Well . . ." Melissa popped a magazine into her rifle, her expression as stoic s ever. "Should the worst happen, there's no better cause to die for."

Theo gave her a wan half-smile. "There's no better person to die with."

Melissa kissed him just as the second shield fizzled and hundreds of Jades dropped like stones onto the final barrier.

Theo switched the safety off his weapon and blew a heavy breath. "Shit."

For the very first time since the endwar began, Ioni Anata T'llari Deschane opened her eyes in wide alertness. A single word escaped her lips, but it had been said in such a hushed and airy voice that no one in her circle, not even the closest thermics, realized she'd even spoken.

But her intended target, a lone Irish traveler on the other side of the barrier, heard her command as clearly as if she'd shouted it in his ear.

"Now!"

Peter jumped to his feet from his meditative position and waved a new portal in the air.

Theo and Melissa caught a glimpse of it from outside the cafeteria: a vertical disc large enough for a jet plane, hovering fifty feet above the ground. The breach was so bright and fiery around the edges that Theo had to wonder if Peter had ripped a time portal.

But then he heard the familiar *whoosh* of swifters, several of them from the sound of it. Before Theo had a chance to process what was happening, the portal disappeared in a blink.

Melissa was the first to notice the jarring change that Peter had made to their status quo. Instead of bringing in some much-needed reinforcements, he'd sent thirty of their heaviest hitters away.

Melissa's mouth went slack. "Amanda . . ."

"Huh?" Theo glanced up at the tall diamond platform where the aerics and swifters had been standing until just a moment ago. "Oh no . . ."

Theo hadn't been privy to the plans of their aer force. It was the one part of the war effort that had been kept from him, by order of Ioni herself. She'd told Theo that his involvement would . . . complicate matters, her genteel way of saying that he'd screw the whole thing up if he knew about it.

So he let Amanda and the others have their secrets and meetings without prying too hard. He didn't even know until just now that Peter had been part of the cabal.

Except now the future was finally tattling on them, and Theo didn't like what he was seeing.

He rushed across the plaza to Peter. "Where did Amanda and the others go?"

"Theo—"

"Where did you send them?"

"Lárnach," Peter replied with a maudlin sigh. "They're taking the fight to the Pelletiers."

"What?" Melissa caught up to Theo and followed every one of his logical thoughts. Peter didn't have the range to draw a portal to Antarctica. He lacked the power to jump blind to an unfamiliar location. And he'd never been able to rip a door in midair, like Mia and Ofelia could.

But all of those limits had been thoroughly shattered, through measures that were easily guessed. Peter's shiny new headband, a gift from Ioni, was clearly giving his talents a kick.

That only left a final question, one Melissa had to field by herself. Theo's foresight had already given him the answer, enough to fill his eyes with tears and make him understand why Ioni had kept him out of the loop.

"Peter . . ." Melissa's fingers trembled around the handle of her rifle. "How is Amanda getting back?"

Peter only met her gaze for a moment before looking away in misery. He paused for so long that Theo had to answer for him. "She isn't."

FORTY-ONE

There hadn't been much room for secrets at Sergelen. With everyone living on top of each other, and every mouth chittering over the nebulous war to come, the rumors had flown like machine-gun fire through the corridors of the Chinese base.

Most of it, of course, had been pure anxious hokum: the tempics would be the first to die, the Jades would all come rigged with nukes, the Pelletiers would turn their captured timebenders into an army of zombie soldiers. There had even been talk that Ioni's real plan was to revert the whole world back to 1912, where she could craft an all-new chain of history that didn't include temporis.

Though Theo had tried to squash the bad gossip, there had been one bleak rumor that simply refused to die: that Ioni had assembled a clandestine team for a game-changing suicide mission.

For the orphans and Gothams of Sergelen, all still traumatized from their losses in the underland, it had been the perfect theory for self-torment. What if their spouse, sibling, parent, or friend had been secretly recruited for a sacrificial task? What if they weren't allowed to talk about it, even to their closest loved ones?

Amanda, ironically, had been one of the first to fall prey to the paranoia. For her first three weeks at Sergelen, she'd lived under the compounding fear that Zack was one of Ioni's kamikazes. He'd been spending a lot of time with the woman, and had been disturbingly vague about their discussions. And wouldn't it be just like him to jump headfirst into the volcano?

On the twelfth of September, twenty-two days before the war in Prior Circle, Amanda finally confronted Zack about it, in a manner that even she could admit was somewhat less than hinged.

"Just tell me the truth already!"

"I've been telling you all night! You just don't want to hear it."

"If you're going to throw your life away—"

"Amanda—"

"—then it better not be for me," she cried. "Don't you *dare* do that for me!"

The look that Zack had given her, a mawkish blend of pity and concern that she hadn't seen since her miscarriages, had been enough to send her ou of their room, off the base, and into the wilds of Mongolia.

She cut a brisk path across the moonlit plains, fighting every screaming urge to fly. The cloakshield that Ioni had thrown around Sergelen was only third of the size of the underland, turning any attempt at wingflight into constrained and annoying hassle. It was a nice enough night for a walk, anyway. The air was exactly as cool as her tempic arms, a thermal equilibrium that felt as pleasant as an evening swim.

After fifteen minutes of circular ambling, a curious sight snapped her ou of her thoughts. Someone had set up a pair of plush red recliners in the middle of a patch of needlegrass. A small oak table filled the gap between them and on the surface of the table: two wineglasses and a bottle of Cabernet Sauvignon.

Amanda picked up the bottle and studied the label. The fact that the win was her favorite brand—a Santa Rosa vineyard that didn't exist on this world—was enough to answer her most pressing question. Someone had pulled her into the God's Eye, and it didn't take a wizard to figure out who.

"How long have I been here?"

"About ten minutes," said Ioni. She relaxed in the seat of the leftmost recliner, as if it hadn't been empty a moment ago. "You were having a nice brood. I didn't want to interrupt."

Instead of her usual Sergelen gear, the same LUCKY WOMAN T-shirt and drab blue jeans that everyone wore around the base, Ioni looked ready for a night on the town in her white satin dress and stiletto pumps. Her hair was done up in a high side ponytail that was popular in modern Europe but had long gone kitsch in Altamerica.

Amanda took a seat in the other recliner and turned the Cabernet bottle in her hands. "Let me guess. You're here because you're worried about me."

Ioni eyed her stoically. "Are you in danger of hurting yourself?"

"No."

"Then I guess I had another reason." Ioni gestured at the wine. "Have some. I've been told by a reliable source that it tastes just like the real thing."

"No thanks." Amanda put the bottle back on the table. "I went a little crazy on Zack earlier. He probably told you."

"He didn't," Ioni said. "But if it's about what I think it's about—"

"I know he's not on your suicide team."

Ioni bristled at her choice of words. "Even if I had one, which I currently don't, I wouldn't ever call it that. It's ghoulish."

"It's not about that anyway," Amanda said. "At least not much."

Ioni nodded thoughtfully. "Your sister."

"She's out there somewhere, suffering—"

"Amanda . . ."

"—because of me! She made that sacrifice for *me*."

"Amanda, *stop*."

Ioni craned her neck at the stars, or whatever passed for stars in this realm. "You remember our first talk in the God's Eye, when you were on your way to London?"

"Of course."

"I told you the Pelletiers would come and take Hannah, but I also told you about the futures where she comes back."

Amanda was tempted to chug some wine before Ioni could break the ba news. "And?"

"At the time, it was just a handful of strings," Ioni said. "Last week, it became a couple of thousand. Today, it's in the millions."

Amanda leaned forward, wide-eyed. "Oh my God!"

"That doesn't make it a certainty," Ioni cautioned. "Just a stronger possibility than it was before."

Though her body was merely a psychic image, Amanda felt tears in th corners of her eyes. "Thank you."

"Don't thank me. If she does come back, it'll be all her doing. Bu remember—"

"I know. I know. It might not happen."

"And it might be moot," said Ioni. "If my plans go to shit, there'll be n saving anyone."

Amanda studied Ioni carefully. "You're tense."

"I'm always tense."

"But you're showing it more. What's going on?"

Ioni paused a moment, expressionless, before pouring two glasses of Cabernet. "I'm not really a wine person. How is this stuff?"

"I love it," Amanda said. "Or used to, anyway. I haven't had much alcoh since, uh . . ."

"Since Evan drugged you at an Indiana hotel and you went nutso."

Amanda cringed at the two-year-old memory, the first time her temp made national news. "I almost killed Zack and Hannah."

"*He* almost killed Zack and Hannah."

Amanda didn't like the way Ioni was stalling. Whatever she'd come her to talk about, she clearly wasn't eager to start.

"I don't mean any disrespect, but—"

"I know." Ioni nodded obligingly. "You're right. I'm sorry. I'm just little . . ."

She sat back in her chair and took a wary sniff of the wine. "Amanda, I' about to give you some privileged information, stuff that even Theo doesn know. If you share a word of it with him or Zack or anyone else, you'll be jeopardizing everything I've worked for. Every life on Earth. That's not hyperbol It's fact. Do you understand me?"

Amanda nodded anxiously. "I understand."

"All right then." Ioni sipped the Cabernet, then crinkled her nose in revulsion. "This is literally the hundredth wine I've tried and failed to get into."

Amanda wound her finger impatiently. "Your news?"

"I've been lying to all of you these past few weeks."

"About what?"

"About our chances of beating the Pelletiers," Ioni said. "From the moment they brought down the underland, they more or less sealed our fates. We only have half the army I expected to have, while they have an infinite supply of Jades."

"Infinite," Amanda said with a shudder. "How is that even possible?"

"Anything's possible if you have the right resources and you know which corners to cut. These mass-produced Jades won't be as autonomous as the ones you fought. They'll mostly be controlled by computer."

That news didn't comfort Amanda one bit.

"But they'll sure as hell know how to eat through my shields," Ioni added. "They'll find me and kill me before I can heal the Earth's damage. I've checked he math from every angle. There's no way to avoid losing."

She looked up from her lap and locked her heavy eyes on Amanda. "Except one."

Amanda suddenly recalled an exchange from their first talk, a cryptic varning about the future. *We may have one more conversation in the God's Eye*, Ioni had told her. *If things don't go entirely as planned. If that happens, uh . . . well, let's just hope it doesn't.*

"There'll be a split-second window about twelve minutes into the war," Ioni explained. "A once-in-a-lifetime opportunity to sneak a team into Lárnach undetected."

"Lárnach?"

"The Pelletier home base."

Amanda narrowed her eyes. "You mean the place they're keeping Hannah."

"We can't help her," Ioni insisted. "By the time this window opens, she'll either be back with us or she'll be dead."

Amanda's spectral stomach lurched with stress. "So what's this team supposed to do?"

"Take down their power reactor," said Ioni. "It won't be easy, but it's still very doable. And if you succeed—*once* you succeed—the Pelletiers will be hindered for the rest of the fight. They won't be able to make more Jades, and they'll have less control over the ones they have."

While Amanda enjoyed the thought of Semerjean's reaction, Ioni remained dead-eyed. Grim.

"What happens at Lárnach will determine the outcome of the war," she plainly told Amanda. "If we miss that window or if we fail, it's over for all of us. Done."

Amanda looked to the grass for a brief, quiet spell before raising her head again. "Obviously, I'm in. I just have to ask—"

"Why you?" Ioni smiled wanly. "There's no walking path where you'll be going. I need all the flying tempics for this. But the reason I need you to lead them—"

"What are our chances?"

"—is because you're the very best of them."

Amanda shook her head. "I'm not looking for flattery."

"I'm not buttering you up. I knew you were in before I came here."

"Ioni, what are our chances?"

Ioni tapped her thigh, her eyes never leaving Amanda's. "Success-wise, I'd say your chances are good. I wouldn't be asking you otherwise."

"You know I'm not talking about that."

"I know." Ioni lowered her head. "If there was any way around it—"

"Just *say* it," Amanda snapped. "I need you to say the words."

"You won't survive it," Ioni replied in a thin, flat voice. "Win or lose, you'll all die in Lárnach. There's no other future. I'm sorry."

After what felt like a small and silent eternity, Amanda finally tried the Cabernet. Sadly, it was nowhere near as good as she remembered. There was an added hint of bitterness that, as far as she knew, had been entirely placed there by her mind. And who could fault her? One of the ugliest rumors that was going around Sergelen had just turned real right in front of her, as the universe demanded yet another sacrifice.

The portal jump to Lárnach was a new kind of hell for Amanda and her flying squadron. The moment they crossed into Pelletier territory, a spatial malaise punched them all through their forcefields, throwing their bodies into topsy-turvy chaos and twisting their senses into braids. The transition left them all so disoriented that they could barely tell up from down. Twenty-six Gotham and four orphans dropped through the air in shielded pairs until, one by one, the aerics regained their bearings.

"Holy hell," said Stan Bloom, the Gothams' most experienced wing-flyer. He climbed back to his starting altitude, then hailed the rest of the team through the comm. "Everyone okay?"

Amanda didn't give anyone a chance to respond. "Shields off. Save your power."

Without their individual barriers, they would have all been rifted to death upon arrival. The Pelletiers kept Lárnach in its own temporal continuum, a wavering spectrum of accelerated speeds that ranged from 20 to 400x. Though the tempo made for a rough and awkward entry, it added a welcome amount of time to the mission clock. The squad had at least fifteen minutes to find and destroy the power reactor before the Jades overwhelmed Ioni.

Amanda was the last to rejoin the flock, mostly due to the bulk of her passenger. While the other aerics had harnessed themselves to smaller and lighter swifters, Amanda had chosen a partner twice her weight to serve as her human speedpack.

"Sorry," Caleb said from behind, as if he just became burly overnight. "I was afraid of this."

Amanda was too busy marveling at her new surroundings to offer him any assurance. Their entry point in Lárnach was like nothing she'd ever seen: a seemingly endless corridor with hexagonal walls of chrome. To call the place a tunnel would be stretching the word to the breaking point. It was enormous. The team could have arrived in their own jumbo jets and still had room to move. Or at least they *would* have, were it not for the thousands of alien obstacles that floated all about like asteroids.

"What the fuck are those?" asked Fleeta Byers, the veteran swifter who rode Stan's back.

The obstructions were completely identical: all oblong blocks of dull gray metal, each one the size of a minivan. Only their trajectories set them apart. They drifted serenely in all directions without ever hitting the walls or each other.

A delirious laugh escaped one of the aerics, the sixteen-year-old redhead named Sky. "This is trippy. I just want to get high and stare at it."

Amanda sighed. Everyone on the team had been given three weeks to come to terms with their impending demise. Some had adopted a desperate *joie de vivre*. Others had become incurably morose. A few of the younger ones, like Sky and her boyfriend Sweep, were afflicted with a glibness that bordered on nihilism: the same grating black humor that had made Amanda slap Zack within half a minute of meeting him.

"Let's stay focused," Amanda said. "We still have to cross this thing."

"Preferably without touching anything," Stan added.

That was obvious enough. Every time two of the floating blocks came within ten feet of each other, they exchanged a loud kiss of lightning before flittering away in opposite directions. The walls also weren't shy about zapping anything that came too close to them.

Pair by pair, they proceeded down the corridor: fourteen aerics on wide white wings and one on a floating platform. Sky had never gotten the hang of birdlike travel, but she could steer her disc better than anyone. Between her nimble maneuvering and Sweep's acceleration, the two Coppers were in no danger of falling behind. If anything, Sky's lack of voluminous plumage gave her an advantage among all the floating bug-zappers.

Caleb flinched at a crackling bolt in the air. "You think this is a defense move?"

Amanda shook her head. "Just part of their power system. They still don't know we're here."

"How did Ioni pull that one off?"

The more pressing question to Amanda was why she didn't pull it off sooner. The first twelve minutes of the war had been agony: being forced to play spectator from a high, shielded perch while the people she loved got rocket-bombed. Worse, she had to stand and watch helplessly as Hannah and Mia nearly died a dozen times right above her. By the time they'd finally escaped their predicament, Amanda felt ten years older. She wouldn't have been surprised to undo her helmet and see her red hair washed to gray.

After a minute of aerial zigzagging, Amanda got her first good look at the juncture ahead: a huge white chamber that was free of floating obstructions.

"We're almost there," Stan said over the comm. "Keep your eyes straight."

Caleb scoffed in Amanda's ear. From their very first training session, Stan had carried the airs of mission leader, despite the fact that Amanda was in charge. For him, it was habit as much as ego. He was one of the last surviving primarchs of the Gotham clan, and wasn't accustomed to taking orders from orphans.

But for all the man's faults, he was certainly skilled. Stan could tell just by aeric sense that one of their teammates was faltering. He fell back to her position with uncanny agility, his wings dodging every obstacle, even in reverse-flight.

"Sparrow . . ."

"I'm okay!" the petite young flyer insisted. "I'm all right."

Despite her assurances, she was clearly on the verge of a panic attack, for reasons no one could fault. She'd been a prisoner of Lárnach for months on end, until Hannah helped her escape. Now, after seven days of freedom and one rough childbirth, her fate had circled back on itself. She was destined to die here after all, and that wasn't even her biggest concern.

"Just promise you won't let them take me alive," she tearfully implored Stan. "You can't let them capture me. Please."

Sparrow's gangly twin brother, the aeric called Finch, decelerated his pace and flew next to her. "We talked about this, Katie. I *promised* you—"

"Look out!" Stan yelled.

Finch's right wing brushed against a passing metal brick, sending fifty thousand volts through his shoulder blade.

Amanda turned around at the sound of Sparrow's shriek, only to catch a glimpse of a new problem behind her. "Oh no . . ."

While the bolt had killed Finch in a tenth of a second, the swifter on his back, Persephone Kohl, managed to survive through the insulation of her warsuit. But without Finch to save her from the hard pull of gravity, she had little choice but to activate her bubble shield.

"Wait!" Stan tried to catch her in a large tempic claw, but her barrier was too slippery. Worse, the forcefield bounced against two metal blocks, sending them both on a frenetic new course. They each collided against a sibling with a snap of electricity. Suddenly there were four blocks in a tizzy.

Before Amanda could even formulate words, the cascading chain of fast-moving obstacles had created a kinetic lightning storm.

"Everyone move forward *now*!" she shouted. "Swifters, shift to maximum!"

Even at peak acceleration, the flyers could barely keep ahead of the bedlam. The electrified blocks seemed to come alive with malice, and there wasn't a living soul on Earth who could outfly lightning.

Caleb activated his barrier around him and Amanda. "Turn it off," he said.

"What?"

"Your shield has too much wind resistance. It's cutting our speed."

"It's better than us getting fried!"

"I can get us out of this," she promised. "You have to trust me."

"Ah, shit." Caleb switched off his shield. "I hate it when you play that card."

She swerved between two spinning blocks before they could collide and swap lightning.

"Wow," said Caleb. He peeked back over his shoulder at the floundering aerics in their barriers. "I'm starting to see your point."

Amanda had another reason to be frugal with their shield time, but she wasn't quite ready to tell Caleb. She was just relieved to see some of her squad-mates move ahead of the storm. Sky and Sweep soared past her on their disc, while two of the Gotham flyers took a winning chance on the lower, less encumbered route.

A scream on the comm link threw her off balance and caused a hiccup in Caleb's speed.

"Oh God," he muttered. "That sounded like Esmé."

"I know," Amanda said.

"I hate that we can't—"

"I *know*." Amanda clenched her teeth as she hooked around a twirling hunk of metal. There was no time to go back and save the wounded. Everyone on the team was expendable.

After a seemingly interminable minute of dodging, Amanda passed through the translucent screen at the end of the corridor and landed on the floor of the juncture. The electrical mayhem seemed to stop at the wall of light, their first real blessing at Lárnach. The second one was Stan Bloom and Fleeta Byers, who'd been at the back of the queue when the storm first began, but nonetheless managed to escape.

Stan retracted his wings, then counted the survivors. "Twenty-four. Who else did we lose?"

"Hank and Esmé," Sweep said. "Saw them smack into a wall."

Amanda looked to Stan. "Sparrow?"

Fleeta shook her head. "She went for Finch. We couldn't stop her."

"Shit." Amanda closed her eyes. They'd lost a fifth of their team in the very first leg, and had used up enough shield time to make the next part a gamble.

Worst of all, the chaos they'd caused in the corridor had loudly announced their presence. If the Pelletiers hadn't been aware of the intruders in their house, they sure as hell knew now.

. . .

"Would you rather be alone?" Ioni asked again.

Amanda had heard her both times without answering. Even if she could get a grasp on her feelings—a king-size "if" in her muddled state—she wouldn't have the words to express them. All she could find within reach were numbers, one of them in particular.

Twenty-two, her mind kept repeating. *Twenty-two days. Twenty-two days to live.*

In her four and a half years as an oncology nurse, she'd seen hundreds of patients grapple with a terminal prognosis. A week. A month. A year. It barely mattered. A ticking clock was a ticking clock. But for as many times as she had witnessed the process, she'd never understood its strange effects until she fell on the receiving end. Who would expect the news of her impending death to create such a sense of . . . numbness?

Amanda leaned atop a fake metal railing and gazed out at the illusive vista. Here in the God's Eye, where senses and perceptions were completely elective, there was no point looking at Mongolia. Amanda had Ioni change the scene to Paris at sunset. And not just any Paris: the *good* one, the long-gone wonder from Amanda's Earth that she'd seen for herself on her honeymoon. No holographic ad projections. No lumbering aerstraunts in the sky. Just a gorgeous old city that stretched on forever, with the silhouette of the Eiffel Tower holding up the sun.

Ioni joined Amanda at the railing and gazed at the orange sky. "Why don't I just—"

"You can stay," Amanda said. "I'm sure I'll have more questions."

The sight of Ioni's white dress, which couldn't have been more appropriate for the location, brought an immediate query to mind. "You knew I'd ask for this scenery, didn't you?"

Ioni shrugged nonchalantly. "Augurs. What can you do?"

"But you don't seem entirely comfortable here."

"I have a complicated relationship with this city," Ioni admitted.

Amanda wouldn't learn until three weeks later that Ioni had inflicted her very first Cataclysm on Paris, in another world's 1980. The devastation had triggered enough cold war panic to ensure that no one lived to see 1981.

"We can change it," Amanda offered.

"No, no, no. We're here for you, not me."

"Why?" Amanda tensely inquired.

"What do you mean, why? You got some devastating news—"

"What, that I'll die in the war?" Amanda scoffed. "I already knew there was a chance."

"There's no maybe about it," Ioni said. "You *will* die. And before you say—"

"That hardly makes me unique."

Ioni closed her eyes, exasperated. "You said it."

"It's true. A lot of us will die in twenty-two days. You're the augur. You see it."

Ioni grabbed Amanda by the shoulders. "Listen to me. This brave face you're putting on? You're going to need it real soon. But right here, right now you're free to cut loose. Yell at me. *Hit* me. Tear this city down. You have more than enough reason to."

"*Do* I?" Amanda wondered, to Ioni's frustration. "Ninety-nine people survived the end of my world, and I'm one of them. There are less than thirty of us left, and I'm one of *them*. The odds of me still breathing at all are literally billions to one. But now I'm supposed to scream and cry because I didn't get a fair shake?"

"Yes," said Ioni. "That's exactly what you should be doing."

Amanda looked back out at the Eiffel Tower, still impaling the sun on its spire. Ioni must have hit the temporal snooze button, because the sky should have changed already.

A bleak chuckle escaped her. "You want to hear screaming? Wait till Zack finds out."

"You can't tell him," Ioni cautioned.

"Of course not. He'd lose his mind. But he'll find out after it happens. And when he does . . ."

The mental image of Zack's grief was enough to rattle Amanda's bravado. She calmed herself with a deep, loud breath until her lower lip stopped quivering.

"You're right," she told Ioni. "It isn't fair. He's the love of my life and we barely had a year together."

Ioni nodded. "And it wasn't exactly a quiet year. All those forced complications with Peter and Mercy. Your arms."

"My miscarriages," Amanda said pointedly. "Don't think I've forgiven you"

"If I hadn't done that, you would have died in Lárnach."

"I'm going to die there anyway."

"You would have died without a reason," Ioni said. "There's no worse death than that."

Amanda examined her wriggling hands: still pure, frosty tempis, even here in the psychic fringes. "I can't even remember what it feels like to touch him with warm fingers."

"Want me to change them back?"

"In real life or here?"

"Here," Ioni said. "I don't have the tech to do it in real life."

Amanda considered it a moment before shaking her head. "Not much point without Zack." She looked at Ioni, inspired. "Unless—"

"No."

"Time doesn't move here. I could spend a week with him in Paris. A month, or . . ."

"You can't," Ioni said with lament. "Not without him learning our secret."

Amanda eyed her cynically. "Right. And you don't want him ruining your precious plans."

"I don't want him dying needlessly."

Amanda didn't have to be an augur to see that future happening. As good as Zack was, as strong as he was, he was still just a bad day away from becoming the next Rebel. His unhinged fury would put him on a suicide course with he Pelletiers.

Just like me, Amanda bleakly thought.

She turned to face Ioni again. "There has to be another way to stop them."

"You think I haven't looked?"

"You're the only one they want now," Amanda reminded her. "You couldn't give them a clone or a thousand brain scans?"

"I can't do the former and they won't accept the latter."

"And you never made a sacrificial offer," said Amanda. "'Just let me save he world and you can do whatever you want with me.'"

Ioni shrugged defensively. "I've been up and down those futures more imes than you can count. They never hold their end of the bargain. They always attack us in San Francisco."

"That doesn't make sense."

"Sure it does," Ioni said. "They've been zealots of their own ambitions for s long as they can remember. Hundreds of years of hard work and hope, all uined. They're scared and they're pissed and they're looking to hurt people. 'm just a pretext for their war."

Amanda closed her eyes, sickened. "Sometimes I think Caleb's right. We're a fundamentally broken species."

"It's not just our species."

"No," Amanda agreed. "That's the system we were all born into. The only one we know. The living eating the living so they can keep on living. One of the reasons I found faith was to try to make sense out of all of it."

"Did you?"

Amanda stared out into the frozen sunset, her thoughts bubbling with memories both recent and old. "It varies. On most days, yeah, the framework fits. Other times, I have to remind myself that we're not equipped to see the whole picture. Even if God Himself came down to explain it, it would still go over our heads, like trying to explain property law to the ants in the backyard. We're too small, too young, too isolated to understand how it all works."

Her train of thought was momentarily derailed by a negative-space image of the future: a pair of silhouette cutouts to represent the children she'd never have with Zack. She struggled to keep her emotions inside her, Ioni's intentions be damned.

"And then there are some days," Amanda continued, "where my trust in God just hangs by a thread, and the only thing that keeps it from snapping is the fear of what I'd be without it."

She forced a droll little laugh. "I expect to have a few more of those days before I die."

A cool silence passed before Amanda spoke again.

"But I still have faith that there's a world beyond this one that's a lot less savage. No wars. No pain. No sickness or violence. No death at all except for those who are ready for it."

Ioni snorted bitterly. "You just described my Earth."

"And you *left* it?"

"Eagerly," Ioni said. "It's not the utopia you think it is. We . . ." She rapped her knuckles on the railing until the right words came to her. "We all lost something on the road to progress. Something crucial."

She wagged a finger at Amanda. "Something you and your people have in spades."

"Yeah? What's that?"

"I don't have the words to do it justice," Ioni confessed. "All I can tell you is that you'll see it for yourself one day with crystal clarity: all your strengths all your grace, all your hard-earned wisdom. You'll see the true you on that day, and you'll understand why you've always had people to love you."

Ioni's compliment threatened to smash all the scaffolds that were holding Amanda together. If it shattered now, God help her.

All she could do was chuckle again. "That day better come soon. I only have twenty-two left."

Ioni kept her brooding gaze on the Eiffel Tower. "It's coming."

It was easy to forget that Lárnach was in Antarctica. Without any windows or decorative markers, the Pelletier stronghold could have been anywhere. Amanda may as well have jumped to the dark side of the moon for all the visual clues she had.

Only the juncture at the center of the power reactor served as a reminder of the local environment. The chamber was a tundra unto itself: a frigid white vacuity that was large enough to fit a stack of ten shopping malls, but had been furnished with absolutely nothing. No consoles or gauges. No floating metal whatsits. Not even a potted plant. Just a circular wall of twenty-four shielded entryways, each one connected to a long electric corridor like the one that had killed Finch and Sparrow.

Caleb craned his neck at the twenty-fifth exit, way up high in the distant ceiling. If Ioni's intel was correct, that vertical passage led straight to the reactor core.

"That's a hell of a climb," he said. "I hope you wingfolk had your Wheaties."

While most of the squad kept a lookout for enemies, Amanda, Stan, Sky, and their swifter partners fixed their tense eyes upward, at the final round of obstacles between them and their final destination. A revolving metal cylinder filled the center of the corridor, its surface flecked with giant white protrusions that looked like flattened fan blades. Though they revolved far too slowly to pose a threat, the sheer size and number of the jutting obstructions made straight upward flight an impossibility. They'd have to zig and zag their way to the core, and that was just half of the problem.

Amanda gloomed at the projection in her visor, an energy readout that confirmed Ioni's dark prediction. Unlike the electrical tunnels that ran horizontally in every direction, the upward passage was a giant solic generator. As soon as the aerics came within ten feet of it, their wings would pop like overfilled balloons.

Stan checked the digital gauge on the inside of his wrist. "I have forty-three seconds left. How about the rest of you?"

The answers weren't encouraging. Ioni had loaded each of their warsuits with a minute's worth of forcefield power. But between the portal jump to Lárnach and the fracas in the electrical passage, nearly half of their collective protection had been spent.

"We're going to have to divvy up," said Amanda. "Split our remaining shield time among the swifters. If we do it right, each two-person team should have sixty-one seconds—"

"Hold it," said Fleeta Byers. She was just one of many swifters to sense a new aura in the air. "I think we may be—"

"Run!" Sweep yelled.

While Caleb cast an acceleration field around himself and his nearest teammates, Amanda covered the group in a thick tempic dome that drowned them all in darkness. The lights of their warsuits barely had a chance to flicker on before Amanda felt a blunt force impact on every side of her shell. The enemy had come at them from nowhere, and struck them hard and fast. She would have never gotten her tempis up in time if Caleb hadn't shifted her.

Amanda flinched in pain at the attack on her dome, a corrosive assault on the northern side that burned like acid in her thoughts. Unlike Ioni's barriers, her tempis was fully susceptible to the withering power of solis. Before she could even cry Stan's name, he used his own tempis to reinforce the melting wall.

"Jades," he said. "At least nine that I can feel."

"How the hell did they sneak up on us?" Sky asked.

Amanda didn't know. Their warsuit visors were supposed to filter out lumic illusions, making cloaked attacks impossible. But experience had taught her more than once that the Pelletiers were crafty bastards. Indeed, they'd rendered their Jades invisible through good old-fashioned nanotech, without a hint of lumis to be found.

Fleeta climbed onto Stan's back. "We have to go now. We don't have time to—"

"I know!" Amanda activated the temporal converter on her comm link, then hailed the squadmates outside her bubble. "Get back to your partners as fast as you can, then fly up into the generator. Save as much of your shield time as possible. You'll need it for the solis."

She willed her wings back to life, then shot a quick look over her shoulder. "Ready?"

Caleb buckled the last strap of their harness. "Go!"

Her tempic dome split open at the top, hatching three different pairs of aeric/swifters. Only Stan and Fleeta stopped to check on their Gotham kin. Amanda, Caleb, Sky, and Sweep shot up toward the ceiling like twin missiles.

Caleb was the only one among them who dared to look down. "Ah, shit. It's a bloodbath."

Amanda sighed. "Caleb—"

"They got Mack and Brenda."

"Caleb, *listen.* I need you to stay focused." Amanda pointed at the generator entrance getting closer by the second. "You have to get your shield ready or we'll be dead too."

"Even if we somehow make it to the core—"

"Caleb."

"I have it! I'm ready!"

Amanda wasn't sure if she wanted to hug him or smack him. He'd been so opelessly depressed at Sergelen that the augurs had declared him a self-harm isk. He came out of the Protection ward two weeks later, only to be recruited y Ioni for the most ironic mission that she could have possibly given him: the ne-way trip to Lárnach. A suicide run.

"Thank God for all that therapy," he'd quipped to Amanda. "I feel like a ew dead man."

At three hundred feet above the ground, Amanda could start to feel the olis from the generator. Her wings bristled with a faint static tickle. "Okay, aleb. On three . . ."

"Screw that." He activated his bubble shield. "I'm not taking any chances."

Amanda hissed a curse as the countdown began. "It was too soon!"

"What's the problem? If my shield runs out, we still have yours."

"No we don't!"

"What do you mean?"

Amanda flew them through the mouth of the generator, her aeris grumbling from the back of her senses. Her wings didn't like being trapped in a ubble, where they couldn't feel the wind against their skin, or taste the auras f the nearby flyers.

Caleb stared at her intently. "Amanda, what happened to your shield time?"

She weaved through a slit between fan blades before answering. "I gave it way."

"*What?* To who?"

"What does it matter?"

"It matters to me if we break our necks! How did you even get through the portal?"

"I kept five seconds for the portal," Amanda said. "The rest of it's gone."

Caleb's whole body tensed up in the harness. "Oh my God."

"I know. It was stupid."

"Stupid?" Caleb laughed. "No, I'm from Florida. I know stupid. What you did was *idiotic.*"

Amanda glanced down and saw Sweep and Sky in close pursuit. Beneath them, four pairs of flying Gothams crossed into the generator shaft, their wings enclosed in shield bubbles.

Thank God, thought Amanda. At least some of her team had survived the ambush, and the Jades didn't seem to be following them into the solic dead zone.

Caleb checked his shield timer. "I'm down to forty-five seconds."

"We'll make it," Amanda insisted.

"How do you know? We can't even tell the height of this thing."

"Just trust me. Please."

He breathed a hot sigh. "Amanda, you know I love you. And I'm willing to forgive you. But if you invoke your faith right now—"

"I won't," she promised.

She knew better than to play that card with Caleb, the one-time rabb turned born-again atheist. On most days, he wore his lack of faith with civil ity and quiet conviction. Other times, he could be a real prick about it.

On a few rare occasions, he wavered on his hill, or at least wavered o what to call it. "I might be more agnostic than atheist," he'd recently con fessed to Amanda. "But I guess it doesn't matter. Even if God exists, I'll neve trust him again. Not after the shit he's pulled."

Amanda spied some light between the next ring of fan blades and mistoo it for an early win. "I think that's the core," she told Caleb. "Straight up ahead.

Her second glimpse of the light nearly caused her to crash into a turbin She was wrong. It wasn't the core. Just the next spinning level of the generato But the Pelletiers had added something to make the experience worse. Muc worse.

Amanda ascended into the next segment and balked at the giant image naked people, naked *friends,* all splayed out like standing corpses. The vert cal dead.

Caleb's eyes widened. His skin turned white. "Oh no . . ."

Hannah had told them everything she knew about the Pelletier archives, a horror she'd seen for herself. Even her secondhand description had been enough to give Amanda nightmares. To think of all those poor souls: kidnapped, paralyzed, and then thoroughly computerized until they were nothing more than organic template files. The only thing that kept Amanda from weeping about it was the fact—or at least the assertion—that none of the victims were suffering. If Ioni was right, then the archive was a morgue, not a prison.

Still, seeing the bodies of friends on display was like a knife in Amanda's concentration. She hated herself for letting such a cruel trick get to her. She hated the fact that she was even surprised. The Pelletiers were veterans at using her love against her. To them, her compassion for other people was just another weakness to exploit, a way to punch her through her shield.

Caleb's body quivered against hers. "Those motherfuckers . . ."

"Don't look."

"It's Mercy," he said in a broken voice. "Oh my God, baby. What did they do to you?"

Try as she might, Amanda couldn't miss her. The Pelletiers had made her nanotech illusion ten times larger than all the others. Worse, they'd put her right in front of the gap of the upper fan blade. The quickest path out was straight through her ethereal midsection, the vine tattoo that looped around her navel.

Amanda tried to speak Caleb's name, but it barely came out as a croak. The sight of her friend Mercy—her *proud* friend Mercy, who would have died a hundred deaths before suffering this indignity—was agonizing.

Her face broke out in patches of stress tempis. "Caleb, you have to keep your speed up."

"Those sick motherfuckers."

"Caleb!"

"Go to hell," he shouted. "You'd be just the same if it was Zack or Hannah!"

"Yes, I would. And then you'd remind me that we still have a job to do!"

Amanda passed them through the illusion of Mercy and into the topmost chamber of the generator. The fan blades were finally behind her, providing her first clear view of the reactor core. But it still looked so far away: at least four hundred yards of straight upward climbing, if not more.

"How much time do we have?" Amanda asked Caleb.

He raised his helmet visor and wiped his teary eyes. "Who the hell cares?"

"Caleb—"

"Why fight for the fucking future if it only leads to people like Azral?"

Amanda heard overlapping shouts on the comm link. The squadmates behind her were getting their first taste of the archives. From the sounds of it, they were reacting just as poorly as Caleb.

The thought was enough to cure Amanda's distaste for cursing. "Goddamn it, Caleb! We don't have time for this! You think Mercy would put up with your whining?"

"Don't you dare use her—"

"Just be a fucking man!"

Amanda wished her wrath was merely a motivational strategy, but she could feel every word she was yelling at him. Maybe that was the real goal of the Pelletiers' attack: to tear up every partnership and watch them fall in fragments.

Caleb gritted his teeth, his forehead mottled with sweat. "I swear to God, Amanda—"

"I don't care if you hate me," she said. "If we fall now, we'll have come here for no reason. We'll have *died* here for no reason."

"That's—"

"We didn't survive the end of the world just to die here for no reason!"

"Fine!"

Caleb pushed his power to its terminal limit, the same hot red zone that had ended Hannah's days as a swifter. If he had checked the inside of his visor, he might have seen his warsuit's measurement of what would prove to be his final speed burst: 217.43x, a brand-new record among the orphans and Gothams that was destined to go unmarked.

Amanda's field of vision turned a cold shade of indigo, enough to drown out the last of the Pelletiers' nasty images. She only briefly registered the hologram of Eden with her throat cut before it was obscured by all the strange artifacts that came with high-speed shifting: the floating lights and pixie streaks, the swirling moiré patterns. A fluttering white anomaly crossed Amanda's view like a moth made entirely of sunshine. God only knew what creatures lived here in the temporal margins of existence.

The sight of it brought a faint smile to Amanda's face, despite all her stress and anguish. The universe was so beautifully complex, with layers upon layers of splintered realities, each one more fascinating than the next. Amanda figured she'd need a million more lifetimes before she could even begin to process how all the pieces fit together.

All she knew at that very moment, all that *mattered*, was that Caleb had bought them the time they needed to reach the top of the generator, and then some.

Amanda passed through a gap in the final fan blade, and then ascended into the heart of the reactor core. She couldn't waste a moment looking around. She had to touch down somewhere beyond the generator shaft before her exhausted wings gave out.

As she cleared the span of the yawning hole, Caleb's shield finally died with a fizzle. The residual solis from the generator turned Amanda's aeris into putty, forcing her into a clumsy landing on the polished steel tile of the core.

"We did it," she said to Caleb. "*You* did it. I'm sorry for everything I—"

Caleb cut her off with a half-conscious mumble, a word that sounded like "Jesus" but with a slightly Irish brogue. *JAY-sus*.

"Caleb, what—"

They were hit from behind by a concentrated blast of heat, enough to sear them both through their warsuits. Even with Caleb and her wings to shield her, the temperature was so intense that Amanda blacked out of consciousness.

Her very last thought, before hitting the floor, was the realization of what Caleb had actually said to her: a warning. *Jades*.

FORTY-TWO

Somewhere deep in the muddy waters of her mind, between her waking thoughts and the chaos of her subconscious, there was a small but welcome pocket of air where Amanda could move about freely. If she'd been there before, she couldn't remember. And if she knew how to get there on her own, she would have gone there at least twice a day. It was wonderful. There in the space between memories and dreams, she could pick and choose the best of both, and experience them as if they were real.

Maybe it was her own personal God's Eye. Or maybe it was the sweet spot that people experienced just before they died. Amanda didn't care. She was too busy enjoying a taste of an alternate life, one where she got everything she ever wanted, and then some.

In this dream/not-dream, she was the Angel of London: a global celebrity and high-flying icon whose words and deeds inspired benevolence across the planet. She could end wars between nations with a televised speech, bring comfort to millions with an empathetic anecdote. Her boundless love for her husband and children was so exalted that families around the world found joy just by mimicking her.

As she walked the red carpet of a charity gala, her backless white dress accentuating her wings, she heard a familiar laugh over the shouts of photographers.

"Is that a serious question?"

Amanda turned around, confused. She knew the sound of Zack's voice better than anyone, but she couldn't see him. He was speaking to her from a different part of her psyche. But where?

She left her fantasy behind and followed the voice to the memory side of her fiefdom. There on the wall of a thousand happy screens, between her college graduation and her first successful wingflight, she found the movie-in-progress of her second honeymoon, just eight months ago in the floating inns of Croton-on-Hudson. Though the place didn't hold a candle to Paris, their aerial suite had given Amanda and Zack all the privacy they wanted. Better still, the bathtub had been large enough for two tall lovers to comfortably canoodle.

Amanda watched in silent fascination as Zack caressed her younger self beneath the bubbles.

"Of course I'm serious," she said to him in the amused but sober tone that she often took with him. "I mean let's say circumstance threw us together—"

"It did," Zack said.

"On the *old* world. Before any of this happened."

"Okay. How?"

"I don't know," Amanda said with a shrug. "Maybe you had an aunt named Esther with a carcinoid tumor, and you came to see her at the hospital where I work."

"Fucking Esther. I told her not to smoke."

Amanda laughed. "Anyway, there I am and there you are."

"I assume we're both single in this scenario."

"Yes. Let's not overcomplicate it."

Zack nodded thoughtfully. "Well, I would have found you pretty. That's or sure."

"Thank you. I'm sure I would have pretended not to notice how cute ou are."

"But then I'd make a real bad joke," Zack guessed.

Amanda held up the golden crucifix on her necklace. "Or you'd see this."

"Or Aunt Esther would mention that I'm a cartoonist, and you'd run the ell away."

The present-day Amanda smiled at the screen as the newlyweds giggled ike children.

Once their daffy humor faded, the younger Amanda sighed from Zack's rms. "Guess we would have passed right by each other, like ships in the night nd all that."

"Probably for the best," Zack replied without a trace of humor.

Amanda turned to look at him. "Why would you say that?"

He rested his chin on the ball of her shoulder, right where her flesh and empis met. Even back then in the early weeks of her new arms, he had never nce treated them any differently than her old ones. Never complained about he coldness. Never flinched at the moments when her train of thought flick-red and her limbs turned soft as dough.

"I was different back then," Zack said. "Without a doomsday to worry bout, or assholes who keep trying to kill us, I just . . . I don't know. It left a lot f room for the mundane shit, like health insurance, hair loss, all the artists ho were doing better than me. There was so much noise and static in my ead that I never would have seen you the way I do now."

Zack ran a slow finger down the length of her arm. "On this crazy world, y eyes are wide open. Every time I look, I see a thousand new things to love bout you. They just keep coming."

As the past Amanda flipped over in the water and kissed Zack, the present-ay version found herself crying—crying with joy, crying with pain, crying ith loss and regret.

Is that what your people lost, Ioni? Is that what you think we have in spades?

A loud machine hum overtook Amanda's thoughts and sent waves of vi-ration through her body. She came awake with a gasp, her fluttering eyes med at the ceiling.

She lay flat across the tile of Lárnach's reactor core, with Caleb sprawled on top of her. Before she could even check on him, she heard the loud shouts of conflict in the near distance.

Amanda turned her head as best she could, but all she could see were the blurry hints of an aerial dogfight, fifty yards away. Closer to her, and six times clearer, was the headless corpse of a stocky male Jade. Best Amanda could tell, some teammates had arrived in the nick of time to save her. But what about Caleb?

She struggled to move beneath the weight of her partner, and immediately paid for her hubris. The skin on her hips and back practically wailed with every gesture. A faint overlay on the inside of her visor told her that she had second-degree burns. A lot of them.

She reformed her arms, along with two extras, and then used them to pull herself out from beneath Caleb. While her main limbs lifted her to a kneel, the spares cut through the straps of her harness, then gently lay Caleb faceup on the tile.

"Oh God," said Amanda. His suit was charred from neck to toe, enough to mess with its functionality. The wavering data from its sensors couldn't tell if Caleb had third-degree burns over thirty, fifty, or seventy-two percent of his body.

But he was alive. He was most definitely alive. He moaned and writhed like an unsettled ghost, his large hands struggling to undo his helmet.

Amanda removed it for him and caressed his cheeks with white fingers. Though his face was as red as a cherry tomato, only the skin around his left ear was blistered. His helmet had saved him from the worst of the thermic blast.

He struggled to speak through stammering lips. "S-s-scouts."

"What?"

"Scouts."

"Oh, right." Amanda had forgotten all about the mini-drones Ioni had stashed inside their pocketed belts, the ones they were supposed to release the moment they got to the core. She pressed a button on her belt buckle, then did the same for Caleb. Soon twenty crystal orbs, each the size of a gumball, rose two feet into the air and turned invisible before dispersing throughout the reactor core.

Caleb chuckled weakly. "Godspeed, little dudes."

Amanda couldn't understand how he was functioning, much less joking

Her injuries were just a fraction of his, and the pain was enough to make her want to die.

"I'm so sorry," Amanda told him. "For giving away my shields. You were—"

A cry in the distance turned her attention back to the dogfight, a battle she ould see more clearly as she continued to recover from her blackout. The eric Anne Hollowell and her swifter cousin Mindy had tackled a Jade in midair. Unfortunately, they flew too close to the generator shaft, enough to drench all three of them in solis and send them plummeting into the pit.

"Go help the others," Caleb told Amanda. "I'll catch up when I can."

"But—"

"You gonna die here for nothing or something?"

Amanda must have still had Zack on her mind, because she suddenly had more love than she knew what to do with. She could have hugged Caleb for the rest of her life, soothing his burns with her cool tempic touch until the nevitable end came for both of them.

Instead she wiped her tears, kissed Caleb on the forehead, and rose back to her feet.

"I'll come back for you," she promised him.

Amanda tried to unsheath her wings, but the burns on her back wouldn't let her. The skin was too raw. Her nerves were shot. Though it broke her heart to realize it, her flying days were officially behind her.

But her arms were just as strong as they ever were, and they were aching to cause some damage. Amanda had come into this world as a hard-hitting tempic. It seemed a fitting enough way to go out.

Unlike everything else she'd seen of Lárnach, the core of the Pelletiers' power reactor didn't look like it had been built for giants. The room was only as large s a high school gymnasium, with enough pipes and catwalks and other metal obstructions to make Amanda feel better about losing her wings. The only good place to fly was near the mouth of the generator pit. And as Anne Hollowell just tragically proved, that wasn't a good place at all.

Amanda peeked up at the high dome ceiling and got her first look at the ore's main attraction: an obsidian sphere the size of a cottage, spinning high bove the pit in a state of magnetic suspension. Between its bone-rattling um—like a chorus of a thousand air conditioners—and the continual sparks f static that crackled across its surface, Amanda didn't need her scout drones to tell her what she was looking at: the catalyst, the beating heart of the Pelletiers' power station.

A white-winged Gotham quickly looped around the orb, with a pair o flying Jades in hot pursuit. Though he was moving too fast for her visor to ge a read on him, Amanda could tell from his unmistakable girth that she wa looking at Stan Bloom.

He caught sight of Amanda. "There y . . . are! Thank God! I thought yo w . . . dead!"

The temporal converter on her comm link must have been damaged, because he was speaking at least twice his normal rate, with snaps of dead air i between. She was still trying to form the first question in her head when Sta hit her with more accelerated half-garble.

"They only sent nine Jades aft . . . us but they're all mean bastards . . . too out most of us in . . . juncture. We managed . . . kill some of them. Maybe fou or five left."

Fleeta Byers cut in. "Passed Sky and Sweep . . . generator. They wer having . . . ious trouble."

Amanda closed her eyes. "Guys."

"Not sure if they made . . . out. Where's Caleb?"

"Guys, *listen* to me—"

A thin black tendril whipped around Amanda's left arm and dissolved ha of it in an instant. In the good old days of flesh and bone, the injury woul have sent her into fatal shock. But even the loss of her tempic limb came wit excruciating pain, as if someone had thrown acid onto her frontal lobe.

She barely had a chance to react to her wound before a second tendr lashed the top of her right shoulder, searing flesh and tempis alike.

Amanda screamed in two directions. While her voice carried far enoug to traverse the generator pit, a geyser of tempis exploded from her back an shoved her assailant into a wall.

Cursing, Amanda re-formed her severed arm, then sealed the gash in h shoulder with tempis. She didn't have time to do a better job. The Jade who' attacked her was hurt but still alive. Amanda could feel him or her strugglin in the craggy folds of her tempis. Breaking free.

"No you don't," Amanda growled. Though she couldn't turn around t look at her enemy, her tempis gave her all the tactile information she neede The Jade was almost certainly a woman from the size of her: barely five fe all and as skinny as a rail. She could have been Mia in another life, a twisted tring of history where the Pelletiers had corrupted the San Diego orphans nstead of the ones from Calgary.

But this was no time to empathize. Not with everything at stake. Amanda pierced the Jade's head with a twelve-inch spike, feeling every bit of softness nside her skull. Her tendril even brushed against a dozen metal gadgets that had no business being in her brain.

She retracted her tempis into her back and nearly passed out from the pain. The skin back there must have been hopelessly burnt and shredded. There wasn't even enough of her warsuit left to gauge the extent of the damage.

"Shit." She compressed her back wounds beneath a tight tempic skin, then took another look at the catalyst. The sphere was held aloft by twenty magnetic projectors, all suspended from the ceiling on metal poles. The Pelletiers, n their overconfidence, hadn't built their reactor to withstand an enemy ttack. There weren't any defenses that Amanda could see aside from the surviving Jades.

Unfortunately, the two that were left were quick enough to undo her teammates' progress. Every time Stan and Fleeta broke a magnetic clamp, a Jade quickly reversed the damage.

With most of her team dead, and without Caleb to shift her, Amanda was ow on options. The best she could do was serve as a distraction while Fleeta nd Stan finished the job.

She extended her arms upward and punched out two magnet clamps at nce. "Come on."

The Jades in the air didn't acknowledge her. They remained obsessively ocused on the elusive Stan Bloom who, even in their shifted state, even in their cramped surroundings, flew literal circles around them.

Amanda knocked out two more clamps in the most conspicuous way possible. "Come on!" she yelled. "I'm right here!"

Something hit Stan and Fleeta from the invisible margins, knocking them both off their trajectory. They crashed to the floor on the far side of the generator pit, and tumbled three times before falling still.

"No." Amanda looked up to see a third Jade in the air: the short-haired blonde who'd rifted Zack's arm and nearly killed him and Melissa in two countries. The only Jade who didn't wear a helmet. The only one her enemies knew by name.

Joelle flashed a sneering smile at Amanda, her fists encrusted with hard white tempis. "You wanted our attention. Now you have it."

Consequences.

The word was practically an expletive to the augurs of Earth, who knew just how fickle a chain of causality could be. A small deed done with good intentions could trigger the death of thousands, while a well-planned act of hostility could end up saving an enemy's life.

Even the Pelletiers weren't immune to the occasional backfire, like when they taunted a pair of teenage orphans with the image of a lost sibling.

Sky and Sweep had already been having a hard time in the generator shaft. An ill-timed pain in Sweep's left knee, the byproduct of a crippling swifter accident, had hindered his speed to a mere 20x, while a power strain migraine had given Sky double vision and undermined her control over her flying disc. She'd nearly crashed into the blade of the first major turbine, then needed an extra twenty seconds to fumble through the gap of the second one. If the pair hadn't been blessed with a copious amount of shield time—a full minute and forty-nine seconds between them—they would have never reached the generator's third segment, where they were greeted by the ghostly countenance of their orphan brother Shroud.

By all accounts, Azral's plan should have been the end of Sky and Sweep. The sight of their dearest loved ones, fresh from the archives, had been enough to impede three pairs of Gothams until their barriers lost power and they plunged to their deaths.

But the two young Coppers had the opposite reaction. They were mad. *Really* mad. Mad enough to ignore their infirmities and shatter their personal records. By flaunting Shroud's fate, all Azral did was remind Sky and Sweep that everyone they'd ever lost—every single person from two different Earths—had died at the hands of the Pelletiers.

Consequences.

They shot upward into the reactor core, their shield barreling into Joelle and her two fellow Jades. One of the men crashed into a magnet clamp, destroying it, while the other one recovered just in time to have Sky shove him into the catalyst.

She held him in place with her barrier, shrieking incomprehensible curses at him as electricity coursed through his shuddering body.

Joelle did a half-turn in the air, then set after the Coppers. She'd barely managed to fly five feet before a tempic tendril harpooned her through her ankle and yanked her down to the ground.

"Not so fast," Amanda said. "I'd still like your attention."

For a woman who'd just had her leg impaled, Joelle didn't seem very bothered. Either the Pelletiers had given her a flipswitch on her pain receptors or they'd replaced her entire leg with circuitry. In either case, it was another advantage that Amanda had to work around.

She turned her free arm into a bladed tendril and then cast it at Joelle, only to watch it pause in the middle of its journey and loop back around at its creator.

Oh no. While Amanda struggled against the force of her own left arm, Joelle climbed to her feet, yanked the tempic harpoon out of her ankle, and then threw it back at Amanda as well. The woman seemed dead set on killing her with her own appendages. From the nasty little curl in the corner of her lip, she was clearly enjoying the effort.

"You're stronger than I expected," Joelle admitted. "But I had better teachers."

As hot sweat dripped into Amanda's eyes, she suddenly realized why the Pelletiers had only sent nine Jades after her team. These weren't the mass-produced automatons they'd dumped on Prior Circle. They were the original orphans of Calgary: conditioned, augmented, and battle-trained to best serve their belligerent masters.

But apparently they still had emotions. Joelle's bright green eyes turned damp with rage as she looked to the corpse of her female teammate, the one Amanda had killed a minute ago.

"I'm going to hurt you for that," Joelle swore. "I'll make your last seconds feel like years."

Thirty yards above them, Sky's barrier finally reached the end of its run. With nothing left to support him, the electrocuted Jade slid off of the catalyst and plummeted into the generator shaft. Sky was just about to move on to Joelle when Sweep gripped her by the shoulder and whispered in her ear.

"Two o'clock and ten feet up."

Sky reached out with a tempic fist and immediately latched onto an invisible head. The last male Jade had wisely cloaked himself, but Sweep's senses were second to none. As Sky reeled in their next and final victim, Sweep pulled out a knife from his hip sheath. "Save some for me."

Oblivious to the murder that was happening well above her, Amanda groaned in strain and agony as her overwrought tendrils moved ever closer toward her face.

"Who are you avenging exactly?" she asked Joelle through gritted teeth.

"Her name was Maeve. Would you like to know more about her?"

"No," said Amanda. "I'm more curious about the people you loved on the old world. Your parents. Your siblings—"

"Why?"

"Because I know the people who killed them." Amanda glared at Joelle. "So do you."

"You're wasting my time."

"If you're going to avenge anyone—"

"You're wasting my time!"

"Yes I am." Amanda nodded her head exhaustedly. "Thanks for noticing."

Joelle's head arched back in shock as she was impaled from behind with a tempic sword. It burst clean out of the center of her chest before retracting into the hand of its wielder.

For all of Amanda's strength and will, she knew that she'd only had seconds before Joelle got the better of her. The only way to beat her was to try a new trick.

New for her, anyway.

As Joelle crumpled to the floor, Amanda looked into the eyes of the creature that had killed her: her first and only tempic minion. She wasn't even sure it would work. Heath had been consistently terrible at explaining his wolves and Jonathans, and no amount of self-taught practice could get Amanda to ape his gimmick.

But then along came the Majee named Meredith Graham, a woman so smart and genuinely delightful that Amanda wished she'd met her sooner. Like Heath, Meredith knew the ins and outs of crafting a tempic golem. But unlike Heath, she knew how to articulate it.

"It's not a matter of concentration," Meredith had told Amanda. "Too much thought actually gets in their way. You just have to go to a safe place in your head, one so warm and comfortably familiar that you barely need to think at all."

Indeed, from the look of Amanda's personal creation, she knew exactly where she went in her mind. Her savior of choice was a long-haired woman who was easy to recognize, even when bleached of all color.

Amanda smiled at the sight of her spectral sister. *Hannah . . .*

As Amanda's tendrils reverted to arms, the tempic Hannah vanished, and er thoughts fell back onto the mission. She scanned Stan and Fleeta through er visor, only to have their warsuits confirm her worst suspicion. They'd oth snapped their necks when they'd crashed into the ground, as quick a eath as they could have prayed for. Amanda only wished that she could tell 'arrie how heroic her father had been.

She looked up at Sky and Sweep, still floating in the air on a wavering disc. We have to finish off the catalyst," she told them. "If we break the last of the ıagnets—"

A cold gust of force suddenly changed the world on her, as if she'd been ıcked into a tornado. She couldn't see. She couldn't breathe. She couldn't feel ıything but a strong, icy wind that lashed at her from every angle. For all she new, someone had thrown her into a blender and was about to make a frozen rink out of her.

Her back suddenly slammed into something cool and hard, enough to ıake her cry in pain. She drew a coughing breath of air, then looked around ırough wet, blinking eyes.

She was back where she started in the corner of the chamber, not far from here she'd left Caleb. If he was still there, Amanda couldn't see him. Her eld of view was eclipsed by the man who'd abducted her.

The very *angry* man, from the looks of him.

Azral pinned her in place with one strong arm, his eyes moving in thought. ɔr all Amanda knew, he was stuck between the simple choice of saying ɔmething eloquent or cursing at her.

"I believe . . ." He defused himself with a faint little scoff. "I believe I've ıd quite enough of the Givens."

e'd pumped enough solis into her body to keep her tempis suppressed for ɔurs. No arms. No wings. No self-made compresses. Amanda felt her wounds :ibbling all the way down her back. Even if Azral suddenly decided to play ce—a thought so far-fetched that Amanda could barely picture it—she'd most surely die of blood loss before her powers returned.

She opened her mouth to speak, but Azral shushed her with a finger. "The st thing you can buy is a quick and painless death. The price of that—"

He waved a glowing hand to his left without taking his eyes off Amanda. "—is silence."

A flash of light forced Amanda to close her eyes. She heard a loud and

messy crash nearby, like a bookshelf full of plastic bowls that had bee
abruptly overturned. She looked to her right and saw a smattering of huma
bones on the floor, along with two empty warsuits.

"Monica Brand and Dae-Hyun Park," Azral said. "In case you were unsure

Amanda didn't need him to tell her who he just killed. Sky was the onl
one on her team who wore a cherry red warsuit, while Sweep's leg bones sti
had metal pins in them.

"I believe they were looking to hurt me more than they were hoping t
help you," Azral teased.

Amanda turned away from him, sickened. Even if he was right about Sk
and Sweep's intentions, the fact that he could be so glib after murder wa
enough to make her queasy.

Azral let go of Amanda, for all the threat she was. Without her powers c
her upper limbs, the worst she could do was kick him.

"All these cruel and avoidable fates," he lamented. "If my mother and fa
ther had listened to me, none of you would have set foot outside of Lárnac
You would have lived here for years in unprecedented comfort, with eve
indulgence at your fingertips."

Right, thought Amanda. *Because you treated Hannah so fucking well.*

Azral's expression turned bitter and resentful, as if he could hear Ama
da's every thought. "Your sister squandered all the goodwill she'd earne
from us. She went out of her way to become a petulant nuisance, just like th
rest of you Silvers."

Amanda tried to speak at last, but Azral cut her off. "We asked you all
help us for the benefit of humanity. But you spat at our feet out of a vain sen
of pride. You refused to be pawns in someone else's game."

Azral sneered at her shoulder stumps. "Yet here you are now, the dispo
able soldier of Ioni Deschane. You sacrificed your life for a petty act of va
dalism, and you didn't even succeed."

A new portal lit the air behind him. Amanda's heart thundered at th
sight of Semerjean and Esis as they emerged from the disc. Like him, the
looked mad enough to tear Amanda to pieces. Yet behind all the wrath, sh
could see a new weariness, especially around their eyes. For once, Semerjea
could have passed for a man in his thirties. Esis wavered on her feet like sh
hadn't slept in weeks.

Semerjean scanned the bones of the Coppers, then took a quiet step t
ward Amanda. "I told you Ioni would be the death of you. Did I not warn you

Amanda had several responses to that, but she kept them all to herself. merjean seemed surprised by her silence until Azral muttered something in ry'an.

That's right, Amanda thought. *Tell him I'm quiet because I want a painless eath. Tell him I'm dumb enough to believe you.*

Semerjean processed Amanda's woeful state: a Venus de Milo, all blood nd singed flesh.

"It's all right to talk," he told her. "You have no more illusions about the ture. No Ioni or Theo to delude you. I'm curious to know, as a one-time iend and an observer of humanity, if your vision works as clearly in the ther direction. Do you have any regrets at the end?"

Amanda pretended to think about it, then accidentally stumbled onto a al answer. "I wish I'd spent more time with Zack," she admitted. "Instead of asting months worrying about what you'd do to him. We've seen your worst. Ve survived it."

She shot a defiant glare at Esis. "I shouldn't have been so scared."

Esis clearly didn't like her answer. "S'laïna no-kiesse!" she hissed at emerjean.

"We will," Semerjean assured her. "But she responded honestly to a diffi-lt question."

He gave Amanda a wavering smile, with just a hint of the trademark con-escension that made her share every bit of Mia's hatred for him.

While the Pelletiers conversed in their native tongue, a tiny green light ame to life on the inside of Amanda's visor.

Finally, she thought. *Thank God.*

Semerjean looked to her. "Any final words before we—"

"Just one," said Amanda. Her face lit up in a savage grin. "Mercy."

The Pelletiers only had a moment to express their confusion before a chain f explosions rocked the upper core.

The attack on the catalyst had been a sleight-of-hand deception, a way to eep the enemy occupied while the true expendable soldiers did their work. ven the name that Ioni had given them—*scouts*—was deceptive in itself. The ttle glass drones did more than look around. They found the weakest struc-ural points of the core and attached themselves to them like magnets.

All they needed was time and a trigger word to fulfill their final function. hey each exploded in a miniature Cataclysm: thirty-eight inches from edge edge. Between Amanda and Caleb's twenty scouts, plus the forty that the

Gothams had released into the chamber, the drones had damaged the ceilir
enough to bring half of it down on the catalyst. The great black sphere brok
out of its moorings and fell tumbling into the generator shaft.

The Pelletiers watched in slack-faced silence as the ever-present hum o
the reactor fell silent and the overhead lights all throughout their domai
went black at the same time.

In the darkness, Amanda enjoyed a brief sense of serenity as she thougl
about the victims in the archives. Despite all of Ioni's assurances that the
were dead, she wasn't exactly a spiritual woman and couldn't account fo
their souls.

But now, with Lárnach's systems down, Amanda knew for sure that Merc
Shroud, and all the others had been freed from captivity at last. She env
sioned their spirits taking flight, ascending through the earth and snow, the
on to the next big phase of their eternal adventure.

Her pleasant thought died when the emergency lights came on, an
Amanda once again had to reckon with the Pelletiers. The dim red glow fro
the ceiling panels made them look demonic. Their eyes had vanished into th
shadows of their furrowed brows, while their hissing foreign language coul
have come from the throats of goblins.

Semerjean grabbed Amanda by the folds of her warsuit. "What di
you do?"

"Temporal explosions," she explained. "The damage is irreversible. Or s
I'm told."

"Shïi-ja!" Esis thrust a tempic blade from her fist and made a furious das
for Amanda.

The only thing that stopped her from driving the blade into Amanda
neck was the sound of bellowing laughter from the darkness: a man in th
throes of wild amusement that teetered on the edge of hysteria.

The Pelletiers and Amanda turned their heads in synch, but all they coul
see in the shadows were the flickering lights of a warsuit on the floor.

Amanda smiled, her face streaked with tears. She should have known th
Caleb was still clinging to life. She should have certainly recognized his laug
It had become all but legend to the orphans of the underland—this boomin
kingly cachinnation that could have thundered from the top of Mount Olym
pus. While it had triggered its fair share of eye rolls, and had once compelle

len to cover his mouth, Amanda had always found his laughter to be an in-
ctious mood-lifter, even when she had no idea what it was about.

Now, as he lay in a state of dying agony, Caleb's humor seemed more cryp-
: than ever. Maybe he was simply mocking the Pelletiers for losing. Maybe
: was tickled by Amanda's choice of trigger word. Maybe he was relieved
at Mercy was finally at peace.

Or maybe, just maybe, he was deliriously happy to have his death mean
mething, when so many people he knew and loved had died so senselessly.

Whatever was tickling Caleb's funny bone, it flew right over the heads of
s enemies. The Pelletiers weren't even remotely amused.

"Enough!" Semerjean thrust his hand and launched a tempic projectile.
he bolt hit Caleb's temple with enough brute force to silence his laughter
rever.

Amanda eyed the remains of her partner-in-war, her thoughts teetering
ı a bladed precipice. She couldn't think of a less deserving death for a man of
aleb's strength and kindness. It was worse than cruel. It was petty.

She looked to Semerjean through hot tears. "Monster. Hannah was right.
ou really are the worst of them."

The Pelletiers once again turned their attention to her, and they all had
e nerve to look affronted. For Amanda Given—the Angel of London, the
sabler of Lárnach, the last surviving member of her sacrificial strike team—
e'd finally had enough of the universe's savagery. It was time to take leave of
l the violent brutes and predators and move on to a better place.

She stood up as straight as she could, then bounced her stern gaze be-
veen her enemies.

"These worlds," she began. "These lives. They're just one stop on a never-
ıding journey. Yet here you are, fighting and killing and destroying whole
anets so you can stay in this tiny little part of creation. What small lives
ou live."

She narrowed her eyes at Semerjean. "What small people you are."

Though she fully expected Esis to finish the attack she'd started, it was
zral who approached her with his trademark eerie calmness. When he
pened his mouth to say something, Amanda sighed in anticipation of one
st taste of ugliness.

But then, in the miracle to end all miracles, he abandoned whatever he
as going to say and simply pressed a gentle finger to Amanda's chest.

Thank you, she thought to her divine Lord and savior, as Azral rifted t
heart inside her.

Amanda fell to the ground in a clumsy heap, her eyes wide open, h
breath coming in gasps. From her tilted vantage on the floor, she watched t
Pelletiers disappear into a portal without a single look back in her directio
Another blessing. Another mercy.

She turned her head toward the lights of Caleb's suit. "We did it," s
creaked in a soft and dwindling voice. "We won."

As her vision went dark around the edges, Amanda fell back into th
blessed little pocket of consciousness, her own personal God's Eye, and b
came lost in an all-new fantasy. In this dream/not-dream, all her pai
stopped in an instant and her arms grew back to full length. Her *real* arm
not the cool white sticks of solid will that had been mimicking flesh f
months.

Despite the limits of skin and bone, Amanda managed to stretch her ne
arms halfway across the world, until her hands found their way into Zack
and Hannah's. But it wasn't enough. More arms split off from her elongate
wrists and connected with the rest of her kin: Mia and Theo, Melissa and P
ter, Heath and Liam, even Meredith Graham, whom Amanda had only know
for three weeks but could have easily become a friend for life. She could fe
the warm touch of each and every one of them, the love that flowed back a
forth across oceans.

It's okay, Amanda assured her family. *All of this happened for a very goo
reason. Everything that we did mattered.*

Contented, she closed her eyes, retracted her arms, and surrendered he
self freely to time. Somewhere deep in the shrinking beam of her consciou
ness, she registered a curious new wind on her skin: a strong but pleasant ru
of air that lovingly caressed every part of her. The sensation was so une
pected and wonderful that she wanted to laugh just like Caleb did. It felt ju
like the first day of spring.

It felt a lot like flying.

ORTY-THREE

he secret war in Lárnach had occurred in its own continuum. From the oment Amanda and her teammates infiltrated the stronghold to the final estruction of the power reactor, the facility had been shifted at 21x, condensg twelve and a half minutes of bloody conflict into thirty-five seconds of al time.

For the surviving combatants of San Francisco and the three billion peoe who watched them, those thirty-five seconds hadn't passed quietly. The des had all but seized control of Prior Circle, forming an impenetrable pemeter around Ioni's final barrier while an inner ring of a hundred and fifty ldiers drilled at the shield with lumis.

Mia looked around with increasing dread at the scant, chaotic resistance. here were barely two hundred allies left alive, only a fraction of them in ghting condition. The rest were either exhausted (like her), wounded (like obby), or so utterly demoralized that they weren't of much use.

Evan could have been president of that last club. He'd left his squad a mine ago, purportedly to scrounge for more ammo. But from the tense and skitsh look in his eyes, Mia wouldn't have been surprised if he'd fled to a far less opeless timeline.

Not that she could blame him. Even worse than the Jades' advantage of umbers was the creepy hivemind conformity that kept them all moving in ckstep. The outer soldiers stood as still as palace guards until a timebender ied to attack them. Then dozens would spring into action as one, and annilate the threat within seconds. Mia had nearly vomited at the fate of Audra rlowski, who'd beheaded a Jade with a well-placed portal and was shredded a pulp by thirty tempic tendrils.

"Do *not* engage the front lines," Theo had desperately ordered his people. Those of you with long-range attacks need to take out the ones at the shield."

Easy enough for him to say. For every inner Jade that got shot, sliced, or fted, another one took its place. The Pelletier portal just kept spitting out einforcements. The pool of enemies around the barrier was only getting icker.

"We have to do something," Bobby said to Mia as he wrapped a fresh roll

of gauze around his thigh. One of the Jades had pierced his leg with a temp
spike just as he was escaping the shield dome. If the projectile had struck hi
an inch to the left, it would have sliced his femoral artery and made Mia a
only child again.

She crouched with her brother on the bomb-scarred asphalt and struggle
for ideas. "I could open a portal to the bay and flush the fuckers out."

"You'd drown us all."

"Obviously we'd have to clear out first."

"Yeah?" Bobby gestured at their scattered army. "How long do you thir
that would take?"

"Too long," Mia meekly admitted. There were too many wounded and n
enough travelers. The shield would be breached before they could even try.

Mia checked on her other teammate, standing quietly near the wreckag
of a corporate security office. "What do you think we should do?"

Hannah didn't hear a word she'd said. Her eyes and thoughts were stuc
on the high crystal platform where her sister had been standing until just
few moments ago. She'd watched Amanda and her team disappear into a po
tal, but where did they go? Where on Earth could they possibly be neede
more than here?

She's gone, said a voice from the pit of Hannah's psyche. *You've been feelin
it in the wind ever since she left. You felt it in the way she hugged you earlier.*

Hannah tensely shook her head. "No."

She knew she was saying goodbye.

"No!"

Mia rose to her feet, alarmed. "Hannah, what—"

Just at that moment, thirty-five seconds after Amanda departed for Lá
nach, a bright, strobing light turned everyone's attention upward.

Mia craned her neck, dumbfounded. "Holy shit."

The giant Pelletier portal, the one that had been raining Jades for thirtee
minutes straight, had abruptly flickered out of existence, leaving nothing be
hind but clear blue sky and the plummeting remains of a dozen clones. Th
sputtering gate had cut them all to pieces like a spring blade.

Bobby shook his head, both dumbstruck and skeptical at the same tim
"It's a trick."

Mia tugged his arm. "Bobby . . ."

"There's no way they'd willingly give up their—"

"Bobby, *look*."

He followed her gaze to the Jades on the ground, and reeled at their new isarray. They'd lost their poise at the exact same moment, as if a hypnotist ad snapped her fingers and brought the whole legion out of a trance. Some of iem looked around confusedly. Some fled the scene in shifted haste. Some esumed their work on the shield. And some of them attacked their nearest iemies, for lack of a better plan.

Mia cut a Jade in half with a portal before he could reach her. "What the ick is going on?"

"What does it look like?" Evan said from the periphery. "They lost their nk to the Borg collective. Now they're all just winging it."

He returned to his team with a duffel bag full of goodies, all looted from ead Scarlet Sabres. New weapons. More ammo. A few premium grenades. Ie'd even made room for some gifts.

He dropped a medkit at Bobby's feet, then gave Mia a vim for her fatigue. Something must have happened at Pelletier Central," he said. "Not entirely ire what, but, uh . . ."

Though Hannah never liked having Evan's eyes on her, she suddenly beame disturbed by the opposite. He only looked at her for the briefest of moients before turning away with an expression that, in the wrong light, seemed n awful lot like pity.

Hannah took a nervous step toward him. "Evan, look at me."

"Don't."

"You've been to the future," she said. "You know something. Where is ie?"

"It's not my place to—"

"Evan, where the fuck is Amanda?"

All the action around Hannah froze in an instant, a sweeping still-frame iat affected everything she could see, from her nearest friends to the newsrones in the distant sky. She barely had time to list the possible culprits efore the scenery around her turned dark and gray.

She took a sweeping scan of her new surroundings, a small concrete chamer with mold on the walls and a high, slitted window near the ceiling. It ooked exactly like the typical room at Sergelen, except for a floating glass orb irectly above her.

Hannah examined the spherical oddity, as smooth and compact as a tanerine. It could have been one of Ioni's weird gadgets, but how—

"Hi, Hannah."

She gasped and turned around. Sometime in the last few seconds, th room had become furnished with two folding chairs. Only one of them wa empty. The other one . . .

Hannah dropped to her knees at the sight of Amanda—the *past* sight o her, from all appearances. She was once again dressed in her shabby cloth from Sergelen, while cradling a bundled infant that Hannah easily recognize as her own.

She looked to her sister, bewildered. "What—"

"I can't hear you," Amanda said. "I can't see you. But I know you're ther and I need you to . . ."

Amanda closed her eyes in anguish before collecting herself. "I need yo to sit down."

She'd wanted to leave notes for the people she loved, but Ioni had told her no to bother. There was a better option available: a dime-size chip that could b stitched into any warsuit. It would activate upon Amanda's death, pull th wearer into the God's Eye, and then play them a holographic recording of he choice.

"I was initially hesitant about it," Amanda confessed to Hannah, after ex plaining the chip and the floating orb that was filming her. "It feels wrong t drop this bombshell on you in the middle of everything. But you were alread going to hear it at the worst possible time. You might as well hear it from me

"Stop," Hannah cried. And mercifully, Amanda did. She paused in eeri stillness while a glowing placard above her head told Hannah to say "resume when she was ready.

"Fuck you!" she yelled, her face drenched in tears. She already knew wha her sister was going to tell her, but she'd never be ready to hear it. She'd onl gotten pregnant to save Amanda's life. It was the one thing that had kept Han nah sane in Lárnach: the knowledge and comfort that her sacrifice had ma tered.

But now . . .

Hannah huddled in a corner and wept into her hands, only occasionall peeking at Amanda. In freeze-frame, her sister was something less than hu man. Not even a ghost. Just an ethereal middle finger from a universe tha seemed to thrive on cruelty. As much as Hannah was loath to continue, sh couldn't stand to see Amanda like that anymore.

She wiped her eyes, got back in the chair, and told the playback orb to esume.

Though Amanda immediately snapped back to life, she didn't finish her entence. She looked to her nephew in anxious rumination before turning in Iannah's direction again.

"Okay, now I can see you," Amanda said. "I don't know if it's prescience or ıst me imagining you, but I definitely know the look you're giving me. You've lready figured it out, and you are . . ."

A tear ran down Amanda's face. She quickly wiped it away. "I know what feels like. I was exactly the same when I lost you. A total wreck. Devastated."

"Except I came back," Hannah replied with venom.

"But you came back," Amanda said, a half-second over her. "With this aby boy who is so, so beautiful. Seeing him, seeing you again, has made ıe . . ." She turned her head away, grimacing. "I was *this* close to accepting my ıte. But now all I want to do is tell Ioni to screw herself. Let someone else die ɔr the greater good. I want to grow old with my sister and nephew. I want to ıake kids with my husband."

Hannah wept again. "You *should* have!"

"But Robert's a reminder of everything we're fighting for," Amanda said. The thought of him dying in San Francisco, or having the sky come down hen he's two and a half . . ." She glumly shook her head. "That's all the reaɔn I need to go."

The baby gurgled from his aunt's tempic arms. Hannah could tell from his ght little squint that he was the Robert Given of two days ago, before his eyes opped open in boundless curiosity.

"I'm sorry I had to keep it secret," Amanda told Hannah. "From you and ack and everyone else. It was one of the hardest things I've ever had to do, ut Ioni insists that it's necessary. And when it comes to putting my faith in er . . ." Amanda shrugged exhaustedly. "In for a penny—"

"—in for a pound," Hannah said in perfect synch with her.

Amanda laughed. "You're talking over me now. That's not prescience. hat's just me knowing you."

Hannah smiled, despite her grief. "You know me better than anyone."

"It's so crazy," Amanda said. "How close we've become after all those years f stupid fights. When I look back at the sister I was—"

Hannah shook her head. "Don't."

"—I feel so ashamed. I misunderstood you at every turn. Misjudged you. had nothing to do with you. It was all my issues."

"*Our* issues," Hannah insisted.

"I was miserable back then," Amanda said. "I was in the wrong job an married to the wrong man. I didn't even know how wrong he was until th right one came along."

While Hannah cried at the thought of Zack's pain, Amanda kept her eye on the sister in the empty chair.

"I'm sorry it took the end of the world for me to finally see you," she tol Hannah. "But I'm glad it happened, because you are truly extraordinary. Th things I've seen you do on this world. The absolute miracles. Just having thes past two years with you has been one of the greatest gifts of my life."

Hannah had to pause the playback for another five minutes to vent he sobbing bereavement. She wouldn't have been able to hear Amanda other wise, and she was determined to take in every word before her sister wer away for good.

Amanda heaved a sigh as she debated her next words. "I know you'll tak this with a grain of salt, because you're not a Christian, but I believe we'll se each other again in a better place."

Hannah sniffled and scoffed at the same time. "Assuming I get past th bouncer."

Amanda smiled as if she'd heard her. "You're definitely going where th good people go. Just not anytime soon. That's more than just my hope for yo Hannah. It's my final wish. You *survive* this war. You pull off one more mira cle. Because I'm not giving my life for the world. I'm doing it for the peop I love."

She glanced down at Robert again. "And God knows this boy needs h mother to raise him."

Weeping, Hannah reached out for her sister's hand, only to pass righ through it, as she'd feared. It seemed particularly unfair, with all the power o the God's Eye and all the wonders of Ioni's tech, that she couldn't touch he sister one last time.

Amanda wiped her own tears away. "When this recording ends, and whe you say 'exit,' you'll be back where you were on the battlefield. Take as muc time as you need to deal with this, because once the clock starts up agai you'll have to stay focused. You can't let your grief get in your way. You unde stand me?"

Hannah nodded her head, sniffling. "I love you."

"Just remember how much I love you." Amanda laughed in sudden remi-
iscence. "You remember what Mom used to call us?"

Hannah laughed with her. "The Great Sisters Given."

"The Great Sisters Given," Amanda said. "Seemed so cheesy at the time."

"*So* cheesy."

"But very appropriate now."

After a brief and contemplative pause, Amanda gave Hannah one last
nile: the soft, wise grin that had practically become her trademark.

"We'll see each other again," she promised Hannah. "We'll find each other
n every world, and make it that much better."

She looked up at the floating glass orb and tossed it a curt nod. Both
manda and Robert faded from view, leaving only the chair behind.

"Fuck!" Hannah jumped to her feet, her thoughts bubbling with rage. She
idn't know how her sister died, but she sure as hell knew who did it. No Jade
ould take down the mighty Amanda Given. It had to be one of the Pelletiers.

"I'll kill you," Hannah said through tears. "Whichever one of you did it, I
ill fucking end you."

Save your hatred, warned the Amanda in her head, the voice of her highest
onscience. *You'll need it soon, but someone you love needs you sooner.*

"Shit." Hannah took one last minute to gather herself before looking at the
lass orb. "Exit."

The cement walls melted away to Prior Circle, and the flow of time re-
umed with a vengeance. Hannah barely had a chance to reorient herself be-
ore Mia fell to her knees, crying.

Bobby looked to her, baffled. "Mia, what—"

"It's all right," said Hannah. She kneeled at Mia's side and lifted her chin.
ook at me."

Mia locked her wet brown eyes on Hannah's. "She's gone."

"I know."

"She talked to me."

Hannah hugged her tight, her tears spilling onto her hair. She thanked the
tes and stars that she still had a sister to touch, even if time was their enemy.
he'd give herself five more seconds to share her grief with Mia before forcing
hem back onto business. Amanda's sacrifice would all be for nothing if they
idn't finish this war.

FORTY-FOUR

Ever since its construction in 2001, the Katcham Corporate Commissary-named after Larry Allen Katcham, the founder of Prior Chronolectrics—ha been a versatile asset for the company. Its wide-open layout and adjustab furnishings had enabled the space to become virtually anything it needed t be with minimal preparation: a banquet hall, a concert chamber, a bloo drive center, even a gladiatorial combat arena. For the past twelve years, o the first Friday of August, Prior hosted a Summertime Smackaroo, where em ployees dressed in department team colors and had a go at each other wit sponge swords.

Of course, no one could have predicted what the cafeteria would becom in its final incarnation: a strategic command center in a war to save humanit plus a makeshift infirmary for timebenders.

As the Jades had first started running amok in the plaza, Sean Howell-one of the Gothams' best healers as well as one of their last—enlisted dozen of people to move the wounded out of the combat zone and onto the dinin tables. While volunteers brought water to the injured, Sean hurried abo from patient to patient in a desperate attempt at triage. Luckily, their warsui did the heavy lifting, conveying their data to Sean through his visor and mak ing it easy to see who needed help most urgently.

The dire health readings of Meredith Graham had moved her straight t the front of the queue. Had Sean not reversed her when he did, she woul have died in ninety-two seconds. Instead, her ruptured spleen repaired itse and her eardrums mended flawlessly. The burns on her skin faded away int faint discolorations that, through the fickle nature of chronoregression, woul never entirely go away.

Unfortunately, Meredith had lost too much of her right eye to have properly restored. A milky white cloud had settled behind her iris, leaving incurably blind. If she somehow survived the rest of the day, she'd have to g shopping for eyepatches.

"You're lucky you didn't lose more," her sister Charlene told her.

Meredith looked to the dead Gotham on the neighboring table, a youn tempic who had died during reversal. She'd helped the tempics build a shiel

uring the collapse of the underland. Meredith wished she could remember he poor girl's name. Susan? Suzanne?

She held Charlene by the hand. "I'm not complaining. I'm still alive and I ill have you."

"Thank Yasmeen for that second part," Charlene said. "When those rock-ts first hit us—"

A dozen people screamed as a clone of the smallest Jade, the one named laeve, smashed into the cafeteria through a window. The glass barely had a hance to settle around her feet before a fast-moving tempic cut her head off.

"Oh my God." Meredith gripped Charlene's arm. "We better get back out here."

"Not you."

"I'm *fine.*"

"You're half-blind and timesick," Charlene said. "And luck only goes far."

"But—"

"If you really want to help, put some of your white boys at the windows. Ve don't want more trouble in here."

Meredith looked to the other side of the dining hall, where Felicity and ee worked tirelessly inside a floating ring of data screens. It would certainly e bad for business if something happened to the brain trust.

"All right," she said. "What will you do?"

Charlene unsheathed her hunting knife. "Yasmeen saved my sorry ass. I've ot to save her back before she gets smug about it."

She kissed Meredith on the forehead before moving for the exit. "Stay ucky."

"Stay *alive,*" Meredith called after her.

Sean Howell stopped Charlene on the way out the door, his handsome face renched in sweat. "If you see Zack Trillinger, tell him to get his ass in here. Ve need more healers, *now.*"

Charlene tossed him a cursory nod before hurrying back into the war zone. Vhatever mudheaded madness was afflicting the Jades seemed to be gradu-lly wearing off. They were getting organized again. Aggressive. And they ill outnumbered their enemies, even without their portal of reinforcements.

She stabbed a Jade in the neck at 30x speed, then caught sight of new trou-le in the distance. That good-looking Gotham with the Irish accent, Peter

Something, was slicing up Jades left and right. But his guillotine portals we
drawing a spotlight on him, pulling more enemies into his orbit. It was just
matter of time before they cut him down.

Charlene rushed to his aid, only to trip on a tempic tendril that had bee
hidden in the grass.

She tumbled across the lawn at high speed, her knife flying out of he
hand. If her swifter-class warsuit hadn't been reinforced at the shins, sh
would have broken her ankle instead of just twisting it.

Charlene had only just managed to flip onto her back when a large Jac
descended on her.

"Shit!" She channeled her temporis into an invisible blade, one that jutte
from the knuckles of her right fist. But before she had a chance to drive it int
her attacker, someone pulled him off of her with savage force and threw hi
faceup onto the lawn.

"Fuck you!"

The man crouched atop the Jade and hit him hard enough to loosen h
helmet.

"Fuck you!"

His second punch came with a loud metal *clang* and knocked the helm
clean off. If Charlene had been better situated, and if her savior's face hadn
been contorted in rage, she would have immediately recognized him. Instea
she had to wait to see his black right fist: a million-dollar prosthetic from
company that the Majee half-owned.

It seemed Charlene had found Zack after all, and he'd completely lost h
mind.

Zack's third punch broke the nose of the Jade and drove a bone fragme
into his brain. The man's thrashing limbs fell still in an instant, but th
hardly deterred his killer.

"You like that?" Zack hit his face hard enough to pump a spray of bloo
onto his warsuit. *"You want some more?"*

"Zack!"

Ofelia shouted at him from the edge of the lawn, with Heath standin
close behind her. Charlene limped toward them as fast as she could whi
keeping a wide berth from Zack. "What's with him?"

"I don't know," Ofelia said. "He just went crazy. He took a bad blow to th
head, but—"

"It's not his head," Heath said in a dismal voice.

On first look, Charlene thought the boy was merely exhausted. It had only een a couple of minutes since his great tempic frenzy and the rough reversal hat followed. All things considered, it was miraculous that Heath was standng at all.

But up close, Charlene could see the tears in his eyes. He was grieving.

"It's Amanda," said a voice to Charlene's left. "She's gone."

In the chaos, Charlene had forgotten all about Peter, though he had hardly uffered for her oversight. All the Jades who'd attacked him lay in bloody ieces on the grass.

Ofelia's heart skipped a beat. "Gone? As in . . ."

"Afraid so."

"Oh no." Ofelia looked to Zack. "When did he find out? I was with him the hole—"

"Fuck you!"

By now, the face of Zack's victim had been mashed to a pulp, to say nothng of the fist that did it. His thumb and ring finger had broken off its hinges, hile the other three dangled from wires. That didn't stop him from landing nore blows.

"Zack!"

The sound of Peter's voice snapped him back to awareness.

"You!" He made a furious dash toward Peter, his gritted teeth flecked with lood. "That was your portal. You're the one who sent her there!"

"I did," Peter grimly acknowledged. "If there was any other way—"

"Shut the fuck up!"

Charlene slowly reached for her backup knife, just in case things got even glier.

"I know it hurts," Peter said to Zack.

"*Hurts?* You have no idea. You only had her on time-share."

"Listen to me—"

"What if Liam had been with them?" Zack yelled. "Would you have served im up like—"

"No," Peter replied. "If it was my boy or Mia, they would have kept it from ne, for the very same reason they kept it from you. And nobody served up manda. She knew what she had to do and she did it."

Charlene could see Zack struggling to get mad again, for reasons she unerstood. Rage was the armor of the afflicted. It was the shield you wore inde your head to keep the pain from devouring you.

Though she assumed that Zack had only just heard about Amanda, he’d been dealing with her loss for six hours. Six long hours in a little cement room in the God’s Eye, with nothing but a chair and a recording. It wasn’t enough. Like the time he’d had with Amanda in life, it wasn’t nearly enough.

He looked to Peter with quivering wet eyes. “What if she’s still alive?”

“Zack . . .”

“What if they’re keeping her in a mirror room, or—”

Peter gripped him by the back of the neck and rested his forehead against his. “Zack, you know it as well as I do. You *feel* it. She’s gone.”

Zack broke away from Peter. “Amanda. Caleb. Carrie’s dad. All sacrificed and for *what*?”

Ofelia approached him. “Zack—”

“Don’t.”

“I’m just saying that your left eye is bloodshot,” she told him. “You have no color. Whatever Stitch did when she hit you—”

“I don’t care.”

“*I* care. You need to get healed or you’ll die.”

“She’s right,” said Peter.

“Fuck you both.” Zack unscrewed his broken prosthetic and dropped it to the ground. “I’m not going to lose my last memory of her.”

“You should go see Sean anyway,” Charlene said. “He needs more healers.

“Who gives a shit?”

As Zack started back toward the central plaza, a Joelle clone rushed him at high speed. Zack rifted her to her skeleton, just as he’d once done in Scotland.

“That’s all we’re good for,” he said to Charlene over his shoulder. “Killing and dying.”

Peter stopped Heath before he could follow him. “It’s all right. He’ll come around.” He sighed at the broken mechanical arm on the grass. “At least I hope he . . .”

Ofelia eyed Peter worriedly as he trailed off, distracted. “What is it?”

“You don’t feel it?”

“If you’re talking about a portal—”

“It’s coming,” Peter said. “A big one.”

Charlene groaned and readied her knife. “This shit never ends.”

The disc burst from the ground like a spring trap: a bright half-circle, thirty feet wide and connected to a faraway continent. It cut a diagonal line through the grassy patch between the cafeteria building and the hard diamond shelter that housed seven newborns.

Rosario hurried out of the nursery and aimed her double-barreled shotgun at the portal, just as Charlene, Yasmeen, and five other swifters got in prime position to strike.

"Hold your fire!" Theo yelled over the comm link. "They're *our* people. Ours!"

Charlene's eyes went round at the shadowy figures that stepped out of the portal—all familiar to her, even as silhouettes. "Oh my God. Finally!"

They came through the light a dozen at a time: the remaining timebenders of the Majee clan, plus the young male orphans from another world's Osaka. Sixty-one reinforcements in total, all at the peak of health and with full shield power in their warsuits.

Akio dashed across the lawn to reunite with his fellow Rubies. "About time," he yelled in his native tongue. "You have no idea what I've been through. These Americans are crazy."

Auberon Graham was the last to emerge. He hobbled through the portal on his mahogany cane, the only one of them dressed in a business suit instead of battle gear.

"You all know your jobs," he said to his people. "Get to it."

While most of the Majee and Rubies joined the fight, three of their healers proceeded to the infirmary. Four swifters rushed to set up thin metal poles around the perimeter of Ioni's shield.

Charlene hugged Auberon. "Grandpa!"

"You're limping."

"I'm fine. Just wrenched my ankle a little."

"And Meredith?"

"She's alive, but—"

They flinched in synch at the sudden burst of gunfire. Theo and Melissa were halfway across the lawn when they saw a Jade moving fast toward Rosario. They both shot him in the head with their assault rifles while Rosario perforated his chest with her shotgun.

"Get back in the shelter and seal the door," Theo told Rosario. He lowered his weapon and gave a tense nod to Auberon. "Glad you finally decided to join us."

The old man looked to the fallen, twitching Jade. "I only chose this as much as you did."

Melissa put one last bullet in the head of the enemy. "Well, you certainly chose the timing," she bitterly said to Auberon. "Very wise of you to wait until the fight turned our way."

Theo sighed with resignation at her new hard edge. While he was still puttering in denial over the loss of Amanda, Melissa had jumped straight ahead to the anger phase. She was livid, and nothing—not even Amanda's beautiful last words to her in the God's Eye—could ease her spirit.

Auberon's expression turned cold. "I come here as a friend—"

"A *fair-weather* friend," Melissa snapped.

"Perhaps you should wait to see what I offer before judging me."

He gestured at the strange new contraption that his swifters had erected around the shield dome: twenty-four metal poles connected to a titanium-plated generator.

"There's a reason the Jades have been using lumis on the barrier," Auberon said. "It works three times faster than any other form of temporis. This machine takes that option away from them."

"How?" asked Theo.

Melissa figured it out before he could explain. "A solic disruptor," she said. "Specially calibrated to affect only lumis."

Auberon nodded. "My people helped bring it to the world. We know its weaknesses better than anyone."

Theo studied the device carefully. If it worked as well as Auberon claimed, then it was a brilliant way to buy time for Ioni.

"Thank you," he said to Auberon. "How did you know about the Jades and their lumis? Was that your, uh . . ."

"My future self," the old man replied with a soft grin. "He's never let me down."

"Did he give you any other info?" Theo asked.

Auberon's smile flattened. He peeked at Melissa out of the corner of his eye. "Admittedly, he told me the best time to come here. Any sooner and there would have been . . . casualties."

"There *were* casualties," Melissa scornfully informed him. "Hundreds of them. But of course you're talking about your people."

"Can you fault me for putting my family first?"

"With all life at stake? Yes. I very easily can."

Auberon sighed. "I'm sorry for your losses. I truly am. But as an agent of the National Integrity Commission—"

"Former."

"—you're hardly in a position to judge."

Charlene moved between them. "Okay, stop!"

"Stop," Theo said. "We're on the same side and we have the same goal. So let's just—"

He was cut off by the loud din of gunfire in the distance, a fracas on the other side of the plaza. Theo looked across the rubble to see Hannah and her teammates engaged in conflict with a group of Jades. She rifted the heads of two of them before briefly catching Theo's eye.

His heart broke to pieces at her heavy expression, a grief he hadn't seen since Jonathan's passing. But that pain had been a trifle, a mere bump on the knee, compared to what Theo was witnessing now. He wanted to run across the battlefield and wrap his arms around Hannah until everything felt right again. Screw the game plan. Screw Ioni.

Melissa saw the tears in his eyes and had to fight to suppress her own emotions. "Theo."

"I'm sorry," he said in a choked-up voice. He looked to Auberon. "We just lost someone very special to us, and, uh . . ."

"No need to apologize," he said. "If anything, I owe you one for putting my trust in Azral. He's every bit the monster you said he was, and worse. However . . ."

Auberon held up a folded sheet of paper. "This is a message from me at the end of the war—the *victorious* end, just a few minutes from now."

He gripped Theo's arm. "The future you've been fighting for is right around the corner."

An overwrought laugh slipped out of Theo's throat before he could stop it: a paradoxical mixture of joy and disbelief. He'd been chasing that string for two long years: that one rogue continuum in a wall of stunted timelines, the elusive golden future where life on Earth continued. What had started out as a myth in the head of Peter Pendergen had become a world-size reality that was close enough for Theo to smell.

But if his time as an augur had taught him anything, it was that any one future—near or far, good or bad—could change at a moment's notice. There was no point celebrating a single thing while the Pelletiers still lived and breathed.

He called up some stats on the inside of his visor. Ioni's last shield was down to twelve percent capacity, and she still needed four minutes to start her great machine.

Theo looked to Charlene. "You good to run?"

"Yes."

"No," said Auberon. "She obviously hurt her leg."

"I'm *fine*, Grandpa."

"Good," said Theo. "I need you to gather all the tempics and swifters we have and get them around the shield."

Melissa nodded in agreement. "Gothams, orphans, Majee. It doesn't matter. Double up in shifted pairs and keep the enemy away from that barrier."

"You got it," said Charlene.

As she sped off in a dusty blur, the new orphans and Majee on the battlefield made the combat look more like a slaughter. The Jades fell by the dozen to their swifters and tempics, while the lumics blinded half the remaining horde in a swirling cloak of darkness. A heavyset man with a salt-and-pepper beard—the vice chair of the Majees' board of directors—waved his mighty hand at a cluster of Jades and robbed them of all their temporis.

A solic, Theo thought with wonder. *We finally have a solic again.*

Melissa's blistering expression was enough to flip the notion on its head. They could have had a solic this whole damn time. To think of all the lives he could have saved.

Auberon directed their attention to the Rubies in the lower sky. "Watch this."

Four of the Japanese orphans, including Akio, had ascended into the air on a platform of aeris that looked like an upside-down iceberg. From the speed at which they moved around, they must have had a swifter among them.

Akio stood near the edge of the floe, his fingers clutched around the shoulders of their tallest teammate. With a burst of light, he boosted the temporal ability of his friend.

And then something extraordinary happened.

One by one, the Jades disappeared: the living and dead alike. They vanished out of existence so fast that Theo wondered if he was watching a new power at work. Maybe it was some kind of invisible super-mortis. Or maybe the kid was just a wizard.

It wasn't until the concrete swallowed two Jades that Theo recognized the magic at play.

"A dropper," he marveled. "They have a dropper like Jonathan."

Melissa tensely shook her head. "Not like Jonathan."

She was right. This dropper was augmented and shifted at high speed, combination that turned him into a weapon of mass destruction. Even as an ally, the kid terrified Theo. No one person should have that kind of kill power. No evolutionary system should have allowed it.

Twenty-two seconds after the aerial assault started, the plaza fell into an overwhelming hush. There were no more Jades to be found anywhere, not even as cadavers. They'd all been dropped to the earth's fiery core. If there was a cleaner, more thorough way of purging an enemy, Theo couldn't think of it. He could barely wrap his head around the fact that the Jades had recently outnumbered them, ten to one.

The silence was soon broken by the Rubies on the ground. They raised loud cheers at their four flying brothers, who wasted no time cheering back down at them.

"Amazing," said Auberon. "As you can see, our young friends have been quick learners in the art of—"

"Get them out of there," Theo said with sudden urgency.

"What?"

He couldn't even begin to describe the horror to come before it already started. A hideous tempic formation, like mutated elk horns, popped out of thin air and impaled the four Rubies in multiple places.

Auberon's eyes went wide as their agonized cries filled the plaza. "No . . ."

The aeric platform evaporated, leaving Akio and the other Rubies dangling from tempic hooks. Worse for them and for everyone watching, none of the spikes had pierced any vital organs. The tempis had been created to inflict maximum suffering and make a show of their shrieking misery.

The Majee solic attempted to help them from the ground, but was immediately eviscerated by . . . nothing. He flailed about in bloody chaos, as if an invisible bear was mauling him.

Theo hailed his people on the comm link. "We're being attacked by people we can't see! Everyone get to safety! Protect each other!"

Melissa fumbled for his arm. "Theo."

He followed her wide gaze upward, just in time for Akio's torturer to make his presence known. His cloaking field had vanished only for a moment, enough for his enemies to recognize his grin.

"Semerjean," Melissa said. "He's here."

Theo closed his eyes in misery as a new black shadow enveloped the future. "They're all here."

FORTY-FIVE

Ever since his miraculous reunion with his sister, Bobby Farisi had fielded a lot of questions about her. More specifically, he'd fielded a lot of the same question from people who only knew the latter-day Mia: the girl who'd cursed and yelled and screwed her way around the underland, the one who'd acted so violently in Mexico that the director of America's most ruthless government agency had to bench her.

For them, there was only one thing to ask: *Is it true that she used to be timid?*

In each instance, Bobby plainly confirmed that, yes, Mia had been the quietest girl in the town's loudest family, the honor roll student among a clan of dumb jocks. Her bedroom had practically needed a fifth wall for all the academic ribbons and plaques she'd amassed, while her indomitably kind nature and precocious intelligence had kept umpteen family arguments from devolving into fistfights.

Of course, Bobby had omitted the other part of the story: the once-in-a-blue-moon incidents when his sweet baby sister had reached the end of her tether. When one of her brothers' jokes went too far, when someone upset their grandmother, when anyone dared to insinuate that Mia was a budding lesbian . . . *boom*. Thunderclouds would gather over the roof of their house and Mia would get a look on her face that made even her father step back. Though the girl was too young to remember her mother, the rest of her family wasn't. And when they all saw the storm in Mia's eyes, they'd feared she inherited the same black rage that had made Lucia Farisi a terror.

Though Bobby had certainly seen Mia get mad on the new world, he had yet to see that lightning stare. Not until just a few moments ago, when four Japanese orphans were gruesomely murdered above the ruins of Prior Circle.

The bodies of the Rubies had barely hit the ground before Mia screamed in feral rage and fired six bullets from her handgun. Bobby looked to see what she was shooting at, but all he glimpsed was the empty patch of air where Akio and his friends had just been.

Mia kicked over a small pile of debris. "Motherfucker!"

Bobby eyed her worriedly. "Mia, what—"

"He's here!" She turned to her other companion and sibling. "It's Semer-ean! He's here right now!"

Hannah had missed the whole spectacle, thanks to Evan. While the Ru-ies had still been flying around, one of his future selves snapped back into im with a warning and a plan.

"We're about to get swarmed," he'd told Hannah. "We need to get as many eople around us as possible and get them in a temporal field, fast."

Luckily, Charlene Graham was already in the process of gathering fight-rs. By the time Hannah waved her over, she had eighteen tempics and swift-rs in tow, including Stitch and Yasmeen.

"It'll have to be enough," Evan said. "Go!"

Once again, Hannah had created a doughnut ring of slowtime around her eople, allowing them to function at normal speed within a barrier of tempo-al protection. No enemy could penetrate their immediate space without get-ing fatally rifted.

Oblivious to all that, Mia tugged at Hannah's arm. "Did you hear me? I aid—"

"Holy shit." Hannah looked beyond the wreckage of the marketing build-ng and finally saw what Evan was worried about. All around the war zone, nvisible enemies were attacking timebenders, disemboweling them where hey stood. It was as if the Jades had all come back from Hell as vicious ghostly pirits.

Yasmeen blanched at the carnage all around them. "What the fuck's go-ng on?"

"Those Jades must be cloaked," Bobby said. He tapped his helmet visor. "I hought these things could see through lumis."

"It's not lumis," Evan said.

"And those aren't Jades!" Mia shouted. "I'm telling you, the Pelletiers re here!"

At long last, the others caught up with Mia's frenzy. Stitch's arms frosted ver with spikes of tempis. She cursed aloud in Hebrew, then made a mad ash for the action.

"Wait!" Hannah yelled.

Yasmeen stopped her before she could run into Hannah's temporal field. Are you crazy? Do you *want* to get rifted?"

"I want to hurt them!"

"We all do," Hannah said. "But if you take another step in that direction you'll be dead."

Stitch threw her arms up. "We're not helping anyone by standing here!"

"She's right," Mia said. "They're slaughtering us!"

Evan shook his head. "We can't fight them if we can't see them."

"Oh, shut the fuck up. You only care about yourself."

In a better state of mind, Hannah might have defended him. Without Evan's warning, they would have all been cut to ribbons.

"We'll just have to hold tight," she told Mia. "Until Theo or someone els finds a way for us to see them."

Mia could have cooked her alive with her glare. "They *killed* her."

"I know," Hannah said. "I want to hurt them as much as you do. But th reason you saw Semerjean at all—"

"Hannah—"

"—is that he *wanted* us to. He wants us to lose our heads. You know him Mia. *Think*."

Bobby couldn't help but marvel at the sudden change in his sister: a reversal of momentum, from hard-browed fury to flinching guilt. The fact tha Hannah was able to reach Mia in her berserker state was nothing short of incredible, a feat that no one in his family had ever been able to accomplish Maybe Mia had acquired some temperance in her accelerated journey t adulthood. Or maybe the chemistry was simply different between sisters.

After a tense, collective silence, punctuated by the near and distant crie of allies, Evan's head snapped back in sudden alertness. He looked to Hannah bright-eyed.

"I think I know how to see them."

Evan wasn't the only one on the battlefield who received hindsight wisdom i advance. Twenty-nine seconds after the invisible assault started, a mousehol portal opened at the feet of Auberon Graham and produced a handwritte note from the near future.

Actually, "handwritten" was a generous term for it. From what Theo coul spy over Auberon's shoulder, the etchings were pure chicken scratch. Aubero had developed his own form of shorthand that would stump all but the world best cryptographers.

"We have to get to your command center," he told Theo and Melissa. "Now

One comm call to Peter gave them the quick transport they needed. Withi noments, a portal opened onto the wall of the cafeteria, and Felicity and See vere joined by Theo, Melissa, Auberon, Peter, Ofelia, and Heath.

Meredith approached them from the infirmary and cast a ring of tempic oldiers around them, prompting Heath to follow suit with his own Jonahans. Though both sets of minions only operated at half-strength, due to the ecovering state of their creators, they formed a tight enough circle to keep all loaked enemies from creeping into their midst.

Soon Auberon gave Theo enough information to allow him to update the roops—what was left of them, anyway. As he activated his comm link, Theo rieved at all the timebender status screens that had gone black in his abence. The display looked as grim as a late-night office building. Just a handul of scattered lit windows in the darkness.

"Okay, here's what's happening," he announced to the survivors. "As some f you have seen, the Pelletiers are here, just as we feared and expected. They rought fifty-one Jades with them."

He heard the groans and cries from the infirmary, all the poor, dispirited ouls who'd suffered enough combat for twelve lifetimes and couldn't take nymore.

"This is their last wave," Theo promised. "Thanks to the sacrifice of manda Given and her team, the Pelletiers can't make any more clones. The ades we kill will *not* be replaced. That's the good news."

He looked to Melissa and Felicity, both toiling away at a pair of liquid netal computers. They were the only ones who'd been trained on Ioni's alien perating system, which seemed to rely on thoughts and gestures as much as eystrokes.

"The bad news," Theo continued, "is that we can't see any of these people. ot on infrared. Not with any filter we have. But Auberon Graham has found way around it: a combination of thermal and electromagnetic imaging that e're programming into all your visors. It'll take about a minute for this uprade to kick in. Hopefully less."

Five more status screens went dark. Theo turned away from the display, ckened.

"Look, we're all at the end of our rope here. But the fact that there are *any* us still standing right now is both a miracle and a testament. We've fought gainst overwhelming forces today and, against all odds, we've made it to the nal leg. Don't lose hope. Stay as safe as you can until you see the enemy. And ien do everything you can to protect the shield."

Theo checked the countdown clock. "We have three minutes and fourtee
seconds before Ioni's machine is finally—"

A dozen people screamed from the infirmary as an unseen assailant stabbe
Monty Melford through the chest. By the time Theo looked, the young Plati
num was dead and the violence had spread to three different parts of th
cafeteria.

"No!" Theo stopped Heath and Meredith before they could send thei
tempic men into the infirmary. The Pelletiers had no interest in the wounded
The attack was just a chessman's ploy to leave their enemy's strategist
exposed.

But that was hardly an excuse to let other people die. Theo snatched th
.44 pistol from Melissa's side holster and pointed it over the shoulder of
Jonathan.

Ofelia and the others watched him, horrified, as he closed his eyes an
waved his gunsight around the infirmary.

Soon the barrel stopped in the direction of Sean Howell. "What are yo
doing?" Peter asked Theo. "That's a friend! He's a—"

Theo pulled the trigger with a thunderous *bang*, swung the gun to th
right, then fired two more bullets into the crowd.

Everyone in the cafeteria froze in shock as the action came to a halt. De
spite all logic and rational reasoning, the spectral assaults had stopped.

A Jade turned visible right in front of Sean Howell, then crumpled dead t
the floor. A second Jade lost her nanotech cloak before collapsing onto a tabl
Ten feet to her left, the third and final enemy apparated into view, the
slumped to the ground against a blood-spattered wall.

One by one, the survivors of the attack threw their dumbstruck gaz
onto Theo.

"How in God's name did you do that?" Auberon asked him.

Though his heart pounded fast enough to make him light-headed, The
could only shrug. He'd nearly died more than once at the hand of Reb
Rosen, a gun-wielding augur who'd mastered the art of prescient aim. Th
man could shoot a person dead without even looking, or take out someone
eye with a three-point ricochet. The trick was to ignore all the ramblings
the future and force it to answer a simple question: *if I fire a bullet right ther
right now, will it kill my enemy?*

"When it says 'yes,' you pull the trigger," Rebel had told Theo last year, n ong after the Gothams and orphans had made peace. "Doesn't get simpler han that."

Of course, the future could have changed or misled Theo, creating conse-quences that he shuddered to think about.

Felicity finished her task at Ioni's console and pushed her chair back. Got it!"

"Still working," Melissa said. The visors had to be upgraded on two differ-nt spectrums, and Melissa only had a fraction of Felicity's computer skills. oni's console was especially maddening, like wishing on a genie who'd only ust learned English. When the computer wasn't overthinking her complex equests, it was dramatically overindulging them.

Theo checked the health status screens and saw three more windows go lark. "Melissa . . ."

"I'm hurrying."

One of the Jonathans twitched in sudden discomfort. "There's another ade in here," Heath muttered.

"Two," said Meredith. "I can feel them skulking around."

Melissa finally got the results she wanted. "It's ready."

"Do it!" yelled Ofelia.

With a press of a button, every warsuit visor in Prior Circle received its nuch-needed upgrade. The daylight view turned an evening shade of indigo, while the friends and allies all around them became blue photonegatives.

As jarring as the transition was, it succeeded in its primary purpose. The isors painted every hidden enemy in a sparkling green tint, giving their skin nd armor the appearance of sculpted gemstone. The Jades looked more like meralds now, but at least they could be seen.

Theo didn't have time to fire his weapon before the two enemy soldiers in he command center were slaughtered. Peter cut down a Jade with a well-laced portal while a trio of Meredith's tempic men killed the other one with heir bladed hands.

Melissa nodded graciously at Auberon. "Your intel saved us."

"Not all of us." The old man pointed at the Majees' health screens. "I lost wenty-two people in the last few minutes."

"I'm sorry."

"I don't want condolences," Auberon said. "I want to ensure a long future or the rest of my clan, and a very short future for the Pelletiers."

Theo scanned the camera screens, which had been upgraded along with the visors. He caught a brief glimpse of a tall, thin man moving elusively among the Jades.

"We're working on it," he promised Auberon. "We're working on both."

As her vision flipped from day to night and her enemies lost their cover, Hannah willed away her temporal field, allowing all the allies around her to spring into violent action. The swifters charged toward the shield dome in a procession of blurs, while the tempics dispersed in multiple directions to take down the nearest Jades.

Bobby sighed from his spot on the shattered asphalt, hobbled. His thigh wound had already bled through its newest bandage, while the muscles in that leg had quit in angry protest. "Great. I'm useless."

Hannah lifted her visor to study him. It was hard to get a read on her friends when their highlights and shadows were reversed. "We'll help you t the infirmary."

"Don't waste time on me. I'll be okay."

"It won't take long," Hannah said. "Especially if Mia—"

Hannah looked around and saw that both she and Evan were gone "Oh no."

"What?" Bobby peeked over his shoulder and noticed his sister's absence "Goddamn it."

"She's not in her right mind."

"No shit. She's going to get killed." Bobby grabbed a broken piece of reba and used it to prop himself up. "I'll get a leg brace from the infirmar Can you—"

"I'll find her," Hannah promised. "I'm not losing another one of us."

"Thank you." Bobby raised his visor to look at her. "I'm sorry about you sister. She was a real force of nature. You both are."

Hannah squeezed his arm. "Stay safe."

While she and Bobby parted, Evan reunited with Mia on the roof of th cafeteria building. He'd just managed to make it through her portal before closed, enough to prompt him to check himself for missing pieces.

"Holy fuck." He caught up to Mia at the rooftop's edge. "You almost Kun Kinted me."

"Shut up," she said. "I never asked you to follow me."

She peeked over the railing and magnified her view of the shield dom

The enemies she spied through her new visor filter were all merely Jades from he shape of them. So where the hell were the Pelletiers? What better place did they have to be than right by the dying shield?

Evan aimed his sniper rifle and felled a Jade down below with a headshot.

"What are you doing?" Mia asked him.

"Protecting Ioni. We still have a job to do, don't we?"

Mia pointed at the far corner of the roof. "Well, go shoot from over there. don't need you drawing attention to me."

"Do you even have a plan?" Evan asked her. "Or is it just *kill kill grrrr*?"

Mia shot him a murderous glare. The only plan was to spot Semerjean efore he spotted her, and then cut him in half with a portal. She didn't need o make any speeches. She didn't even need him to know who killed him. She ıst wanted the satisfaction of ending him.

Unfortunately, Semerjean was being as elusive as ever. Was he toying with er, or did the Pelletiers find a less obvious way to mess with Ioni's barrier?

Evan took down another two Jades with his rifle, his head twitching oddly efore each shot. Mia assumed that he was rewinding over his many misses. he almost admired his patience.

"Don't get me wrong," he said. "I'm rooting for you to kill him. I just want o make sure you do it right, because you'll only get one shot."

"What do you suggest?"

"What did *you* suggest?" Evan countered. "You'd think Future You would ave broken her embargo and sent you a note by now."

In point of fact, that exact thing had happened, just a few hours before eaving Sergelen. But the only advice that her elder self had for her was to "let im go."

That was not an option. Not after what he and his family did to Amanda.

"She wasn't helpful," Mia told Evan. "And if you don't have any useful dvice—"

"Look out!"

Evan yanked her down as a thermic blast flared up from the central plaza. rom her stinging pain, Mia assumed she'd caught the edge of a fireball. ut the rooftop railing had become covered in frost. Her breath came out s steam.

A coldburst, Mia realized.

She peeked over the edge and surveyed the damage down below. The biggest change to the scenery, besides the flash-frozen corpses of a few friends and foes, was the solic disruptor that the Majee had erected around the shield. The machine had been completely destroyed, giving the enemy carte blanche to resume their lumic attacks.

Fuck, Mia thought. She didn't have time to wait for Semerjean to show hi face. She had to draw him out of his rabbit hole, fast.

Unfortunately, she could only think of one way to do that.

Evan eyed her guardedly as she closed her eyes in concentration. "Wha are you doing?"

"You may want to run."

"What?"

She cast her consciousness onto the portal network and unleashed a psychic roar.

DAVID!

Mia knew that the Pelletiers were all master travelers. Strong enough t jump anywhere in the world. Stealthy enough to hide their auras from eve the keenest observers. If Mia banged a few pots on the telepathic web, the would hear it. And if she used the right name—or in this case, the right *wron* name—she would poke at the vanity of her chosen target, enough to flus him out.

But in her haste and fury, Mia had miscalculated. More specifically, sh forgot about the other Pelletier who had unfinished business with her.

"Hello, child."

Mia screamed as an electrical charge hit her square in the back, drivin her down to the floor in a fetal ball while paralyzing her muscles.

Esis descended onto the rooftop as gently as a moth, a sprightly grin o her face. Between her smile, her soft landing, and her sleeveless white dres the newsdrones could have mistaken her for a benevolent fairy godmothe the Good Witch of the South.

Evan, of course, knew better, and he'd come thoroughly prepared. Befo Esis could even look his way, he slapped a button on his wrist and activate his warsuit's forcefield.

Esis chuckled at his protective bubble. "You've recharged your supply."

Evan nodded nervously. "I like to keep my options open."

Indeed, while scrounging for ammo, he'd managed to leech thirty-fiv seconds of unused shield time from the warsuits of dead allies. It wasn't lik they needed it.

Esis approached his barrier and traced a finger along its surface. "Impre ve. You've been miserable for centuries, yet you scheme and fight to extend our time on this world."

"What choice do I have?" Evan replied with forced aplomb. "It's this or othing."

"One of the few things you grasp that Amanda did not. Contrary to her ying assertion, there's no existence beyond this one. No Heaven or Hell."

"Just a big fat void," Evan anxiously offered.

"If even that." Esis's grin went flat. "You sadden me, boy. Of all the little ubs we spared from death, you had the most potential to evolve."

"What do you want from me?"

"I want you to die and stop disappointing me."

Evan stepped back in his forcefield and checked the gauge on his wrist. Well, in twenty-nine seconds, you'll have your chance."

"You have seventeen seconds," Esis countered. "And an explosive device ehind your back. Even now, in the face of your inevitable end, you still cheme to survive." She nodded approvingly. "I respect that. And despite all e headaches and setbacks you've caused for us, I still like you. I may be the nly soul on Earth who does."

Evan struggled to keep his eyes off Mia, who was finally starting to re-over enough to cast a fatal portal. "You know, it's funny that you mention—"

Esis cut him off with a wave of her hand: a dismissive little gesture that nt a tempic spike flying behind her back. It flew a straight path toward Mia nd nailed her right hand to the floor.

Evan flinched at the sound of the poor girl's cry. Esis had partially cruci-ed her without even looking.

"Now *that* one," Esis said to Evan, "I never liked. That cloying little child led entirely by emotion."

At long last, she turned her attention to Mia. "Did you think I forgot your sult to me? Did you believe I would let it go unpunished?"

"What insult?" Evan asked. "I don't—"

Esis flicked her hand again and covered Evan's forcefield in a sheet of ice. 'm done with you. You bore me."

She crouched down to Mia and dissolved the spike in her hand. "Come ith me on a journey of remembrance. It'll take but a moment. I promise."

Between all the pain and bedlam in her body, Mia felt the touch of cool ngers on her temples. And then suddenly, the whole world changed. Every-ing around her. Everything inside of her. It all got worse in an instant.

Before Mia could even begin to get her bearings, she caught a horrifie look at her physical state. Her legs had been melded together and rooted int the ground, as if the lower half of her body had morphed into a tree. Her arm had been removed all the way to the shoulders, while her mouth was entirel gone. She stood as still and helpless as a potted plant.

Her thoughts shrieked with panic as she struggled to adjust. *This isn't re-ally happening,* she insisted to herself. *It's all just a sick illusion.*

The notion gave her just enough strength to process her new surround-ings, which she immediately recognized. She was back in the tunnels of th dead Gotham village: the *under*-underland, where she'd suffered more tha once. It was somewhere in these warrens that she'd severed Peter's feet, the searched around for Carrie while the whole world crumbled.

But of course Esis didn't care about that recent trauma. She had broug Mia back even further in time, to June 12 of last year: Red Sunday. The da Integrity invaded the underland and killed a hundred and twenty Gotham The day Jonathan died.

The day Mia lost the version of Carrie Bloom that she had known ar loved.

Esis stood behind her and stroked the stumps of her shoulders. "You re-member this moment, do you not? The pathetic end of Rebel Rosen."

She pointed to his bloody corpse, sprawled just beyond the door to a sto-age room full of mirrors. Beyond him, Mia saw Semerjean and Esis in ten conversation with Zack. That was where they'd forced him into a mating a-rangement with Amanda, Peter, and Mercy, a twisted little square dance th had tormented them all for months.

Mia's heart hammered as two teenage girls came sneaking down the co-ridor: a younger Mia and an older Carrie.

Oh God, no, Mia thought. *Don't.*

Esis smiled as Past Mia perched at the edge of the doorway, her wide ey locked on Rebel's discarded revolver.

"I've reconstructed this scene from my own memories," Esis admitted Mia. "So I can't replay the silent exchange of words that you and Ioni had."

The present-day Mia tried to look away as her younger self picked up t revolver. Unfortunately, Esis had immobilized her neck and removed her ab-ity to close her eyes.

"What lies did she tell you?" Esis idly wondered. "Did she promise a vi ry free of consequence? Did you think that my husband would do absolutely othing if you shot me dead in front of him?"

In point of fact, Ioni had promised to take Mia and her loved ones to a fe, distant place where the Pelletiers couldn't hurt them. For all Mia knew, e'd been talking about Sergelen. But given the ugly turn of events, it was vious on hindsight that the woman had simply fibbed.

I know this is hard, Ioni had said to Mia at the time. *But you have to believe e. Inside that gun is the bullet that kills Esis Pelletier. I was hoping that Rebel ould be the one to fire it, but he's gone now. It has to be you.*

"And here it begins," Esis said. "Your most foolish mistake in a very long ain of them."

The window's closing! Ioni had told Mia. *Do it!*

The past Mia aimed the revolver with wincing hesitation, then fired it at is's head. The bullet tore through the skull of the mother Pelletier, splatterg her brains onto the nearest mirror before sending her body to the ground.

The present-day Mia cocked her head in confusion. *What?*

"My goodness," teased Esis. "That's not what happened. That was just hat you wished would happen. Let me amend it."

She rewound the scene and played it through properly. The other Esis rned her head and deftly caught the bullet in a two-inch time portal.

"Ah, yes," said the present-day Esis. "That matches up much better with y recollection."

Tears spilled out of Mia's eyes. She struggled in her rooted spot. *Please,* she gged Esis in her thoughts. *Please don't show me the rest.*

Esis crossed in front of her and eyed her in brief debate. "You have the eedom to move your head again, so answer my question, if you will. Do you member this moment clearly?"

Mia nodded, crying.

"Do you regret listening to Ioni?"

Mia nodded again. *I've regretted it every day,* she thought. *Every fuckg day.*

Esis smiled contentedly. "One last query before we return. Do you remember what I said to you next?"

In the wake of Mia's third head-nod, Esis traced a finger across the lower lf of her face, reforming her lips and mouth.

"Then say the words," Esis demanded. "Exactly as you remember them."

Mia coughed the choke out of her throat, then looked to Esis, wet-eye
"You said that bullet I fired would come back one day, and it would kill som
one I loved."

Esis nodded with a hint of reservation. "I technically said, 'You won't li
where it goes,' but that was the implication. Yes."

"Listen, please, I'm begging you—"

"Hush." Esis sealed her mouth again. "As you've no doubt gathered, th
day has come. I always keep my promises. The only question now—"

The memory of the underland quickly gave way to a still-frame view of t
present.

"—is which loved one of yours will pay the price for your folly."

Esis ferried Mia around the ruins of Prior Circle on a floating disc
metal. She stopped at the frozen battle scene in the center of the plaza, th
peeked through the shield at Carrie.

"Your pretty young love would be the obvious choice," Esis said. "But sh
still under the aegis of Ioni Deschane, and I don't have the patience to wait.

She flew them north to the edge of the campus, where a familiar m
kneeled at the side of a dead Gotham and pressed two fingers to her wrist.

"Zack Trillinger," Esis said with a laugh. "Irrevocably broken from the lo
of his wife. He mutters to himself like a lunatic and checks the pulses of alli
who are clearly beyond healing. Though his death by your hand would ser
a most fitting punishment, he's become far too pathetic to kill."

Mia continued to struggle in her immobilized state as Esis moved the
again. She caught a brief glimpse of the cafeteria rooftop, and the motionle
forms of their doppelgängers.

Wait a second, Mia thought.

Before she could finish the notion in her head, Esis took her to the sti
frame of Hannah.

"Now *this* one," said Esis, "deserves to die. The troubles and frustratio
she caused us in Lárnach. She was a horror. The fact that my husband let h
leave with her child has been a thorn in our marriage ever since."

Esis chewed her lip in thought before shaking her head. "No. A bullet
the head is too good for that one. Too quick. And it would deprive my son
his own vengeance."

Mia was barely listening anymore. The sight of her other self on the ro
and the faint little traces of energy that emanated from her, had set her mi

ı spinning motion. This wasn't the God's Eye, and it wasn't quite reality. hat could only mean—

"Of course!"

Esis had expressed her inspiration so loudly that Mia fell out of her ıought. The disc looped south across the campus grounds and stopped at a rge, wounded orphan.

Mia's eyes teared up at the sight of Bobby. *No* . . .

"I've been so occupied with your surrogate siblings that I forgot that you ill have a real one." Esis studied Bobby closely. "I have no feelings for this ıf, but clearly you do. How fitting that he should die by your hand."

Mia screamed inside her head, her body rocking on rooted legs.

"You had no cause to trust Ioni when she commanded you to kill me," Esis ıid. "Even a young and foolish mind like yours had enough information to ıoose better. But you were determined to ignore all the warning signs. They ent . . ." She laughed to herself. "What's the expression of your era? 'In one ır and out the other'?"

She waved her finger in the direction of Bobby's left ear, creating a new virl of energy in Mia's senses.

"And so we reach the end of a string," said Esis. "With a perfectly fitting ›itaph."

Mia shook her head, weeping. *No* . . .

"In one ear . . ."

Please . . .

"And out the other."

NO!

A time portal opened. A bullet launched out. And the whole world ıanged all over again.

onsequences.

If Esis had learned anything from her debacle with Ofelia, it was that anyıe, no matter how inexperienced, could become a threat on the travelers' ane if given half the chance. Had Esis been able to do it all over again (and certain strings of time, she did), she would have girded her mind from Ofeı's worst memories and inflicted her with an overwhelming sense of helpssness, enough to keep her from closing Esis's portals.

But live and learn, as the ancients say. When Esis brought Mia into the

realm, she took all the wise precautions she'd neglected before. With the me
power of suggestion, she'd pinned Mia's legs, removed her arms and mout
robbed her of every last bit of agency. Perception was power on the traveler
plane, and illusions were stronger than chains.

Unfortunately, Esis had made two new mistakes with Mia. The first o
was letting her see their own counterparts, the real-world Esis and Mia, c
the cafeteria rooftop. In addition to cracking Mia's psychic fourth wall, it or
ented her spatial senses to Esis's true location.

Esis's second mistake was her choice of illusion: the removal of Mia's arm
an infirmity that Esis had inflicted in real life on one of Mia's most belove
companions. But in reminding Mia of Amanda's plight, Esis had inadvertent
reminded her of Amanda's recovery: a heel-spin turn from helplessness to s
perheroics that had been so incredible, so inspiring, so very *Amanda*, that M
had never once thought of her tempic arms with anything other than pride.

So when Esis opened her portal of reprisal, just a few inches from Bobby
ear, Mia's panic brought about a startling change. A pair of strong white arm
unhindered by the limits of flesh and bone, grew out of her shoulder stum
and reached out toward the portal at the speed of thought.

Though Mia's first reflex was to slap the disc shut, a new plan sudden
occurred to her. Call it instinct. Call it vengeance. Call it divine inspiratio
Whatever it was, the notion overtook Mia before she even had time to que
tion it.

Instead of closing the portal by Bobby's head, she simply picked it up
her great white hands . . .

. . . and moved it to a better location.

All of it happened so fast and unexpectedly that Esis barely felt the pre
ence of her own time portal, six feet above the cafeteria roof, just a few inch
from the head of her physical self.

In her very last moment of lucid awareness, Esis suddenly recalled som
thing her husband had told her on more than one occasion: a warning not
underestimate the smallest and youngest Silver. But his words, like the bull
had passed right through her.

In one ear and out the other.

Mia crashed back into reality, her mind reuniting with all her body's ne
problems. Her temple was throbbing from where she hit the ground. H

uscles still reeled with disruption. And her right hand sported a new and oody hole that was wide enough to shove a pencil through.

But Esis had come out of the travelers' plane in even worse condition. Mia ruggled to process her crumpled heap of a body, her brown hair matted in a iick pool of blood, her coal-black eyes forced open in shock. Unblinking.

Did this really happen? her frozen expression seemed to ask. *Did you really 'll me?*

A loud crackling sound snapped Mia out of her stupor. She turned her ead and saw Evan punch his way out of a globe of thin ice. He stumbled out f the construct before it could collapse on him, then took a dazed look at the adaver on the roof.

He lifted his visor, just to confirm that it wasn't a glitch in its filters. Jh . . ."

Mia was glad to see him just as dumbstruck as her. Otherwise, she'd know iat this was just another one of Esis's mindfucks.

Evan blinked at Esis, stammering. "How did you . . . ? I mean . . ."

Mia struggled to her feet, then peeked over the edge of the roof. Fifty yards the east and two stories down, she saw Bobby limping toward the infir-iary with a piece of rebar as a cane.

It had all really happened. Her brother was still alive. And Esis wasn't.

Mia swallowed a shrill, maniacal laugh as she caught up with Ioni's mach-iations. The woman had been setting up this moment since June of last year, multi-link chain of causality that was convoluted enough to elude the Pel-tiers' foresight.

But was it even that complex in the end?

Inside that gun is the bullet that kills Esis Pelletier, Ioni had plainly told lia at the time. She hadn't been lying after all. She'd merely failed to mention iat it would take sixteen months for the projectile to reach its intended rget.

"Holy shit." Mia blinked at Esis in stammering awe. "I killed her."

Evan wasn't nearly as euphoric. "Mia . . ."

"No, no, no. This isn't a trick. I thought it was, but it's not."

"I know it's not."

"But?"

Evan looked away in misery before meeting her gaze again. "You only lled one of them."

Mia's face went white as she remembered the painfully obvious. It wa
entirely possible to kill a Pelletier, but not without—

"Look out!"

—consequences.

Something barreled into her from the unseen margins, grabbing her wit
inhuman speed before tackling her into a portal.

Mia's physical senses went topsy-turvy as she tumbled through the fol
of space. She came out blind on the other side, and was immediately ove
whelmed by new stimuli. The smell of salt water. The screech of hungr
seagulls. A pair of strong hands on her shoulders. She felt a soda-pop tingle a
over her skin that she immediately recognized as solis.

"No!"

Mia barely had a chance to open her eyes before a hard palm smacked h
to the ground. As the taste of blood filled her mouth, she looked down at th
dull brown wood beneath her and saw her right hand bleeding onto the plank

"Look at me," said a stern voice above her.

Mia recognized it immediately and had to fight back a bitter laugh. Fro
the moment he came to San Francisco, she'd been trying to catch his eye.

Now at last, she had Semerjean's attention. And all she had to do was ki
his fucking wife.

FORTY-SIX

"Which kind of pain would you prefer, physical or emotional?"

Nearly two years before the war in San Francisco, on a cool autumn nig
in Brooklyn, Semerjean had asked Mia a most peculiar question. But it wa
perfectly in line with the character he was playing: a brilliant but quirky Au
tralian boy who, like the rest of the Silvers, had been rendered an orphan b
the Pelletiers. After three months together on the strange new world, David
companions had gotten used to his social eccentricities. Mia in particular ha
been repeatedly subjected to his out-of-the-blue hypotheticals.

She turned onto her side with a wry little grin. "I'm sorry. Are you offering
hurt me?"

"You know what I'm asking," David said. "I'm curious to hear your answer
ecause I'm conflicted on it myself. If I was forced to choose between those
vo kinds of pain, I'm not sure which one I'd pick."

Mia eyed him quizzically. "I assume you mean a lot of pain, not just a pa-
er cut or—"

"Unbearable amounts," David confirmed. "The kind that breaks the heart
r body."

She rolled onto her back again and gazed up at the crescent moon. It had
een a week since they'd moved into Peter's four-story brownstone, and they
ere still getting used to its layout. The garage was in the attic, of all crazy
aces, with a sliding roof that opened to the sky. Against Peter's advice (they
ere still federal fugitives, after all, and the Deps had cameras flying all about
ie city), Mia and David draped a blanket over the top of Peter's aerovan and
ad their own little campout under the stars.

For David, it was just a way to fight his growing case of cabin fever. But
r Mia, who'd survived more shit than any teenager had a right to, it was a
iance to embrace the miracle of life with the world's most wondrous boy.

"Huh." Mia retreated into her thoughts. They'd already covered every other
pic, from the subjugation of droids in *Star Wars,* to the identity of Jack the
ipper, to the suspected root cause of Zack's snoring. But the pain question?
oy, that merited some thought.

"I once woke up in the middle of dental surgery," Mia said. "Not my hap-
est memory."

David cringed with sympathy. "I imagine not."

"That same year, I found out that one of my friends was only pretending to
ke me so she could cheat off my math tests and stay out of summer school. I
as in a bathroom stall when I heard her. She was, like, 'Oh God. I can't wait
ntil finals so I can be done with Mia. She's *so* boring. It's like talking to my
randparents.'"

Mia scoffed at herself. "Just thinking about it makes me want to cry, even
iough I've been through so much worse. That thing at the dentist? I was over
in a day. But what Laura said will probably keep on hurting for the rest of
iy stupid life."

She looked to David with a self-effacing smirk. "There's my sad and ram-
ing answer."

He smiled at her with enough reverence to make her whole body tingle. " wasn't sad or rambling. It was wonderful."

"Wonderful?"

"I could pose that question to a thousand people. None of them would b as thoughtful and honest as you just were. To get so much insight from a pe son so young is just . . . extraordinary. You have no idea how special you are

While Mia's spirits could have floated up through the roof, past the star and straight on to Heaven, David merely shook his head. "That girl was wron on every level. You're a brilliant conversationalist."

He rolled onto his side with a doleful look. "Talking with you is one of th few things that keeps me sane."

That night, as Mia slept in her ruddy little bedroom and dreamed a drea of sweet romance, a half-inch portal opened high over her bed and deposite a note from a future self:

> That night with "David" that you cherish so much is going to hurt like hell within a year. It'll be the most agonizing fucking memory you have, and it'll never stop playing in your head. Because you'll know full well that he never found you special. He sure as hell never thought you were smart or interesting.

Like all the notes that warned Mia about Semerjean, the Pelletiers ha burned it in transit. The paper snowed down on her as a hundred black flake while the Mia Farisis in a billion dark futures continued to howl in rage.

Semerjean hadn't wasted any time on greetings. Upon teleporting Mia Fisherman's Wharf, two and a half miles north of Prior Circle, he'd squelche her power with solis, torn off her helmet, and then examined the sorry state her right hand. Though he wasn't a doctor or augur like Esis, he saw the cop ous amount of blood she was losing and knew full well that she could pass o at any moment.

He couldn't have that now, could he?

With a wave of his finger, he sent a small but intense blast of heat into h hand, enough to cauterize the wound from front to back. Her scream cause every seagull in earshot to flee.

Mia clutched her hand, her thoughts bubbling over with fury.

"Look at me," said Semerjean.

Mia kept her dark, wet eyes on the pier planks. "Fuck you."

A tempic tendril extended from his hand and clamped her face like a vise. Vhen it forced her head upward, she didn't resist. If she struggled, he'd only nake it hurt more.

"The people of my era live a multithreaded existence," Semerjean informed her. "We don't just experience one string of time. Our consciousness xpands simultaneously across millions."

Mia hocked a gob of spit onto the base of his tendril. Semerjean shoved er head against a wooden post before retracting his tempis into his arm.

"My point, dear Mia, is that my wife's still alive in the majority of these trings. I can see her, touch her, *love* her whenever I want. Do you understand hat I'm telling you?"

He advanced on Mia, his perfect teeth bared in a snarl. "You took *nothing* om me."

Mia met and matched his seething gaze. "Then why are you so pissed?"

"Because . . ." Semerjean stopped himself, then chuckled. "I forgot that we aven't spoken in ages. It feels strange considering all the time I spent with Iannah."

He retreated a few yards down the pier and took in the surroundings. Unl recently, Fisherman's Wharf had a been garish little tourist trap: nearly iree dozen food and souvenir stands using lumic and aural gimmickry to ompete for attention. But the proprietors had been quick and thorough in eir evacuations, leaving nothing behind but the empty wooden husks of eir businesses. Now the wharf had returned to its quaint historical roots. ist the seals, the seagulls, and the sound of lapping waves.

Semerjean stuffed his hands into his pockets and rocked on his feet in ontemplation. "I bet you think that they were all lies," he said to Mia. "The ompliments I gave you."

"Of course they fucking were."

"They weren't," he insisted. "It's only the worst actors and politicians who uild their myths from scratch. The rest of us start from a foundation of uth, and the truth is that I adored you. You were preternaturally wise for our age, and you were a consistent voice of reason among our more . . . imulsive friends."

While he gazed out onto the water, Mia slowly reached for the gun in her olster. The bastard may have ruined her dominant right hand, but she'd ent dozens of hours in the underland's gun range learning how to shoot ith her left one.

"Still, you had your issues," Semerjean said. "Your woeful lack of self-esteem got tiresome rather quickly. You wasted months on surly notes from the future when you could have taught yourself how to teleport. Imagine al the trouble we could have avoided in those early months. I could have quietl guided your portals."

Mia winced when she popped the latch on her holster. *Too loud. Be carefu*

"And then, of course, you developed a crush on me," Semerjean contin-ued. "My wife found it amusing, but I knew it would inevitably lead to trouble Your bitterness. Your resentment."

He did a quick heel-turn and cast another line of tempis at her. It yanke the gun out of her left hand, breaking her index finger while hurling th weapon into the bay.

"Your bad decisions."

Mia shrieked again as a new pain overtook her. Semerjean was determine to crack her into pieces before killing her, and there was little she could d to stop him. All her wrath, all her training, just to have it end this way. wasn't fair.

Suck it up, said the Zack in her head. *The universe gave you a freebie wit Esis. There's no way in hell it'll let you kill two Pelletiers.*

At least not without consequences, Mia thought. She still had a grenade o the back of her belt, and enough working fingers to pull the pin.

But she'd have to wait for him to get real close. This wasn't a trick she' survive.

Semerjean sighed at her. "You ask me why I'm *pissed*, to use your crud vernacular. I'm pissed because you had the most potential."

Mia shot him a baleful look. "To get knocked up by a Gotham boy."

"To understand our mission!" he yelled. "I explained it all to you last Jun Everything we were planning. All our hopes and aspirations."

"I don't give a fuck what you want!"

Semerjean nodded with a bitter laugh. "Of course you don't. It's just ever life on Earth."

"*Your* Earth," Mia shouted. "How the hell did you expect me to care whe you didn't care about mine?"

"Grow up," said Semerjean. "When we explained it to the Jades, they un-derstood perfectly."

"Your Jades are nothing but slaves."

"I'm talking about the originals. The ones who just died in Lárnach. They oined us of their free will, because they were able to—"

"Oh, shut the fuck up already," Mia said. "You'll never get me to see you ne way you see yourself. And you want to know why?"

"You're in no position—"

"It's because he doesn't exist!" Mia hollered. "This noble man you think ou are? He's even less real than David!"

Here he comes, Mia thought as she gripped the grenade behind her back. *'m sorry, Carrie.*

Semerjean dashed back into her personal space, livid. "As opposed to this ew role you're playing: the angry and indomitable veteran."

"My anger's *real.*"

"I have no doubt."

He snatched the grenade before she could pull the pin and dissolved it in a stful of mortis.

"But after all this time, you're still just an amateur."

He grabbed a metal bar with a tempic prong, then raised Mia's right arm bove her. She barely had a chance to protest before he bent the bar around er forearm, securing her to the wooden pole behind her.

Mia shrieked as the pressure threatened to crack her bones. "You mother-ucker!"

"This salty new language of yours is not an improvement."

"Fuck you!" She laughed through tears and agony. "Your bitch wife let an *mateur* kill her!"

"And this is what you're reduced to." Semerjean shook his head. "A scream-ng, helpless mass of rage, no wiser than an infant. If Amanda could see you ow, she'd weep."

Even in her frenzied state, Mia could see his hateful strategy. It wasn't nough to kill her for what she did to Esis. It wasn't enough to break her bones nd cook her hand from the inside. No, Semerjean was determined to smash very last scaffold that was holding her together. He remembered exactly hich kind of pain she dreaded more.

But he hadn't done himself any favors by mentioning Amanda. All it did as remind Mia of her noble last words, delivered by holographic recording n the God's Eye.

"I was tempted to talk about Semerjean," Amanda had said from her little

gray room. "The anger you feel and the effect it's had on you. But you've hear
it a dozen times from other people. You don't need to hear it from me. And i
the long two years we've known each other, you've proven to me again an
again that you can take care of yourself. The last thing anyone in their righ
mind can call you, after everything you've been through, is a child."

At the time, Mia had been too busy crying to fully process what Amand
was saying. But when played back in her memory, she could parse and fe
every word.

"Do what you think is right for you," Amanda had concluded. "You war
to keep hating him? You have more than enough reason. You want to forgiv
him? More power to you. My only hope—and this is completely hypocritic
considering what I'm about to do—is that you don't throw your life away ju
to stick it to the Pelletiers. You may not be a child anymore, but you still hav
decades left to you."

She'd given Mia one last smile before the recording ended. "If you're th
good at sixteen, just imagine how you'll be at sixty."

Semerjean tilted his head, confused by Mia's new and inexplicable pois
She looked to him with calm brown eyes, her voice as steady as ever. "Are yo
the one who killed her?"

"Who, Amanda?"

"Yeah. Who else?"

"Why does that matter?"

"I'll take that as a yes."

"I was not," Semerjean flatly replied. "My son committed the final deed. B
if he hadn't done it, I gladly would have, especially after what she said to me

"Why? What did she say?"

Semerjean paused in brief debate, as if Mia were employing a canny ne
strategy. In reality, she had no plan or secret knowledge. No time to wait f
the solis to wear off, and no more hidden weapons. She fully expected to d
on this wharf.

But she needed one last bit of information before she could finally clo
the book on Semerjean.

"She called me the worst Pelletier," he admitted. "As if I hadn't saved h
life a dozen times over. As if I hadn't freed her sister from captivity. I'm t
only reason that any of you ever got to see this world and travel it. I gave yo
freedom. I gave you *life*. And how am I repaid for it? With nonstop insults ar
invective. Certainly not gratitude."

Mia suddenly flashed back to Daphne Jones, a senator's aide from Con-
ecticut. The poor woman had suffered her own monster nemesis, the stepfa-
er who'd done far more harm to her than Semerjean had ever inflicted on
lia. Yet somehow Daphne had managed to make peace with him, even when
e'd failed to show a hint of contrition.

"Forgiveness," Daphne had told Mia, "and I mean the honest-to-God,
oul-cleansing kind, doesn't ever come on demand. You just have to wait for
e moment to find you. And when it does, you can't fight it. You have to let it
ı or you'll never be free."

At long last, Mia could feel the moment knocking, an emancipation that
ad nothing to do with absolution. Just pity. She was finally ready to let Se-
ıerjean go, and all it took was to see him at his lowest point. To whine about
eing unappreciated by the Silvers, after helping to destroy their world, was
bout as pathetic and deplorable as a person could get. He was broken on a
early cosmic scale. Hopeless.

And *this* was the man she'd declared her mortal enemy?

Mia nearly laughed at how simple it all seemed in the end. Semerjean
asn't worth her wrath *or* forgiveness. He wasn't worth another moment of
ıought.

"Okay," Mia said in a staid and even tone. "You can kill me now."

Semerjean blinked at her in bewilderment. "What?"

"I'm all out of moves," Mia admitted. "You're the one in control. You can
ill me right now or let the Cataclysm do it. Or you can stay here with me and
e can both die. It's your call."

Semerjean shook a finger at her. "Okay. You're stalling. You must have
eard something from Ioni."

"Semerjean—"

"You are *not* this calm without a reason!"

"I have a reason," Mia assured him. "It's just none of your business."

"Quiet." Semerjean looked around in sudden apprehension, then chuck-
d. "Oh, I get it now. It's not Ioni. It's *him*."

"What? Who?"

"Don't be coy," said Semerjean. "He's even more transparent than you are.
nd as usual, he's failed to think things through."

He extended a tempic blade from his fingertip, pressed it to Mia's neck,
ıen yelled at someone that neither he or Mia could see. "I can feel your aura,
ou idiot! If you even try—"

The blade suddenly retracted from Mia's neck as Semerjean bounce around the boardwalk in a shifted blur. From Mia's perspective, he almo looked comical: a cartoon character whose foot had been set on fire.

But on closer inspection, she could see what was really happening. Seme jean was struggling to stay alive amid an onslaught of floating portals. The opened and closed all around him, threatening to tear him apart like sa blades.

Ten seconds after it started, the barrage ended. Winded, sweating, Seme jean crouched on the pier, his fierce blue eyes locked on Mia. "For a man wit no feet, he sure is spry."

She'd already suspected that he was talking about Peter, but she hadn been sure until now. Had her senses not been smothered under a blanket solis, she would have felt every bit of his energy signature, and the enhance amount of power behind it. Whatever Ioni had infused into Peter's headban it was strong.

After another high-speed round of portal dodging, Semerjean de-shifte and aimed his howling rage at the sky.

"Coward! Show yourself! Let me kill you in front of your—"

Peter dropped down onto Semerjean from seemingly out of nowhere. Th portal came and went so quickly that Mia had barely caught a glimpse of it.

Before she could even say his name, Peter pinned Semerjean to the plan boards. He broke his nose with a well-placed punch, then pressed a thum into his right eye.

Mia flinched at Semerjean's unholy shriek. In a better mood, she mig have felt sorry for him, but she was too busy worrying about Peter.

"You wanted me?" he asked Semerjean through gritted teeth. "Here am, *boy*."

Like Mia, Peter had spent months in the company of "David," enough spot a weakness behind his acting performance. When Semerjean had lo two fingers in a gunfight, he'd cursed and yelled at everyone around hi even the friends who were trying to help. At the time, it had seemed like a ra tantrum for David, but on hindsight it made perfect sense. Semerjean cam from a thoroughly advanced society where nobody bled or lost fingers. Th were too smart, too prescient, too cushioned by technology to suffer such a archaic infirmity.

Simply put: for all his strengths, the man was a real wuss about pain.

His thumb still embedded in Semerjean's eye, Peter placed his other hand n his chest.

Mia's heart hammered in excitement and dread. She knew that all Peter eeded was one last moment to open a portal inside Semerjean's heart. But if er experiences on this world had taught her anything, it was no grand deed ver came too easily. There was always a hitch. Always a consequence.

Indeed, the very same portal assault that had worn down Semerjean had so exhausted Peter. His arm and his power moved one second too late to revent his enemy from attacking.

Mia blanched as Semerjean stabbed Peter through the chest with a three- ot tempic blade. It popped out the other side of his warsuit, its white tip overed in blood and shredded fabric.

"No!" Mia struggled against her makeshift manacle, her bones shooting ghtning bolts of pain up her arm.

Don't, Peter told her from the back of her thoughts. His psychic voice was faint and distorted that she could barely make it out.

"Peter—"

It's all right, darling, he silently assured her. *I got this.*

Mia couldn't even imagine the strength it took for a dying man to reach er from the portal network, punching all the way through her solic haze. But en what was Peter if not a man of miracles? The last survivor of his Irish an. The indomitable conscience of the Gothams. A man who'd kept Mia d her friends alive for months when no one else would help them.

Peter pressed his thumb deeper into Semerjean's eye, enough to make him ream all over again and turn his tempic blade rubbery. He then waved his ee hand in a circle, a shaky little gesture that nonetheless triggered a portal.

Mia's face went white. "Oh no . . ."

Peter's disc came to life like a brand-new moon: a twelve-foot vertical hole the air, with a ring of white fire around the edge. All the loose papers and od wrappers within thirty feet began to congregate toward the portal like orshippers.

A time door, Mia thought. *Peter's making a time door.*

From the way he struggled, Semerjean realized the same thing. But the umb in his eye locked the rest of his powers behind a thick glass wall of gony.

Please apologize to Hannah for me, Peter told Mia through their psychic

link. *I wanted to help her raise our boy. But there'll be no future for any of u*
while this bastard breathes.

While the nearby litter flew into the portal, the two men had yet to mov

See my sons through this, Peter implored Mia. *None of this will mean*
blessed thing unless they get a chance to grow old.

Mia wept from her shackled post as, at long last, the vacuum of the port
began to shake its creator.

Peter looked at Mia through tight, wet eyes. *I'd feel a damn sight better*
you lived, too.

"Please!"

Daughter of my heart.

"Peter!"

That's what you are.

Semerjean let out one last cry before his body lifted up from the whar
Before Mia could shout or even think, she watched the two men wash aw
into the portal, first as silhouettes, then as nothing.

Mia fell limp at the base of the pole, weeping as the gateway swirled shu
If time kept on moving and the war kept progressing, she couldn't feel a hi
of it. She had seconds, minutes, *hours* to reckon with everything that had ju
happened. Yet her mind refused to take comfort in Semerjean's fate. Not wit
the cost that came with it.

She heard the distinct whirr of an aerocycle engine and saw its blur
streak in the sky. It landed on the wooden planks, just fifteen feet away fro
her, before its rider de-shifted and took off her helmet. Mia didn't need to s
her face to recognize her. She was the only one on the battlefield who wo
coveralls instead of a warsuit.

Felicity rushed over to her, a crowbar in her hand. "Brace yourself, kidd
I gotta work quickly, not gently."

"How did you—" Mia shrieked in pain as the crowbar put more pressu
on her fractured wrist.

"Peter," Felicity explained. "He told me where you'd be. Said you'd need
ride back, and fast."

Her expression went dark as she pried Mia loose. "I saw what happene
I'm so sorry."

She caught Mia in her arms before she could hit the boardwalk. "Whoa.
got you."

Mia wrapped her arms around Felicity and cried over her shoulder. In nore perfect world, Peter would have been her ride back to Prior Circle. Did e know that he'd die fighting Semerjean, or did he just call Felicity as a ackup measure?

Mia had no idea. But she just figured out where he went.

"The party," she said through choking sobs. "He jumped all the way back the party."

"What are you . . ." Felicity's mouth dropped open as she caught up with Iia's thought process. "Oh my God."

Ten weeks prior in the underland, at the two-year anniversary of another orld's apocalypse, a pair of charred and unrecognizable men had burst into e clubhouse through a time portal. Though Mia had felt the aura of a future eter behind the temporal breach, she'd only partially opened her mind to the ossibility that Peter had also been one of the casualties.

"It's not worth dwelling on," Peter had told her at the time. "It's just one ture out of many."

Except that one future had become Mia's present, and she would have one anything to avoid it.

"Come on," said Felicity. "We have to get back."

It wasn't until they lifted off the ground that Felicity fully processed Mia's ews. "So Semerjean died ten weeks ago, and we didn't even know it."

Mia held her from behind and nodded. "I don't even think he knew it."

"Well, if anyone deserved to die by portal—"

"No," Mia said over her. "He didn't."

"Wow. You're the last person I'd expect to hear that from."

Felicity had misunderstood Mia. She wasn't talking about what Semerjean eserved. She was merely disputing his cause of death. Mia had been right ere on the clubhouse floor, ten weeks before, when Semerjean opened a gray id cloudy eye and grabbed Mia by the wrist. He might have even managed to urt her, too, if a quick-acting tempic hadn't stabbed him through the head ith a bladed tendril.

Felicity turned her head in bafflement as Mia laughed deliriously. "What?"

Mia didn't have the mind to explain it. But on the short trip back to Prior ircle, she chewed on the notion like candy.

It wasn't the time portal that had killed Semerjean in the end. It was manda.

FORTY-SEVEN

In her thirty-six hours of prewar preparation, Melissa had placed a lot of strang objects around Prior Circle. Ioni had provided her with hundreds of mystify ing gewgaws from her era: crystal spheres, metal cubes, a couple of rods pure white stone. None of them came with labels or instructions, just mini ture global positioners that told Melissa precisely where each one needed go, right down to the vertical inch.

"They're just seeds," Ioni had said. "All you have to do is plant then They'll do the rest."

Indeed, at first light on Thursday, just two hours before the start of th war, all the cryptic little gadgets of Prior Circle came to life at the same tim Some of them grew into geodesic shelters, while others evolved into higl functioning computers. Several of them formed the framework of Ioni's pro tective shields. A few became mere water fountains, a transformation s mundane and anti-cathartic that Felicity had laughed herself hoarse.

But there was still one seed that had yet to bear fruit: a black metal or that was large enough to hold two people, and heavy enough to make crack in the concrete. The moment Melissa had rolled it into the heart of the centr plaza, the grass swallowed it like quicksand, and it was never seen again.

Not in that form, at least.

At 9:21, nearly sixteen minutes into the conflict, and seventeen second after the death of Peter Pendergen, the ground of Prior Circle began to quak The asphalt shattered as twelve narrow spires emerged from the earth in clockwork circle that encompassed the central plaza. Like the sphere they' all hatched from, the towers were made of a cloudy black metal that didr provide a hint of reflection. They merely bloomed into the sky as monolith cylinders, until they were each ninety feet tall.

Melissa watched unblinkingly through the monitors of the commar center as the spires became the dominant new eyesore of the battlefield.

"Please tell me those are ours," Auberon implored her.

"They're ours," Melissa confirmed. "But you still won't like what they do

Auberon didn't need a second hint. "The Cataclysm."

"Shit," said Meredith. "When's it starting?"

Melissa pointed to Ioni's countdown clock, which had just reached the vo-minute mark.

"Oh my God." Meredith clutched her grandfather's hand, her one good e fixed on the timer. "We're all going to die here."

neo didn't share her bleak view of the situation. After checking in with Evan d Felicity, he had enough good news to warrant another broadcast.

"Esis and Semerjean are dead," he announced over the comms. "It's not a ick. They're really gone. They've been erased from every possible future, d no one's going to miss them."

He lifted his visor and rubbed his aching eyes. The thermal/electromag-tic filter was giving him a migraine. "But we can't celebrate yet. Azral's still it there, and he's real mad. There are also ten or twelve Jades still running ound. If you're as sick of them as I am, please, do whatever you can to take em down."

He looked for Hannah on the monitors and found her just outside the feteria, holding Yasmeen in a field of extreme slowtime. A Jade had cut the ifter's carotid artery. She would be dead in seconds without reversal.

Fortunately, Hannah had bought her the time she needed for Charlene to t a Majee healer to her. Theo could already feel the storm clouds moving ay from Yasmeen's strings.

But she wasn't the one he was worried about.

Theo opened a private radio channel. "Hannah . . ."

She kept a vigilant watch on Charlene and the healer as they tended to smeen's health. "I'm here. Is Mia okay?"

"She's fine," said Theo. "She's on her way back with Felicity."

"But?"

Theo dipped his head in sorrow. Even his closest friends on the old world d complained that he was hard to read. Yet Hannah was able to draw a nole tale from the tone of his voice and his pauses. The only blank left to fill s the name of the main character.

"Oh no." Hannah shut her eyes and pressed her fingertips to her temple. eter or Zack?"

"Listen—"

"Peter or Zack?"

"It was Peter," Theo said, his voice flecked with grief. "He's gone."

Hannah's knees buckled. She struggled to regain herself. It had bare
been four minutes since she lost her sister. Now she had to face a future wit
out the father of her child. She couldn't let the news sink all the way into h
She had to put it on ice, put it on ice, just put it on ice so she didn't fall
pieces.

"I'm so sorry," Theo said. "There was nothing we could—"

"But Zack's okay."

Theo checked Zack's health screen for the hundredth time. "He's alive,"
said. "He's not answering anyone's calls."

"Is he hurt?"

Theo vented a deep and doleful sigh. "You know exactly how he's hurt."

Hannah fought back another flood of tears. "Where is he?"

"You can't help him," Theo said. "Just keep doing what you're doing. We'
so close, Hannah. It's—"

"I have to go."

She disconnected the link, then steadied herself with a breath. *One mc
hit*, her ailing mind warned her. *One more loss and you're done. Finished.*

"Hannah!"

She barely had a chance to register Ofelia's voice before a burly male Ja
barreled into her, knocking her to the ground and cracking her visor.

Hannah's vision flipped back to its default setting, rendering her attack
invisible again.

"Shit!"

"No!" While Ofelia could still see the enemy on top of Hannah, her o
tions were frustratingly limited. If she'd still had her portals, she could ha
cut the brute in half with a thought. But her magic had seemingly left h
forever, without so much as a goodbye.

Desperate, she pulled a throwing knife from her holster and chucked it
the Jade's head. It merely bounced off his helmet and embedded itself in t
grass.

Luckily, Hannah had seen where the knife careened, and cast a narrc
cone of slowtime in its direction. The Jade turned visible and fell over dea
his face rifted black inside his helmet.

"Christ." Ofelia helped Hannah back to her feet. "You okay?"

"Yeah. Thank you."

"Don't. That was pitiful." Ofelia took a glum look at her discarded knife.
should have learned how to shoot a gun."

"Guys!" Rosario beckoned them from the nursery shelter. "Get in here. urry!"

Oh God. Hannah's thoughts turned white in motherly fear, even as she ckoned the obvious. If there was a Jade in there slicing up babies, Rosario ouldn't be waving at the door. She'd be at the creature's jugular with her eth fully bared, like any sane mother would do.

Hannah rushed into the crystal dome and was relieved to see all seven fants resting safely in their bassinets.

"Just get inside," she urged Ofelia. "Quickly!"

The moment Ofelia crossed the threshold, Rosario sealed the nursery. The oor blended into its diamantine surroundings without even a hint of a seam.

"What's going on?" Hannah asked Rosario.

"You saved my life. Now I'm saving yours."

"What are you talking about?"

"Azral," said Rosario. "When the last Jade dies, he'll come down hard. nd he'll come for you first. I've seen it."

Rosario looked to Ofelia. "And you don't have your portals anymore. ou're safer in here."

"With the babies?" Ofelia crossed her arms with a surly pout. "Is that what u think of me?"

Rosario shook her head. "I think of you as my sister. Why else would I this?"

"But—"

"We won the war," Rosario insisted. "It happened the moment those tows went up. What's started now can't be stopped. The only variables left are 10 lives and who dies."

Hannah didn't feel comfortable with Rosario's plan, as prescient as it ight have been. "There are still people out there who need us."

"And what about the ones in here?" Rosario gestured at the bassinets. Ialf these children have already lost their mothers. You want yours to next?"

Hannah hesitantly moved to Robert's crib and pulled him into her arms. ne sight of his bright blue eyes—his *father's* blue eyes—was enough to break e levee inside of her and drench her face in tears.

Robert Peter Given, the boy said in her thoughts. *I've heard worse.*

"Just stay here," Rosario begged her. "Both of you. Please."

Ofelia crinkled her nose at the bassinets. "Smells like shit in here."

"They're *babies*," Rosario said.

Hannah's earpiece hissed with a new connection, a faint and crackli
voice that was distorted by temporal conversion.

"*—you hear me?*"

Despite all the aural artifacts, Hannah easily recognized the caller. "Mia

"I'm almost back at the circle," she said. "But in case we don't conne
there's something you need to know."

Hannah closed her eyes. "I heard. Theo told me."

"I'm not talking about Peter," Mia said. "I'm talking about Azral. Som
thing Semerjean said about him."

"What?"

Mia's response was obscured in a rash of static garble. Hannah raised h
voice. "Mia, I lost you. What did you just say?"

"I said *he's the one who killed Amanda.*"

Hannah felt a cold squeeze around her heart.

"If I'm not back in time, you kill him," Mia demanded. "He can't get o
alive."

"Mia—"

The line went dead. Hannah yanked off her helmet and threw it to t
floor, a loud enough gesture to make Eden cry.

"Sorry," Hannah said.

Rosario cradled her daughter in her arms. "You don't have to be sorry. Yo
just have to stay."

Hannah sat on the edge of a squat crystal chair and held her son close
her chest. She could tell by the way his tiny eyes crinkled that he was mo
than a little tense. Maybe he already knew that his father was gone. Or may
he was just sensitive to his mother's hot dilemma.

Your father and aunt would want me to stay with you, Hannah said in h
thoughts.

Sounds about right, Robert Peter replied. *But if you had a chance to sa
Liam and Zack, I'm guessing they'd feel otherwise.*

"Fuck." Hannah's tortured thoughts swung back and forth in confli
Somewhere between all the *shoulds* and *shouldn'ts*, she imagined Azral Pel
tier, his face as cool and dispassionate as ever as he snuffed the last spark
life from Amanda.

Hannah's fingers clenched around the folds of her son's blanket as s
slowly began to ponder her third and worst option.

· · ·

y all reckoning, Theo should have been jubilant. The enemy horde had been duced to single digits, two godlike menaces had been neutralized forever, d Ioni's machine was finally coming to life. It just needed ninety-nine secds to finish its start-up process.

Yet the strings of the near future were filled with grief and peril, a nonstop ray of terrible visions that played in a high-speed montage. Worse, his foreght sported a strange new shadow around the edges, as if all the darkness of e next few minutes had become centered around him.

You're getting ahead of yourself, said a stern inner voice. *Focus on the probms right in front of you. Focus on* Azral.

By the time Theo checked the monitors again, the Jades had become nearly tinct. Thanks to the coordinated efforts of a dozen timebenders—a motley sortment of orphans, Gothams, and Majee—only two of the enemy grunts mained.

Well, one and nine-tenths. Stitch had caught one of the Jades on a bladed mpic tripwire and sent him tumbling across the concrete without the comny of his feet.

The young Copper followed him as he tried to crawl away, her boots leavg prints in his blood trail.

"Where you going?" Stitch asked him. "The foot store's closed. I checked."

"Just kill him already," See pleaded over the comm. "Don't drag this out."

"He's the one dragging," Stitch dryly replied. "I just want to hear him ream."

Melissa broke into their connection, livid. "You're a human being. *Act* e one."

Stitch yelled a Hebrew curse at Melissa, then stabbed the Jade in the head th a tendril.

"Don't talk to her like that!" See yelled at Melissa. "She's grieving!"

"We *all* are. It's no excuse."

As the last Jade fell to the sword of a Gotham swifter, Theo felt a flash of arm in his foresight. Rosario hailed him on the radio.

"Get down!" she told him.

"Take cover!" Theo yelled to everyone around him. "Now!"

The campus was rocked by a deafening *boom*, enough to shatter every winw in the cafeteria. Ceiling panels fell and broke against the floor. A light xture dropped onto the head of a Majee healer, knocking him unconscious.

Theo would have taken a blow to the head himself if a Jonathan hadı tackled him at the last second.

Melissa and Heath helped him back to his feet, while Meredith assiste her grandfather. "Is everyone all right?" Auberon asked.

Charlene burst into the command center in a windy dash. "What ha pened?"

Theo brushed the dust off his warsuit and looked out the broken windo "He's here."

If anything, Theo had understated the problem. Fifty copies of Azral floate around Ioni's shield, their hands glowing green with bright, withering lumi

"He's still after Ioni," Auberon noted. "Even now with his family dead."

Melissa reloaded her assault rifle. "He's always been a single-mind creature."

See looked to the health status screen of the shield. The Jades had alrea whittled its battery to a nub. At this rate, it would be gone in less than thir seconds. Azral would have nearly a full minute to extract his vengean on Ioni.

"We have to stop him!"

Stitch tried to impale one of the floating Azrals, but her tempic harpo passed right through him. The swifters didn't have any better luck with the weapons.

"They're lumic ghosts," Theo told them over the radio. "They can't hu you, but they can still hurt the shield."

"So what do we do?" Charlene and Meredith asked in rare unison.

Melissa looked to Auberon. "A lumic could potentially disrupt his ill sions, but all of ours are helping Ioni. How many do you have left?"

"None," said the old man, his dark eyes fixed on the health screens. "V just had three a moment ago."

Theo cursed under his breath. "He took them out in the sonic explosion. was strategy."

"Son of a bitch." Charlene grabbed an assault rifle from the wall mour "I'm going to kill him!"

"How?" Meredith asked her. "They're just phantoms."

"One of them has to be the real one!"

Theo shook his head. "They're all fake."

"How do you know?"

Melissa peeked out the shattered window and saw exactly what Theo was
oking at. "Because the real one's right there."

Azral stood on a burnt patch of grass, looking as dapper as ever in his gray
usiness suit. If he was nervous to be alone in enemy territory, he didn't show
. He merely loomed like a statue on his new stake of land, his arms crossed,
is harsh blue eyes locked firmly on the command center.

Theo was more thrown by his kinetic adornments: at least twenty metal
rbs the size of grapes, all orbiting around him at different trajectories. At
rst glance, he looked like a parody of science: the man-shaped nucleus of the
orld's largest atom.

It wasn't until the timebenders attacked him that Theo understood their
urpose. The spheres deflected everything his enemies could possibly throw
 him, from tempic spears to rifting cones to good old-fashioned gunfire. It
ll bounced off of Azral with ease.

Auberon cocked his head at Azral's curious choice of protection.
That's new."

"Yeah," said Meredith. "I would have expected him to use that aegis stuff
e showed us."

Only the augurs could see the strategy behind Azral's decision. Theo's
yes went wide as Stitch made a running leap toward Azral. "Wait!"

"No!" See shrieked.

Stitch had come at him in her finest regalia: a plate mail suit of tempic ar-
ior that was covered in spikes and surrounded by spinning blades. She was a
ving white blender, impenetrable and fierce.

But the moment her tempis came within a foot of the metal orbs, it all
ielted away in an instant. In Azral's presence, she was just Olivia Bassin: the
xteen-year-old Israeli extremist who'd been taught her whole life to fear de-
ions. On hindsight, all the talk of Palestinians had been nothing but propa-
inda. She hadn't faced true devilry until she came to this world.

Unfortunately for her, Azral was in no mood to hide behind a bubble
iield. He'd come to war in a new form of protection that allowed him to
ght back.

The flying spheres expanded their orbits as Azral grabbed Stitch by the
eck. He lifted her slender form off the ground, then drained all the color
om her skin.

See wept as Stitch continued to transform, from flesh to white flesh to a glimmering mineral substance. The girl had been crystallized from head t toe, all the way down to her bones.

Azral dropped Stitch's hardened corpse to the ground, where it broke int four jagged pieces.

The sound that came out of See's throat then—a banshee scream of over whelming grief—was enough to draw tears out of Theo. Truth be told, he' never much liked Stitch. The girl was combative and often cruel, and had shaky grasp of ethics at best.

But to See, she was a sister. The last of her Copper kin. Now the family tha Mother had built in Seattle had been reduced to one shattered young augur.

See fell to her knees, then sobbed into her hands. It wasn't until she hear a familiar voice that she dared to look up again.

"Nadiyah."

Heath met her gaze with big, wet eyes, his hand extended out to her. She' told him her real name more than two months ago, and he'd never said since. But he remembered it, just as much as he remembered his pain at be coming the last of the Golds.

See threw her arms around him and wept over his shoulder. "I can take this."

"I know."

"I can't do it anymore."

"Yes you can," Heath insisted. "If I can keep going, then so can you."

Theo was so lost in his own maudlin thoughts that he didn't hear Meliss and Charlene shouting. Before he knew it, he and Auberon were engulfed i thick vines of tempis and yanked through the window like dolls.

Charlene raised her rifle. "Grandpa!"

"Don't!" yelled Melissa. "You won't hurt Azral. You'll only hurt them."

Theo already felt like he was dying. Azral's tempis was constricting hi like a giant anaconda, making every breath a chore. It had only vaguely oc curred in the back of his mind that Azral had once been weak with tempis.

Not anymore, apparently. Not even a little.

Azral pulled Theo and Auberon into his field of swirling orbs, then stuc ied them both curiously.

"We had an agreement," he said to Auberon. "You broke it."

Auberon moaned and wheezed in his grip, his creased brow dripping wit sweat. "Point of fact . . . we never . . . signed anything."

"I don't care about contracts," Azral flatly declared. "I care about hono

g promises. So this is now my promise to you: after I kill you and your be-
ved granddaughters, I'll go to Japan and slaughter the rest of your kin, the
-called Majee who were too genetically weak to matter."

Auberon's eyes went round. "Are you truly so cruel?"

"No worse than those who have ruined my life's work," Azral said, "over
eaningless moral objections."

"Meaningless," Theo mocked. "You're worse than cruel. You're clueless."

He jerked his head at the nearest black tower. "You hear that noise, Azral?
hat means the damage you caused to this world is being fixed. Even you
n't stop it now."

Azral scoffed. "The fate of this Earth is of no concern to me. Haven't I
ade that clear?"

He turned Theo toward the shield dome, which had finally begun to
cker under the assault of Azral's doppelgängers.

"I reserve my wrath for the people who've wronged me," Azral said. "Start-
g with Ioni, and ending with you. If you're lucky, I'll let you live long enough
watch—"

Theo cut him off with an unexpected laugh. Both Azral and Auberon
ed him strangely.

"Have you gone mad?" Azral idly inquired. "Or is this another one of your
olish gambits?"

It was actually neither. Theo was just getting ahead of himself, as usual,
d laughing at a joke that hadn't been told yet.

Soon, Azral began to get wind of the gag, though he didn't find it funny at
. "He dares?"

Theo nodded, still laughing. "Guess so."

Soon enough, a willowy woman came tumbling off the roof of the cafete-
building. She landed on the ground with a loud, messy *thump*, her eyes
ide open, her hair matted in blood.

Azral looked to the mangled body of Esis, then upward at the man who'd
rown her.

"There's my Yelp review for your mirror room," Evan shouted. "Asshole."

Under any other circumstance, Theo wouldn't have laughed. He would
ve considered it savage to defile the corpse of a man's mother, even if that
an was indeed an asshole.

But on a day like today, when so many good people had died for bad
asons, it had just seemed like a perfect response. It was the kind of mean gag

that would hit a man through his armor. The kind that would shatter his str
tegic reasoning and leave him stammering with rage.

More important, and more hilarious to Theo, it was the kind of gag th
would seize Azral's attention while his defense system crumbled to pieces.

Before the first metal orb could even hit the grass, a tempic spike hit Azr
in the shoulder blade and drilled halfway into his collarbone. He holler
in pain and dropped his two captives, just in time to dodge a second flyin
spike.

Azral resummoned his defensive metal orbs, then spun around to face h
new assailant.

Ioni glared back at him from the center of the plaza, with thirty-six lumi
and thermics behind her.

"I was aiming for your heart," she admitted to Azral. "My fault for assum
ing you had one."

She squeezed her right hand into a fist and stopped the clock of the worl
"So now I guess we have to do it the hard way."

They had finished their task thirty-two seconds ahead of schedule, a feat th
even Ioni had never dared to predict. She had hoped to have her machin
powered up at least ten to twelve seconds before the barrier fell, but *this*? Th
was a windfall. This was Christmas in October.

Ioni's hardworking team of timebenders had exceeded her wildest expe
tations, enough to make her feel even worse about the way she'd treated ther
Instead of cracking a whip when they fell behind, she'd brought their battere
minds into the God's Eye and showed them the death of a loved one. Flyn
Whitten got a front-row view of a witchstick killing his brother. Sage Lee w
forced to watch a Jade run a tempic blade through his boyfriend. Matt Ham
blin had received a posthumous recording from Caleb, informing him in a
vance that he was now the last Platinum, and that he better not fucking die.

While any sane leader would question Ioni's tactics, she'd gotten exact
the result she wanted from her helpers. In each case, their grief had harden
into rage, and their rage had become raw power. For Liam Pendergen a
Carrie Bloom, Ioni's two strongest thermics, the news of their fathers' viole
deaths had turned them both into raging novas. Their hot and cold vengean
could have brought down half a city if it hadn't been properly channeled.

But from the way they'd dropped to the ground and wept, Ioni feared th
she'd gone too far.

"I'm sorry," she'd told them fifteen seconds ago, while Azral was murdering citch. "What I did was an act of abuse, and no good intention can excuse it."

Liam glared at her through drenched blue eyes. "Fuck yourself."

"And twice for me," Carrie said. "We don't care about your apologies. We ıst want to get out there and fight."

Ioni glanced out at the plaza. "Azral's all that's left."

"Then let us kill him!" Liam yelled.

Ioni had already been working on it, but it was easier said than done. Even ı his unhinged wrath, the man's prescient instincts were just as sharp as ers, maybe sharper. Ioni had to approach him just right or he'd see her coming from a mile away.

While Azral had been occupied with the ill treatment of his mother's ɔrpse, Ioni had popped her own shield dome, then made a shifted attack on is true form. She'd had a split-second chance to sneak around Azral's foreght, and an even smaller window of opportunity to land a fatal blow.

Unfortunately, she'd hit one mark and missed the other, leaving Azral ive but wounded. Ioni didn't need her prescience to know the consequences f her failure. There were more casualties coming in the last minute of the ar. More sacrifices.

rom Theo's perspective, the entire fight had occurred in a nanosecond. One ıoment, Ioni and Azral were facing each other. The next, they were flying in ɔposite directions, as if an invisible bomb had exploded between them. They ɔth writhed on their backs in agony.

"Ioni!" Theo rushed over to her. "Are you okay?"

Though she looked as clean and healthy as ever, she cried like she'd just een eviscerated. Her breath came out in shallow wheezes. She struggled to eak through quivering lips.

"I missed my shot," she told Theo. "I had one chance to kill him and I ew it."

"Ioni—"

"You have to get him out of here!"

All the thermics and lumics had already advanced on Azral, but it was too te. He'd finally swapped his floating toys for an impenetrable dome of aegis.

From the way Azral teetered inside his yellow forcefield, it seemed Ioni ıd hurt him as much as he'd hurt her.

"What happened?" Theo asked her.

Even if she'd had the time to explain it, she couldn't have. Her battle wit
Azral had taken them all around the existential spectrum, from the God's E
to the travelers' plane to a dozen realms of existence that had yet to be disco
ered in this era. She and Azral could have been at it for days, *weeks,* chippin
away at each other's defenses while expressing their mutual loathing. The
was no common ground for them to find, no frame of reference that coul
help them understand each other. All Ioni got for her trouble, aside from
thousand new cuts and contusions on her psyche, was the firm belief that th
people of Azral's world were just as broken as the ones from hers.

Ioni clasped Theo's arm. "You have to push him out beyond the tower
fast. If he's still here when the walls come up, he won't leave any survivors."

"Shit." By the time Theo checked on Azral again, a crowd of two doze
timebenders had formed around his barrier, attacking it with every pow
and weapon they had. If Theo wasn't so harried, he might have stopped to ap
preciate the flipped dynamic. Azral had taken Ioni's place as the primary ta
get, while Theo's allies chipped away at the shield with all the quiet ferocity
the Jades.

On Theo's command, his allies all moved to one side of Azral's forcefie
and concentrated their power attacks. They soon succeeded in pushing bot
the bubble and its occupant a few inches toward the edge of the plaza.

The hum from Ioni's black towers was only getting louder. "We have
pick up the pace," Theo said. "Time's running out."

Melissa had been watching the effort from the beginning and could easi
see which timebenders were making the best progress.

"Tempics and lumics only," she ordered. "Thermics and turners, you kee
your energies on his shield. We can't give him a moment of respite."

While Meredith and Heath sent their tempic men to assist, Charle
joined Theo and Melissa in the center of the plaza.

"Is that it?" she asked. "After all the shit he's done, we're just going to sho
him the door?"

"He's lost everyone and everything that matters to him," said Theo.

Charlene crossed her arms. "It's not enough."

"Not nearly," Melissa agreed. "But our first priority—"

"Hold it," said Theo. He turned around to check on Ioni, only to find h
back on her feet, and then some. She sent a giant lumic copy of herself into th
sky, drawing all the nearby newsdrones into her orbit.

Though they assaulted her with questions from every corner of the world, er booming, godly voice brought a hush to the entire city.

"Anyone on Earth who's still in the air needs to land their vehicles now," she ecreed. *"A big change is coming very shortly to the planet. If you're still flying hen it hits, you will crash and you will die. This is your only warning."*

By the time her specter dissipated, nearly everyone in the infirmary had ome outside to either help or watch the effort to move Azral. Bobby and Yaseen, the last of the Violets, leaned on each other for support as they joined e chorus of jeers.

"Just die already, you piece of shit!"

"Hope you choke in your stupid bubble!"

"When you get to hell, say hi to your mom!"

"My son was worth a thousand of you!"

Azral merely stood motionless in his impregnable barrier, his eyes closed ut in concentration. Whether he was maintaining his shield, his composure, a combination thereof, Theo had no idea. He just prayed that the bastard dn't have any more tricks up his sleeve. The war had gone on for seventeen inutes and it already felt like a year.

The moment Azral was pushed beyond the perimeter of black towers, Ioni ldressed the troops. Her voice touched them all as gently as a whisper, as ear as a loving thought.

"I'm going to need at least eight of you to stay with him," she said with laent. "Keep your powers on his shield and hold him in place so he doesn't ome back in here. I don't make this request lightly. Once the walls come up, u'll be trapped on the wrong side."

Ioni lowered her head in sorrow. "I'm basically asking you to die."

Despite the gravity of her request, more than twenty people volunteered to ay and guard Azral, despite the consequences.

"Oh for shit's sake." Ioni extended two tempic arms and pulled Liam and arrie out of the crowd. "You two don't get a choice in the matter. You're stayg alive."

"No!" Liam struggled in her grip. "It's my decision!"

"Not anymore," Ioni said. "I made a promise to your dad and I'm going to ep it."

She turned her hot gaze onto Carrie. "And *you* still have an amazing girliend. Do I even need to remind you?"

Carrie stared at her with a mixture of hope and skepticism. "Wait. She alive?"

"Of course she is. You should have asked."

"I was afraid to! I didn't see her anywhere. I thought—"

Ioni directed her attention upward, to a fast-approaching aerocycle. "That Mia right there. You still want to die?"

Carrie shook her head, crying. "No."

"I didn't think so."

The number of volunteer sacrifices had dwindled to eight—five Gotham two Majee, and the last of the Dutch Opals—when Theo stopped trying coax people back. At the end of the day, he could understand their reasonir better than he would have liked. They were all spent on an existential leve and ready to move on to whatever came next, if anything. Theo might ha even joined them if he didn't have one last task ahead of him.

He looked to the shield bubble and saw that Azral's eyes were open agai and fixed right on him. The serenity on his face was downright unnervin He wasn't just calm. He was confident.

What the hell are you planning? Theo wondered.

Melissa tugged his arm. "Come on."

The moment they returned to the safe side of the perimeter, Ioni wave her hand. The twelve black towers lit up in synch, each one forming an energ wall with its neighbors. The central plaza of what used to be Prior Circle be came enclosed in a glowing red dodecagon.

Melissa examined the strange new barrier, a much different beast tha Ioni's other shields. Its discernible depth and perfect refractions made it loo more like glass than light. And it crackled with a powerful energy that Me lissa hadn't heard since she was a little girl, visiting her uncle's old power sta tion on the outskirts of Khartoum.

"All electric," she noted. "No temporic components."

Ioni nodded her head distractedly. "It's sucking all the power out of Sa salito. They'll be blacked out for a while."

"Why not use the local grid?"

Ioni's expression darkened. "Because we'll still need this shield after th city dies."

"Why?"

"Hang on."

Twenty feet beyond the barrier wall, Azral's forcefield exploded in a bur f light. By the time it subsided, he stood alone atop a pile of eight skeletal orpses.

Azral dashed toward the wall in a windy streak, then pressed his hands gainst the barrier.

"You miscalculated again," he said to Ioni. "You built this shield to withtand a Cataclysm, not me."

Ioni glared at him through the wall. "I can do both."

"Surely even a woman of your limits—"

"Oh, shut the fuck up."

Theo's heart hammered as the barrier began to crack around Azral's ands. Though Ioni worked hard to reverse the damage, Azral seemed to have n easier time breaking it than she did fixing it.

"Is there anything we can do?" Theo asked Ioni.

"No."

"We still have some turners—"

"No!" Ioni said through clenched teeth. "We got this!"

"We?"

Melissa was first to see who was she talking about. She looked past Azral. Oh no."

"Hey, shithead," said a voice in the near distance.

Azral only threw the briefest of glances at the man standing twenty feet ehind him. "Go away. I have no time for your foolishness."

Zack leaned against a broken wall, his lip curled in a smirk. "That's okay. I an talk while you work."

e'd been keeping a low profile these past few minutes, sticking to the corers of the battlefield where only the dead remained.

The friends and foes who did manage to see him had assumed, with good ause, that Zack had lost his mind. He'd taken a blow to the head from one of is own people, after all, while the love of his life had died violently beneath e Antarctic tundra. Given that, it was sad but hardly surprising to see him andering aimlessly around the ruins of Prior Circle, muttering to himself ke a crazy person while checking the wrist pulse of allies who, from the eer bloody sight of them, were clearly beyond saving.

But if the others had looked more closely at Zack, they would have seen at he wasn't checking pulses at all, merely leeching unused shield time from e warsuits of the fallen. And instead of rambling to himself, as some had surmised, he was apologizing to his dead companions for looting their earthl remains.

"You deserve better," Zack had said to them all. "I wouldn't be doing thi if I didn't have a reason."

By the time he finished, he'd amassed two and a half minutes of shiel time, more than enough for his purposes.

"So what's the plan?" Zack asked Azral a moment ago, from the safety c his personal barrier. "You still hoping to get Ioni under your microscope, or i this just a straight-up 'fuck you' killing spree?"

Beads of sweat trickled down Azral's temples as he continued to crac away at Ioni's wall. All he needed to weaken it were the bladed edges of a bil lion micro-portals, each one as small as a hydrogen atom. But he had to forr them quickly enough to counter Ioni's resistance, and that took dedicate concentration.

"I'm just trying to understand," Zack said. "If it's vengeance, I get it. Be lieve me. I was fixing to go all Rebel on your ass."

He looked to the eight rifted corpses near Azral, all of the bastard's late victims. Like Amanda and Caleb and so many others, they had sacrifice their lives to hold a bad man back. Now they were all just food for the crows

"But then I figured it'd be more fun to annoy you," Zack said. "Stick wit my talents and all that."

Azral kept his hard attention on the barrier. "A pathetic attempt to di tract me. You're as transparent as you are childish."

Zack chuckled. "Well, that's just downright . . ."

He flinched at a sudden shock of pain, yet another flash headache in never-ending chain of them. To think that it was Stitch who'd killed him i the end. His own ally.

Azral took a moment to scan Zack's grim future. "You're dying."

"Aren't we all?"

"And you choose to spend your final moments on a failed, buffoor ish ruse."

"'A failed, buffoonish ruse'?" Zack furrowed his brow. "Who writes you dialogue, Stan Lee?"

"But then what more could be expected of you?" Azral asked. "You've bee a tragic clown your entire life. You revel in it."

"Ouch," said Zack. "That's no way to talk to one of your own."

Azral looked at him over his shoulder. "You think you're my peer?"

"Sure," Zack calmly replied. "I mean you just lost both your parents." He shot Azral a nasty smile through the light of his shield. "Guess that akes you an orphan."

Thirty feet away, on the other side of Ioni's barrier, a small crowd of peo-le had gathered. While most of their attention was fixed on Ioni's struggle, ome were determined to hear what Zack had to say.

"Can you amplify his voice?" Theo asked Matt Hamblin, the last surviv-ng lumic among the orphans.

Try as he might, Matt couldn't look away from the cracks in the shield. What happens if that thing—"

"We all die," Ioni curtly informed him. "Just do what Theo asked."

Azral sneered at Ioni through the web of cracks. "This is why you fail, eschane. You put your faith in people like Trillinger."

Ioni shrugged as casually as she could. "I thought what he said was funny."

"A testament to your weakness."

Zack rolled his eyes. "For fuck's sake. You know, dialogue coaches aren't at expensive."

"I'm done with you," Azral snapped. "Your plan has failed. Now go away."

"Now *that* was good villain patter," Zack admitted. "Though a little hypo-itical, all things considered. I mean, think about it. Even if you manage to kill veryone here, what's next? You gonna fly back home, alone and empty-handed, r are you gonna jump to a timeline that went a little less fucktangular?"

The chuckles Zack elicited from his people made Azral grit his teeth. You're a fool."

"No doubt," Zack said. "I've made my share of boneheaded moves, but not n the level of yours. Trillions of experiments in trillions of strings and not a ngle one of them gone right."

Azral's face flushed with rage. "You know *nothing.*"

"I know that you wasted your life," Zack said. "That's sad enough by itself, ut the fact that you wasted everyone else's life is what really pisses me off. ou destroyed a whole world for nothing. You hurt *this* world for nothing. nd now here you are, the last Pelletier—"

Azral spun around to face him. *"Enough."*

"Having a violent little tantrum because your whole life's a sham." Zack ashed a mocking smile at Azral. "A failed, buffoonish ruse."

Ioni breathed a sigh of relief as Azral finally abandoned his efforts. He let the barrier behind in a shifted blur and sped straight to the edge of Zack bubble.

Melissa looked at Zack in wonder as Ioni fixed the fractured shield. "H did it."

Theo wasn't nearly as relieved. His best friend was still out there all alon his life slipping away on three timers. If the brain damage or Cataclysm didn kill him, it would certainly be the man he'd enraged.

Azral pressed his glowing hands to Zack's shield, draining its power i gulps. Zack checked the gauge on his wrist and saw the countdown movin faster than time itself. *99 seconds. 96 seconds. 88 seconds. 80.*

He looked to Azral glibly. "I sense I have offended."

"On the contrary," said Azral. "You've helped me decide my next course c action. I'll take you back to Lárnach, restore the power, and then lock you in mirror room before I leave this timeline forever."

Try as he might, Zack couldn't hide his fear. "You said I was dying."

"It doesn't matter," Azral assured him. "By the time the end comes, you' believe a thousand years have passed. Two thousand, if I leave you in the com pany of your dead wife."

Azral smiled at Zack's pained expression. "It must break your heart t think of her dying alone and in agony, as she did."

Zack shook his head, his pale face streaked with tears as his shield time continued to dwindle. *45, 41, 36, 30 . . .*

"Not alone," he said in a barely audible voice. "She was never alone."

"A childish delusion to comfort yourself."

"Maybe," Zack admitted. "But there's one thing about Amanda you're fo getting."

As the clock on his wrist reached its final ten seconds, Zack took a ste forward in his dying shield bubble and narrowed his wet eyes at Azral.

"I'm not the only one who loved her."

Azral's eyes opened wide in alarm as he processed a sharp temporal au approaching. If Ioni hadn't already hobbled him, if Zack hadn't so thorough flustered him, he would have managed to activate his shield in time. He' only been a few nanoseconds away from flipping the mental switch when cold metal blade plunged into his back and sent a sharp wave of pain throug his body.

Gasping, Azral turned around at the edge of the shield, only to feel the h ting of a second blade in his heart. He looked down in horror at the jutting rotrusion before making eye contact with his killer.

Hannah stared back at him, her voice a guttural rasp. "Nul'hassa e'nul."

Azral raised his hand to rift her, but his mind played one last trick on him. s his consciousness bled away, he brushed the trigger on the wrong power. He ppled backward toward the asphalt and then fell through it like a ghost. Iis intangible corpse continued to plummet—through the earth, through the tone, and all the way down to the fire deep below.

While his allies cheered from the other side of the wall, Theo pressed his ands against the barrier, crying.

"We have to get them back."

Ioni shook her head. "Theo . . ."

"We have to get them back in here!"

"Theo, *listen* to me. The Cataclysm's coming in just ten seconds. We an't . . ."

Her voice washed away into faint, garbled noises as Theo came to a horri-le realization. In addition to making her poor son an orphan, Hannah had ome to the inadvisable decision to play the swifter one last time. The neu-ologists had warned her again and again what would happen if she risked nother speed run.

And now there they were. The consequences.

Hannah looked to Zack with bloodshot eyes as her legs gave out be-eath her.

"Hannah!" Zack caught her before she could hit the concrete, but with only ne hand to keep her steady, he was forced to topple to the ground with her.

Zack held Hannah in his arms as her body seized in mayhem. "It's okay," e said. "It's all right. You did great."

While tears rolled down his stubbly cheeks, he suddenly laughed at some-ing on her thigh: a half-empty holster of throwing knives, freshly borrowed om Ofelia.

"Guess they came in handy after all," he said. "You really got him good."

Hannah writhed in his grip, struggling to form words. "Amanda . . . she ld me . . ."

Zack rubbed her arm. "It's okay."

"She told me to stay alive."

"I know," Zack replied. "She said the same thing to me. We can't, uh . . ."

He slowly shook his head. "We can't always give them what they want."

The thought of Amanda brought a twitching smile to Hannah's fac
"Gonna give us both . . . a real earful . . . when she sees us."

Zack laughed. "Oh boy. Will she ever."

Ioni's towers began to glow on the outside. Zack looked beyond the barrie and smiled at his friends in the distance.

"They're going to make it," he told Hannah. He lifted her arm and held he by the hand. "I guess you and I are the last two . . ."

He was going to say "casualties," but then became distracted by somethin on the inside sleeve of Hannah's warsuit. A bright red gauge. A number.

"Wait a second . . ."

Ioni grinned from the other side of the barrier. "Now you see it."

Melissa eyed her curiously. "See what?"

"Doesn't matter. Get ready."

She summoned a spectral pair of shades, then activated a black screen fi ter on all the timebenders' visors.

"Brace yourselves," she said. "It's about to get real bright."

At 9:24, Pacific time, Ioni changed the world all over again.

The news media had set cameras as far as thirty miles away to capture th Second Cataclysm in all its magnitude, and they weren't disappointed. Th conflagration swallowed San Francisco in a heartbeat before reaching a heigh of two and a half miles. Every cloud above the central western seaboar swirled away in a fit of mist, while the waters of the bay were so jostled by th blast that all the rubbernecking witnesses on the shores of Alameda had t run from a thirty-foot rogue wave.

The billions of hang-jawed viewers at home only had a few seconds to watc the destruction on their lumivisions before something entirely new happene a secondary wave of powerful energy that Merlin McGee hadn't warned the about. Unlike the Cataclysm that had set it loose, this force was imperceptib to human eyes, and it wasn't content to stop after five miles. It expande across the western United States at a hundred times the speed of sound, pas ing through mountains as easily as air. Nothing, not the highest satellites i orbit or the deepest subterranean vaults, could escape its ethereal touch.

Roughly twenty seconds after it was unleashed, the spectral wave of e ergy had blanketed the entire planet, to noticeable effect. In the business di trict of Yokohama, every lumic sign and hologram went dark at the sa time, stripping the streets of all illumination except for the moon and a fe ectric bulbs. In Greenwich Village, New York, all the floating aeric tables of ke's Humble Tavern crashed to the floor at once, while the tempic walls of e nearby Faith Mall bled away to wires and dead circuitry.

And, just as Ioni had emphatically warned, all the last few aeric vehicles in e sky fell to earth like scattered hailstones.

With the death of every lumivision, people all over the world had little oice but to speculate among themselves while the citizens of the planet's rk half began to scramble for their old electric flashlights. *What happened? ho did this? How is it even possible? How could that madness in San Fran- sco affect us all the way over here?*

After thirty more seconds of unprecedented quietude, the same question gan to pop up in every pocket of the world, in every language: When is the mporis coming back?

The answer, as they would slowly come to learn, was "never." That was the ice of their world's salvation. That was the cost of the future. The Temporal ge that began with the first Cataclysm had come to an end with the second.

here wasn't a single camera drone left alive that could document the new n Francisco. The city of hills had been reduced to a flat circle of ash. All the t-behind remnants of the once-great metropolis, from the buildings to the ter to the stubborn human beings who'd insisted on staying, had become distinguishable from each other in their final incarnations.

They were all just little gray flakes in the wind.

Had anyone managed to withstand the Cataclysm, and had they dared to nture into the heart of the former city, they would have noticed its one last cket of life: the central plaza of what had once been called Prior Circle, mly secured in an ominous-looking structure of black towers and red, assy barriers.

After trying for three seconds to undo his sunglass filter, Theo merely lled off his visor and dropped it. All around him, his shell-shocked com- nions followed suit. While some kept their eyes on the radically altered ndscape, others aimed their bewildered gazes at Theo.

"Is that it?" Melissa asked him. "Did we do it?"

Theo wished to God he could answer that but his foresight had gone snow- ind in the wake of the Cataclysm. The future was all just little gray flakes, t there was still someone in the vicinity who could set him straight.

Ioni kneeled on her hands and knees by the barrier, sweaty and short of

breath. She held up a trembling finger to Theo as she struggled to colle
herself.

"Ioni—"

"Wait."

"We have to know."

"Just wait!" she yelled. "Please. I need to do this."

Ioni climbed back to her feet and pressed her palms against the barri
She gritted her teeth in monstrous strain, like she was trying to push t
whole wall outward.

Soon the last remaining souls of Prior Circle formed a loose crowd arou
Ioni, every one of them equally clueless about her struggle.

But then the snowfall of ash began to clear outside the red glass wa
enough to reveal the hints of a light in the void.

Stunned, Theo and Melissa cupped their eyes against the barrier.

"Dear God," said Melissa. "Is that—"

"Yeah." Theo brushed the tears from his eyes, even as he found hims
laughing. "Guess we know what she's doing."

Twenty feet beyond the edge of the plaza, among the ashen remains
Prior Circle, a seven-foot shield dome radiated soft white light against t
backdrop.

At the rear wall of the bubble, down on the ground, Zack and Hann
nestled together, half-awake and three-quarters dead. From the matching w
their drooping eyes fluttered, they were just about to start the final leg of the
stuttering race to the next world.

But the reaper hadn't claimed them yet. And from the resolute look
Ioni's face, she had a much brighter view of their future.

ORTY-EIGHT

wenty-two minutes before her death, Amanda had made a quiet and more timate sacrifice.

As the timebenders had gathered on the plains of Mongolia, waiting for e portal that would bring them to San Francisco, Amanda took her sister by e hand and pulled her into a hug. Only she had known that it would be their st real moment together. Hannah had merely suspected it from the ominous tle clues: the backbending strength of Amanda's embrace, the ripples of ress in her tempic arms, the tingle of emotional energy that carried an air of nality.

Though Hannah had been right to suspect something, the tingle had acually come from her warsuit. While embracing Hannah, Amanda had made e spontaneous—some might say reckless—decision to donate fifty-five secds of shield time to her sister. It had seemed a meager gift in light of everying Hannah had done for Amanda. And if that extra protection gave her a ance to survive and be a mother to Robert, then there was no downside as r as Amanda was concerned.

The ensuing fight had been so chaotic for Hannah that she'd never even ecked her shield status. It wasn't until the last seconds before the Cataclysm at Zack looked to the little red gauge on her wrist and saw her unexpected unty. Even in his addled state, he didn't have to wonder where it came from.

You incredible woman, Zack marveled to his wife. *You just can't stop lping.*

Several yards away, three dozen people watched Ioni intently as she willed extension to her barrier. It protruded from the wall as a closed red tube, no icker than a sink pipe.

"They won't fit through that," Heath matter-of-factly attested.

"Yes," Ioni said, her face contorted in strain. "I'm aware they're not rbils."

"Why not just lower the wall?" Felicity asked. Yasmeen had already filled r in on everything she'd missed while she was rescuing Mia, but there were ill several holes in the narrative. "I mean the Cataclysm's over. Isn't it?"

"I'll explain everything," Ioni promised through clenched teeth. "Just give e a little time."

As the red tube continued to extend across space, a yellow tube bulge from Hannah's suitshield. With twelve seconds left on her barrier, the protru sions converged in a glowing orange juncture.

Ioni exhaled with sharp relief. "We're linked up! Theo!"

He took Melissa's hand. "We're ready."

"For what?" Melissa asked.

Theo sometimes forgot that she couldn't see what he saw. "Just follo my lead."

Both barriers were thoroughly portal-proof, even for a woman of Ioni talents. But now that the two environments were linked, a small new sphere physical space opened up in her traveler's senses.

The moment Ioni formed the entry portal, Melissa caught up with th plan. She and Theo hurried through the disc and retrieved Zack and Hanna before the bubble shield ran out of time.

Ioni closed her portals with a gasp. "Oh, Christ. That was close."

"I still don't get it," Felicity said. "Is the air out there toxic?"

"For some of us," Ioni replied. "Not you."

"That makes no—"

"Hang on." Ioni opened her fist to two glowing white spheres, then se them floating through the air like spores. They fluttered their way into Zack and Hannah's mouths, turning the skin on both their faces into bright, vein masks.

"Those were my last two menders," Ioni confessed. "I'm sorry to those you who are still injured, and I'm sorry for the people we lost in the infirmar I just . . ."

She looked to her remaining soldiers in sorrow. "This has been costly day."

From the shell-shocked expressions of all the survivors, she had unde stated the matter. More than eight hundred people had lost their lives in th fight. Good people. *Their* people.

"Just tell us it's done," Melissa implored Ioni. "Tell us this world has future."

"*A* future?" Ioni laughed with overwrought emotion. "That string we've been chasing has already split into trillions. Branches upon branches, grow ing every which way."

She brushed away her tears, her face lit up in a wavering smile. "This Eart has *infinite* futures, Melissa. And they all go farther than I can see."

. . .

'hile Ioni had depleted her supply of menders, she still had plenty of other ;eful gadgets. The splints on Mia's finger and wrist appeared to be made out ' sentient apple juice. The clear brown liquid knew exactly where it needed to •read before solidifying into crystal. The braces secured Mia's bones so well ıat she almost forgot that they were broken.

Of course, that comfortable feeling could have come from her other new ft: a little glass disc on the back of her right hand that killed all her pain and .en some. Even her grief had lost its jagged edge, a reprieve made all the bet-r by the loving caress of her girlfriend.

Carrie held her from behind and traced a finger down Mia's bandaged ılm. "I bet it'll still look better than my frost scars."

"I don't know," Mia said. "When this is over, we can have an ugly hand ›ntest."

"When *is* it over?" Carrie bitterly asked. "I want to get out of here."

Mia understood her anguish all too well. After everything that had hap-ɜned in the last twenty minutes—all the triumphs and losses and near-death .periences—her brain felt like it was on the verge of its own Cataclysm. Only flimsy veneer of glibness kept her from falling into complete hysteria.

"We'll leave soon," Mia promised. "Ioni's still getting her ducks in a row."

"Her *what* in a *what*?" Carrie laughed. "Tell me you didn't just make ıat up."

Mia shook her head somberly. She'd had the exact same exchange with the d Carrie last year. "Just a stupid expression from my world."

"It doesn't even make sense."

"No, I guess it doesn't." Mia looked at Carrie over her shoulder. "I'm sorry ›out your dad, by the way."

"I'm sorry about yours," Carrie said. "I always loved Peter. He was every-ıing our clan should have been."

Mia could feel her sorrow poking through the palliative haze. She rested ɜr head against Carrie's. "I don't know what your people are doing after ıis—"

"My people." Carrie scoffed. "There are only sixty of us now. I counted. 'e're not a clan or a tribe or anything anymore. We're just scattered survi-›rs, like your people."

My people, Mia thought. There were only sixteen orphans left. She'd ›unted. And three of them were Rubies who she couldn't pick out of a lineup.

"I guess what I'm saying," Mia awkwardly began, "is that whatever ha pens from here—"

"Yes."

"—I hope we stay together."

"Yes," Carrie repeated. "Was that even up for debate?"

"Not in my head."

"Or mine." Carrie kissed Mia on the lips, then gave her a wry grin. "Ou two ducks—"

"Oh God."

"—are completely lined up—"

"Stop."

"—in a beautiful row."

"This is abuse," Mia said. "This is flagrant abuse of metaphor and—"

A flash at the edge of the portal network made her jump to her feet i alarm. Apparently Semerjean's solis was finally wearing off, but not th trauma that he'd inflicted on her.

A spherical portal opened in the center of the plaza, bringing dozens new objects to the scene. Mia saw at least forty shiny warsuit helmets to r place the ones that were lost, plus a hundred weathered brown travel bags th could have come from a previous century.

Ioni teleported into view in front of the accessories and motioned for e eryone's attention.

"All right," she said. "Now that we've had a chance to catch our breaths, w need to talk about the immediate future."

She met Auberon's gaze for a cool half-second before awkwardly lookin away. "The news isn't all good."

Within moments, every living soul inside the barrier—every soul in *Sa Francisco,* Hannah grimly realized—had assembled in a circle around Ion The seven infants of the nursery had either been reunited with their mothe or passed off to the next-of-kin guardians who'd be raising them from now o

Hannah sat on a folding chair with Robert in her arms, her brain still r covering from its hemorrhage. Her vision and hearing had become tho oughly muddled, as if she were processing the world from inside a fish tan Her memories were blunted to the point where she had to keep remindin herself that Amanda and Peter were gone.

Ioni took a deep breath before addressing the timebenders. "First off, l e say this as plainly as I can: the people of this world will never thank you r what you did today. They'll try to understand it for the rest of their lives, ut they'll never know the whole story. It's just how history works. But for ose of us here, the truth is real simple. We saved this Earth. Every one of us ho survived the fight and every one of us who didn't. We're all messiahs to-y. Don't you ever forget that, not even in your darkest moments."

No one in the crowd had the strength of mind to cheer. They were too red. Too battered. Too mournful.

"This world is saved," Ioni said. "But not unscathed. A beautiful city is ne forever, and a powerful new form of energy has overtaken the planet. It's ot like solis but . . . stronger. And crueler in some respects."

"Crueler?" Melissa asked from the front of the audience.

Ioni sighed. "There are ten different species of algae that are vulnerable to is energy. They're going extinct as we speak. That'll create some environmen-l and food chain issues that will negatively affect everyone. There'll also be ore lightning storms. Bad ones. Even in places that don't usually get them. hey won't destroy the human race, but they will make life more difficult."

"For how long?" Bobby asked.

"Until humanity learns how to control the weather," Ioni said.

She waited for the murmurs to quiet down before continuing. "More im-rtant, and more immediately, this energy spells the end of temporis. None those devices will work anymore. Not now. Not ever. Not anywhere. In ct, this little patch of land right here is the last place on Earth where time n bend."

Melissa swapped a horrified look with Felicity. If Ioni was right, then to-y would prove to be the greatest one-day disruption in human history, a ousand times worse than the first Cataclysm. The infrastructure of every tion's economy would collapse all at once.

"That's horrible," Felicity said. "It's like we traded a quick death for a ow one."

"No," Ioni sternly insisted. "There may be chaos and famine—"

"*May* be?"

"*Will* be," Ioni said. "But it won't be the death of humanity. I promise you."

Theo stood at Melissa's side, his arms crossed tight. He'd gotten a pre-ient glimpse of Ioni's next bombshell, one that rendered all the previous ews moot, at least for his people.

Ioni caught his nervous expression. "Don't get ahead of me."

"Then say it already."

"Say what?" asked Charlene.

"The fourth effect of the energy," Ioni replied. "The reason the barri walls are still up. This planet's now poison to people like us. If this shie cracks, even a little, every single timebender will die in an instant. Only M lissa and Felicity will survive."

Carrie clasped Mia's hand. "Oh my God."

Sean Howell shot up from his folding chair. "I have a cousin in Texas," l told Ioni. "He's a tempic who left the clan years ago. Is he—"

"He's already gone," Ioni said. "I'm sorry."

"What about our people?" Auberon asked. "We have more than four hu dred relatives with chronokinetic DNA."

"But not chronokinetic powers," Ioni stressed. "Without the cerebral m tation, they have nothing to fear. They're all fine. They'll *stay* fine."

Charlene and Meredith exhaled with relief. Their parents, their cousin their twerpy little brothers. They would live, though God only knew how t family and corporation would handle the upheaval that was coming.

"Why did you keep this from us?" Zack pointedly asked Ioni. Though l looked far healthier than he did a minute ago, his skin was still white and h eyes remained cracked with red veins. "Why all the secrets?"

"I'm sorry," Ioni told him. "I had to, for the sake of the war. If you had to much knowledge—"

"I don't care," Hannah said. "When Merlin said this was the end of t road—"

"I told you he was wrong and I meant it," Ioni insisted. "There's a reason asked you to bring your baby to a war zone. There's a reason I brought a these travel bags. More than that . . ."

She fiddled with a handheld console until everyone felt a vibration in the wrists.

"There's a reason I just gave you all three more seconds of shield time Ioni said. "Because the road's not ending. It's just taking a sharp turn."

Mia double-checked her wrist gauge, dumbstruck. Why would they nee a barrier to get to where they were going, unless . . .

"Are you sending us through *time*?" she blurted.

Ioni nodded. "Time and space. There's a place out there where you'll l safe. No one will come looking for you. If you play your cards right and lea to adapt, they won't even know you're a stranger."

She cut off Rosario before she could ask her question. "No, there won't be nporis where you're going. Once the energy reserves in your body are de-ted, your powers will be gone forever."

Mia nearly cried at the very thought of it. Her portals were one of the best ngs to ever happen to her. They defined her as much as they empowered r. How the hell was she expected to live without them? What if trouble *did* d its way to her?

Ioni checked her analog watch, the one she'd bought from Freedom Wil-ms. "Look, these barriers are coming down in fifteen minutes. We don't nt to be here when that happens. Get a new helmet if you need it. Find the vel bag with your name on it. And then get ready. You're leaving this world d you're not coming back."

She looked to Auberon. "I need to talk to you right away. You too, Mia."

While most of the others prepared for departure, Mia and Auberon joined ni in the cafeteria. Meredith and Charlene insisted on tagging along, while rrie and Bobby flanked Mia like bodyguards.

Before anyone had a chance to speak, Ioni pressed a crystal coin to Mia's earm.

"What is that?" she asked.

"It'll kill the last bits of solis that Semerjean put into you," Ioni explained. need you at full power for what's coming."

"That being?" Auberon asked.

Mia wasn't encouraged by Ioni's dark look.

"I was planning on handling this portal by myself," Ioni said. "But Azral lly knocked the wind out of me. I'll need every last traveler we have to sup-rt me."

She gestured at Mia and Auberon. "Unfortunately, you two are all at's left."

"What about Ofelia?" Bobby asked.

Ioni shook her head. "Ofelia was brilliant in her fight against Esis. But it me with a cost, and that cost was her power. She's no more of a traveler than u are."

Charlene narrowed her eyes. "What are you not telling us this time?"

"That it'll be rough," Ioni admitted. "Mia, you're young and strong. You'll nost certainly survive it."

"Almost?" Carrie and Bobby asked in synch.

"She'll live." She turned to Auberon, grim-faced. "You, on the other hand—"

"No!" said Meredith. "You are *not* sacrificing him. We lost enough peo today!"

Ioni sighed. "If there was another way—"

"*Find* one," Charlene snarled.

"It's all right," Auberon told them. He took a cleaning cloth out of his s pocket and wiped the lenses of his glasses. "I was informed by one of my elc selves that I wouldn't need my warsuit today. Now I know why."

"But, Grandpa—"

"No." Auberon held Charlene's hand. "What have I told you from the b ginning? My credo."

Charlene looked away. "Your family is your nation."

Auberon nodded. "And I will continue to do whatever it takes to keep safe and thriving."

Meredith turned to Ioni. "Just let us talk to him alone. Please."

"Make it quick."

As the Grahams moved to a distant corner of the dining hall, Ioni look to Mia. "Like I said, you're young—"

"I don't care." Mia jerked a thumb at Auberon. "I'm right there with hi Whatever it takes."

Ioni smiled. "Just one of the many reasons I admire you."

"You knew I'd kill Esis," Mia said. "You've been setting it up since last yea

"I planted the seed," Ioni replied. "But an augur never truly knows. N until it happens."

"But it seemed probable," said Carrie. "Otherwise, you wouldn't have do it, right?"

The awkward look on Ioni's face didn't fill the others with confidence.

"You bet her life on a long shot," Bobby griped.

"I bet all our lives on long shots," Ioni countered. "That's all I've been d ing these past two years."

She shook a finger at Mia. "But for what it's worth, I had faith that you beat her. You were stronger than her in all the right ways."

As touched as she was, Mia couldn't shake her bitterness. "There are st strings out there where they won and we lost."

"They never won," Ioni said. "They may have killed us all in other tim lines, but they never got the cure they wanted. Not once."

Carrie didn't take any comfort in that. "Is that really worth celebrating?

"To me it is," Ioni insisted. "A world without death is a world witho

·aning. If the Pelletiers wanted to learn that, they should have come to my ghborhood."

Soon Meredith and Charlene left the cafeteria in tears. Auberon took a ›ment to compose himself before rejoining Ioni and the others.

"My granddaughters have come to terms with my decision," he said. "Tell : what I need to do."

ter five more minutes, the surviving timebenders were ready to make their ›dus. They gathered on the grass of the central plaza, muttering nervously ıong themselves as they waited for the final holdouts.

Theo stood in the kitchen of the old cafeteria, his hands tightly clasped ›und Melissa's. They'd slipped away for a private conversation that neither e of them wanted to start. Yet the crowd was waiting. Another deadline ›med. Even now at the juncture of infinite futures, time continued to be a ·rciless enemy.

"You think I would enjoy having a choice in the matter," Melissa said. "To y on my old Earth, or to go off on a grand adventure."

Theo lowered his head. "I don't think it'll be all that grand."

"And I don't think I have the option to go," Melissa said. "This is my world, ıeo. The only one I've known."

He nodded understandingly. "It'll need people like you more than ever."

"Well, I don't know how much sway I'll have. All my areas of expertise ve just become painfully obsolete."

Theo cupped the side of her face. "You're still a brilliant, unstoppable ·ce. If anyone can fix this world, it's you."

Melissa pressed her forehead to his. "I was hoping we could fix it together. we've proven anything, today of all days, it's that you and I make quite e team."

"I'm sorry for all the time I spent away from you," Theo said. "The secrets ept. I—"

"Theo . . ."

"I could have been a much better boyfriend."

"Theo, you were perfect." Melissa stroked his hair. "We were never the ne and roses type. We never needed to be joined at the hip. We built someing that was perfect for you and me, and . . ."

Theo could see from the quiver in Melissa's eyes that she was fighting ck tears.

"I'm just grateful for the time we had together," she said.

"You're going to have an incredible life," Theo told her. "You'll do amazi
things."

"As will you, I expect."

Theo nodded uneasily. "I'm nowhere near as good without you, l
I'll try."

"Just please make sure to take care of the others," Melissa said. "I'm tru
ing you to guide them, with or without your foresight."

Ioni's spectral voice cut into their conversation, as somber as she e
sounded. "It's time."

Of all the ironies of the day, Melissa found it especially curious that she a
Felicity had been strapped into a pair of cafeteria chairs that Ioni had fused
the concrete. They were the only two people in the area who *weren't* about
go on a journey. So why were they the ones who had to buckle up?

"It's for your own safety," Ioni said. "This portal will have a real pull to i

Felicity jerked her head at the assembled crowd of timebenders. "Will th
be okay?"

"They'll be fine," said Ioni. "They'll have one last bit of unpleasantness
take care of. But after that, they're home free."

"What kind of unpleasantness?" Melissa asked.

"The unavoidable kind," Ioni cryptically replied. "They'll be fine, and
will you."

While Ioni made her final preparations, Mia stood with Auberon at t
head of the crowd. Given his future, she would have expected him to be mc
nervous. Yet he scribbled in his notebook with a serene expression, as if
were merely making a shopping list.

Auberon caught her watching him. "You of all people should understa
what I'm doing."

"Writing a note to your past self," Mia surmised.

"Indeed."

"But why?" Mia asked. "If your situation is, uh—"

"Unchangeable?" Auberon smiled and kept writing. "Theo told me th
you've had a rocky relationship with your future selves."

Mia scoffed. "That's putting it mildly."

"I had a similar problem at your age," he admitted. "It took hard work a

nmitment to develop a good rapport: one simple rule that I've religiously
ıered to for close to sixty years."

He wagged a finger at Mia. "Always pay the favor backward. Whatever
ws I get from the future, I send it right back to the past, usually with addi-
nal context. That's been the one key to harmony with my temporal coun-
parts. The secret to my company's success."

"Wow," said Mia. "I guess I should have figured that out."

"As I said, I was older than you when I had my epiphany."

He tore a blank scrap of paper from the back of his notebook and handed
o Mia. "Go on," he said. "Send her one last message."

Mia suddenly realized where her future self had been when she'd mailed
ıt final note to Sergelen. She'd been right here at this very moment. And all
ıt other Mia could say was simply: "Let him go."

In the end, Mia wasn't sure how helpful it had been. She supposed it was
ot, anyway. Her right hand had been stabbed and burned. It'd be weeks, if
r, before she could work a pen again.

"It's okay," she told Auberon. She figured the best thing she could do for
younger Mias was to simply let *them* go, and forgive them for their mis-
es.

We did okay, Mia would have told her past self if she could. *Considering
at we were up against, we did pretty well.*

Soon Auberon sent off his final words, and Ioni stepped between him
d Mia.

"We're ready," she told the crowd. "Don't worry about your shields. They'll
itch on automatically. Just hold your travel bags tight. You'll need them.
d for those of you with babies, you'll want to hold them extra tight. These
rriers are a little more snug than usual."

Ioni looked to Auberon guiltily. "You're a good man. I'm sorry it had to
d like this."

"So am I," he said. "But I've lived longer than most. Who am I to com-
in?"

"Just know that your family will live on," Ioni said. "The people you have
this world, and the ones who are going elsewhere."

"I'm more concerned with the latter right now."

"They'll be fine," Ioni promised him. "But we have to work fast. Get ready."

Mia and Auberon barely had a chance to prepare themselves before Ioni

opened the floodgates of her mind and drew them both into her tempo
exertion.

Mia screamed as the universe tore open in front of her, then swallowed
into its folds. She didn't have the framework to even process its spatial co
figuration: a shape that expanded well beyond three dimensions and i
something that she was convinced she wasn't meant to see.

You're breaking the rules, said a panicked voice in her head. *You're bre
ing the rules and there'll be consequences.*

It's all right, said a second inner voice: her beloved Gotham mentor,
father of her heart. *You're doing fine, darling. Ioni just skipped you a couple
lessons ahead.*

Mia had to close her eyes to keep from vomiting. The universe kept sho
ing her colors and shapes that had no place in her tangible world, while
body kept twirling in paradoxical directions that she barely had time to p
cess, much less name. Downward-up? Outside-middleward?

Worse than that, her travels hit her with a whole new sense of magnitu
that nearly cracked her mind to pieces. Every molecule of the universe w
a universe in itself. Every moment of existence came in infinite layers a
varieties.

You think that's vast? the universe teased. *You're barely getting a speck
the big picture. You're only seeing what your little mind can handle.*

I can't take it, Mia cried in her thoughts. *Ioni lied. This is killing me!*

She could almost see Peter shaking his head. *You're not dying. You're si
ply retiring from the traveler's game. So drink it in and take some pride at wh
a brilliant run you've had.*

Mia was half-convinced that Ioni was merely faking Peter's voice to ca
her down. Real or not, it was working. She peeked an eye open and took in h
surroundings as Ioni made a sharp turn sideways.

It's a memory leap, Mia suddenly realized. *We're going somewhere s
used to—*

A sharp cry knocked her out of the thought as she felt the last gasp of A
beron Graham. His aura turned to mist in her psychic senses, until Mia w
alone with Ioni.

No. Not alone. All her fellow timebenders must have been pulled into t
portal, because she could feel every one of them in her mind. Zack and Ha
nah, Theo and Heath, Bobby and Carrie, all the miraculous survivors who

›ven more than once that life by itself was unkillable. It was a universal ›stant as much as death, and yet the two forces would never stop trying to ›eat one another. The conflict would play out *ad nauseam* in every string of ›e, every pocket of creation: a battle between two certitudes, a war of two ›ens.

Mia had no idea where it all would go from here. All she knew was that she ›s done fighting. She was retiring from more than the traveler's game. She ›s finished with the whole struggle. Let life and death do their own soldier-›. She was moving on to new pastures.

Who knew? Maybe she'd try writing fiction.

From an external perspective, the departure of the world's remaining time-›nders occurred over three seconds. Melissa and Felicity watched through ›inting eyes as the brightest portal either one of them had ever seen—a ›tical disc nearly ninety feet wide—sucked dozens of people into its maw. ›ly Ioni, Mia, and Auberon remained, secured in Ioni's tempic web.

But sometime during that final moment, Auberon's silhouette had van-›ed from the tableau. Melissa's eyes stayed open long enough to watch Ioni ›ease Mia into the vacuum. Then the portal swirled shut, and the wind ›pped howling between the barrier walls.

Melissa and Felicity unbuckled their chairs, their mutual attention fixed Ioni.

"You're still here," said Melissa.

Ioni nodded her head exhaustedly. "I never said I was going with them."

"But if you stay—"

"I didn't say that either."

Ioni flicked her hand, triggering a sweeping change among her remaining ›ls. The crystal structures, the liquid metal computers, even the water foun-›ns melted into puddles of opaline gel. Only the twelve black towers and ›ir eerie red barriers remained. Ioni studied them a moment before facing ›lissa and Felicity.

"Well, it all started here with you two," she said. "And that's how it'll end. case I didn't say it, you were both brilliant. We couldn't have done it with-t either of you."

Felicity looked beyond the shield at the vast gray void that was once San ›ancisco. "Still won't be putting this on my résumé."

Ioni nodded with empathy. "Nineteen hundred and four."

"What?"

"That's how many people died in this Cataclysm," Ioni told Felic "Would you like to hear how many lives you helped save?"

"No."

"That's good, because I don't have the number yet."

Ioni approached Melissa and placed a small velvet bag in her hands. "Th will be okay."

"He didn't seem to think so."

"He never thinks so," Ioni said with a grin. "And he's always proven wro It's part of what makes him so endearing."

Melissa smiled wanly. "If you see him again—"

"I won't," Ioni brusquely replied. "My future lies elsewhere."

"Where?"

Ioni laughed. "I have no idea. First time I felt that in almost a hundr years. It's kind of nice, actually."

She opened a new portal that was just large enough for one person. I was a temporal breach, then Melissa couldn't tell. It had no white fire arou the outer edge. No vacuum pull.

"Ioni . . ." Melissa struggled over what to say next. It was her very l chance to get wisdom from a prophet, yet her brain refused to face forward was officially on sabbatical from all things future-related.

"You were the true messiah," Melissa said instead. "This world would ha never been saved without you."

"Or doomed," Ioni reminded her. "But I appreciate it all the same."

She took a half-step into the portal before turning around. "I can't e come back here, but this world's still my baby. Take good care of it. Help back on its feet."

Ioni gave them one last smile before disappearing into the unknown. "T future's all yours."

The moment the disc swirled shut behind her, the barriers died a sputt ing death. The metallic smell of petrichor immediately filled Melissa's no trils as the flakes of a dead city snowed down on her.

Felicity watched the last of the towers as they crumbled into ash. "Ho crap. I'm spent."

"Me too." Melissa checked her watch. "And the day's barely just begun."

"How are we getting out of here?"

Melissa looked to their aerocycles, now thoroughly obsolete. Without t

ıeshifters in their engines, they wouldn't even start. The only way out of
: great ashen plains was to walk due south toward San Mateo. It would be a
ıg trip by foot but, without any newsdrones and flying government vehi-
ːs, it would certainly be a quiet one.

Felicity noticed the velvet bag in Melissa's hand. "What did she give you?"

"Oh." Melissa opened the drawstring and reached inside. When she
ened her palm, she found seventeen perfectly cut diamonds, just a fraction
the windfall that Ioni had bestowed upon her.

"I guess you could call it start-up money," Melissa said.

"For . . . ?"

Melissa had no idea. Her future, like the world's, had suddenly become a
bulous thing, all swirling clouds and question marks. But after living for so
ıg in the shadow of death, she suddenly sensed a hint of promise beyond the
ıcertainty. The future was anyone's game from here on out.

It was everyone's game.

"I'm not entirely sure," she replied to Felicity. "We have a long walk ahead
us, and plenty of time to figure it out."

ORTY-NINE

mewhere in the folds of time and space, a mere half-second before blacking
ıt, Hannah took a moment to marvel at the circular nature of history. It had
en just two years, ten weeks, and five days prior that ninety-nine people
ːre thrown across the multiverse—each one a survivor of an unimaginable
lamity, each one clueless as to what came next.

Now the very same thing was happening again, right down to the number
refugees. Hannah had conducted an idle headcount while waiting for Ioni's
ırtal: sixty-six adults, twenty-one teenagers, five children, and seven in-
ıts. Another ninety-nine souls on a transdimensional odyssey to stay one
ːp ahead of death.

There were even two Givens in the mix again.

Hannah woke up to the sound of Robert's cries, just one of a chorus
babies. While her head throbbed in pain, she forced herself up to a sitti
position, then examined her son closely. If the trek through time had knock
her out, then God only knew what it had done to poor Robert.

To her relief, she couldn't see any injuries. As far as she could tell, he w
just really pissed.

Hannah wrapped him back up in his little blue blanket and took a curso
look around. Her vision was still blurry from her recent brain trauma, but s
could tell from the clues—the trees and the grass and the looming shapes
brownstones—that she was in the middle of a metropolitan park. The sky abo
was a deep and starless indigo, but the clouds beyond the rooftops were g
ting brighter by the second. It was almost sunrise in the city, but *which* city

Hannah only had a moment to check on her people, still writhing a
moaning on the manicured grass, before Robert cried for attention again.

She held him tightly in her arms. "It's okay," she whispered. "It's all rig
We made it."

"Speak for yourself."

Hannah smiled at the familiar voice behind her. Two years ago, Zack h
been the very first orphan to greet her on the new world. Now here he w
again, an ever-dependable ally.

"You okay?" she asked him.

"That a serious question?"

"Are you *physically* hurt?"

"No," said Zack. "Those menders Ioni gave us are working pretty well."

He took a sweeping glance at his people, still waking up in dribs a
drabs. "They probably gave us a leg up on the trip."

"Zack."

"I don't see Ioni. Did she ditch us?"

"Zack, come here and hold me."

"Why?"

"Because my arms are full," Hannah said. "And I really want to hug you

After a moment of hesitation, Zack hooked his arms around Hanna
waist and rested his chin on her shoulder. Robert stopped crying at the sig
of his uncle and processed him with a crinkled brow. *Hey, I know you*, h
little eyes said. *Where do I know you from?*

Hannah turned her head, pressed her lips to Zack's cheek, and kept the
there long enough to feel his tears on her mouth.

"Stop," he said in a cracked and distant voice.

"No," said Hannah. "I know how you get when you're in grief. I won't let u pull away."

Zack rose to his feet in a surly huff. "I shouldn't even be here."

"Why not?"

"Because I was ready to die!"

"Well, you didn't," Hannah said. "You're going to have to deal with it, be- use you still have family who love you and need you."

Zack froze at the sight of a stranger in the near distance, a young Black an in a tweed cap and jacket. He clutched a suitcase to his chest with sweaty speration, as if his most vital organs would come spilling out if he let go.

The stranger took a step back at Zack's approach, his eyes round with ight.

"It's okay," Zack said. "We're not going to hurt you. I just . . ." He blinked the stranger, mystified. "Where are we? And why do you look so—"

Zack was about to say "familiar" until a weak hand gripped his shoulder.

"It's all right," said Theo. "I know where we are."

Zack turned around and studied him, a sorry sight if he ever saw one. en with a forcefield, the strain of time travel had bleached Theo's skin to a alky white shade and drew dark rings under his eyes.

As the artifacts in her vision began to clear, Hannah joined Zack and heo, and then took a bleary look around the area. "This looks like the place ni showed us."

"Winthrop Park," Theo confirmed. "She showed it to us for more than one ason."

"What do you mean?" asked Zack.

"I mean we have a problem," Theo said. "It's not just the place. It's the me."

Hannah and Zack bathed him in the same blank look as their memories itted together.

"You mean 1912," said Zack.

"1912?" Hannah echoed. "Right before the—"

"No, no, no." Zack shook his head in denial. "She wouldn't save us from e Cataclysm just to drop us into another."

Theo kept his tense gaze on a nearby tree. "She's not trying to kill us. I ow how to—"

"Mia!"

The shout had come from Bobby Farisi, just ten yards away. He crouch down at his sister's side, his large hands compressing her chest.

"I need help," he said. "She's not breathing."

Forty-five seconds after their abrupt arrival, nearly all the timebenders Winthrop Park had found their way back to consciousness. While some them, like Carrie, Liam, and Heath, remained committed to watching Bob perform CPR on Mia, the others gravitated around Theo as he explained the urgent new problem.

"What the fuck was Ioni thinking?" Yasmeen demanded to know.

Theo sighed. "If you let me finish—"

"She said we'd be safe here!"

"Just let him talk!" Meredith yelled at Yasmeen.

"Thank you," said Theo. "As I was saying, Ioni never does anything wit out a plan. She wouldn't have sent us back to this moment if she didn't thir we'd survive it."

"But how?" asked Ofelia. "I was right there with you when she showed the Cataclysm. She never told us how to stop it."

"There's a way," Theo assured her. "You're the one who gave it to me."

"What do you mean?"

Though he knew it would raise more questions than answers, he took out of his pocket and showed it to everyone: Ofelia's silver bracelet, the o that had insisted on its own significance from the moment Theo had first la eyes on it.

At long last, he knew its true purpose.

Zack anxiously checked on Mia before looking back at Theo. "Anoth forcefield."

Theo nodded. "The last one we'll need."

Even Hannah couldn't follow his reasoning. "You expect us all to in that?"

"It's not for all of us. Just me."

Charlene's eyebrows rose. "*Excuse* me?"

"I don't mean . . ." Theo palmed his face, flustered. He pointed to a tr just forty feet away, a twelve-foot sapling that had yet to change color with t autumn season.

"The Cataclysm starts right there," he said. "A floating orb of light, no bi r than a baseball. It stays like that for four or five seconds before it destroys lf the city."

"How do you know that?" Sean Howell asked.

"Because Ioni showed it to some of us," Zack replied on Theo's behalf. "In ving color."

Hannah finally understood the plan. "You want to put that baby Cata-ysm in the forcefield."

Theo nodded. "It'll hold the light. Keep the damage contained to just a nall radius. It . . ."

He chuckled at the sight of the bracelet. "The future kept telling me that is thing would save millions of lives, not billions. Now I finally know why. this trick works, we'll be saving the whole city."

Ofelia eyed the bracelet suspiciously. "So she sent us here to fix her biggest istake."

"Who knows?" Theo said with a shrug. "I just know that time's run-ng out."

"That forcefield won't turn on by itself," Hannah said. "Someone has to ear the bracelet."

"I know," said Theo.

"Meaning someone has to stand in that bubble and take the full force of e Cataclysm."

"Hannah . . ."

Charlene looked to Theo with new understanding. "You're sacrificing urself."

"It has to be someone," he insisted. "We don't have time to—"

"I'll do it," Meredith offered.

"*I'll* do it," Yasmeen said.

Theo groaned as three more people volunteered. "This bracelet only works r certain people," he yelled over the din. "Just the Silvers from San Diego. o one else."

He pointed a stern finger at Hannah before she could speak. "Don't you en think about it."

"He's right," Zack told her. "You have a kid."

"I can do it," Ofelia offered. "It was my bracelet anyway."

"No," Zack said. "You've been through enough."

"And you haven't?"

"Oh, I have," Zack replied. "More than enough. That's exactly why should be me."

Theo stepped back at his approach. "Zack, listen to me—"

"Ioni showed that thing to *all* of us," Zack reminded him. "Every sing person who could get that shield working."

"That doesn't mean it has to be you," Theo said.

"Or you," Zack said. "Our work is done. You're not the messiah anymor

Theo closed his eyes, his voice choked with grief. "The last thing Aman asked me to do was to help see you through this."

"And the very last thing *I'm* asking you to do is to let me be with her," Za said. "Let me do this last bit of good."

Hannah cried from the periphery, voiceless. There was no tiebreaker vo that she could cast that wouldn't leave her shattered. How could Ioni do thi After all the blood they'd shed for her, how could she demand another sac fice?

Theo suddenly glimpsed a quick premonition, a bit of good news in t middle of the bad.

"She'll be okay," he told Zack.

"Who, Mia?"

"Yeah."

"Great," said Zack. "We'll slap the bracelet on her and go out for so eggs."

Theo laughed. "You've never been quite right in the head. You know th don't you?"

Zack only smirked for a moment. "Let me do this."

"I can't," Theo said. He slipped the bracelet over his own fingers. "You ju proved why."

"No!"

Zack reached for the bracelet and clutched it before it could pass ov Theo's wrist. The others watched their struggle with breathless dread until t two friends stopped in synch. They both looked utterly horrified, as if they accidentally stabbed each other.

Hannah had no idea what they were reacting to until she saw the remai of the Pelletier bracelet in their hands. The cursed thing had broken into tv pieces.

Sean Howell blinked at the fragments. "Did you two idiots just kill us al

Theo shook his head, dumbstruck. "That's impossible."

"He's right," Zack said. "These things are—"

"Guys."

"—indestructible."

"Guys." Ofelia pointed to a nearby patch of trees, where a seven-foot orb of llow light cast a soft, pulsing glow.

In the center of the globe stood a smug-faced man, the black sheep of the lver family.

Evan shook his head at Zack and Theo, his tongue clucking in admonish-ent. "Now I remember why I don't hang out with you guys."

He twisted the silver bracelet on his wrist. "You're all way too dramatic."

ıere was a reason Ioni had wanted him alive, and it had nothing to do with e war. From the moment Evan joined their ranks, she'd befriended him, unseled him, even bedded him on occasion.

But mostly she'd groomed him to take on a task that would have other-ıse fallen onto Theo.

It hadn't been easy to convince a man like Evan to lay down his life for her people. And not just any others, the people he'd considered his enemies. ıere were times that the future had become so tenuous that Ioni was afraid give Evan the real silver bracelet, the one she'd pilfered from Theo in the iddle of the night and replaced with a cheap duplicate.

By the time the war in San Francisco had finally begun, Ioni was confi-nt that Evan would do his job. She refused to let Theo suffer the same fate Rebel and Merlin, two good men who'd served her needs, only to earn pain d death for their troubles. This time, the karmic scales would balance just ght. This time, her helper would live.

As for Evan . . . Well, at least he'd get to blow the minds of some of his big-st detractors.

Ofelia pressed up against the light of his shield. "What did you do, you son a bitch?"

Evan met her hot gaze with a smirk. "You know, you're a lot less pretty up ose. Have you considered using moisturizer?"

Ofelia threw her hands up. "He's saving himself at our expense."

"No he's not," Theo said. "He's standing in the right place."

"That makes no sense!"

"Not to you, *chica.*" Evan smirked at Zack. "What about you? Is your head inning?"

"It is out of character," Zack glibly admitted. "Then again, you're dying."

Evan nodded. "I have a year left to live at the very most." He glanc around with distaste at the nearest tenement houses. "And I'd rather that ye not be 1912."

Hannah cut her way through the throng of onlookers until she stood wi Zack at the shield's edge. "Is that the only reason?"

"No," said Evan. "Ioni told me we wouldn't have our powers where we' going. That was a dealbreaker. I've been living with my rewind button for long that . . ."

He fell into thought for a moment before chuckling. "This just feels li the place to tap out."

Evan ran his finger along the edge of his Pelletier bracelet, his expressi dark and distant. "Funny. The whole thing started with one of these fucke Now here it is again at the end."

He snorted in dark humor. "My life just keeps moving in circles."

"Not anymore," Hannah said.

"Yeah. Great. Now I get to be nowhere."

"That's just one belief," Zack reminded him.

"Don't you start with that Heaven shit."

"I wouldn't," said Zack. "Even if there was one, I strongly doubt—"

"Yeah. I know." Evan briefly laid eyes on Ofelia again before looking aw "I never pretended to be a nice guy, and I don't expect what I'm doing to wi the slate clean. But . . ."

He forced a flippant shrug. "It doesn't matter. I'll just be atoms in t wind."

Evan turned to Hannah, only briefly stopping to study the infant her arms.

"One day, you'll tell him the story of us," Evan said to Hannah. "I mean of us. The whole shebang. I just hope that when the time comes, when you' done talking about the pranks I pulled . . ."

"Pranks?" Ofelia sharply inquired.

"The bad shit," Evan grudgingly acknowledged. He looked to Hanna "Just make sure you tell him this part, too. Give him the whole picture."

Hannah nodded. "I'll tell him everything."

"He'll probably have you committed."

A fierce new light suddenly appeared behind Evan, a three-inch orb th floated under a tree branch like some divine and holy fruit.

Evan peeked over his shoulder at the nascent little Cataclysm. “Oh shit. it!”

Hannah pressed her hand to the shield. “Evan . . .”

“I’m not ready! I don’t want to do this!”

“Evan, *look* at me.”

He forced his wide, trembling eyes back onto Hannah.

“This isn’t the end of the road,” she told him, echoing Ioni’s words. “It’s st a sharp turn.”

“Into *what*?”

“I don’t know,” she admitted. “But you don’t need to be afraid.”

Evan pressed the palm of his hand against hers, his expression warm ough to make Hannah cry. He’d been lost in the woods for so very long, urting himself in life after life, to say nothing of his many victims. But in e end, he’d finally glimpsed the alternative that had eluded him for centu- es. A better way to pass the time.

“You had a million chances to kill me in Lárnach,” Evan cried to Hannah. But you saved me.”

He took another quick peek at the light. “You *saved* m—”

The orb exploded inside its cage, forcing everyone to cover their eyes. Un- er different circumstances, the Cataclysm would have erupted for five miles every direction, from the western edge of Forest Hills to the eastern shore Hoboken. Here, it only grew eighty-four inches at its widest.

In another chain of history, the explosion would have taken nearly two illion lives.

In this string, it only claimed one.

After three seconds, both the light and shield melted away in unison, leav- g no trace of their existence but a ring of smoldering grass.

Theo watched the final wisps of smoke as they dissipated. With the Cata- ysm neutralized, there would be no flood of timebending energy to push the orld in a wild new direction. The only temporis on the planet rested inside e bodies of ninety-eight aliens. Just dying little embers of biological wiz- dry.

As the lid on his foresight began to close forever, Theo took one last impse into the strings, and got more than he ever expected. He could see ead for miles, from the Great War looming right around the corner to the reat Depression at the end of the next decade. The future looked a lot like story, a revelation that elicited a dumbstruck chortle.

Theo looked around at his fellow survivors, then focused his attention o
the orphans.

"This is our world." He took in the view through a slow, twirling circ
before letting out another laugh. "It's back."

Even the companions who followed his line of thinking didn't join him i
laughter. They merely stood together in the crown of old Brooklyn, expre
sionless, until the sound of Mia's coughs cut through the heavy silence.

EPILOGUE

Ioni had gone to dizzying lengths to prepare them for a future in the pas
Their travel bags, all custom-packed with care and devotion, had everythin
they needed to start their new lives right: cash and clothes and identificatio
papers, all thoroughly era-appropriate. Medical supplies for the injured. Di
pers and lotions for the newborns. She'd even stuffed a pouch of diamond
into every bag, to hold on to for a rainy day or to fund whatever twentieth
century ventures her good friends wished to pursue.

More curious was the space-age garbage bag that Ioni had included i
each pack, composed of a thin and silvery substance that refused to stretc
or tear.

Theo was the first to glean its true purpose: to dispose of their warsui
and helmets, at least eighteen pounds of anachronistic future tech that wou
likely be dangerous in the wrong hands.

Indeed, a mere five seconds after sealing his gear inside the bag, The
watched the whole thing disintegrate into crystal powder. His companion
quickly followed his lead.

By the time the sun peeked up over the tenement roofs, and the early-bi
locals began to emerge from their homes, the survivors had fully blended int
their surroundings. Just a normal crowd in Winthrop Park on a quiet an
lazy Saturday.

Of course, even inconspicuous people couldn't travel inconspicuously vhen there were ninety-eight of them. After an endless round-robin of hand-hakes and hugs, the crowd broke up into splinter groups. The last three Ru-ies took a cab to the Brooklyn seaport and were on a steamship to Tokyo by ightfall. The sixteen Majee headed south in two clusters, with a plan to re-nite in Atlanta. The five dozen Gothams split up eight ways, forming brand-ew families out of the fragments of the old ones before bounding off in eparate directions.

Only Carrie and Liam chose to stay with the orphans, a motley band of wice-displaced migrants that included four Silvers, three Pearls, two Violets, Copper, a Gold, a Platinum, and a pair of disoriented newborns.

After convalescing for a week in a Midtown hotel, the group ventured north ıto the heart of the New York suburbs. There at the crest of Rockland County, ear the western bank of the Hudson River, stood a quaint little hamlet of ine hundred souls that was formally known as Congers. In another string of me, the town would be renamed Quarter Hill in honor of those who'd pro-ided food and shelter to the homeless refugees of the Cataclysm.

But in this chain of history, the name would stay Congers. And for Han-ah and the others, it was as good a place as any to settle. They'd spent a part f their fortune building four custom houses on an empty gravel cul-de-sac. y the summer of 1913, their haven was finished: their own little Freak Street, ; quiet and secluded as any of them could have hoped for.

Though they gradually coalesced into the local community—new jobs for ›me, new friends for others, and the occasional new lover for the more dar-ıg among them—they kept an airtight lid on their secrets. The only strange ıing about them, to hear the townsfolk tell it, was the ethnically diverse akeup of their brood.

"We're orphans," Hannah said to anyone who asked. "We grew up together tough conditions, and it made us into a family."

Over the next four years, as a Great War raged on the other side of the tlantic, Hannah's clan began to suffer its first defections. Matt Hamblin, the st of Caleb's Platinums, migrated south to Ocala, Florida, where he started a uit and vegetable farm that would grow into a national conglomerate. Lau-n Iniguez, a one-time Pearl of Guadalajara, found both love and God with a aveling preacher, and started a church with him in Texas. Yasmeen left for dia on a thirty-year mission to alter the course of history. She bought her

way into high society and, true to her cause, played a vocal role in the birth c
her native Pakistan.

In 1918, after a near-fatal bout with influenza had prompted a catharti
reassessment of her life, Rosario bought an apartment in Spanish Harlem. Sh
wanted her daughter to grow up with a cultural identity that the white-brea
suburbs simply couldn't offer.

The others were saddened but hardly surprised when Ofelia decided t
leave with Rosario and Eden. She had fallen in love with a certain one-hande
Silver, and was sure that the feelings were mutual. But even six years after th
death of his wife, Zack refused to let go of Amanda.

"If he won't move on, then I will," Ofelia told Hannah. "I'm done waitin
for him."

As much as it pained Hannah to lose Ofelia's company, her heart was sha
tered three years later, when it became Heath's turn to go.

In July 1921, Meredith and Charlene drove up from Georgia to make hi
a special offer. Their corporation, Auberon Enterprises, had done extreme
well in the technology sector, enough for them to purchase a thirty-stor
building in midtown Atlanta.

But after the recent horrific massacre in Tulsa, Oklahoma, in which a
entire Black business district had been burned to the ground, the Graham
tripled up on their security. Their new tower had become both a fortress an
a haven, with more than five hundred employee-residents working together
help improve the world.

"We want you there with us," Meredith told Heath. "Things are bad o
here for people like us. You and See—"

"Nadiyah," Heath and his wife corrected in unison.

"You and *Nadiyah* need a safer place to live, especially now."

She wasn't wrong. Heath and his Moroccan-born partner had never ha
the easiest time in Congers. And with their very first child on the way, the tw
of them had more reason than ever to think about the future.

Hannah cried for days after losing Heath and Nadiyah, even though th
called her once a week and mailed her endless photos of their daughter. Th
strings were pulling her family in different directions, and Hannah didn't li
it one bit.

The biggest exodus came in 1925, thirteen years after the orphans mov
to Congers and three years after Mia's career exploded. While her first tv

novels had garnered rave reviews but mediocre sales, her third book—a pulp adventure story about a stubborn but dauntless Irishman who traveled the world, righting wrongs—had sold well enough to warrant several sequels. By the fifth book, the series had become an international sensation. By the sixth, it seemed like half the world was waiting with bated breath for the next adventure of Peter Pendergen.

Soon enough, a team of Hollywood executives came to Mia with a business proposal. Thanks to recent innovations in the motion picture industry, much of it sparked by Auberon Enterprises, United Artists was starting to dabble in full-sound "talkie" pictures. As such, they wanted Mia to adapt her own novels into the studio's first fully voiced film franchise, with Douglas Fairbanks in mind to play the starring role of Peter.

Though Mia was initially hesitant to take the offer, her family threatened to harangue her to the grave if she didn't at least try to live her dream.

Within a month, she had packed up a pair of Ford Model As, and headed out west with her coterie: Bobby and Liam and their new wives, and of course her partner in all things: Carrie Bloom. Though the Hollywood community would know her as Mia's inseparable best friend, the story of their secret lifelong romance would become the subject of its own movie in 2011, a semi-fictionalized account at best. Neither the film's screenwriters nor the world at large would ever learn the true and more interesting story of how Mia and Carrie had met.

With the vast majority of her people gone, Hannah cleaned out the last of her street's vacant houses, then put it up for sale on the market. They were down to just one dwelling, with mostly strangers as neighbors.

And there was still one last departure to come.

In the winter of 1926, after a long, dark night of contemplation, Zack went to Spanish Harlem in search of Ofelia and got a slammed door in the face for his trouble. It took three months, ten apologies, and a special cartoon in *The New Yorker* for Zack to finally earn Ofelia's forgiveness, and then another four months to prove to her that he was ready to move forward.

When Zack told Hannah that he and Ofelia were getting an apartment together, he could barely look her in the eye.

"I wouldn't blame you for being mad," he said. "She was your sister. I mean—"

"Zack . . ."

"It still feels like I'm betraying her."

Hannah hugged him tight and whispered a word in his ear, the very sam one that the Amanda in his head had been saying to him for years. "*Live.*"

As Zack drove away with his last belongings, Hannah sat on the fron porch swing of her house, teary-eyed.

"Not you," she said to the man sitting next to her. "You don't get to leave.

Theo smiled and held her hand as he watched the giggling mayhem o the lawn. Robert was trying to teach his little sister how to fold and thro paper airplanes. Unfortunately for him and the planes' imaginary passenger Amanda was much more amused by the crashes.

"Don't worry," Theo said to Hannah. "I'm not going anywhere."

True to his word, he remained a stable and loving constant in Hannah life, all the way till the summer of 1974, when the one-time messiah reache the end of his string.

When Evan sacrificed his life to save New York City, Theo had made an e roneous assumption. He figured that without the upheaval of the Cataclysn history would proceed exactly the way he remembered it, without a sing deviation or hiccup.

What he'd failed to take into account that day were himself and th ninety-seven other temporal refugees, each one a new variable in the tim line. Their every decision, even their indecisions, created ripples of change a throughout the strings.

Some of their impacts were patently obvious. Mia's novels splashed lik boulders in the waters of the world's culture, while Zack's political cartoons- always sharp and historically prescient—had altered the decisions of mo than a few lawmakers. Sean Howell developed a vaccine for polio four yea before Jonas Salk. And books had been written about Yasmeen's wise infl ence over Indian/Pakistani politics.

Most notable for music fans were the upbeat tunes of Ahmad "Heat Bradshaw, which helped accelerate the dawn of the rock-and-roll era, an which John Lennon cited as an early influence on the Beatles.

But none of them held a candle to Auberon Enterprises, one of the mo paradigm-shifting corporations in history. Their technological innovatio had jump-started the progress on dozens of industries, from movies to roc ets to personal computers, while their ceaseless investments into Black-own

usinesses had triggered enough racist backlash to draw the civil rights move-
ıent from the sixties to the fifties.

By the middle of the twentieth century, there were more differences in the
imeline than similarities. And by the early 1970s, the collective historical
nowledge of the orphans had officially become moot. The world had evolved
nto its own unique entity. New actors. New products. New presidents. New
rises. An entirely new generation of people who'd never come into being on
ıe old Earth.

Hannah would have found the notion beautiful were it not for the dispirit-
ıg counterthought: all the long-gone souls of her native world, overwritten
y cascading changes. In 1972, eighteen years after her parents were supposed
) be born, Hannah hired a private investigator to look for them. As she'd
eared, there was no record anywhere of Melanie Winwood or the original
obert Given. They didn't exist, to Hannah's sorrow. She'd been holding out
ope for sixty years that she'd live long enough to see Amanda reborn.

While that never happened, Hannah did survive to see the day itself: Feb-
uary 11, 1982, nearly seven full decades after she'd crashed into Winthrop
ark.

At ninety-five, Hannah was a silver-haired wonder: the sharpest old lady
Congers, New York, and one of its most celebrated residents. Though she'd
ever set the world on fire with her acting and singing, she'd lived a rich, full
fe of a thousand little triumphs, with barely a hint of regret. She was crucial
the people of her beloved community, crucial to her children and grand-
ıildren, crucial to the orphans who still lived and breathed, and crucial to
ıe patrons of her theater. She'd built the Imperial Street Playhouse back in
926, though her trustees and family had conspired behind her back to re-
ame it the Hannah Given Theater in 1980.

The building would continue to bear her name for another two hundred
ıd eighty-five years, not that Hannah would ever know. After three heart
tacks in the past four months, it had become clear to her and everyone who
ved her that her time was running short. Robert ruled over his younger sib-
ngs from California, making sure that if he couldn't be there with her, then
ıe of the others would.

Even Heath joined the circus of worrywarts—an old man, half-deaf, fly-
ıg all the way from Georgia to keep a watchful eye on her. Though Hannah
ıd repeatedly told him not to bother, she knew that he wouldn't listen, and

part of her was glad. He and Carrie were the last of her orphan brood, th
ones who could corroborate the stories that she'd told to her children an
grandchildren behind closed doors. They'd been right there with her in tha
fantastical world. They remembered. And if Carrie and Heath were anythin
like her, they were remembering it more and more.

At sunset on Sunday, February 11, Hannah draped a duvet over Heath'
sleeping body and planted a kiss on his forehead. Though she had three bed
rooms and a den to accommodate him, the stubborn old fool insisted on tak
ing the couch. From the way he stirred, his nap was nearly over. He'd no doub
want a cup of his favorite tea.

As the kettle heated up, Hannah looked out the kitchen window and onc
again became lost in old memories. She remembered a New York City tha
had glimmered with flying traffic, their shifted headlights making brigh
streaks in the sky. She remembered her first step into the underland, with a
its illusive wonders. She remembered kissing Jonathan for the first time in th
elevator of a hijacked, out-of-control aerstraunt.

And she remembered the look on Azral's face as she plunged a silver kni
into his heart.

Hannah gasped at the sudden pain in her chest, as if Azral had someho
flipped the script on her. She collapsed to the floor in agony, her eyeglass
sliding across the tile.

"Oh God," she moaned. "I think I . . . I think I . . ."

"Shhhhhhh."

Hannah registered a blurry white form above her, a woman she couldn
recognize. The stranger silenced the whistling tea kettle with a wave, the
took a kneeling vigil over Hannah.

"Hang on," she said, in a voice that rang bells in Hannah's recollectio
"You're about to feel better."

True enough, she pressed a finger to Hannah's sternum and abrupt
ended her pain.

Hannah sucked a sharp breath from the floor, baffled. "Who . . . wh
are you?"

"You don't recognize me?"

Hannah fumbled around the floor. "My eyes aren't what they used to b
I . . ."

"Hang on." The woman fetched Hannah's thick bifocals and put the
back into place. Hannah blinked at her three times before gasping.

"You're shitting me."

Ioni smiled down at her, as young as she ever looked. She'd cut her hair to
short and wavy bob, as red as a tomato, with little blond streaks at the top. It
as a trendy style in the 1980s—*these* 1980s—and it went fashionably well
ith her sleeveless red summer dress.

Hannah examined her ever-present watches before goggling at Ioni again.
)h my God. Do you ever age?"

Ioni smiled humbly. "Short answer, no. But I should point out that it's only
een twenty-one years since I saw you in San Francisco."

"Not for me," Hannah said.

"Not for you," Ioni echoed. "You've had a hell of a run here. Not that I'm
ırprised."

Hannah tried to examine herself, but didn't have the strength to lift her
ead. "I feel . . . weird."

"I only stopped your pain," said Ioni. "You're still having your heart at-
ck, I'm afraid. I can buy you a couple of days at the most. Give you time to
y goodbye. But I won't be around when the next one hits. So if you're look-
ıg for a painless exit, this is it."

Hannah closed her eyes. "How much time do I have?"

"To decide?"

"To live."

Ioni checked her watches. "Two minutes, give or take. Though I can stretch
out a little for conversational purposes."

"Conversation." Hannah laughed. "Most of my kids think I made you up.
hat we suffered a collective delusion."

Ioni shrugged. "When you look at it their way—"

"I know. I never blamed them." Hannah squeezed Ioni's arm. "Thank you,
the way."

"For what?"

"For letting me have Theo, instead of making him die in the Cataclysm."

Ioni shook her head. "You set up all the dominoes. I just gave them a flick."

Hannah suddenly flashed back to Melissa Masaad, a woman she hadn't
ought about in ages. No doubt Theo had dwelled on her more often, but
'd never made it obvious, bless him.

"How's that world doing?" Hannah asked. "I mean without temporis."

"It's still going," Ioni said. "I can only view it from a distance, but I've been
ıtching every day. They had a lot of hard years after that second Cataclysm.

A *lot* of hard years. There was a time I feared that they wouldn't make it. Bu
the good people of that world pulled together and they found a way to adapt

Ioni smiled at Hannah. "They named a school after Melissa and a com
puter after Felicity."

Hannah chuckled. "Just tell me they were happy."

"They were happy," Ioni confirmed. "They never lost sight of the preciou
ness of life. Every day was a well-earned gift."

"I agree," said Hannah. "Which kind of makes me a hypocrite."

"What do you mean?"

"I made my decision," Hannah said. "I'm ready to go."

"That's not hypocritical," Ioni insisted. "You had yourself a hell of a lif
You deserve to go out on your terms."

"When will *you* be ready?" Hannah idly inquired. "You've lived so muc
longer than us."

The subtle change in Ioni's expression would have jolted Hannah's heart
she could feel it. Ioni may not have been aging, but she was certainly evolvin
There was something new and different behind her eyes. Something entire
more than human.

"It's still not my time," Ioni confessed. "I don't know if it's a strength or
flaw, but I've become pretty comfortable in my existence. I still like bein
here, and . . . I don't know."

She shrugged her shoulders listlessly. "I still like changing worlds."

Hannah drank her in for a long, quiet moment before recalling som
thing. "You once told us that your people got temporis too soon."

"Wow." Ioni chuckled, impressed. "You *remember* that?"

"I remember everything," Hannah said. "My body's a mess, but my minc
still sharp."

"I'll say." Ioni scratched her chin in contemplation. "We came by tempor
naturally, but yeah. We weren't ready."

"Well, then I have a new project for you."

Ioni shook her head. "Oh, no no. Wait a second."

"You already know what I'm about to ask."

"It's not a *small* ask."

"I don't care," Hannah said. "I love this world and I love my family. I wa
them to have a good future."

"Hannah—"

"You make sure they get temporis when they're ready for it," Hannah de-anded. "Not one minute sooner. *Promise* me."

Ioni shook a stern finger at her. "You're a sneaky old gal."

"Not as sneaky as you," said Hannah. "You still have foresight. You knew ere was a chance I'd ask. And yet you came here anyway, because I think on me level that you wanted me to give you something new to do. A new world take care of."

Ioni grinned at her with awe. "Does anyone ever say no to you?"

"Not often," Hannah weakly replied. "The privilege of being a stubborn d—"

She felt a sudden cold grip around her consciousness. The edges of her vi-on turned dark.

"It's starting," Ioni said. "I can't hold it back anymore without—"

"Don't."

"—saving you."

"You don't have to," said Hannah. "I'm ready. I'm scared as hell, but I'm ady."

Ioni held her hand. "I'm here, hon."

"I remember . . . I remember one of the last things you said to us before nding us to Winthrop. You said, 'It's not the end of the road. It's just a sharp rn.'"

"I did say that, didn't I?"

"And then I said it to Evan," Hannah confessed. "I don't think it helped."

Ioni smiled. "If I could tell you what comes next, I would. But that's the e road I can't see down. If I had to guess . . ."

Her words faded into the periphery as Hannah slipped into a tenuous new ate of consciousness. Instead of moving forward, she found herself lost in a stant old memory, a giant white prison cell beneath the snows of Antarctica. e and Rosario had been the last two prisoners of Lárnach. All they had left do was bide their time and shoot the breeze until their waters broke and the lletiers archived them. It had been one of the scariest times of Hannah's e, but also one of the simplest. Her thoughts about everything had been ystal clear, from the dilemmas of the past to the mechanics of the afterlife.

"I don't think it's just one world," Hannah had speculated to Rosario. "Not ter everything we've seen. Maybe our souls split off into parallel versions, d we each go a trillion different ways."

Hannah hadn't thought about her theory in at least fifty years, but now soothed her like a warm blanket. If the system worked the way she hoped did, then she already had a teeming list of people and places to visit. A billic of her would find their way back to Theo. Another few million would sp their time between Jonathan and Peter. Heck, a few Hannahs might even visit Jury Curado to see what all the fuss was about. And some would fly c all by their lonesome: a happy phantom, bouncing around the universe ar drinking in all its wonders.

But across all the infinite Hannahs that she was about to become, all the infinite plans for the future, there was still one unifying constant among ther

One given.

Ioni looked at Hannah curiously as she chuckled from the floor of t kitchen. "What is it?"

Hannah kept on laughing in simple bliss, her bright eyes flowing wi tears. "I'm going to see my sister again."

More than a hundred and twenty years after Hannah passed on, a curio thing happened in Portugal. A brilliant young scientist at the University Lisbon was attempting to invent the world's first true cold laser when she a cidentally breached the temporal veil and summoned a molecule of temp Unfortunately, her nanoscope had malfunctioned at just the wrong momen preventing her from noting her own discovery. She'd go to her grave nev knowing about tempis. But she did get to conquer that laser.

Ninety-two years later, a British weapons research analyst came to the o sessive belief that time itself could be used to accelerate just part of a hum body, causing massive amounts of damage to the vascular system. After se eral years of failed experiments, three firings, and two divorces, the analy finally developed a machine that caused a banana to rot at 1.004 times t normal rate of entropy. Or *would* have, anyway, if an errant piece of du hadn't found its way to a microcomponent and forced the whole machine in system failure.

Dejected, the analyst abandoned his lifelong plans and began his next c reer as a drug addict.

On and on, the failures continued. All around the world, in century aft century. Whenever anyone got close to discovering temporis, the univer threw them a mean-spirited curveball that either nullified their accomplis ment or removed their ability to notice it.

By the start of the thirty-first century, Ioni found it difficult to keep up her romise. It seemed like every egghead with a physics degree was on the verge f a temporal breakthrough. The veil was all but begging to be breached, and oni's engineered setbacks were becoming less and less of a deterrent.

More vexing still, the human race was starting to surprise Ioni in all new ays. Every time she expected them to fall back on old patterns: all the selfish reed and animal instincts that had collectively kept them stunted, they dem-nstrated a willingness to learn from past mistakes. They'd even managed to a full century without a single bloody war.

And so it was in the year 3182, almost exactly twelve centuries after Ioni arted her project, that an international consortium of thirty physicists—ost of them carrying at least some trace of orphan, Gotham, or Majee in eir DNA—set about to test the theory that light from the recent past could replicated.

Somewhere deep in the corner of the lab, invisible to human and me-anical eyes, a girl with two watches observed their experiment, her hand ipped tightly around a remote trigger switch that would sabotage their ef-rts for good.

But then, at the last second, Ioni released her hold on the trigger and con-dered her oath to Hannah fulfilled. Humanity had come so far in the past elve hundred years. They had learned so much. They were ready for the xt big phase of their adventure.

It was time.

.CKNOWLEDGMENTS

'on't read this.

Seriously. If you reached this page the long way, and just finished the story ; Hannah and company, then close the book and save this part for later. To ·llow the end of this doorstopper trilogy with a page and a half of author rattle seems gauche and discordant, like playing a kazoo over the rolling end 'edits.

But credit comes where credit's due, and I'd be a real schmuck if I didn't ıank the many people who helped bring *The War of the Givens*—the longest, ɜaviest, and most labor-intensive book of the Silvers series—into creation.

Are you back from your little post-finale siesta? Good. Let's name names.

First up are Mark Harvey and Leni Fleming, my longtime friends and al- ıa readers who've been providing me with spiritual guidance since the ɔening chapter of *The Flight of the Silvers*. This house of cards would have ɔllapsed at the first floor if it wasn't for their support and encouragement. hank you, Mark and Leni.

Then there are my beta readers, who were fewer in number this time ound due to the book's chaotic schedule. I remain eternally grateful for the edback of Craig Mertens, Jennifer Gennaco, Mike Tunison, Craig Aikin, ıd Ysabelle Pelletier (who thankfully bears no moral resemblance to Azral, ɜis, and Semerjean).

Huge thanks to A. J. Sass, my friend and fellow novelist, for his expert edback. Be sure to check out some of his amazing works, like *Ana on the lge* and *Ellen Outside the Lines*.

I can't say enough good things about the people at Dutton, who were so ıtient and kind during my many illness-related delays. Everyone there was ɔnderful: Stephanie Kelly, my original editor, who moved on to greener pas- res during the book's long inception; Dorian Hastings, my two-time copy litor, who even caught me misspelling some words I'd created; Sydney ɔwler, expert consultant and spackler of plot holes; Tiffany Estreicher and son Booher, who made the book look pretty both inside and out. And last ıt certainly not least: Lexy Cassola, my superpowered editor, who helped me ɜan up this manuscript in record time, with unfailing grace and wisdom.

As always, I thank my agent, Stuart M. Miller, who's been pulling off mi-acles on my behalf for nearly a quarter century, and who refuses to rest unt the Silvers hit the movie or TV screen.

You might have noticed I dedicated this book to Ricki, as in Ricki Ba Zeev, as in the woman who gave birth to me. Not only did she make me pos-sible, but she was the very first person to encourage me to stop daydreamir about the Silvers and start putting them down on paper. Twenty-two hundre pages later, here we are, Mom. Thank you.

And of course there's Nancy Price, my partner in crime and everythir else. Without her love and the occasional ass-kick, I'd still be floundering i the book's middle chapters. She held me together through some of the tough-est years I've ever had, and I'm grateful for her every day.

Finally, a big, fat THANK YOU to all my wonderful, patient readers. I lo count of the number of emails and tweets I got from you folks, many of whor have been waiting six years to read the end of the Silvers saga. Now that we' here on the other side, I hope *The War of the Givens* brought you a measure joy. Whatever happens, I'm thankful for all your kind messages over th years, all the words of encouragement that pulled me out of the muck. I ma not have the world's largest readership, but I do have one of the best.

Rest assured my next novel will be a stand-alone story. After ten long yea in Altamerica, I'll be taking a break from trilogies for a while.

BOUT THE AUTHOR

aniel Price is the author of *Slick*, *The Flight of the Silvers*, *The Song of the rphans*, and *The War of the Givens*. He lives in Gilbert, Arizona, with his ırtner, Nancy. He cannot actually manipulate time.